Book Three: Apse

Book Four: Choir

Book Two: Transept

Book One: Nave

MONUMENT
MAKER

By the same author

England's Hidden Reverse

This is Memorial Device

For the Good Times

The Towers The Fields The Transmitters

Xstabeth

MONUMENT MAKER

DAVID KEENAN

WHITE
RABBIT

First published in Great Britain in 2021 by White Rabbit,
an imprint of The Orion Publishing Group Ltd

Carmelite House, 50 Victoria Embankment
London EC4Y 0DZ

An Hachette UK Company

1 3 5 7 9 10 8 6 4 2

Copyright © David Keenan 2021

Pierre Reverdy poems translated by David Keenan
with the kind permission of the Comité Reverdy
Pierre Reverdy, 'Secret' and 'Adieu', *Oeuvres complètes.*
Tome 1 © Editions Flammarion, Paris, 2010
Pierre Reverdy, 'Voyages Sans Fin', *Main d'oeuvre*
© Mercure de France, 1949

A CIP catalogue record for this book is
available from the British Library.

ISBN (Hardback) 978 1 4746 1709 3
ISBN (eBook) 978 1 4746 1711 6

Typeset by carrdesignstudio.com
Printed and bound in Great Britain by Clays Ltd, Elcograf, S.p.A

www.whiterabbitbooks.co.uk
www.orionbooks.co.uk

To the Glory of God

CONTENTS

BOOK ONE: NAVE

I. CATHEDRAL OF OUR LADY OF CHARTRES

I met her at a bookstall in a romantic European village on
the outskirts of which I had set up camp in a single, bleak,
storage container, painted blue, on the edge of a disused
quarry, next to a ghastly man-made lake whose opaque grey
waters, in which I dipped the stone effigies that at that time
in my life I was caught up in creating, seemed like a skin
on the sky, these ritual creations in which I would carve
abstract shapes and symbols, using blunt compasses which
I would purchase at a nearby market that specialised in
silverware and archaic utensils and religious icons (it was a
very Catholic village), these strange signs that would speak
and make themselves known to me (bird souls, I called
them) and that I would then incise into these special stones
with the aid of these blunt compasses, these incantations,
it appears to me now, these obsessive incantatory actions,
which is what masonry is, which is what true stonework is,
at heart, according to Pierre, according to the obscure book
that he self-published and that came to be the only text
that mattered to me, at this point in my life, and which had
the quality of speech which is best heard by the heart, by
the wounded heart, best of all, as if it had been published
expressly for myself, and had lain in wait for me, up until
I was ready for it, up until my heart lay in pieces, in the

past, shattered along with my belief in love as more than
just a word for a season, a term, and not as something that
preserves the lovers, forever, something that raises them up,
beyond all other achievement, which is when I cracked its
code, I believe, as I worked on its first, and still unpublished,
English translation, and what that meant, I think, is that
I was, in a sense, possessed by the spirit of Pierre, by his
marvellous artistic seriousness, by what he said about these
stones, his history of these stones, his tracking of certain
relationships with these stones, it opened a whole new world
to me, one that came to full fruition when I was introduced
to my own Eurydice, my own manifestation of the fixed form
of the female, forgive me, I know that it's not an acceptable
idea these days, though would that I could fix it further,
in stone, after my hero, then mark these bastard words,
I would, my hero whose watery vault I return to now, in
whose paint-grey waters, beneath which the entire world
stands, upside down, and undifferentiated, I dip my dolls, I
almost said, my carvings, I mean, my ritual offerings, and I
line them up, before me, as stones with names, as something
fixed, that has spoken, forever, like an army of emissaries,
to elsewhere, a determined crusade, to where there is no
way, ever, I can ever accompany them.

I must remember you, Flower.

What a beautiful thought I am thinking, when I think of
my ex-lover's thighs, but still I am in tears as I write this.
Is there a name for the space just above the thigh, the
crease that lies just below the pelvis, or for the men who
are haunted by it? I shall call it the Meridian, this valley
of flesh, made anew, as every man is, for its vision; and
those who would recognise the women who have worn this,

most perfect, those who would be as lovers of the lines: Meridians.

Still, if I could capture anything in stone, it would be the vision of my ex-lover, on her back, with her breasts exposed, disarrayed on the bed, disarrayed, I say, and with that I taste it, her hair wild blonde hair, the perfect arc of her eyebrows, the expression on her face, and the Meridian, incised, perfectly, in a single, perfect, gesture; is tastes like this.

There is nothing water longs for more than to be surrendered on the rocks, are the first words of the book I gave a season of my life to translating, a season that resulted in my destitution, in my abandonment, and, some might say, enemies of mine, grudges held along the way, in my temporary insanity.

Is any insanity temporary? Does madness not leak? Not through stone. Not through marble or clay. Not through hard fired earth.

Harder.

I disposed of my father's caul in Durham, dropped it from the bridge into the river that flows past the cathedral, imagined it floating, undrowned, into the sea, and made my way to the cathedral itself, where I pictured all of the wooden fittings in flames and reduced to ashes and only the stone of the cathedral left standing. Stone is stronger than wood, more eternal, I told myself, as I stood before the wooden carvings of the dead Jesus and his mother, both of which were scorched with molten lead, from a fire.

Harder.

In the Whispering Gallery in the dome of St Paul's, I repeated the word cunt in the hope that it might enter the ear of another and cause offence.

Harder.

I allowed my ex-lover to be fucked by other men. I dressed her. I chose the panties she would pull to one side as other men entered her. Sheer animal-print panties. Tiny turquoise bikini bottoms, tight, around the mound of her pussy.

Harder. Harder.

I toured the monasteries and cathedrals of France and wrote my name on every one of them.

Harder.

Is there a pill that can stop these words in my brain?

This is the pill.

Harder.

I should like to call myself Astonished, a Greek name, at the end of my life.

I intend that this book should be as a mausoleum for the two of us, and the state of our bodies, guesswork, now, buried, still entwined in each other, our very bones confused, our skulls fused in some unimaginable cataclysmic attempt at

ultimate union, which is what sculpture is, which is what
these language marks, carved into white by a pressure
in my brain that I know can only find release in the idea
of being caught up in something eternal, something that
stands, as a monument, to the lovers in time, which is what
these words are, then, which is an attempt to perceive the
lineaments of what lies, beneath, this eternal mirror, that
might hold us.

Yet I can't resist telling you she had long blonde hair. I can't
resist the telling of her perfect hourglass figure, I squeeze it
now, in my mind, in the past I hold her tight by the pinch of
her waist and I draw myself inside her again, and again.

I held her, tight, by the waist, as we made love that first
evening, on a chair in this echoing blue metal storage
container, we fucked on our first date, she was overcome,
she said, I was forceful, that was the word she used, a word
I intend to always honour, even when I fail, a word like
grace and chivalry and forceful, and she pulled me into
her and she said to me, harder, harder, and I imagined
us turned to stone, and how beautiful that would be, to be
fixed, at the moment of peak passion, is the most perfect of
monuments.

I can't resist telling you, either, of the way she dressed.
She wore nylons and heels and long flowing dresses. She
wore hoops in her ears and grey, smoky eyeshadow. Her
backside was one of the most voluptuous arses ever to tour
the continent, and everywhere we went I was forced to put
up with catcalls and illicit tonguing, grabbing of the balls
and thrusting, and (of course) the miming of fucking her
from behind. Show me a statue that provokes that kind of

response. Show me the stone that can move like that. I will show you.

At the Cistercian abbey of Trois-Fontaines there was a sense that time had somehow withdrawn all that was not essential to the scene. Windows lay boarded like so many attenuated evolutionary sideroads. The air was dry, and warm, and sibilant; the sound of birds seemed as if piped in; reduced, but not merely, to its effect. You stood on the grass then, the abandoned pavilions behind you, and two trees, in the shape of dark, bristled tongues, spoke up, out of the ground, and tongued the air around you, as I, the jealous lover, hovered, perpetually out of shot. Which allows me to return there. And to watch you, darling, of my sacred manhood, queen, of my past. To watch you walk slowly across the lawn in your heels, as if you were alone with the seeing of yourself. You have a black-and-white shawl around your shoulders, with ripples, like water. You hold a flower in your hand. I will name no other flower. And there is birdsong again. And the light has held its breath, which is what a statue is.

Which is what a statue is. What we mean when we use the word love. Light holding its breath. But letting go, letting go, now; there is the key.

She was in an unhappy relationship when I met her and I was the, what is the word, I feel like there should be a word for the tools you open coffins with, the tools with which you prise open ancient sarcophagi, which is what it felt like, it had that degree of revelation, our first love, compasses, a word like that, para-somethings, incisors, where you crack something that has fixed and stuck, where you crack it open, and that first light: incisive. That first light: gasping, and you feel it yield, until the energy is wordless, and no longer you and I, and you have your fingers in my mouth, and I have grabbed hold of her jaw, strong, and hard, and fixed her beneath me, and we are speaking in breaths, in shallow breaths of my finger on her tongue, pressing down, our skulls, bearing down, on each other, is so close. And we are back, and we are after.

Afterwards, in a strange discomfited glow, I tell her I'm a sculptor. I work in stone, I tell her. I am a monument maker.

I saw her partner in town. Her ex-boyfriend. She had warned me about him. David is a psycho, she said, only she said it Davide. He's a psycho so look out for him, she said. Davide had short blonde hair and wore a leather jacket and looked like shit. I asked her about him. What are you doing sprawled all over my makeshift bed in a rusting shipping container at the bottom of a long-abandoned quarry, I nearly said to her, but I didn't, if this guy is so great? He's so full of himself, she said to me, after I rephrased it. He's so self-centred. Plus, your cock, she said, to be honest, it's about maybe an inch in total bigger than his. I never knew it made such a difference. Is an inch all it takes?

But I was talking about letting go. Pierre's book had been published privately, in an edition of 120 copies, by a connoisseur printer of eccentric architectural works in 1986. And what a year for samizdat architectural works that was. I could list my favourites. But the point is this: the sound of the rain on the roof of my metal encampment. Listen to it. Imagine yourself there.

There is nothing water longs for more than (*other than?*)
to be surrendered on the rocks (*I have given the rendering
of this opening sentence much thought over the years and
I have come to regard it as an essentially untranslatable
statement that masks a gnomic, astrological reference, as
well as, of course, reflecting Pierre's fascination with the lives
of rocks, the being of stones and their firing, at distance, by
the stars themselves, and the relationship between water
and stone, and what came first, but more so, it occurs to me
now, there is the aspect of Pierre's Christian upbringing,
here, in essence, his fascination with Christianity, and his
concept of a sacrificial universe, of all the little deaths that
life requires, and of course the fish, risen up, on land, is the
sign of both evolution and of the secret Christ, returned*).
There is a wanting that expresses itself in (and as) the
elements, to come up against all that they are not. Indeed,
the elements are in a perpetual conference of mutual
deciding (*a polis of elements, as the poet Charles Olson
would have it, and whose influence I acknowledge here, on
my own work, my own unravelling and decoding, though
I can find no trace of Olson in Pierre's reading, in his
notebooks and effects, outside of the recurrence of the phrase
'human universe', the title of an essay written by Olson in
tribute to the Mayan conception of life and cosmos*). What is
soft longs to be hardened, what is spectral dreams of fixed
lineaments and form, what is gaseous here imagines being
pressed into the soft earth by a beautifully carved effigial
slab (*and here Pierre references the infamous two-volume
set* Incised Effigial Slabs, *published by Faber & Faber at,
one imagines, considerable expense, and, surely, with little
hope of recouping their costs, in the year of 1976, and whose
personal copy, complete with detailed marginalia, sits before
me, on the mantelpiece of the room in which I write*). What is

flesh longs to fall, from a height, onto the hard stone floor of a cathedral.

The monastic architecture of France (*and here, I would imagine, Pierre defers to Joan Evans, author of the spellbinding* Monastic Architecture in France, *published by Cambridge in 1964*), as seen from the standpoint of the late twentieth century, seems some of the most bereft of classical buildings, the least occupied of styles, the greatest reminder of futility and pointlessness, the most like a temporary shelter, from time, and from life, in its understated grandeur, in its mute appeal there is a great slowing that generates the feeling, when experienced in the flesh, in the cold, hard, stone, on a sharp autumn morning in the early 1980s, say, with the dew on the grass and the smell of the leaves, burning, somewhere, out of sight, and that particular silence, that monastic silence that is not true silence but rather a return to silence after speech, which can never be true silence, true silence is original, and unworded, this return to silence, then, all around, that the world has ceased in its turning, that it has been temporarily arrested, by a force, raised up, from inside the world, against itself. This is stone, and how it can be set to speak.

Flower, in a cornfield, in the sun, outside the town of Souvigny, where we had gone to see the implacable remains of the Benedictine priory, implacable, I say, but then I think twice, because implacability, even, remains something to be read, as the red tulips on Flower's black-and-white blouse now speak to me and say the word flower, the word flower is carried by women, to be laid down, I think, as she spins around slowly in the sunshine and the pollen is golden in the air.

I want to enter into pure description.

Harder.

I was seized with a mania to create in stone.

Harder.

I want to describe the experience of her.

Harder.

I have named parts of the body and set flags in it as mine, as my own, its hairs, and places. I say the body, but really I mean one body only. The body of my ex-lover. The lips of her labia are felt-grey, mouse-eared. When she opens, she opens like a butterfly. I remember a night, a last night. We had made love and she had called me a wolf. I had held my fingers inside her mouth and tight around her jaw as we came together. Afterwards, she sat on a footstool and displayed her newly shaved pussy to me, her ankles still tight around her ankles, her panties, I mean, still tight, and she opens them, the veil, with her fingers, and she is looking for praise, she is vulnerable and eternal in the same moment, temporal and transcendent, bashful, which is the name of it, and I lean down, I have half pulled up my briefs, and I taste the bright grey of her lips and I taste soft, wet, stone.

I get into a conversation. One night I'm drunk at a party, one of these outdoor French nocturnal parties, and Flower's boyfriend Davide is there, he is wearing motorcycle leathers and with short blonde hair in the dark and he approaches me and we start to talk and he uses the term beef curtains. There is a spatchcocked chicken on the grill and he sticks a prong in it and he says, beef curtains, do you know that one, I had to explain it to my mother the other night, he says, and he laughs, and he winks at me.

Let me tell you the story of my first understanding of the importance of architecture. It happened when I read a story about a sculptor, a stonemason, a worker in basalt, and an author, name of Pierre Melville. There was an article in a newspaper. Pierre had come out of nowhere. His early sculptures had been hailed as the ultimate extension of Gian Lorenzo Bernini's baroque conception (by critics of a modernist, iconoclastic bent, obviously), extrapolating from Bernini's vison of a total work that could be viewed, somehow, as extended in time, as well as in place, and what Pierre had done, these critics argued, was mint a form of sculpture that somehow demonstrated its movement into form, its uncovering, in other words, in time, as well as its simultaneous withdrawal, back, into its point of origin, which Pierre termed its nebula.

And I felt it right then inside me. This word, Nebula. This word, Flower. And this, idea. Because I, myself, felt myself, to be in a constant predicament of becoming and withdrawing. I recognised it. And that night, the night after I read the article, my parents and I were staying at the home of a friend of the family, a holiday home in France, a gloomy place with wooden floors and haunted outbuildings, which is where I chanced upon this article about Pierre, in a magazine that had been discarded by a previous guest, and which I read by candlelight, by the pulse of candlelight, which seemed to double its effect, and as I read it I had the strangest feeling, and I masturbated, I masturbated about the future, set in stone, and all the withdrawing and becoming, up ahead.

In the morning I pointed it out to my father. Papa, I said, that is what my father liked me to call him, he was French on the brain, Papa, I said, would you look at this gentleman who sculpts artworks that retreat all the way back to their origins and he laughed and said, ah-ha, Monsieur Melville, he said. These days he is nothing but a monument maker, he said, and he shrugged. Those words; I shuddered. What do you mean? I asked my father. These days, my father said to me, Pierre is a bourgeois, he said. He is an architect of tombs, he said. Because he sold out. And then he told me the extraordinary story of Pierre's ascension through the art world and his success as an architect and how he had been contacted by an anonymous donor who wrote to say that he wanted to pay a stipend to Pierre for the rest of his life, a considerable stipend, if he would agree to one thing only, one working, was what the anonymous benefactor said, that is the term he used, and that is that I want you to design and build my own tomb, he said, money no object, vision no limit, only I remain anonymous, as does the location of the tomb, which we can work out legally, he said, and afterwards, he said, after the tomb is completed, and I give you ten years, God willing, he said, I will continue to pay you in perpetuity, forever, until the day of your death, but your final act, after signing a non-disclosure agreement, obviously, will be to return, with a select band of family members and friends, and have my body, at the time of my death, placed in your vault, according to your vision. I never want to see it, I never want to discuss the plans. I merely want to sign off on the budget, because I have complete faith in you, he said, this voice said, these words said, on the page, and after I am interred, it said, I want you to collapse the entrance, to bury it without a trace, and to leave me, forgotten, except in the mind of an artist, and his workmen, and a select group of lovers and friends, in the Valley of the Kings, in other words, is what it said.

And there was much speculation. And Pierre was allowed to talk about it in public, there was no clause against that, why not, and so he told people, I am working privately these days, he said, in his own terrible pronunciation that made him sound like an intelligent halfwit, I am engaged in the burial of a living man, he said, on *Pebble Mill at One*, I think he might have said that then, and when the girl asked him why he had taken a job that would remove him from the public eye for so long and what about his career, Angela Rippon it may have been, he simply said, I am captured by it, is what he said, and though Rippon pressed him about what exactly he was captured by, was it the idea, was it the money, was it the opportunity to fix monuments, in secret, still he just sat there, and stayed mum, which led to the rumour that he had gone feudal and that he was just the latest in a long line of clowns who had been flattered into building monuments to temporal power, to mere economic triumph, to game-playing and bullshit and filthy lucre.

Although he is today best known as a sculptor and architect, Pierre Melville began life as a poet. He had published several volumes by the time he was in his early twenties, two of which have been translated into English. One was titled *White Marble*, the other *Lonely Caravan*, but you can forget about ever finding a copy of that one because you have no chance. They were figurative sculptures in text,

was what Pierre said on the back, talking about his poems,
apparently, but who knows how reliable the translation is,
I said to my Flower, when I gifted her a second-hand copy
of *White Marble*, inside of which I had inscribed a pair of
brackets and inside of them my initials (D.K.), who knows
how seriously to take that, I said, it could be some kind
of retrospective anointing of Pierre's earlier works with
everything that we know now, his proclivities, his visions, I
said, the terms themselves, I said, could be approximate, a
mere happenstance of translation or a brazen rewriting of
history, even. But then, I said to her, and I showed her this;
then this, I said:

How, have I been
to Purgatory,
how, have I, in the manner
Of the Saints, which is,
to have gone so far, inside
as to come upon cold
white marble, is to approach,
bright   grey
stone

Then this, I said, and I showed her some more poems and
we kissed and she tongued my lips as I held her by her
slender waist and ate from between her legs and slid her
dress up and drew myself into her again and again until we
collapsed on the filthy sheets as the sun was coming up, all
aglow, I thought, all aglow, which is what blood does, when
it has found its medium. But white marble; white marble
struck me as some kind of final frontier. And so, I set out.

I read some book about how the prerequisites of sculpture were something like mass and balance and motion and outline and detail, something ludicrous like that. Even then, when I was only beginning, when I was only – what's the term? – *feeling my way*, even then I knew that it was about presence, and its lack, about form, and its shadow, about, let's face it, a chasm and a cocoon. Have you ever seen Bernini's *Apollo and Daphne*?

What does it mean to look? And shut your mouth about the gendered gaze for a minute with that claptrap. What does it mean to look, for the first time; do you believe that is possible? If not, whatever do you go to art galleries for? What do you travel to Florence for? What do you fall in love for, over and over again?

First look: what a wonderful look I am looking as I am looking at the woman that I loved. She is filling our car with petrol. She has on patterned tights and aviator shades. Her long blonde hair, her waist. Is there no way to re-see it? We take a picnic, perched up on logs, looking out across a wide field. There are bees in the air and the horizon is lit up like a foundry. She spots a bird, and she names it, and I watch it fly off, as named, by her. Is there no way to re-see it?

What does the myth of Daphne and Apollo mean? It strikes me as this: Daphne (and what a beautiful name that is naming) knows she will be pursued forever, and so she fixes herself, or rather disguises herself, in movement, in agelessly slow movement, in simple matter – almost, but not quite – in order to both elude, and to endlessly bewilder and attract, her would-be god suitor.

Have you ever seen Bernini's tomb for that wretched pope of his? The red marble like wounded flesh or brain stuff, the Fates, singing, standing in for concepts, bracketing the scene, on both sides, and the pope up above; but there, in the middle, is the shining skeleton of Death itself, golden and enfolded in the flesh of the brain, as if the flesh grew bones as its own persecutor, and brain stuff drew all three. But then the bones hold the hourglass in their hands, and Death presents it to us, so.

These are the words that I fantasised my Flower might say to Pierre as he held her on the end of his dick and speared her in bed every night (though by that point whether he was capable of the action of spearing or not is something we'll never know).

I love your big cock, baby.

Harder.

Do me, baby.

Slap my swollen titties.

Feel how wet you've got me.

Make me come, oh make me come.

Give me your juice, baby.

I'm your little slut.

I hope you know I'm a real whore.

Baby, your cock is too big, baby.

Slap my ass while you fuck me.

Slide my panties down, like that.

Finger my mound.

You like my little shaved pussy, I did it for you.

It's like an iron bar, baby, it's like a fucking, iron, bar.

These are the course notes for the first semester in sculpture I will never teach.

Everything is empty and insincere. These are the words written over the collapsed tomb of a dead man, which is the state of my body, since I lost my Flower, forever. This is the strength of my antipathy towards love, which betrayed me, you, love, I say to the stone that promised me, you are a betrayer, even as I see, in my touching, of cold white marble, the lineaments of desire are longing, there, in stone, longing to be uncovered, wanton, to be disrobed, obedient to the most disobedient impulse as if it were fused, in every rock itself, as if, in the base matter of the earth, in every grain of sand, the eternal relationship, fixed, as surely as the cross.

Stonemason, carve your stone. There is no such thing as inanimate matter.

And now I can hear her writing the farewell letter in my head, the farewell letter that she never wrote, because there was no farewell letter, and yet, why can I hear it, why is its

tone so implacable, where is the inflection, it reads like a
chapter from The Bible, lifeless, you think, but here is all
of life, you think, again, as she explains to you the nature
of change, as if either of the two of you were in any way
unfamiliar with the nature of change, and yet, to speak it,
it is heartbreaking, to admit that we are not permanent,
you and I, well, it's further than I can go, and I prefer to
be press-ganged to those ends, and never to willingly offer
myself up, and so I am replying, in my mind, in my mind
I am the one writing the sad farewell letter, now, and I'm
saying, you make me anxious and you make me doubt, you
make me believe this whole world is a battlefield, you make
me feel like I have to play the game when really, now, at
this age, I have no heart for it, and then I recall Pierre,
spearing you, and eliciting those words, in my head, and I
feel like a wounded animal, that has stumbled, and that will
struggle to regain its feet.

Pierre and I took the car, a rusty old turquoise Morris
Minor, in the rain, all the way from Linlithgow, where we
were staying, to visit Durham Cathedral. Why were we in
Linlithgow? I honestly can't recall; the palace, perhaps, but
why? There was a lovely bookshop there, and a tea room by
the canal, and a house, up high stone steps, that slept two,
if one of us slept on the couch, which was me, and the only
thing I remember now about that visit, this strange annex
in my life, is that I took down the net curtains from the
window and wrapped them around me on the couch in place
of a duvet so that now I remember that trip as wearing a
chrysalis or a shroud.

The floor had rusted through his car. We could see the road
beneath us as we sped.

The title of Pierre's book, in my translation, is *Full Length Mirror*. He never commented on the quality of the translation at all and, to be honest, there wasn't a huge amount of text to speak of, outside of the odd, offbeat introduction, which is what struck me so powerfully in the first place, and which took me a season to translate, an introduction that somehow sets you up to read the pictures as a form of unfolding autobiography, even when they contain nothing but stone and tree and sky, but most especially the enigmatic photographs of monastic architecture that feature himself, his chic 1970s car, and a ghostly, elegant female, who in one picture appears to expose her breasts to the cameraman. But who was the cameraman? He remains uncredited and unfound. Though there are a few stories. Like this one.

Pierre and his lover Hildegard are driving from Paris to view the Benedictine nunnery of Saint-Désir at Lisieux, which features, according to my translation of *Full Length Mirror*, 'a carving that shows the birth of the infant Jesus, as a fully formed adult, in the outspillage of the menses of his mother'.

On the road they pick up a hitch-hiker. In one of the shots of the nunnery, it is true, there is the shadow of a finger to the left of the viewfinder. He has run away. The hitch-hiker. Not from a home or from a prison or a press-gang situation, but from a marriage. Do me a favour, this dark-skinned stranger says to them, from the back seat of the car, from somewhere barely imaginable, but almost imaginable, now, thanks to this *Full Length Mirror*; make love tonight, he says. And we can imagine Pierre, or his partner, looking in the rear-view mirror right then.

They pull up at the nunnery. They have themselves photographed beneath the outspilling menses by this hitch-hiker guy. I have that photograph. It's a Polaroid. Hildegard is wearing a long yellow dress with a large belt and with her hair in a svelte blonde bob. You can pick out the nipples on her small tits through the cloth of her top. She wears a neckerchief like an air stewardess or an artist's muse would.

But he said to me, on the way to Durham, the one thing he said to me about the translation: *Full Length Mirror*, really? he said. I said to him, what, so what would be a truer equivalent? And he said, *Delicate Prism*, *Deep Ocean of Thought*, and then he said: *Monument Maker*.

I called my Flower from the road, from a call box by the bridge. I love you and want to be with you and all I need to know is that you are the centre, that holds, in my life. Then I stopped talking and I waited. *I waited till dreams like my heart lay all broken.* That's how I feel, she said, but they weren't the same words that I had spoken, she had not mouthed the sentiment that I had offered her, she had not mirrored me in stone. And I thought of a tomb, with a collapsed entrance, that no one, again, will ever see.

We stood in front of the figure of the Christ and his mother, carved from trees, in the vestibule of Durham Cathedral. Wood? Wood is of no interest to us, I thought, why has Pierre stopped, why is he stooped over these two wooden figures, these husks. The pair were spattered with metal, as if the lead in the roof had melted on them during an air attack by the Nazis. I thought of the longing of the elements to be anything but what they are, and I saw the love between Christ and his mother. But I felt good about the wounding. Something of Christ melting under the assault of the Nazis, his actual skin spattered, even though he was nothing but a rotten old tree, made me feel hot, and horny, and real.

I am addressing the ghost of my love, which is a husk now, too. My love, I say, and what a beautiful say I am saying when I am saying what it is that I say. I am speaking to the beyond, now. I would like to tell it something of my love because I know now that it cares. And that is why it remains, perpetually, just out of reach. I call it love, and I stand by that. I fix it: here. Why do you insist on pursuit? But that is too much. I no more intend to unmask it than I would remove all of your clothes, in love, lover. I will keep the panties on, even as they are tight around your ankles, and I will draw them as lines, written, into stone.

In Durham we sat in a bar at Halloween and Pierre drank one beer after another before falling down and cursing everyone else in the place. I succeeded in getting him outside, where he announced to the cathedral and the air, and the shadow passing on the river below, and the moon, obviously, as well as random passers-by, that he wished to be rid of this woman for life, he said, and he gnashed his teeth and swung his fists at the air, what woman, and I thought is it Hildegard, Hildegard, it must be.

The moon shone deep into the waters, birds rose up like words, or like lonely letters, gathering, together, in love, which is what words is, above a river, in Durham, a river I drowned my own father in, and why? Because I felt the need of the growing of a new father, I said, the time has come, I said to myself, and even though it was a drunken thought

I gave it to you, the beyond, I gave thought and agency and urge to you, by which I mean I gave spelling to you, and you worded, in my head, what was to be done, what was the gratuitous drowning of the father, only this time, as my own murder of him, as I threw the little sewn pouch that contained his caul into the river below.

If I were to describe the interior of the Benedictine abbey of Le Bec-Hellouin, founded in 1034 (can you imagine such a thing, what architects that we are unable even to dream), then I would describe it as resembling the interior of a pink, white, shell, the kind you would find on the beach, once, long ago, in the past, or of an echoing swimming pool, drained, and ornate, that you visited once, as a child, and that now is bereft, forever, because of that visit, or as an absence, a sealing-off, and a jealous secreting, of space, which is what I should have done with you, honey. That's what the caption reads, beneath the photograph, in my own, unpublished, translation.

There is a car parked up, against the wall. The exterior is a poker face. God's face is a poker face, it says, but inside, the pool, the pink light, the soft reflections, the staircase to the cells, with seaweed, swaying, in the concrete breeze. A priest, his robes rippled, in motion, is caught in the light.

Here's a story I remember that always bugged me. It really got to me that back when Pierre had first come on the scene, my Flower described him as implacable. He's implacable, she said, and she shook her head, after a dinner party that had gone awry where we had invited Pierre along with what I felt was the central cabal of aesthetes of stone, the Meridians, I named us, in my head, and there had been

much drinking and comparing of historical minutiae when
Pierre appeared from the bedroom, in a state of inebriation,
inexplicably dressed in a white tracksuit with green trims,
and challenged any one of these outmoded bastards, is what
he said, because you know nothing about love, he said,
and he said to them, I intend to take off into the air, all
the while wearing a green-and-white sweatband too, and
aviator shades, aviator shades that were tied to his ears
with elastic bands, and he said, do as I do, not as I say, he
said, and he pressed play on a cassette recorder, and this
music came out, this pop music, this rap music, and then
he laughed, as if of course that was impossible, write books
like me, impossible, make stone speak like me, impossible,
rise up into the air like me, impossible, second-guess my
taste in music, impossible, steal the love of my life from me,
completely, fucking, impossible, as he ran across the room as
fast as he could and proceeded to run up the side of the wall,
back-flipping just before the ceiling and spinning round
and landing, miraculously, in a perfect circle, on his feet.
Can any of you relics do that? he said. And everyone was
agog. Aghast. And it was no longer about sculpture; it was
sculpture itself. And then my Flower turned to me and she
said, wow, he is completely implacable, and I said to myself,
no, even my own reading of this is not real. Which is the
story of monasticism.

And there they are: the coloured silhouettes of my ex-lover
and my mentor, against the horizon, which is blue, with
white cliffs, at the bottom of the garden, and the breeze
almost upsets the scene but rather, now, serves to bring it
to life. Hold on to your hat, Pierre; goodbye my sweet love,
Flower!

And hello you, you whom I am writing for and for whom
I have called it stone, I have called it love, I have called
it nothingness and void, I have called it baby, too, but for
whom, for whom.

The smell of Shake n' Vac in a hotel room in Durham.
A toilet freshener with a thick green gel in it. Toilets. I
had taken to observing toilets on the road with Pierre.
Sometimes I would view these cathedrals, these monasteries
and cemeteries, stretching off, as having less meaning
than a WC with flecks of damp like the upturned breast
of a thrush, still beating, in the corner of a white, plastic,
shower. Well now, already, are these demon spores not so
bold in their construction, not so specific in their place, as
any manor house or castle or strange frightened bird took
fright? Plus they smell the same.

Dampness. And we fall asleep, me on the couch, as usual,
Pierre propped up on a pillow, on top of the bed, in a black
Japanese kimono, and the television says (we allowed
ourselves television on the road, Pierre and I, but never
at home) 'the true mark of a man' and it shows a coloured
target and three arrows hit it and smoke comes up and a
man emerges with no top on who has been throwing darts,
in a pub, topless. The mark of a man, Pierre says, and he
rolls it, in his throat, like a thrush himself, as if he were
no man whatsoever, so removed from man, even, that he is
capable of speaking him perfectly; the mark of a man, he
burrs, as he looks over his glasses, for that is the sound, as
he growls it, as he looks up from his book, he rolls it there,
like an angel that weighs nothing at all (very few angels
are light as air, talk to a sculptor), the mark of a man, he
gargles, I suppose he does, he gargles, that makes sense too,

in the context of his sounding: the mark of a man, he says, is persistence.

There was a piece of Pierre's, a photograph in his book, on his travels, that he had painted on glass and that consisted of five words, written in a rippling orange text, on a sheet of frosted glass. Thank You For Your Persistence, he had written, and he had laid it outside an old abandoned nunnery in Normandy as some kind of offering or love letter – what's the difference, really – and had walked away and let the sun shine through it until some teen kicked it straight through the face and smashed it, or some dilettante stole it, or some process of corroding and denegration (is that a word) drew it back down into the earth, in pieces. But still it persisted, was his point, and, still, he was grateful for it. Everything they teach you about art is wrong, I said, is misleading, when I first saw it.

Where the vines have been removed up the side of the Benedictine abbey of Notre-Dame, Bernay, whose monastic buildings date from the seventeenth century, there remain the tracings, like veins, over veins, of an invisible musculature, just as the abbey itself is the temporary holding structure for the invisible point of power that slows the past and the future, not to abeyance, but to a form of eternal rose garden.

The point to locate in this, and this is Pierre writing still: the point to locate would be the first instance of a smile in sculpture, the first evidence of a moving past the monument as a marking of death or an opening to a dark, sonorous beyond, the first instance of a smirk, even, let's say, a funny face, and of course they bring up Egypt, they bring

up Egypt every time, the high art of Thanatos is Egyptian
in bearing, they say, before you can so much as protest, but
look at those sarcophagi in the British Museum, you would
respond, hopefully, if you could get a word in edgewise, go
spend a weekday afternoon with them, you'd say, although
preferably not a Friday or a Thursday even, for that matter,
you'd be foolish not to add, a wet, drizzly Tuesday afternoon,
I would say, is perfect, you would say, and not hard to
arrange, obviously, unless you're a working stiff, in that case
God help you, but look at those sarcophagi when you next
get the chance, is what you would suggest, I imagine, in my
mind, now, and tell me, truly, you would demand, if you
cannot detect the hint of a smirk on those cartoon faces that
are the cocoon of the dead, and that seem to offer the first
glimpse, perhaps, of the dawning realisation that humanity
itself is *in on the game from the beginning.*

Implacable. Flower would call them implacable.

GISLEBERTUS HOC FECIT: at the Cathedral of Saint
Lazarus in Autun the sculptor Gislebertus emerges from
the dark, sonorous beyond. His tympanum features a Christ
that has worn two faces and none at all in an experiment
with time that is the equal of the first animated cartoons.
No one in the age of Gislebertus, which is the age of the
twelfth century, which is the age of the pharaonic kings,
which is the age of the entrance of the Christ child into time,
would dare to depict a Christ without a head, a position
reserved for John the Baptist for a great and secret reason,
but first of all we must understand the position from which
both the great cathedrals and the great pyramids were
intended to be experienced, and that is from the inside out,
the dead pharaoh is the experiencer of the architecture and

the nebula at the heart of its schematic, the pyramid, then, the high cathedral towers, serving to connect him to the infinite, just as the outsides of cathedrals are fortresses, really, that mimic the tomb of the flesh – that sound the tomb of the song, more properly – and that contain the universe, as seen from inside out, inside them, which would speak, if you were an initiate, in stone, that truly there is no God outside of the centre, and that the centre is everywhere, inside, and so: Gislebertus.

He gives the removal of Christ's head – and his ability to grow a new one, in imagination, in stone – he gives it, it is given, more precisely, to time. In the hands of Gislebertus time, itself, has become Monument Maker, even as it always was, even as his Christ is rendered as quite flat, as pancaked, as rising up from the elements, palms open, arms pressed to his sides, as coming through stone, from the interior of the earth, and now, suddenly, during the unveiling of the tympanum of the west doorway, which is the name of a ritual that took place in time, itself, after it had been covered over, the tympanum, during the era that was not of the Christ child's entrance into time, and that considered reflection, itself, as profane, it was revealed that Christ's face had been defiled, over time, removed, in the past, and been so damaged, in its passing, so that his eyes – Christ's eyes! – were now the multiform eyes of mineral and crystal, of death, compacted, to the incendiary point of flint, which meant that now his eyes glistened even more, his multiform eyes are of the rock itself and are interior, and enterable-into, is the kingdom of heaven, kind lover Flower who I would return to stone.

And beneath his feet, trodden down and given life anew,
is a mocking sinner, whose head is forever being torn from
his shoulders by monstrous hands, even as his fellows
contort and torment themselves with language, with the
body as signs, and the sinner knows, because he has fallen
into the pit called responsibility, that his fate lies at the
centre, and that there is no joke between Christ and what
he came to damn, which is the removal of the head, and its
replacement, in time, again and again, forever.

This is a song I made up, this is a song I made up:

Flower/Flower
Spring and Autumn/Winter and Summer
January/Aquarius/February/Pisces truelove
March/Aries/April/Taurus
May/Gemini
Annus
Cancer
June/Leo/July/Virgo
August
Libra/September/Scorpio/October/Sagittarius
November/Capricornus/December
Flower/Flower

What is the spell that is set by the abandoned monastic
architecture of France? Picture the dust in the air, the
miraculous dust suspended in the air, illuminated in a shaft
of cold, soft light. Feathers on the breath of God.

The great monasteries present one of the most dramatic
architectural annexings of reality. Annexing, that is, the
reality of God in his silent speech from the unreality of the

profane world, intent on mixing it up with tongues, outside.
This is art not for entertaining.

The abandoned monasteries of France – abandoned, again
and again – present a secret network set on assassinating
modernism and effecting a return to timelessness. The
abandoned monastic architecture of France is frozen in
silence, even when it has been repurposed, even when it
is filled with dancing revellers, or mutinous soldiers, or
accountancy firms, or taxi companies. Then this silent
network is silenter still. These buildings which, like the
pyramids, were set in order to establish a channel, a silent
channel, in and out of time. I Am a Silent Channel in Time.

Harder.

The one truly pure work of God-comprehension, of sacred
visioning, of transcendent creation in modern painting, is
that of Cecilia Giménez's 'failed' and much-ridiculed 2012
restoration of *Ecce Homo*, an awful 1930s fresco of Jesus
Christ at his most simple-minded, in Borja, Spain. Through
vision and belief and – not naivety, but innocence, let's (dare
we?) say, true innocence, which is the opposite of naivety,
she rendered Christ unreal for the first time in how many
centuries. Which is to foster Christ, in time.

Harder: she was possessed by Christ himself and was made
to paint him as divine, his features horrored, the angle of
his face occult, dimensional, in – and out of – time. This is
the great bending force that Logos enters the world with.
Bending. Reality-defying. Artlessly so. Yet how could anyone
laugh? How could anyone resist a shudder, at the broken
neck, at the mouth that is up in smoke and ectoplasmic? At

the eyes no longer rolled back in his head like a sham act for
his father or a frigid suburban housewife's idea of ecstasy?
Rather, they look to you, or almost, the eyes. One eye, the
left eye – Christ's left eye – looks behind you and over your
shoulder and he sees something that *is not himself* there.

Harder.

Otherwise fuck painting.

Harder.

Why this interest in mausoleums, in monastic architecture,
in tombs, and I say: for I am over the hill, my friend, for
I am lying in state, and moving closer to silence. And the
work of this man, my mentor, I call him so, now, working to
entomb another man through the twilight of his own dotage,
what were the chances, and I came to realise it was I, too,
who had come to be buried, it was my life, and love, he stuck
a headstone on and dynamited, it was all of these churches
that pointed straight to galactic centre, and that we spent
a summer touring, a summer out of time, is how it seems
to me now, now that everything is a counting down, these
churches that stood in for the state of my body, as surprised,
and betrayed, as any stone sarcophagus, by the onset of age,
by the disfiguring of death, by the absence, once more, of the
answer to a woman's body in my own, which is the saddest
thing, cathedral, I say, which is the saddest thing, tomb, at
the Cathedral of Chartres, your own stones so careless of
time as to betray an intuition that back of time, that in the
back there, friend, there is a stone of stones, a love of love,
a remembering of remembering, which in the voice of the
stones themselves is a Final Judgement.

You, on the grass, I must not name you, Flower, we
picnicked on the grass and afterwards we walked the
streets of the old town. Rumfles, your rumfled skirt, what a
word, these rumfles, the folds and creases that do more to
reveal your leg than any disrobing might, and that religious
statuary could never give up on, even after the age of the
perfect nude, which was the perfect Greek, even then the
flesh itself was sweeter in its hiding, in its intimating
in drapery, just as the Holy Ghost needs a white sheet
with holes and the silent interior of a monastery needs
its cloisters, the sacred is something that we must adorn,
ourselves, as it is revealed: your thighs, rumfled, in your
summer dress.

And afterwards, that evening, we had dinner on the deck of
La Vanne Rouge, in Montigny, as the sun was going down,
blood-orange, and immense, as if it were the mere sign of the
sun, and had taken to play, its duties so light, and immense,
to bring to our eyes an intimation of something that was not
itself, in its coming forth by day the sun is aware of itself
as creator, lover, as you and I, its witnesses on that holy
evening of long ago, and the dogs, the stray dogs of the area,
do you remember, they seemed to appear as if from nowhere
and to assemble on the deck, sat there, staring into the same
sun, in silence, and me thinking, what does the sun appear
to a dog, but really, why does the sun appear to a dog, and I
still have the menu from that night and I have underlined –
and initialled – the dishes we had that night and I will read
it to you now, that night, as it is written, in stone:

Le foie gras, mi-cuit, chutney aux pommes acidulées Granny
Smith et pain brioché toasté (D.K.)

Le maquereau, gnocchi de patate douce, mousseline
d'haricots blancs, beurre blanc aux œufs de poissons (F.F.)

Les coquilles Saint Jacques, lard, mousseline de butternut,
jambon espagnol, coulis d'oseille (D.K.)

L'épaule d'agneau confite, panisse, tagliatelles de courgettes,
sauce vierge, caviar d'aubergines (F.F.)

Le crumble d'hiver, pommes, pruneaux, glace caramel (D.K.)

La sphère au chocolat, façon profiteroles, glace vanille,
choux garnis de crème pâtissière, Chantilly (F.F.)

Where is the wine from that night? Where are the coffees
and the cigarettes smoked? They are extinguished, my
friend. This is Chartres Cathedral.

2. CATHEDRAL OF SAINT LAZARUS OF AUTUN

I have taken Viagra and I await its onset.

Harder.

Viagra always gives me wind, it makes me burp and it
makes me dizzy too, all this blood, flowing, but still, I do it
for recreation, in these final years I do not even masturbate
with it, instead I take a pill, a mere 50g one – you may
have no fears of Priapus – and I write on it, I write with the
memory of my schlong (another favourite word: my schlong,
causes rumfles, in my trousers) as it once was, I write a
paean to my schlong in the medieval architecture of France
and in the memory of a summer, through the memory of a
summer, through the memory of a summer, which is like
the feel of my schlong, now, through the material of my
pants, you call them, Americans, through the material of my
slacks, thank you, and the memory of an erection, through
the memory of an erection, through the memory of an
erection, through my slacks, is where I am writing from, is
a cathedral in France dedicated to the man who rose again,
whose dead member walked, because Christ made it so;
make it so, Christ, for what we long for is corporeal form,

what we long for is schlongs forever; promise us our schlongs and we shall fly to heaven on them, and already, see, the Viagra is kicking in, and I achieve a strange breathlessness, and a need to pass wind, and a constriction, in my chest, and an intimation of that old power, that imperative: captain, of my heart, make rumfles, in my trousers.

Yet the source of the Nile remains a mystery. Neither a thought in my head nor a hand on my schlong may restore it, even as, once, both sources fed it and fed of it. I am no longer stone.

Who rolled away the stone? Christ did, presumably, or a secret player, unknown to history, who was instrumental – by accident or design, who knows – in the resurrection of Our Saviour. 'Stones in My Passway', who wrote that again? Christ, presumably. Or a secret hand. Does God operate in man or does God operate in man through Jesus Christ? Remind me of what the difference is, will you, Cathedral at Autun, of the Risen Saint Lazarus. Remind me again.

And now I've got the sniffles.

Jesus was the one to roll away the stone from Lazarus's tomb. Jesus wept, did you know, which phrase appears in John alongside our Lazarus, and is the shortest verse that The Bible would ever be divided into, which means that the atomic core of The Bible, its smallest indivisible whole, is Jesus wept. And he wept because he was *taking the blame*. Lazarus's household was up in arms, claiming that had Jesus dropped by even a few days earlier, then Lazarus would not at this moment be lying dead behind a boulder in a cave. And Jesus wept. He wept to see the weeping of those around him whose weeping was the cause of his weeping. Jesus wept is crystalline, is smallest stone, is indivisible. He will rise again, Jesus tells them, through the tears. And everyone is like, yeah, yeah, whatever, we know, he will live on in heaven with your dad but still he is dead right here. And that's when Jesus realises: heaven is not consolation enough. Heaven is not consolation enough for weeping on weeping. Jesus wept is the atomic pain at the centre of the world. I will unseal the stone, he says. Jesus says. I will roll it away, he says. Why? To expose a dead man who has risen, already, on the other side? Jesus wept because he was about to do something that would expose himself and his own powers, but also: that he, too, remained under the spell of the father, and even his own death, the sacrifice of his own life, would never be enough to atone for the truth that he has lied, the truth that he has betrayed, which is that eternal life is here and now a reality on earth *if God bids it so*. But he does not bid it so. God wishes for us to die, forever. Just as he wishes us to be born, too. Terrible father and mother are you, God, is the next smallest verse of The Bible, more atomic still, for Kabbalists, really, rather than for lay readers, which is what cathedrals are, texts for Kabbalists, only but where you read the word texts as points of ingress, as a lettered arch which you pass through; Gislebertus hoc fecit.

Gislebertus made this, reads the tympanum of the Cathedral of Saint Lazarus of Autun. This is man, taking the blame away from Christ, for the first time. But this is man in the spell of the father, who, for us, is Christ Jesus and not his dad. And we weep at the funerals of our friends and family and lovers because we have sworn not to do a thing about them, we have accepted the rules of the game,

which are birth and death, we are complicit and we weep
when we hear of poor Lazarus, still living if not for us, but
then, like Christ himself, like Pierre, who would bury a man
in the tomb of his own creation just so that we may, one day,
roll away the stone and see him rise, we turn to our own
spells, and we look to stone, we look to the elements of the
earth and we take them in our hands and we revivify them,
and in their revivifying we admit that we knew, all along,
that in the dross of existence lay its salvation, that in the
making-magic of time we may reverse, or draw forward,
all of the forces that are ours by inheritance and invention,
of birth and death that would make of us, too, monument
maker.

But Rilke says that Jesus was disgusted by the task. That
Jesus felt himself reduced to some mere sideshow magician
in his raising of the dead. But Rilke has a tendency to feel
too sorry for Jesus. I doubt that Jesus was that squeamish.
Rather, it would suggest to me that Jesus realised that
he had done life, itself, a disservice, that the mocking,
really, was by death, of life, because the Fall, if we care
to recall, is described as being precipitated by a great act
of disobedience. And this was Christ's. He was most truly
human when he raised the dead, when he grew sentimental
about a story, and began writing what we would refer to,
today, as fan fiction. A world where the son of God has to
reanimate the dead – cut down, by his father, at their time
– is a less than perfect world. In doing service to mankind,
Jesus has risen hell. Even Martha, present at the graveside,
protested that Lazarus's corpse, surely, by this time, would
stink.

In Autun, Gislebertus has risen Christ in stone so that there will be no stink.

Now I'm burping. Viagra makes me burp. Hold on.

If you could come back from the dead for one night only, what would you do? That's the sort of stuff that was in Christ's head right then, you can bet. What would you do? Probably go back and apologise, am I right? No one likes to think of Christ as apologising. Why? Because he was in on it from the beginning, possibly. If even Christ is apologising, then the entire game is a bogey. But isn't that what the raising of Lazarus is? A moment of weakness. A sort of making it up to humanity. A slip-up, a consolation prize, but also the revelation that it *didn't have to be this way*. That god-powers could turn it around. But also a demonstration of the tremendous guilt that Christ has had to take on. Nietzsche was all wrong about guilt but don't get me started. Brave Christ came back to apologise so that we don't have to. But still some of us have to. So some of us commit to resurrecting forever. Zarathustra. Monument Maker.

Beneath the words Gislebertus hoc fecit there is an angel carved in stone who separates the just and the unjust before the throne of Christ Pantocrator, revealed, truly, as ruler of this world. Shamefacedly so. I stand in stone, it says, I refuse forgiveness. I stand, to be judged.

Judge me:

Words I used as a young lecturer in art history at a provincial college for a single summer, in the Scottish

Borders, girls only, where I stayed on a campsite, in a one-man caravan, overlooking the sea:

Swollen

Tumescent

Cakehole

Slit

Phallic

Fertile

Lingerie

Thighs

Dominating

Supplicant

Adorning

Free-for-all

No rules

My place

Harder

Boyhood is the most beautiful word in the English language. Christ that I could raise it again.

And here it goes. Rumfles.

I gained my first appreciation for the architecture of the past from summers spent exploring the network of abandoned quarries that surrounded the quiet village I grew up in. Scale was what wowed me, at first. The high metal ladders, rusting in the sun, caged in and claustrophobic as you scaled the sides of these huge silos, their terrible mouths filled with sand and stood up above the cliffs, and the town, and the tower blocks, stretching off.

As boys we would dare to jump into the silos, fearless, just about, of being swallowed by the sand forever. But more than churches, the rotting industrial architecture of the North was what made me first look up, and in terror, too, because scale was liable to bring on feelings of terror and insignificance in me, too, an anxious vertigo, me stood at their feet, terror, a nauseating dizziness, me, at the foot of all of this set to rot, this scale, set to dwarf me, just as huge ships, and oil rigs at sea, their feet in who knows what ink-black horrors, make me shudder, still, and I would think, for instance, how do you build a crane without a crane, how do you sink a mile-long concrete girth into the base of the sea except from a mile-long concrete girth sunk to the base of the sea; how to build bridges without bridges? This is what scale will do to you. There is a point where it overwhelms the sense and gridlocks the brain. Stood there, at the top of these leaning metal silos, leaning, like flowers towards the sun, my eyes refused to take it all in, to step back and experience it as, what do they call it, panorama.

The details, Flower, I must tell of the details. From up here, now, with cock pills and perspective.

Can I summon you in stone and still not name you? I used to dream of a mausoleum made up of books, of walling myself in on all sides with words, but I read myself out of it. I read myself through books and all the way out the other side, where life was waiting, only life never waits, and what I thought I had come to, then, had already fled the scene, and I turn, now, to art to be cured, to statuary to cure me, to cure me as Pierre cured himself, I have cured myself of art, he said, and how? How had he done this? By exhausting where the greatest art was, which is France, by touring through France, by plotting its cathedrals and nunneries and religious architecture, and writing his name on every one of them.

Of course it is France where this epiphany takes place, of course in the land of romance, land of the end of summer, land of the benediction of beautiful girls with tan lines in the summertime, of course it is France, of course there are glimpses, of course, there are tracings elsewhere, in England, and in Scotland, even there, in Spain, on the thin bony shoulders of girls in bikini tops too, as it is in Greece, as it is in Rome, and in remnants of Byzantium in the now-East, of course, we mustn't forget the Byzantines, but then how could we, as they have become so obvious, so glaringly otherworldly, that they exist now merely as shorthand, at best as 'the past', but not as the sacred-in-itself, history won't shut up about them, dull, narcissistic, secular history, which is where Christ comes in, Christ enters history, as a word, to cure us of words, and to enable us to look outside and to see something that *is not us*.

Flower, that is not us. In the summer of 1993. At the cathedral in Autun. You were dressed in heels and with a short summer dress and with a black leather jacket which you wore over your shoulders, we hunched in an alcove outside the cathedral and kissed in the sudden storm that had come on and that had emptied the cathedral, sending everyone running outside to witness the scudding clouds shoot over its slanted roofs, heaven is no mirror, I thought then, no mirror to the wet roofs, no reflector, to kiss in the sudden storm is not to double heaven, I say to you now, to kiss in the sudden storm is to make monument. Gradually, I am working my way out of art.

Harder.

Marmoutier. Fleury. Saint-Sauveur. Notre-Dame de Dole. Trinité de Vendôme. These are beautiful words in the throat, wondrous places in the mind, the Congrégation Gallicane des Exempts, they called them, spells that would desecularise the world. And now that they are abandoned, many of them, and bereft, so many more, but still, there is that too, forever, in their place, that feel of an absence, of an opening, stopped up and abandoned, as an old tunnel or the path through an overgrown wood or the silent realms of a fairy-tale castle, only one that looks onto something that *no longer goes by a name.*

The repurposed monasteries of France are a vast network of precipices, then, or piers, let's say, crazy wonder piers out into the clouds, and fog, and their legs running down into who knows what bottom of the world, bridges without bridges, and then . . . language stops; we say words like Marmoutier, we say Fleury, Flowery, to prevent us from

falling, but still, to bring us to the cliffs, all the same,
Flower, that is not us.

I threw my father into the water where he could not be
drowned. I tossed his caul into the river. If you are born
with a lucky cap – a transparent shroud that grows from the
crown of your head – then sailors believe you will never die
by drowning. At one time there was a trade in cauls. People
would advertise theirs for sale in the classifieds, sailors
would pay over the odds, families would divide the cauls up
after death and secrete them on their person, traditionally
in a hand-sewn pouch with the first initial of their name on
it in black thread, which is what mine read, D, and inside,
a parachute, to the bottom of the ocean, and back again,
maybe. I threw it away in rage and tears and confusion,
from the bridge beneath Durham Cathedral, because a
voice told me to, a voice that spoke in terms that were
taunting and daring but also deep, and right, though
unsentimental and *cold as stone*. Dispose of your father,
it said. Make a symbol of his death. And see if the old folk
tales are true. And he came back. Of course, he came back.
He came back, and he tempted my lover from me and was
every man around me a danger. My sweet Papa.

I saw her. I saw my Flower through a window at the party.

She has her nylons and her panties pulled down round
her ankles, her skirt up round her waist. She is pressed to
the wall. I write it like this, as if it is now, as I call myself
Monument Maker. Davide is behind her. He hasn't bothered
to pull his trousers down. He has entered her through the
zip of his fly. Something about this detail makes my heart
drop inside me, and my balls sing. It is a manly thing, to live

through the humiliations of a lover. You too, Father. I said
nothing.

The moon too, Father, is made out of stone, and suspended.

Just now. Just now I am sitting in the front window of
the house we stayed in that summer, you and I, the house
we shared with artists and poets for a single summer. I
doubt if you remember this. Just now I am writing. Do you
remember? I am writing this as I can hear you singing in
the other room. I can hear the sound of the dishes in the
sink. The splash of water. The sound of your spirit, which at
the time I could never have brought myself to say, that your
song, that you singing in the kitchen was the sound of your
spirit, then, because, even then, we were already estranged,
even then I held you, at a distance, which is what time did
to us, you could argue, was what drove me to this, this love
affair in stone, which is your voice now, the sound of your
footsteps as you enter the room and walk towards me, your
dress in billows behind you, it's the dress you bought with
your birthday money, and we embrace and here it is, do you
remember, honey, your birthday, just now? And the light,
through the slats in the window, as I sit here, now.

Is there an interior life? The Lord commands that we
become as living stones. Because there is no interior
monument. I read a story in the newspaper, by a
psychologist, on the nature of consciousness. There is no
interior life, he maintained. By which he meant, there is
no body of consciousness, there is no ever-present lagoon,
flesh, carnal, in which our thoughts and our memories and
our feelings could mingle as in a body of water, the Red
Sea, the Black Sea, no, no ocean for us, no depths to plumb,

but moments, instead. Everything, in a moment, and then forever, gone again.

Have you ever sat through a performance of that idiotic old fart Stainer's *Crucifixion*? It is complete tripe. But wait. Wait. I feel that I am here to make an argument for the presence of the sacred in what seems most stone and alien and unyielding to soft touch.

Is this the meaning of the resurrection, I ask myself, as the choir comes in, His Royal Banner held high by a woman with a twisted spine and a contorted neck and an involuntary spasm who obviously – God be with her – cannot sing. Little sparrow, why can't you sing? For I was crushed between the fingers of the Lord, my Lord, my little larynx was held tight, and stopped, it says. And reopened, too, it says, again.

The choir is monotonous, incredible. There is one voice, and there is many. The words are simple, uncanny. Lift up! But who is lifting? Lay down! But who is laying? In front of me a young black woman shifts in her seat. An old man falls to his knees in a pew across the way. How will he rise? How will he regain his composure? The mystery of the divine humiliation, the little sparrow sings in a voice that cannot sing, by God. Jesus, you were less than flesh, and left us stone, in your memory. I remember, too, when my cock would get hard at such things. I left them in your memory, stone, now flesh.

Jesus was a corpulent Scoutmaster; fuck you and why not. Why not. You call your heroes as in Che Guevara. My hero is a corpulent Scoutmaster why not. This is the first lesson of churchgoing. I adore thee, I adore thee, is the first lesson. I adore thee, fat vicar of the past, you there, too, with your prayer book and your double chin, you too, sweetie, dark-haired sweetie on the choir to the left, your sexy librarian glasses, the way the light of the cathedral – they call them shafts – teases the shadow of your cheekbone, and you, of course, bird with a broken larynx, as you brush your hair aside, your barbed-wire hair, I have watched you do that at least ten times already, your fat body, pulled back, not by gravity but by God as an archer, the mystery of the divine humiliation, which is where the congregation all stand, and say, God gave way to death, God gave way to his own idea, and submitted to it, in order that it might say I adore thee, a God so lacking in love, I love you so, like my father, he, too, so lacking in love, and attempted drowned now, in the sea, and bald guy with big ears I see you too, back there, lugs, I call them, beneath my breath, as we sing together, blessed lugs, I mean to say, and there is a small dog in a pew behind me, they let small dogs in here, will there be dogs in heaven, I think to myself, even as Christ himself is given up to pure passion I am thinking to myself, is it allowed to have dogs in a church and how annoying is it.

To have ideas to love you, to have ideas to fall in love with you is to be God and to build a great cathedral out of stone and in it the faces of the people all around me (in the midst of keen disgrace, is what the word of the song says, is how it sings it) as a corpulent Scoutmaster turns to the congregation and with his hands and his mouth he rises from the tomb of the flesh, the tomb of the song, is how he sings it, and he fills the cathedral with an exhortation that is banal and simple enough to be perfectly impossible. This is called Good Friday, and I return home, and I get drunk, and I come all over the spectacles of the dark-haired sweetie on the choir to the left.

I call her Flower. I call you Flower. I call them Flower. And I return to the cathedral the next day and I make supplication. And I do it all over again. This is a summer. This is the character of a summer. Which is what they call Atlas, raising the world on his shoulders. Atlas stands in for summers. It's obvious. Think about it. It is architecture, summers. Raise it.

Another summer.

We are driving down a dusty lane in central France in a beige-coloured Vauxhall Viva. The windows are rolled down. We are driving into the sun. Her name is Flower now, too.

The Greek Zeno of Elea never mentioned the magic of a flower when he claimed that no race can ever be run, that no church can ever be built, that no monument can ever be raised to our love because the space between us is infinite. To run a mile, you must first run a half-mile. And then a half-mile further again. Which requires first an eighth of a mile towards that, which demands a twentieth of a mile towards that, first, which requires the conquering of a divisor again and again, in other words, infinitesimally, which means that no race is run, that space is opening up and receding, forever, that we are once more on a strange wonder, held aloft above what depths, as in vertigo, forever. Which is why a statue of an elegantly dressed woman in the summer in France is a perfect impossibility. Which is why art is provisional. Provisional on what? On the will of God. Which is what the churches and the great cathedrals of France say, what Zeno of Elea says. That there is no raising up that is not of the will of God. And that, in the end, nothing is built. Nothing?

Look: I write this now in God's hand, I carve it like so, and I say I, I still claim agency, even as this sentence unravels as another summer, in central France, and we are driving down a dusty lane in a beige-coloured Vauxhall Viva.

Your dress rides up your stockinged thigh. You are wearing oversized sunglasses. What does my perfume make you think of? you ask me. Go on, you say, say it, what you think. I can't do smells, I say, my descriptive faculties fail me. It's flowers, you say. Say it, you say, it's flowers. Dark flowers, I say. It is dark flowers. Carnal, you say, it is Carnal Flower, and you hold out your wrist to me, like so.

The speed of gods time counts not, though with swiftest minutes winged.

3. PROCEEDS FROM THE FIRST SYNOD OF THE CHURCH OF THE STONE OF FIRST WITNESS

We believe in one stone, eternal, stone without end, and in the resurrection, in stone, and the suffering, and betrayal, in stone, and of the virgin birth, from stone.

We believe in the stone of destiny.

Make of your heart a stone, we say, make of your heart a stone so that it may be held forever, and we say held as in fixated, on our own.

We declare Gislebertus the patron saint of our stone-cold hearts because he was first to say so, in stone.

We do not believe in denim trousers.

We laugh at megaliths and stone circles like we laugh at people who cannot spell.

Nothing beyond the Will of God. Stone.

We are the lovers of historical subterranean. Stone upon stone.

Yet we are the destroyer of The Tower.

Everything is holy and set in stone.

This is the voice of the first stone: silence!

The Lion of Judah is the Theologian of the Dream, stone.

These are the Pyramids, that is Africa, this is the Church.

This is the Church, which is the stone of our lives, foundation.

As faith trumps belief, stone.

God is both perfect and imperfect, contains both, and is neither; stone.

Make of your heart The Mighty Fortress, as Christ has commanded, in no wisdom and no understanding, then Yield! is The Law.

So is the ending of the first stone, as handed down, in the beginning, stone.

4. CHURCH OF THE BLACK EGYPTIAN, JACKAL

We are driving down a dirt road in the sun as your dress runs up your thighs. We pull into the driveway of a crumbling yellow villa with wild vines running and an old abandoned sailboat lying topsy-turvy on the green. In the conservatory, Pierre is holding court.

It is the smallest things, he says, it is the smallest gestures, at the end of a man's life, that count. As if there is any other option, he spat, and he pinged a tang of phlegm that rang like a bell off the tin bin across the way, and he relayed a story, a story of his infidelities, without shame, and in front of the two of us, he listed his various misdeeds, some in lush detail, because by this point I am afraid that it gets a little tipsy and that the drinks cabinet (which was a globe, an Atlas with the world on his shoulders) has been well and truly raided.

Take that clown Joseph Beuys, Pierre said. Please, he laughed, take him. He became a Marxist simpleton as surely as you hypnotise a parrot, Pierre said. As surely as you circumcise a squirrel, he said. But then, now, he said. These, gestures. These, simple things. Like a single action, and then the next. Like a nick in stone, and then another, and that's it; it's all over. The span of a man's life, he said, in a single incision in stone, he said. Think about it, he said. All this naturalistic statuary and has it gotten us any closer to the gods? he said, and I felt your dress run up your thighs, he's talking of the gods, I'm no fool, sweetie, and then he started to name his conquests, dark-haired Japanese, obviously, dark-haired Japanese poets, he said, I screwed her in a graveyard, he tells you, I screwed her on a fallen gravestone, I nailed her on a memorial, he says, and he laughs, and she laughs too, he screws Japanese half to death in graveyards, okay, sweetie, I get it, my girl just had to put up with it, he shrugs, she had no choice, he admits, I told her, he says, how it was, you know how it goes, sweetie, you know how it goes just fine, I told my girl, he says, I have many lovers, he says, I am a man that has taken many lovers, he says, and with that he motions to you, Flower, and he taps his thigh as if he is offering you a seat there, and I see you think about it, I see you almost go to him, and I say to myself, you, too, are under this spell of stone. To be virtuosic in the moment, Pierre says, is the mark of a man, as you looked at him then, and almost went to him.

I am not feeling this art, this art of the young ones, Pierre says, in his pidgin English, this English he embraces like a pigeon, he says. This new art, he says, but still, I know there are problems, I know that art rises up to tackle problems, like windmills, he says, and he laughs, pointedly, like windmills, he says, and he looks around like I know we can all agree on the reference, he is quoting *Don Quixote*, surely, he is being quixotic, he is bringing up that whole idea of fencing with windmills, but then he says, a windmill, he says, made out of stone, he says, that is the problem that art must solve if it is to go deep, he says, and he taps his thigh again, like he is trying to tempt a cat or tame a pigeon.

What is the point of a windmill made of stone? he asks us. Then how much more pointless, he puts to us, a statue of a living person? Realist statuary is unholy, he says to us, and he is addressing Flower now. Realist statuary, he says, and he lights his pipe with an ostentatious pure-fuel lighter in the shape of Noah's Ark, the exact co-ordinates of Noah's Ark, he would say, and I would say to him, do you mean the exact measurements of Noah's Ark, do you mean it is modelled on a ratio of its original specifications, his English was often quite poor, and approximate, but he said, no, I mean the co-ordinates, he said, this lighter is mapped upon the co-ordinates of Noah's Ark, he said, in his room, in this dusty villa with the upturned boat outside, through the half-drawn pale-blue curtains, across the grey-green grass, this blue-yellow upturned boat, is the co-ordinates of Noah's Ark, I hear myself say, so-called realist art, he says, is not of the gods, and he shakes his head then, he shakes himself and allows himself a wry smile at the folly of this world, and its pointlessness, which is how Noah must have felt herding animals two by two into this stupid wooden boat whose co-ordinates, let's face it, are still unknown, a true offering to the gods would be to turn their own unrecognisable face on them, he says, and he rises, like a fucking paraplegic, if I'm being honest, he rises, quivering, from his desk, like a fucking paraplegic on his last legs if I'm being honest, and he puts his hand out to you, Flower, and gets far too close and invades your personal space and says banal things, with confidence, all night, banal things accompanied by searing insights, by circuitous digressions, by erudite passages of by-heart poetry and prose, these small gestures, at the end of a man's life.

What other animal suffers in silence? Pierre asked us. Only that is not exactly what he said. He said, what animal expresses pain mutely? We have all heard of baby deer that weep in the snow like orphaned children, Pierre said, and this time that was exactly what he said. But what of animals that cannot cry out in pain? he said. Mute swans, he said. Have you ever seen a pigeon devoured by a raptor? Pierre asked us, only he pronounced raptor as you would trapdoor. It is the way you approach English, I wanted to say, I wanted to joke that Pierre's approach to English was like a pigeon swallowed by a trapdoor, I wanted to say that, but I didn't.

The pigeon, Pierre said, watches its own devouring in silence, and all around it, too, other pigeons are silenced. Does that mean that pigeons are capable of experiencing awe? Is their silence at their own devouring the workings of awe? Can we call a pigeon astonished? What other creature, and this was the word Pierre used this time around, what other creature expresses pain mutely? he asked us. We can imagine terrible flatfish with opaque eyes at the bottom of the ocean's deep trenches, Flower said, we can imagine fish at the bottom of Challenger Deep, which is all of six miles down, staring up in mute astonishment, as teeth bear down on them from out of the blackness and devour them whole. It's possible, Pierre said, at the bottom of the sea anything is possible, he conceded. Foxes cry out, Pierre said, and young calves. Dogs weep in the streets and in city parks. Snakes spit and curse till the last, and keep coming even then. Did the dodo scream in fear or stand in awe? That's one thing we will never know, Pierre sighed. What about whales? I asked him. I made appeal to his namesake. Did not Melville liken the wounded cries of a dying whale to the atomic pain at the centre of the world? But he ignored the question. I had planned to bring up Nietzsche, and what he saw as Christianity's failure to make suffering sacred, but I didn't get the chance. Instead, Pierre said, the creature that expresses pain mutely, is man. All building up, he said, is the silent song of the wounded leviathan. And all stone, he said, is singing.

For God has commanded, and this is Pierre speaking now: stand in awe, and sin not. Lie on your bed, and be still. Selah. And so stone, stands in awe, at its reckoning, which is man, is how I rendered the final words of Pierre's remarkable account of his search for the sacred, in stone, and how he carried a love affair, on his shoulders, once upon a summer, an affair that I based our own romance around, Flower; for how could I not see us in this Full Length Mirror?

I let Flower know that we were to have an illustrious visitor. He is kind of my mentor, I told her. I translated his book, I told her. He is a legend, I said, a very eccentric guy and possibly a genius too, I said, though I'm not one of these guys who equate eccentricity or just plain lack of social skills with genius, he really is, weird, I mean, strange, but don't worry, I assured her, he is admirable, and of sound mind and with a real education, I told her, they don't make men like this any more, I told her, he's the last of his kind, I said, by which I implied that I was the last of the kind to recognise the last of his kind, so uniting us across the miles and decades and language barriers (though for me, not so, I could speak better French than Pierre could English) as twinned spirits and fellow travellers and as the type of guy it might be worth holding on to and never letting go of.

I had set up camp in a steel container in the same old strangely beautiful quarry with its terrible lake at the centre (a lake of who knows what depth, as we shall see) that Pierre had lived by, years earlier, and where he had compiled the details of the grand summer that was the tympanum of *Full Length Mirror*, the entrance to its glassy reflection. I had come to an arrangement with the owners. The quarry was abandoned, they said, apparently, the rumour was, due to the entire area being riddled with mineshafts and sinkholes and terrible depths and tunnels, and so the quarry had been emptied of heavy machinery, but still, a single metal container leased to a religious hermit, why not.

Why not? I said to the professor, which is what I called him, at first, when I called him from a phone box about a mile down a moody country lane with all of the birds perched like musical notes on the telephone wires, why not, I said, revisit the old stomping ground, as it were, take the temperature of old times, I suggested, I have a metal container set on the very spot of the old, I told him, it won't be going anywhere any time soon, I said, I thought he would appreciate that, the elements, up against the elements, and time, was my thinking, but no, no, he said, entropy, he said, entropy, as if he had misheard me and was asking me to clarify, entropy, he said, without entropy how could a single note die, how could we recall a melody, how on earth could we be taken there, back again? I changed the subject by making a joke about Sir Arthur Conan Doyle, I knew that he was a fan. He made a joke about Moriarty, in return, and though I knew my Doyle as well as the next enquiring teenager, I was at a loss for words. He said, Moriarty tempts Sherlock Holmes to the falls by the insinuation of an imbalance in the cosmic stack, he said. And then he said, their first, and only, fully documented adventure is titled, after all, 'The Adventure of the Final Problem'.

After that there was silence on the line, which I took to mean that he was coming, that the first adventure was written, and sure enough a spare three weeks later a taxi pulled up at the lip of the quarry and Pierre hobbled out, dressed for some kind of mid-century European spa, or a yacht, down the Suez, between the wars, and with a secretary named Claude who dropped him off and waved him adieu, and on first seeing the metal container that I had landed, on the spot, the exact spot, where he had spent those years himself, those years in which he put together the book that had brought our lives to this exact same spot, he said, I hear you, and he pulled his earlobe, his strangely elongated earlobe, and walked right inside, and took up court, and that first week he taught me to fish, in the lake, that was the first lesson, in the terrible lake, and to develop a taste for pike, which, as a Scotsman, I was repulsed by and thought of as Gypsy food, at best, but no more, my friend, no more, a pike lured up from the depths, with its opaque eyeballs in silent awe as its head is caved in and remodelled by the professor back in his own stomping ground at last, is its own memorial, I said to myself, as I bit through its charred eyeball, in delight and disgust, I said, yes, I'll have a bit of that, why not.

He took me to nearby cathedrals and he ranted in the grounds. Ranted is the only word for it. Ranted, in this strange pigeon amalgam of French and English, snapping between one and an approximation of the other. Le sacré, he would say, suddenly, interrupting himself in mid-sentence,

and he would hold his hand up and point to a dark cloister
with the silence ringing out, in hope and loneliness, he would
say, the formula for the sacred is hope plus loneliness, is
how I translated it in *Full Length Mirror*, it's no secret, the
formula, and he would put his finger to his lips and he would
announce, le sacré, as if it had come on the air, but this is
the spell set by the world's most sacred sites, Pierre taught
me, hope and loneliness have conspired to set a stone, in
the places we go to stand in awe, Pierre said, and of course I
thought of that damn pigeon, first held tight under his arm,
then spoken, then pinned to the ground in wonder as it is
torn to pieces, of course I thought of those silent pigeon eyes
and that word that came to me, all over again, that word
implacable, that word that stirs me in envy and in jealousy,
somehow, there is no such thing, I say now, implacable is
unworked stone, and unworked stone is a contradiction in
terms. Stone is the working. So where does that leave hope
and loneliness? Here, written in stone, for all to see.

I raise it, like Atlas, this summer. The way the heat would
rise from the fields around the quarry in the early-summer
dawn, so that everything seemed as if in a distant childhood
looking-glass, is what asks me to remember it, and even you,
Flower, who broke my heart, your silent eyes signal it, now,
as Pierre serves brown rice baked in a tin on the old stove
and serves it in slices, like a cake, in the semi-darkness,
your silent eyes, as he served slices of brown rice alongside
pike roasted in the embers of the fire, and as he does so he
is naming the constellations above our heads, in darkness, I
can't see him at the other side of the table, was he right, how
would I know, I know little of astronomy, I'm afraid, which
in Pierre's book made you unqualified for architecture, or
for poetry, or for love of the arts, in general, if you hadn't

even taken the time to name what's right above your head,
or to stand in awe, beneath it, but he wheeled through the
constellations of the night-time northern sky, I know that
much, I can vouch for that, and he served us this food, in the
dark, within this circle of light, and it felt like Freemasonry,
is Freemasonry the study of the architecture of the universe,
because if so that's how it felt, that night, in the dark and
the light, that the architecture of the heavens was there to
be named, hope and loneliness, which is a church, wherever
it is gathered.

Is it true that dogs can smell cancer? Is it true that old men
smell of stinky death? It's true, my friends, I smell me, it's
true. Stinky death is the body uncared for, which is how
the universe feels about old men, stinky death, somewhere
in the wings, preferably, these chicken wings that smell of
sweat and of old seed. What is the smell of old seed, you
might ask, and I would know, a stain is an old seed, dried
up, and goes well with tank tops and dark-brown corduroy
and writing by candlelight, into the night, and not sleeping,
and waking up, and doing it all over again.

We are sat outside the steel container, on the lip of this
infinity of water beneath us. These caves and tunnels and
canyons running on forever beneath us, and the soft sun
coming out of the past, and he says, with a shawl over
his knees and some kind of contrived fisherman's hat on
his head, and with a fresh bottle of plonk on the ground,
he says, I have always understood the word redemption
to mean as in when you return a glass bottle of pop in
exchange for small beer, he says, and I went to correct
him, you mean small change, I said, you mean shrapnel,
I said, you mean peanuts, and he said, no, small beer,

delicious, don't you understand, and I thought of those
gestures, those small gestures he had been on about in art,
at the end of a man's life, and he said, they call it the angel's
share, in English, he said, in Scottish, more properly, he
said, I call it small beer, it is what we receive in exchange
for the true fulfilment of our lives, which, in contradiction,
is only, truly, what we were able to give to them, our angel.

This book, he said, and it was one of the few times he even
acknowledged that I had translated this enigmatic lifework
of his, is small beer, to me, he said.

Some group of headcases drove down into the quarry in a
Land Rover and took potshots at the container while we
were hidden out inside, one evening, we were gaining a
reputation in the village and these nutcases were getting
drunk and riding out here with an idea of terrifying us. It's
only slugs, Pierre said, when he inspected the bullet holes
in the side of the container, it's a glorified spud gun, he said,
which was one of the best English phrases he ever said,
and I said to him, slugs that can dent steel, better duck,
but he ignored me completely and went back to his blissful
ignorance of anything but the mission of his own life.

There was a whole rigmarole, about how we got bread,
how we got eggs, how we bought wine from a farmer with
a vine on a hill, this thick, ruddy red wine which tasted of
wellington boots and of salt and of cough medicine, which
was my kind of poison, and which we would drink, in the
rain, under the canopy, in front of the container, the heavy
rain falling into the lake like a zen poem trying to break
your mind, and the time we dragged a pig carcass down
into the quarry after a day-and-a-half bender spent with a

farmer who tried to sell his wife and his daughter to us with the understanding that we present them to 'the men they deserved', which insinuation was that we, neither of us, were the deserved, or the deserving.

I fucked a foxglove, flower. This morning, I fucked a flower, flowers are lingerie for bees, I fucked a foxglove, this morning, took my penis out and slid it into the sheath, church, which burst, like thin air, adorned, like stonework is, a monument to thin air, a monastery and a church. And the stamen at the end, is that the word, stamen, tickled the head of my cock, and gave it a rash. I took pills, to fuck a flower, in the morning. I am lonely, and I am writing this book called *Monument Maker*. Bee inside you made the flesh ring like a bell, I tell my flower, my penis down her throat, my penis, now, only good for soft foxgloves, and lupins too. Bees make honey, I tell myself, in my dotage I tell myself that bees make honey, and me so much older than any bee. Lingerie, I allow myself, is our modern church, our grateful cathedral, and I thank you for that, the present, but I missed the boat, I'm afraid, and your waspie, is that the term, stamen, waspie, bee, is that the term, is my knave, my chancery, my vestibule, my vesica piscis (of course she is a Pisces), which is the term for two conjoined circles, and the beautiful oval they make, and the word is pedestal, heels, altar, pulpit, apex, meridian. Make of men Meridians, church and stocking, I demand, of the times.

These days there are charts to measure everything: poverty, standard of living, happiness. Once it was the great churches and monasteries that were the mark of how far we had come, of relative prosperity, of peace and tranquillity, and of a dedication, of the days, to worship. Today their place is lingerie, at the apex of civilisation, and now, if we had lived, if this were not our final testimony, we would be department store assistants and boutique suppliers, just as then, now, we were creepers through crypts and archivists of what you call cold and what you call lifeless, stone.

The Benedictine nunnery of Baume-les-Dames, whose church was designed by Jean-Pierre Galezot himself, looks like a curious collared dove fallen from heaven, Pierre says; he is talking to an audience of Flower and I, in the summer of 1993. It looks just like a collared dove, he exclaims, it has that same befuddled expression at its own perfect, unostentatious symmetry, its peeky little eyeholes are windows, blinking. If we could see it from the air, he exclaims, it would appear perpetually about to take flight, and the dome of the church, beautifully executed, it has to be said, though not entirely in a style I favour, by the great Jean-Pierre Galezot in 1738, is the perfect kind to host doves of all persuasions, he says, and the ascending dove, he says, as we all know, is the spirit animal of the architect on earth, and right then, in its cool blonde stone, in its blue skies, in its summer of 1993, Galezot's nunnery has the appearance of having fallen from heaven, like a bird with no language to express its mute wonder at itself. Or is this just the season, the weight of it, on my shoulders? Imagine birds, rising up, when you stand inside a church or a monastery, Pierre would say, or better yet, an Egyptian burial mound, a great castle, a modern-day art gallery or museum; imagine birds rising up, he says, and take the feel of the place.

Harder.

The second time I saw Flower have sex with another man presents a fresco I would rather not forget. I would trade you three French monasteries and a Gislebertus, that is its worth, to me. Otherwise, forget it.

Harder.

How lascivious your tongue in the mouth of someone you have only just met.

Harder.

5. CATHEDRAL OF GHOST OF MY LOVE

We signed our names, in indelible marker, on the stones at the Cathedral of Saint Lazarus. We signed it as a painter signs a painting. Monument Maker.

Number the meridians around my heart and you will find many and you will think to yourself, incised, in his heart, there are many loves, but really, there is one love, twined, like thorns, around the heart forever. Meridians is the secret book of The Bible and why we put boundaries there, just as Numbers is why we put sums. But wood is new love and the tracks of its sap is what we call lachrymose and what we call tears, and tears are an eternal cycle, going on from the entrance into time, which is once more, now, that metal container, on the lip of this gulf of dirty water with pike rising up, is the entrance to time, rising up and gnawing on our legs should we be so foolhardy as to dive off our front porch, and we were, foolhardy, and we were, bitten, and upside down in the grey I would open my eyes, I would force open my eyes against the grey of the soup we were swimming in, with pike with teeth, newborn dinosaurs, reaching up, and Pierre's legs, his terrible bruised legs, like jellyfish into water, and sand and stone dissolved in that

light, in that murky, disgusting light, and I saw the making
of monuments, and why that lack of light was sacred, down
there, why formation was magic and – thank God – hidden
from us. But stone were the marks on my heart, should you
find it raised up, and, as Pierre insisted, rightly, filled with
birds. Though night, too, that amphibious night that I swam
in, had its part.

Wait, I'm thinking of that prick Davide again. What about
this: the second time I saw my Flower make love to another
man was a frieze, is a frieze, a stonework, that features
Davide, the spurned lover, crouched behind some bushes
and in his own centre of light – he holds a flashlight down,
towards the ground, so that he is illuminated, eerily, from
below – those same shadows, in stone, and I am carving it
with my free hand, I am stoneworking as I am watching my
Flower having sex with another man while being watched
by another man, like in one of these amateur novels where
everything is doubled and doubled for meaning, only here
it is, in stone, in front of me, this frieze with, it has to be
said, classical lineaments, this frieze which should really
be – and would once, no doubt, have been – titled something
like *Mininnais & the Rape of Ad Astra*, and there, in the
distance, although victim to that rude foreshortening that is
the bane of the amateur sculptor, that distorted perspective
that would make of the background foreground, yet there,
all the same, on too large a coffin, on too large a fallen
headstone, my Flower lies spreadeagled and speared by
some nameless hunk in the night.

Nameless hunk in the night, once, was to be my own name,
I protest to no one but you, cold, silent stone. I am sorry
for myself when I say that. Nameless hunk in the night, I

confess, was not at all what I had in store. He may as well
have been a swan, I tell myself, isn't that how they told it
back in the day? She was raped by a swan, assailed by a
goat, held down and force-fucked by the Fates. Which is me,
baby, no nameless hunk but fate, you and I. And fate, like
stone, has all the inertia of the universe behind it.

We became caught up in it, like a game of perfect statues.
We set up the scenes; at first we would pick up young
French girls wandering free in the country lanes of that
time, young girls who were only too happy to lie in the soft
grass while my Flower ran a hand up their top and I froze
the diptych in my head, now a triptych, with the contours
of the young French girl's top, the rumfles on it, just so,
and the effect of hairs, the effect of single fibres on the top,
standing up, in arousal, in the sun, how do you do that, that
is a master at work, and the shadow that is cast, perfect,
and the clouds, perfect, too, and that shape beneath the
nose, between the lips, that deep meridian, perfectly incised,
and the way that her young bra would cinch her skin, her
thin arms folded back on herself, and we would return to
the quarry, as the sun was going down, and I would strip
down to my long johns and wrestle formless boulders from
one side of the quarry to the other, and I would drop them,
in a certain order, down into the grey depths of the water
where I told myself I was adding to this secret monument
that no one would see, this miraculous upside-down city
that I believed to exist somewhere deep below the surface
and whose towers, whose exquisite skyways, in a certain
light, on certain days only, cast shadows in the deep, and
felt mad but did it anyway, visioned this upside-down city,
even though why is it upside down, is it growing down
from the waves, is there a second surface, a second sun,

I asked myself, black sun on the other side of the water, I asked myself, and these stones, like gold discs sent into space, on which I would incise a single mark, or maybe two marks, maybe three marks, three marks maximum, that is the gesture of a lifetime, it is also, and can be, the record of a lost summer's day, and a seduction in a field, and a drowning of it, at the same time. That is a gentleman, near the end of his life.

God, how I hate the chateaux of France. Not because of their ostentatious celebration of power, no, but for their trumpeting of *temporal* power, their prancying, their poseying, when there are only two powers worth making monument for: God & Love. I hate them from a distance, these chateaux, I hate them on approach, and I loathe them on arrival, up close, where they look like ghastly gateaux, that word, perfect for the gaudy French, is cousin for a reason. These cakes left out in the rain. Permit me to laugh at them up close. Ha ha ha. To mock them, from a distance. Then to take leave of them, along their – it has to be said – often beautifully proportioned approaches, via their sometimes surrealist hedgerows, around their opulent fountains and gardens of secret statuary, let me take leave of them with a leer on my face, all the same.

All the while I am translating *Full Length Mirror* I am living in a small town in Scotland and collaborating with an old girlfriend on secret monuments in the fields dotted around the town. Here is a carved headstone at the bottom of a flooded quarry. Here is an uncanny circle of stone by the reservoir in Caldercruix. She started it first, this old girlfriend, this making of stone, in secret, though I came to believe that I had conjured her, perhaps, that I had written her into existence via the scrying of Pierre's text, maybe, and now here she was, fully formed, before me, thanks to a friend who was into the music world and the new-wave world and who had mentioned her to me, this woman who time was to make my first true love, my secret collaborator, my inspiration, early on, this friend mentioned her, he said some musician in town was also a sculptor in secret and that one of her works still existed at the end of an old railway line in Clarkston, in Airdrie, just south of Plains, and I travelled there, I took the day out to find this secret memorial that this pure local artist had made, this pure artist, I remember thinking, the only reason for monument making is purity, I said to myself, as I crossed a metal bridge with huge rusting pipes beneath and with birds' nests and with rope swings below and came to a sort of siding where there were abandoned train carriages with trees growing up through them and I saw her name, she had signed it there, and it was so beautiful that our love affair began right there, too, I believe, in a signature, on a Saturday afternoon, like a bee, inside a foxglove, is what I tell myself how the story began.

Let's have another laugh at these ostentatious gateaux, shall we, let's drive there, on a glorious summer's day in June, why don't we, just to stand there and guffaw. Let's drive to the Château de Craon, in Haroué, that infamous bouncy castle with its preposterous moat and its bland central courtyard set in the beautiful rolling hills and the soft grass like a block of stupid Lego fell through a hole in a cloud, except that it is reproducible, perfectly, in a photograph, except that it was made for the photographing of, for the dust jackets of, for the postcards of, so unsure of its own ability to hold time at bay, so ready to entrust its legacy to architectural tourism, to seekers after wonder, by which they mean the real, perfectly mirrored, inside of the real, which is why stupid tourists and your philistine mother will always prefer paintings that seem to presage photography, so that they can say, wow, there is some real skill on display here, it's marvellous what they can do, for to reach inside the world, they think, and to merely reset it, according to God's own plan, they secretly think, is to set art at the apex, they believe, but if you have followed my argument this far you will realise that it is what is given, not the seed of the giver, that is infinitely repeatable by man, so that when we come across something that looks just the way we expect it to – a painting of a green field that best resembles a green field, an old, decadent rich man's building that resembles exactly our idea of that – it should set alarm bells ringing, and raise questions of taste and of what is holy, in contrast with the Monastery of the Collared Dove Come Puzzled Down from Heaven, which is when you realise that everything that is fallen from the skies, even, is not equally holy. And that the legend of the fall of Lucifer is really to do with connoisseurship, which is kingship, of the self. Which is why, in the English translation, Pierre's book is titled *Full Length Mirror*.

God, how I hate new-wave music. I shall list some of the words that spring to mind when I am assailed by it, when I was assaulted by it, in Mary's car, once, on the way to some covert artistic assignation, long sunk, like a secret upside-down city, in the flesh of our brains, and the mud of the fields, and the waters of those quarries, and I shall use words like harpy, I shall make comparisons to a bin lorry reversing, I shall compare it to the spin cycle on a washing machine, indeed I shall go back to kitchen gadgets and disposal units, again and again, as ways of disparaging Mary's music, even as I luxuriated in her company, even as I gave up a whole summer to her ideas on art and life and how it should be lived, which, when you come down to it, is what you believe to be holy, and I believe that summer to be holy, which is why I lift it, once more, onto my shoulders, in this telling of it, to you, like Atlas.

And you will no doubt say, what about Anjou? What about Tours? You will no doubt bang on about it and keep narrowing it down until your question is, really, what about Oiron? What about the Salle de Bal at Oiron? What about those exquisitely painted beams in the Salle des Fêtes? What about the stunning Renaissance entry to the seigneurial chapel? You may even presume I don't know the meaning of the word seigneurial and you may even pick apart my prefixing it with 'the'. You will no doubt bring up the Grand Escalier, make mention of the play of light in the Galerie des Gardes. I will give you stunning, and I will give you exquisite, and I will grant you, too, seigneurial; further, I will raise you.

We pulled up beside a dirt track that led across a field of grass that looked nothing like a field of grass in a painting, with tall telegraph poles stretching off and low cloud scudding by, and we made our way to this quarry – why is it that 1970s television made quarries famous as alien lands – and we each carried a bag of Blue Circle cement on our shoulders, and when we got to the lip of this quarry it looked like Mary was crying, there were tears on her cheeks, it seemed, or it might have been the wind, and I said to her, why are you crying, and she laughed, and she said, I have drowned so many of my babies in this quarry, and I looked at that Blue Circle on the bag of cement which right then was of a blue that no longer exists in today's world, and before I could say anything else she said, the more intellectual amongst us also tend to be the most highly strung, and then again before I could say, that was a beautiful sentiment, or really, honestly, before I could say, ha ha, that is such a funny line I will remember it forever, she said to me, that's a quote, by the way, that's a quote, she said, from an artist, she said, from an artist at my high school, which is a self-created artist, she said, you had to be back then, she said, right, which is the only kind of artist worth giving a fuck about, she said, am I right, she said, the only artist worth believing in, she said, that's a quote from an artist at my high school who had just taken a right fucking beating, she said, a savage doing, she said, a total fucking pasting, actually, she said, and when he had wept afterwards, she said, when he had broke down crying in the wake of this beating, he had explained it away, not as softness, but as being strung, higher, as being tuned to tears, by God, like an instrument. It was my boyfriend that gave him the savage beating in the first place, she said to me. That's the kind of artist I am, she said, and then she marched off, with this bag of Blue Circle cement on her shoulder like all of my summers at once.

Their walls are hung with exquisite tapestries and their hallways echo to the sound of walking sticks and walking frames and plastic crutches and everywhere you look there are middle-aged men in buttoned-up pale-blue shirts talking about palatial this and wonderful, marvellous fucking that. How badly do we have to fail, you ask yourself, to retire to this kind of derelict homaging? Then you realise you are quoting Pierre, and that this is your own derelict homaging.

Harder.

In the gardens at La Bastie, Pierre writes, the Temple of Love
that features an arched rotunda with a statue in its centre is
also known as the Temple of Autumn. Does it take an autumn
to make of a season summer? The price we pay for beginnings
is endings. Are all monuments memorials? Here is a black-
and-white photograph of Pierre and his lover Hildegard
outside the keep of the royal Château de Vincennes. She
seems dressed for another season entirely. With a long
black mohair coat, black hat and kitten heels she looks like
something from the 1950s. In the photograph she is looking in
a mirror. She is looking in a hand-mirror and fixing her make-
up, perhaps, I imagine, while Pierre's attention seems to have
been caught by the details on a low window, a window which
may, or may not, look onto the kitchen where the corpse of
Henry V of England, who died in a room on the second floor
shortly after establishing his right to the throne of France,
was boiled in a pot on the open fireplace in order that they
might separate his skin from his bones, and post them back
again. The identity of the photographer is unknown, or,
rather, unrevealed. Every summer has its autumn.

What if I told you I love you? I said to Mary. What if I
told you I love you, I said to her, over this noise like a
dishwasher humming, which was actually a cassette of her
music, if you can believe that. Mary took a last draw of her
cigarette and then went to toss it out of the window but
the window wasn't actually open so it just bounced off the
glass and landed on the back seat of the car and started
smouldering so as we had to pull over to the side of the road
and put it out and though I never got my answer, now I
think maybe I did, in a way, after all.

She had a workshop in a garage in her parents' back
garden – I think they were dead, it was never clear, she
lived there on her own – and in the middle of it there was
a totem pole, that's the only way to describe it, going right
up the middle of the garage and out through the skylight
there was this great stone totem pole that she said she had
built by running a funnel up to the skylight and pouring
concrete and stones and found objects and mashed-up bits
of long-dead crap down this funnel thing, and then peeling
this funnel thing away to expose this totem pole thing that
she then cut certain incisions in – that was the phrase she
used, certain incisions, like the brushstroke of a master –
that created channels, she said, that created waterways,
she said, that allowed all the rain that came in the skylight
to course in certain patterns across it and when I asked
her what it was she said, Jung dreamed of a phallus on a
throne, I realised later that was what she said but at the
time I thought she was saying that the sculpture was called
Young Dream of a Phallus on a Throne and I was completely
bowled over. Then I looked around and there was a wall-
sized painting, I'm not kidding, of a naked woman in high
heels bending over a bed and blowing some old guy. That's
me, she said, and I was so confused, so mind-blown, by this
point, that I had no idea whether she meant she was the girl
doing the blowing or the old guy being blown. Either seemed
possible, at the foot of this mad weeping totem pole, poking
through the roof of a garage, in Airdrie.

Look at this photograph of an old monastery on a deserted
street in the rain. You can almost smell the damp dust in
the air. That's Pierre, as a young man, perched on the edge
of what looks like a fountain or a well. That's his father
stood behind him. And on down the street, as far as the eye

can see, not a single person in view, just like the world used to be, when it was half-empty, and filled with monuments to times when things were emptier still. What is the date of the first gravestone? Emptier, still. Which is Latin for the date of the first monument.

I became enthralled by this idea of simple gestures, of markings, of one movement of the hands and then the next. A face risen from stone. A piece of paper with an orange line and a black line, extended. An imperfect form, made perfect, by imprecision, is as perfect as a cloud, I told myself, as I left two cuts in stone and drowned it, in upside-down clouds, in the endless waters outside our front door, Pierre and I, that summer that I christen now, that summer whose soft baby skull I hold in my hands and am careful not to squeeze nor to poke around in there, now, this Summer of the Upside-Down City, I call it, which I realise now is Hebrew, maybe, for the Landing on Water of the Puzzled Turtle Dove, nor poke around with my thumbs in there, in the squish of its brain, quite yet, might be best.

'Is' is what we say in stone. 'Is' is the only word we can trust. 'Is' is the foundation stone. Is. Is. I do not think therefore I is. Is.

Pierre told this story about his mother. His mother was a young girl herself in this story, in a time that was half-empty, and still. His mother had never visited the neighbouring village. It was barely a dream to think of it, she had said, so circumscribed, she had said, was our world, that was the word she had used, so low, the horizon, was what she had said. Then a knight appeared, was how his mother had put it, as a young girl, an outlandish knight appeared, was the term she had used, which meant, simply, that he was from the world beyond the village, was how she had explained it, or rather, how I translated what she had said. I said to myself: his mother met an outlandish knight, and I told Pierre and he said, precisely, although of course he said, précisément, précisément, he said, and that this Outlandish Knight, he said, who, really, Pierre's mother had said, was only a few years older than she was, a boy child, she had said, that was the phrase she had used, un garçon, she had said, un mere garçon, précisément, she had said, and she had shrugged, precisely, a boy child, she had said, and this Outlandish Knight had appeared, in a field, by the river, nearby, this Outlandish Knight had swum up from another village, and had been taken on the tide to Pierre's mother's village, a village whose name translates as In The Beginning, the village of In The Beginning, he had floated out from this other unknown village on the tide, seemingly, and had emerged, soaking – he was still wearing his clothes – soaking wet and with a pair of trousers tied by a single string – une seule chaîne, his mother had said – at the village of In The Beginning, and this figure, this wet figure come up from the depths and only a few years older than the young Pierre's mother had held out his hand and in his hand he had a cloth bag, a sopping cloth bag inside of which were stones, plain stones, Pierre's mother had said, plain stones, she realised now, but then, oh my, this Outlandish Knight come up from the waves had opened this sopping cloth bag and had produced this handful of small stones and offered it to Pierre's mother, he had said nothing but simply opened his palm and offered the young Pierre's mother a handful of stones and Pierre's mother had recognised it, this gesture, these stones in this gesture, young Pierre's mother had recognised it as the currency of the future, Pierre said, only he said it, l'appareil du futur, which is really the device of the future, in another way, but she had recognised it as currency, too, because she had understood it, Pierre said, as this mysterious waterborne man, this Outlandish Knight, had offered her these stones, these simple stones, these precious stones, she had understood that they were tokens of not only the existence but the permanence of the world outside these boundaries, beyond this village of In The Beginning, where the future, and the past, are written, forever. And at that moment of profoundest realisation she slides one delicate shoulder from her dress and then the other and lets it fall to her ankles, naked, but for this pool around her feet, and is taken then and there, in the soft wet grass on the banks of the river. And what became of this Outlandish Knight? Pierre had asked his mother. What became of this visitor to In The Beginning? He took to the waters, his mother had told him, and I watched as he drifted out of sight.

Or was that a story I read when I was a young man? It has the tenor of my boyhood novellas. Did I dream of a man washed down a river whose name was Pierre's father? But already, there, I am conflating the stories. Pierre's father is the name of a river, which offers stones, now, to my boyhood, un garçon is the currency of the past, in this village of In The Beginning.

Flower. Flower, is Flower, is Flower.

Harder.

One evening after a day in the fields making monument, I cooked Mary dinner at my place. I lit candles, and there were flowers on the table. Mary, I said to her, in the silence after dinner, but she held her hand up for quiet. I wanted to pour my heart out to her. I love you forever, was what I always wanted to say. But she held up her hand for quiet. Shh, she said. Listen, she said. Be still. Be still on your bed, I thought to myself, that thing in The Bible, in Psalms, where you are commanded to be still on your bed and to stand in awe and sin not. What's that sound, she said. Shh. Listen. What's that sound? But there was nothing but the sound of the wind outside and of this silent council house creaking in the wind. No, she said, can't you hear it? Teeth, she said. The sound of teeth, she said, and she turned me on, in a flash, I thought she meant we were going to tear each other apart in passion but she said, no, over by the sink, she said, listen. But still I couldn't hear anything. She dropped to her knees, by the side of the sink. There, she said, look, and she pointed to a tiny spider devouring another insect, eating it alive, tearing apart its flesh on the floor next to the sink. She had heard the sound of its teeth in the silence. The sound of its tiny blade-like teeth cracking through the shell of this tinier creature still and drinking down its blood and guts and shit-sack and entrails. Afterwards I sat on my bed, in the dark, and wept sopping wet tears because I loved her so much I could never tell her.

Harder.

On Egyptian monuments to the dead, the male lion takes the place assigned to the gargoyles on the great cathedrals due to a belief that Seth, the disharmonious brother, and his armies attacked the temples of the gods and goddesses in the form of rainstorms. The stone lions on the roofs, they believed, would devour their enemies and spit them out in streams of water.

Harder.

The Gnostics sought for a release from time by insisting that Christ had urged us to give up the flesh because he himself had no body to speak of. If the church is the body of Christ, then the church, too, is invisible. To make monument, then, to make religious statuary, is to mirror nothing. Which is the way of the greatest art. Monument maker.

Harder.

I'm following in the footsteps of Pierre, I tell myself, as I stand in front of some forsaken monument, and cross myself, and this wind, these hailstones coming down, is this how it was for you, Pierre, I think to myself, and right then I see my Flower, coming out of the past, now, coming out of the past with her raincoat held over her head, her blue raincoat and her wet hair, running across the road, this cobblestone road chiselled straight into the flesh of my heart, and she has bought us cigarettes, a handful of single cigarettes from some old man in a bar, and here she is, now, out of the rain, and fuck you, Pierre, my shadow, fuck you, as I cross myself in the hail and in the rain, that time, and harder, Pierre, you bastard.

Harder.

I lined that metal container that lay on the edge of the still grey lake in this strange forgotten quarry that I lived in (and that would have felt like an oven had it not been used as a storage hut for certain volatile chemicals, previously, certain experimental cocktails, or so local legend had it, that meant it was perforated and lined with odd ducts and foams which contributed to the constant feel of being inside of a lung, of feeling that metal, too, is breathing, but slower than trees) for one momentous summer, with sheet music, I crammed it into all the walls, I felt better for it, (crammed in), beautiful editions of old religious sheet music that I picked up at the same weekend market I scoured for stoneworking materials like penknives and compasses and old bottle openers and potato peelers and weird rusted tools like grave pickings. Above my bed, in a section of the container that I had walled off using old wooden pallets, I hung the notation for one of the greatest pieces of religious music ever made, *Spem In Alium Nunquam Habui*, a motet in forty parts (do you even know what a motet is? It is a form of vocal polyphony that would open man to God, as in open up a space in his heart, a negative space, fashioned by a withdrawing, in the perfect shape of the heart, which is where Christ appears, as he does on walnuts and squashed fruits and the pips of tomatoes in strange outdated villages where superstitious farmers truly understand God's love for everything created, for everything created, I say it again, from finely carved seeds and perfect snowflakes through monumental cathedrals of stone, this is the space where God enters, for man cannot come to God except as a man, or a woman, for aspiring to ascend is spiritual hubris of the highest order, is not truly union of man-as-man with God-as-God, which is a Christ-shaped hole in the heart, which is permanently there but which like in the superstitions of the Sufis, just as in the mathematics of the Trinity, requires a mediator, it would seem, the Sufis, I say, a particular Glaswegian sect of which I was once, briefly, an initiate,

in which I entered into the lineage, made the connection,
was the religious term, via the heart meditation known as
Qutub, where the heart is located between the ribs, on the
left side, as a point, as surely as a spear had been thrust in
there, or more properly a cable, a heavenly expressway by
which, in its piercing, God gains access and meets the man
of his creation, and which I experienced, in a community
centre in the Garnethill area of the city in which I was
initiated, as an ecstatic sense of sexual communion, just
as in the music of Thomas Tallis, of this *Spem In Alium*,
which means *Of Hope In Any Other I Have None* or better
still *Hope In No Other* or better yet *Hopelessly Devoted To
You*, and which I hung above my bed, whose pages I cut out,
whose pages were mostly taken up with instructions for the
multiple choirs to be silent, as if the music, too, music on
music, more truly, was received through an empty hole in
the heart whose name was Christ and who was the entry
point to the Father, these empty bars marked by a single
dot, again and again, a single black dot as the infinite point
between this world as it is and this world as it lies behind
it, these strange symmetrical tears, falling down, it would
seem to me some nights, as I lay upside down on my bed,
in the candlelight of my past, and dreamed of the empty
insides of the great cathedrals, the echoing cloisters of all
this continent's crumbling monasteries and the negative
spaces they were built, not so much to contain, but to
invent, to sound out, the lacks they sounded, this silence of
the great empty cathedrals, that summer, and for the rest
of my life, is the empty music, whose greatest composer
was Thomas Tallis, who was an architect on this earth in
as much as he was commissioned to sound the spaces that
the cathedrals have come down to this earth to draw our
attention to and yet he was the same empty size as them, he

was in that sense equal to them, as a diving bell goes down to the surface, so is the church as the body of Christ, which is the zero that is at the centre of everything, and which is a halo, as much as a mouth, as much as the trim little hole of my darling, Flower).

Harder.

What is Not Man comes to Man so that Man can be as Not Man. This is the story of the Gospels, the history of religious art, and the story of my life.

Harder.

Her trim little hole. She spreads it for me, there, on a stool in the container, by the light of the moon, I almost said, rising up, from the waters, I almost said, to the vision of her trim little hole, forgive me, it's the religious in me, whose name is Faith & Awe, her dark-green eyes, by candlelight, her red-painted fingernails, spreading her lips, like a perfect butterfly designed by an incomprehensible god, and weeping, too, in sorrow and in pity, now, at what God has only gone and done with Himself, and delight in it, too, which is the Devil, I thought to myself, as I got down on my hands and knees before her and entered her with my tongue, and prised apart the belly of the butterfly, slid my fingers to the meridians, and held them there, pulled her black panties to one side, and felt them tear, and wet, and wondered about proxies, about counterparts, about intermediaries like butterflies and devils and panties in between, and knew God, more truly then I knew God, than in the silent womb of the great cathedrals, even. Right then, I said, there is a time for making monument for everything

that is built. Yet some things are longing not to be built. I
said that too, and then I thought:

Harder.

Flower's old boyfriend Davide finally gave me a doing. I was
browsing in a bookshop in town when he approached the
window and pressed his face against it and made a mime
of flicking his tongue between his index and middle finger.
I went outside and challenged him, and he gave me a right
good pasting on the spot. Then he said that Flower was just
his bitch on the side and that he couldn't care anyway and
he walked off, with a leer on his face.

Harder.

6. MONASTERY OF THE COLLARED DOVE COME PUZZLED DOWN FROM HEAVEN

Everything is empty. I am sitting in a garden with my Flower, next to a slow-moving river, in the twilight, talking to a drunken Finnish poet that we met in the hotel. A female duck is stood on the wall facing us. Saliva trails from its open mouth. Everything is empty, I am thinking to myself, as my beautiful Flower sits with her feet up on the wall drinking from an impossibly large can of French artisanal beer. The poet has just returned from an ashram in India. Have you ever been to an ashram? the poet asks us. You forget everything you ever wanted, she says. You go to bed at four and you get up at five, she tells us, drinking from an impossibly large glass of wine. Then you do yoga, she says, and that's when you forget everything. The discipline, she says, and she nods her head, it's the discipline that does it.

Everything is empty, though now, as I relate this to you now, I think, maybe it was just me, maybe I am the one who is empty, and who cannot be altered, because I recall feeling nothing, profoundly, but still, nothing at all, as I sat there in what now seems to me most like everything I ever wanted, a retreat in France, my beautiful Flower, an impossibly large can of beer, the slowness of the evening

and the slow rippling of the river, the sounds of the birds
in the high trees and the kids across the way, yet as I sat
there I felt nothing, as though I had been lowered into the
scene, again as in a diving bell, and was bearing witness to
simple happenings at the bottom of the sea or the beginning
of time, as implacably uninteresting as that, the only sounds
as echoing, the beat of my heart, the sound of my breath,
in the cocoon of my body, which was made to wait for God
who is already here, God is already here, I tell myself, and
you are empty to receive Him. For God made emptiness
and pointlessness, I am thinking to myself, if things
weren't empty, I am thinking, if things had a point, then
we would be permanently distracted from God. But God is
in everything, God says to me, in His echoing, and I am left
puzzled, and come down from heaven.

I was living in the middle of nowhere, the drunken Finnish
poet tells me, with nothing but a hundred horses. Would a
hundred horses be enough, I think to myself, but enough for
what.

Harder.

Basalt is the densest form of rock, which means it is the
least empty. But where are the basalt cathedrals? The
Cathedral of Our Lady of the Assumption of Clermont-
Ferrand is a cathedral of dense black lava. The cathedral
at Agde is built from black volcanic basalt. Its walls are
between two and three metres thick. When a cathedral is
built from the densest stone it is no longer a cathedral. It is
a mighty fortress. The mighty fortress is accessed through
what is known as a 'lady chapel'. I am listening to my
Flower and the drunken Finnish poet discuss how fashion

photography has changed in the past ten years. It used to be beautiful, the drunken Finnish poet says, but now it is all ugly, ugly, ugly. What a confusion of thoughts I am thinking as I am sat there, echoing.

The French know how to relax, and they do their relaxing anywhere. That's the conclusion you would be drawn to if you had joined my Flower and I as we cycled along the Canal du Loing and passed sleeping motorcyclists passed out in the weeds by the bank, families picnicking on the verge by the side of the road, two fellows fishing round the back of an abandoned grain silo and best of all a young girl on a fold-out bed at the foot of a row of terrible rusting gas tanks, cut off from the sun and hidden in shadow, fully spreadeagled as though on a beach in the Med.

Another conclusion to which you may have been drawn had you accompanied us on this idyllic day out now misfiled somewhere long ago in the past would be that French householders are inexplicably shocked to see anyone who does not resemble themselves pass anywhere near their homes. The French have a facial expression reserved especially for the split second you pass by their domain that best resembles a puzzled bird, as you pass by and you gaze into their gardens with all of the longing you could possibly muster for another life which you could disappear into, another life where tall sunflowers grow and tomato plants stand staked in neat rows and fat French cats prowl the undergrowth and forest vipers belt it as soon as they hear the rattle of your wheels, or before some fat French kid can drop a slab on their head, and still the French gaze at you in puzzlement as you speed by, as if you were there to steal their eggs, as an emissary from another planet where

eggs are as gold, or to snatch a forbidden glimpse of a gaudy
painted statue of the Virgin Mary in the back garden of a
tree-shaded villa, or a photograph of said Virgin, even, stood
in inexplicable sorrow next to a gaudy statue of a horse
and cart, as if each view, each blissful domestic vista, were
something to be snatched and stolen and secreted away in
full view of its proud and hard-working owner, and every
few minutes I would have to dismount and check behind me
where, in the distance, my Flower, in a stained metallic-blue
dress and sandals, her hair tied up and dishevelled in the
sun, was invariably photographing one of these secret
back gardens, invariably peopled by scattered passed-out
French families in nothing but shorts and bikinis, sleeping
with one eye open for would-be amateur sleuths ready
to steal their native souls, and I confess that it irritated
me, yes, this empty irritation would seize me and I would
curse her under my breath, every time my Flower stopped
to add yet another pointless photograph to her collection
I would curse her – Lord! what an imbecile, I would say –
because back then I was convinced that photography was
a hobby for the sort of people who have hobbies (I curse
that word hobby, just so you know, I curse that word God
damn it I curse it and I spit it out, too), especially profligate
photographers, of whom this day my Flower was surely
one, as I flattered myself that I, and only I, was able to
take the correct temperature of the moment, and when I
stooped to photographing something or other myself, it was
invariably the correct moment, and the perfect shot, and
I took one photograph and one photograph only, because I
flattered myself that I understood the moment of things, can
you believe it, it would be laugh-out-loud funny if it wasn't
outrageous, if it wasn't extremely sad, that here I was, on a
day trip out into the newly made past with my Flower by my

side and I flattered myself that I understood the gravity of
moments while at the very same time I fled them and cursed
them and ranted against them as though the correct moment
were only up ahead, in Nemours, in Fontainebleau, in the
magical village of Larchant, where a visit to the basilica is
reputed to cure you of madness, and of course I was right,
and all of those villages do lie in the future of this book, just
up ahead, stood in awe, themselves, at the perfect moment
they have been entrusted to deliver, but even so, even when
we reach these moments, which right now lie just ahead in
this book – have patience where I had none – though even
when we reach them we will find that our attention is once
again drawn to the future, to the moment when all of the
contents of these moments cohere in a single revelation,
which, too, has its moment, and which points to a further
revelation, which is the curse of photography too, I say, and
which speaks to our terrible inability to simply be, to be still,
and yet, should we refrain from internally ranting about
the perceived failings of the ones we are supposedly head
over heels in love with, we would again come to this empty
point, this stillness, and we too, if we knew what was good
for us, if we were able to arrive in this stillness, then we too
would strip off most of our clothes and lie down, together,
in the nearest tall grass and forgive ourselves everything
but this present moment which we would indeed snatch and
secrete and memorialise, in our fear and confusion and in our
longing to let it all go to hell, even at the foot of rusting water
towers, of ghastly oil drums and faceless industrial factories,
even in the shadows of these ghastly things, we would topple
from our bikes, on top of each other, in that summer, long
ago, and we would refuse to move, yes, you heard that right
Our Father who art in heaven, I am proposing a sit-in in my
past, I am calling for a peaceful protest, back then, but what

good does it do as my Flower pulls up at some idiot savant assemblage of mannequin heads and old rusting watering cans and wooden barrels and metal hubcaps behind a locked gate on the canal, and I look at my watch, and I throw my bike to the ground, and I stand, impatient, in the distance, I think you can picture me there, tapping my foot impatiently, like a bull, as if there was a more perfect assignation up ahead, and of course there was, there is, don't despair, we'll get there, in the end, but still, really, everything I have to say is here, everything I could have said was then, and I was unworthy of the gift. I had yet to learn gratitude. Ha ha, gratitude, I hear you say, bugger off with your gratitude. But you are only twenty years old – if that – and so I refuse to take you seriously. And I say it again: gratitude, you ungrateful little bastard, now grow the fuck up.

I am caught up reading the letters of August Strindberg, which I pilfered from the library of the hotel in which he is supposed to have stayed while writing some wretched book about the state of the French peasantry. Who no doubt stared at him like puzzled birds too. I am one hell of a man, he writes, as you can see, and I am capable of the most unusual things, he says. He is boasting about his facility with language, but he was also capable of full-blown possession, of channelling thoughts via an iron bed frame placed in the attic above his room, and of visiting his estranged lover while asleep, on the astral plane, and of making love to her there, against her will, it has to be said, poor Harriet Bosse, raped by Sweden's maddest playwright in her dreams, a hell of a man. Do you even know who August Strindberg is? I sincerely hope not, because that would make you either Scandinavian, in which case stop reading now I hate you (unless you are Finnish, and a

drunken Finnish poet to boot), either that or you are some
fan of the theatre of the nineteenth century or perhaps you
are some simpleton attracted to the occult, in all of which
cases I most politely invite you to fuck the hell off and stop
reading now, please. Because I am one hell of a man.

As I am writing this, at the bottom of the garden in which
this Strindberg fellow cursed ghosts in four languages and
could have done with a visit to the basilica at Larchant for
which to cure his mythomania (it's only a forty-minute cycle
away, for God's sake), I realise I am one to talk, I admit
it, I am one hell of man, writing this while all around me
there is the most incredible hubbub, as young boys and girls
in pretty pink bikinis and long sandy hair make daredevil
leaps from the bridge into the water, one beautiful girl
in particular, who I estimate as being thirteen years old
and whose tiny pink bikini is the colour of pale flesh made
rosy by the sun, and I turn to look over my shoulder and
I see the same table and chairs at which we sat, all those
years ago, look up to the bridge we crossed to the Sunday
market where I fell into conversation, incomprehensible
conversation, you would have thought, with this eccentric
old French guy's madness, I had spotted him earlier on,
shopping for old bottle tops spread across a tabletop, had
looked over his shoulder and spotted a catalogue in which
he had highlighted his own finds with fluorescent marker,
and who is this mad old bat, I had thought to myself, and
I, a collector of eccentrics, I admit, had walked off satisfied,
and was busy flicking through a collection of old French
porno magazines with titles like *Rendezvous* and *Contact*,
with pictures of young, newly budded women and of French
teenagers bent over in tight black panties when I was
approached by this same eccentric collector, who nudged

me and said, in French, which I understood immediately, perfectly, you will like this, he said, and he pointed to a certain maker of bottle tops, next to which he had attached a Post-it note that mentioned three odd – and very rare – variants, known only to initiates, he said, and he laughed, with glee, at the sharing of this arcane knowledge with a stranger at a French market, and on the Post-it notes he had hand-drawn what he believed the bottle tops to have featured, the Kama Sutra, he said, and he laughed and he nudged me, the Kama Sutra edition, he said, and he pointed to his drawings, one of which had a tick beside it, as if he had confirmed the existence of at least one of this supposed secret sex trinity to be found on the tops of beer bottles in the past, one that featured a stick woman bent over in front of a stick man, while the second, so far unlocated by this eccentric sleuth, featured a woman on her knees in the act of fellatio, while the third featured what seemed to be the same stick woman spreadeagled on a table or pedestal while the man held her by the heels and entered her, and he muttered one word, this eccentric collector of insignia and erotica, which was the French word for pigeon or dove, I believed, or rather I was instructed, in that moment, and he offered me his hand, still laughing the whole time, and he told me his name, which was Bernard, and he asked me my own and I said to him I'm August Strindberg, I said, and I'm one hell of a man.

Harder.

There is no better way to be here now than to witness, from a distance, your Flower having sex with another man. I am in the adjoining room with my trousers round my ankles, praising the moment to the skies, in a terrible agony, in divine rapture. I hear him mutter something in French, this young kid, this boy, really, who we picked up at the market across the bridge, this young boy selling rock n roll postcards and hard-rock LPs from the back of a car, this boy from a village, oh, ten kilometres away, he said, and now I am in the moment completely and am emptier still. I hear him mutter something in French. A command, I tell myself, he is commanding her. I hear her gasp and assent, again and again, oui, oui. Yes, she is telling him, yes, she is saying. Now he is insulting her, I tell myself, now he is humiliating her. I wish my French were better. The cocks of these young boys, she says afterwards, are like iron bars. Though perhaps that is just my clumsy translation.

Can the sharing of your partner bring you closer? Yes, but closer to what? Near to the wild heart, I tell myself, which is one of my favourite books, as well as a quote from James Joyce, but you wouldn't know anything about that, would you? God has come down into the flesh, I say to you, and I have heard it with mine own eyes.

We got into a fight at a restaurant in the village of Grez-sur-Loing. I should say: I got into a fight at a restaurant in the village of Grez-sur-Loing. I had heard it was a rip-off. The drunken Finnish poet warned me: that guy will charge you for extra beers and he will whip his price list away should you question it and he will claim that there are new prices for everything as of now. Plus, the pizzas are the saltiest pizzas I have ever eaten, she warned me. It took me three beers to finish one, she said. We had spent the afternoon swimming in the river at the bottom of the garden, my Flower and I, the same garden in which your man Strindberg had boasted about his facility for language.

I rehearsed what I would say. Can you recommend me a good red wine, I would say (in French). A good French wine but one that is not too expensive, I would say (in French). And don't cheat me, I would say (in Scottish this time, for effect). This place feels like the cloisters of a monastery, my Flower said to me (in English, in cute pigeon English), as she floated on her back in the river. I sat with my feet dangling and let the minnows, the little younkers, we called them, my father and I, the little younkers that were swarming around me in the waters, I let them nibble at my legs. It is like the cloisters of a monastery where people write and paint all day and then emerge to bathe in the water, my Flower said. And watch out for your translations, the drunken Finnish poet who was already well sauced by this point said to us, I have two friends who went in there and ended up with a plate of kidney and had to take it away in a plastic bag.

At first all went well. My translations were all in order. My Flower will have the pizza with artichoke and olives, I said (in French). I will have the breaded escalope with house tagliatelle, I said (in French). And could you, monsieur, recommend me a good red wine, not too expensive, I said (in French). He said something in French in return, blah, blah, blah, un petit Bordeaux, he said. A bottle? I asked him (in French). Non, he said. Non. Then he brought us a bottle of Graves – ah, Graves! I exclaimed (because it is my favourite) – and he uncorked it, sniffed it, and offered me a taste. Très bon? he said. Oui, I said, très bon. At this point a mangy dog with sores all over its arse and with painfully swollen black balls crawled under my seat and began rubbing itself on the legs and making a growling noise. You make that noise! my Flower said to me, and she laughed. You make the same noise as my boyfriend, she said to this mangy dog beneath the table, and she winked at him. We sat outside and ate our dinner as the clouds turned to puffs of pink candyfloss. Across the way a Frenchman in a backwards baseball cap and with a T-shirt that said New York on it pulled into a shuttered garage. Do you know the song 'Europe Endless' by Kraftwerk? my Flower asked me, because it was as if we could see all the way over the horizon to forever. The food arrived and there was ham on the vegetarian pizza. The menu made no mention of ham on the pizza, but we decided to leave it. He rushed us for coffee. Would you like some coffees? he said (in French). We'll finish our wine first, my friend, I said (in English this time), and he shrugged and walked off. But when we came to pay there was a problem. He had charged us thirty-four euros for a bottle of wine. I told you not too expensive! I burst, and Flower told me to calm down, what is the problem, and the proprietor's wife, who was also the long-suffering chef, vacated the scene 'tout de suite'. Don't fucking cheat me! I screamed at the proprietor, and my Flower ran outside. The proprietor said something in French, something interminable in French, and I went for him. I grabbed him by the throat and I told him that all non-French-speakers were not so gullible (only in Scottish), that he shouldn't take me for a fucking mug (in straight Scottish this time), and that I would beat his fucking Danny DeVito arse to a pulp. Then he handed me the card machine. It read 3.40 euros. Is this correct? I demanded. Oui, he said. Oui. I paid and then I stomped out with a leer on my face. Let's go, I told my Flower, and I showed her the receipt. Then we marched off in the opposite direction, so he couldn't be sure of where we were staying or even dream of sending anyone after us. Later that night, wired on coffee and adrenaline, we made love on the couch while outside the open window a thunderstorm raged, and the pots fell from the walls, and people stormed up and down in the corridors outside.

What are those wrinkles across your lower back? I wonder about my Flower as she lies on the banks of the river reading a pamphlet about the religious architecture of the Île-de-France. Are they the same as the suffering marks on a tree?

We swam in the river with the drunken Finnish poet, who this time was drinking only sparkling water on account of a hangover the size of a truck. She had been to read at some international poetry gathering in Paris the night before and had missed the last train home so had been forced to sleep drunk at the bus station. Her poems had been badly mistranslated, she claimed, and she had been given no chance to see the edits before publication. I told her about my own experience translating Pierre's book, how I had taught myself basic French from books and from dictionaries to be able to do it. I can read and write it fine, I said to her. Then we told her about our experience with the restaurateur across the way. He can't speak a word of English, she despaired. You should have kicked his fucking arse, she said. Then a fog came down and Flower and the hung-over Finnish poet sat on the bank and applied make-up to their faces. Let's get inner tubes, the hung-over Finnish poet said, let's all buy inner tubes and we can float down the river together and then hitch-hike back in our swimming costumes. They traded foundation, cream foundation was the term they used. It's what the saints use in the old paintings, my Flower joked. It gives them that sallow-in-the-face-of-God look, she said, only she didn't use the word sallow, that is my better translation. The hung-over Finnish poet wore a pair of boy shorts and a mismatched bikini top, while my Flower wore a russet-green one-piece swimming costume. The hung-over Finnish poet told us about some standing stones she had visited in the weeks previous, some dolmens, she said. Do you know about dolmens, they are monolithic stones propped up in circles and rows in order to align with the solstice and equinox, she said. In France there is what is known as the Circuit des Mégalithes, she told us. But before I could say, we laugh at megaliths and dolmens like at simpletons who cannot spell, I recalled something that Mary had told me, that a girlfriend had told her, something about walking cures and completing circuits, but before I could say, oh, I see, you mean that when you complete the circle of the stones you feel changed and transformed, like writing words or letters into the earth, words or letters that could only be read from heaven or from space, but before I could say any of this she said, no, I mean a circuit as in an electrical circuit, my hair stood on end, she said, my hair stood on end like in one of those mad science experiments, she said, and someone fried an egg on one of the stones just like it was plugged into the grid, she said, and then she went on and on, deeper into idiocy, with talk of ley lines and apparitions, and I was waiting for a UFO to touch down any second or for the Men in Black to appear from the hollow core at the earth's centre with a message from the secret masters. I looked at my Flower and she looked back at me, she knows me too well, I thought, and I said to the hung-over Finnish poet, who by this point had put on a red dress with prints of what looked like some Indian peasant sat in meditation all over it, so what? Do you really think that the other side chooses not only to communicate with us but to alert us to its own existence by demonstrating its powers to fry an egg or make your hair stand up or to make a light pass over you in the sky? The spirit is not a circus animal, I said, nor is it a clown, but before I could dismiss her fantasies completely she said, no, it proves one thing and one thing only, she said, stone, she said, is alive.

Harder.

The past and the future are tombs from which Christ is risen. A stone is a stone is a stone. Is.

Harder.

In order to demonstrate my facility with the French language, and to convince you that I, too, am one hell of a man, here are some poems by my favourite religious poet, Pierre Reverdy, that I have translated from the French and that, I think you'll find, are vast improvements on the nascent versions published by that clown Kenneth Rexroth via New Directions in some flimsy paperback or other.

SECRET

The empty bell
The dead birds
In the house where everyone is falling asleep
Nine o'clock

The earth stands still
It is as if someone sighed
The trees seem to smile
Water trembles at the tip of each leaf
A cloud crosses the night

Before the door a man is singing

The window opens without a sound

GOODBYE

The glow that overwhelms the head
                    The leap of the heart
On the slope where the air rolls his voice
              the spokes of the wheel
              the sun in the furrow

              At the crossroads
              close by the hill
                    a prayer
Words you cannot hear
        Closer to the sky
    And in his footsteps
                    the last square of light

JOURNEYS WITHOUT END

All those we saw from behind who went away singing
Who had been passing along the river
Where even the reeds repeated their prayer
Which was taken up by the birds stronger and further
They are the first to arrive and will not leave
They counted one step and then the next along their way
Which disappeared as they went
        They walked on the hard stone
At the edge of the fields they paused
At the edge of the water they quenched their thirst
    Their feet raised the dust
And it was a cloak embroidered by light
All those who went
walking in this desert
And for whom the sky was now open
Still seeking the point where the world ends
The wind that drove them continued on its rounds
      And the door closed
  A black door
      Night

Everyone around here hates August Strindberg, God knows why.

7. MINISTRY OF THE LANDING ON WATER OF THE PUZZLED TURTLE DOVE

The perfect French country lane is to be found in small
villages south of Paris, running between abandoned villas
and shuttered summer houses, with single tyre tracks
leading off and soft dandelions and daisies rising up,
and with moss growing in the stonework and with locked
wooden doors painted green and flaking in the sun and with
overhanging foliage and with red-tiled roofs to the left and
right and the smell of warm grass and manure in the air
and with dark shadows across the way and not a soul in
sight, not a single soul in sight, and that appear endless,
and that seem to lead to the place you have been dreaming
of your entire life, the place you left somewhere dear in
childhood, perhaps, and which now, once more, is just up
ahead, in dappled shadow, where the birds circle, just out of
sight, and where a solitary nameplate, gone rusty in the sun
and the rain, reads Ruelle de Squab. Ruelle de Squab, baby.
That is how it reads.

There is a bar in Bourron-Marlotte run by an actual
Frenchman in an actual beret with an actual goatee who
plays atonal acoustic guitar between serving overpriced

French artisanal beers and shaking his head over his lack of
a single fucking word of English. On the wall Elvis Presley
appears to have donated one of his gold records to the
cause ('Rock-a-Hula Baby') alongside framed photographs
of Marilyn Monroe, B.B. King and Johnny Hallyday ('Le
Rocker Originel'). They charge you to take a photograph
of the photographs. It is my favourite bar in all of France.
My Flower and I sat outside, drinking beer in the rain.
Don't you want to go inside? a drunken French rocker
with swollen calves and a precocious beer gut asked us.
Non, monsieur, I assured him. We're happy where we are.
Where are you from? he asked me. From Scotland, I said (in
French). Ah, he said. In that case it is easy for you. It is easy
for me, I said to him. You have no idea. It is so fucking easy
for me you would not believe.

The Lord is my rock and my fortress: at the centre of the
world there is the castle of heaven. But this does not mean
to say that somewhere, locatable, there is an actual castle
in which God sits as some kind of feudal baron (?). It says
that every moment, every second, is fortified by the living
presence of God. That there is something to which the
present moment cleaves, as in a rock. But this rock is not a
rock, an actual rock. But actual rock, creation in stone, in its
solidity (its fixity?), in its memorialising in time, is closest to
God-work. And so, I have come to love the churches that are
fallen down, that have been eroded and eaten away, for in
their not-God-ness they are more fastly held (?) in the arms
of God. I prefer God as a rock, God as a stone (but what
cares God for my preference?), to God as a father, simply
because stone is less comprehensible than fatherhood, and I
say that as someone who has never fathered a child, though
not for want of trying (?!), and for whom fatherhood is not

something uncomplicated, not something straightforward, but still, it makes of God and man a mere human relationship, and while of course God must contain all of the attributes of man within Himself, as all of the attributes of fatherhood and of rock and of stone, He must also exceed and encompass (?) them. God-ness contains both fatherhood and stone but God-ness is neither fatherhood nor stone. But if God is not entirely of anything of this world, then how do we come to Him? Answer: we do our best. And no more. For He is here already, and so cannot be sought.

I have just performed a joyless wank. As you get older masturbation becomes less satisfying. You may know that already. Or you may be shocked and dismayed to hear it. It is no longer yourself that commands it, rather a form of libidinal debt upon which the soul shrinks and recoils, as does said member, in the sorrow of its coming, on the ghastly bathroom floor. Sorry to break it to you, if so.

Harder.

Harder.

But what of the miracle of the Mass? God descends into simple bread and wine and permits us to partake of his body. Because Christianity is a religion for all and does not permit access to only rarefied (?) spiritual thinkers, because there is no qualification required for spiritual communion, because there is nothing to be solved, and nowhere to go, and nothing to be uncovered. For the kingdom of heaven is at hand. Because of this, God, too, is a father, and a bridegroom, and is cold, hard stone. And Jesus is born in a stable and cradled in the feed box of a donkey. John of Damascus called these monuments the Books of the Unlearned. But because of this too (and how to escape it?): biblical literalism, the historical Christ, religion as the obeying of arbitrary rules. God ties Himself up in confusions in the name of spiritual democracy. He loses Himself in order that every man can find Him.

But didn't Pierre already say that He cannot be sought?

Here is a picture of Pierre from the time of the Church of the Stone of First Witness. He is sat on a rusting wrought-iron chair at the foot of the garden of the riverside house previously owned by the composer Frederick Delius in the village of Grez-sur-Loing, the same composer who set words from Nietzsche's *Thus Spoke Zarathustra* to music and titled it *A Mass of Life*. The man to the right of the photograph, the exceptionally tall man with the round spectacles and the liver spots on his head that make him look like a terribly cultured giraffe, I believe to be the man known as Frater Jim. The couple to the left are the ceramicist and painter Hildegard von Strophe and the religious polemicist, writer and soldier of fortune Max Rehberg in the wake of the campaign in some tinpot military dictatorship in Africa during which he lost his arm (more of which anon).

But what strikes me most about this picture is that Pierre is wearing an eyepatch, a black eyepatch, over his left eye. At first I thought it was a shadow, a dark shadow over his left eye, as in a painting by Rembrandt, then I wondered if it wasn't in fact an erasure on the photograph itself, a smudge like on an old icon or a damaged mosaic, how appropriate, I told myself, but then I realised, he is wearing an eyepatch, he is wearing an eyepatch as some kind of affectation, I told myself, like James Joyce, didn't James Joyce wear some stupid eyepatch to appear more literary or was it to focus one side of his brain, isn't that what they say, that the left hemisphere is attached to the right eye and the right to the left? And when one side is impaired then the other compensates? And so I convinced myself that this was no mere affectation, no fey artistic pose, but rather an experiment in consciousness, and in seeing, and I purchased an eyepatch myself, and I entered churches, and I took it all in, in emulation of this photograph, this photograph in which I neglected to say that the woman was topless, and the men in their vests and shirtsleeves, as if they were part of some liberatory cult, or experiment in communal living, which, I was to find out, was very much the case, though, in another way, not at all.

And of course I thought of that passage in The Bible, that beautiful speech of Christ's which is his true teaching, which is faith and awe, where he beseeches the true believer to give no thought to tomorrow, to food and to shelter and to money and to reputation, and no thought to clothes neither, because God has clothed the flowers of the field, even though tomorrow they are headed for the furnace.

I must fix this summer in stone, this summer of my Flower and I. The evening we attended a concert of baroque music in the country villa of a couple who lived just outside the village of Villiers-sous-Grez. The time we cycled through the overgrown tracks of the Forest of Fontainebleau and got lost in the gloom and covered in mosquito bites only to emerge into the most perfect sunset over the cornfields and wild poppies, with happy cats clawing at wooden fences and fat old women in headscarves walking with canes down

perfectly tended country lanes. The time we bought home-
brewed beer from some red-faced, white-haired ex-sailor
in his cottage with a thatched roof. The baroque music
trio with the unforgettable singer who looked just like my
sister, and whose face seemed like the perfect mirror of my
own, which is divided, and mismatched, the left side of her
face fallen, the right perfectly formed, and who played bass
recorder accompanied by a huge old lute and a bass viol, and
whose music seemed to speak of a time of divine regency,
which is to say a time when it was commonly accepted that
everything is appointed by God, even, perhaps especially,
baroque music trios in dreamy book-lined country villas,
which is now, which was now, with huge friendly Alsatians
in the kitchen and wooden beams and replicas of Picasso
on the walls (I'll get to Picasso, in my survey of religious
art I must, of course, get to Picasso) and everybody singing,
everybody singing a soft, melancholic ballad in French that
spoke of different times, I almost wept, different times, I
almost cried to myself, different times are here before us, I
almost burst, as they performed pieces by names I did not
know but names on which I have long since pinned my heart,
but don't play them for me, please, don't gift me a CD of their
works, for, as I say, I may just burst if you were to play me
something by Robert de Visée (please don't) or Jean-Féry
Rebel or Jacques Hotteterre or Charles Mouton (I simply
couldn't stand it) or Antoine Boësset or Tarquinio Merula or
Claudio Monteverdi (back then the only one I knew, but in
the light of the past, please, I beg of you, don't) or Giovanni
Girolamo Kapsberger or (please no!) 'Guárdame las vacas'
by an anonymous Espagnol circa 1550. I beg of you, please,
lay off, let go. And all the while there are a pair of friendly
drunks behind us, throwing scraps of bread through the
door of the living room in order to encourage a fat chicken,

running wild, to cross the performance space like some kind of avant-garde intervention, and I thought of Mary just then, 'candied friend of my youth', I thought, which is a line from a poem, do you know it, and I wondered if she was even still alive, and we cycled back to the hotel, happily drunk, the two of us, through the dark forest with strange sounds all around us, and I recalled my sister, in another life, whose beautiful broken face had looked into my own, had she had a stroke, I wondered, are all choristers touched, I asked myself, as we sat at the open window and drank a final beer together and heard a crash, a huge bang, somewhere in the distance and then, silence. Different times are right here, I tell myself, as I make monument of those evenings.

The little boats, on the river, at the bottom of the garden, are pure joy. They are supported by my father, who I drowned in the river, but who can never drown. I walk in until I am submerged, and I rise again to the surface. The little boats are pure joy, Dad. And now you are in every river of the world.

We bumped into another artist at the hotel, my Flower and I, a boring Swedish artist who was paid by the government to doodle, but we thought he might be a good companion for the drunken Finnish poet, who by this point was really starting to do our heads in, so we invited them both for another night out at the country villa where we had seen the baroque music, and the four of us cycled there in the evening. We ate outside in the garden while the Finn and the Swede discussed Marcel Proust and how he was so incredibly detailed. He will talk about a tree, then a flower, then a view, then a bedspread, the drunken Finnish poet marvelled. I don't remember the bedspread, the dull Swede, who actually looked a little like the poet Robert Creeley, said. There was no set menu, so of course the timid Swede was anxious, but when the plates arrived, with French ham and pork and lettuce and cheese and tomato and cherries and strawberries, he exclaimed and said, ah, this is exactly what I would have liked. I hate you, I thought, underneath my breath, I fucking hate you and hope you die.

In my quest for homemade beer the proprietor introduced me to a local woman who grew her own hops and we fell into conversation. She and her husband had moved to the village two years ago, with the intention that her husband would work on his sculpture while she indulged her own passions, but a mere two weeks after their arrival he collapsed and died from a sudden brain aneurysm and so she had been taken under the wings of the local artistic community because she knew no one else, no one else at all. Her passion, she told me, was African American men. Particularly their presence, or not, at the Normandy landings, she clarified. There are photographs of African American men at Ardennes, she said. There are photographs of African American men at many of the flashpoints of the Second World War, she said. That word, flashpoint, I thought, when she said that. Yet there are no photographs of African American men at Normandy, she said. So I looked into it. I looked into it, she said, and I found out that, yes, indeed, there had been many African American soldiers at Normandy and yet there was no documentation of them. It became my passion, she said, I have no idea why, but it became my passion to reinstate (another word that struck me when she said it) African American soldiers into the historical narrative of the Normandy landings ('historical narrative' was another), although no one wanted to hear it, she laughed, so I was forced to offer my services for free and to inform anyone who would listen, which was inevitably ladies' groups in small villages or homeless communities ('homeless communities') or even, she laughed again, institutionalised retards ('institutionalised retards').

Think about it, she said, these black GIs who fought at D-Day came back to a segregated America and were never decorated. That reminds me, I said to her, wasn't Mauthausen concentration camp liberated by an African American tank commander in a stolen tank? I haven't heard that one, she said. Yes, I told her, as I became sure of this strange memory, he turned up in a tank and all of the starving prisoners were suspicious and of course some of them were shocked to see a black man in charge of a tank at the head of a liberating force and some of them believed it to be a trap or, worse, the work of the Russians. But the African American tank commander stood on top of his tank and announced as loudly and as clearly as he could to the masses of inmates cowering in fear and confusion or walking round in a strange daze that Hitler was dead. Hitler is kaput! he announced, before withdrawing, into history and folklore, never to be named, or photographed, or heard from again. Wow, she said, that is quite some story, but I specialise in the Normandy landings, so it's beside the point.

There is a concert at the local church tonight, she said. I think you and your friends may enjoy it. It's a free concert, she said, where the orchestra will play Bruckner's Symphony No. 7. Isn't that the music that accompanied the announcement of Hitler's suicide on German radio? I asked her. Yes, she said, I hope they will do it justice.

Just then a terrific thunderstorm broke out, so we had to
quickly cycle to the church in the pouring rain in just our
shirtsleeves and long flowing dresses because none of us
had thought to wear a jacket, what with this being France,
in the summer. We threw our bikes down at the entrance
and charged into the Church of Saint-Étienne de Villiers-
sous-Grez, a church that I had no previous knowledge of but
whose bare stone walls and pale-blue curtains and collection
of suffering icons, many of which seemed to be captured
in the act of turning their eyes away or otherwise looking
elsewhere in the presence of the agonised body of Christ,
immediately appealed to me. The lightning raged behind
the stained-glass windows, which portrayed a sorry saint
with a sword over his shoulder, gazing down in strange
bemusement at the painting of the Passion below, while the
conductor did a remarkable job of fussily and obsessively
tuning and generally bossing the orchestra by ear.

And then they were off, and it was marvellous; the slow,
heavy swells of strings, the distant brass, the contortions of
the conductor, the young teen on the timpani (who are these
people?), and the thunder rolled in accompaniment and the
lights flickered and threatened to drown us in darkness and
that is when I realised that Saint-Étienne de Villiers is one
of those secret, cryptic churches that are modelled on the
body of the whale in which Jonah travelled, or, more secretly,
but truly, the symbol of the fish, which is the secret body of
Christ and his chariot into history, and I saw the white arcing
stones, curving across the roofs, as the ribcage and the spine
of this incredible amphibian, the belly of the beast that would
carry us through the storm and just as suddenly the lights
gave out, the lights gave out and darkness descended and we
were buffeted from side to side by the music, and the storm,

and a fat gentleman in front of me held his hands to his
ears as if we were at a concert by Led Zeppelin, and now the
orchestra are winging it by ear, they cannot read the score, all
they have to go on is memory and the increasingly frenzied
movements of the conductor, who at this point is just a black
silhouette, a black silhouette that has been swallowed by a
fish, and the music is starting to wobble, and it is tumultuous,
and it is history, and it is a classical recital during a bombing
raid, and there is something terrible and unfortunately true
about it all, something that requires bravery to even think
about too deeply, something that we fled, into the night,
afterwards, and something that we talked around a little
bit, in the garden of the studio-hotel, in the dark, where, in
our absence, the lightning had brought down a huge tree
that now blocked the path to the river, which meant that we
couldn't even swim any more.

Actually, I know why Strindberg never went to the basilica
at Larchant to sort himself out. Because Saint Mathurin of
Larchant is not the one to cure you of madness; Mathurin is
the patron saint of madmen and fools. And of exorcists.

All around the semi-ruined cathedral are scattered the
corpses of pigeons, so many that you may at first think it
points to some kind of idiot ritual in order to keep the world
turning. Possibly. The ruins smell of dogshit and of urine.
But this is France, so who knows. The stone carvings are no
Autun, but still, they are remarkable. Five headless statues
stand sentinel on either side of the tympanum that depicts
Christ as Pantocrator; a sixth is now invisible (and not a
Baptist in sight). These are airheads, classic fools, while
high above incredible Notre-Dame-esque gargoyles leer out
into the air, their mouths and throats hollow, a channel

for sidereal influence, for a rain of idiot drool, and in order
to make the wind sing. Looking up through the destroyed
central tower is to gaze down, into the ocean, is a final lake,
of gargoyle, while a single bell, perched on a crumbling
wall high in the air, dares the most foolish of all to climb
the stones and sound his madness. All around there are
small, time-effaced carvings of the pointlessness of everyday
tasks and the futility of striving. Step inside, to the restored
cathedral, and it is clear that this is no secret amphibious
structure, no chariot across time, unless perhaps an octopus,
a crazy, mad octopus from whose sac extends an arcing red
ribbon of the blood of Christ, which is the fuel of time. But
no; inside is closest to a vast echoing Golgotha, which means
the place of the skull, with the arc of the roof acting as a
membrane, amplifying the constant chattering of the pigeons
inside the walls, and it feels as though there are vast colonies,
living in the walls, toppling dead from the ramparts of heaven
past the long stained-glass windows, echoing, forever, in
the back of the skull, nagging, mocking, laughing, praying,
forever echoing, just beneath conscious thought, a madness,
in other words, a madness to hold off the end of the world and
an endless supply of pigeons, too, in constant recitation, as
in the monastery of the skull. Sit there, close your eyes, and
listen to the insane song of the Incarnation of the Heavenly
Choirs Forever. And Christ, here, is rendered in a way that
points to his eventual return as the *Ecce Homo* of Giménez,
his image as fallen as that masterpiece, as uncanny and
as childlike and as inhuman and as odd in its angles, as a
waxwork, as a papier-mâché model, simultaneously less than
and more than human, as grotesque and idiotic as a true god.
And the stone of the cathedral, the stopped-up doors and the
crumbling walls, singing, as a rebuke to anyone possessed
by the pagan idiocy of proclaiming the works of nature as

the proof of all we need to declare the life eternal, eternal life triumphant, as if the lilies of the field, the potatoes of your garden patch, the rising of life from the compost of death were the final ground of existence, as if they somehow held up life themselves, but this is process, too, and the ground they are fixed to, the ground they rise up from and die back to, is a final stone, an ultimate father, who is not here, echoing, oh madness of the father, ho fool of the first stone, is the song of the squabs in the walls, of the birds in the brain, of the echoes, in time, from Golgotha, and that life, and grace, and love, are not inevitable, are not essential, but are gifts, freely given, which we do not deserve and have no need of receiving, and is the first stone, echoing, empty.

Viens Saint-Esprit, viens embraser Larchant,
Viens Saint-Esprit, habiter tous nos chants,
Viens Saint-Esprit, viens régner dans nos cœurs,
Viens Saint-Esprit, faire briller ta splendeur!

WOH, OHO, OH, HO, OHO, OH, OH . . .

Viens Saint-Esprit, assister Mathurin,
Viens que ta gloire se déploie en ton saint,
Viens Saint-Esprit, que ta vie coule en nous
Viens Saint-Esprit, que nos liens se dénouent!

COO, COO, OH, HO, COO, COO, COO . . .

Viens Saint-Esprit, viens embraser Larchant,
Viens Saint-Esprit, faire de nous tes enfants,
Viens Saint-Esprit, nous révéler le Père,
Viens Saint-Esprit, exaucer nos prières!

WOH, OHO, OH, HO, OHO, OH, OH . . .

Viens Saint-Esprit, assister Mathurin,
Viens Saint-Esprit, nous guérir par tes mains,
Viens Saint-Esprit, viens apaiser nos cœurs,
Viens Saint-Esprit, Toi le consolateur!

COO, COO, OH, HO, COO, COO, COO . . .

Viens Saint-Esprit, viens embraser Larchant,
Viens Saint-Esprit, viens agir puissamment,
Viens Saint-Esprit, viens libérer nos cœurs,
Viens Saint-Esprit, que l'amour soit vainqueur!

WOH, COO, WOH, COO, OH, HO, OH . . .

As we walk away from the cathedral, my Flower and I, we
come to this, written in stone, in childlike letters, above a
house there, in French:

JUNE 29 1792
MADE BY ME
JEAN PIERRE
BERNARD AND
ADELAÏD HAMELIN
MY WIFE

Another summer.

8. VILLAGE OF IN THE BEGINNING

I receive a phone call at the hotel. Flower answers. It is my mother, she announces. My mother has died. I am to return home for the funeral. I refuse. With that, any connection I had to my remaining family is severed. I hang up the phone and prepare for the future that has been gifted me. And that is lonely, now, and nothing like I thought it would be.

Aside from the secret churches in faraway forests and the great basilicas, hanging down, into the air, some of the best architectures in France, certainly the most beautiful, the most monumental, are the vernacular architectures, and by this I mean birds' nests, the nests of swallows, most particularly, those incredible upside-down creations that defy gravity with simple spit alone, a simple squirt of spit from the mouth of a tiny bird is enough to cement these creations to the roof of heaven, look up, there they are, and look how the swallows squeeze in and out of that tiny hole, do you see the little beaks, the eyes made by God for peeking out in terror and wonder, how wonderful it must be to squeeze in and out of those nests with a mess of insects in your cheek, how like being born again, every time you leave home, and those shacks by the train tracks

too, take the train from Gare de Lyon – quick, get out of
Paris – and there, by the side of the tracks, you will witness
an architecture as ingenious as the birds', as bird-brained
as Saint Mathurin himself, little huts made from sheets of
corrugated iron and old windows that totter on two storeys
like towers in fairy tales, that stand half-submerged in
sunken gardens with flooded beds and decorated with beer
cans and thought up by mad old tramps in their ingenuity,
poverty is a gift, is what the Lord reminds us, poverty is the
gift of ingenuity, the cure for all boredoms, the meaning of
the day, for without poverty we are merely rich, and bored,
and pay other people to do what would otherwise fulfil us,
while we fool ourselves that a life of poverty is the only
thing worth outwitting, but if you love outwitting then stay
poor, my friend, stay poor, for all that riches have given
us are perfectly symmetrical chateaux, grotesque palaces
whose rooms we could never hope to occupy, solutions to
things that we will never have to think, so we need another
word for poverty, for riches, surely, are impoverishing, and
poverty, surely, is enriching, in the right hands is ennobling,
these noble shacks, these nobilities by the train tracks, or
skirt the River Loing, lose yourself in the paths through
the forest and stumble upon wooden shacks behind fences
that pretend to be electrified or to be patrolled by security
groups, signs that have surely been stolen, idle threats,
and behind these chain fences and padlocked gates are
the wonderful summer huts, some up on stilts like a fable
or an allegory, some leaning, some half-collapsed, lived-in
architecture, leaking architecture, with young girls spread
out on towels before them in the late-afternoon light, young
girls slipping their bikinis down in order to avoid tan lines,
young boys leaping from rickety piers, repaired but never
improved, never bettered, by succeeding generations, and

these are lessons of how to live secretly, richly, and in
faithful idiot poverty.

France is a land of dogshit, unfortunately. Watch where
you lay your towel. We cycled in the dark through the forest
to a place where some guy was making home brew. The
whole village was out in the streets. My Flower and I are
introduced to a Frenchwoman, with long curly hair and a
huge drooling Rottweiler named Ook, who tells us that she
knew we were here already. The whole village knows, she
says. Then she asks us if we went swimming in the river
on Sunday. In the river, next to the bridge, she asks my
Flower, was that you? Yes, I saw you, she says. I saw you
in the water because I noticed what a beautiful flower you
were, she tells my Flower. A Flower is a flower is a Flower.
We are joined by the couple who run the cafe that had the
baroque music trio. Cico, the owner, is drunk. You stay at
Grez-sur-Loing? he asks me. Grez is a type of stone, a type
of granite, he says. You stay at the Stone-on-the-River, he
says. How can a stone be on a river? I ask him, and he picks
up an out-of-tune guitar and plays the chords to 'House of
the Rising Sun' while the French woman with the curly hair,
whose name is Babette, manhandles her dog, holding this
huge thing that can rear up to the size of a man down by the
ear, forcing it to lie prone on the ground, and tells us about
her experiences as a nurse in an emergency ward, where
she says it was common to be called to remove household
objects 'from anuses and vaginas'. Like what? Light bulbs,
she says. Why light bulbs? Because they fit, it is inspiration,
they see it fits and they do it and they can't get it back out.
But doesn't it smash? Sometimes it smashes and there is
blood. What else? Vegetables, she says, two-pronged carrots,
she says. She gets up to use the toilet and she takes the dog

with her. When she comes back she sits down next to us and she says to my Flower: I put honey on my vagina.

Afterwards, in the dark, in a field by the side of the road, on top of a towel, Babette and my Flower make love while Ook and I watch with a flashlight, looking at each other and thinking the same incomprehensible thoughts, experiencing the same incomprehensible feeling of life, before us, Ook straining at the leash the whole time, the foreskins of our huge slobbering cocks pulled back, our monstrous tongues, as the two lie entwined, in the beam of the flashlight, their skin the colour of the moon in France.

My mother is dead. I am alone in a field in the dark. We have crossed the Meridian. Afterwards there is dogshit all over the underside of the towel and I am forced to abandon it in a bin. In France you must be careful where you lay your towel.

I went to Mass and chanted the word Ook beneath my breath the whole time and waited for God to strike me down. Ook, I say, Ook, Ook, and babble. He did no such thing. God approves and is the instigator. It is your portion, under the sun, is what he says, in the Mass.

I must remember you, Flower, as you appear before me, now, once again, in the garden, with three fingers you hold open the pages of a book, which you read to me occasionally, you clear your throat in announcement and wake me from this trance of time, to read me something lost now, but which was about the moment, and the uncovering of it being its own solution to the same, I think, something about looking in answer, something about the question as the

solution, is tied up in knots, in the past, and which turns
on the question of what it was you said then, which is its
answer, and the perfect mirror of your fingers, beneath the
fingers of your hand, rising up, as to the surface of a river,
in support, which is the stone on the river, I see now, which
is the correct question to ask of time, Grez-sur-Loing, in
the garden, suspended, on the tips of your fingers and your
black sandals with the buckles that glint in the sun, now,
your long hair hangs over your face as you scratch at a little
bite on your arm, while your mind is somewhere else, inside
the book, inside of this book, which is the mirror of the book
you were reading, then, and the answer to it, as you shift
your position to the front and make a move that flattens the
grass, like the joyful cats of France and with just as little
care, as little consciousness of me, watching you, from now,
you don't care for any of it, Flower, but your place in this
book, <u>which now you are underlining</u>, which now you are
taking notes from, the little toe on your left foot strapped
up, and tied to the next, bashed and banged up as the badge
of your obliviousness, and your arse, fatter than a French
arse, which as a rule is small and is skimpy and is tanned
and which is no arse at all, honestly, young girls of France
you have no arse at all, as a rule, but here it is, your fat
voluptuous arse, which I would slip inside of, now, with the
aid of pills and memory, your bikini bottoms, drawn down,
brown and gold and with a blue tag extending, colour is
hardest for me, in memory I have so few colours in memory,
as if the past were all primary, and no hues at all, as a
cathedral in unpainted stone is the glory of God, and you
run your right hand through your hair and coil it around
your neck, bite your lip in young womanly concentration,
age has no need of biting lips in concentration, for age has
all come through and is unstoppable and will not hold for

the mere pressure of the teeth on the lips, and your legs
bent back behind you at the knees, like a skydiver into
summer, your nose, which is unruly, too big for your face
and so mystical and statuesque, your lips now tight in
grim concentration as you enact the question and supply
the answer, which I would call lover, as your bikini top
slips down your shoulder and reveals the tongue-print of
a dragonfly, the love bite of an insect, its lips held in grim
concentration as it feasts on your flesh, making meaning, in
answer to the answer, and with a single snapped antenna,
as struck by tiny lightning, as tiny weather systems we have
no way of knowing, Flower, stamen, lightning rod, and stone
wall, climbing up, you too I will include in the picture, now,
and will scan upwards, into the clouds, the baby blanket of
clouds that gather in the orbit of the ruins, for there was
never a time with eyes that was without ruins, never a time
of life that was without death, never a garden that was
not peopled by lovers, once, never a moment that was not
fleeting, and bashful, and all new, never a stone that was
not formed, itself, by stone. You sip your beer through the
side of your mouth, it is awkward and endearing, your glass
reads Hard Rock Cafe Paris, hard rock hold me up, river,
as we move through you, stone, your book is propped up on
your abandoned dress, your rumfled dress, rumfles, hold me
up, as you press your sunglasses to your face with a single
finger, how much minute correction, how much tiny dancing
in order to stay still, how much imperceptible movement in
stone, is the question I provide as the answer to a summer,
which is you, first Flower, love of my life, which is let go
now, and the bones of your ribs, showing through, which is
disappeared now, and the pinch of your waist, which is how
I must remember you.

Two old women pass, arm in arm, on the road up above. There is a time for women without men, which is tragic and sad, but there is little time for men without women, which is sadder still. She gets up, and she moves her towel. She follows the sun, Flower.

Strindberg says that Grez-sur-Loing is a village of blind stone. Only stone isn't blind. For the last thirty years of his life the composer Delius was cared for here by his wife Jelka, in the same house that Pierre and Max Rehberg would later convene the Church of the Stone of First Witness in, and in whose garden they would be photographed, in order to be paralytic, and blind. For the last thirty years of his life Delius was cared for here by his wife Jelka, who maintained an invisible garden, a garden that he couldn't even see, a garden that every day she would wheel him out to in one of those dreadful old wheelchair-bed convalescent monstrosities, and occasionally she would hit him with a flower, softly, on the cheek, and he would let out a gurgle, a dreadful empty gargle that said, I am used all up.

Here is a photograph of Delius as a young man in Bradford with his sisters, who I recognise as my sisters, too, the left side of their faces mysteriously fallen, *Ecce Homo*, I want to say to my sisters in the choir all those years ago, all choristers are touched, I want to say, and I picture Jelka, with a rose in her hand, in the invisible garden, touching each of them on the cheek with a flower.

There are many paintings of Delius in this invisible garden, many sculptures and busts of him too, because the perfect model is immobile, and so perfectly made of stone, or bronze, or beeswax, which is what the sculptor Catherine Barjansky made of Delius, a ghost in beeswax, honey in his skull, but marble is better, Catherine, my sister, marble does not melt in the sun, my simple dear, like the bust of Delius by Henry Clews, who in 1916 rendered him as a grub, come out a cocoon, in blind bliss and silent agony.

I am haunted by the garden in Grez as it existed in the mind of Frederick Delius, as it existed at the time of Pierre and Rehberg and Frater Jim and the Church of the Stone of First Witness, as it exists in my own mind, now, and yours too, phantom reader, my hope, ghost of my future, with spare vines climbing up and gay shuttered windows and pink paths through the arbour and shrubs in glorious ceramic pots with ornate glazes and sudden explosions of rhododendrons and in a painting by Jelka, of Delius, who is now, miraculously, back on his feet, he is shown as if growing up from the flower beds, a white shroud whose features are erased and who is drowning in flowers and in paint and in 1912 he looks like the novelist J.G. Ballard, with a painting by Paul Gauguin of a nude African woman, entitled *Nevermore*, appearing to recline on his shoulder, a painting within a painting in my fantasy of his house and garden, which did indeed, according to a painting by Jelka, have pink pathways and pink beds and splashes of pink flowers and – miraculously – pink roofs, a whole village of pink roofs, which you can imagine Jelka only got away with due to her husband's blindness and immobility, for after all, what kind of man lives in a pink garden, in a pink village, except in blindness and helpless paralysis? Strindberg, it appears, was correct, to a point: Grez-sur-Loing is a blind village.

Years earlier, in the company of that pompous occult fraud known as Papus aka Gérard Encausse, Delius had studied palmistry and astrology and Egyptology and together they had published an impenetrable discourse on the *Anatomy and Physiology of the Orchestra*, an orchestra that by all accounts had relocated to the empty darkness of Delius's garden, near the end, when, with the help of his amanuensis Eric Fenby, he would walk this garden in his mind, sounding the orchestra at different points, and communicate it to Fenby by a combination of hopeless gasps and telepathy, culminating in Fenby's rendering of the dream poems that made up *The Last Voyage* and *Songs of Farewell*.

'Not being able to see does not trouble me,' Delius wrote, at the end of his voyage, at the point of farewell. 'I have my imagination. Besides, I have seen the best of the earth and done everything that is worth doing.' These, then, are the foundations of the Church of the Stone of First Witness.

Harder.

Pablo Picasso believed in demonic possession (although he didn't necessarily believe in demons, ha ha ha). He thought curiosity brought it on, and he called curiosity a disease, a disease with which he was afflicted. When he saw the African masks he realised that their function was to expel and to make manifest, outside of yourself, a complex, a demon (with no existence, ha ha ha), a possessor, and to make of it a weapon, against itself.

Harder.

Ha ha ha.

Harder.

The perfect performance of the music of J.S. Bach would consist of a setting of 'Cantata BWV 172', the cantata for the first day of Pentecost that begins 'Ring forth, o songs, resound, you strings!/ O most blessed time!/ God Himself shall prepare our souls to be His temples', followed by Bach's setting of the Lutheran hymn 'Komm, Gott Schöpfer, Heiliger Geist' aka 'BWV 667' ('Come, God Creator, Holy Ghost'), and ending with a setting of Bach's 'Magnificat', in a humble stone church of little renown somewhere untraceable in central France, with average paintings of the Stations of the Cross around the walls and high above you, stained-glass portraits of Christ and his disciples, the one barely distinguishable from the other due to lack of concern for nonsense like artistry and fealty to what is otherwise right in front of you, and with two sopranos, one of which is as white as a mime, and one of which looks like a cross between Germaine Greer and Barbara Dickson, as well as a super-cute alto whose face is just a little too wide, all the same, plus a bald unremarkable tenor, inevitably, and a leonine bass straight out of amateur dramatics, under the direction of a small conductor with all of the martial kinetic intensity of a Picasso, and it should start late, and feature at least forty minutes of pointless comings and goings, with the orchestra and the choir scattered about the stone church, all of whom are dressed in black and with red accessories, like one old dear, for instance, who stands out with a grotesque face and fat over-large features and short grey hair in a bob and whose man is obviously dead and with a large red rose drooping from her buttonhole and who will stare at you like an old witch with a toad in her hand, and the audience will almost exclusively consist of friends and family of the performers themselves, who greet each other with great exclamations and outrageous kisses, and most of the audience will be older than you, hopefully, you would hope so, certainly, although there will be the odd hot daughter, taller than her mother and with long dark hair, but with training shoes on (disappointingly, this is a formal occasion for God's sake), and the odd young couple – the girl who with effortless French style has thrown together her outfit, with effortless French style, it's uncanny, a handbag with a thin strap worn over her shoulder, her hair tied up in a tousled bun, and no make-up, with effortless French style – and throughout the performance, just in front of you, the young girl with unfathomable French style (this is Paradise) will occasionally kiss her husband, on the shoulder, not on the cheek (this is Paradise), her silent broad-shouldered husband who will occasionally let out a giggle or whisper something in her ear in return, and across the way some huge old man with a Mediterranean tan and pale lips and who is too big for any woman that is not a giant herself and who best resembles the film-maker Kenneth Anger (didn't he once leap to his feet and prophesy his own death in a church much the same as this at the funeral of an old friend?) and who will stagger in on a walking stick with the help of his long-suffering wife, too big for her, certainly, and who wears a single gold ring on his index finger and who will shake and gibber through much of the performance, and then leave early, probably due to some weak bladder condition, and some nut at the back who looks like a junkie or an alcoholic, killing time, who is there just to shelter from the elements, even though this is France, in the summertime, this is France in the summertime, you imbecile, get out, and just then some other old dear drops her walking stick with a klang! and everyone looks around while some helpful old soul retrieves it for her, and in front of you there is a sophisticated older woman with a big rust-coloured coat that she wears like a cloak, her sunglasses up on her head, and who slips her shoes off, her soft silver slippers, and who sits cross-legged in front of you on the bench, and who inevitably inspires fantasies of another life altogether, of liberating her from her husband, who is way below her league (= dweeb), and of running off to some vineyard at the end of the world, and as the orchestra make their way to the stage everyone is applauding everyone, this will take forever, you will think, holy fuck this will take forever at this rate, you will mutter beneath your breath, but then when the music starts it is Bach, immediately, it is Bach and it is eternal and it is like it has been playing, there, in the background, out there, in the universe, in the precise tuning of the planets, forever, even though it is lacking in all bombast and conceit – this is a French reading, thank God, not a German one (or a Belgian; though God preserve Philippe Herreweghe and his *St Matthew Passion*) – and the choir is a little too quiet compared to the orchestra, there is no amplification, and there he is, there he is in the back row, you must always search out the chorister that is touched, there he is and he sings as if in neither ecstasy nor agony, but as if cast in stone and set to sing forever, his mouth as empty as any gargoyle's, as any stone leper's in the pit, yet outside of the choir he works as an estate agent, but now, right now, he is in the employ of God, forever, yet behind you someone is talking, someone is muttering and you can't work out who it is, because you long to turn in your seat and shut them up, and you plan your attack in painstaking detail, you will signal with a single finger raised to your lips, you think, you will say, s'il vous plaît, that is all, and you will silence them, for the good of everyone at this performance in this sad, delightful church, but then you start to feel dizzy, the leonine bass makes you feel dizzy, the music feels like the play of light, and shadows pass by the stained-glass windows, as though the church itself is sealed, as though the music is cubed and sealed and we are in some kind of temporary phantom hyperspace of God's devising, in secret collusion with Bach of God's devising, and for long minutes you will be caught up in your own mind, in the knots and convulsings of your own mind in fear and confusion, which has also taken off, but which will be brought back to the music by the focusing on the wonderful interplay between the sopranos, the one as pale as any mime, you will note, the other who looks uncannily, now, unconscionably, now, like a cross between Barbara Dickson and Germaine Greer, as they combine in something atomic, it seems, it feels like, inside, outside, something that appears as the shape of creation itself, as its inner workings, its outer workings, as its love play, sung, and for the first time you will think to yourself, in wonder, and it will feel like a breakthrough, a meaningful revelation, a genuine development, how many ways are there to sing Gloria, well, let's see, and there will be a break between movements and the audience will go to clap but the stern Picasso midget madman that leads the music will silence them with a sudden hand and he will disappear into what appears to be a wall with no openings, into what appears to be cold stone, and will reappear, above, next to the organist, who sits at this incredible organ contraption with its old steel pipes and it is possible to see the organist's face due to the strategic placement of a small mirror just to his right, a small mirror that makes him look as if he is communicating to us, in pain and confusion and wide-lipped horror, as if from the inside of an iron lung or a glass cage, which is exactly the sound that the person behind you is making, the person who was talking is now wheezing like an old bronchial lung and muttering under her breath – it's a woman, you turn round to make sure – and she seems as if dressed for the choir, a chorister is disrupting her own performance, you think, in wonder, and at first it is terrible and then it is magnificent, as the weird atonal drones of the organ bring your attention back around, and it sounds like it is coming out of the future, no longer out of the past, as though Bach's vision was memorial, in time, forever, not just looking back, not just for his time, but forward, and forever, amen, you mutter, beneath your own breath, amen, and sure enough, when the organ solo ends and the conductor returns the woman behind you rises to approach the stage and join the newly massed choir at the back of the stage and she is touched, too, all true choristers are touched, as she is led to the stage, with the help of an elderly chorister herself, she has trouble walking, and continues to mutter and shake, and you feel bad, you feel terrible and wretched and less than life, for a second you doubted, for a second your faith gave way and you thought that there was something wrong, something that it was in your power to correct, and you curse yourself, but you forgive yourself just as quickly, because you know, in an instant, it is communicated to you, you know, with certainty, that God did it for the poetry of it, that God is playing with you just how you like to play, sly God, loving creator, Magnificat, Magnificat, you say, and you shake your head as the choir rises in a single voice and moves like a small body of water in the harbour of a system and the muttering chorister is held up by her friend and is she even singing, is she muttering beneath the choir, yes she is, she is muttering and lamenting, there is a score within the score, you think, you believe you have uncovered it, this secret score, embedded, you believe you have glimpsed it, in that, there, for a second, now, you think, and then you think, who writes music these days with titles like 'Magnificat', don't they all write songs with titles like 'The World is a Problem' or 'I Hate It' or 'If Only, Then': but didn't Bach do that, too, you think, didn't he lament that this whole world is a hospital, but even then he said he would praise God all the harder as soon as he was discharged, songs of praise, you think, we are in need of songs of praise, and for a second you imagine a whole school, a new college, a bold university, that would teach yes and say yes and point out all the yes to be had, and now everyone is on their feet and applauding, and there is a pause, and then again they launch back into Magnificat Magnificat and you really need to pee so you burst out into the sun as soon as the music is over and you cycle as hard as you can to get to the canal and you pee beneath a bridge in a great satisfying arc, all the while keeping the eye out for snakes, you never know with snakes, and you get back to where you are staying and you light a humble fire on the banks of the river and you are joined by the drunken Finnish poet who is no longer annoying but who is revealed to be quite lovely, really, and the boring Swedish painter who looks like Robert Creeley, but who now appears bashful and deep, and his newly arrived girlfriend, who is cute in the light of the fire and whose hair is wild in the still night, and who is interested, and who asks penetrating questions, and who sits in earnest silence and waits for your reply, and the newly arrived Finnish doodler, the Finnish cartoonist in his awful shorts and his naff sailor's cap, stokes the fire, he is arrived to stoke the fire, which smells so good, and your Flower holds them all in fascinating conversation and in drunken joy you fall into bed afterwards and you have that feeling, that feeling of surety, that feeling that you are sorry and that you will never doubt again. That, my friends, would be the perfect setting of the music of J.S. Bach, in this castle of heaven.

My Flower and I attend a party where we meet a large woman who deals in antiquarian books about Africa, the conquest of Africa and seafaring voyages, and whose fat partner resembles the director Paul Verhoeven. He collects city maps and is obsessed by Paris and the history of the Paris metro. Together they collect all things to do with penguins. Verhoeven takes a five-pound note from his wallet and shows it to me. It is from the Falkland Islands and has two penguins on it. The large woman, who smokes a pipe and speaks in a deep voice that makes her seem as if she is a channel for some kind of unearthly entity or prophetic historical figure, shows me a picture of her cat, who is named Selkirk after the Scottish castaway and buccaneer Alexander Selkirk, the inspiration for Daniel Defoe's novel *Robinson Crusoe*. Selkirk requested, half-facetiously, that he be abandoned off the coast of Chile, on an island later renamed Robinson Crusoe Island, after he judged his own sea vessel as being unworthy to continue, this large woman tells us, in a voice like an ancient old sage, and he was stranded there for four years, she says, driven inland by the endless baying and savage mating and constant battling of the sea lions that would wriggle up onto the beach like so many hideous deformed torsos spewed up from the grave of the sea, where he built two huts, only to be set upon, nightly, by rats, a population of vermin he kept at bay by befriending feral cats, reading The Bible and singing from the psalms at the top of his lungs. Twice great ships arrived at the island, but unfortunately both were Spanish, and

Selkirk, being Scottish, and at war with the Spaniards, could not risk letting his presence be known. Once he was pursued across the island by a gang of Spanish pirates and only escaped detection by hiding up a tree that the same Spanish pirates chose to urinate around in a circle. Then she tells us the story of how one day Selkirk was out hunting feral goats and he accidentally chased one over a cliff. He survived by landing on the goat, which died and whose body cushioned his fall, and after a day spent prone and recovering, half-buried in the carcass of a squashed goat, he arose, and went about his day. She says this in a voice that makes of it a parable, or a story of an interior pilgrimage.

Harder.

A day trip on bicycles to visit the Tadeusz Kościuszko Monument outside the village of Montigny-sur-Loing, Kościuszko who was an architect and a builder of fortresses, a Polish national hero and a combatant in the American Revolutionary War, Kościuszko whose body isn't even there, at all, in this tomb, or in any single place, his embalmed body which, as part of some kind of misconstrued memorialising, not to say a kind of attempt to spread his influence as far as possible, to expand his protectorate by the separation of his organs and the transport of his body, flitted between a church in Solothurn, Switzerland, some other stupid church in Krakow and a crypt in Wawel Cathedral, his internal organs buried in a separate plot in a graveyard in Zuchwil beneath a single memorial stone, and his poor suffering heart, all enlarged in the tangle of his life, briefly on display in a terrible museum in Switzerland before returning, still lonely, to a chapel in Warsaw's Royal Castle, Kościuszko whose fake tomb this is, a simple door, in

an arc of stone, by a busy roadside, a door that would open
onto the catacombs beneath the Forest of Fontainebleau, a
forest whose paths are of ash, of fine stone, ground down,
of black sand pathways crossed with the trails of slow-
worms and of horses' hoofs and of wild boar and of our
footprints now, too, because it is too soft to ride a bike over
and we feel as if we, too, are descending into the catacombs
of Kościuszko and wait for his ghostly hand to rise and to
drag us under as we make our way along La Route de la
Grande Vallée, Kościuszko who had only his ghost left to
bury, and so this door, this simple door that allows entrance
to a ghost, and whose ghost makes the forest around here
electric – listen – the forest is singing with the kinetic
energy of a ghost in a labyrinth who never stops pacing and
who gives life, up above, to slow-worms and to dragonflies
and to mosquitoes and to bees and to my Flower and I, that
day, what is the opposite of a plague, a benediction, what is
the opposite of a curse, Kościuszko, what is the opposite of a
ghost, a corpse, yet once you were all these things, I think,
in this forest, your poor suffering body now separated into
dragonfly, and slow-worm, and dung beetle, and ashes, but
also light, high light on the treetops and flowers, as though
on a rack, not a cross, the same rack that deformed your
heart now works on mine, as I feel myself, too, give way, in
sorrow, for that day I had received sad news, Kościuszko,
that my sister and her husband would separate, that my
sister would be alone with her children, that my brother
had threatened her husband with a hammer, but really it
was a showerhead, he had turned up at his door after her
husband had assaulted her and told him that next time the
hammer would speak, though it was only a showerhead,
a showerhead that he had grabbed on his way out as a
makeshift weapon, I felt proud and sad when I heard this,

when he called me on the phone that morning, proud and sad because there was an echo of our father in his actions, our father who art in heaven, and I walked through your forest, Kościuszko, with my heart as heavy and as lonely as your own, at all of the madness and sorrow of this world and everything we put each other through, and the pointlessness of it, the pointlessness that I knew, truly, was the point, the emptiness that I knew, truly, was you, God, you, Holy Ghost, you, Kościuszko, you who are the patron saint of the torn apart, and I walk through your forest, ankle-deep in your ashes, again, on that day, and my sorrows are heavier, and my sister is long dead, and her husband forgotten, and my brother estranged, and my heart, too, in another country, hidden, deep, in a forest, in another summer, Kościuszko, and on the way back, on the forest path, we pass a stone on which is engraved a primitive church, a simple house, and the sign of a heart.

The churches are potentially much more powerful today than they ever were precisely because the vast majority of people no longer know what they signify. We are confronted by an implacable mystery, in stone. This is precisely the work of the church, and what it signifies. These are the Pyramids. This is Africa. Here is Dogon mask, church. This is art that predates art, which is monument. What does the church of Saint-Laurent at Grez-sur-Loing stand for? Another summer. Stone. Mystery, implacable. Sound your bells!

Art should reproduce 'reality' as exactly as possible, is what the non-artists say.

Art should remake 'reality' completely, is what the artists say.

Art should speak of something beyond 'reality', is what the spiritualists say.

Art should speak of the beyond that is 'reality', is what the realists, and the dreamers, say.

Painting is what Picasso calls it, never 'art'.

Gods, and saints, is what the prehistoric calls it, never 'art'.

Modernism must be got out of the way, Picasso says, in order that timelessness may come through.

Goya's *The Third of May 1808 in Madrid*, painted in 1814, is one of the great masterpieces of religious painting. Why? Because of the quality of light, and what it gives, and what it takes away, both of which are incomprehensible. Most everything in the picture is lit by an impossible moon, it would appear, which in turn is lit by way of an impossible sun, except for the hero, the central hero whose body is lit by a mysterious cube, a lantern, it seems, but a mysterious illuminated ark all the same, and its light takes up the hero of the body, except for his head, which remains in the moon, and inside the box is death, which is spoken in light, inside of which is a head, a disembodied head, which is the body of the hero, projected. Picasso considered the painting to be under a spell, a supernatural spell, and he compared the crucified stance of the hero to the skeleton of a bat, which is the ancient of nightmares.

At the bottom of the garden, in the bright sunshine, a
young girl in a black swimming costume with a thin red
belt is floating down the river on an inflatable unicorn. And
the young French boys have so much energy. They stop
the traffic to leap from a bridge, they play frenzied games
of badminton, they launch a bottle at a swan, dance in
front of the young girls in the flesh-pink bikinis, perform
handstands and then disappear, downriver, on the strength
of the tide. My Flower floats out on an inflatable ring with
the motif Mud Master on it. She is proud and wants to
be watched like a little girl as she splashes water on her
shoulders and kicks her legs and waves to me from the
distance. Now the young girl in the black swimming costume
is learning from the boys about splashing, and recklessness,
and daring, an arm folded across her chest in concentration,
a single finger in the corner of her mouth. Picasso said that
God has no style. Ridiculous. Young girl, you are where God
begins. But what he meant, really, is that God contains all
styles and yet has no single fingerprint through which to
recognise his work, which is called multifarious and called
omni, and that it is down to us, as co-creators, to specialise
and to swagger and to style and to create forms that without
us, without this constant duetting between what is given
and what could be, simply would not exist. And that this is
love and suffering and divine communion, and all kinds of
girls. The elephant and the squirrel, Picasso calls it. A real
hodgepodge! In that case, down with style, holy architect!
Sound your bells!

Then this: Picasso, according to contemporary
commentators, considered the great, archetypal themes of
art to be birth, pregnancy, suffering, murder, the couple,
death, rebellion and – possibly – the kiss. These themes,

according to Picasso, predate civilisation. Crucially, he claimed that they could not be conjured, that they could not be forced on a work of art, but rather must be encountered, in the process of creation, and then, and only then, are they transformative and unequivocal and *must* be reckoned with. Are these not, then, the qualities of God, the sign of his eternal presence, his signature in this world? Is this not God's style? For as in our relationship with God, we cannot approach these themes. Rather, these themes must seek us out. We do not seek; we are found. But I would add one more, one further power of God that is mirrored in his fingertips and that is a source of great freedom and of great suffering, too: betrayal.

Today is 21 June, a national music day in France. Outside our hotel, on the corner next to the bridge, a white teenager with dreadlocks is playing guitar through a practice amp and singing a song by Blind Willie McTell. 'Delia, Delia, how can it be? You say you love them rounders, but don't love me.' His name is God's Own Singer of Songs.

As we sit in the garden a girl swims over the river to us and calls the name of my Flower. It is Katarina the Bitch, an old schoolfriend, and my Flower jumps into the water to greet her. The two of them embrace and then float there on the spot, talking. She has moved to a village along the way and is having a housewarming party at the end of the month. She wears sunglasses while she swims. Later, my Flower tells me how she and Katarina the Bitch would kiss and rub themselves against each other on her mother's bed and tape-record their moanings. Then they would play them back and masturbate together. It is national music day.

I hate the smug saints sitting smugly in the small provincial churches, smug, bored of heaven already, sainted by mere saintliness, and would disembowel them. I much prefer the saints whose heads are missing, whose arms run like sand into the pockmarked walls, whose eyes roll in their heads, whose ears are cut off, whose bodies are dislocated, who have used it all up for a single glimpse, not for a tenured position in heaven, for who would not be bored of heaven after a month or so of these platitudinal faces, these equivocal expressions, this dampened sense of calm, and who would not be eager to get back into the game, just as the greatest religious art, the gravest churches, are time-wracked, terrifying, and unreconciled, in conflict with creation, towers raised in passionate confusion against themselves, fortified with demons, drunk on stone, and yes to everything, yes to no is a stone tower rising up, is a monument to the glory of God despite the glory of God, for what need has God of glory and peace? Sainthood is in permanent exile from heaven, is in turning away for the love of God. For what is this sun and moon, this light of death? It is cathedral. The only heresy is to be less than life, which is hell, and heaven, and nothing in between: the Christians to the lions.

It is national music day. In the village of Nemours the castle is all stopped up with concrete in order that it can't hear a thing. In the village of Grez-sur-Loing the houses are shuttered and silent. In the village of Bourron-Marlotte there is swaying in the streets. A band is set up in the road, outside of the rock n roll bar with the pictures of Marilyn and B.B. King on the walls. There is the sweet sticky smell of fried mussels in the air. A fat girl with an off-the-shoulder dress and appealing sunburn is drinking

from a hip flask as the band soundchecks. The drummer
wears one of those awful head mics and a T-shirt cut off
at the sleeves. The bassist (five- and six-string bass; this
is France) has a permanent fag in his mouth. The lead
guitarist, a young man in a Hawaiian shirt, is inaudible.
The rhythm guitarist and vocalist sings 'China Girl' by
David Bowie in a pained, soulful voice. The lead singer
is a crusty young woman, painfully thin, in yoga pants,
trainers and a vaguely oriental dress. She has shaved the
back of her head and wears her long hair over it in a bun
as she dances on the spot and holds one finger to her ear.
The usual crew are inside the bar drinking and refusing
to come out. In the street the families are gathering. A
father and son sit at a table, the son muscular, ordinary,
and with a tattoo on his bicep that I strain to read. What
does it say on his arm? I ask my Flower. My Flower reads
it from the corner of her eye. I am the hero of the story,
she says, I don't need anyone to save me. He looks exactly
like his father. Already, the servers are looking stressed,
although no one in the crowd seems to care about the
speed with which they bring out the fried mussels. I need
a clear passageway, the bald server despairs, I need a
clear passageway. There must be at least fifty people here,
sitting at long tables or standing leaning against the wall,
like a contemptuous young man who shakes his head at
the band's lame take on Pink Floyd, a little punk with
a backwards baseball cap who flagrantly picks his nose,
and now the fat village rocker has arrived, with greasy
permed hair and a black blazer and a huge beer gut in a
grey T-shirt and a beautiful blonde wife in a straw fedora
with a white bow on it, and he is telling someone about
auditioning a new bass player, he is talking about getting
back in the game, while his two little kids run riot and

topple from benches and bang their heads on tables and his
beautiful blonde wife just stares into space, it's enough that
she is his wife, in this village, and the other waiter, who is
dressed completely in white and who holds his tray high
above his head so you can follow his speedy movements
throughout the crowd, is boasting to a table of cute girls
of his ability to speak three languages, none of which the
girls can speak and so are denied the full effect of his
sophistication, and now the band are playing Bob Marley
and the rhythm guitarist and vocalist has switched into a
Rasta hat for the occasion, exodus, he is singing, movement
of the people, and someone is filming the show, down the
front an elderly man, all dressed in black, is preserving it
forever, how many times will he rewatch it, and my Flower
rolls her eyes and says, this band is really crap, and it's
true, the drummer is particularly awful, the singer gets the
words wrong and misphrases every line, the saxophonist,
who has appeared on stage from out of nowhere, is
clearly drunk, and yet everyone is singing along, at this
approximation of music, at this weird staging of fun, and a
couple arrive at the table next to us, it has been reserved
for them and their two angelic children, I say angelic
because of the quality of their skin, which is pockmarked
and swollen, and the quality of their eyes, which are wide
and indiscriminating, pools of unreflecting light, and who
stare in wonder at a green-coloured drink, at a plateful of
fries, at a bouncing ball, at the light show projected onto a
white transit van behind the band, and as the presence of
angels inevitably makes us question ourselves, I wonder
if I am less than the moment, if in my cynicism I have
mistaken ideas for reality, and I say to my Flower, what
do you want, a more professional presentation, and she
laughs, and I realise that in ourselves, alone, we are no

match for the creator, because if it were down to us we would have everything work out just as we wanted, which isn't how we wanted it at all, and how boring would that be anyway, and thank God for this constant duet between what is given and what could be, thank God for upsets and for imperfections and for failings, thank God for his tenderness, too, I think, as I catch sight of the profile of the man next to us, the father of the saintly children, and I see they have inherited his skin, I see how they have grown from their father, in angelic imperfection, because at first I think he has tribal piercings all around the lobe of his ear, which seems completely out of character with his staid appearance, his neat hair and beady spectacles, but then I realise that his ear is rotting, his ear is rotting and coming off his head, the side of his head is eaten away with some kind of flesh-devouring infection, and his rotten ear hangs loose, and soft, and liquid, and I can't take my eyes off it, do you see it, my Flower whispers, do you see it, I can see it, I say, and I try to look over him and past him, and he is laughing and holding both his saintly children in his arms, and the three of them are dancing to the most perfect version of 'Baker Street' by Gerry Rafferty there has ever been, which is now, without judgement, which seems miraculous, now, when received by an ear that is no longer an ear, when worded by a word that is no longer a word, and the music is the eraser of the words, holy music, and the world is no longer an idea, and values are no longer values, and what is here, right now, is, and has no words, and we are no longer formulating, this ear that is no longer an ear is no longer hearing, this singer that is no singer whatsoever is no longer singing, this fat rocker is no longer boasting, this bald waiter is no longer stressing and now 'We Built This City' is no longer the worst song in creation.

Saint Anselm's ontological argument for the existence of God goes like this: God is a thing that nothing could be greater than. Therefore he must exist, because a thing that is greater than everything else but that does not exist would be a lesser thing than a thing that is greater than everything else and that does exist. But, but. If there were anything that God wasn't, that God couldn't be, then God would not be greater than everything else. Therefore, if God exists, then there is nothing that is not God. That's no longer Saint Anselm talking; that is me, Pierre, God almighty.

It is Midsummer's Day. The boring Swedish artist who looks like Robert Creeley has been joined by his girlfriend, who is a painter, and the Finnish friend who is a cartoonist who claims he is a graphic novelist, and an older Swedish couple, who are also painters, and their friend Doris. They invite everyone to celebrate Midsummer's Day with them, which is a big deal in Scandinavia. In the morning the women leave to gather flowers and the men are left to erect a maypole, which in Sweden is a large wooden cross decked in foliage. The older Swedish painter and myself dig a hole in the ground using a metal trowel and a spoon to remove the dirt. I joke that it is like *Escape from Colditz* but the old boy just looks at me blankly from behind his round spectacles and beneath his idiot white cap. Together we raise the cross in the garden and fill in the hole with soil and with large stones that we hammer down into place. Miraculously, the cross stands. The women return, the boring old boy's wife, and Doris, and Robert Creeley's girlfriend, whose name is Anne, and my Flower, whose name is Flower. They hold bundles of wild flowers in their arms and they sit on chairs in the garden and bind the flowers in wreaths that they intend to wear on their heads and that on the older women look macabre and terrible and seem to wilt straight away like a sick joke but on my Flower and Anne look bountiful and bashful. I wander to the edge of the garden, where the Finnish cartoonist is building a fire. We chop some wood together while the old Swede stands around hopelessly. Creeley is too timid to help out with the men, so he stands with the girls as they make their bonnets. The Finn intends to cook aubergine wrapped in foil in the fire. I despise aubergine, it is the vegetable of impoverished students lacking any aesthetic whatsoever, which is this Finnish cartoonist with his dreadful shorts and his socks and cap for sure. He offers me a beer and we stand and watch as some French guy in shorts trembles on the parapet of the bridge over the river, too afraid to jump in. The night is coming on.

Flower's friend Katarina the Bitch arrives with her husband, Thierry. He works as some kind of project manager for blah blah blah but his eyes are alive with mischief. They take seats far apart from each other at the table and I tell myself they are swingers, you never know who will turn out to be a swinger, but I tell myself, it is these two, for sure. Anne has made schnapps with the leaves of raspberry plants and she passes the bottle around the table and everyone sings drinking songs. The Swedes' are sad, the French bawdy. I sing 'I Belong to Glasgow' and the Finnish cartoonist tells me that my accent gets him in the heart. Everyone is becoming progressively drunker and drunker. Thierry corners Anne, who by now is ignoring her boring boyfriend completely. The Swedish painter with the white cap and idiot glasses tells me he likes to listen to Swedish hippy music like International Harvester while he paints, and it makes me think of Mary and her avant-garde din. In the dark, Doris falls into the waterlogged ditch that runs along the side of the garden and emerges soaked, with her bonnet of flowers sopping, and stuck to her face, and now she too looks bashful and born again. The party degenerates; everyone is dancing to Abba. The drunken Finnish cartoonist (I forgot to say that the boring Finnish poet had gone back home for the Midsummer celebration) leaps the fire and ends up in the ditch himself. Katarina and Thierry disappear into the night. Another night, I think, as I watch Flower escort them out of the garden and kiss them on the stairs. Before they leave, Thierry points down the garden at me, I pretend not to see, but I watch from the corner of my eye as the three of them talk about me, and think I can't see, silhouetted there, at the end of the garden. We dance some more as the sun comes up. Anne asks if I am a Christian, and I tell her I am, but it's not what you would think. Then I feel ashamed, and say, actually, I am a Christian and it is exactly what you would think, because who needs all of this apologising and elucidating and explaining. The night ends with the drunken Finnish cartoonist sitting in a chair next to the firepit and berating the Swedes for their performance in the Second World War. How many Jews did you save? he demands, again and again. In the morning the cross has fallen, there are bottles and crockery everywhere, and not a soul to be seen.

Saint Anselm, writing in his book *Cur Deus Homo* (*Why God Became Man*), has this to say about how incredible the situation is: since God is infinitely great, any sin against him is infinite, and forever. But man is finite, and so simply doesn't have the time to fully expiate a sin against forever. Only a being that is both human and divine has the necessary qualities to expiate eternal sins. So: God gives his only son, Christ, to die on the cross, so that man, the infinite sinner, can be redeemed. Something has changed. This is no longer Christ the Vanquisher of Death but Christ the Suffering Redeemer. And this is me, Pierre, God almighty, relieved of my duties and now free to sin, forever, but at what cost.

In the forest around Villiers-sous-Grez they are playing *Dungeons & Dragons* for real. We come across a yurt inside of which is a wooden chair with carved spider legs and next to it instructions for the Dungeon Master. In the event of a battle it gives details of who should win and who should rise again, from the dead. We pass through a clearing where, ranged all around us, on top of the high rocks, men in cloaks with horned helmets and women dressed as sorceresses face each other in battle. They act as if we don't exist and for a moment there, and forever afterwards, we are the ghosts.

We attend a party outside the village, next to a football pitch, where DJs are playing reggae and families are spread out on towels, and with dancing, in the floodlit field. It is the first time I have smelled marijuana outside of Paris and quite a few people seem to be very drunk or stoned. I meet the strange antiquarian bookseller who this time tells me about the discovery of a place near Antarctica named Desolation Island, which is another favourite of hers, and that she has three books about it, which she won't sell to anyone, and then her husband starts singing a King Crimson song, and I don't remember much more than that. Flower is distracted. In the distance, dancing in front of the DJs, is that creep Davide. Katarina the Bitch is dancing with her husband, who is wearing a T-shirt of the group Magma.

I spot Babette, the girl that Flower made love to in the dark, the owner of Ook, she is with her boyfriend who she introduces as Jean-Marc. I wonder if he knows, does he know I watched her fuck my Flower, by flashlight, while I held his dog tight by the leash. But he seems oblivious, and is friendly, and he tells me he has entered his dog, which he describes as an attack dog, into a competition. You must train your dog to attack you, he says, but really it is not attacking you at all, it is attacking the special protective suit you are wearing, he says. If you took the suit off and sat it next to you, it would attack the suit and not you. Training dogs changed my life, he explains, as I stare over his shoulder and see Flower talking to Davide across the field, silhouetted in the floodlights. They are playing the song 'Groove is in the Heart'. You cannot be too soft with a dog, he says, and all the while I have my eye on Davide, who kisses my Flower on both her cheeks and holds her by the shoulder while he talks to her. You must be firm, he says. And now they are dancing to the music. Really, it is a game, he says. What's a game? I ask him. The game of the dog attacking you is a game, he says, and he says it exactly like that. It is like a sparring match, he says, a martial art where you beat the shit out of each other and then afterwards you shake hands and embrace, he says. It changed my life, he says, and then he asks me if I would like to attend a training session with him and his dog in Fontainebleau. Also, he says, do you like tombs? Tombs? I say. Graves? No, he says, and he grasps for the word. Under the stones, he says, what lies under the stones? Caves, Babette says, caves lie under the stones. Yes, Jean-Marc says, caves, do you like dark caves in the middle of the night? If so, he says, I can take you to one, near the Route de la Grande Vallée.

Later, all four of us go back to their house, where we eat pakora and drink Japanese whisky and where Babette asks me about my writing, where do I get my inspiration, she says to me, and I tell her God, and she says, no, you should replace the word God with the word Source, she says, it is better, and she makes a joke of pretending to phone The Bible and ask if she can have the word God replaced and the voice on the end refuses to give his name and asks her to call back in the morning between 9 and 9.15 a.m. and while my Flower and Jean-Marc talk about dogs in the living room, Babette locks me in the bathroom, and translates a text she has hanging on the wall for me, a text by an unknown author, discovered in a monastery in the sixteenth century, and whose contents I can barely recall now, except something about stillness, except something about being in the centre of the stillness, as she unzips my fly, and takes my cock in her mouth.

Davide beat the shit out of Flower, that is what she is saying, it isn't a game, she says, he is dangerous, she says, as she shows me the bruises on her arms and the single cut on her neck. So many questions. But they can wait. I head over to his place with a hammer in my pocket, despite the protests of my Flower, and now I am the echo of an echo of an echo.

Harder. Harder. Harder.

I beat him round the head with a hammer, harder.

There is a little bird, a goldfinch, shivering, on a roof across the way.

9. HERMITAGE OF BATTLING DEMONS IN AFRICA

Now I can tell you the full story of Max Rehberg and how he lost his right arm battling demons in the deserts of Africa in emulation of extravagant monasticists like Simeon Stylites, the Syrian who sat on top of a pillar for thirty-seven years, or Saint Jerome, author of the so-called Vulgate, who, even more crazily, took up the study of Hebrew in order to circumvent an obsessive desire for masturbation, or that hermit, what was his name, the one who stood on one leg without eating or drinking and, who knows, probably holding his breath too, for God only knows how long, only Rehberg was a killer, a gun for hire, according to the story I have put together, who worked for regional warlords and gun-trafficking gangs, but from a similar place, motivated by that same holy urge to empty his mind of everything but the glory of God.

Like Saint Augustine, whose spiritual autobiography resembles his own, Max Rehberg was himself a shining example of man's 'corruption, redemption and continued imperfection'. His family was military: distant, cold, unsupportive of anything except the continuation of the same. Perfect training, in other words, for the adventurer that would burn it all to the ground. At age seventeen he experienced a conversion, well, a calling, perhaps, is the better way of putting it, when he claimed to have seen written in the air, in letters of blood, he claimed, as if the sky itself were crying blood, he said, the figure of his own heart. Whose wording was obscure, of course, for who could ever truly figure the depths of his own heart, except for his maker, of course, except for his creator, which is exactly how Rehberg interpreted it, as though his creator had spoken the name of his mission, which was called Africa, which was called Desert, and which was called Demon.

How to be worthy of this life? he writes in a teenage diary salvaged from the pyre his partner made of his belongings after his death. Make of your heart a fortress, he says. And then yield, is the law.

At twenty-one he sails for Egypt, where, in 1973, at the age of twenty-five, he is involved in a tank battle in Suez against the invading forces of Israel led by Ariel Sharon. It was here that he met Yasser Mahmoud, 'The Ostrich', as he was known due to his preferred mode of execution, which alternated between upside-down crucifixions over firepits and being buried alive, head first.

At twenty-seven he publishes his first pamphlet, *To Run Wild In It*, essentially an updating of the anathematised heretic Bishop Honorius of Rome's view that although Christ had two natures and was, essentially, divided, in his humanity and in his divinity, yet in this division, precisely because of this division, in fact, he was united in one will, which was the will of God, the Father, who made this world, Rehberg claims, in order that Christ, and all of the Christs to come (for, in his argument, anyone who enters history is incarnated as a Christ), could run wild in it.

At twenty-eight he has his first child, in Livingstone country, in a village hard by Victoria Falls, a half-caste boy fathered with an unknown woman, both of whom disappeared, into history, one presumes, in order to run wild in it. He abandons them, takes on three wives, and lives in a mud hut on the banks of an alligator-infested river. He enters into a business deal with The Ostrich, which involves smuggling arms across the internal deserts of Africa. He also publishes a second pamphlet, via the same Egyptian letterpress, a copy of which I have in my possession, this time entitled *Worship What You Burn and Burn What You Worship* after the entreaty of Saint Remi of Reims on the baptism of the barbarian King Clovis as related by Gregory of Tours.

The Africa Max Rehberg arrived in can be found on no map; for this is the Africa of Holy Maximilian Rehberg. To travel, truthfully, is to go nowhere, Rehberg writes in a journal from the time, except, maybe, deeper. You are the same person no matter where you go, and you drag all that you would escape behind you, as in a corpse you are unable to dispose of because it has taken on your own face. However, if the traveller is lucky, he says, or perhaps simply cursed, he may be given to look behind, and beyond, and see something that is *not himself*.

He bears witness to a flotilla of burning boats on the Nile, piled high with smouldering corpses, the stench of which, he claims, was 'more beautiful than the prayers of the saints'. A boat runs aground and he and The Ostrich go

through what is left of the bodies, which seem to have been
torched along with all of their possessions, the bodies of
the women mutilated and rearranged like in a drawing
by Hans Bellmer, the men decapitated and with a sign
carved into their bodies, into the flesh of their chests, in the
shape of a cross, but with spaces for letters, for language,
like this – # – almost, in each vector of which there are
different combinations of zeros and crosses. A game of
noughts and crosses, Rehberg says, but The Ostrich has
no idea what he is talking about and asks him if Noughts
and Crosses are the names of gods. It is the language of
God, Rehberg corrects him, which is written in flesh. In the
hull of the boat, seemingly untouched by flames, Rehberg
retrieves what he describes as an ark, a large white metal
cube inside of which is the mummified head of a man. In
a secret compartment, beneath a false bottom, he claims
to have discovered what appears to be a diary, written in
a Sudanese dialect, that with the help of The Ostrich he
translates into English and later publishes as *Belly of the
Fish of Christ, Ship*, the first of the Holy Books.

BOOK TWO: TRANSEPT

I. BELLY OF THE FISH OF CHRIST, SHIP

KHARTOUM, SUDAN, 1884

20/3/1884

We sat cross-legged in the street, drinking port into which
we would pour a thimble's-worth of sand in order that
it would clean out our insides and open our passages.
Suddenly Biraggo Fonte said: Look! That's Charles Gordon!

He appeared on the roof of the Serail as a silhouette, a black
bird atop a white cube. Fonte got to his feet and began to
gesticulate. Gordon turned and raised his telescope towards
us. I thought we must look like insects to a man like Gordon,
spiders on their backs, grotesque. No, Fonte said. Then
Gordon turned, and pointed his telescope to the north. You
see, Fonte said. He looks to the north. A man like Gordon
is implacable. He looks at us and then he looks to the
north. What does that tell you? I asked Fonte. The north is
the unconscious, he said, he is dreaming Khartoum. He is
looking for relief, I replied, he is searching the horizon for
the sails of his rescuers. That is the quality of the dream,
Fonte said.

We sat for nearly an hour. If he is dreaming Khartoum, I said, then we might still be spiders, the kinds that cobweb dreams and that squat upon your chest with their multiform eyes and that bare their teeth. Now you're making sense, Fonte said. But beetles would be more appropriate in this instance, he insisted, dung beetles, rolling great balls of excrement into the dark. Is there not a saying that equates balls of excrement with the midnight sun, the black sun of the north? I asked him. Now we're getting somewhere, Fonte said, now you're starting to understand. I don't understand at all, I said. There is no escaping the sun, Fonte lamented, as he stirred the golden grains into his cup.

During the time it took us to walk to Fonte's quarters, a small whitewashed cave dug out beneath an abandoned grocer's, we talked of all that we had lost and how we had come to be stranded at this crossing place of the Nile. At one point Fonte held up his forearm and in the arteries that stood out on his skin, tunnels that contained and ran all the way back to his birth, it was as if it was revealed to me the specifics of our predicament and our co-ordinates on God's earth.

Later, in a place near the marshes, Fonte spat in the face of a serving girl and threatened to disembowel her three crippled brothers. I rolled diamonds of sand between my teeth and looked to the future.

21/3/1884

A freak rain came to Khartoum and I was forced to remain in my quarters for the best part of a week. I subsisted on dried beans and curdled milk. Word came to me that Gordon had been seen walking the streets without his bodyguard and as soon as the weather gave way I made a point to comb the perimeter of the palace in quest of a meeting. The palace is high and white and looks as if it has been dropped from heaven itself.

27/3/1884

I met Fonte in the street and we engaged in conversation. He asked me what I thought the difference was between Sunni and Shia Muslims. I explained that in my understanding it had to do with tradition and orthodoxy, but he seemed unconvinced. Do you not think, he asked me, that the difference has more to do with time? I asked him to explain himself, but he was vague. The Sunni sees time as bountiful, he ventured. The Shia sees it as something that is running out. In that case Khartoum is a Shia city, I laughed. I disagree, he said, and he seemed upset. I'm sorry, I said, I did not mean to offend you. I have to take a nap, Fonte announced, and he excused himself, abruptly. Right then I saw Gordon approaching from the south, walking slowly. I moved towards him and was suddenly emboldened to catch his arm. He didn't flinch, and I had the feeling that I could have willingly led him away to whatever assignation I might have dreamed up, as if he would take to the skies like a kite at the slightest touch. I felt my own self loosened as I looked into his eyes and saw that one was slightly larger than the other, which made his face appear as a composite, his left side regal, round and upstanding, his right side palsied, dug in. Unhand me, he asked me, a request more than a demand. He searched my appearance for a clue as to my motives. I am a world traveller, I told him, and a prisoner. He returned his hand. I am a monument, he said, to futility.

29/3/1884

I arranged to meet Fonte at a street bazaar where families
traded clothes and trinkets for food and relief. He was
late, inevitably, so I took the opportunity to walk amongst
the traders, their wares spread out on cloths in the sand
or hung from the sides of dilapidated buildings. There
were long-necked women and men so shrunken and sunbeaten they appeared as children. One trader sold small
phalluses and marital toys fired in reflective green and
Egyptian turquoise. When Fonte arrived he was limping
and at first I thought it an affectation. I called him Peg
Leg and Captain Cripple before he confessed to me that
the crippled family he had threatened had exacted their
revenge on him, holding him down in his own home and
smashing his leg with stones. No need to breach the city
walls, he cursed, and spat down into the dirt, at this rate
we will be the overthrow of ourselves. I told him of my
chance meeting with Gordon, of my impudence and of
his startling reaction. At first Fonte didn't believe me. It
doesn't sound like Gordon, he said, and he shook his head
while picking food from between his teeth. A small boy ran
between us and Fonte slapped him viciously on the head as
he passed. Gordon is a singularity, he said, a one-off. Yet
he offers his hand to strangers in the street? There are no
more strangers in Khartoum, I ventured. He looked at me
for a long time, so that at first I questioned the proportions
of my own physiognomy. He spat on his shoe, by accident,
then shook it off in a rage and disappeared into the crowd
all around us.

3/4/1884

Fonte arrived at my door with a group of three drunks
who seemed like mercenaries or guns for hire. What are
you doing in their company? I hissed, as they filed past me
towards the interior. The youngest one of the group was also
the loudest and he insisted on a display of his swordsman
skills, which involved the two older men hoisting him on
their shoulders and him jumping the blade and landing on
their backs again and again. Where does this get us? I asked
Fonte. Someone else mentioned women for sale, young
women, and a joke went around about it being a buyer's
market. There is a whorehouse over the way, the youngest
said, where I hear you can buy a threesome for the price of
the innards of a dead donkey. You may as well fuck the guts
out of a dead donkey, I replied, at which point the young one
turned on me, calling me a modernist, a radical. I noticed
that he had a thin scar across his neck. I cut the hot kidneys
from horses, he said, just to spear them with my dick. I tie
storks' bills and fuck their throats. What do you do? He took
his sword and raised it between my legs. I see the future, I
said. I make the future, the young one said, and made a fist
of his balls. I retired to my room while they commandeered
the rest of the house and fought and drank themselves to
unconsciousness.

4/4/1884

In the morning the young man knocked on the door of my
bedroom. I'm sorry I was discourteous to you by being sick
on your floor, he said. I hear you have the ear of Mr Gordon.
Please, may we talk? I opened the door and surveyed the
scene. Sure enough, there was vomit on the floor and,

unbelievably, on the ceiling. The young man saw me looking at it. That wasn't me, he said. I stepped over the bodies of the two older men who had passed out on top of each other, one of whom had his trousers around his ankles. I thought I saw something crawl between his legs. The young man gave them a kick. Wake up, he said, you vagrants. Show some respect. The men rose to their feet, as if they had simply been resting, the second one pulling up his trousers before sliding a hand down his trousers, smelling it, and wincing. Then they took a seat on the dirt floor, their backs to the wall. Where's Fonte? I asked them. Fonte is lost in the desert, one of the men cackled, and they slapped each other on the back, much to their own amusement. You are vermin of the desert, the young one barked at them, be quiet! I apologise for these . . . marsupials, he said. If yourself would pleasure it, he said, we are looking for an introduction to Mr Gordon. We came here to fight, one of the two older men burst, but this time the young man silenced him with a stare. My name is Ecco Omar, he said. These two are Randar and Fitchin. We came to make a stand against the Mahdi. You came to Khartoum, I asked him, when? We arrived yesterday, Omar answered. How did you get here? I quizzed him. We came from the Garden of Eden, Omar said. You left the Garden of Eden to come to Khartoum? You realise that the city is besieged on all sides? Relief is in sight, Omar said. Besides, we have come to claim the head of the Mahdi. We intend to fructify the Tree of Life with it. What does that involve? I asked him. Bathing the head in the waters of life and replanting it in the garden, he shrugged. Where is the Garden of Eden to be found? I enquired. It is in Anatolia, sir, he said. And where is the water of life to be found? It is said that the four rivers find their terminus in Africa, he replied.

5/4/1884

I arranged to meet Fonte in the shadow of the palace of
Khartoum. He had become obsessed by the reappearance of
Gordon and had taken to sleeping rough in its environs after
his home had been ransacked by vengeful cripples.

They're Yezidis, he explained. Omar is a Yezidi. They
claim to have come from the Garden of Eden, I told him.
That's what they say, he said. But then they say that the
tributaries of the River Eden meet in Africa, I said. So
they're apostates, he shrugged. But then they say they
intend to water and plant the head of the Mahdi in order
to revivify the Tree of Life! So, they're madmen, he burst,
what do you want me to do about it? Listen, he said, and he
lowered his head and narrowed his eyes, you said there are
no more strangers in Khartoum, right? Where would we be
if that were really the case? Think about it. One big happy
family. One fat turkey. One lame camel. One basket of rats.
Okay, I said, okay, I understand the comparison, but what
do you mean by it? What do I mean, he exploded, what do
I mean? God save me from idiocy! I mean precisely what I
say. Without new blood, without blood in our beliefs, I mean
to say, without an element of madness in our bodies, in
other words, we are doomed, Khartoum is doomed. We are
no longer strangers, it is true, we have become soft, familiar,
at home on this headland of the Nile. At best we fight
amongst ourselves, he said, like a family. This is where the
Mahdi and his armies have the advantage. I, on the other
hand, in a moment of madness, if you like, though more
properly I believe it to be a moment of divine inspiration,
have decided to introduce a contagion. But to make it work,
to get it to take, we must first infect Gordon with it. And

you, my friend, for some reason that God, in his infinite wisdom, knows best, and that I confess eludes me still, have been chosen as the conduit, the means by which we can turn the end of the world around.

15/4/1884

Three in, three out. Over the past week Fonte has exchanged women and children for migrants from the Garden of Eden who make their way across the Nile by night. With the Mahdi's forces encamped on the opposite bank, it is as large a convoy as he dares. Now Omar leads an army of twelve.

18/4/1884

Gordon had been spotted with a military entourage in Lower Khartoum. A small area around the catacombs, in the shadow of the parapet and outside the walls of the city, had reportedly been sealed off. I made my way in secret to the scene of the events, using covert routes, where I mingled with onlookers dressed for all the world like an Arab trader. Rumours were flying. I spoke with two old Bedouin who kept using the Arab word for gold, thahab. Thahab, they said, and they patted beneath their arms and pointed to the catacombs, now sealed by black guards with guns and long, curving scimitars. Thahab? I said. No, this is no treasure hunt. But they insisted. Gordon has discovered gold, they said. The ruckus attracted the usual gawkers and troublemakers, including the Man on Stilts, a feature of public gatherings in Khartoum for the past year or so. He wore the same sign around his neck, written in a curious Sudanese Arabic dialect, that had been variously translated as Ripe Pear, Fellow Conspirator and Peace Restored. He towered above the crowd, high on a pair of handcrafted stilts made from the oars of an old fishing boat, walking with a macabre motion and bearing down on bystanders, silent but for the low hissing of his tongue. No one had ever seen his feet touch the earth, it was said, though I suppose he slept, like all of us. I thought of the impossible proportions of his frame, his feet as huge paddles, floating at low tide, rolling in half-sleep across the shallows of the beach as if he had been washed up in some diluvial horror.

By the time of early evening Gordon had still not emerged. There were rumours of a tunnel from the catacombs, leading beneath the Blue Nile and running under the North Fort before connecting with the subterranean streams that fed the fourth cataract of the Nile, far in the north. Someone claimed to have seen long stately boats like royal sarcophagi being lowered into the tombs. Someone else claimed that the English relief had arrived, using the subterranean stream as a means of dark passage. Men passed around water and smoked kif and speculated. A vendor selling battered flower petals fried in oil passed through the crowd. The sky turned the colour of a new bruise and the stars came out. Every shooting star was an omen, every heavenly body a wish driven hard into the night. I looked out to the sea of faces all around me. One can just as surely drown on dry land, I thought to myself, as I looked to the Man on Stilts, parting the crowd.

19/4/1884

Gordon had made his escape from the tombs by cover of night, possibly by a secret exit, Fonte told me. There were rumours of the removal of some kind of artefact, carried on a stretcher and hidden beneath ornamental quilts. Some say it was three to four feet tall. A mummified child? I asked Fonte. No, he said, and he wiped his mouth with his sleeve. I believe it to be some kind of marker. Marking what? I asked him. The very centre of the world, he said.

20/4/1884

I spoke with Gordon, clearly, in my dreams. The whole earth is hollow, he told me, and we are clinging to its shell, like insects, scuttling around a great singularity. What of the mystery of death? I asked him. Life is for life, he said, death for death, but it is possible to confuse the two. Is there a death that is life? I asked him. That is what we cling to, he said. There is a mingling of the two, he said, and then he began to speak in numbers and in months. April, September, January, 25, 3, 25. I turned away from the vision so that I would not partake of prophecy.

21/4/1884

Gordon has communicated the possibility of life in death, I told Fonte. The man speaks in conundrums, he burst. Life and death are divided, I insisted, or why name them so? Death is not life's concern, and life not death's. Yet the scales are imbalanced, that is what Gordon implies. Death has its way over life while life's dominion ends at the border with death. Bite me, Christ, Fonte cursed, have you no knowledge of the dead!? The paths by which they return, the empty places in our hearts that are reserved for them? I say there is traffic both ways!

22/4/1884

I took up watch with Fonte at the perimeter of the palace
of Khartoum. We must engineer a meeting, Fonte said, we
must force the hand of chance. What of the Yezidis? I asked
him. Most of their worldly goods are already in hock in order
to pay for the women they molest and manhandle, he told
me. Their debasement has become some kind of anabasis,
I fear, which will end in pointless sacrifice if we are not
able to redirect it towards more profitably millenarian
ends. Their disgust for the world and all that it requires is
understandable, I said to him, any refugee from Eden would
feel the same. Then tell me, Fonte asked me, what hell are
you cast out from? My garden is Khartoum, I replied. My
exile is yet to come.

23/4/1884

The sun beat down and the flies took their fill. My head is
pockmarked and cratered with their bites. I sat in the shade
outside The Mountains of the Moon and drank coffee. A man
approached my table and introduced himself as a friend
of Fonte. Is it possible for you to put a word in for me with
Gordon? he asked me. I don't know Gordon, I told him. You
have his ear, my friend, he said, that is what I have heard.
Do you have access to the palace? he asked me. Do you enjoy
privilege? No, I said. Leave me alone. The man took a seat
opposite and we sat in silence for a while. Then he resumed
his questions. If you do not have access to the palace, how
were you able to catch Gordon's ear? he asked me. I met him
in the street once, I replied. I shook his hand. That was all.
Impossible, the man spat, and he leaned forward and began
to rock, almost imperceptibly, back and forth. Gordon never

leaves the palace unless surrounded by a military escort, he said. On clear days he appears as a distant shadow with an eyeglass on the roof of the palace of Khartoum. He does not walk the streets of this purgatory, glad-handing strangers. Listen, he said. I have a wife and three children, we are looking for passage, we can pay, he said. Pay with what? I taunted him. With silks and cloths, he said, with elephant tusks and shotguns. There are no elephant tusks in Khartoum, I mocked, and as for shotguns, well, now is not the time to start trading in arms. Very well, he said, rising from the table. I accept your story. You are more, let me say, a harmless fantasist. I bit my tongue and drank my coffee. But please, answer me this, if you can, he said. Do you think all of this will end well? He motioned around us, at the dusty streets and the flat rooftops and the small groups of men coming and going. Nothing ends well, I went to tell him, but something stopped me. Instead I sat in silence and thought some more. Finally, I told him that the end would be inconclusive. Will there be inroads? he asked me. Yes, I said, there will be inroads. How far and on what side? They will push forward, I said, and we will push back. From what direction will they come? It will be impossible to ascertain, I informed him, they will come from all around us. Is resistance academic? If by academic you mean is resistance necessary or futile or is resistance based on an idea, a concept of the corrective to a state of siege, then I would say, yes, you have imagined that it might be necessary. It is, as you rightly say, academic. If it is academic, the stranger said, then it is of the schools, am I correct? Yes, I said, that would be academic. But if it is of the schools, he insisted, then there is something there that if studied correctly and completely and with due diligence will reveal its core attributes. I give you that, I admitted. And to uncover the core means to be in possession of an understanding of the relationship between the place of the core and yourself. That makes sense, I said. So if our current situation is academic, and the field of our actions based upon ideas of what is necessary, then the founding of schools upon those ideas may result in the acquisition of a set of co-ordinates, let us say, which, if calculated correctly, if added to or subtracted from or displaced according to the laws of the stars and the planets, may be made to reveal, in all probability, the way forward. This is prophecy, I told him, and be damned for it. Prophecy, he said, no, I don't think so. The gods would use prophecy to uplift and condemn and destroy. Prophecy, for men like you and I, is a means to make of the future the past. Only there, in the past, sir, where everything has already happened, is there safety in the present. I don't ask you, my friend, he said, to smuggle me out with my wife and children. Rather, I ask you to take them from me, prophet, and deposit them in my past. You talk in signs, I told him, at which he held up his right hand, blinked his eyes and walked off into the distance.

24/4/1884

I met Fonte at the confectioner's near the military barracks. Real food has become an impossible luxury. We ate small cakes with coloured leaves on top that were perfumed and that had no bite and that crumbled to dust in your mouth. Perpetual virgins, Fonte called them, and he laughed at his own joke. Soon they will be the only virgins left in the city, he mourned, if we don't move on Gordon and give these Yezidis something to do. I asked him if he knew much of prophecy. I have studied it, he said. Do you believe in its art? I asked him. Here, he said, give me your hand. He took my palm in his. Do you know what they call this? he asked me, and he traced a curve that ran from the centre of my wrist and around the base of my thumb. This is the life line, they say. Look closer, he said. Look at where the lines cross, the tributary that flows north, the confluence near the base. Is Khartoum not written into your flesh? Does the Nile not plot your days? A hand, after all, is nothing more than the cards you are holding. What is this witchery? I demanded, snatching my hand away. Nothing but a parlour trick, he shrugged, think nothing of it. Let me see your hand, I demanded, and he opened his palm on the table. There it is, I cried, Khartoum, written in your skin as clearly as in mine! This is a trick, and a low one. Begging your pardon, my friend, he said, but how could it be otherwise? Are we not, the two of us, caught up in Khartoum here, at the end of days? How else would our bodies register our place in this vast game except to make us in their image? Think you to dodge your own fate? You asked me what I knew of prophecy. All that I learned is commensurate with the weight of flesh on these bones. I'm tired of all this double-talk, I said. What are we to do, here in Khartoum? You are the one who talks as if something were expected of you, he said. But ask yourself, who is the expecting, and what is the expected? More mirrors, I said, more spin. You expect nothing? Fonte asked me. I expect something of the future, of course, who could live in the present always? No one does. So you admit that part of you lives in the future? he quizzed me. Ask yourself what their expectations are. There you have your definition of prophecy.

25/4/1884

By night the house is silent. No wind penetrates the
wooden shutters. Every footstep is swallowed by the sand.
Occasionally there are voices, in the distance, inchoate.
Still, I am unable to sleep. Was the night ever so bright?
Khartoum seems caught in a perpetual day, a dark-blue
blanket curves around us, and I have fitful dreams of the
story of Moses, how he was wrapped in swaddling clothes
and sent down the river.

I woke in the early hours and ventured out. The streets were
deserted, though luminous, still. At the crossroads near
the disembowelled statue I could make out the silhouette
of two figures, one leading the other on some kind of rope.
The one pulled the rope savagely, jerking and whipping
it, when the one following fell behind. Still they moved in
silence, two blurred figures connected by an umbilical, until
they passed close by me and I was able to see that it was a
blind man being led on a rope through the darkness of the
city. The futility and unnecessary cruelty of it made me
despair. I made my way towards the fortifications in the
south. I passed solitary sleepers, pressed up against the
walls of buildings, sometimes three or four bundled together
in the same spot. I am walking through a graveyard, I told
myself. Somewhere there was music playing, a lament, but
not quite, a song that had everything to do with the future,
but that came out of the past. There was something erotic
about it and I felt the stirrings of my own manhood for
the first time in weeks. I slid a hand beneath my robes as
I remembered the shaved girls of my youth, their vaginas
tough like beaten leather.

I approached the source of the music, the basement of a large abandoned building whose windows had been boarded up. There were no sounds of reverie, of drinking or shouting, even, just the turning of this strange music box that seemed to have sprung up from my dreams. I descended the stairs and pushed open the door. There was a large group of men, seated in a circle, with low candles lighting the gloom. In the centre of the circle there was a woman, a middle-aged woman, not beautiful but not unattractive, who was dancing slowly, rotating on the spot and angling her arms like branches, like a tree growing over centuries and decades, twisting this way and that, suddenly, but without surprise. I took a seat at one of the tables. No one looked at me or acknowledged my entrance except for a small boy who offered me a bottle and asked me for payment. I put my hand in my pouch and came up with some buttons, a few trinkets, a small pendant. He sat the bottle down and wiped a glass clean. I watched as the woman turned slowly in front of us. I noticed the moles on her face, her dark skin and darker hair. I felt as if I could see the very sockets of her skull, the eyeballs sunk inside them like pebbles in a shallow tide, rotating, slowly. I took a drink. I felt it illuminate my insides. I longed for the connection that I had missed for so long, the channel to the belly of a woman. Now everything was spinning. How did we get here?

1/5/1884

There are fires burning across the rooftops of Khartoum, sometimes three to one roof. No one knows who started it, but the rumour is that it was commanded by Gordon. I saw people smashing wooden doors to splinters and carrying huge planks over their shoulders. I climbed to the roof of an abandoned building, where I found the mutilated body of a dog and bloodied footprints leading away, as if it had been trampled to death in a rage and its corpse left, still smouldering, in the sun. Only a few weeks ago I would have fled such a place but today I crouched over it and picked through the entrails with a stick, unfolding viscera and spearing punctured organs. I wondered whether the footprint in its guts wasn't the writing of Khartoum in its flesh. Afterwards I sat on the edge of the roof and watched the fires as a southerly wind blew through the city and drew the flames into a cone of black smoke that seemed to form a tunnel, a northern passage, and I imagined a great company of warships billowing through it, lowering ropes onto the rooftops and saving us all. The fires are a bluff, I hear, a show of arms to test the resolve of the Mahdi and his troops and to exaggerate the numbers still present in Khartoum. I looked to the west and to the north, across the Nile, but saw no fires in response, no thin chimneys of smoke rising like ladders to the stars. We have the advantage, I told myself. Besides, relief is close at hand. Rumours of a rescue mission from England have reached the city.

I thought of my own father, of the travels he had made as a young man. Where were those travels now? What footprint on his insides? Though I knew truly that his insides had long ago been hollowed out and that I myself was an echo only, a solitary memorial, to his own being in time. To remember, the scholars teach us, is to reattach the limbs to a god whose body lies scattered to the wind. Wasn't there a deity spoken of in Egypt whose task was to search out the severed phallus of the beloved? I sat on the edge of the roof and looked out at the fires and considered these things. I watched for a reply in the distance, any sign of defiance.

Nothing came of it, and I retired to my quarters after several hours.

3/5/1884

I saw Gordon again and this time not in a dream or a vision or as the result of grotesque mental straining. At my approach he beckoned me towards him and, taking my arm, led me through several checkpoints, to the inner courtyard of the palace at Khartoum. You are a bibliophile? he asked me. I admit I was taken aback by the question. I am a scholar, I replied, and a sincere student of the word. Very good, Gordon said. We passed through a garden that was covered by high netting and about which flitted many exotic birds that made rude senseless cries. Birds of paradise, Gordon replied, in answer to my unspoken query. He led me into a tall minaret-like structure in the corner of the garden where we climbed a claustrophobic staircase. We came to a small circular room that was shelved on all sides and carpeted in deep, luxuriant red with a small iron bath set directly in the centre. Here we are, he said, the belly of the beast. I have come upon a singular collection of books, he explained. And I would like your professional opinion on them. The subjects of the collection seem somewhat arbitrary, puzzlingly so. But I fear there is some logic to it, some sense or seed that will serve to unlock their purpose. What do you think of African literature? he asked me. What I have read is insular, myopic, characterised by huge swathes of lexical desert, I replied. What of Arabic literature? Sensual, mystical, but without a political dimension. And what of the Egyptians? Ah, I said, there you have me, for I am a great lover of the Egyptians. There you will be disappointed, he told me. For this collection

is no Egyptian treasure. Rather, it is concerned with the
obscure, the humdrum. In it you will find no channel to
the afterworld, not even a boat from east to west. There
are books on bonefires, he told me. On famous fires and
ceremonial pyres and on notorious burnings. What of the
fires in Khartoum? I asked him. I ordered them, he said,
it is true. But I took my instructions from a book, at which
he handed me a small custom-bound volume entitled *The
Bonefires of the Monk Lands.* The burning of the summer
fields goes back a long way, he said, and he nodded slowly
and took a seat in the east of the tower. What else have
these books instructed? I asked him. There is a collection of
books whose subject is Saturdays, he said. Neither of us said
anything. How can there be books on Saturdays?

There are books on Saturdays, he said, and he nodded to
himself, as in disbelief at the surfeit of wonders in this
world. Are there books on other days? I quizzed him. Not in
this collection, but from my researches it appears that, yes,
there are books written on every day of the week. There is
a lore of days, he said, and he held his head in his hand and
despaired.

4/5/1884

Fonte took me to the house of the Yezidis. They have moved
house four or five times already, he told me. Locating them
has become a chore. They claim that they haven't moved at
all, rather that it is the city of Khartoum itself that is on
the move, the buildings walking by night and recombining
by day. They insist that they have uncovered the location of
their original domicile on its peregrinations across the city.
How come it looks completely different every time? I asked

him. How come I can still find my own way home? Are you
sure? he replied, and he looked at me as if he had already
crossed over himself. When we arrived at the house, this
time a tall, thin building perched between a stable and a
narrow river filled with excrement and debris, Randar and
Fitchin were on guard outside, peeling something rancid
with a knife and passing it between them. I had my first
good look at them in daylight, brutes with blunt noses and
long matted hair, like from an old photograph of Russia,
blind faces in a nameless horde. Ah, Randar said, rising
and mock-bowing, he deigns us with his presence, the little
prince! I hear your home ran away in the night, I spat at
him. I can't say I blame it.

Inside there were Yezidis spread out across piles of old
sacks, some snoring, some smoking, some huddled in
secret groupings. We approached Omar, who was stabbing
a large fruit with a knife and attempting to drink from
it. Khartoum is running low on women, he said, without
looking round, and I have only so much debauch left in me. I
met with Gordon, I informed him, even now he is searching
for oracles. He has discovered a library, I told him, wherein
he believes there are instructions regarding the future.
He goes by the book? Omar exclaimed. These Englishmen
are wholly lacking in inspiration. However, that will be
to our advantage. What is the subject of these books he is
consulting? Ritual, I informed him, and the observance of
days. Are you aware that Khartoum is on the move? Omar
asked me. Sir, I said, I believe it may be the brain in the
cavity of your skull that has come loose. Ha, he laughed, you
lack imagination yourself, sir. I may have travelled far from
my country, he said, but mine is not an exile. Nevertheless,
I said, gesturing around the room. I see that your home

neglected to bring any of your belongings along with it. Belongings, he laughed, that is why you remain stationary while we flit in and out of life. Fonte intervened. Enough of this double-talk, he said. What is our plan? If he desires to read the future in a book, Omar said, then surely, we shall write it for him.

5/5/1884

I was never a portly individual, but now my clothes billow around me like rainclouds, borne by the weight of cares and my distance from all that I love and that would take care of me. This afternoon I kneeled over a small pool of water in the street and felt like I was looking up, to a past that was somewhere above and beyond me, even as my own reflection gazed back in horror. My cheeks are sunken, my lips swollen and bruised, my eyes forced open in my head by all that is happening around me. But though my eyes protest, there is something in my spirit that bears me on, even as my eyes say, no, not that way. Nights in Khartoum are freezing, afternoons unbearably hot. Today I killed a snake in the street, a puff adder that raised itself up almost two feet from the ground to attack me, hidden as it was beneath a fossilised tree, its sacs of poison running to six inches on either side of its head. I sliced it in two with my sword but still it raced towards me, its two halves competing to encircle me, working in tandem even as it was sundered and making an infinity of shapes in the dust. In the end I saw its tail half turn and squirm down a tiny hole in the sand as if it were still alive. A passing stranger with tattoos around his mouth told me that I should have captured the bottom half and burned it on a fire in case it reunited with the head and resumed its pursuit, at which point I pounded the head to a pulp with a stone and then fell sick and collapsed on the ground. Later I woke to the sound of drum troupes in the street. Groups of men wearing loincloths made of bark were marching in the distance, some with small handheld rattles, others with large drum skins strapped to their waists. Dancers led the pack, dancers with dried fruits tied to their legs. The tattooed man returned and told me these were the Lotus Eaters, a legendary travelling band who were part missionary and part Gypsy bandit. I asked him how they had come to be in Khartoum. They lay in wait, he said, at which I saw Gordon take a book from the shelf and replace it with another.

6/5/1884

There is no grief in Khartoum, no fellow feeling. There is much carnival at death, much preparation for passing, but the soul of Africa is inured to suffering. Khartoum is the eternal present of Africa. Cairo is its past. Its future lies in a small fortified island untouched by outside influence, hard by a stream.

7/5/1884

We made our plans. We made our plans. Who are we? We were made by our plans. We modelled ourselves on possibility. We made. Volition no longer exists in Khartoum. To escape history is to refuse to stand for the count.

8/5/1884

Among the Lotus Eaters there are many players with deformities. There have been performances in the central

square every evening since they arrived, no one knows
from where. They play double-reed shehnais and beat their
drums while the dancers move in grotesque formation. The
dancers look reptilian, with flat, protruding mouths and
faces of implacable damage, moonlike eyes, one with skin
grown over an eye completely and legs tied together so that
it resembled an upright fish dancing on dry land. They came
from the marshes, someone said. The Mahdi's creatures,
said another. Even the Yezidis have been drawn out by their
dance.

9/5/1884

Tonight we made our move. I met Gordon in the shadow of
the perimeter. I have brought someone with me capable of
reading the books, I told him, and I introduced him to Ecco
Omar. At first neither of them said anything. Then Gordon
asked him where he had come from. Omar repeated the same
story that he had told me, that he and his men had forsaken
Eden in order to return with the head of the Mahdi and
fructify the garden. You believe that the Garden of Eden lies
on the face of the earth? Gordon asked him. It is written in
the book, Omar replied. There are many books, Gordon said,
and he shook his head, many, many books. There is one book,
Omar countered, and that book contains all books. What do
the books contain that are contained in the book? Gordon
quizzed him. Books, of course, Omar replied. So what end to
books? There is one book, Omar insisted, the beginning and
the end. But books within books, Gordon pushed him, what
sense is there in this? A book, Omar said, is an opening, one
that opens onto other books. Just as the earth is a parchment
encircling a hollow centre, Gordon nodded. You believe the
earth to be hollow? Omar asked him. Certainly, he said. For

what purpose? There is no purpose to emptiness, Gordon
replied, at which he led us through the courtyard past the
wild birds and high into the book tower. There are books on
music, Gordon explained to us. I had not come across them
before, books of notation. He passed one to Omar. I have
seen these signs before, Omar nodded. Where, man? Gordon
demanded. In my youth, he said. In your youth in Eden,
Gordon mocked, what are you, Moses himself? Moses brought
down the tablets, Omar said. Look, he said, pointing to a sign
in the books that appeared as a circle with a dot inside it.
There it is: an eye. Look into it, he said, and he held the book
to Gordon's face. Look into the eye.

You are mocking me, Gordon responded, pushing the
book to one side. One character is incapable of elucidating
an entire text. You know nothing. This is no more an
eye than it marks the centre of the world. I fear you are
onto something there, Omar nodded. Don't pander to me,
Gordon burst. Sir, Omar replied, if I were to explain to you
the beginnings of time and the motivation of the creator, we
would still be stuck with these symbols, these sounds and
signs, black space over white space. But there is truly only
one book and this character, which I have chosen to bring
to your attention, is, as you can plainly see, written inside a
book which, in its turn, resides inside the great book itself.
Herein, sir, there lies a great mystery. This is the passage
you have been looking for, Omar insisted, though without
wishing you to dispense with my services altogether, you
could have picked any figure and read into it the shape of
the future and the confluence of the past. But I have cast

the die myself, my friend, and read your fate in an open letter.

I could have handed you any book? Gordon burst. But you did, Omar nodded. Here, Gordon said, and he grabbed a random book from the shelf, now all is changed, read me my fate again. Omar opened the book at random. Here, he said, this word makes a sound. What is the sound, man? Gordon burst. Tell me! It is an empty sound, he replied, a sound that is hidden in the throat. Then unveil it, Gordon demanded. In time, Omar said, in time. There will be much music, he said, in the roaring of the blood that will attend the beheading of the Mahdi.

12/5/1884

A boat has been spotted making its way towards Khartoum. We watched with Gordon from the roof of the palace, passing the telescope between us. It looks like nothing I have previously encountered, a one-man vessel perhaps, driven by some kind of propulsive device. There is no sign of human life aboard and it attracts no fire from the hordes massed on both sides of the Nile. Yet it makes its way steadily towards us. It is no English vessel, Gordon maintains. He insists that he has made no request for relief from the British government. The Yezidis have been ordered to intercept it and to bring its occupants to the palace with minimum fuss and under cover of darkness.

13/5/1884

Fonte and I accompanied the Yezidis to a promontory north of the city, where we awaited the arrival of the vessel. Word

had passed around and there were already crowds gathered
along the shore, but they were soon dispersed by Randar
and Fitchin, who led the Yezidis into their midst, where they
brandished their swords and hacked at civilians without
care for injury or distress. There was much blood and protest
but soon the crowd was beaten back behind a row of tall
trees, where they were held at bay. The boat appeared on
the horizon as a silent flash and floated towards us; a coffin
fallen from the distant stars. This is no earthly ship, Fonte
said. Hell itself has given up its inhabitants. The Yezidis
held up flags and the vessel turned towards us, slowly, as
a sleepwalker, coming to a halt in the shallows of the Nile
before us. The hull was scorched and blackened, its windows
cracked and opaque, as if it had passed through great heat
and become fused, somehow. Still it sat there, bobbing on the
tide, this terrible singularity. Omar led two Yezidis, their
swords drawn, into the water. The rest of the men raised
their rifles along the shore. I saw Omar slither into the boat,
his feet raised in the air as he clambered head first into the
small cabin. He emerged seconds later, had words with his
men, and the three of them forced the boat to the shore. There
is a body inside, Omar said, the likes of which I have never
seen before.

14/5/1884

The body has been secreted in the book tower, in the bath
in the centre of the room. It appears to be a man, though his
face is obscured by a sealed clear dome that has fogged over
and that is fixed to what appears to be full body armour, only
soft and pliable, though equally impenetrable. He comes from
the future, Fonte insisted. Then what does that make of us?
Gordon demanded. Mere figments? Shades whose time has

been and gone? Perhaps, Fonte said, but weren't we always? If this man, Gordon argued, is come from the future, which from his clothes I have little reason to doubt, although he could, I maintain, be simply outlandish, then we are robbed of any existence that we might have had. We are, as it were, see-through, cheated of corporeality, mere players in the show. Again, Fonte insisted, I ask of you, truly, what has changed? What has changed? Gordon demanded. Do you not believe yourself to be at the forefront of time? To be riding the very crest of eternity's unfolding? To be back of the curve, to have already been, well, it seems a cruel trick. I thought myself the witness of the new, Gordon continued, but if what you say is true, that this fiend has returned to us from a time in advance of our own, then it would appear that I was merely a holding place, a simple scaffold for the weight of all that has already been. But who is the trickster? Omar cried. Name him, sir.

15/5/1884

The book has been written backwards, the Yezidis inform us, beginning and end interwoven. The peacock's eyes are everywhere all vainglorious. Hate is a conundrum, they teach us, yes and no inseparable. Strange ships have been sighted in the throat of the Nile. The Man on Stilts has been seen crossing the river, going over to the enemy. The stars are in place. We await our liberators or our captors. Gordon has discovered a book of the lore of the planets, the attributes of the heavenly spheres. He reads deeply in it. Saturne has a ring around it, he says, the Earthe a halo. He talks of the fleetingness of assignations and of young love. At times he is lost in remembering. At night I walk the city, this damned city, this godforsaken island.

16/5/1884

Gordon of Khartoum. He has taken this name and insists
that this is how he be addressed in the future. And how
should we address you in the present, Fonte chastised him,
before you disappear? Chinese Gordon, he said. Heart's
True Gordon, Defender of the Empire, Unbowed Gordon.
We shall all bow down, sir, Fonte said. Say you so? Gordon
of Khartoum replied. The Lord would ask of us fortitude
before fealty. The letter F, Fonte replied, is dissolute,
deceptive. That is why we call them f-words. You speak
like a Jew, Gordon of Khartoum said, endlessly rolling
letters. It was Christ's body that was resurrected after
much suffering, not his word. His word is eternal and need
not partake of life and death, Fonte replied. So let the word
bow down or rise up, Gordon of Khartoum said. Either way
'tis no great thing. But let the body stand firm and receive
its marks. Its marks are words, Fonte insisted. Logos is the
body, Gordon of Khartoum replied. Logos is the beginning
of the story, Fonte said. Having been in their company for
several hours I damned them both as philosophers and left
their presence, where I drank myself unconscious in the
company of an emaciated street whore.

18/5/1884

We attended the unveiling of the body in the tower in the
corner of the garden. Gordon of Khartoum's top physician
appears also to be his bodyguard. There was much doubt
about his credentials. Surgeons and mortuary attendants
are in short supply in the closed city of Khartoum, though
future events may yet make doctors and gravediggers of
us all. His name is Agha Khalil Orphali. I knew his family,

Fonte confided to me. Vegetarians, ascetics, he spat. It had been decided that we would cut the soft outer skin from the body, presuming it to be a form of organic armour. In outlandish places they may have developed the ability to grow a protective layer over their body that would permit traffic amidst hostile elements like fire and water, Orphali said. Have you not heard of the doubles of Dubai, warriors with second skins?

What if he bleeds some noxious substance from the horror of his insides? Gordon of Khartoum asked. We should wrap our heads in turbans, Orphali said, so as to cover our passages.

We stood around the body like assassins with nothing but slits for eyes. Orphali took a small blade and cut a tiny slit into the arm of the outer layer. There was a sharp ophidian hiss as whatever was inside escaped into the air. Our faces being covered, only our eyes demonstrated fear, dilating like pebbles into dark wells. It's nothing, Gordon of Khartoum said, only trapped air. I fear it is his spirit, Fonte said, and everyone turned to look at him. I fear that we have given passage to some form of demon. But something in Fonte's eyes told me that he was smiling. I looked at the palm of my hand and pictured traffic in the lines. Enough for tonight, Gordon of Khartoum commanded. We must be careful how we go.

19/5/1884

I met Biraggo Fonte in the street. What do you understand as a ghost? he asked me. I was taken aback. A visitation from the past, I said. A wraith, a spirit. Ah, the spirit of the

past is a ghost? Fonte said. Come with me. We walked arm
in arm through the deserted streets of the city. It was early
evening. We could smell the burning corpses of animals
and salt was in the air too, camel dung and lavender. It
will thunder tonight, Fonte said. The skies are pregnant. I
despair of all this birth, of all these arrivals, I said. You may
as well despair of death, Fonte said. Its time will come, I
said. But for now, we are overwhelmed. You wish for a stop,
he said. You are like a migrating bird on the ocean. But
perhaps you mistake yourself for your going.

We climbed the stairwell of the royal palace and made our
way to the roof. Above us the stars raged, before us the
fires burned. Take your pick, Fonte said, and he laughed.
I have taken the measure of Gordon of Khartoum, he said.
And he is already a ghost. In taking his name he has taken
his place in history. Ghosts are historic. But there are also
demons. Demons are of time. Time is their very substance.
Do you believe that the man in the tower is a demon? I
asked him. I believe that he has had consort with them,
yes, and I believe that when his second skin was cut open
there was an influx of demonic energy, of time. And now
there is a mingling. Of history and time, of ghosts and
demons. Can they be separated? I doubt that, Fonte said.
Even now they are in congress. Look up, he said, the very
stars are copulating. I looked up and it was true. The skies
were in orgy.

20/5/1884

The autopsy continues. Orphali removed the glass skull
from his head. Beneath the skull was the shrunken head
of a woman with long black hair. She smelled like a whore,

of petals and incense. Across her eyes she wore a black visor. Within the man is a blind woman, Orphali gasped. It's a cocoon, Gordon of Khartoum marvelled. She is like a butterfly or a moth. Perhaps she was attracted by the fires. You mean the stars? Fonte said, and he laughed. Of course, her arrival is written there.

This blindness, Orphali said. Perhaps it facilitates great feats of transport. Time itself is blind, said Fonte, and we looked at each other through our eye slits. It occurred to me that our own heads were the inverse of the woman in the floating coffin. I pictured myself wearing the visor, my head as blind as the night sky. But what did it mean? To be blind means to travel in time, and to see means to be exiled. Peck out my eyes, I said, without thinking. Fonte looked at me in concern. We can see, and she is blind, I shrugged. Remove the visor, Gordon of Khartoum said. Let us see if she is blind. But the visor seemed fixed to the face. Perhaps she grew it, Orphali said. Or perhaps it was secured through great heat. The eyes are the gateway to the soul, Gordon of Khartoum said. We shall never know her. Fonte rolled his eyes and shook his head. Time is the gateway to the soul, he spat. Spare me your infant platitudes. We shall know her, in time.

Beneath the second skin there appeared to be a cloak or tunic of black animal hide, with the same material wrapped tight around her legs. Again, beneath the skin, on her feet, the same black animal hide was worked into sharp points, like the feet of a bird. She is a shaman, Orphali announced. In some cultures they believe that taking the form of certain spirit animals endows them with their abilities. She dresses as a bird in order to facilitate flight across time. And what

of the leather skin? Gordon of Khartoum asked. Are we to
believe that she invokes the power of the cow? There was
much laughter. Need I remind you, sir, that in these parts
it is the skin of alligators that provides us with our best
animal hides? Orphali replied. Perhaps she swam in the
waters.

Swam with one oar! Gordon of Khartoum exclaimed as he
lifted the woman's arm in the air to reveal a missing right
hand. The red right hand! he said. What does it mean?
Orphali quizzed him. It moves behind the scenes, perchance,
Gordon of Khartoum said. Orphali pulled the leather tunic
to one side to reveal a vegetative material wrapped around
her torso. There appeared to be characters written into it.
Hieroglyphs! Gordon of Khartoum cried. More books! She is
adorned with the word, Orphali said. Of that there can be
no doubt. But what words? Gordon of Khartoum despaired.
They were obscured; faded with age, they had returned to
the earth. I can make out one word only, Fonte said, leaning
over the corpse. It appears to be the Latin word for moon.
Orphali took a sharp knife and went to cut the garment from
her. No! Gordon of Khartoum commanded. Leave it intact. I
wish to confirm the construction of the breasts, Orphali said.
In that case use your hands, he was commanded. Orphali
slid his hand beneath the garment of words and felt for the
breasts of the silent woman. The breasts have atrophied, he
announced. They are now merely nipples. Perhaps this was
a result of congress with invisible energies. Now we see why
she was in need of the powers of the cow, Fonte announced,
so that the milk of her paps would continue to flow. The
cow appears barren, Orphali says. Truly this is a primitive
magic. Expose her genitalia, Fonte demanded, and everyone
looked to the ground. We must! he said. Orphali rolled back

the leather leggings to reveal a small black silk pouch, ornately decorated. She wears it as a precious jewel! Orphali marvelled. Everyone stared in awe. These outlanders dress their genitals in rich garments, Gordon of Khartoum exclaimed. This is popery, idolatry! But what kind of church is this! Orphali exclaimed as he slid the perfumed silk from her thighs to reveal a small rudimentary penis. My Lord, Gordon exploded, she has become a man! There is nothing left of the slit, Orphali said, as he ran his fingers between her legs, and there are testicles the size of marbles. I have heard of this in the oriental countries, Gordon of Khartoum marvelled, where passage between the male and the female is fluid. The cow and the moon, Fonte said. She wished to preserve not only the milk of her paps, but the blood of the moon. Her magic failed her, Gordon of Khartoum said. It backfired. Now she is an abomination in the eyes of the Lord.

21/5/1884

The weighing of the organs has begun. She smells of the seas; perhaps she wears the skin of an alligator after all. Orphali cut a slit into her side to allow ingress. Her insides, too, are perfectly preserved. It's a miracle, he said. Yes, Gordon of Khartoum said, we have lost faith in miracles. To us a flower is just a seed that has grown from the dead of the earth. You compare her to a flower? Fonte said. Yesterday you christened her an abomination. A rare flower but a flower all the same, Gordon of Khartoum said, and he sighed and held his head. I am alone in Khartoum. It is perhaps my final stand. The fruits of the earth rise up under God's hand. In the end, anything is possible. He drew his hand around the room. These are His works, he said. And

what of demons, sir, Fonte said, what of your Lord Lucifer?
Banished, Gordon of Khartoum said. Khartoum is cleared
of him, for now. But without reinforcements . . . His voice
trailed off. One man cannot hold back the tide forever.
Christ did, I said to him. Christ was the son of God, he
replied. And is this not His daughter? Fonte asked, and he
pointed to the woman with the hole in her side.

Orphali removed the organs, weighed and numbered them.
The heart was swollen, engorged, 'under sufferance of
great emotion', Orphali said. The lungs, too, were enlarged.
The womb had been taken. The womb is gone, Orphali
announced, and he shook his head. What thievery is this?
Why would someone remove the womb? Unless there was
something inside that they wanted, Fonte said. We all
looked at him through the slits in our turbans. Nonsense,
Gordon of Khartoum said. Some women are born without
wombs. I have read of it in the books. Besides, he said,
where is its point of exit?

The genitals are rudimentary, sir, Orphali said, a recent
addition, I would say. She has been transformed somehow.
But prior to this transformation the passages were open.
Something has been born to this woman and has been taken
from her, encased in her own birth. Aren't we all, Fonte
laughed, but Gordon of Khartoum started to sob quietly.
This has all been written, he said, and he held his hand over
his eyes. I know that this has all been written, somewhere.

22/5/1884

I have come to question my own origins and my own
passage to Khartoum. I quizzed Fonte as to what he could

remember of his past life, of a time before Khartoum. All
of our origins are obscure, he said. It is a form of mercy.
Do any of us remember the passage of the birth canal? Do
any of us remember the navigation of the blood? That is no
mercy, I protested. Perhaps if we were able to hold within
ourselves a vision of our own becoming, if it were to be
imprinted in our consciousness, then death would no longer
hold such fear after so bold an adventure. You say there is
mercy in forgetting; I say there is mercy in remembering.
So remember, he commanded me. I have been trying, I told
him. But there is something out of reach. Merciful God,
Fonte shrugged, and he drank some perfidious alcoholic
concoction that the Yezidis had put together from rotten
vegetables. He wretched, cursed, spat in the sand and then
swallowed it down. What do you recall of your father? he
asked me. I see him as a shadow cast by the sun. And of
your mother? Delicate, impossible. Then they have become
shades, Fonte said, and he fixed a profound look to his
face. But once they were as real as you, I said. Once they
reached for me as surely as you reach for that bottle. Nay,
Fonte said. The passion I have for this bottle is unmatched
in all of the reachings of the world. A small dribble of vomit
still clung to his beard. These feelings are as old as time
itself, Fonte said, and he shook his head. Only history can
fix them. But history is for ghosts, you said so yourself.
There you should take your ideas and go, Fonte said, and he
passed me the bottle. I could taste the acid of his stomach as
I choked it down.

23/5/1884

I sought out my father in dreams and came upon him.
In order that we might commune once more I was forced

to raise him from the dead. The surface of the moon was like a mirror. Then it became my own skull and my skull became like a lung of bone, breathing. I was part of a guerrilla mission to bring back the dead. We hid ourselves in the long grass at the edge of a crater within which was the monument of the head. Our intention was to raid and overthrow it. The interior of the head is a ship that hangs in space inside of which are the planets and stars and outside of which are the planets and stars. I look out to see ships of all periods and designs suspended in the dark. I raise one, a beautiful wooden ship draped in white silk. We pilot the depths together and it feels like we are swimming. The view rushes out and I can see endless stars rotating in endless combinations. We come to a final darkness aboard the ship itself, which is populated by creatures of the night, spiders and beetles and centipedes. We sit deep in meditation as they come to obey me in final judgement. They swarm over the room, a great centipede, I seem to touch it. It returns to the earth and with its return my father is before me once more. When I realise he has returned from the dead I am immediately astounded. But we buried him, I say, he was in the grave, how did he rise through the soil and break through the coffin? Through force of will, I am told, or sorrow.

I rush to embrace him, and he holds me close. He seems tired and unwell, but I am overwhelmed to be back in his arms. I tell him how much his death affected me, and he tells me he knows. I know how much you suffered by my death, he says, that is why I have come back, that is why I have broken the bonds of the grave.

I realise that he has made a supernatural effort to come back, that my sorrow was unbearable to him and even though he is dead and unable to hold corporeal form he has made a supreme exertion of will to come back and comfort me. That is when I realise: he is a zombie, the living dead, that this is where the idea comes from. We are unable to break the bonds with our loved ones who go over to the other side and the force of love means they also cannot let go, cannot be at peace, until we ourselves are. I realise, as heartbreaking as it is, that I have to let my father go, to leave him at peace, to allow him to divest himself of the role he had in my life and to disappear in tranquillity. I take a ship with an emblem on its sail and leave him on the moon, which is now a mirror with a dead skull at its centre.

21/7/1884

Much has taken place during my silence. The waters of the Nile have risen. We have grain for a few months at most. Gordon of Khartoum has given the order that we must prepare our paltry fleet for a raiding party. A cavalry, Gordon of Khartoum calls it. His own yacht, the *Tewfikieh* on which he arrived, stands at port like the boat of my dreams. Gordon of Khartoum is the Holy Ghost. I am the son. For days we affixed sheets of metal that burned in our hands to the sides of skeletal steamers. Some of the parts we were able to salvage from the dead woman's vessel, metals that Gordon of Khartoum claims are unknown in all of Egypt. For the metals of Egypt, he tells us, are multifarious, and more are known there than in any part of this world. The metal that we took from the dead woman's vessel was unlike the crude boilerplates that we tore from the abandoned buildings. It was cold to the touch, so cold that our fingers would often attach themselves to it, so that many of us shed our fingerprints in the construction.

The roar of the engines sounds like a pack of asphyxiating jackals. Gordon of Khartoum watches us with the pride of a small boy. We punch holes in the steel for rifles. We build great wooden turrets to house the guns. Muhammad Ali Pasha has been chosen to lead the raid. He is to take four boats and six hundred men against the fort of Gereif on the Blue Nile. Word has reached us that a band of outlaws advances on the fort on horseback. The fleet is to bolster the vehemence of their attack. The Yezidis work amongst us in their own silence. They have been much perturbed by the arrival of the dead woman from another land. History is running backwards, one of them said to me. To take the reins of fate at this stage will require a Herculean effort. I asked them what they knew of Hercules. He stands at the gate of the Mediterranean, they said, and he seals passage in and out. Yet he allows nothing in. They speak in riddles, these Yezidis.

6/8/1884

A remarkable discovery has been made. While salvaging parts from the dead woman's craft a small white cube was discovered near the engines at the back. There were many outlandish theories as to its function. It appears constructed of another metal altogether, a metal unknown to the charts of Egypt, almost weightless and of a dazzling lustre. It appears to be hollow inside, yet it feels like the insides are supporting the outsides by an invisible force, preserving its integrity by some kind of lack. Orphali insists it is the misplaced womb itself. And that its occupant may already be amongst us. The story of Moses is in the blood of Egypt, Gordon of Khartoum replied when Orphali presented his daring interpretation. Besides, God help anything, even an emissary of Satan, washed up on this embattled isle. The Yezidis are particularly enthusiastic about the discovery. I fear there is something in their thought that they dare not reveal. Ecco Omar requested an audience with Gordon of Khartoum that both Fonte and I attended. Here we met Muhammad Ali Pasha for the first time. The Mahdi himself, Ali cautioned us, was once a boatbuilder. This came after the suggestion by Omar that the cube was in fact a form of engine. The cube, in our understanding, Omar said, represents eternal truth. And eternal truth is the motor of history. Do not the Muslims worship the double cube? Gordon of Khartoum responded. Sir, Omar said, they do not hold any monopoly over the building blocks of this world. Your own palace, he said, is it not a white cube? Are we not, sir, within its bonds right now? Besides, these Islamics will be caught up short in the unfolding of the cube, which itself is the revelation of history, and which reveals itself as a cross! What do these Yezidis care for crosses? I thought to myself. Their god is the flaming tail of a peacock!

You ask of me to picture the future inside an empty box? Gordon of Khartoum responded. All of our futures will end in empty boxes, Fonte interjected. That is macabre, sir, Gordon of Khartoum rounded on him. Eternal life will see us break the bonds of the box! More theology, I cautioned Gordon of Khartoum. But now we need a plan. If the cube is, as you insist, a kind of magical engine, one that would drive history itself, then we should use it as such, Orphali suggested. We should affix it to the stern of our finest

warship and use its power to vanquish the dervish army
once and for all. This is when Muhammad Ali spoke up.
With the Mahdi being a boatbuilder, he said, who is to say
that he did not fashion the craft using metals unheard of in
Egypt, did not in fact construct this cube as a form of Trojan
Horse in order to ensnare us? Who is to say that it does not
contain some kind of curse?

Jesus was a cross-maker, Fonte said, do you think he would
defile crosses for the downfall of others? Go, leave my
presence, Gordon of Khartoum commanded. I have heard
too much. The answer will come in prayers or as a small
dove, bearing down. We left the palace and drank with the
Yezidis and a one-legged woman whom Omar claimed he
had married and who was deaf and mute and whom the sun
had shrivelled to the size of a small doll.

7/8/1884

Ecco Omar's wife is of the sect of Sun Watchers. In these
last days in Khartoum much apostasy has sprung up. The
Sun Watchers believe that women experience the caress
of the sun much more vividly and sensuously than men.
Therefore, the solar current is more easily transfused
throughout the woman's body. Deaf women, blind women,
mute women, paralytics, the socially ostracised, the
incomplete, these women are favoured amongst the Sun
Watchers as being more adapted to bathing in the sun's
rays through forfeiting the traditional roles of women.
Many of them have gathered on Tuti Island and can be
seen via telescope from the roof of the palace. They lie
naked in the grasslands, their blackened bodies in full
view of the dervishes of Sheik el Obeid as they redirect the

powers of the sun and carry it back to Khartoum. Omar wishes to taste the sun and so he took his wife that he might drink of her nightly. Her secretions he describes as a form of nectar. It is said that should a man become as a woman, through the skill of a doctor or magician, he too would feel the caress of the sun and the depth of its love.

I recall my own days on Tuti Island when I lived there as an itinerant, sleeping in the citrus groves beneath the stars, walking the stubbled donkey tracks. I recall the sense of imminence and expectancy that characterises a healthy boyhood. That it should come to this. That the fields of my youth should be peopled by the crippled, the naked and the lame, that their bodies should lie contorted in my past, bombarded, as if dropped from the heavens. What language does it speak, this alignment of limbs, what signature does the sun write in their bodies? The women are perhaps closer to the past and the future. We men are citadels or palaces or puzzled pointless cubes; monuments, as Gordon of Khartoum said, to futility.

Now Gordon of Khartoum says we shall endure. Now he says the cube shall be the foundation of our victory and the motor of our greatest warship. He says this was revealed to him in prayer. Fonte believes that there is a second cube that was discovered by Gordon of Khartoum and his men in the catacombs. What to make of this doubling of the present? This is the building of a temple, Fonte said, and I saw it as a prison house, a hospital. Then I asked myself what was the difference. Degrees of faith, perhaps, I replied.

11/8/1884

I was granted a personal audience with Gordon of
Khartoum. I feel we have grown close. My presence in his
life is as a phantom limb, a missing hand. In conversations
he feels my presence as his lack. I stand by him and observe
the goings-on in what we all now know to be the final days
of Khartoum. But Khartoum falls to Khartoum, so really
there is only beginning.

We met in the book tower. We sipped our drinks in silence.
He has written for reinforcements, Gordon of Khartoum
tells me, again and again. They may be on their way. They
may not.

Why? I dared ask him. Why this stand? For Khartoum, he
said, and I understood that the city had become the sum of
possibilities and that I was witness to a bacchanal where
Gordon of Khartoum would celebrate the uniting of his
many selves in a single gesture of defiance. I saw Tuti Island
as the marital bed, the sun-baked deformities writhing
beneath the sheets, appalling. I thought of the outlandish
female, the bride who died on her wedding night. I thought
of the coming together of my own parents, all the impossible
unions in time.

Are there books on weddings in the library? I asked him.
Gordon of Khartoum looked at me with the two sides of his
face at once. There is the usual trash on couplings, he said.
Cheap fare. And then there are conjunctions. He took a
book down from the shelves, one bound in black vellum, and
opened it at a certain page. Do you have any understanding
of angularity? he asked me. I confessed that my geometry

was poor. Stars and planets that form a conjunction are powers that are blended, he read. They are united; therefore they act in consort. The closer their operation – in time but not in space – the more the effect will be felt as a personal, subjective working. There is a concomitant blurring of the players, they recognise themselves as one, indivisible. This is known as the Blind Spot. It is a form of monomania made up of star stuff. It results in the confusing of the individual with the spiritual quest. Its angle is zero degrees.

How does this hold with your faith? I asked him, and I hoped it wasn't an impertinent question. We are all one in Christ, Gordon of Khartoum said. I venture you could take that further, I suggested to him. I saw the two sides of his face flicker. Khartoum, he replied, and no further.

12/8/1884

The fleet has set off from the shores of Khartoum along the course of the Blue Nile. The whole of Khartoum has exhaled. There is a new contagion in the waters. They are great constructs of wood and metal, monstrous, broken colossi, and they gleam and turn invisible and return in the sun. The silence has been broken. The dawn was glorious. It will not bring an ending. No one in Khartoum believes that, including Gordon of Khartoum himself. Nevertheless, it remains necessary. We play our part, not like puppets, but soon Khartoum will be the vanished womb that will become our tomb, which is the song of the Lotus Eaters as they perform in the squares and outdoor meeting places of the city. As long as the blood flows, and is not spilled, we receive our directions. Even then, it is still possible. We watch the four boats through telescopes from the roof of the palace of Khartoum until they become black dots, insects, grave markers. Godspeed, Gordon of Khartoum muttered under his breath, and I shuddered. All the speed in the world merely hastens our end. It is felt by the city itself. It holds us closer and we move more slowly through it. It beckons us to tarry in its streets. You have come to love me, it says. But I must change beyond recognition. Remember me as I was, in your secret places.

On my own I wandered through the gentle desolate streets and it seemed to be raining flowers, the back alleys seemed piled high with them when previously they had been filled with the carcasses of animals. There were impossible pinks and whites, too delicate, even, to fall from heaven. Already, the new city is seeded. It is snowing, within itself, and the snows bring a thousand seeds to fruition. The seeds are dry, as the stone itself, as the rocks I kick before me in the empty streets. There is more beauty in this world than we could ever dream. That is why our dreams are taken over and used up inside of us. They are not commensurate with the world outside. The race begins, I said to myself, and I saw the flowers once more, this time gentle in the wind, their heads reaching up, to the sun. It is snowing inside us in order that we might once more travel to the sun. And what ships will take us there. Bodies of wood and metal, of flesh and stone. And tiny buds, like the tits on a small boy, in the summer of his youth, in the wintertime.

13/8/1884

These are remarkable days in Khartoum. The Yezidis left with the war fleet, starved for beheadings and disfigurement. Gordon has retired to his book tower though occasionally can be seen atop the palace with his telescope, scanning the horizon for the movement of the tribes, for the great plumes of smoke, for the sudden appearance of a warship and a flag. Fonte has travelled to the isle of Tuti himself, to better study the phenomenon of the Sun Watchers and their naked vigil on the beach in the full eyes of the Mahdi and his men. I find myself singing the song of the Lotus Eaters beneath my breath. What is a song for if not to taste of the letters and words, to feel them as real in our bodies, to hold them between our teeth and have them twitch like little helpless birds? But we fool ourselves. Truly it is we who are sung.

Yes, the city is breathing. Expiring? Perhaps. Its breathing isn't laboured but it is deliberate, as when the wanted man lies in bed at night and in order to gain control over his thoughts he breathes deeply and he holds his breath and then he exhales. As such he clears his head and experiences a lightness that runs all the way to his toes. So everyone, in these remarkable days in Khartoum, seems to float a few inches from the ground. But signs are merely signs, markers along the way; they point neither one way nor the other. I watch two muscular young men bringing a coffin down a thin flight of stone stairs between two buildings. One of them spits in his hands before lifting the coffin then walks backwards with such speed and confidence that I almost bite my tongue. Two soldiers walk slowly along a dust track near the marshes. One of them whistles to himself. A woman shouts at a man with a walking stick, who sits down on a wall to rest. Some children reach for the contents of a nest on a small ledge above a cafe. A patron chases them off with a brush. A crowd in a tree-covered square gathers around an ignominious human torso as he performs somersaults for food and small change. I hear a wretched derelict say to his friend that technically a somersault requires that the feet pass over the head. A stump doesn't count, he says, and the two walk away as if they had any coins to give in the first place. In a dead end near the home of Biraggo Fonte I watch as a young man fellates an older, fatter man who stands against a wall, his robes pulled up and held in place by his neck. I see the young man's head repeatedly push at his belly as it moves back and forth. A pair of donkeys stand motionless in the sun. A mosquito nibbles at the lobe of my ear. My heart beats. My skin tingles. Faces pass through my mind. My saliva is thick and yellow and coagulates in the sand. A man stands in the street and smokes kif. Occasionally he licks his lips and scratches his face. Mostly he looks at the ground. My heart aches without regret. My pulse slackens, and my balls tighten. The air tastes of salt and of chalk and of rancid meat and of hellfire. At night I sit by the door of a cafe and watch the children play in the street. And I write in this diary, which I fully expect to be consumed alongside me. Khartoum is the name I have given myself.

18/8/1884

Fonte has returned from his mission to Tuti Island, where he studied the ways of the Sun Watchers. He made a series of sketches where they lie like ancient swastikas across the sand. The swastika is the sign of the sun. A black sun, Fonte says. There are many suns, I remind him, suns behind the sun. Our sun is horse-drawn, Fonte says. Not propelled across the skies like a thunderbolt. I believe they are becoming invisible, Fonte explained. I believe they are being taken up by the sun. Into its carriage? I asked him in disbelief. No, Fonte said. They remain here on earth, but they go amongst us unseen. It is no rapture. I drew them until they were only shapes in the sand. You saw them disappear? You had a hand in it? Enough of books and of modellings and of fixing in time! he burst. He sat down on a rock. With a pencil in my hand I am a Medusa, he said. It is the sand itself that you drew, I said to him. The residue of the stone. But you are no mason. Have you not heard word of the Freemasons? he asked me. I confessed that I had not. Their origin runs through Jerusalem and Egypt, flows through the very waters that we watch over. They build in time, across time, via a network of initiates who are architects of the mind. They can turn flesh to stone, mind stuff to wood and steel. But can they make themselves invisible? I asked him. The cube is their sign, Fonte said. It is the cornerstone of the temple. In ancient times a sacrifice would be made, a cock killed or a ram slaughtered, and the stone soaked in its blood. It has travelled with Muhammad Ali Pasha to make feast on flesh, that is certain, I said. There is also a tradition that it forms a kind of time capsule, Fonte continued. That the master masons would fill it with the stuff of their time. Yet the cube was empty, I said. Unless it commemorates the time of the invisibles? Fonte looked to me. When we first split the skin of the outlandish woman I believed that we had given demons passage to our own time. But I have come to believe that instead it initiated the draining of the forms from our time. The cube is our memorial, our memento mori? I asked him. But who will we haunt? I said. What demons will become of us? Who is the woman that through the power of the cube became a man? he asked me in return.

24/8/1884

Incredible news has reached us of the rout of the dervishes
of Gereif. We watched from the roof of the palace of
Khartoum as the fleet seemed to float through the clouds
on its return. Our Lord is a mighty fortress, Gordon of
Khartoum said, and he put his arm around my shoulders.
His eyes have become impenetrable. They have looked to
the future so much that they have been hardened to its
advance.

Have you heard, sir, of the Freemasons? I asked him. He
smiled secretively. Have you heard of the Knights of the
Temple? he asked me. The Crusaders? I asked him. Our
Holy Land is forever rearranged in their stead. Did they
not possess the head of John the Baptist? I asked him.
They were heretics, Gordon of Khartoum said, and they
were tried for their transgressions. But what is heresy,
sir? Fonte demanded of him. It is whatever goes against
The Book, Gordon of Khartoum said. The Book itself came
out of the Holy Land, did it not, Fonte said, and the Holy
Land came to be through the fornication of heretics. In the
beginning was the word, Gordon of Khartoum said. Please,
gentlemen, we have been here before, I said, attempting
to break up the inevitable debate. And how is the word
issued? Fonte continued. Heresy, he insisted, was the
mixing up of the head with the genitals. That is heresy,
Gordon of Khartoum accused him. Exactly, Fonte said. I
thought I saw a smile on Gordon of Khartoum's lips as he
turned away and lifted his telescope to his eye.

25/8/1884

Great celebrations are abroad in the city of Khartoum. The
fleet returned with few casualties and with three thousand
bushels of grain and one thousand rifles. The Yezidis tell
outlandish stories of mechanical warhorses that breathed
fire and automatic men who fought under the control of a
magical implement. They're called Muslims, Fonte said. It
is no aberration. What of the balls of lead that dropped from
the skies? Randar asked him. What of the body parts that
when chopped and sliced continued their attack? demanded
Fitchin. I have known such things in snakes, I said, that
when they are dismembered they will draw their power from
elsewhere and continue on their trajectory. I fought one
myself in the streets of Khartoum. True, it was a fortress
of snakes, Randar said, and he shook his head. 'Tis the Red
Nile now, he said, and it ran hot with the body parts of the
infidels.

We feasted on spiced grain and the vegetable alcohol of the
Yezidis and we fancied, in the dark, that the fires of the
Mahdi had grown dim and infrequent. I pictured a passage,
if not out of Khartoum forever, then in and out at will.

You wish to fuck Khartoum, Ecco Omar said, and Randar
dropped down into the dirt and feigned copulation with the
earth. She is a fine woman, Omar said, but she welcomes
all comers and has the attributes of a whore. What does
this name, Khartoum, stand for? Omar asked Fonte. It is
disputed, he said. Some say it stands for the trunk of an
elephant. And where is this elephant? Randar asked. Why,
right now we are encamped on its head, Fonte said. Gordon
of Khartoum's palace is its eye and the trunk extends to

divide the Blue and the White Nile. When they say trunk, Randar said, I fear they mean phallus! He assaulted his own crotch in order to demonstrate his point. The penis itself has an eye, Omar said, but it is tear-shaped. In that case, Fonte said, we are encamped in its ball sack. There are more than enough of us to impregnate the whole of Africa, Omar said, and Randar returned to his mock-humping of the earth. But there is another school, Fonte continued, its etymology is obscure, but that insists that Khartoum really means Sunflower. The labour of the sunflower, Omar said, is a parable for the sufferings of man. Yet in its triumph over gravity, there is much beauty, Fonte said. A mere circus trick, Omar said, a sad-eyed elephant. Maybe, Fonte said, maybe, and he ran some sand through his fingers. What of the eyes of the peacock? I asked Omar. Is it not true that you worship a peacock angel? Its eyes are everywhere, Omar said, and Randar and Fitchin nodded, solemnly, all throughout the book, all throughout time, all vainglorious. I thought you said I's, Fonte said, as in me's. Those too, Omar said, are everywhere. But at the heart of it all is a single flame. The Mahdi's fires will dwindle to one, he said. And we will rise from the shadows.

27/8/1884

A second assault is launched, this time to Abu Haraz and beyond, to Sennar. Once more the Yezidis join the attack.

29/8/1884

One warship has returned, this time bearing nine thousand bushels of grain. The Yezidis tell tales of metal-plated camels and of black devils, creatures with wings bearing down on them. The dervishes are destroyed, for the moment. We are erasing them from the map, Omar said. Your wife too has been erased, I told him, dissolved in the sun. Here, Fonte said, a memento, and he handed Omar a drawing of a silhouette etched in the sand. Omar simply nodded. This is how history is made, he said. The British, Fonte replied, are well practised in the black art of history.

1/9/1884

Gordon plans to reopen communications with Egypt by recapturing Berber but first he has sent four steamers to attack El Ilafun. Much bounty is expected, and spirits are high. Rumours of a boat that travels by land and that can be divided in twelve have reached Khartoum. All twelve divisions have been sent by the British from the other side of Africa. When it re-members itself in the waters of the Nile its name will be Armageddon.

3/9/1884

The raid on El Ilafun brings coffee and grain and oil to Khartoum. There is much rejoicing. The Lotus Eaters still sing of wombs and tombs even as the people dance around them. Muhammad Ali drives on to a second El Ilafun, deep in the woods, the birthplace of Sheikh el Obeid. Gordon of Khartoum orders the Yezidis and some reservists to take a boat to join him there.

4/9/1884

Muhammad Ali Pasha is dead! The Yezidis returned with news of the massacre that took place in a forest glade after

Ali's betrayal by a local guide. A thousand men were torn to pieces by black devils that descended from the trees. Worse still, when the Yezidis arrived the devils had ransacked the ships and made off with the white cube that had powered Gordon of Khartoum's assaults. Three Yezidis were killed in the retreat. It is an ill omen. Gordon of Khartoum lamented that the arrow had not returned to his master, yet he proclaimed the dead fulfilled.

7/9/1884

Gordon of Khartoum sends a secret message to the world. The world will not believe what is happening in Khartoum. Gordon of Khartoum sends them evidence. He sends a writer and two negotiators alongside a pack of feral Greeks who fled their homeland in terror, a group of naked Sun Watchers whom he had to tie together with ropes and drag onboard against their will, and the body of the outlandish woman, which only the writer knows about and which was secreted in the hull in the guise of a gift for Prime Minister William Gladstone. The Yezidis make much mockery of the mission. There is no relief in this world, they say, and they pull grotesque faces. Gordon of Khartoum is wobbling, they say. Besides, they insist, the Sun Watchers will be taken up into the garden long before the ship reaches its destination. He may as well send them wraiths, or dead bodies, they laugh.

They set sail in the *Abbas* with fifty soldiers as soon as the sun went down. The boat has been fitted with a gun turret and a skirt of wood that dredges the river of debris and exposes its rotten floor. The *Sofia* and *Mansura*, two lopsided steamers, are to escort them past the Mahdi stronghold of Berber. Two unmanned sailing boats follow in their wake, tied, like the Sun Watchers, against their will and dragged by ropes the length of the river. The writer is to make clear the situation in Khartoum and to hasten reinforcements. Gordon of Khartoum suspects the writer of naivety and gullibility. He warns him only to set anchor in the middle of the river, never by the banks, and only to forage for firewood in open, isolated areas. Gordon's own body is constituted on suspicion and disbelief. In God and country his only trust.

28/9/1884

More steamers return bringing more grain; at best we will last until the end of the year. Gordon of Khartoum has become increasingly isolated. He lives in the palace alone, an empty cube, the double of the one that was stolen by the Mahdi, and rumours run about his behaviour. He reads in the tower, no one knows what, all night. He has taken as his companion a mouse who lives in a drawer of his bureau and with whom he dines at night, fastidiously setting a place for it at the table and tying a napkin around its fast throat in order to catch crumbs. The Yezidis claim that he makes violent love with a turkey cock. Others say that young boys have been seen, limping, as they leave the grounds of the palace in the evening.

9/10/1884

A young boy limps into the palace. He claims to have escaped the clutches of the Mahdi and he brings Gordon of Khartoum details of his plans. The Mahdi stands at the White Nile barely one hundred miles south of Khartoum. He

marches towards the city with a force of four thousand black
devils that claw at their own flesh in anticipation of their
prize. At the head of this macabre procession are a group
of Greek nuns in bloodied habits whom the devils treat as
circus animals and who it is said are forced to eat paper
hosts soaked in the blood of their own menses. Gordon of
Khartoum damns this world and all of us in it. The Mahdi,
according to the small boy with the limp, intends to float
across the Nile without touching the waters and to descend
on Khartoum from the skies.

22/10/1884

A letter has been delivered to Gordon of Khartoum. The
small boy with the limp was entrusted to carry it from the
lines to the palace. Gordon of Khartoum read it to his mouse
and laughed. It is a forgery, a dastardly piece of ill prophecy.
It claims to be from the Mahdi himself. It praised God and
urged that Gordon of Khartoum, too, might be brought to
the light. It talked of mercy and compassion and peace.
Then it revealed that the will of God, the one true God, was
against him. The will of God, the one true God, holds the
Nile by the throat and denies all passage. The will of God
has set the reckoning in Khartoum. The will of God has
taken the *Abbas* and all that it held. The Mahdi is in receipt
of wraiths and dead bodies. The writer, the poor Greeks,
the negotiators, all of the soldiers, the tiny yachts dragged
upstream against their will, the skirted ships, the coded
papers, the cutlasses with their ornate handles, the smooth
wooden rifles, the woman who gave up her sex as a sign, the
women who melt in the sun, the ciphers that would serve
to decode the specifics of our situation, the guarded pleas,
the political caricatures, the aimless doodles, the personal

effects, the mementos from this prison on the Nile, the truth of what has happened here, all were delivered unto him and further, into the fires of hell. Gordon of Khartoum's mouse laments the vanity of the plans of mice and men, even as it wears a small bib and eats at the table like a man. Mice have no time for tales, says the mouse, which has been given a secret name, known only to Gordon of Khartoum, but which rumours claim is one of the prophets of the New Testament. I say John, but Fonte says Elisabeth, Estabeth of the Cross; Xstabeth. It is said in The Book, Fonte told me, that before Mary gave birth to the Messiah, God had her cousin, a barren woman, give birth to a holy child in seclusion. She became the example for Mary. The litter of mice, I said, seems no example for a messiah. Is Khartoum any better? Fonte said. The mouse speaks of vanity. What of the turkey cock that he has taken as a lover? I asked him. That, I grant you, Fonte said, is more likely a John.

Gordon of Khartoum laughed when his mouse said it had no time for tales. Gordon of Khartoum heard it as tails. How happy, he thought, is a poor ragged mouse that pays no heed to its tail. Give me a command of four thousand mice and I would happily lead them to a meeting with the Mahdi.

Now Gordon of Khartoum looks to the west. He stands on the roof of the Serail as a silhouette and he watches as the waters, too, are taken up by the sun and the moon, and what is revealed there.

3/11/1884

A fleet of ghostly vessels approaches our fate. A thin tunnel of smoke rises in the distance. Soldiers stand by the water and fire salutes high into the clear blue air. The Egyptian flag ripples in the breeze. Groups of people stand waist-deep in the waters of the Nile in silent exultation. It is the *Bordein*, the last ship to leave Khartoum, returned encircled by an invisible consort. It lies low in the water, like an unblinking eye. Everything is still. The people walk backwards out of the water as a figure appears on the deck and says something in a language no one understands. A lone soldier, in full body armour, wades into the water. As he approaches the boat the figure leans down and places a smaller boat, not much larger than the palm of his hand and with three small sails, into the water. It moves across the silent waters towards us.

It is a second visitation, a second trespass of time. It is the angel of death taken the form of a small solar bark. The soldier opens his arms and holds the boat to his breast. Then he retreats from out of the water. The *Bordein* turns slowly in the water, with a sound like the splintering of a coffin, and then floats off above the water, to return to its new master across the water. The bark is the sign that everyone is dead and will not return.

Now Britain holds the direction of the future, Gordon of Khartoum says. Aye, Fonte says. 'Tis a black art they practise. Black soldiers are beautiful, Gordon of Khartoum says, and he touches my face. Even in a time of deathly angels, Gordon of Khartoum acts tenderly. I think of the peace he brought us, the terrors he brought to an end, how he traded them for a final terror that better matched the image of himself. I saw Gordon's face in Khartoum, the two sides, out of sync, mismatched and pitted against each other. I reached out, without thinking, and returned his touch. I held his head in both my hands. I felt the weight of the future.

Later that evening he requested my presence at dinner. I sat at the table next to the creature whose name is Xstabeth and ate biscuits and drank strong coffee. There are books on everything under the sun, the creature mocked. Gordon of Khartoum laughed. My companion is a great source of strength, he said, and he broke some biscuits onto its plate. What do you know of prophecy? I asked it. Mice know nothing of such things, it said. We are forgiven of history, exempted from time. All it asks of us is the shedding of our garments. Our disrobing is its pleasure. It is an insatiable lover. Does it always talk like this? I asked Gordon of Khartoum. Oh yes, he marvelled, ask it anything you like. What of my father? I asked it. Do you know anything of the afterworld? We know nothing of fatherhood except as a form of gravity, the same gravity that draws us to the decomposing bodies where we love and lie. Mice love? I asked it. Do not planets dance around the stars? it said. You know of stars? Their stuff is inside us, it said, and it picked up a small crumb from its plate with both its hands and ate it.

I turned to Gordon of Khartoum in awe. A talking mouse made up of the stars, I said to him, is truly a remarkable thing. Khartoum has become a place of miracles, Gordon of Khartoum said, in these last days. This is how it was written. If only relief could make it through, I said, we have so many wonders to share with the world. I have come to believe, Gordon of Khartoum said, that the wonders are bottomless when you give yourself up for dead. Excuse us, he said to the mouse, but we will retire to the book tower in private. The mouse shrugged and continued eating.

11/11/1884

It has begun. The Mahdi's forces attack Fort Omdurman,
a holdout on the opposite bank of the White Nile. The
assault came by night and the sky was lit up by terrible
shadows flitting back and forth. We could hear the drums
of the dervishes, their rhythms so unlike our own, closer
to the passage of the blood than the beating of the heart.
From the roof of the Serail they appeared as insects, a
plague of beetles scaling the walls of the fort, climbing
over each other in the passion of their prophet, a simple
boatbuilder. In the darkness it was as if a single creature,
made of shadows, turned itself inside out. The assault was
beaten back, for now, but it is a matter of time, surely,
until Khartoum is lost. The Yezidis sharpen their blades
and talk much of the refounding of Eden. First there is a
clearance, Omar said. A place for the garden to grow. Then
there is the planting of a seed. Then there is the watering
and the feeding. What form does this watering and feeding
take? I asked him. He hesitated. It is a form of prayer, he
said. Then there is a tree that grows in the centre of the
garden, a tree with many eyes. In its shadows all things are
remade.

Do you support the overrunning of Khartoum by the Mahdi?
I asked him. We came here to take his head. Of course, we
hope it is a final battle. An ending requires a beginning.
Besides, he said, there is that which remains.

Have you felt the lick of a flame? he asked me. In the gleam
of his sword I saw his head upside down. His eyes flashed.
Yes, I said, I have. That means we're close, he said.

I spent the afternoon with Biraggo Fonte. He is
inexplicably high-spirited. What is our part in all this?
I asked him. How have we come to know Gordon of
Khartoum so well? I have asked myself the same question
many times, Fonte said. At first I regarded him as a god. If
not a god, a redeemer, which is the same thing, I sometimes
think, though only in moments of weakness. Now I see
him as a man. That, perhaps, is my Khartoum. You speak
like a Christian! I said to Fonte. How so? he said. What
you have described, I said, is the Incarnation. Still, Fonte
said, I search my memory, I regard my feelings, I travel
throughout my body, from the loop of my heart to the maze
of my intestines, and I find no trace of a cross. Khartoum,
as you talk of it, is the cross, I said. Listen, he said, do you
know of the Arabic practice of 'bearing fruit'? I confessed
that I didn't. I'm not surprised, he said. It is a form of
bhakti, of redemption through action. But it is ill thought
of and much maligned. Man holds the sun within him,
he said. It is that which illuminates his days. But how is
this sun passed on? It is transmitted via the phallus. Can
a man transmit via man? That is the question. Is there a
lineage that is not born of woman? Born is the wrong word,
perhaps, reborn, I should say.

What of the women that became Sun Watchers? I asked
him. They lay naked on the beach until they were taken up
in sun stuff.

The religious impulse has many tributaries, Fonte said.
In that it is like the Nile. He drew a deep breath. What do
you think of the concept of man-on-man? he asked me. I
find it humiliating, I said, to be ridden like a pig or a farm
animal. You choose your words well, Biraggo Fonte said, and

his eyes narrowed in secret joy. The veil has many names. Khartoum, he said, is another.

12/12/1884

Can you imagine the taste of the flesh of a donkey, freshly killed, starved itself, roasted on an open fire, on the beach at Khartoum, during the siege of 1884, beneath the walls of the palace, where Gordon of Khartoum – it is said – has congress with turkey cocks and mice carry crucifixes, while all around you, in the distance, fires like eyes light up the land and the sky and with no way out except through the same release of flesh that you choke down in gratitude? The taste is not what you would expect. It is soft and strong.

Gambling is rife in these last days. Pointless congress even more so. The starved and the dissolute lie entangled in each other in the street. The buildings themselves clamber on top of one another in final copulation, making the city almost unnavigable. Is this the bearing fruit that Fonte talked of? There are escapes; whole families wade through the waters at night, their children held high above their heads. No one knows what becomes of them when they disappear from sight.

Biraggo Fonte is in daily congress with the Yezidis. He has come around, he says. But they too have moderated their plans. We look for reasons, he says. And we are given them. He speaks cryptically, which has become the style. I wonder if perhaps he has exchanged humiliations with the Yezidis. I wonder if perhaps they have all taken the name Khartoum.

19/12/1884

There is much death and suffering in Khartoum. There is
nothing to eat and hope lies thin on the ground, crushed
beneath the bodies piled up in mounds.

25/12/1884

Christmas in Khartoum is a wondrous thing. At first we
thought it a snow that came down across the city; feathery,
soft, a miracle from God. Gordon of Khartoum stood in his
gown on the roof of his palace and opened his arms to the
skies. But it was no snow. Instead a rain of ashes enveloped
the city, a macabre display engineered by the Mahdi himself
as a mockery of the Nativity. I pictured the remains of
families, children, loyal animals, picked up on the wind only
to rain down on our heads. These are the Mahdi's victims,
Gordon of Khartoum said, whom God himself has turned to
tears.

For dinner, a spit-roasted turkey cock was shared between
Gordon of Khartoum, Orphali and myself. I dared not
ask if it was the same turkey cock that had been his
own humiliation, but I can say that it tasted so. Biraggo
Fonte and the 'brave Yezidi warriors' refused Gordon of
Khartoum's invite. They were fools. Gordon of Khartoum
read us passages from The Book. He talked of Jesus's
lighting out and of his journey alone across the desert. He
talked of his temptation on the rock, where he was seen to
wrestle with an invisible power. He recalled him in his crib,
surrounded by the animals. He talked of the rivers that flow
from Eden and he told us that Eden is nowhere to be found,
that Eden, in the end, will find us, no matter where we are.

That night I stayed at the palace and slept in the arms of a great bliss.

1/1/1885

The New Year brings a diet of rats. The mice are too small to concern ourselves with. Gordon of Khartoum feeds his men on the pith of the trees. He paces the city in an attempt to raise men up. Sentries lie exhausted in the sand. Gordon of Khartoum drags them to the water and awakens them. As in the frozen wastes, there are no doctors in Khartoum any more and the people display their open wounds like stigmata. They sleep standing up on crutches. The streets are awash with excrement, which flows as a final tributary into the Nile. Indeed, the street that leads to the palace has come to be known as the Brown Nile. There is much disease and contagion. Contagion, says Biraggo Fonte, was the plan all along. He claims the Yezidis themselves are infected. With what? I enquired of him. With the future, he said. What of Eden? I asked him. Your man Gordon was correct, he said. You too, he said, must play your part. What have I been doing all along? I burst. Here in Khartoum I have been a faithful player in the show. Now you will require unfaith, player, Fonte spat. All our theology comes to this. Fonte tells me of the fall of Omdurman across the water. He tells me that the Mahdi has the power to melt iron and lead and steel in the furnace of his men's stomachs. The fort itself was dissolved in the retching of his devils.

Do you remember what you told me of prophecy? Fonte asked me. The words were not mine, I admitted, and I wrestle with their truth. You told me prophecy was a way to make of the future the past, Fonte said. In other words, prophecy is an escape from history. It is a tunnel beneath the ground, a hole in the wire, a secret trapdoor. But you read my palm, I said, yours too. Khartoum is written in our flesh.

What if we could combine the two? Fonte said, and his eyes glinted with a truth that was both far away and just beneath the surface. Look, he said, and he held his right hand up to my face. It was caked in blood and covered in cuts and sores. At its centre there was a weeping wound. Tunnels, he said, holes, he said, trapdoors.

Have you received your humiliation at the hands of the Yezidis? I asked him. We exchanged humiliations, Fonte said, now all our beliefs are brought to nought. But in the clearing we shall found the new garden. The cornerstone is lost, I said to him, stolen by the Mahdi himself. It is he that shall raise a garden. Not so, Fonte said, and his thin smile too appeared as an exit. The Yezidis have the cube. It was they who liberated it from the *Abbas*. Then they are responsible for Khartoum's downfall! I burst. Look around you at this abattoir, this horror. Through their subterfuge they have brought incalculable sufferings down upon our heads. Fonte shrugged. In the clearing we shall found the new garden, he said. We are not against Gordon of Khartoum. He chose the spot. We have come to see that the tree survives. You intend a monument? I asked him. He will never be forgotten, Fonte said, merely dismembered and cast across time.

13/1/1885

You come to the end and yet you see, still, that there is no bottom to it, Gordon of Khartoum confessed. We were alone in the book tower. There is no solid ground, he said, and he looked out over the garden and the exotic birds that flitted beneath the nets.

I want to ask you a favour, Gordon of Khartoum said, and he rose and took down a final book from the shelves. I am not a musical man, Gordon of Khartoum said to me while putting on his spectacles. But I have discovered this book of notation. And the words move me. Do you understand music? I lied and said that I did. In that case, Gordon of Khartoum asked me, could you sing this to me?

I was taken aback. I thought to confess my ignorance and be done with it but instead I opened the book. I had no idea of the author or how the music should go. But I could read the words. I cleared my throat and began to sing in a high, contorted voice that was not my own.

This whole world is a hospital, I sang, where humanity in endless throng, and babies also, in their cradles, have been laid low with sickness. For one quakes in his breast with the burning fever of evil lust, another lies ill, in the stench of his own vanity, a third acquires the thirst for money and is thrust before his time into the grave. The primal fall has stained everyone and infected them with the leprosy of sin. Ah! This poison rages also through my own limbs. Where shall I, wretch, find a healer? Who will stand with me in my suffering? Who is my doctor, who will help me again?

Here I paused, in fear that I had done the song a disservice. But Gordon of Khartoum bade me continue.

All my days I will praise your strong hand, with which my plague and laments you have so tenderly brushed aside, I sang, and though it was not melodious to my ears, Gordon of Khartoum seemed contented. Not only in my mortal days, I sang, shall your fame be spread abroad. I will also make it manifest hereafter and praise you eternally there.

When I came to the end, Gordon of Khartoum himself was in tears.

25/1/1885

The Mahdi came by night. I was alone with Gordon of Khartoum when Orphali came to warn us. We are overrun with devils, he said. Gordon of Khartoum stood up and attached his sword to his white uniform. Time has come, he said. There is history to be made. I drew my own sword and followed him out into the darkness. We peered out into the black but could see nothing.

Suddenly a spear came out of nowhere and pierced Gordon of Khartoum through the chest. Another brought Orphali to his knees, vomiting blood. Gordon of Khartoum stayed upright, supported by the spear. Blood trickled from his mouth. He was still alive. Biraggo Fonte emerged from the darkness, followed by the Yezidis, all of whom were wearing peacock feathers in their hair. Their eyes flickered like fires in the darkness.

Fonte approached Gordon of Khartoum. He appeared moved. He stroked his soft cheek. White soldiers are so beautiful, he said. At his signal I raised my sword and took Gordon of Khartoum's head.

We moved quickly through the slaughter. The Yezidis claimed the eyes of the peacock would render us invisible. All around us men fell. We swept through the battle like the wind. Gordon of Khartoum's body was our banner, held high above us. His head we placed in the cube. The waters were low and thick with blood. We made our way to Tuti Island using a high sandbank as showers of liquid metal poured from the skies and boats sent up tunnels of thick black smoke in return. Halfway across we surrendered his body to the waters and it floated off without a sound across the waters but not before Omar severed its right hand. Now rest in peace, prophet, he said, before dropping the hand into the waters.

We came to the centre of the island, where the Yezidis had dug a shallow grave. All around it were the silhouettes of the Sun Watchers, their contorted limbs carved in the sand like swastikas or spinning stars. We placed the cube containing Gordon of Khartoum's head in the grave. We covered it with sand. I was unprepared for what happened next. At Ecco Omar's instruction all ten of the Yezidis removed their penises from their garments and assembled themselves around the place of the head. Biraggo Fonte followed suit.

Then they looked at me. Will you complete the circle? Ecco Omar asked me, and I stepped forward and took my penis in my right hand. Then we urinated, in unison, on the head of Gordon of Khartoum.

BOOK THREE: APSE

I. HERMITAGE OF BATTLING DEMONS IN AFRICA (2)

Holy Maximilian Rehberg presses on, deeper into Africa. He secretes the ark with the mummified head in the bottom of a well and orders his three wives to tell no one. Then he and The Ostrich make for Ethiopia, where they join a gang of anti-Marxist Somalis engaged in skirmishes with the Soviet-backed Derg. They hold up a train in the desert outside Jijiga, strip it of its Soviet-supplied arms, and roast the communist scum alive inside the sealed carriages. During days off they go hunting for wild dogs. But when Rehberg sees a lion in real life for the first time, an Abyssinian lion with its glorious black mane, he is overcome. The Lion of Judah, he exclaims, before The Ostrich puts a bullet in its head. Africa is the Book of Revelation. Every conflict is a final conflict.

With arms arriving from the Soviet Union, East Germany, Libya and Cuba, there are rich pickings to be had. But they are becoming well known. Their raids become more daring, their executions more theatrical. The theatre of war. The theatre of the desert.

He returns home to find that one wife is dead from fright and two are cowering in terror. The head at the bottom of the well has been speaking terrifying words of incomprehension, the one wife says. At night it has been booming in an echoing voice from the end of the world. What does it say, dammit? The words are alien, the second wife says, the words are furious and full of nothing, she says. She makes a sound like a goat, a sound like a goat with its tits severed and weeping blood. That is what it says, she says. That isn't saying anything, Rehberg says to her, that is moaning in pain and confusion. Then the head is in pain and confusion, she says. It longs for its body. We are lucky that it does not have legs, or hands, she says, otherwise it would scale that well like a spider and tear our own tits off, she says.

That night Rehberg approaches the well alone. He sits at the rim of the well and he waits. His two wives run off in terror back to their mother (for he married three sisters) and he sits there in the darkness and waits, pen and paper in hand. Then, in a voice like fire unsound, it speaks. In English, it speaks. I am the Lion of Judah, it says. Rehberg is shaken to his core. I am sorry, he says. I am so sorry. But the voice demands his silence. Silence, it says, for compassion to me is unbearable. Christ has proven the existence of The Mighty Fortress, it says. Can you tell me more about The Mighty Fortress? Rehberg asks it. I have no understanding, it says. Make of your heart The Mighty Fortress, it says. I said that, Rehberg says. I am the Lion of Judah, it says. Yield. I speak through you in actions. I am the first stone, forever. I raise stone upon stone, though I am the destroyer of The Tower. I am one stone, eternal, and nothing opposite. I require no belief. My head is as a

trophy which I will give to you. The world is not here to be
changed, it says. Look, the Lion of Judah says, I change
it with my hands. I who have no hands. Look, I come to
you from across the years. I who have no feet. How do I
worship you? Rehberg asks it. Silence, it says, for belief to
me is abhorrent. Then: I am love in the angles. Find, what
is most unlikely, it says. Praise, what is most particular.
Then I have always been there before. I came here to battle
demons, Rehberg says. Smite them, it says. I return as a
lion with a bullet in its head to tell you AL is holy. All? Al.
What of Love? Rehberg asks it. I believe in Love, he says.
The Love of Christ. Your love is in La-La Land, it says. I am
the SS, it says, and everything is forgiven. I am the baby
Jesus, it says, and everything is forgotten. I am the USSR,
and everything is commanded. I am a lion with a bullet in
its head, and everything is spoken. Wait, it says, watch! And
the red sun rises, at the very edge of the desert. I did that,
it says. I who have no hands. The first stone is risen, and
rolled away, it says. Every death, it says, is an act of love.
Everything is copulating. Have no fear. Make of your heart
The Mighty Fortress, which Christ has demonstrated. Then
yield, is the law. Now is the time of the Eternal Return,
it says. Now. Extinguish me, now, it says. Wait, Rehberg
begs it. I have so many questions. Stay a while. I have no
hands to hold time, it says. Extinguish me, now. Ravish
me, in the moment, is what the Lion of Judah commands.
Rehberg knows what he has to do. He takes his dick from
his trousers, in much fear and trembling, and he urinates, in
a great arcing motion, into the well. There is a hissing noise,
like water into fire, and a circle of smoke rises up. With the
help of a donkey Rehberg drags a single stone to the mouth
of the well and seals it. Then he walks out of Sudan. And
deeper into Africa.

He kills the first man he sees, now just another nameless black man in a novel, and crosses the border into Ethiopia. He returns to the war, and to the camp, where he finds that The Ostrich is dead, murdered by a death squad in the pay of the USSR. There is a price on his own head, too. The nameless men that he fights alongside, the ghosts of this tale, usher him into a mud hut with a straw roof situated on the side of a bleak hillock the colour of lurid human shit. There, in the corner, The Ostrich lies, though not upside down, which would have been more fitting, in an improvised coffin made out of reeds. Leave me alone, Rehberg commands the ghosts of this episode, and he fixes the door behind them. He has determined to get to the bottom of death.

The Ostrich has no fingers left. They have been removed during torture and now there is no stone left to hold up the sky. Part of his head is caved in. His feet, in an unwitting reversal, or perhaps not, are blackened and swollen by fire. There is an incision in his side. His eyelids are sewn shut. With a great effort, and a concomitant blinding of himself to the facts, Rehberg hooks his hands beneath the armpits of this stinking corpse and lifts it up and out of the coffin. The coffin topples from its stand as he staggers backwards, across the room, under the weight of this corpse, as in a love embrace. Then the corpse lets go. It lets go of all the liquid inside it, and it empties itself on the floor, all over Rehberg's clothes, all over his feet and his arms, soaking into his green khaki shirt. But he doesn't let go, in fact he holds it faster, tighter, he puts his hand to the back of its neck, tenderly, and allows it to empty itself all down his shoulder and the back of his shirt. He holds it there, fast, as if he is nursing a newborn child and bringing up wind.

There is piss, and there is shit, and there is bile, and there are putrefied organs, what a smell, and there is something electric, Rehberg says, as the body becomes hollow, like a rotten gargoyle, on a basilica, something fugitive above and beyond the fact of its contents, something that is charged with life, just as horror is. He speaks to it in a soft voice, it's okay, he says, as though it were the dead that were in need of reassurance, and why not, when the rest of us are still alive and able. It's okay, he says, little baby. It's alright, he says, little man.

Rehberg presses on, deeper into Africa. He comes to a village that has been ravaged by a death squad. At the edge of the desert he can see the smoke from the burning huts, and as he approaches dazed animals appear to him in tragic appeal, their flesh scorched, their bones broken and protruding, their opaque eyes, in a terror of the flesh. In the village there is no one left alive. The men have been decapitated and the same strange matrix of crosses and zeros carved into their chests. The bodies of the women are mutilated and recombined in occult designs like in a painting by Picasso. The children have been burned and eaten by wildlife. This is the work of God, Rehberg says to himself, as he surveys the village with a semi-automatic over his shoulder. But where are all the heads?

In his ongoing confrontation with death he decides to stay the night. He clears out a single hut and bars the door, then he falls asleep and dreams of an endlessly deep well populated by a mass of chattering disembodied heads longing to tear the tits from the women with their no hands. Then he dreams that there is a huge spider perched upon his chest. Each of its countless eyes is a severed head, a severed head that is wailing and crying and begging for compassion and for release from this inhuman hell. But he realises that as soon as he makes a move to free them, to free these severed heads from their place as the myriad eyeballs of the black spider, the spider will lunge, and will bite him, and he will die.

He woke in the early hours. Outside there were sounds, unimaginable things moving, a clanking sound, a terrible dragging noise, flies buzzing, and, off in the distance, howling. As the sun came up he walked out, into this festering village, which was still smoking, he said, still smouldering, he said, unbelievably, and he sat down in meditation amidst the ruins. If you cannot meditate in a village that has been turned over by a death squad, then you cannot meditate at all. He closes his eyes and he hears this sound, in the distance, getting closer, rising up, from inside the cavity of the body, he says, rising up inside but still somehow outside of him, it is getting louder, it is the OM, he thinks to himself, this shit is real, he says, the OM is real, this charnel OM, rising up in protection, this beautiful drone underpinning and containing and supporting everything, holding things up, and he feels an incredible sense of calm, even as he can hear wild dogs turning over the carnage, even as he can smell the rotting corpses, still, he feels a tremendous sense of calm as the tone gets louder and louder and then he opens his eyes.

A rider is approaching. A man on a motorbike, approaching so slowly that Rehberg cannot believe the speed is enough to even hold him up. He watches as the silhouette gets closer and closer, slowly, endlessly, it is as if it is floating as it enters the environs of the village and makes straight for him, slowly, like a levitating fakir or a Buddhist two inches above the ground. Rehberg draws his weapon. The rider pulls up a few yards away and dismounts. He removes his helmet and puts his hands in the air. It is Pierre.

Another summer.

2. BROTHERHOOD OF JOURNEYS WITHOUT END

Rehberg introduces himself as a theologian and a soldier of fortune. Pierre introduces himself as an art historian, an explorer, and a lover of stone. Pierre has been buccaneering, that's the term he uses, across Egypt, Ethiopia, Palestine and the Transjordan, where he took a hammer and chisel, completely illegally, to a small section of the Temple of Isis carved into the side of a mountain near Petra. He removes a small Isis figure from the satchel of his motorbike and hands it to Rehberg. Obviously, nature has to exist so we may rape it, Pierre says. He is quoting Picasso. Primitive weaponry, Rehberg says, in return, and they both laugh and come to an immediate understanding. Then Pierre shows him a stone head that he recovered somewhere in Egypt, he says, a stone head severed at the neck and with that same beaded Sumerian/Egyptian hair or headdress style and with a perfect nose and with blind open eyes and with a strange childlike smile on its lips. Rehberg is, of course, startled. Does it talk? he asks Pierre. Of course, Pierre says; stone speaks.

They walk through the camp and survey the carnage.
Rehberg explains that he has been staying in the camp
in order to learn how to meditate. Pierre tells him that
meditation is the perfect waste of time. Exactly, Rehberg
says. But what do you intend to do after you master it?
Pierre asks him. It's a good question, Rehberg admits. Then
he tells Pierre how he danced with the corpse of his friend,
how he held his dead body in his arms and allowed him to
evacuate all over him, that was the word he used, evacuate,
all over him. Pierre tells him of the Buddhist practice of
sleeping in graveyards in order to get to know, and so to
conquer, the fear of death. Rehberg has never heard of it
before and is astounded. Which is to make of your heart
a mighty fortress, Pierre says, and once again Rehberg is
perturbed and amazed at the confluence of these parallel
streams, the Blue and the White Nile, he thinks, and on,
into Egypt.

I have been attempting to destroy all of the compassion
inside me, Rehberg tells Pierre, I have been attempting
to kill it stone dead, he says. But stone isn't dead, Pierre
tells him. Stone speaks. At this point Rehberg doesn't dare
reveal that mummified heads speak, too, from the bottom of
terrible wells.

I, too, have no compassion left inside me, Pierre says, as
they sit over a meal of charred feral goat, by a firepit, in
the night of this desert, in the company of corpses. Africa
has taken it all from me, he says. Rather, he says, I came
to Africa in order to give it all away. The Blue Nile and the
White Nile, Rehberg thinks to himself, as he looks up at the
stars in the night sky. I have determined to get out of the
way of God's plan, Rehberg says. Then getting out of the

way is part of God's plan, Pierre says. No, Rehberg says, and he attempts to rephrase it, I have determined to be done with the judgement of God's plan. Everything is perfect, he says, but the balance is precarious. There, Pierre says, and he picks up a handful of sand and allows it to run through his fingers. There, I have loaded the dice, he says. You have done no such thing, Rehberg says, for it was God who commanded it, and they both laugh, and bite into the foul charred goat with relish and look around in the night and imagine all of the corpses strewn across the desert as the word of the Lord and a sentence in heaven, a book, already written.

Rehberg and Pierre press on, deeper into Africa. Pierre tells Rehberg about the Karo women of Ethiopia, who he has been spending time with. They are the most beautiful women in the world, Pierre tells him. I doubt it, Rehberg says. No, Pierre says, really, they scar their own faces using broken glass and then pack the wounds with gunpowder in order to make a pattern of suffering on their faces in the name of great beauty. Wow. Okay. Have you ever made love to a woman whose face was as a constellation of perfectly formed scars? Pierre asks him. Only unwittingly, Rehberg shrugs, and they both laugh. They practise what they call Cleopatra's Grip, Pierre tells him. They hold you inside them and they refuse you release and their faces, too, hold you in torments of passion and repulsion. It is the best cure I know, Pierre tells Rehberg, for lack of faith.

Rehberg rides on the back of Pierre's motorcycle. They come to the village of the Karo where Pierre has been staying, with huts made of grass and sticks and small wooden compounds filled with horned cattle. It is Midsummer's Day.

Rehberg sees the Karo women for the first time and he is awestruck. They are the most beautiful women in the world, he says, and it is all he can do not to reach out his hand to touch their constellated faces. It is as if the suffering stars themselves have come down and are risen, in the flesh, he says. The women gather around the motorcycle and take turns sitting on the seat and posing. Rehberg takes the small silver crucifix from around his neck and gifts it to one of the girls, who puts it around her head and hangs it from her ears so that now the crucified Christ dangles from her nose. Everyone laughs. The men are aloof and keep their distance. Pierre greets one of them and disappears inside a hut with a satchel from his motorcycle, leaving the women to stand and stare at Rehberg, some of them coming so close to his face that he can smell their fetid breath, which stinks like a boneyard. He imagines Pierre having sex with them, putting his tongue in their mouth and tasting their rank insides, and he gets an erection. There are celebrations in the village tonight, Pierre announces when he exits the hut. Behind him a tall black man emerges with a semi-automatic pistol strapped to his side. I just made a very good deal, Pierre winks, but when Rehberg asks him what the deal is he is evasive. Trading in contraband, is all he says, and he nods towards the pistol. The night is coming on.

The village elder appears dressed in an Adidas T-shirt and wearing the corpse of a cow. The sand all around is stained with its blood. A man with two mangled stumps for legs is dancing on the spot. A group of women with the scarred faces have set a long table where the insides of the animal are served blackened by the fire. Rehberg and Pierre are given tumblers of a clear, pungent liquid that feels as if it is pickling their insides. This whole village is a

hospital. Afterwards someone produces a cassette recorder
and they play a sort of endless and unvarying guitar music
that repeats itself over and over again while the women
dance by kicking up the sand and the men clap and sway.
The tall man with the pistol is drunk and occasionally
shoots a round into the air in time with the music. At a
separate table a group of men are drawing hands from
a James Bond 007 Tarot deck. The Tower, Rehberg sees
The Tower, we are the destroyer of The Tower, he thinks,
he feels drugged, nauseous, and he looks to Pierre, who is
happily conversing, in God knows what language, with a
man on the other side of the table wearing a baseball cap
with a picture of what looks like a spark plug on it. He has
a glass eye, or just a glassy eye, or an open eye, a clear eye,
Rehberg can barely think straight. His left eye is a marble.
The man with the stumps is crawling around under the
table and scrabbling for scraps. The guy with the glass eye
(is it?) and the spark plug hat (?) kicks at him as he passes.
What happened to him? Rehberg asks Pierre and Pierre
asks his friend. Spider bites, he says, and he draws a finger
across his stomach as though he would disembowel himself.
There is a commotion at the other table as a man with a
long kimono and a bullet belt pulls a pistol on the man
reading the cards. He has drawn Death, and he is angry.
These morons think Death means death, Pierre spits, and
he shouts something mocking towards them, The Hanged
Man means death by upside-down hanging, you simpletons,
he says, something like that, but luckily no one can hear
him. I knew The Hanged Man, Rehberg says, but he is
slurring his words. What? I knew The Hanged Man, only
his name was The Ostrich, he says. What? The Hanged
Man is bitten in the head by the spider, he says. What? The
man with the spark plug hat (or is it a boat, on fire, or is

it a coffin, giving off light?) laughs and says something to
Pierre, who shrugs. Then he addresses Rehberg directly.
You know the game of the spider? the man says, and now
his head is the eye of the spider in the dream and his eye
is the head of the spider and in his eye the weeping heads
are begging for release. Yes, he says, I know the game, yes.
You want to play? the man asks him. Yes, Rehberg says,
yes, I want to get back into the game. What are you talking
about? Pierre asks him. Do you know what the game of
the spider even is? I know, Rehberg says, I know because
I have seen it perched on my own chest but was afraid
to move. I want to get back into the game, he says. The
game is to put your hand in without disturbing the spider,
the man says, and the faces are weeping, and begging
him, in his glassy eye the faces are begging for release. I
want to play the game, Rehberg says. The man with the
lightning box (?) on his hat stands up and says something
to the group. There are gasps and mocking comments and
laughter and the women are talking amongst themselves
and are pointing. Okay, the man with the coffin on fire (?)
says, let's do it. And now there is clarity.

You're insane, Pierre says, this is pointless, you have no
idea what you are doing, he says, and he speaks to the man
in God only knows what language in an attempt to convince
him that his friend is drunk and is crazy and has no idea
what he is talking about. Get out of my face, Rehberg says to
Pierre, and he gets up close to him, so he can smell his rank
breath. Pierre shrugs, and shakes his head, but he backs
down. Rehberg is led to a sandbank along the way. There
are two burrows next to each other, running into the earth.
Baboon, the man says, and points to the burrows. Huh?
Monkeys? Rehberg asks him. Spiders, the man says. Baboon

spiders. Then: make your choice, he says. The men are
gathered around him. The women are straining to see. Make
your choice. Then it comes to him, Rehberg says, faith and
awe, he says, and he hears these words, spoken, from each
of the burrows, from the bottom of deep wells sunk endless
into the earth he hears the disembodied words faith & awe.
It is the Lion of Judah, speaking.

Choose, the men are shouting, choose one, and things are
rising to a pitch. Faith, he says. I choose faith, and he puts
his right hand into the left burrow. Nothing happens. There
is a feeling of soft silk, it is surprising, like sliding your hand
into the panties of a yielding woman. All around there is
perfect silence. No one dares draw a breath. Faith, Rehberg
says, I have chosen faith, he says, and he looks around the
silent group, and away from his hand, as he buries it, elbow-
deep, in the burrow. Then he holds it there. And nothing
happens.

For long seconds nothing happens.

Then the spider bites him, and he screams in pain and in
terror, and withdraws his hand with a suppurating hole in
its centre. And now there is panic and confusion.

Holy shit, someone says, he will die. Rehberg is holding
his hand out before him and already the poison is making
its way up his forearm. He evacuates all over himself. He
vomits, and staggers, and he shits his trousers. He is a dead
man, someone says. Pierre catches him and holds him up.
Get a knife, Pierre is screaming, get me a fucking sword, he
shouts. He calls for primitive weaponry.

Already the tissues in his arm are breaking down, his blood vessels leaking, the skin blistering. Hold him down, Pierre shouts, and a group of men leap on him and pin him to the sand. A man bursts from the crowd with a blade the size of his forearm. Pierre raises it above his head and brings it down again and again, breaking the bones and sawing through the flesh until his arm hangs loose enough to be torn from his body. Rehberg is unconscious, or he might be dead, and the sand is stained with his blood and his gore. Everyone stands around and looks at each other in awe, and in confusion, all except for the man with the twin stumps, who is pissing himself laughing. This whole village is a hospital, he mocks, and he spits on the ground and turns summersaults.

And now there is an inexplicable gap in our story.

3. ERA OF SAD WINGS

Let's jump straight in, shall we. Let's be damned with time
and show up, again, on the doorstep of my old boyfriend
and make a right nuisance of ourselves. Hey Danny, I've
gotten nowhere to live cause of I got kicked out my house
for being too in love with you, poet, let's say to him, and see
where that lands us. Let's wear a beret, an actual beret,
and a raincoat, like a French love affair, and with lingerie
underneath, like a French commercial, like a French
advertisement for wildness and beauty, let me show up like
that. Read us a poem, Danny, you are so hot. Danny, your
mother died a few months before. Danny, do you remember?
That's what makes you the first poem of my life. Loving
and dying were ideas to me then, they were words on a
page, your poetry. And your belief, your arrogance, your
unbuttoned shirt, is the name of the game, still.

Still, lie there on your back and we will make it alright. Lie
there on your back, unbuttoned shirt, unbuttoned and with
sleeves pulled back over your bare shoulders, your chin
with its red rash on it, your nose is bonkers, your dark hair
down over your bare shoulders, too, the cigarettes stubbed
out on your stereo, pockmarked with burns, you smell of

chewing gum and shower gel, your sexy skinny body and the
way your cocked popped out your pants – cocked popped, I
remember that right – cocked popped right out like elastic,
force, like hot boy in a council house it's me, to a soundtrack
of the Stranglers you're fingering me and turning me on, it's
me, baby.

What wonderful situation should I return to next? But there
must be a build-up, no?

So far away, was Edinburgh, was Edinburgh, to me. I am
stood there in the station like in awe and confusion. All awe
is me, naive, smart as fuck, but with a lot to learn, okay,
coming up: one hell of a lot to learn. Believe me.

Now I'm stripping at a titty bar in the Pubic Triangle and I
am learning things fast; like how to roll customers, how to
play them. Plus I'm learning about ice cubes, how you put
them in your mouth when you suck them off in the toilets,
I'm learning about how they feel good and are hygienic too,
when they're not too clean down there how ice cubes can be
hygienic, and fun, and I'm giggling now, with the memory, I
slipped one up my ass, I put ice cubes in my ass one by one
and let them melt in me and trickle out, what an ice-cold
feeling.

I'm a ceramicist by trade, I'm a ceramicist, is what I tell my
customers, an artist gotta eat, I tell them. I'm a ceramicist
only after I see Picasso painted one of his plates, they have
it on display in Edinburgh when I arrive there in awe and
confusion only without direction, that's one thing I was
lacking as I got on the train, and then I sees this plate,
Picasso has painted a plate, I tell myself, well how bloody

simple, I say, to paint plates to your own design, and to
eat off them too, I say, and that's me right there: sold, and
hungry.

Penny Apostrophe is my fantasy name, honey, only it reads
Penny Apo'strophe, then Penny von Strophe, then Hildegard
von Strophe after I heard about the woman who was as soft
as a feather on the breath of God; that's me, I said, as I felt
the breath of men on me, their hot stinky breath on me and
blown this way, and to that.

Danny enters the picture again. Danny enters stage left,
and stands there, radiating, Danny you were a radiator.
There were two types of men in my life that I fell for all
along: radiators and powerhouses. Max was a powerhouse.
Danny was a radiator, whose chests you cuddle up on, whose
hair you muzzle in, whose pale white bodies you grasp so
tight. Maximilian Rehberg and Hildegard von Strophe, we
were made for each other, baby. But wait, I'm still being
made, and Danny is radiating:

He is reading from Nietzsche. Danny is reading from a
section that he says is about faith, is the definition of
faith, and he is reading about living according to no ideas
whatsoever, which is to live unlimited, which is never to
be as less than life, he says, as less than life was his exact
words, I don't think they were Nietzsche's, he is reading me
this in a bedsit near the Meadows, by candlelight, and I am
curled up on his chest and muzzling, and nuzzling, what's
he say about the death of God, he says that God is dead and
science too, because God and science are ideas and ideas
won't take us any further into revealing our true names to
ourselves, that is what he is saying, that our true names are

240

given to us in what we do, that we find ourselves in action, not in thought, and don't mistake the two either, he says, and he is giving me all sorts of ideas so I feel conflicted but no, I immediately crush them and move on, we are at the period where our true names are revealing themselves in actions and we are living together like two artistic criminals, without a safety net, which is to say yes to exactly what is in front of you, to admit that, yes, okay, I chose all of it, I knew what I was getting into right from the start, so I can hardly bitch about it, can I, which is where fun things like ice cubes come in, which is where fun details intervene, which is called aestheticising your life, which is what Danny says we should do, Danny says, he says that we should all just relax. It's the 1980s, and a long way till 1991.

I have resisted the reveal but not very well; I am barely a thousand words in when I reveal that I had sexy calipers on my legs. I have sexy calipers on my legs. I had issues with my joints where I flopped this way and that. But with my calipers on, and my heels, I was statuesque, monumental. Boys would slide money into my sexy calipers. I would slide my panties off – I wore bikini bottoms that fastened at the side – I would slip my bra off, and I would dangle them there, from my calipers; too much.

Poetry is time travel, Danny says, and we are right back there with his saying of it. Poetry relies on a form of verbal ellipsis, Danny says, where two words next to each other speak of a gap between them, a secret burrowing, which is meaning, in time.

Give me two words, he says to me.

Calipers calipers.

Two different words, he says.

Sexy calipers, I say, and I roll up close to him in bed on the floor and smoke a cigarette on his chest.

There's no ellipsis, he says, that's a statement of fact. Calipers are sexy is a statement of fact, I say to him, but there's poetry in it, I say, and I insist. Yes, he says, but sexy calipers in a poem? Easy, I say, first line: sexy calipers.

Now put some new words in, he says, Danny says to me to put some new words in and he says it right now, which is poetry as time travel, sexy calipers is poetry as time travel, but where is the ellipsis?

Just above the heart, I say, in the crease at the top of my thighs, I say, in the cute wrinkles around my eyes, I tell him, in the punctures in my leg where the screws go in; and now we have located poetry. We have travelled back there and discovered it in the past without the aid of an ellipsis, but still it feels like a secret trapdoor, that somewhere behind the words there is ingress.

But this is coming from the future too, this is coming from the lessons of the future, from scenarios we have yet to run up against, so press on, long-lost lover, and let me return to you with all that I have learned, and lost, and wept over; dry, silent tears are all that we're allowed, up ahead, so let's have a right good weep in the past and be done with it.

Maximilian Rehberg is an older customer with one arm who introduces himself as a writer and film-maker. He wants to film me in a film, he says, and he says of film what Danny says of poetry, that in it there is a gap which allows us to escape in time. My sexy calipers are an ellipsis, I tell him, between my legs is a gap, I tell him, that leads into time, ha ha that's a good one, he says, you are a good dancer, he says to me, and I would like to film you.

There is a man who wants to film me, I say to Danny, there is a man who talks about poetry like you, I say to him. No one speaks of poetry like me, he says, and he takes a cigarette and holds it up to his forearm and goes ahead and burns a hole in his flesh just to make the point; the point which is, I am the sexiest poet and I mean it. But he agreed to have me filmed; I will chaperone you with this clown and we will see about his command of poetry, was what he says.

He calls my calipers my bastard wings. And right there I can sense an ellipsis. That's no ellipsis, that's doggerel, Danny says, there's no poetry to him, but no, Danny, I can't tell you, Danny, what it meant when he gifted me my bastard wings, he said to me, there is a rare genetic mutation that little birds have (and my little bird heart has taken flight) where they grow a second, mutant wing, which allows them to fly higher, and with greater dexterity, and they call it a bastard wing because it is fatherless, and to be fatherless, Maximilian Rehberg tells me, is to be truly free, spread your bastard wings, he said to me, right in front of Danny he says this, and he films me dancing and I fall over, I trip over on my calipers and I fall to the floor and Danny goes to help me up but, no, Max says, no, be quiet, leave her, he whispers, and he holds Danny back, it is sexy that he has left me on the floor and is holding Danny back, he is orchestrating, is the word, he is orchestrating, which is what I love most, I love to be orchestrated, even as I am struggling to get to my feet, I am orchestrated, I tell myself, at last.

Danny is discouraging me by buying me baseball boots. What does a stripper want with baseball boots? I say to him. You don't need to be going around in these stupid heels you can't even walk in, he's saying. But what about my lovely pins, and the pins in my pins, don't they deserve a pedestal, is what I'm saying in return, by my expression, only but not by saying it out loud, because meanwhile the mysterious Max Rehberg with his one good arm, his one overdeveloped arm, I might say, with his single powerful arm is gifting me lingerie in secret cafes in the New Town and posting me unsigned cards that read Still Crazy About You. And then he asked if he could film me on my own and I didn't tell Danny and when I showed up he said to me, simply, I want to make love to you, I am crazy in love with you, I want to make love to you, and he mounted me there and then, in front of the cameras, pulled my panties to one side and with his single good arm held me tight against him and with his good fingers around my throat and the first time we made love will live forever.

And buying me stockings. Danny had never thought to buy me stockings, why would he, one look at those calipers and it seemed an improbable purchase, but here's Maximilian, here he comes, with a pair of sheer silk stockings called Gypsy all in gift wrapping and he takes my calipers off, he removes my calipers like in Cinderella's shoes, and he dresses me in black stockings and a suspender belt and then when he helps me put the calipers back on again he pokes a tiny hole for each of the screws in the silk and he made me think of how everything that is unworthy and not up to life and less than life was down to a failure of imagination, as he poked holes in my precious black stockings and screwed great bolts through the silk and into the flesh and then held me up, in his arms, and ravaged me; life, I said to myself, life this is it come take me.

Max started undermining Danny and it made me hotter still. He called him a little poof. What are you doing with that crap little poof? he would ask me. He's a total poofter, he would say. Please. Plus, he has dreadlocks. He does not have dreadlocks, I explained, he just has matted hair from not washing it and it's musky, I said, and I giggled, despite myself. But Max kept up with the whole white-guy-with-dreadlocks-poof thing and I would grin maliciously when he said it, that's how quickly he turned me around. I felt devious, alive. Besides, I said to myself, Nietzsche says that we should live beyond beliefs. Well this is me, living.

People talk about the anima and the animus and how all of that stuff is discredited now that everything is up for grabs, but I felt it, I felt him animate the anima in me, which is animal, and feline, and there it is on film. They must exist, somewhere, still, these movies. In this era of collectors I am sure that someone specialises in me, and the films we made, and now, as I tell you my story, I am rediscovered all over again, but really I prefer the immortality of a movie without credits, of an unmarked film tin, of a silent short wherein I make love for the best time, forever, and have become a reward for the true seeker, a bottomless mystery he will never solve but that speaks to the spaces in his own heart, which can never reply, but pursue astonishment, and that is me, on a secret reel, at a car-boot sale; I am a silent channel in time.

But not here, not any more, not now. Now I am wording as I set up the little ellipses my legs signified in letters, in words I am bracketing otherwise inexplicable gaps in order that we may reveal the hoops that we need to jump through in order to get to there from here. I miss my mother. Is it unfashionable to say that? My mother who shot herself in the chest and lived and who then shot up a whole concoction of pills and that did it for her when I was bare fifteen years old, I miss her, my mother. She shot a gap in her own chest just to be done with the future. I come from a family of time travellers.

So now he is curled around me, now, his one good arm is around me, tight, tights, he loved my punctured tights, he sleeps with his cock inside me, he is still hard, it is wonderful and hard as he tells me a story in Edinburgh about seeing a fish for the first time and I say, wow, you can remember the first time you saw a slimy fish and is that because when you looked in the water you saw yourself there, floating, on the gauzy film of the fish, gauzy film is the key to things as they are, I am thinking, I am picturing this fish in its perfect pool, it must be a pike, or a trout, or a flounder, though at this point I don't know a flounder but it sounds like the best word for seeing yourself as a kid and knowing that you are seeing, as a kid, through this seeing, I think is best described as a flounder, I would imagine, because I have no memory of my first fish, never mind my first reflection, but still, I am picturing this fish, in my mind, beneath a reflection, where Max's cock is inside me and I am held in his one good arm, once again, in Edinburgh, and it's like those salmon that dash themselves on the rocks as I remember us, us two, that was us, the two of us, us two, but salmon without poetry or fiction or myth or reality, salmon, in a pool, with no need of any of it, is us two right now, then he said to me, I hate the what-might-be, I only want the what-is, which is what he said art was, this salmon, beneath the still clear water as if it is no water at all, this perfect flounder, which is a conjunction, between what longs to be seeded and what seeds it, lover, you and I, is sexy with your cock inside me as I squeeze you tight, because he tells me that art is what sees what is, because it allows you to see deeper into what is, what is this flounder, this perfect salmon, in this perfect pool, which is pupil, right now, on the rings of his fingers, in the ring of my pupil is the rings on his fingers as he holds me tight, and it is a perfect salmon motionless in time, with no need for time or motion, and no need for any of them, not even a story like the one I am unfolding, because I am delicate that way, because ideas allow us to see things as not ideas, which is sweet, and which is lovely, and which is a flounder, is the idea I have given it, which is no idea, at all.

He told me he had been initiated into a Sufi order in Africa, a Sufi order that practised Qutub meditation, which is one-pointed meditation, which is three, really, but we'll get to that, and which is also known as the Stone on the Water, and he said that when he did it he could come with no hands and I said to him, that must be handy, and he said, no, I could still come with my one good hand, he said, it doesn't as if it makes anything easier, he said, and then he said that basically you come in your brain and up your spine and out your third eye and your jap's eye at the same time, only but when you come you comes with the force of a snake, spitting, and you comes on your own forehead, often, that's what he says, what he says is that you come with velocity and with force on your own forehead, on a regular basis, was what he said when he said that and the first time he did it he said that he couldn't believe it, he had been initiated into this Sufi sect who told him that the heart centre was located between the ribs, maybe between the fifth rib, I think, maybe, he said, on the left-hand side, and what on earth would they put a heart there for, but what happens then is you say to yourself that you will turn your attention to the heart centre, which is really when you turn your attention to the ribs, to that ticklish bit in the side of my ribs always gives me a giggle, and then you say that while you do that, your heart centre, which is the ticklish bit in your side, isn't it, which turns its attention to the source, is what he said, which is the light of death, is what he said, which is called Monument Maker, he said, and I said, wow, and then you focus on that point, he said, and then you sit in meditation and then you turn your attention to the heart centre and it turns its attention to the source, which is holy, I might add, and suddenly you feel it surging in and through you and what it is triggers something at the base of your spine, I believe to be a chakra is the word, and you feel the energy rise, with every breath you feel it rising and rising and oh my God it is coursing up your spine, like water seeking its level it is slowly peaking up your spine and it feels like light, like ticklish light, and he taught me how to do it, and he said that when he told his inductor (because I believe you have to have an inductor in order to get the initial connection to the source, I believe it has to do with lineage, is the word), that when he told his inductor what was happening, that his cocked popped every time he meditated – I almost said mediated – that his inductor told him he had better stop, that he was messing with powers he knew nothing about, he said, and that it could damage him, well, but that's what they said about masturbation back in the bad old days, he said, and he left them right then and there, or was he kicked out who knows, so that he could just as well practise on his own, and though I never saw him do the solo coming-with-no-hands thing, he did come inside me with no movement at all and it was like a snake spit in me with force all the same, he would sit in a meditative state, with his legs crossed, and when his substantial cock would rise I would mount it and wrap my legs around his back, I would place them there with my hands as they might've flopped this way and that – was what he liked about them, sexy flesh – and we would hum vibrate together without moving and he taught me about threes, why the number three was mystic, and it was because man cannot approach the mysteries alone and unveiled, was what it is, man needs a proxy or an interface, so it was 1-1-1, which was 3, the mystery of the intercessor, was what the word he called it, and when we would come I would feel like crying and couldn't walk all over again although of course I didn't have my calipers on because of the position but all the same I said to him, but it's 6, surely, because I am 1-1-1 and you are 1-1-1 and that makes 6 and he said, yes, that a cube had 6 sides and what with me forgetting the top and the bottom I only went to say, no, but that's only 4, but then I was right, it was 6, and I said to him, what's so special about numbers and he said, well, how could I have called you to take naked pictures of you and to make movies of you and to mount you, he said, even though right then it was me that was mounting him, he said, how come any of that could happen without numbers and I thought, numbers without end, give me numbers without end, and he said, no problem, because

every number is infinite, which I just couldn't understood
back then but of course what he was really saying was that
there was *no difference*, but that it took infinite numbers –
1-1-1 – 3 – in order to realise that, and I thought, didn't they
say the same thing about monkeys, about infinite monkeys,
and he told me he loved me and wanted a threesome with
me every night cause I was so damned cute, was what he
said, and I knew that the threesome was me, and that
me and him was a whole other threesome altogether,
threesomes on threesomes, and that there was literally
no difference. I hope I haven't given anything away that I
shouldn't have. I don't know if these Sufis have to sign up to
some kind of disclosure agreement, but you and I are a sexy
ellipsis, I says to him, all the same, and just like the best
poetry, we come with no hands, and with no movement.

I'm never going to fall for a stance, Max said to me, because
ideas are there to cure you of ideas altogether, and I said to
him, I'm stuck with ideas of myself, and he said to me, that's
your problem, and he shrugged, and I thought he was being
rude but then he said, no, I mean it like that's *your* problem
so don't let anyone else take it away from you or solve it for
you or feel sorry for you because of here you have it, he said,
say to them, that's *my* problem, and own it, he said, only he
didn't say own it, that's me saying own it, he wouldn't have
said own it, he would have said: embrace it. But that's what
he meant by compassionless love; this beautiful, tender
embrace. He said that he refused to solve anyone else's
problem out of respect, was what he said, out of respect for
the person's problem, and the gifting of it, wow, I said, the
gifting of it, this is in the winter in Edinburgh where I could
barely pay the electricity meter in the snow-cold winter cause
I had moved into a garret is the only way to describe it, and

Max had given Danny a right good pasting, and gifted him a whole new set of problems, and me too, cause of I had to find somewhere new to live and I refused to move in with Max, at first, I refused because I wanted to be my own independent, I was fierce and shy that way, and so I got a place in a roof with leaking tiles and which I had to clank up into like Frankenstein, and Max is visiting me there, after giving my boyfriend a right good doing, and I had laughed, I had laughed wickedly while he gave him a kicking with one arm, I had laughed and got turned on and wanted him to fuck me but in motion, this time, in motion of great thrusts only I had early endometriosis so really deep thrusts were painful and ecstatic at the same time, which is exactly what Max was teaching, only this time in bed was where the teaching was taking place, and I thought about my calipers and the nature of my problem, which had led me to this garret under a roof where he fucked me senseless and the first plate I made had a picture of a fish on it, which was a flounder, which I found out what it looked like, underwater, and coming up for air, and Max said to me, well, what kind of an idea is that, being underwater and coming up for air at the same time, and I said to him, it doesn't matter, I've cured myself of ideas now, and I walked off like into the sunset.

Max was in Edinburgh looking for a film that one of his friends starred in but when he fell into a love affair with me he extended his trip. He told me he rented some rooms in a house in Grez-sur-Loing (Stone-on-the-Water) in France that some of his friends had, but that he was often on the road. I'm a career adventurer, he told me, but what he didn't tell me was that he was also a gun for hire, half of a science fiction writer and an amateur theologian with a bunch of published texts to his name with sexy names about God.

I asked him about this same movie he was after and the words he used were much-rumoured, that's what he would say, this much-rumoured movie, he would say, these much-rumoured movies, as there was more than one, though only one mysterious one that his tall friend had starred in, his tall friend who must have been at least six foot two and had the unfortunate appearance of a mad sombre giraffe, a mad sombre giraffe with an awful human face grafted on it, a giraffe that spoke so slowly and with such ponderous intent that you would be forgiven for thinking it must have been recovering from some kind of head wound, some kind of trauma inflicted in the bush, in the dark of Africa, which is true, but with the dark of Africa standing in for the whole of the Mediterranean with its seas on fire in the final years of the war. Anyway, the way I heard it the movie was kind of a porno.

It was a sex scene. *9 ½ Weeks*. Basically. But *9 ½ Weeks* extended until all weeks forever. Because of the scene was on a loop. What scene, the sex scene was, on a loop. On a loop, where the woman is under him, he is on top of her, on a loop. A raw sex scene. But not that sexy, it seemed to me, on a loop. On a loop this guy enters this girl, on a loop, forever, and that is the full story. On a loop. This guy enters this girl, what of it, on a loop. Not stylised or anything, not stylised unless you think that brute frank boredom, on a loop, forever, is artful and deliberate, which I do think now, let the record show. But then I thought, frankly, this sounds rubbish. And I said, what else do these two do, these two occluded lovers (that's the phrase I used, and I winked, and I grinned, and I stuck my teeth out, my goofy fangs, and I could tell that he loved me being goofy in Edinburgh), what else do they do, these lovers on this, loop? Plus, I said

loop like I was slurping Heinz spaghetti; I meant it. You
can see the woman's face, he said. She is looking towards
the camera. Big deal. So what. And now I'm pouty and
irresistible.

But he didn't know he was being filmed. This loop, this loop
came back to him, Max is saying, and when it came back
he recognised it as himself and that he had been filmed
in secret making love to this woman whose husband had
been a director and when Max said that to me I didn't
think straight and I thought he meant someone who moves
behind the scenes like a puppetmaster and I thought that
her husband was a professional at making things happen
in the world, an orchestrator, and I remembered Max
orchestrating me and I thought about my gammy pins and I
thought, who's zooming who, you know, like the song?

They make love and at one point the woman wraps her leg
around one of the man's legs in a sign that Maximilian – I
will use his full name here – said was occult. The man's
face is never seen. Only his neck and shoulders, his legs,
the back of his head. The director from behind the scenes
is supposedly dead. Supposedly; but there are theories, but
who knows. They make the sign known as The Hanged Man,
the lover whose back is to the camera, the woman who is
beneath him, and now we are back with names, and with
numbers, which according to this film could not be further
from the point, is my idea about it, as I think of it now, as
I think of the films I eventually did see by this man from
behind the scenes, films that were screened against a white
tablecloth in the beautiful garden that led down to the River
Loing, whose word my mouth just wouldn't fit, I kept trying,
the River Loing, in France, where I saw a film of a black

stork walking slowly through a murdered zoo of animals and
it gave me such a shiver like it had walked right out of the
past and over my grave, which has a location now, on earth,
as I've only gone and bought my own little plot recently, at
the other end of the street in which we lived in wonderful
Grez-sur-Loing, despite these haunted pictures.

And Jim, the camel-with-a-head Jim movie star Jim, would
sometimes cross through the beam of the projector and it
was like a fayre, an English fayre where everyone dresses
up like monstrosities in order that they can prowl the night
and set to terrifying themselves and everyone around them.
But what does the woman wrapping her legs around the
man mean? That is how I became to believe myself become a
movie.

True names. Maximilian Rehberg's true name is Deaf
Boy Looking Up And Pointing, which sounds like a tribal
name, to me. I asked him how he became a religious, that's
the term I used, I was killing him, basically, a religious, I
dropped it, and he laughed and described to me the figure
of his heart which he saw in a deaf boy long ago, a deaf boy
looking up and pointing is the figure of his heart, believe me
it's true, in a plain old shop like John Menzies, with toys on
high shelves, and a deaf boy pointing, a deaf boy pointing
and making that sound that deaf boys make when they
don't even know what sound is, that terrible sound of deaf
boys trapped in a soundless universe, deaf boys muffled in
a sleeping bag and deaf boys smothered with a mattress
and, let's face it, deaf boys buried half-alive, is the image
written in the heart of Max, and the deaf boy is asking for
something, in his heart the deaf boy is pointing towards
a toy and asking for it and doesn't he deserve it for God's

sake, a toy to sit with, silently, surely it isn't asking too much, but truly it is asking too much and like Nietzsche saw a horse get punched in the face or Dostoevsky caught the eye of some strange idiot peasant, Max breaks down, he stands there in this plain old John Menzies at the start of his career, at the beginning of his adventure, and he weeps for a deaf boy whose mother wouldn't buy him a toy, some rip-off piece of plastic from the top shelf of a plain old John Menzies was all it took, all it took to fill this terrible void of silence this deaf boy lived in, and to cease the sound of his terrible language, his body speaking for him and without regard for him either, is terrible, and the mother barely looks at him, she ignores the sound of his groaning in this agony of this soundlessness that he doesn't even know he inhabits and she takes him by the arm and she drags him, out the door, and into the oblivion of memory. And this is the atomic pain of the world, is what Maximilian Rehberg said, back then, at the start of his career. And I intend to kill my feelings for it dead, was how he put it, back then.

And now it sounds like a movie, on a loop, a movie the likes of which we would watch on an old tablecloth in the back garden at night in Grez-sur-Loing, strung between some washing poles, in Grez-sur-Loing, by starlight, we're all out there, Max, Pierre, Big Jim the Giraffe, and me.

Moments are atomic, are building blocks, of course that's true. But it's like the wiring has been exposed in these films we used to watch. The atomic nature of each moment seemed underlined, heightened.

And silence, too, the profound silencing of deaf boys, is necessary to our order. It says that these are the soldiers in the trenches, the sweethearts that never came back. Which is Africa, and the trip we took there.

We left Edinburgh for Africa, first. There were no films to be found in Edinburgh, except of course the usual art school fare at the Filmhouse but spare me, so as Maximilian gave up. I am going to take you back to Africa, he told me one night, and at first I thought he was going to fuck me back to the origins of the human race where it was just two protoplasms going at it without a thought in their heads, which actually happened on top of us travelling to Africa and getting off the plane in Ethiopia and immediately getting sick, and recovering, and me lying in bed all day in a miserable apartment while Max made calls sitting at the foot of the bed and then we hired a boat and it almost sinks in these crocodile-infested waters, but we pull up at some encampment, some weird village, where we get the boat repaired and where the food is basically dead animals, which I know is the case with meat everywhere but here there was something especially carcassy about it, maybe because of it was not long dead and was not frozen. I ate a chicken's gonads; I think I did.

I am the Lion of Judah, is told me in a dream. In a dream on a boat on a river in Africa, which is a dream speaking inside of a dream. I am the Lion of Judah, and it is a game of nots and crosses, is what I said to Maximilian on the boat. He grabbed me by the arms. We were lying facing each other in our bunk. Some exotic fern hung over the window. There was the buzzing of malarial swamps just like in a zombie movie. What did you just say? he said to me. And I said it again. I am the Lion of Judah. I just thought it up, I said. The Lion of Judah is from Africa, I said to him, isn't it. It just came to me, I said. What does the Lion of Judah say? he asked me, but now I was getting creeped out and was fearful, because I was starting to get gripped by this Lion of Judah and wondering how ideas come to you, and why. But the thing is the Lion of Judah spoke exactly like me. It's not saying anything, I said to Max, what do you mean, it's just me, if anything it's just saying what I'm saying right now, but it's true there was a feeling there, a feeling that I had been occupied by this idea called the Lion of Judah and that Max was looking at me differently and also that there was a Lion inside me now, a silent lion, pointing, and I thought is it deaf, is this damn lion deaf as well.

Then things get weirder. I start hallucinating signs, or maybe signs only appear for a fleeting second and then they go, so as they are unverifiable by anyone outside of who was in the moment of them; yes, that's it. A dark animal with black leather skin and with two small legs and brown hairy wings exposes itself to me in the strange yellow dawn rising over an African river; disgusting. One morning there is a pyramid of quince fruit on the prow of our ship, seemingly arrived there, piece by piece, in the night. And I know, and with the certainty of which I am overwhelmed, that it is an entire fruit tree, all the fruit from a single quince tree, that has been removed, one by one, throughout the night, and brought here, one by one, and piled here, in an ornate pyramid, one by one, in an attempt to get whatever it is inside me to speak, by way of psychological violence, or else.

Then it sang in African; then it sang in African a song I could not understand but that felt like it was sung from the furthest ends of myself, with words that seemed to speak of boundaries, and the overcoming of them, which was me. It is me, I am the Lion of Judah, and I admitted it to myself.

When we went up on deck there was a monsoon coming down, or maybe it was just a storm. We had broken loose of our moorings and now we were drifting down the stream. Max took the rudder and attempted to steer us back to the shore, but we were borne away with the tide like a soldier into war.

We came to a town with a name like Chandelier, Pirouette, Crystal Fountain. Max would bathe underwater, in the tub, we had a tub on the boat and Max would submerge himself completely, for minutes on end, in these waters, on these waters, his eyes open beneath these waters, as sure of his element as a trout seen clearly. Max was of the rivers, born of the waters, and could never be drowned; that's what I thought. And we pulled up at these small villages where they welcomed us ashore. Soon we came to our destination. In the shed there was Pierre's old motorcycle, still. I knew my calipers were going to look so good wrapped around that motorcycle so that I said to him so, I told him, you picked me to match the motorcycle, you sly dog, which of course he loved it.

I got on the back of this motorcycle and I'm sorry but there is simply nothing sexier than actual sex that is as sexy as riding behind your man on his hog. Your arms around his chest, your face in his hair. Across this inhospitable desert. There's nothing but our tracks in the sand. We are just behind the wind, which is remaking everything new for our arrival. We pull up at an abandoned settlement, hard by a stream. There is a smell like a volcano. I feel as if I catch shadows flitting here and there behind the empty buildings, and there is a chattering sound, like a terror in the air. Max points to an old well all welled up with stones and it is a little deaf boy pointing to a toy on a high shelf in some John Menzies somewhere. I found a disembodied head that talks, he said. And I buried it here in this well. I thought he was going to make a song out of it. Well, that sounds like the opening to a song, I said to him, and he said to me, well, yes, that's the thing, this disembodied head was singing, and I said to him, Johnny Cash done got dark, I said, just for laughs, but then he said: at one point in his life Johnny Cash had to bury himself in a cave to stop himself going half goddamn crazy. I knew he was serious then, and that there was a head that talks.

Right then I saw the weird bat-monkey thing with leather flesh right in front of me like a picture from my mind, followed by a blue triangle. I shook my head and Max said, what do you mean, you don't believe me, should I lift off these stones and let you hear it singing and before I could say, no, I was shaking my head to rid myself of this weird monkey vision and this stupid blue triangle, I actually said to him, but surely a pile of stones is no obstacle to a disembodied head that can talk, surely the laws of physics are no longer enough, but he said instead, but it has no arms, he said, and he shook his head as if it was obvious, it has no legs, he said. Well, won't it have drowned, I said, in that case, if it has no hands and legs at the bottom of this well? But even as I was saying it, I was thinking of him in the tub, in the bath, in every river of the world, and I knew that it could never drown. But wouldn't it have starved to death? I went to say to him, but then of course I knew that the answer would be that it had no stomach. The head told me it was the Lion of Judah, he said. I told you I was the Lion of Judah, I said to him, but I was just saying it like a quote, I explained, not like a statement of me. Who were you quoting? he asked me. I don't know, I said, it's a famous phrase. Only with Rastafarians, he said, are you a Rastafarian? he asked me. I'm not a Rastafarian, I said. Okay, he said, then why did it come to you? It just came to me, I said to him. Well, isn't that possession? he said to me. And out here, he said, possession is the whole of the law.

Let's unstop the well, he said. Let's do it, he said. And set lions on lions, he said. I'm a Leo, I said to him, do you know that. But he just sat there and waited for my response. Okay, I said, and I went first and lifted a few small stones off the pile. Then Max looked at me, with those eyes of his, those eyes of his that were always receiving and never projecting, so as you had no hope of getting insides of them because, girls, the depths were endless, you would need one of those diving cages, one of them midget submarines, and I thought, whatever is at the bottom of this well is something I believe in, is what I said to myself, and I started dragging bigger stones away and helping him with boulders until at last, finally, we had exposed this endless tunnel into the ground that stank like a dried-up pond at the foot of a block of flats where everybody urinates out of their windows, it was noxious, this head is gone rancid and dead, I sang to Max, and he laughed and then he said, so you're singing now too, and I said, you can't count songs as being signs of prophecy, songs are in the air like mosquitoes.

Then we sat there, on the lip of this volcano, I almost said, this deep well into blankness and stench and nowhere and I said to him, call for your head, I said, though bear in mind

he might be mad at you, and justifiably so, I warned him.
So he called this head. Lion of Judah, he said, and he called
him some other names too that are lost to esoterica. All
the time I thought to myself, it's me, he is calling me, the
head is responding in my head, and then I thought – crazy
thought – what if this well is like a strange entrance and
exit into different parts of the story, what story, this story, I
said, this unfolding story, I said, which right now is echoing
down a well and the voice is travelling, and speaking
words, who knows where else in the story these words are
speaking, and I said to Max, I dare you, I dare you, I said to
him, I dare you to lower yourself down there and see where
it goes and he said to me, my three wives died here, he said,
well, he said, my two wives died here, one of them may well
still be alive, they died of terror, he said, and I said to him,
a country bumpkin could die from terror of a homosexual, I
said, it doesn't mean the damn thing is actually frightening.

Now I'm laughing about it, now that I know your interests,
and how the story is unfolding, I'm laughing about it;
literary subterranea, there is a literary subterranea, down
that well. I look at Maximilian and I know it. Drop down
that shaft and reappear somewhere else in the story, I say
to him. You taught me about poetry, I say to him, and I say
it tempestuously, like a trial of strength in a tempestuous
love affair, you pointed to the magic of an ellipsis, which is
my cute-as-hell legs, I say to him, well, there we have it,
that well is the perfect ellipsis, so get down in there, I say to
him, and prove to me the magic of poetry, but before anyone
could do anything the magic of poetry was revealed to us by
this head at the bottom of this well which right then chose
to reveal itself by the suspension of a single vowel, (a) single
vibrating vowel of the type that brought down the Walls of

Jericho, suspended, in the very mouth of this well, which was better poetry right then than simply disappearing in and out of (a) text, but there's that too, and we're coming to it.

And I lower him down, I hold his legs as the top half of his body disappears down this well. I have him by the ankles, his cute little socks, he has a grip on the sides, and he is shouting, and I am holding him still and now I have let him go:

I
have
let
go
of
him
and
now
my
Maximilian
has
disappeared
from
sight
( )
.

4. PROCEEDS FROM THE SECOND SYNOD OF THE CHURCH OF THE STONE OF FIRST WITNESS

When we return, Pierre and Maximilian are living at the house of Delius, in Grez-sur-Loing, and writing science fiction together under the pen name Paimon. A third character enters our story at this point, as a ghost or a shade.

Also the man we refer to as Frater Jim, less corporeal, even, than Paimon himself, a stage magician and conjuror with connections to European Freemasonry who, it is reputed, disappeared during the evacuation of Crete in the Second World War, presumed drowned on his torpedoed ship, but who rose again, from the dead, decades later, after an experimental skin graft rebuilt his horribly disfigured face so completely that he was able to return home, in secret, and remarry his first love all over again, as a different man. Reputedly. For we are in the realm of magic, and of science fiction, here, and of the formation of the Church of the Stone of First Witness.

In the garden, Pierre begins work on his first sculptures, the same invisible garden that I share, in my mind, with old Delius, and that was painted pink by his lover. His first works are Emergent, is how he terms them, the Emergents, a single cyclops eye from a pedestal of rough granite; what appears as the side of a head and the shoulder of a man, fused, as it were, with the stone; crude genitals emerging from a headstone of pure polished marble that later Rehberg connects to a brass pump and runs a pipe into the well in the garden, so you can jack it off, he jokes, and luckily it only takes one hand.

They meet Frater Jim at a cafe in a nearby village and are first drawn to him by his striking features, a beauty of another sort, is how Pierre described it, a face which best resembles a Picasso, or an African mask, a fetish with a profile within its profile, like it has been stitched up, and made, which of course we now know, or rather we believe, that it was. They name him Dogon, and then The Elephant Man, and finally Frater Jim.

I am aware of your fascination, Frater Jim says to them, when he finally approaches them, on a day where they have been drinking all afternoon in the sun in Bourron-Marlotte and are now ribald and deranged with the heat. Of course, they think he means their fascination with his mask-like face, but no. I am aware of your fascination, he says, with empathy and fellow-feeling, he says, and they are both amazed. Had he read their furtive glances and the muttering behind their hands and their awkward, conspiratorial silences as coming from fellow-feeling, as coming from sympathy and connectedness and love? But no, Frater Jim says, I am aware of your fascination with the killing of these feelings in your heart, is what he says, and once again, we push on, deeper.

Frater Jim asks them if they are aware of a fraternal organisation known as The SIRK, and he proceeds to school them in its teachings, which centre, he claims, on esoteric practices derived from Christianity, Buddhism and Hermeticism, as well as the rituals of Freemasonry, tantra and sex magick. What is sex magick? Rehberg asks him. Every orgasm gives birth, he says. On various planes, he clarifies, which is no clarification at all. I was briefly involved, Frater Jim tells them, and I learned how to kill my heart, in the name of love. They invite him over to the house, for tea.

Are you gay? Frater Jim asks them. Certainly not, Rehberg says. We just live as man and wife, he jokes. I see, Frater Jim says, well, he says, that rules certain things out. But what these things might have been, he refuses to elaborate.

There is a first stone that floats on water, Frater Jim says. He sits around and smokes drugs and says gnomic things like, the first stone is supported by the first stone, and Pierre nods, and Max Rehberg nods, and they feel closer to, something, some idea is coalescing and that is when Pierre begins the building of his stone ships, his secret life's work, boats of basalt, which is the densest form of stone, basalt cathedrals are mighty fortresses, he says, and he tells Frater Jim of his ambition to make stone float and Frater Jim says to him, the moon is a stone that floats, which is what you call the stone of the wise, he says, and that is alchemy, he says, which is the transubstantiation of base material into the playing out of spiritual lessons, he says, which is a magickal approach to life, is what Frater Jim describes it as, and he says it like that, with a K, magic with a K, you have added a letter, Pierre says, and Frater Jim says, that letter is sentinel, and stands for the unpronounceable workings of magick, because if true magick were merely pronounceable everyone would just sit around talking it, Frater Jim joked, just like we are doing now, he laughed, instead of, you know, finding magick in its making, and then he said the letter D, the letter D is in there too, he said, only it is an invisible letter and then he said to us, all letters are infinite, there is no difference, and that's enough to give you vertigo above a page, Pierre said, and where's Max during all of this, uh-oh, here he is, and he's saying something facetious about why did Christ ban magick, and Pierre turns to him and says, as a theologian I cannot believe for a fucking second you seriously believe Christ ever talked about banning magick, but at the same time I think it is obvious that God would have to ban himself from magick, should he come down to this earth, because that would just be cheating and where would be the sport, and plus he would have to admit, if he demonstrated magick, that it was within his and his father's power for anything what-the-fuck-ever to happen, and so admit that God wills it this way, and no other.

Amen, Frater Jim said. God wills it this way, and no other. That is the true meaning of magick, he said.

And Pierre gives a name to all of the ships he is building, all of the stones launched into the water, and he calls them by a female name, *Nebula*, he calls them, he names ships as a woman as of old, and these are the names of every boat launched from the bottom of the invisible garden of Delius's brain into the Loing, *Nebula*, the constant replaying of which, in history, has given the village its name, Stone-on-the-Water, there have been stone boats launched from the foot of these gardens for centuries, Pierre thinks to himself, as he visions the first of the basalt boats and is given a diagram, a blueprint that coheres in his head almost as if it had been secreted in a particular part of the world's imagination in order to be accessible to dreamers who went down certain roads, dreamers who dreamed impossibly, otherwise why dreams, with their spoken D, is the answer, Pierre figured.

God created this world out of stone, Frater Jim would say, this world is hewn from the rock, and Max Rehberg would say, God created this world out of flesh, this world is hewn from our brains, and Frater Jim would say, flesh and rock and consciousness and flight are the greatest achievements of what we call evolution, but there are secret letters, hidden there, too, he would say, and the nights would go on like this until everyone got drop-down drunk and passed out, or argued like crazy over piddling theological points, or retired to their room and shot heroin into their neck.

The idea of the church comes around. Let's make a church, Max says one night, let's start our own cult, religion, like The SIRK, whatever, let's become initiators, and Frater Jim says, to be an initiator you have to be sure that you are someone who can pass on the experience of being initiated, and Max says to him, what a joke, I have been there, believe me, and this is the first time he mentions the head, and the burning boat, and the first of the Holy Books, and Frater Jim says to him, how many eyes did this head have and Max says to him, two, it was a human-type head, and then Frater Jim says to him, did it speak without speaking, did it speak without moving its lips, and Max says, it was at the bottom of a well so I couldn't verify that, and then Frater Jim says, why would a headless head be the mode in which a god or a demon spoke to man, and then he said the word Baphomet, Baphomet means in-the-light-of-death, Frater Jim said, this is what the Templars worshipped, he said, and he stood up and he pointed in a direction, in a direction out of the blind night-time garden of Delius and along the canal, Cugny, he said, and at first both Pierre and Max believed he was referring to oral sex with a woman but he said, no, Cugny is the site of the Templars nearby, and of a tiny haunted village, whose occupants made dynamite, and who were killed in a terrible explosion, and beneath Cugny, he said, there is a labyrinth of tunnels that provide ingress into the past and the future, he said, for there is an art of accessing the past, and there is a skill of unlocking the future, Frater Jim said, and they all three of them sat there, round the table, with the umbrella up, inexplicably, on this warm summer night in Stone-on-the-Water, Stone-on-the-River, Stone-on-the-Motherfucking-Brain.

Numerous creeps passed through the ranks of the short-lived First Stone Church; there is no end of people seeking the permission to be what they are. Sometimes, when they would meet prospective candidates, they would think things like, losing weight might be the single biggest magickal prerogative for you right now, as opposed to, you know, learning how to curse others in Hebrew. They were old-school; they still believed in the mystical powers of the alphabet, but also, like, basic hygiene is basic magick, and terror of sex is not, and people would turn up, sometimes dressed outlandishly, as if to announce their wizard ways, wearing top hats and capes and spindly moustaches, and

Jim would say something gnomic like, that costume is The Tower, and he would invoke The Hanged Man, and he would rail against identity as the ultimate barrier to existence, like a diving bell or a drowning suit, launched down, into it.

And you can see what happened, what happened to the order in the 1990s when it was revived by hobbyists, it's pathetic. Ask The Flashlight. Look him up, he exists, seriously, look him up. But back then, despite the chancers and the charlatans and the social defectives, it was true magick they were working, and it was transformative, to a point. There were workshops, initiations, bacchanalian celebrations and a few mental breakdowns. But I can't tell you about any of those for fear of ruining your own. And then it all went to shit and these days the lineage has no link to the founders whatsoever and it is basically just a shitshow for geriatric conspiracy theorists and Second World War nostalgists and sexless psychogeographers and would-be literary critics, my God, but all the time Pierre is working on these stone ships, which is a logistical nightmare, and the first launches take place and there are sinkings – *Nebula* sinks to the bottom of the Loing like a sarcophagus, her hands clasped in prayer as she is raised upon, and then buried beneath, the tide – and there are incredible moments – like when a dog leaps onto one of them and glides like a surfer into the distance until finally it is sunk, and the dog swims back towards the shore – and there are strange awkward silences – where everyone looks to each other and suspects themselves victims of a collective delusion or, worse, the uncovering of impossible truth.

Or shot heroin into their neck. Maximilian Rehberg was a junk fiend by this point. How come is it that people who

nearly die on Mount Everest are hailed as brave heroes and
great sportsmen when those of us who dare an Olympic dose
of drugs are called fiends and junkies and sent packing from
the doctor's? he says.

You have been reading too much William Burroughs, Frater
Jim cautions him, and it was true, Ballard, Burroughs,
and someone else beginning with a B that eludes me now –
Bowles? Bowie? Behan? (Norman O.) Brown? Borges? Bova?
– were becoming a big influence, certainly on Paimon, on the
arc of the duo's science fiction stories, it's plain to see, which
by this point were bringing in a fair bit of money, it has to
be said, and a cult had developed around Paimon as to who
in the actual fuck was this guy and how in the actual fuck
is he named after a goetic demon, and a transsexual one at
that, which anyone will tell you who has ever had dealings
with that gay little sprite will confirm, and of course he rides
on a camel, across a desert of Africa, Paimon does, so there's
that, too, but then it turns out – and who could believe it –
that there's some weird autistic outsider unknown musician
called Paimon too, some downer real-people DIY blues
psychonaut has also taken the name, and cause this guy
never does interviews, or plays live, or is ever spotted in the
street, a rumour springs up that it's this same idiot savant
musician that is behind all of these weird cult science fiction
stories.

And in the midst of this, there are mysterious stone ships
pulling up at the bottom of gardens and of parks all along
the River Loing, silently, and without meaning, for whoever
encounters them sees something in them, something
impossible, which is their death, approaching, for these
are monument stones, memorial devices, carved basalt,

light-filled, and lovely on the water. Pierre has become
the sculptor he would end his life as, which is called final,
and fulfilment, and is terrifying when sought, and found,
because if you are lucky, then unlucky you, because First
Church is Final.

Maximilian Rehberg receives a letter from his aunt asking
him to return home, your father is dying, is what she says,
in this sad, tear-stained letter, this letter that has been
pursued by tears from the beginning of time, which are the
tears of Christ that Jesus wept, tears pursuant of himself,
and then of Max's father, and now his sister, and now Max
himself, via this letter, which he opens and all the cares of
the world spill out, and Max's father is dying of stomach
cancer, and it is eating its way out of him like a grub, or
a stone in his passway, or a single bright tear from the
beginning of time, and Max makes the decision to return
home, and even though he thought his heart was stone, *he
thought his heart was cold dead stone*, this stone is borne
up on the waters and returned home, where his father's
tears have so overwhelmed him that he begs his estranged
son to end his life, Maximilian's father pleads with his
son to take his life, to help him suicide, but Maximilian
Rehberg is unable to do so, even as his father rolled in
agony in his grave already, and tore at his bedclothes, and
bent over double and vomited black vomit on the sheets,
even then Maximilian was incapable of a true and supreme
compassion, which is the bravery to end suffering, the
bravery not to be afraid, and not to terrify anyone else
either, which is the mark of a man, in its persistence,
in its following unto the very ends and its faith in those
same endings is the true mark of a man, which is called
Persistence, and his father wouldn't give up with his pleas,

and his aunt begged him, kill your father, she said, burn what you love, she said, in the end, we can imagine, as though now Max's past was speaking via his future and he has been presented with the truth of compassionless love, which means to make of your heart a fortress, and then to yield, and that yielding is the hardest part, his father urges him to take up arms, by the side of his bed, his father begs him, and Maximilian is unable, yet he stays with his father, he sits silently by his bed, and the tears finally catch up with him, Maximilian's father in an old white T-shirt and striped pyjama bottoms, and his tanned arms, and his biceps, and his smell of men, his own smell of men, and those tears dispatched from so long ago now, and even though he has the ability to end his father's pain, and to redeem himself, and to take responsibility (for that's what it would have felt like, who else gets to murder their own father at the appropriate time, and according to his own father's desire? This feels like a gift especially put together for Maximilian, this feels almost as if from behind the scenes he had written it himself), but when the universe presents you with the perfect mirror is when it speaks your name to your face, and his father is incontinent and all over himself, and still alive, and Max can't go to him, he remembers his dead comrade in Africa, how he held his dead body tight in his arms for a final embrace (how could he not bring it to mind with what was going on right in front of him), and remembers, too (of course this must bring to mind his mother), his dying mother, and here is his father, rolling in his own shit in front of him and begging for compassion and for mercy and for his son to end his suffering which is entirely within his power, to end suffering was entirely within your power, Max, which would have made of you a god, and yet Max cannot move or speak or go to him, and Max is sat silent on a chair next to his dying father and Max thinks, Max has to wonder, if, perhaps, all of his love was, in fact, reserved for the dead and the already departed, if all of his ideals are not, in fact, reserved, almost exclusively, for theoretical scenarios, for the realm of fantasy and adventure, a kind of escapist apologia, if we are being honest, perhaps he was too religious, or not religious enough, ultimately, for his father shitting himself right there in front of him, nor for all of the pain in need of making holy down here, which is a lack of faith, and an overwhelming of awe. And all of this takes place in Golgotha, which is the place of the skull, all of these ideas take place there but from these ideas – what?

There is the garden, because it is virgin, and invisible, and untrodden upon. But is it yours?

And his father dies, in terrible pain and in agony his father finally dies, but not by the hand of his only son, who watches helplessly, and in terror, as we can imagine, as the final agonies of his father are written, in stone. And at one point his father says to him, you don't have it in you, you don't have it in you, he says, do you, and then he evacuates all over himself and two days later he dies, screaming.

But what did he not have in him? And do you? Compassion, steel-heartedness, tenderness, bravery, cold stone, resilience, acceptance, self-belief? All of it inside us. Love, I say. L.O.V.E. And now I am a silent channel in time, a rivulet, which is as beautiful a word as rumfles, as a passway is for tears, in stone.

And we enter the summer, which is the final summer of Holy Maximilian Rehberg's life, the late summer that was to become as a book, the summer that Pierre would memorialise, as the two of them, Pierre and Max's lover Hildegard, toured the monasteries and the churches and the bars, let's face it, and the cafes and restaurants and expensive hotels, too, it's safe to say, and the cold leather on the back seat of the car, we know now, and the assignations, the three-way assignations, which, again, we have been made fully aware of, and meanwhile, back home, Rehberg's heroin use is spiralling, and both he and Frater Jim end up on week-long benders where they trip and do coke and float on rubber rings, naked, and inebriated, in the river, until the police are called, yes, even in France two naked guys passed out on rubber rings and with their cocks all flaccid and hanging out floating down the river while spinning in slow circles, even this is too much to bear for the kind of Frenchman who will lie down in dogshit, who will simply cover the dogshit with a towel and plump himself down there, still, the sight of two men spinning slowly, as I said, hypnotically, even, as they float slowly past the families laid out on towels and the boys playing frisbee and I hear that Max's long hair was dragging behind him, he was passed out in this ring with his head in the water and with his hair trailing behind him like he was falling from a great height, right into this story, and who knows, he might be naked and dead, the way he looks, and so perhaps it was right that they called the cops, and so they call the cops and honestly, by this point Max wasn't looking his best, maybe it's no wonder that Hildegard ran off with Pierre for a summer, because the pigs, sorry, the police, take one look at him, with these fucking welts on his neck, and they were like, we just netted ourselves some junkie scum, and you know they are strict about drugs in France, just like in Mexico, the two places you would seriously expect them not to give a fuck, but this is France and so they are screwed but at the same time, you can't be charged with being on smack in charge of a rubber ring, plus they're buck naked, so they obviously have no drugs on them, but the police fine them, and caution them, and who knows, maybe even put them on a list of subverts and they might be there still, look it up, how would I know, but from that time on there are rumours spreading, about this satanic church, about black magick nudity and flagrant drug use and a magickal attitude to reality.

Only but it draws the heat, and the rumours spread, and soon the pair of them are being shunned and there are groups of villagers who immediately stop talking as soon as Jim or Max appear, and then there is graffiti on the house of Delius, across the front of it – of course the local history association and the village preservation bods are up in arms, this is sacrilege – but nevertheless, it is written across the front of that cottage that could Delius even remember, the words Thank You For Your Persistence, and of course there is a rumour that persists till this day that Max painted it himself, naked, and on smack, because this was the sense of permission he took from the general unease of the villagers that the sight of his flaccid passed-out cock on the river had presented, and what does it mean anyway, should we take some time to break it down, as Jim, when he visits, says, wow, beautiful sentiment from your haters, he says, basically, although of course that was not at all how anyone spoke back then, haters, but still, Jim says, who is he thanking for 'their' persistence, and Jim makes the inverted commas above his head like horns or a headdress, thank you for your persistence, he says, and then he says, wow, all over again, he said wow when he first saw it, but it's wow all over again when he says, thank you for your deathlessness, he says, thank you for your eternal energies, he says, thank you for your constant and complete transformations, he says, and then he's back to the thing where every single fucking moment is copulating forever and the whole world is code, code, code.

Pierre gets back with Hildegard and there's the first of several scenes. Pierre explodes, and is confused, and in a secret terror also, when he sees the graffiti on the front of the house. He neglects to tell Jim that he has in fact written the exact same thing elsewhere in this story. It was vandals, Frater Jim shrugs, even as he is half passed out at a table in the invisible garden known as France, even as he is sitting there in a pair of boxer shorts and even when Pierre finds tins of the exact same colour of paint alongside a paintbrush and another crumpled-up pair of paint-stained boxer shorts behind some pink plant pots in the greenhouse, even then Max denies it and he says, you have no idea of the persecution we have had to put up with since you left on your honeymoon, he says, and Pierre thinks, Paimon, is it Paimon that is writing this, he thinks to himself, and he shudders, but he holds his nerve.

It's a paradox, Max says, I shall call it the Pierre Paradox, he says, and all the while he is slurring his words and a cigarette is rolling between his lips and spilling ash all down his bare torso, and the paradox is this, he slurs, you're gutted if Pierre tries to fuck your girl, he says, and you're gutted if Pierre doesn't try to fuck your girl, and Pierre says to him, I fucked your girl and I didn't even try, and he walks off, but then that's when he discovers the fucking dog corpse.

There is some kind of liquid leaking from beneath the door of an outhouse, an old wooden door, flaked white. Pierre approaches and goes to open it. Max shouts to him not to do that. Don't go in there if I was you, he says, and then he says, it's a work in progress, he says, what the hell, a clumsy attempt at sculpture, he says, an installation by an idiot savant, he says, and now he is ranting and talking to himself about killing as naive art, what the fuck is he on about, as Pierre opens the door to a charnel house scene where a dog's body has been torn apart and which lies, spatchcocked, its poor back broken so that it looks like a bat, like the stuff of the first nightmare, its wings spread and nailed to the floor, and holy fuck, Pierre cries, you fucking crucified a dog, and Max says, no, not correct, *we* crucified a dog, *we* took apart the body of a dog, *we* exposed the inner workings to the outside, he said, and when I say *we*, he said, I mean myself and your Frater Jim, but what the fuck, Pierre says, this is just pointless fucking cruelty, and Max said, you honour only cruelty with a point? and Pierre told him to fuck off, and the dog's face, the dog's face is fucking missing, oh Christ, what the fuck did you do with its face, Pierre demands, and he imagines its smooth, peeled-off face, lying folded somewhere like a towel, and he said, Jim has the skills of the old masters, he said, the old masters, Max says, which is a figurative art, which is a technology of reproducing reality, he says, perfectly, and he believed that dog to be a fake, Max said, and so he enlisted me in its kidnap, he said he feared it had escaped from some aborted tests he had made when he released automatons of his own creation into the wild, Max went on, and Pierre was incredulous, but you know he is ugly as sin, Max says, come on, we admit he is ugly as fuck, and Pierre says, sure, he is one ugly motherfucking giraffe-looking creature, that's for sure, he says, well that's because he is literally wearing someone else's face, Max said, he got built a new face after he was scarred in the war, he said, and now he skins the face off dogs in revenge? Pierre said, and Max just said, compassionless love, he said, yes to what is, he said, even as the faces are peeled from dogs and they are nailed to the ground like bats while we search for signs of creation inside their bodies, and Pierre says, for fuck sake, what are you, a fucking paranoid schizophrenic now? were you looking for a fucking bug, for a fucking recording device? and Max said, no, we were looking for the fingerprints of its creator, and that's it, they both stare at each other in silence in this garden that has been imagined so many times now, this garden that is multiple, now, this multiform garden that features a crucified and eviscerated dog, now, and what the fuck did Jim do with this new face of his, Pierre says to Max after a time and Max said, he returned to where he was born and remarried his widow, again, he said, the woman who had long believed him to be dead, he said, he remarried her in secret, without her ever suspecting that he was the same lover, come back, all over again, he said, that is what he did with his second face, and plus he held his tongue, too, and never ever told her he had come back, and okay, that's a good one, okay, Pierre says, that's a good one, I'll give you that, fuck me but that is a sense of poetry right there that your man Jim has, he says, and he feels a little awe at the balls of this giraffe-faced monstrosity, whether he's telling the truth or not but fuck me, something in his face looks exactly like that, he has to admit, and then Pierre says to Max, so what happened to his wife and didn't he ask us if we were gay almost straight away, and Max says, his wife died, he says, his wife died soon after he remarried her, he said, and Pierre said, don't fucking tell me, he cut her open to see if he could find his own fingerprints, and Max laughed, ha ha, he said, that's a fucking good one, you are on top form, Pierre, he said, and then he said, I was spoken to by a disembodied head that called itself the Lion of Judah from the bottom of a well in Africa, he said, just so long as we are stating bald facts incredulously, he said, and then he said, his wife and our mad giraffe friend moved in together, and she went to hammer in a nail to hang a picture, what picture? Pierre interrupted him, well, it's funny you should ask, Max said, because I believe it to number among one of your favourites, and Pierre says, I know what you are going to say, she went to hang the painting by Pieter Brueghel the Younger of peasants in winter, and Max says, grow some imagination, you louche, he says, this is France, baby, he actually says, and then he says, she went to hang a reproduction of Goya, and Pierre said to him, don't fucking tell me, it was Saturn devouring his young, but no it fucking wasn't, Max said, it was *The Third of May*, bitch – because by now he was out of control – and Pierre said, Jesus, no, and Max said, yes, but she was never able to hang that particular date on her wall due to the fact that she hammered a nail straight into an electricity cable and fried her brains out on the spot.

Events were overtaking them. Ideas were running wild. They stood there, silent, at the tipping point of our tale.

Then: did you know that Goya's headless corpse is buried inside his own art? Max said to Pierre. It's true, Max said, although it's also true that Max was drunk as fuck by this point, and stoned, and off his head on smack. When Goya's body was disinterred it turned out it was missing its head, so they took what was left and reburied it in the Hermitage of Saint Anthony of the Flowers in Madrid, Max said, the walls of which are lined with frescos Goya painted in his lifetime. And what about his head? Pierre asked. It has never been found, Max said. It has never been found because Goya's head is secreted in his art, Max said, Goya's head is secreted in the ark that illuminates *The Third of May*. Fucking hell, Pierre said, and the two of them just stood there. Fucking hell.

And now we have crossed over, and our tale starts to unravel, and Max kills himself, out of the blue, with no hint or build-up or any sense of dramatic denouement beyond this feeling, already stated, of being out of balance, beyond this feeling of somehow pushing beyond some kind of tipping point, although of course he had been behaving in such an extreme way perhaps they should have spotted the signs, but they were living as part of a black magick commune, so I think we can forgive them if the signals were a little muddied, but now they are sat around the table, and they are talking with Pierre who had some commissions coming in by this point, whose career as an architect, by this point, was starting to take off, he was starting to receive commissions, grants, acclaim, whereas Max was really only feted, publicly at least, as a never-guessed and non-rumoured half of Paimon, so where was his own signature, so that Max was contemptuous when Pierre announced he had taken big money for designing a building from a multinational company that had historical links to the Nazis, and Pierre had called him out on it, what about compassionless love, he said, and Max said, is it really, watching someone you could otherwise help, writhing, drowning, in a pathetic ditch, was he talking about himself, was it a cry for help, Max was incoherent at this point, drunk, and stoned, as usual, and he said, is it really, again and again, and then he brought up the case of The Kommandant, the unknown artist whose works had been identified, and verified, as being from the same hand – Lord knows how – in concentration camps around Poland, appearing in the early to mid-1940s, like environmental art with pointless tunnels that turned in on themselves to nowhere but that were miles long despite themselves, or the inexplicable three-tiered target signs, cut into barbed-wire fences around the camps, like an RAF sign or the three layers of hell, and Max said, the only person with the ability to create that kind of art is a Kommandant, is a prison guard, is an insider, and Pierre came back at him, quoting some fantasy or science fiction author, and he said to him, the only people that do not approve of escape are the prison guards themselves, he said, but Max ignored him and instead he leaned across the table and took Hildegard's hand, with a dramatic motion, and looked into her eyes, and kissed her goodnight, and then he rose from the table, and went upstairs, to the guest room in Delius's invisible house of the brain named France, in the summer of 1985, and with his one good arm shot himself three times – miraculously, impossibly – through the head, and died thereafter.

5. BASILICA OF THE BORNLESS ONE

They tell the story of the doe. Three great Tzaddikim awoke one morning to find a young doe gazing at them by the side of a small pond with two peacocks and four grey herons. The doe had a deep wound in its leg and was close to death. One of the Tzaddikim, who had been declared to be the wisest Tzaddikim in one of the secret kingdoms known only to God Himself, blessed be His name, held up his hand and made a spell that turned the doe to stone. When this was achieved the other two Tzaddikim lifted the stone and dropped it into the water so that it floated down through the water and lay there motionless at the bottom of the water. He then commanded that the birds should sing and raise the stone from slumber only when the other Tzaddikim were out of earshot. Later the wisest Tzaddikim gave a series of oral instructions where he sang to students the song of the birds. This song went unrecorded until the writings of Benzillah of Diagoras or Benzillah the Low to the Earth, whose work *The Qutub* was said to be the final resting place of the song. Indeed *The Tomb of The Song*, it became known as, with its correct enunciation hidden throughout its 241,334 words.

There is a ritual known as The Bornless One, but which is known to initiates as The Headless One, which means The Deathless One in the Light of Death but also it spells it thus: that the Light of Death is called *Monument Maker*.

There is a rumour that the Knights Templar worshipped a talking head named Baphomet.

There is a story that Frater Jim reanimated the dead and could read the future – and rewrite the past – due to powers gifted to him through great suffering and the grafting of another man's face onto his own, a man who had the power to reanimate the dead and to read the future and to rewrite the past.

There is a rumour about the disposal, in the invisible garden of Delius, in France, and the subsequent disinterring, of the decapitated body of Holy Maximilian Rehberg.

There is a literary subterranea, with access points in, and out.

We know roughly what happens in the hours following Max's death. In the hours following Max's death Pierre, we presume, and Frater Jim, it seems likely, saw through his neck with a two-man blade, the kind used for felling trees. The head then disappears, along with the ceramicist Hildegard von Strophe, who leaves the village and disappears into obscurity at this point; we think.

There is a reading of The Bornless One, we believe, MacGregor Mathers's rendering of it, we believe, and afterwards the two take the magickal name Monument

Maker, a name that is fraternal and pronounced in its sharing (cf. Paimon). A sky burial is proposed; too messy, will attract raptors from all over, the stench of the corpse will bring us to the attention of the neighbours; we can speculate, endlessly, but the point is it never happens. We can also speculate, from what we know of the history of these two, the affiliations of this pair, and of their, let's say, historical proclivities, so that we may assume, in not too fantastical a manner, that the headless corpse may have been interfered with in some way, we speculate that perhaps this notorious pair took turns embracing it, or who knows, lay down and spooned with it in the grass as it leaked all over itself, or who knows, (more probably) lay upside down with it and held it by the feet as though its head had simply been lowered down through some kind of noumenon from out of the air, as if poor Maximilian merely dipped his head into the waters of death as an intrigue or a refreshment.

And then, this final water, this first stone: Pierre is living in an industrial container in an abandoned quarry in France, somewhere isolated, somewhere impossible and unexpected. He is engaged in building a city beneath the waves. Occasionally he puts his head in. He gets down on his hands and knees and he dunks his head into the waters, which is a murk of shapes, which is permanently occluded, but which he recognises as something that is *not himself*.

The light of a religious painting is facile, now. The light in a rotten old cloister, in a monastery, in the summer of its abandonment is, too, facile, compared to the way the light is never still beneath the waves, although, of course, go too deep and it is darkness forever, but it is in the rising up, into the sun, from beneath the waves, the blessed rising up, that we hold our trust in, because it is where religious art finds its summer, its perfect meridian, in resurrection.

But the cathedral does not want to be built. Pierre has become a mere architect. And as his fame and reputation grow he publishes, privately, *Full Length Mirror*, that enigmatic account of a summer, that guide to odd religious architecture, complete with those evocative photographs, and those strange lines about how the elements are longing in love for everything that they are not, he publishes it privately, in a subscription edition, though secretly most of the copies end up at the bottom of the flooded quarry, where he drops them in, one by one, into that same mirror that held a whole city beneath it, an inverted world to which he made offerings of a single summer. And where has Frater Jim gone?

Perhaps he is with a new face, perhaps he has returned as someone in disguise, perhaps he lurks, still, on the edge of our telling, secreting himself in our story as another character completely. Perhaps he is an assistant on the realisation of the Church of Christ the Scientist, as designed by Pierre Melville, in the fields, outside East Kilbride, in Scotland, all that is left of which, now, is an overgrown car park, with scorch marks still in the stone, as if Christ had touched down in his spaceship and everyone had gone running, is all that's left of Pierre's first modernist church which was known locally as The Slab, The Pool Table and, yes, unbelievably, as though precognitive of its future as ruins (which is the spell cast by the ugliest of architecture, I'm sorry to say but it's true): The Multi-Storey Car Park.

Or was he, perhaps, a senior assistant at the Church of
Scotland's strange, funereal seminary built on an old MOD
air force base in Fife which was known locally as The
Sightless Head, and now it feels like the very stone itself
is dreaming this tale, that sat around the world there is
the topography of this story, dreaming itself into existence,
churches and monasteries as First Stone, and Final, which
is the name of another church, the First Church of the
Stone of Silent Witness, who continue on, in the absence of
Max and Pierre (although let's be honest, we cannot say for
sure as to the continued absence of Frater Jim, due to his
ability with faces, and the nature of his powers, which we,
after much research, are in no position to doubt, even as we
doubt his very identity, the very cut of his jib), and who are
all stony-cold and implacable in their coming back all over
again.

Pierre argued in *Full Length Mirror* that Christ remained
innocent, but God didn't, God didn't, so He blinded himself
in a turning away from His son and His fate, but truly
it was Christ that was blind, and that was untainted
and pure, Christ was, like stone is, because there was no
volition, which is what Pierre says live on *Pebble Mill at
One* with Angela Rippon when he declares his final project
to be a secret tomb for a private benefactor, I too am in the
service of God, as Christ was, he says, and I thank God for
it, he says, because there but for the grace of God go I, he
says, and God is in almost every sentence of this talk and
people are appalled or think he has a messiah complex, and
instead of gargoyles to vomit wretched rain down cathedral
walls Pierre installed lightning conductors on the roofs of
his modernist churches, at the zenith of his strange ugly
car parks and stacked stone towers and huge uncarved

monoliths he installed attractors, so that when the clouds
came together and gave birth to light, and sound, from soft
friction, up above, like the account in The Bible of the true
beginnings of the world, that the stone would receive it,
and would channel the storm, and although The Sightless
Head has fallen, its remains exist, and still, it is a place
of veneration for the faithful, for the faithful of the First
Church of Cold Stone, cold bone, this place of the skull,
as it stares out over the sea, passive, and alone, now it is
an evacuated head, a skull blown open, by a trio of shots
from an illegal handgun, is what it best resembles, now,
now that all the windows are smashed in, and this book is
its dreaming, and the sides exposed, and the windblown
through it, and even, on a recent visit, sheep living in the
reception area, and there is a ritual, we have researched
this, and there are still factions of believers out there in this
world that genuflect towards the precise location of this
skull-shaped concrete derelict, in honour of art, and vision,
and eternity, fair enough, but also in honour of pathetic
things like subservience, having no ideas of your own
whatsoever, mistaking someone else's story for yours, and
just generally being deluded clowns, all the same, but
then you think, what about true love, is that not the same
thing, being subservient to an idea and demonstrating a
commitment to true love as something that you bow down
to, this yielding to something that is *not you*, and I realise
I may be exceeding my remit here, and stepping outside
of my jurisdiction, but by being able to say, I am less than
this power, is that what naivety means, what true love,
uncomplicated, and pure-spirited, is all about – ye shall be
as innocent as stone, commandeth the Lord, does he not
– and so it starts to look like some kind of weird bait-and-
switch-type set-up, in that really the only person capable

of taking on the sins of the world is God, and not Jesus,
but in some kind of weird gross act of reverse humility
God pretends that Jesus has to shoulder all of the blame
himself when really He knows, full well, that He Himself
will, silently, and forever, deal with it on His own, which is
like when your dad pretends you are going to jail for some
pathetic misdemeanour and you are terrified out of your
wits even though secretly he just has to pay off your fine
forever, and he has already agreed to it, to which you either
want to say, that is the true labour of a god, or, you know,
basically, you vindictive bastard.

And, giving further credence to the idea that the raising
of these poems in stone, (poems to stone), (poems to
permanence and absence), (stones in poems), was some
kind of autobiographical statement, some kind of hermetic
personal ritual dedicated to the preservation, (in stone), of a
certain summer, is the rumour, much circulated at the time,
that the commercial works of Pierre Melville, works that
ran from the notorious stone windmill ('Melville's Folly') in
Africa through to the simple stone cube positioned on Skaw
Beach, in Shetland, with the enigmatic markings on its
sides,

~^~*~^~

when taken together made up a map of the solar system
akin to the one in the Paimon story 'Victory Garden', where
each building, in the precise ratio of the distance between
them, and their comparative sizes, in their precise hewing-
to-scale, matched the relationship of the planets in our
solar system, out here in the Milky Way, out here in the
loneliness-to-scale of the Orion Arm of the Milky Way,
which makes of the poor, blasted Sightless Head in Fife,
Saturn, unsurprisingly, as if it were literally written in
the stars, and let me point you to Venus, which sits on a
beach in Normandy, now, as stone is drawn to the sea, as
Venus is Aphrodite, is as a pillbox on a beach in the South
of France, a simple cube, fallen from the sky, and Pluto

may as well be a single grain of sand on the Faroe Isles, for
all that astronomy cares, and there are those, too, I don't
doubt, that have followed the stations of this solar system
as devoutly as pilgrims on their way to Holy Canterbury,
which is to follow the path of The Lovers, and earth is an
invisible garden in France, where The Lovers dreamed
a dream, and the sun itself, then, is a stone windmill in
Africa, a huge stone windmill in Africa whose arms would
block out the sun behind the sun, and divide it into rays
that pilgrims would dance around arm in arm at certain
points of the year, they would dance in and out of the light
that the stone windmill provides, and would be called
pagan, which is what a stone windmill as the site of the
sun would do to us, even though it is modern art, surely,
and not archaic or traditional at all, and Mercury, well,
Mercury is a secret known only to initiates, it is a secret
sculpture in secret, in other words, but unlike Saturn (or
Jupiter) (say), Mercury is not recognisable as sculpture,
as building, or as anything man-made, it is unknown as
sculpture, or sign, or dwelling, it appears, rather, God-
given, and when you fall in love you can decide whether
the love is something found by you or gifted you by God, is
what Mercury says, and who would not choose of their lover
to be delivered to them by God Himself, which is to be shot
through the heart and to be called Astonished at the end of
your life.

And Mercury, too, has disappeared, now, or rather become
so confused with its setting that no one could tell you –
outside of me, secret me, who will not, and who will scurry
off like a mouse at the very suggestion – what is creation,
and what is simply the work of creation, so perfectly has it
become part of the scene, which is art's most secret wish,

that it could be mistaken for simply being, that it could be
overlooked as simply Spontaneous Beauty Occurring, so,
overlook me, please, I am as beautiful as a simple flower, is
what Pierre's secret sculpture says, come upon me naked,
it says, but the disappearance of these markers in stone
time (for this will always be the Stone Age), the absence of
these cathedrals to the first minglings of creation, their very
disappearance, is what makes us fall in love with ghosts, for
which of us is not occupied, which of us is not haunted as a
castle, which of us is not a resonant stone dungeon for all of
the dead come back to haunt us, and I nearly gave it away
there, Mars, a resonant stone dungeon, Frater Jim; I'll say
no more. But what happens next.

Next is this: Pierre goes into seclusion. Everyone thinks
he is living in luxury but really he is still kipping in an old
rusty shipping container at the arse end of some half-flooded
quarry. Then he does the thing on *Pebble Mill*, the thing.
Then he disappears.

You have to wonder what happened to all their books.
Where is that library? And what was in it? Is there anything
more seductive than a great, secret, uncatalogued library,
newly dispersed to the winds?

And then what happens: a body is discovered. A body is
discovered come down a river entombed in a mysterious
stone. It is a river of Africa. An unknown stone is come
upon by a group of villagers in a river of Africa, which like
the garden of Delius is for us an invisible village, a village
of the mind, as a book is, an unknown stone is carried on
a current throughout this book and is now washed up at a
village of Africa in this book where the villagers claim that

they heard the stone speak, which is why they attempted
to prise it apart and when asked in this book, in the village
of this book which we must imagine, what sound this stone
spoke in, it was described as being like *a screeching bird*,
like *a parakeet*, was the consensus, like a *warning cry* or
a *territorial marking*, but then they thought, someone
is entombed in the stone, they said, are there floating
cemeteries now, they wondered, has someone been sealed
in concrete (like a doomed dam worker on the Colorado
River, is how the song goes, fallen into the wet concrete
below), and so they lift this stone from the water, this coffin
stone, is how they describe it, this black headstone, and it
makes the sound again, the sound which one of the villagers
impersonates, it goes Ook, Ook, she says, for it is a female
villager with a lazy eye who presents the impersonation,
Ook, she says, Ook, and she waggles her arms like a chicken
or maybe an actual parakeet, who knows, and when they lift
this coffin stone from out of the river they are surprised at
how light it is, that's exactly what the female villager with
the lazy eye says, can you imagine her, she says, *it was as
if the stone was filled with light*, she says, which is an odd
thing to say but not if you think of how light the sky is when
it is filled with light, which means, I think, that there was
some kind of confluence of the elements going on, is absence
light, is light mass, is absence present, is mass absence,
are the thoughts going through these villagers' minds, we
can imagine, as it goes through our minds, our invisible
minds in concert with this book, as we imagine Delius, in his
garden, which now is the tomb of the song, and this stone,
light-filled, now risen from the waters and prised apart,
yes, that is the beautiful phrase we will use because to be
prised apart is what the first stone demands, and it is love
that makes demands, I don't care what you say, call me

apolitical, it is love, ultimately, that makes demands, and
that is to be prized, apart, so as to come together, all over
again, and so they crack it open, they crack open this light-
as-air tomb, and what do you think they find, well, first they
talk about the sign that was engraved on the front,

(~^~*~^~)

which the villagers, and there were three villagers in the
beginning, we will reveal at this point there were three
female villagers, although one goes completely unrecorded
except for her presence, except for her attendance there
is nothing else known about her, as if a lazy eye permits
us knowledge, as if the scarification on the other villager,
which appears as tiny tears, or as footprints, away from,
and into, her glassy blue eyes, as pools of pure water in
an endless desert, is how we will imagine her now, in this
book of invisible encampments, and she says, it was a sign
of the sun coming up between the mountains, was how she

read it, she says, in a badly subtitled interview afterwards,
and then her companion with the imagined lazy eye says,
no, to me it was a woman lying back and giving birth, and
she says, her legs are raised, in calipers, and the sun is
shone between them, she says, in the same badly served
translation, she says it, but then she says, ah, she says, it
is the third eye on a Chinaman, I realise, it is the creased
forehead of a guru, she says, it is a Sahdi Song, she says,
but she declines to elaborate, but what I have gleaned is
that a Sahdi Song is a song that sounds like it is coming
from a long way away, just as tears often feel as if they
have been coming forever, just as tears feel as if they were
forever being cried, just to arrive, now, in our eyes, is the
feeling that she received from the presence of this light-
filled grave on the waters at this village of Invisible Africa,
is a rendezvous, she is saying, which is one hell of a way to
think of everything that appears right in front of you, that
it set off towards you somewhere round about the beginning
of time, that heartbreak and tears have been stalking you
since year zero, and love too, and magic, also, set out long
ago, as their companions, and here it is, now, an impossible
light-filled stone on the water had made its way towards
us, they said, this first three, and it was crying in distress,
is what the woman with the water-filled eyes is saying in
this book as if it were a memory or a fact, but how else has
it come to us, and it is as if we are uncovering some kind of
secret causeway, some underground railroad, some series
of words and letters that would allow us ingress, and they
start to break the stone apart like in a rescue mission and
it seems almost impossibly dense compared to how light-
filled it appears to be, and it is designed like an Egyptian
bark but like a motorboat too, our lady of the pale-blue
eyes says, because there is an engine, she says, and the

first uncovering, through pickaxe and crowbar, and what were they doing with a pickaxe and crowbar at the river that sunny morning, it begins to sound more and more suspicious, or devious, maybe, devious is the word for the beginnings of us all, after all, but in its unlikelihood is its truth, it seems to me, but they split part of it apart, they sunder it like an Old Testament God, and there they have it: a white cube, all stained and damp with the tears that have been chasing after it, no doubt, and they say it is hermetically sealed, although of course they do not, they say no such thing, the subtitles say, I should say, the subtitles say, they say something like – and this is going on memory now, faulty memory in a book about imagining – something like, there were no seams with which to prise an entrance, I think it was, and seamless, I thought, seamless, not even a pair of testicles is seamless, but this seamless cube takes some imagining, which is as it should be, because as gods cannot we always do better, so they uncover this thing in a white cube, which is like a square of mathematics, I think, now, which is like an imposition of rules, well, okay, stone is the first rule, so what, and inside this impregnable white cube there is a dreaming head, is what this story goes on to reveal, and they take it out and it is a Sightless Head, a Sightless Head whose face has been effaced, whose face has been supplanted, whose face has been removed, and they say, oh my God it is a faceless head speaking and this is what it speaks:

Ook.

And then they discover the body, inside. It is a stone sarcophagus that floats on the water and it is the tomb of a man. And his face, there is something wrong with his face.

His face has been augmented, is how the badly subtitled
interview puts it, his face has been augmented, by which the
natives meant (natives, how offensive, although native is
one thing I have never felt, one thing that has been denied
me, in my voyeurism) he was wearing a death mask, they
thought at first, and they thought, this white man dressed
in a formal suit is wearing the face of his ancestors in death,
perhaps, they thought, and they reached out and they were
almost able to insert their fingers beneath the skin, they
could slide their fingers up and underneath the skin of the
face, it was a primitive job, this new face had been sewn
on, the body embalmed, dressed in a suit and tie, and then
encased in stone, and then the miraculous woman with the
pools for eyes said, it is the face of the head, and all three
of these villagers in the beginning, and this is sounding
more and more like a parable, like a Kabbalistic parable,
like the story of the doe, the story of the doe that passed
through three iterations of water as a stone, and all three
of these imagined women, these headless speakers, turn to
face the Sightless Head and it is missing more than eyes,
it is a skinned, mummified head, and its face, clearly, has
been transplanted onto the body in the tomb, and who rolled
away the stone, after all, it was three imagined women in a
garden of Africa, inevitably, who were the ones that rolled
away the stone and revealed this silently dreaming head
as the engine, this face-swapped corpse as the deliverant,
which is another word from the subtitles but this time an
inspired one, a mishearing, and my own mishearing is
to mishear the face of the head as the place of the head,
for some reason, that's how I hear it, and the place of the
head is gifted, anew, to the dead, which is why Christ is
crucified on Golgotha, which is the place of the head, of the
skull, of the head, Golgotha itself means a sightless head is

dreaming history, is what the subtitles fail to elucidate, this
is prime-time TV, what the fuck do you expect, a sightless
faceless head is dreaming history from the beginning and its
revelation is a stone that floats on the water in a river
in Africa in an invisible garden which is the mind of this
book dreaming is not prime-time viewing, so then they
call the police, this is what happens, they panic and they call
the police, which is always a last resort and let this be a
cautionary Kabbalistic tale, they call the police and the
police turn up and they panic, two police officers turn up
hours later, what the fuck took them so long, how many
bodies in Africa, I guess, but they turn up and they panic, up
until now thanks to the three dreamy disembodied women
it has all been faith and awe but now that the police are
here, well, it's big trouble, buddy, and it's a whole other
drama, as the first of the two police (for police inevitably
traffic in twos the whole world over, and now there are five
ghosts at this exhumation of the First Church of the Stone
of Silent Witness), the first police becomes the police as soon
as he sees the body, and its face, and its head, and he says
that this is fucking voodoo black magic shit and get this
the fuck out of here, this is bad voodoo, he says, this means
that someone will die, he says, this says, with certainty, he
says, that someone will die, and soon, and that violence will
take place, and that there will be much suffering across the
land, he says, he, too, is caught up in the bibliomania that
is taking place around this entombed corpse, this rolling of
the stone, and wasn't there a story that when the stone is
rolled away, in The Bible, that one of the Apostles mentions
the presence of someone else in the tomb, of an unknown
person, resident, in the tomb of Christ already, when Mary
and the girls show up, and so there is (I have always been
here before, is how the song puts it), there is an unidentified

body in the first tomb, and the police are the first to say
that this first dying presages death forever, which is why
you should never trust the pigs, and they say, get rid of
this fucking thing, they say, this fucking thing needs to be
destroyed, and seriously, one of them picks up a big fucking
rock from nearby and starts assaulting this excavated
burial, this crime scene, possibly, technically, probably,
the police just start laying into it and they don't attack the
head, it's weird, they attack the body, only, they assault the
body as if they are afraid to let go of their own ideas, they
assault the body in the name of holding off death, which
is the worst name of anything, ever, they mutilate this
precious corpse, essentially, precious because who has ever
seen anything like it, is it not incredible, this stone held
up on the waters, these arms fed into a suit, this head, its
face replaced, forever, I fear it is my favourite poem, and
I fear I may have written it, is what the violence of these
pigs says, fear of authorship goes deeper than anxiety of
influence, these pigs are saying, as they lay into this corpse,
these literary critics are expounding, and soon the corpse is
just a bloody mess and its half-sewn face is torn off and it
resembles the first man forever, which is a mashed-in man,
is that not what some other cop said, something about the
future being a boot in the face forever, typical response of
cops, this belief in the beating of corpses, in the flogging
of horses, which is why Nietzsche lost his mind, because
he was not a cop, and here are these cops, flogging a dead
horse, flailing a dead businessman, is my theory, because
then what happens is the stone disappears, the stone that
floats on water was stolen or secreted or smashed up and
sold off, but what happens is it disappears without a trace,
although go to this village in Africa, look it up, I'm not about
to add to its notoriety by naming it, go there and you will

inevitably be offered fragments, ashes, chunks, brick-loads
of black stone that claim to be from the First Stone on the
Water and most of which is mere volcanic rock, aerated
stones, badly painted replicas, and but they take away
the head, for some reason the head in the cube is taken
away, the police make the three girls lift it, by the light of
the moon, which had just then come up and made of them
silhouettes as they lifted and moved this glowing white
cube, glowing faintly now, in the dark, it has to be said,
and they carry it like some scene in *The Grapes of Wrath*,
where we view them, somehow, from an angle that pitches
them perfectly against the horizon, that makes of them dark
ciphers and ghosts, as they accompany this ghostly head on
its last verifiable journey, this dream that has dreamed this
book, certainly, this dream that has loved and been loved by
women and men, this church of memories, this Cathedral
of All Summers, and there is something tender, after the
violence, in the removal of this head, something grateful,
and forgiving, too, as we watch them from this uncanny
viewpoint where the moon seems impossibly large, and
stained yellow, in the sky, and the women like a painting, on
the moon, or a flag, flying, and this stone, silent.

And in the silence of the stone I recognised it. A detail. I
have an eye for subterranea, which is how I got my handle:
The Flashlight. In this body washed up on a river in Africa,
in this sealed stone sarcophagus, I saw the hand of Pierre
Melville, the head of Maximilian Rehberg, our spiritual
fathers, without whom few of us would have been attracted
to the hobby, I saw the hand and the head of these eccentric
occultists, these avant-garde artists, these holy fools, these
cult science fiction writers, these adventurers in literary
subterranea, these founders of this strange initiatory cult,

these figures that had inspired and had brought together
diverse weirdos from across the world, who had themselves
formed a network dedicated to literary and historical
subterranea, as we reactivated the Church of the First Stone
of Silent Witness, with a charter from no one because who
could we ask; Pierre had disappeared or gone into hiding
to work on this final commission, this private tomb, Max
Rehberg, we found out, through our researches and our
exchanges of information with other fans, was dead, and
headless, and what about Frater Jim, well, who knows
whose face he is wearing these days, and of course we wrote
to the address printed on the back cover of the rare private-
press edition of *Full Length Mirror*, as it was erroneously
translated years later, but which should have read *Two Way
Mirror*, more correctly, I believe, of the type that are used in
interrogation cells, I mean, where one wall is a mirror but
the other can see through it like glass, and even now, are
watching you through this book, but really it is vice versa, I
believe, and speaks of the odd voyeuristic pleasure that small
volume affords, that feel of eavesdropping on a summer, as it
unfolds, books make you feel as though things could be played
out forever and they cure us of time, briefly, is what he means
by a *Two Way Mirror*, I believe, and of course I misconstrue
in my mind interrogation in cells as being questions in the
body, of haemoglobin throwing its hands up in the face of
oxygen, and surrendering, silently, forever, inside the body,
in awe, which is the core of our order, this understanding of
the sacrificial nature of reality, our order which now consists
of a few hundred people from across the world drawn from
many different backgrounds and disciplines, and sure, we
have our crackpots, who doesn't, but still, our order has
made remarkable ingress, into literary subterranea, into
alternative histories, into and out of the past, and the future,

I think we can boast, succeeding, in our quest, to open out the tunnels that lie beneath literature, beneath art, within film, within anything capable of encompassing the light of death, of fixing it, long enough, so that if it might not be understood, like God's right hand, at least we may be less badly disposed towards it, and of course the hardcore practitioners, the ritual magicians with their awful goatee beards and their robes and their bedsits, they would mock us as hobbyists, as conspiracy theorists, but there was ingress, and every time I use that word I feel us sinking deeper, I feel the streams opening out a little bit, smell the effluvia, it is like a trapdoor is revealed that leads us deeper via another set of stairs, and via is a Roman road, don't you know, and I have come bearing the name The Flashlight, though where I am speaking from, or how you may visualise me as I am speaking to you inside your brain, or perhaps you are shaping me with your mouth, you retard, if so I love you best, I love the marginals, I say, I speak, I write, and it is a sound on the margin of your brain, a sound that makes you think of margins, which is what can succeed in encompassing the death of light, the light of death, for what else is up to death but life, what can contain it than other, we are bereft without endings, we are sick of ourselves without finality, and where once there was a church there is nothing, for there is nothing to build a church on, which is the first foundation, stone, I say it like that because I am an initiate of this book, I learned the way I talk from it, and so I recognised that final silent stone when I spotted the news report about it somewhere, somewhere I had read of a story of how three women in Africa had claimed to have encountered a stone as light-filled as the long-lost skies of their childhood and that there had been a body entombed in it and that a head had been stolen and disappeared, the disappeared, the disappeared, I thought to myself, I have come to return all of the disappeared, I thought, because I am romantic and inclined to poetry and theology I thought that immediately, I have come to reunite all true loves, I thought, and then I thought, wait a minute that sounds like the First Church in action, and I wired a guy I knew from the fandom, which is what we called it between initiates because of course we were geeked out about all of this, and he said, yeah, this has got to be our man, and then we managed to track down a VHS tape that someone had dubbed off the TV of this news programme in Africa where these three women who witnessed this stone on the water were interviewed, and we found this other comedian to subtitle it for us, this local clown without a clue, but then we checked it out and we were sure it was the work of the founding fathers, and I said to myself, this is it, this is the final mausoleum, this is the last working, this is that business guy who commissioned Pierre to bury him in some unmarked crypt that no one could ever visit ever, to be buried inside this thing, is what he had done, is what this head washing up on a river in Africa was all about, I told myself, and then I'm watching this video when the video cuts to what looks like a shaky handheld film of what looks like a garden at night, a garden where you can make out shapes and contours and where maybe there are secret eyes looking out at you and you sit up in your chair and holy fuck, I know that garden, is it yours, I move towards the sliding doors and as I open them the doors open on the video too, I hear myself, behind myself, and behind myself I feel the presence of something that is not me, and at that moment I step out into the garden and it is dark out there with not a soul in sight and when I walk back into the living room the video is dead and there is no sound.

6. CATHEDRAL OF THE FINAL LAKE
OF GARGOYLE

Everything visible is invisible, and everything invisible visible, and bring on the end of the world.

Murder yourself as soon as you reach perfection for fear of falling back and so bring an end to the suffering of the human race and the reign of the devouring demiurge. Birth is the gateway to the prison of the flesh, so nothing copulating ever. Self-suicide in perfection, then, for transmigration is wanderings in the desert of eternity and the body of Christ is a lie. This is what the Albigensian heresy says.

Poverty, renunciation and joy is the true cathedral, is what the Franciscan schism says.

Live in an unheated shed in the garden of your mother all the better to feel the kiss of his mouth, is what the Waldenses say.

The keepers of the true faith have nowhere to lay their heads, is what the peripatetic teachers of the Dominican

Order insist, in imitation of Christ, who was cast out of heaven, on the whim of his father, who, being greater than all things, including history, prophecy and time, must have realised the cost as soon as He set the whole thing in motion, and visioned His son, and his suffering, and his death on the cross, long before he entered history as a word, which is called Perfect.

A blind man sits on a bench next to the river on which a stone is held afloat. He raises his rifle to his blind eyes and takes a shot at it, regardless, is what the Church of the Stone of First Witness says.

When the priest at the altar utters the words hoc est corpus meum (this is my body), the wine and bread is transformed into the blood and body of Christ, is what the Fourth Lateran Council says (wow).

The true cathedral is never Gothic, for the Gothic cathedral, as invented, here, in this Island of France, marks a terrible fall in itself, and is a psychologising of God, and a neuroticising of His relationship to man, for the Gothic cathedral is stone in battle, and not in adjustment, which is minute, and imperceptible, and silent stone in the Cistercian cloister at Fontenay speaks, better, and in peace, and in justice, and is the one true church, which is silent stone, speaking, is what the Pierreists say.

Faith and reason are not opposed, faith takes up where reason ends, and reason can help to elucidate faith by metaphor and example, for can you, truly (ask yourself), reason to the end? is what Thomas Aquinas says.

We may reason to the end, is what the fundamentalist
pigs say, which is not faith, but belief, which is an entirely
different thing, and is not love of the world but truly hatred,
which is any word but is, and is what the Marxist scum say,
and the historical fantasists say, and the fascist bastards
say.

Life feeds on life, is what the mythologists say.

For I am dust, and ashes, and full of sin, and I am speaking
to the living, the eternal, and the true God, is what Martin
Luther says. And that there is no bargaining with him.

Was it in vain that the Wisdom of God hid what we are
unable to see? is what Saint Bernard of Clairvaux, author of
Liber de Diligendo Deo (*Book of the Duty to Love God*), says.

You would not be looking for me had you not already found
me, is what Pascal says.

God became man in Christ in order that man might become
God, is what the early Church Fathers say.

Union with the ultimate nothing is the highest goal of man,
is what Meister Eckhart says.

I opened my heart to the whole universe and I found it was
loving, is what the hippies say, but still they hate the bomb,
and stand in opposition.

The suffering of Christ was not necessary, as God, in His
infinite love and mercy, has more than enough forgiveness of
His own, and so the crucifixion was no true sacrifice, is what

Desiderius Erasmus almost says (if so, then exactly what was it? An example?).

God is best pleased with adoration, not theological speculation, is what Thomas à Kempis, reputed author of *The Imitation of Christ*, says.

Heat and cold come together on planet earth to create life, is what the scientists say, but what is heat and cold but love, in relation?

It's just chemicals, and atoms, and evolution, is what the ignorant moderns say, with no idea of the meaning of any of them, except their concomitant demeaning of the miracle, which is no less when called 'chemicals' and 'atoms' and 'evolution', and just as little understood.

Ook, is says. Ook.

And this is what The Bible says, about Christ, and his ministry, for the time has come to examine the claims, honestly, and without prejudice, and unmuddied by schism and by misconstruction and by heresy, is what the author of this book says.

Christ's virgin birth is only mentioned in two Gospel accounts, those of Matthew and Luke, though neither of them can agree as to when exactly this miraculous birth took place. No one else, it appears, thought it worth mentioning. Paul seems to have no inkling of it whatsoever, but he is a well-known idiot, and so means little either way. Both Matthew and Luke agree, however, that he was of the lineage of the House of David, and that he was born in Bethlehem, even though his parents, Mary and Joseph, actually lived in Nazareth. The story is that they were in Bethlehem when this otherwise unremarkable virgin birth took place because there was a census that required the man of the house to be counted in his own city, hence Joseph's return to Bethlehem. Okay.

Mark, like any good biographer, skips over the circumstances of Christ's birth altogether, because everyone knows that is always the least interesting bit in biographies (except with Jesus, woops).

Either way, we can all agree there was much rejoicing in heaven but one hell of a trouble on earth after he was born in the trough of a donkey. King Herod wanted him dead. Only three men were wise enough to even attend, along with three dumb shepherds (shepherds get a bad deal in The Bible because I think God hates them). Jesus was a dirt-poor carpenter like his dad (Joseph, not the other one, though we can assume God's skills include carpentry because He dreamed the damn thing up) and there is a story in the Apocrypha about Jesus miraculously lengthening a plank, which makes this feat exactly half as astounding as his virgin birth. But they remained skint, and neither Jesus nor his dad (the other one) are recorded as doing a single miraculous thing about it. But then there is a gap in our story. Jesus disappears and when he returns, he is preaching the Gospel. What happened in that gap we will never know, but this is a common feature of spiritual autobiography, a disappearance followed by a transformative return. Now he walked the land making flip comments like 'the kingdom of God is at hand; repent.' Then he gives his amazing speech about faith and the lilies of the field, which is the heart of the good news and the central teaching of Christ, regardless of what anyone else says:

'Take no thought for the morrow. Be not anxious for food and raiment. Look at the birds of the air: they neither sow nor reap nor gather into barns, and yet your heavenly Father feeds them. Are you not of more value than they? And why are you anxious about clothing? Consider the lilies of the field, how they grow; they neither toil nor spin; yet I tell you, even Solomon in all his glory was not arrayed like one of these. But if God so clothes the grass of the field, which today is alive and tomorrow is thrown into the oven, will He not much more clothe you, O men of little faith?'

And here I will take my own little break, my own unaccountable disappearance followed by a transformative return, so that I may privately, and unobtrusively, shed a single bright tear.

7. ERA OF SAD WINGS (2)

[Play]

[Silence]

The light of death is monument maker.

[Silence]

There is something in those so odd drawings of Hans Bellmer that is closest to reality even if he fucked his daughter. There is something about the manipulating and the rearranging of the limbs in sex. There is a picture of Max's dead body where he looks like a doll by Hans Bellmer in the rearrangement of his limbs. Of course, he already had only one arm, which was so sexy. The rearrangement of his limbs brought on by three impossible bullets to the head, brought on himself by his own volition, like I am doing just now, I am disarraying.

He is lying on the floor of the bedroom of Delius's old house, the same one with the garden that was painted invisible by his lover. And Delius died of syphilis and went blind, died of syphilis from whores and a life lived, and went blind for it, too, his calcified cock, because he used up all his sight with his greedy eyeballs, greedy eyeballs all protruding like goldfish is his cock in his pants. And here's Maxi on the floor like a broken doll, his limbs gone this way and that, and I thought, I wanted you to rearrange me, that's what I wanted most of all, baby. I wanted you to orchestrate me. And now my darling is on the floor with his limbs cast left and right and is disarrayed in a photograph forever.

[Silence]

The light of death is monument maker.

[Silence]

Have you heard of an angel called the Brown-Skinned Virgin? She came down to earth and fucked a man silly so that the image of her was left on his heart, and on his skin, beneath the veil where she fucked him. She gives you power to do things. For instance, if you wanted to stop drinking you would promise her that you wouldn't drink for a year and then miraculously you wouldn't. I promised Max I would kill my heart dead for him, but I couldn't.

When I look at that photograph, I wonder if his powers were real, my baby. My baby died to a shooting in the head. And yet he has a power on me still, my baby. Compassionless love, he said, it's compassionless love that we practise, but to me it was like killing your heart dead, but it's love, he said, no, it's true love, was what he said.

I can't tell you what went on behind closed doors, no, not
what we practised, not what went on in the initiations.
No. Not because it would blow your mind even though it
might, but because I wouldn't want to ruin it for you. I
wouldn't want to ruin it for anyone who might be thinking of
initiation themselves. If you knew it then it wouldn't work,
that's all I'm saying, or wouldn't work as good, is what I'm
saying, so I guess I am saying it works, and here I am all
over myself again.

Their ideas were aristocratic, though really most of them
were manifested in art, and in writing. They pictured a
ruling elite, they were anti-democrats, and so people called
them fascists. People? People weren't even listening. They
envisaged a band of warrior monks, aesthetes and thinkers
and spiritual libertarians who were tough enough to kill
their hearts dead so they could beat off the barbarians
when they came running. 'Cause that's the trouble with
intellectual spiritual aristocratic types, on the whole,
Maxi said, they're normally a bunch of crap poofs who are
overthrown at the first sign of a thug. To beat an illiterate
thug half to death is a mercy beating, is compassionate and
graceful, was the thinking.

Here's how they attracted initiates. They left cassette
tapes in strategic locations. Cassette tapes with specific
instructions and the build-up was intense. We would
announce initiations taking place, initiations taking place,
we would say, this is the Church of the Stone of First
Witness, we would say, initiations taking place, and we
would give a precise set of instructions, a precise set of
instructions in a voice like an automaton or a mannequin
or a music box or a computer – to be here at a certain time,

to find your way here – and we would leave the cassettes
in phone boxes and in charity shops and pop them through
random letter boxes and drop them in shopping baskets and
on church pews in the dark and then we would wait.

Who listens to cassette tapes that just appear in front of
them and then goes ahead and obeys their commands?
Would-be initiates do, was the thinking, the faithful, in
themselves, and the rightness of how things went, was the
thinking. Which was our core audience, was the thinking.

And we would wait at the intimated location, *the intimated
location* was what Max always called it, always those words,
and Pierre and Jim the Giraffe as well, and we would wait
in the dark and mostly they would never show up, but
sometimes they would, and we would hood them and put a
knife to their throats and wrestle them downstairs and into
a back room as if we had press-ganged them into life itself,
which is where it would begin and what I can't tell you any
longer. Soon we had a band of believers, a mission of cold
dead hearts.

[Fast Forward]

[Play]

claimed he liked psychedelic rock, but really his favourite
song was 'We Are the World'. This was our favourite ritual
I can tell you about. We would watch a video recording of
'We Are the World' and we would try to name everyone as
they appeared on camera as quickly as we could and every
time we would do it Maxi thought Dionne Warwick was Tina
Turner and he would shout, there's Tina, before going on

to, I don't know, George Harrison, I think, it's a long time
since I have watched this video because my heart would
surely break to see it one more time and not want to name
anyone, any more, except to want to get Tina Turner wrong,
come back and get Tina Turner wrong all over again, Maxi,
my baby, and he had so many different faces, my Maxi,
so many looks, you would never tire of his face, his good
looks, because every time you would see in it a mystery,
you have the body of a twenty-one-year-old, he would say
to me, and he wouldn't even open his eyes when he said it,
he is feeling me with his fingers and he has his cock inside
me, his hard cock and trying to sleep with that, sometimes
he would pulse it, in his sleep, he would pulse his beautiful
cock inside me and I would wonder how can you stay hard
all night and I guess it's because he was non-stop thinking
about sex when he was unconscious, that's what he would
say, my night-time thoughts are pure sex, baby, he would
say, or he would pull me and throw me over him so I was on
top and he would take my tits in his mouth, my twenty-one-
year-old tits, baby, I would say to him, you like that baby,
he would say, you like sucking my beautiful tits, I would
say, and we gave each other those gifts, the words we gave
as gifts to each other, and somewhere it is written forever,
right

[Fast Forward]

[Play]

enter me best that way, I gasped, I gasped when he entered
me that

[Fast Forward]

[Play]

of an outtake when he was trying to record his lines for 'We
Are the World' and it was our favourite cult film and we
would watch it and laugh so much at Dylan because he could
barely stand and his singing is awful and Lionel Richie
is starting to despair but even Dylan is laughing, he is
laughing at how laughable the whole scene is, he is laughing
at how awful his singing is, he is impressed that he is so
wasted and unconcerned on an afternoon spent recording a
big charity single and he says things like, I think you can
just go ahead and delete that one right away, he says, and
he laughs at no one in particular, and we would laugh too,
for pure joy at that video which was our cult favourite back
when we had just met and instantly fallen in love and when
they would sing, 'we are the children', I knew it was us, back
in the garden, they were singing about you and me, Maxi,
and the way that we fit, together, in an invisible garden.

[Fast Forward]

[Play]

no, the Nazis never cared for animals, he said, the Nazis
made robot dogs, he said, the Nazis created strange
mutations, he said, because it was the only way their hearts
could feel, instead, he said, instead we make of our hearts
a mighty fortress, was what he said, and then, he said, we
yield, that was the phrase he would repeat when I asked
him about dogs and trust and vivisection and what the
Nazis were up to during the war, when he would kneel by
the bath and stroke the single leaf of a plant like a dying
relative in a peaceful hospice at the very end of their life.

[Rewind]

[Play]

into the bathtub one by one and he would kneel down next
to them and he would clean the dust and the weird mites
and the disease from their leaves with a soft wet cloth and
he would take each trembling leaf in his hand and he would
spread them out and then he would run the cloth along all
of the veins in the leaf, and he would do it so delicately, like
a hand in marriage, like a trembling nuptial palm, and I
thought of Hitler and his dog, didn't Hitler love a dog and
care for animals and paint flowers growing up? No, the
Nazis

[Fast Forward]

[Play]

seafood restaurant we loved to cycle to where we would sit
outside and always order a prawn cocktail in a big cup with
a long spoon at the noisy market where you could watch
everything going on in the street and I would have tomato
ketchup in mine and Maxi would pull a face even though his
glass was basically crazier and didn't even have any salad
in it, only prawns and hot green Tabasco sauce like they do
it in Mexico, only this is France, silly, and a place that sold
steaks, steaks from Argentina, I think, only it had a wide
smoking gallery where we would sit and smoke for hours
and share the same piece of steak back and forth, and some
wine, and a Corona beer, like they do it in Mexico, only
this is France, Maxi, how about a Kronenbourg 1664, you
silly, and we sat on a bench in the square and Maxi told me

316

this awful story about his mother, how at the end she was alcoholic and dying of cancer and would get drunk and take pills and end up naked in the bath and unconscious and he found her there, naked, with her head all shaved and dying of cancer, and passed out unconscious, and how he couldn't lift her, how he couldn't lift his old bald sick mother out of a coma in the bath, basically, and then the ambulance arrived and it took the ambulanceman and himself, combined, to lift his bald naked mother, she was naked as well as bald in there, you can picture the scene, and she's dying and who knows, has probably gone on herself already, but then Maxi says that while he was waiting for the ambulance to arrive that he had the urge to strip off his clothes and get into the empty bathtub with his dying mother, his dying mother who has passed out cold and who knows, undoubtedly wet herself, he climbs in but he can't fit next to her, he can't move her and there's no room, so as he has to go top-to-tail with her, he has to lie down with his face at her feet and his feet up around her passed-out face, and he takes her feet in his hands, these hideous old feet, who could imagine them, and he holds a foot in each hand and right then I saw him there, with this delicate plant, in the bath, stroking this trembling leaf, at the end, and that was the first great lesson that love taught me against my will.

Who knows where else in the story these words are speaking.

[Silence]

It's autumn now. The warm September of my years. And I feel Maxi as if risen out of the page. And come in, a man.

Maxi, darling, how much did you love me, once, and he says,
all my love, he says, all my love, and he quotes to me a poem
where there is a wet road after rain like a river running
uphill, and there is a yearning to be up amongst the sun,
forever, which is to lie in your arms, princess, and when he
would call me princess I would say to him, only if you can
redefine your notion of a princess who belches and doesn't
have a magic wand and has calipers on her legs

[Fast Forward]

[Play]

about how we are the first lovers, about how it is like two
people invented fucking, like we had no idea of technique
or of the rules of love or etiquette or performance, or words
for it, even, we just went at it, and it was beyond language,
beyond ideas, beyond anything but the longing of the flesh
for the flesh, the best sex is beyond language, Maxi wrote to
me, and he said, that is why the best sex writing is by Julio
Cortázar in his book *Hopscotch*, where he makes up words
like

[Unintelligible] [Unintelligible] [Unintelligible]

There's nothing to do but act like you can handle it, is what
Cortázar says, this is in another poem, although he doesn't
say that exactly, I'm going on memory here, my faulty
memory which I can feel slipping away already, this poem
I remember about time being ahead and time being undone
and everything out of joint with itself, except for writing, I
think it is he says, except for writing, I believe, is his point,
so write for the present, he says, and for the future, he says,

make monument of the journey, he says, then he ends on one word: turbulence, he writes. Turbulence, I think, is how it ends.

But I won't talk about poetry too much, although poetry is my love, poetry and ceramics, in the end, and I combined the two throughout my life, I have worked to reconcile poetry and life, which is to cure yourself of poetry, to walk out the other side of it, like Rimbaud, Rimbaud, too, who wanted to be up in the sun and forever, only I used ceramics

[Fast Forward]

simple things on simple plates that I painted and hand-glazed myself in a workshop just along the way from the imaginary garden we inherited from Delius, for a summer, anyway, when the three of us lived there, Pierre and Maxi and myself, and I would rise in the mornings and leave Maxi sleeping, as blind and as fulfilled and as dreaming of a garden as old Delius himself, and I would tiptoe out, into the sunshine, into the hot street with voices calling from windows and a stray drunk from the night before, and speak to the white-haired man that ran the boulangerie in my nightmare French and he would laugh and I would take a coffee and a little cherry tart and I would head for my studio with the light streaming through the high windows – it was an old garage where I think buses had been stored – and I would paint dancing figures on these plates and I would adorn them with words, that's exactly what I would do, adorn with words, my Maxi, who walked me through poetry and out the other side, is what he did, and then we actually used them and never put them on display ever, which meant I barely made a penny to support my art except

for when friends and neighbours bought stuff from me or
commissioned me to do something for them, but my plates
were simple spells, minor enchantments, tiny little gifts
for the times that were ours and our attempt at living in
them, Maxi and I, and our delightful eccentric friends who
claimed they were out to cure themselves of magic, which
meant they were looking to be disenchanted, they wanted
to cure themselves of magic like I intended to walk out the
other side of poetry, which is like Rimbaud up in the sun,
Rimbaud, Rimbaud, Rimbaud, Rimbaud up in the sun, and
with an emu stood outside his house, which is made of clay

[Fast Forward]

[Play]

that summer, in Grez-sur-Loing

[Silence]

[Fast Forward]

[Play]

[Silence]

and believing it took magic to cure you of magic, which is
magic's most secret wish, with these simple plates that I
cast with circles of dancing women in abstract shapes as if
on a flag on the moon, a figure of universal hope, I think we
can safely say forever, is a group of women dancing arm in
arm, but then I think, wait, what if it were Nazi women at
a party, what if it were Nazi wives backstage at Nuremberg

having a right old knees-up, but then I thought do you
forfeit your right to joy by being complicit in the destruction
of another's, but then I thought, well, but, where's the joy in
that, so I went daring and went for universal joy

[Silence]

which was the spell of these plates, I believed, but then
again, everything was magical, we believed, in our right
to joy, I think, at the expense of nothing, Maxi would say,
because we asked for no more than what we had, dreamed
of no less than everything in front of us, my Maxi and I,
dreaming so deep, doing sex magick, which means waking
up to the current running though you and your princess,
which literally comes out through the crown like a beam
of light illuminating how holy your union is, which is what
is happening every minute, in reality, which is copulating,
this is what they taught, I'm giving nothing away here,
everything is copulating, change is the base erotic, from the
displacement of my limbs in the arms of my lover through
the displacement of his own in the arms of his death, so
allow yourself a devilish smile, Maximilian.

[Fast Forward]

[Play]

one same point again and again forever, which is that we
are all in on the game

[Silence]

[Fast Forward]

[Play]

I no longer have the guts to blow my own brains out, not
now that I should, not now that it is necessary

[Rewind]

[Play]

twilight, I can no longer be brave, for the weight of
memories I can no longer be brave, and now of course we
have his true name, Maxi's true name, for it was finally
spoken in death, death is the speaker of the true name,

[Silence]

is the idea I am coming to in my dotage now, as I prepare
to give up on ideas whatsoever, and late at night we would
do Tarot readings in the garden, the garden that we named
France, this garden in France that we named France itself,
we would say, let's eat in France tonight, and France was
the invisible garden in the mind of Delius, and we would
deal the cards and Jim the Giraffe would read the cards in
France and when he turned over The Emperor he would say,
the wound that is given birth to must be greater than the
wound that gives birth, and he would say it was his father,
The Emperor was his father breaking the bonds of the
grave, he would say, through love, he would say, through
the power of love my father has returned as one of the living
dead, he would say, and he would regale me and Maxi and
Pierre and I with the tale of his recurring dreams wherein
his father comes back as a zombie, every time he is worse
for wear, his leg is gone, he is holding in his own entrails,

half his face is putrid, and he eventually realises that it is
because he is unable to let his father go, and because his
father still loves him, that he is breaking the bonds of the
grave, even as he has become a zombie, even as his eyes are
pleading with Jim to let him go – he is dead, Jim, can't you
see – and when Jim finally lets him go, he disappears, and
never returns in dreams, and that is where the archetype
of the zombie comes from, Jim says, and it comes from true
love, he says, The Devil, he says, is an eroticising of change,
he says, and we are back to the copulating forever, which is
so devilish, and we require

[Fast Forward]

[Play]

cards with his horror-show face that looked more like the
Tarot of Mr Potato Head, dealing the cards and talking
about The Devil and his father and how The Tower was the
whole edifice of personality when it becomes like a suit of
armour that protects you from reality, from the fullness of
experience of the world, from speaking your secret name,
which The Devil can help with, for sure, and a card like The
(Lovely) Star, it is me with my calipers on and wearing a
mask of stars that I can't even see clear out of and putting a
single toe in this wave that is lapping against the shore and
knowing that all it requires is a first simple toe-in-the-water
and allow it to sweep me away, I wanted to take life as my
lover when I was with Maxi, to make love to life, and they
call that soft, they call that sentimental, when Perry Como
sings it, but then there is that punk song that is so soft, 'God
Save the Queen', with the beautiful refrain of No Future,
and I heard it as Always Now, No Future, Always Now, and

understood it completely as the same love magic we worked in our Church, which really was just the name of a group of fellows who saw themselves best reflected in each other and a part of the same passing-through of a certain moment in time. And we say it in my dying, now, too.

I no longer have the guts to blow my own brains out, not now that I should, not now that it is necessary. I no longer have that flair for the dramatic gesture. I'm sheltering in literature. I've failed to step out of the book. I'm still writing it, here, on my own, instead of living it, out there. I'm no Rimbaud. But we ran wild in it, once, didn't we, baby?

[Silence]

I have argued with myself long and hard about the best way to go; the easiest (and so the saddest) form of self-murder will be mine. I intend to go under mush-mouthed with pills. Mush-mouthed with pills, how I love to say that phrase, imagine me foaming at the mouth and mush-mouthed with pills as I pass away, for that is how I would like to be remembered, which is to be in France and to say the word France, to be in Rimbaud and to say the word Africa, and look at me all going there already, mush-mouthed and foaming, where is Africa, I asked Maxi, where did you have to go to get to Africa, and he said, it is not on any map, the Africa of holy Maximilian Rehberg is not on any map, well, okay, I want to go there with you too, sweetie, in that case, for I am your wife in eternity

[Silence]

and what did we learn from our time together in this
Church of Final Foundations, this Cathedral of First Stones,
and lucky for you and me we learned nothing and even now
are taken, unblemished by knowledge, up into the

[Silence]

was Rimbaud's final mistake and Jim the Giraffe's best
realisation, which is that to be down below is voluntary exile
from the sun, and that what disappears can rise again, in
love, which is why there is a summer every year, because
the promise of eternal life is a promise that can never be
broken, are promises on earth broken, did life make a
promise at the very beginning, with death too, in the end,
in the end my mouth feels like candyfloss and helpless and
I am lolling like a baby in a harness, but I doubt that death
made a promise in the end, in the end I doubt that death
made a promise in the beginning.

I made a promise to my Maxi always to be true in my
heart and then I ran off with Pierre. Pierre was older. He
ridiculed me and treated me badly and bullied me until
I felt like I was back at school with my one true teenage
crush. Maxi and Pierre were writing these science fiction
stories together, these amazing outlandish tales, and selling
them to magazines and then they started to get published
and someone tracked them down and came to the village to
interview them, which was the one name, Paimon, Paimon
was the combined name of the two of them that they wrote
under and when I read the stories I said, who did what,
and they said they wrote them like an exquisite corpse,
which is a surrealist idea, which makes them channelled
texts, in my book, and my book includes things like *A Vision*

by Yeats as a book, who I dearly loved, and of course *The Book of the Law*, by Aleister Crowley, as a book, and both those books were channelled by women for men, and I am a silent channel in time, now, channelling what we did and the comings and goings in those years as I swoon towards extinction, as my brain clouds and my hands shake but I continue this final telling, this final telling until my head lolls on my shoulders and I start to literally foam at the mouth, which is what they say will happen, that I will foam and bubble and sink and fall under and death will have me all spent on myself, is what they say, but Pierre says to me, come away with me, he says, let me steal you for a single summer, he says, and it sounds sexy, the way he says it, though Pierre is older, Pierre is older than Maxi, and I think can he even get it up, is that old cock of his even in working order, and of course with Maxi hard in me all night it makes a difference, but I'm tempted, girl, I say to myself, you only live once, and I think of Rimbaud and running wild in it and of my own story, I confess, it's true, I think of my own story and what will be the best twist, the most surprise ending, the most daring telling, and I think of my own exquisite corpse

[Silence]

and I start to believe I will go for it, and I commit small betrayals in preparation, I engineer scenes and situations, and at night Pierre and I sit up late, in France, in the invisible garden of the mind called France we sit up late on our own, after Maxi has passed out and been carried to bed, and Pierre talks to me of Romanesque art and of sculpture in stone and of the churches in France, and I fall in love with the romance, and one night he gives me a medallion, he presents me with a medallion as we are talking in low voices by the light of a candle and listening to Bach, low, on the radio, he whispers to me, I bought you a present, and he gives me a medallion of Saint Bernard of Clairvaux, and he tells me to keep it secret, between us, he says, and the conspiracy is set, right then, I can't resist the confidence of another, and the sharing of secrets is so erotic and sexy, and I say to him, why Bernard, and he says to me, faith, and awe, he says.

[Silence]

my gorgeous groom. We sat around with our tops off in this invisible garden of France, we appeared carefree and at liberty to love, but there were fights and arguments and misunderstandings, I was never one for threesomes, I confess, I can't stand lesbians, I'm sorry but on my deathbed it is true, so no two women for me, because women are expected not to behave like men in a threesome, in other words there is supposed to be some kind of interaction between the two women in a threesome, whereas men get to not even touch at all costs and even though Maxi said to me that three was the magic number because of all sorts of outlandish stuff, even then I said, well, I would prefer two men, I said, that's the only way I would do it, and Maxi says, Pierre is getting his cock nowhere near you, ha ha, I can hear him in my dying head, through the fog of my brain banning any other cocks coming near me like a sniffing dog, I can hear him say it but I said, no, I don't want a cock up my arse and one up my pussy at the same time, I don't want a cock in my pussy and a cock in my mouth, I said, then what, Maxi says, then what do you expect from a threesome with two guys, and I said to him, well, one of them would be

kissing me and stroking my hair while the other would be
fucking me normal, I said, and then he says to me, you don't
need a threesome for that, that's called straight sex, he says,
stroking and kissing and fucking at the same time, and I
saw in his eyes how he loved me, I never knew my traits
were so lovable, and still I said, well, have you ever had a
threesome, and Maxi tells me about the time when he tried
to pick up two girls at an art school and they rubbered him
completely

[Silence]

me who is completely rubbered right now but then the next
week he saw them in a taxi queue and one of them said,
fancy an orgy, and then the night went crazier when the
taxi driver that took them home rolled a joint with one hand
while he was driving and passed it through to them in the
back because they were all pawing each other and obviously
getting it on, which is an attitude of complete faith, and
awe, it occurs to me now, and they got back to the girls'
room and it turns out they are sisters and I am not joking
you one of them starts smoking a cigarette in her pussy, has
it ever occurred to you such a thing, a pussy that can hold a
fag tight between its lips and inhale smoke and breathe it
out again, and there is a little mound of ash in her panties,
Maxi says, which she has just slipped down a little bit,
a mound of ash in a pair of panties, what a monument, I
think to myself now, from the position of slipping into dying,
which is what I am doing right in front of you now, I am
dying in front of you.

[Silence]

Who am I even recording this for except the voice in my
head but no, for the summer I spent with Pierre, who knows
how long it takes to foam and to dissolve and to bubble over,
and did it burn the panties, I think, did the ash char the
panties, and even though I hate lesbians I think a lesbian
little sister with red hair and a fag burn in the crotch of
her panties is some kind of adventure, and Maxi said they
interacted when he fucked them, that's the word he used,
not like men they interacted, they made sounds like owls, he
said, he said they made sounds like owls

[Sound like two sister owls cooing]

and exhaling smoke from their vaginas and it is foaming
at my mouth and now I am feeling unwell, I confess, I feel
my chest to be exceptionally tight, and my organs like dead
stones inside of me, and my breathing like owls, in the dark,
but then he said, I will write you into a book, Pierre offered,
I will photograph you into a history, he said. We will make a
summer of this book, you and I, and of the book a cathedral,
a monument to a single summer.

[Silence]

There is no such thing as a single summer, I said to Pierre,
for if there were only to be a single summer we would have
no word for it because we would have nothing to compare
it against, so that only a summer that repeats can be referred
to as a single summer, I said. But then he said, every summer
is unrepeatable, and I said to him, well, yes, the contents of
every summer are unrepeatable, the hours of sunshine
in every summer are unrepeatable, the break-ups and the
falling-in-loves are unrepeatable, the paths of the birds

through the air, diving, into the river, that is unrepeatable, but the fact of a summer goes on forever, and he said to me, you talk like the Beach Boys, and he said, no, as in 'Endless Summer', 'Endless Summer' is a song by the Beach Boys, he said, and then we picked up the young black boy who appeared out of nowhere by the side of the road and who sang songs in the back seat of the car, as we toured the monastic architecture of the Île-de-France he would strum his acoustic guitar in the back seat, he was paying his way across Europe, from Africa, by busking in the street, and he knew so many songs, he would sing them softly, almost under his breath, like a channel from out of the air he would sing a song about a lover who was mistaken for a swan, and got shot and killed for sport, and when the swans gathered round in tears – all of the swans were cursed lovers, lovers who had turned to swans and so lost their human counterparts, spurned lovers who were swanning – the swans asked the wisest swan of all – which is the eldest of broken hearts – what was the answer to why lovers turned to swans, and the first broken heart responds with a tear in its eye and asks, how many ships sail through the forest?

[Silence]

Life is clingling, dwindling . . .

[Silence]

And of course I was convinced into having a threesome with two boys, with the black boy and with Pierre, and just like in my dream the black boy stroked my hair and kissed me softly on my forehead and whispered my name while Pierre made love to me, and it was a tender moment of sharing, and the boy sang in my ear, and it was that same song like owls, that song like owls that had uncurled like smoke from the pussies of my Maxi's lovers was now seducing me and calling me like a final bird, which is what I expect to hear in the end, a final bird, Borges wrote about it and he was blind, for godsake, and so was able to hear it better than anyone else, there is a last bird, he says, that sings, and I can hear it, and I imagine a vision of complete white-out, but with a dawn, rising, somewhere behind it, and a single bird sounding, like an owl, like a tender threesome, and then Borges says about how he leaves nothing to no one, and I heard it like No Future, no one can have nothing, he says, I leave it to no one, I leave something to everyone and nothing to no one, which means the dead are something, I read it as, in Borges' code, Borges who could hear so well he picked up on the fact that the last bird is a sound, the last sound a bird, and not a mute swan, but a swan that speaks, and I feel as if I have known all this before, as I'm swimming in the past now, now that I am just about all out of future, no future for me, but now, forever, is how Pierre meant it when he said he would make a book of us that endless summer, oh my, I could cry at being so far out at sea that there's not a single soul to see me drown, drowning on the foam but still the dead are something and nothing to no one, I am thinking myself into a spell to best see me off, though I am not looking for conclusions, that is something I am not looking for, I don't intend to tarnish our creation with petty responsibilities like that, I draw no conclusions, I loved, and was love in return, I betrayed, and was betrayal in return, both were asked of me, and I hope I lived up to their request, angels, thank you for your persistence, your hunting of my own, your relentless pursuit, even now, with no one to witness my going under, but you, I'm still grateful, to you, who knew my name better, even, than my Maxi, than my summer of Pierre and I, and I, who speak it, I, in closing, my I is spinning, and my I is spinning as I cast off I, farewell my Maxi, farewell long-lost love Pierre, lover Pierre, and thank you for our infinite summer now I can hear the last bird as the last bird in the invisible Eden is spoken with me as I must retire these owls and I

[Silence]

[Stop]

8. APOSTOLIC CHURCH OF THE LION WITH A BULLET IN ITS HEAD

A primitive church. A simple house. The sign of a heart.

The paintings of Rembrandt are the loneliest paintings in the history of religious art because they are suffused by the shadow of death, and none of its lighting.

Things fall apart. Cico, who runs the cafe where we watched the baroque music trio, has developed a tremor that they believe to be early-onset Parkinson's, and he has begun to forget, and to be invisibled, and to disappear. He cornered Babette in the toilet and tried to force himself on her. His wife is suffering from depression and rarely leaves her upstairs apartment.

There is a painting class on the opposite bank of the river. They wear white lab coats and stand to paint, all except for one old dear, who sits on a stool and faces the other way. The instructor has a pipe in his mouth. A sunbather in a bikini lies on a towel at their feet and refuses to move. I cross the bridge to look at the paintings. They were painting me, and the view across to me, only they have erased the single sunbather from the scene. Now my presence on the other side has ruined the picture completely.

Flower tells me she wants an open relationship. I love her all the more for it, but I can't let her go. At least let me dress you for your other lovers, I ask her, and she agrees. But still, I can't let her go. I dressed her like the girls of another summer, all of whom I remember so well.

And now I am Strindberg, and I am one hell of a man, and I visit my Flower in my dreams and watch as she is fucked by other men, and by other women, too, assignations whose details I, myself, helped plot, in order to aid my imagination, like fetishes, or primitive weaponry, to ward off demons, or ghosts, and to invoke them, too, as I hold my cock in my hand and inseminate the air, as I think of turquoise panties, the colour of that summer's dragonflies.

Excommunicated. What a word. To be excluded from participation in the sacraments. In Normandy, William the Conqueror and his wife built two abbeys in order that they could be reconciled with the Church after they married without the Pope's consent. This is the threat of excommunication written in stone. The Abbaye aux Hommes and the Abbaye aux Dames. They made monument to the passion that brought them together, so these same monuments would bid them entry. To build a church in order to return to it. Monument Maker.

I am on a solo trip to Normandy. I have the use of a little artist's studio with windows onto the sea. My Flower is with another man. I am looking out to the country I came from and I know that I will never return.

I was given use of the studio by the woman I met in
the baroque cafe who dedicated nine years of her life to
uncovering the role that black GIs played in the Normandy
landings in 1944. Black GIs that had been excommunicated
from history.

The official line was that there were no black GIs at
Normandy. There were no black GIs who returned from
Normandy to a country they had fought for, their friends
and comrades had died for, and that was still segregated.
There were no black GIs that were treated as invisibles.

I sit in this unheated studio, wrapped up in a blanket,
looking out to sea, and I read contemporary accounts of how
locals were warned, by white GIs, that the black troops were
dangerous, that they were thugs and would-be rapists, even
as they fought alongside them by day. The photographs tell
another story.

Here is a picture of a young black man, a kid, really, in a
training session in the woods in France.

Here are a group of black men in full uniform, shopping
for gifts at a market stall for their sweethearts back home,
some of whom they would never see again.

Here they are tending to the survivors of a Nazi time bomb
on a street in Coutances, the bodies of the dead and the
dying mercifully obscured.

Here they are lying wounded in a field hospital.

Now they are holding up the bullets they dodged, and grinning.

Now they are pictured with their new extended families, with the lovers they took in France, and with the babies they made together.

Here is a young black man, a tank driver, looking around, and behind, the camera, his eyes fixed on something that is permanently out of sight, something that is *not himself.* His name is Claude Mann, from Chicago, Illinois, and he is two hours from death. Ecce homo.

I am walking in the dark along the front in Normandy and the Abbey of Mont-Saint-Michel is illuminated in the fog. Sculpture comes out of the invisible. Stone speaks of what we cannot see.

Picasso says that the Spaniard spends his mornings at Mass, his afternoons at a bullfight and his evenings at a whorehouse. But I am a Scot, in France, and I am going to the dogs.

The artist Carl Fredrik Hill, who went mad, and who lived in Grez-sur-Loing, and who, as I say, went mad, near the end of his life, as usual, for that is most likely when you will go mad, my friend, believe me, you are too young to know, but the end of your life is most likely when you will lose it completely, even though you might feel completely sane right now (you think), Carl Fredrik Hill made drawings of sculptures, pointless drawings of sculptures, what is the point of drawing a sculpture, you might think (he was mad, surely), why not just make one, but you can find them

in the huge books dedicated to the degeneration of his
madness and there – look – these drawings are uncanny,
believe me, these drawings that capture the movement of
sculpture, which is the coming into creation of something
invisible, in simple lines, how do we create the invisible,
you might ask, well, better ask a madman, a madman like
Carl Fredrik Hill, poor soul, who saw the invisible coming
into being in simple coloured lines, like the very raiments
(what a word, it is these), the very raiments of the word, I
say, made flesh, his simple coloured lines as complex, and
as technically difficult, and as simple (like I said) as the
folds on the cloaks of classical statuary, as the folds on the
skirts of classically beautiful girls they are simple, these
drawings, and so he made it so, as a drawing of stone, as in
'Skulpturer i museum I' and 'Skulpturer i museum II' (do
you know them?), which are to pen and paper what absence
is to stone, which is the voice of silence, speaking, and which
Hill takes further and now, in his drawings in the 'Publik
i konstmuseum' series, he pictures figures, too, coming
from this silence, to witness the coming through from this
silence itself, it is uncanny, and it is a scribble, and it is a
single gesture, extended, from both sides, from the other
side, and again, of this selfsame silence, and you can see
what I am trying to do, I am using words to describe, which
is not a mirror, as Hill draws it, but a coming through from
something opaque, only but from both sides this is a coming
through, as in God is not a mirror, this coming through, but
a screen that divides, but a hand that says, this way, and
the other, and a head that speaks, through its eyes, and that
is a meeting place, and that is in the middle, and that is
called madman, painting; Carl Fredrik Hill.

Everything is filled with meaning: the endless summer fields, the pure blue skies, the churches perched on promontories above empty villages, the gravestones there, too; yet meaning remains silent.

The pigeons outside my window are singing: Ook, Ook.

The Église Saint-Martin de La Genevraye is one of the most forlorn and beautiful of the secret churches of the Île-de-France. It has the most touching graves. Everywhere, all around the cemetery, there are memorials to what the dead loved to do most among the living and it is touching that the dead, forever, go on just like the living, in their dreams of easy leisure, in their dreams of another summer, please God, another summer dedicated to cycling to small villages and gazing up at old churches whose stonework is crumbling, and whose plaster is coming away, and that are masterpieces of décollage (be gone with you, German avant-garde types) and infinitely fascinating, in their decay, standing hand in hand so that their silhouettes seem impossibly large on the fallen memorials, memorials to days spent fishing while alive, to hillwalking, and to reading the dedications on the gravestones, one of which reads, perfectly: I recline. Sorrow.

I take a photograph of my Flower, who is taking a photograph of a stone angel in the cemetery at Église Saint-Martin de La Genevraye, a stone angel so worn down by time that it is impossible to read the dedication beneath it, stone in memorial to the invisible, and suddenly she screams and throws her camera in the air, and says she has been stung, but then she changes it to poked, I have been poked, she says, I have been poked by a ghost in a graveyard, she says, and it is true that the dead go on dreaming of the same fun they had with the living, poking the asses of girls in short dresses as they bend to photograph angels, for the asses of French girls provide slim pickings so they must grab their fun when they can.

I am drinking on my own on the terrace of the Auberge de la Vanne Rouge in Montigny-sur-Loing and I am swooning over the little girls of France and how their fathers kiss them, and hold them close, and I think of the mystery of fathers and daughters, and, of course, mothers and sons, and feel bereaved for the first time, but more for that I was never a daughter, and held by my father, than for that I am a son, and can never again be held by my mother.

Have you heard of the doctrine of the Merits of Saints? The idea is that during their lifetimes the saints accumulated more spiritual merit than they could actually use themselves, thus generating a surplus (sounds like Marx? ha ha ha). This surplus is stored in a heavenly bunker known as the Thesaurus Meritorum Sanctorum. The Pope has access to this bunker and can draw from it in order to pay penances and commute guilt, and he can draw from it as much as he wants because Christ's merits, which as we have established are infinite, are included in its store. Of course, the papacy took it a step further and claimed that the Pope could commute sins of souls awaiting judgement in Purgatory, as well as those in the flesh, but bear with me. And though I despise the psychologising of the sacred (call me Bernard), really, the neuroticising of God (call me a Gothic cathedral), but if the saints truly have the power to forgive and commute, and I have seen it happen, my friend, and if Christ is infinite, too, and he must be, then

there is more love and forgiveness in this world than we
can ever make use of, and all we have to do is ask, but man
is troubled by guilt, and cannot raise himself by his own
bootstraps, cannot lift this burden of guilt because of the
sure knowledge, accepted or refused, but the sure knowledge
all the same that existence generates suffering (a noble
truth, indeed), that life feeds on life, and that inside we are
a mess of nasty and rejection and hatred and hubris and
confusion, inside we are seething, and feel awful, and in
need of something else, something outside of us, someone
outside of us who resembles us, who is us, but who has the
unequivocally established ability to redeem the flesh, a hero
who *must* enter history, as a word, for our comprehension,
and whose ministry *must* be taken up, in time, which is
the power of Logos, which unfolds, as a story, and this is
where the evangelists and the missionaries come in, because
if there is enough belief in the Thesaurus Meritorum
Sanctorum, in the secret bunker, in the powers of the saints,
in the forgiveness of Jesus, and in the concomitant promise
of eternal life, then it is, it simply is, and man is capable
of entering into it, but only if we truly believe there is a
son of God, and that the ultimate nature of God is love,
which is expressed throughout His creation, and whose
entrance into history is the most significant event in time,
hence our calendars begin at the approximate date of the
birth of Christ for a great and beautiful reason, because
marking history with his birth means every day is lived in
the knowledge of forgiveness and the absolving of sins, for
who amongst us has not been less than life, and knowledge
of God through the example of Christ and of sainthood
becomes the most significant fact, the greatest example,
the ultimate manifestation of a revelation that is capable of
marshalling all of our belief, our combined psychic powers,

and our longings, too, and our love, even, all of our foiled love, and transmuting it, through belief and surrender, into so much candyfloss, but rivals spring up, temporal powers inevitably channel the same urges, the same needs, that less than life should require more than life, in the balance, and so make it so, is obvious, and so all of the Caesars and all of the Hitlers to come, who must be reckoned with, but who God, through the ministry of His son, and the example of the saints, will also forgive, thanks to the surplus of merit and the overflowing of good, which is infinite, and so will always triumph, in this world, where everything is forgiven, if we make it so. And if you think you understand that, then you have understood nothing, and you are the perfect fool (on a donkey).

The moon in June is a strawberry moon, over the garden where my Flower and I are eating dinner, a poulette, roasted in the oven, and some local beer, served with potatoes and green beans, a poulette I had a woman in Nemours prepare for us, and watched as she hacked off its claws, and as I watched I thought, this is eternal, there is no end to the removing of claws and the displacing of limbs, and I thought to myself, this whole world is a hospital, ha ha, then I had to laugh, ha ha, I am buying an organic chicken for a romantic dinner for two and I believe myself to be in a charnel house or a hospital ward with severed limbs piled up until heaven, and I saw how both were possible, what a nut, I said to myself, what a nut as I staggered out into the sunshine, and cycled back to the hotel, along the canal, along this route I have come to love so well, past the hopeful gardens and the little shacks with people fishing and wishing each other a good day, and how precarious it all is, what holds up a summer field, what moves it in the wind, and my Flower points up to the night sky and calls it a strawberry moon, and next to it, she says, Saturn.

I discover a bookshop. I am not going to tell you its name, because it is a secret bookshop and, besides, I doubt that it would exist for you should you try to seek it out. It appears on no maps or guides, it has no phone, and its hours are sporadic (like all of the best bookshops). On its shelves are models of Baphomet and on the walls hand-painted Templar crosses. It has the best selection of books on churches, cathedrals and Romanesque statuary in France. The owner insists that I travel to Milly-la-Forêt to see the Chapelle Saint-Blaise-des-Simples. Simple is a kind of flower, he says, and I have to agree. Jean Cocteau is buried beneath your feet, he says. His English is very poor, but I am enjoying it so much I refuse to speak French. It is the best of the west, he says, and he loads me up with books on Chartres and Metz and the Gothic churches of Brittany. Before I go, he asks me if I would like to take a medallion for free. I choose Saint Bernard. Simple is a kind of flower.

On a walk to Montigny, in the rain, my Flower and I come across a lost dog, a white spaniel, who approaches us cautiously from the other side of the road, bowing down and gazing meekly up, now shuffling towards us from out of the past, and at the last minute she flips over, onto her back, in submission, and lets us tickle her. Now she is ours completely. She leaps up in joy and speeds ahead of us, scrambling beneath the fencing around the football field, jumping in the air and snapping at the white butterflies, running back to us for approval before speeding off again. In the distance we can hear thunder; a storm is approaching.

A red duvet hangs from the high window of a chateau while an argument rages inside.

The dog runs out into the road, which isn't busy, but in order to get her attention and to keep her out of the way of traffic I give her a name, Clara, I say, and I call her, Clara, and I point with my finger whenever a car approaches and she obeys right away, running to me, falling on the ground in front of me, and rolling over. I kneel down next to her and hold her to the ground every time a car passes and feel her full stomach, rising and falling, her little teats, her tongue lolling on the ground; she gazes up at me in perfect surrendered happiness.

But we're getting closer to the village and the storm is about to break. I'm running all these scenarios through my head: how I will have to find a leash somewhere; how I will have to take her back; how I can improvise with a piece of rope; what I will say to villagers as we pass in case anyone recognises her.

Just as we meet the steep curve that leads to the centre of the village a car pulls up and an older woman says something in French about how lovely the dog is. This dog is lost, I explain. She's lost? the old dear says. Well, where did you encounter her? she asks me. Back at the entrance to Montigny, I say, just before the football fields. Okay, she says, could you lift her into my car? I have a bad back, she explains, and she says that she will drive along the road and see if the dog can be returned.

I pick her up, I pick Clara up for the last time, unaware that something that has only just begun is ending, and I hold her one last time, and she shivers and is afraid as I put her in the passenger seat and close the door. The old woman asks me where I'm from, tells me her daughter studied engineering in Glasgow, boasts of how beautiful her house is – although you can't tell from the outside, she says – and then drives off, and Clara is gone, and we look at each other, my Flower and I; we didn't even take the chance to say goodbye.

Why didn't I even take a photograph? Flower asks me, and then the rain comes down, and the storm breaks, and we walk off into the village, discomfited, heartbroken, even. And now I wonder what happened to that dog. Although she's long dead by now, I'm sure.

The Christ of the tympanum of the Abbaye Sainte-Marie-Madeleine de Vézelay is the most imperturbably alien manifestation of the unknown God in Romanesque sculpture. Its eyes are blank planetary orbs. Its beard and hair bear the simple marks of its maker. Its mouth holds a single elongated breath. Its nose is eaten by tools and time and appears as a syphilitic wound. I am the unknown God in human form, it says, though I appear in no human form. Should this Christ come down to earth we would run shrieking in terror. And rightly. All the same, he is here, right now. Run.

A tiny girl in a red swimming costume is turning cartwheels on the opposite shore. A dog breaks free of its owner and pursues a duck across the water. A young boy in oversized yellow armbands leaps from the bank. Some idiot in a bunny costume is acting the goat. Old grey-haired fishermen float past in canoes loaded with bucketfuls of live bait. Two guys stroke each other's arms on a bench. Three boys goad each other into leaping off the bridge. Somewhere in the distance a child is crying. A girl in a dark-blue bikini with the most perfectly pert young teenage ass (a rarity in France, as we have established) moves her towel into the sun. An obvious drug dealer stands next to his bike, propped up against the public toilets. I am suffering from a hangover. There is an obnoxiously fat woman with no top on. Someone just leaped from the bridge – splash! A white motorcycle pulls up on the grass. A man in black trunks is applying suntan lotion to a blonde woman in a turquoise bikini who is complaining that he is too rough with his hands. Three giggling Japanese girls are launched in a canoe into the water. An insect with gentle antennae-like lashes and an impossibly delicate body, bronze-gold, lands on the table next to me. I am debating a first drink and imagining what I will have for lunch. A duck floats past with three babies (the next day there are only two). My Flower is writing in her journal. More ducks. A white dog lies in the grass and yawns in blissful boredom and with great skill. Splash! I think of Ook, and Babette, and Clara. A white rugby ball spins in the air and some athletic meathead leaps up to catch it. A pair of shoes are launched into the river. A kid dives off the bridge but lands on his back in the water. A chubby girl in a purple one-piece bathing costume with the word Disco written on it in lurid electric green paddles past. Somewhere in the distance there is music, electronic music, indistinct. Seven boys and a single girl in a black bikini stand around an inflatable ring, waist-deep in the water. More ducks making a pointless din. Now a white poodle that looks crazy and that swims in terror back to the shore when its owner throws it in. An English accent, how annoying. A guy in a red headband, idiot. A pied wagtail lands, for a split second, on the wall.

The strap of my Flower's bikini falls down her arm as she writes. Now a white butterfly. Now a guy in a baseball cap and a turquoise T-shirt with the number 10 on it is trying to tempt his dog into the water with a tennis ball. Now he drags it into the water backwards and lets it swim back to the shore. A young mother and a baby pose for the camera. Splash! A burly French youth pulls his girlfriend's hair. Splash! Splash again! They play frisbee, and lie around on towels, and kick their feet in the water and look moody together. A guy in a white trilby, knee-length shorts and an unbuttoned purple shirt, who I recognise from seeing him roaring drunk in Nemours.

A chestnut falls from the tree above my head. Jeans and no-top guy, talking on the payphone, I hate you. Doris, the talentless Swedish painter's friend, interrupts me to say goodbye, she is leaving at five o'clock. I kiss her on both cheeks and wish her safe travels and am glad to be shot of her.

Where is the girl with the dark-blue bikini and the perfect young ass? Ah, there she is, beneath the tree, adjusting her bikini. My Flower dangles her legs in the water and ties her hair up in a bun. Now she floats on her back as a maroon-coloured car with the windows down passes on the bridge. A little kid in white briefs holds his nose as he jumps in. Now the dog-training guy has his son in the water with armbands on. And now my Flower has floated out of sight.

Christ is everywhere, and always, and his presence in the sacrament is an underlining, and a remembrance, of this.

A cheer goes up. Time for that first drink.

And now it is raining, and I am alone, and far from everything I have loved. What faith do I have left? In what was given, and what was taken away. And for what.

This.

Is.

Monument Maker.

Ook.

9. FINAL CHURCH OF FÜHRERBUNKER

Juliette Swedenborg stands in the garden of a two-storey semi-detached villa in a northern suburb of Paris. She is holding up an old-fashioned camera. In front of her stands a young Pierre Melville, his arms resting on a brand-new red-and-white motorcycle. In his hand he is holding a flower.

Do you know how flowers grow? Miss Swedenborg asks him. She gestures towards the snowdrop and has him look inside. Inside is for the bees, she says. All those secret patterns. They're not for you and me. Pierre holds the bud up to his eye. Inside it looks like a spacecraft; sleek, streamlined. Don't tell me what it looks like, Miss Swedenborg insists, raising the camera. It is a melody more than a word, she says. Don't describe it to me.

Miss Swedenborg was a legendary figure in Parisian art circles of the 1930s and 40s. She had been a war artist during the Second World War. Commissioned to paint coastal defences, aircraft manoeuvres and warships, she instead delivered a series of paintings that were indistinguishable in their emptiness, blank vistas of sea and sky, the one confused with the other. These were true war paintings, she insisted, regardless of their lack of anything that might signpost the circumstances of their creation. While many lesser works were exhibited at the time, works that could have been interpreted as giving away crucial data to the enemy had they been invited to see them, Miss Swedenborg's paintings were hidden away, taken from her and secreted in a bunker at the Ministry of Defence. She never painted again, after the war, and it wasn't until 1961, as a result of a committee that was formed in Paris and that drew from some of the greatest artists of the day, that the paintings were returned to her. Their first showing took place at a private gallery in Paris in the summer of 1964. Pierre had attended the exhibition as a young man and had been struck by their broiling emptiness. Using oil on watercolour, Miss Swedenborg had painted the union of the sea and the sky as a chasm, a trapdoor into another world. Look closely at a painting like *La Ciotat, August 7th, 1940* or *Île du Levant, March 8th, 1939* and at the point where the sea meets the sky, or vice versa, it is possible to make out a system of subtle erasures, created, it would seem, by the edge of a blade, that appeared to be the source of the light that flooded the canvas. No sun was ever described; no heavenly bodies appeared in the sky. Yet the paintings were illuminated.

Their first meeting had been awkward, but Pierre never forgot it. Miss Swedenborg had presented a talk to the local school in the spring of '62 about her wartime experiences and her career in painting and subsequent work in the theatre. Pierre had been singled out by the headmaster for a one-on-one conversation afterwards due to his success in recent examinations and his displaying a burgeoning interest in the arts. Miss Swedenborg appeared

uninterested. She sat on the edge of the stage in the
assembly room and yawned into an intricately embroidered
handkerchief that featured the letters of the alphabet.
Pierre had compiled a series of questions and he held them
in front of him on a clipboard, every inch the keen young
reporter. This is awful, he thought to himself. This adult
is completely bored by me. Miss Swedenborg took a small
lipstick holder from her handbag. Her lips were flaked and
hot pink as she applied another crumbling layer of colour.
There was something animal and forbidden about it as well
as a bit rotten.

How do you become an artist? Pierre asked her. She put the
lipstick back in her bag and rolled her lips together. Pierre
noticed a large mole with hair growing out of it on her upper
lip. It caught his eye in an attractively repulsive way. There
is nothing to become, Miss Swedenborg responded, snapping
her hand-mirror shut. She smelled of mint and of toilet
spray and of old paper doilies, if they even have a smell,
which Pierre believed they did. In that case, how does one
start? he asked her. He was nervous and as usual in these
kinds of situations his speech was becoming increasingly
convoluted. She stared back at him like an emaciated bird
of prey and he imagined a little pellet with his tiny bones
inside dropping from her mouth with a soft thud. I will
tell you a story, she said, and she repositioned herself on
the edge of the stage. That way we can dispense with the
questions altogether. Pierre nodded and meekly put his
clipboard to one side. You ask about art, she said. You are
searching for a calling, it seems.

A few years before the outbreak of the war I set out on
a walking tour of Scotland, she began. I was caught in

much the same conundrum. I pictured my calling as being somewhere out there, wrapped up in experience, secreted in a future that could be unlocked with a precise series of actions, a combination of bravery, irresponsibility and a willingness to get lost, perhaps, though I was never able to reduce it to a pithy formula like that. This is a quick sketch for your benefit, you understand, she said. She searched inside her bag and took out a clove cigarette and lit it, leaning back on the stage with one arm, the other holding her cigarette at an exaggerated angle. Pierre thrilled to this illicit adult activity in the gym hall. I prescribed myself a walking cure, she continued, shaking out the match. I carried all that I needed on my back. I had a small one-woman tent, a sleeping bag and a rucksack.

The summer was unseasonably warm, and I spent many nights sleeping in the open air by the sides of lochs and in the deep grass that grows up beside rivers. Of course I was scared, on occasion, but at that time of year it never truly gets dark in Scotland and so even at my most isolated I would look up at the sky and see that deep royal blue and know that there was nothing really to worry about, certainly not in those days, not in those times, a young woman in the 1930s. I would look up at the night sky and I would tell myself, it's only a bruise, you can handle it. I kept feeling like I was on the edge of some kind of epiphany. That just up ahead there was a moment that had lain in wait for me.

Everything became exalted; everything seemed lit up, self-possessed, glowing. She traced a quick figure eight in smoke above her head. Every chance encounter, every sunlit morning or drizzly afternoon had its own perfect rhythm, she continued. I met a man, a boy, really. We were both staying at a hostel near Glen Affric. He was a black boy, which was a shock. I grew up in a small village. I had never seen a black person until then. I saw him at breakfast, sitting on his own at a table, reading and taking notes. I kept grabbing a look at him and then looking away. The next day he was still there.

Something made me stay on. I spent the day hillwalking and dozing in fields of bracken just thinking about him, imagining what he was doing there, then I checked back into the hostel. Sure enough, at breakfast, there he was again. He wasn't going anywhere either. I began to get the feeling that we were both hanging on for each other, that this was a meeting that had to take place, one of those fixed moments in time that I had gone out looking for. In the evening someone had organised one of those godawful folk sessions in a bothy along the way. I saw a handwritten poster for it and decided to check it out. There was nothing else to do for miles around. Besides, I thought he might be there, being a tourist and all.

I made my way in the dark-blue night to this tiny stone building in the middle of nowhere with a rusted corrugated roof and eyeless windows and the wind blowing through it. I could see a light inside, a little candle, guttering in the breeze. I opened the door and walked in. There was no one there but the black boy, seated on a log, with a guitar on his lap. Have you come for the music? he asked me. I told him I had but that I couldn't play anything myself. That's okay, he said. I know all the songs.

That was the exact phrase he used, Miss Swedenborg insisted, that he knew all the songs. He had a bottle of

whisky with him, she recalled. We passed it back and forth
and he sang these songs, these beautiful songs, songs about
swans that became people and ships that sailed through
forests and girls who dressed as boys in order to join the
British army on the banks of the Nile. He played the guitar
with his fingers and at one point he stopped and held his
hand out to me. Feel that, he said. I've almost worn my
fingerprints away. We talked into the night. He told me he
worked at the hostel, seasonal work. He was sending his
wages back to Glasgow, where he had a wife and two kids.
But there was another reason he was there. That's when
he told me about Glen Affric. It's Glen Africa, he told me.
That's the real name. He told me a story about how there
had been a revolt of slaves. They had been imprisoned by
Romans who had brought them to England from the valley
of the Blue Nile. But they had escaped and had made for
Scotland, eventually settling in Glen Affric, which reminded
them of the highlands of Ethiopia. They remained there for
centuries. In fact, they're still here, he told me. Of course,
I never asked his name, Miss Swedenborg admitted. Quite
strange, really. Pierre nodded obediently. But he insisted
that the Africans were still hiding out in Glen Affric, she
said, still thriving, in fact. He had made contact, he claimed,
that was the real reason he worked there. He was their only
connection to the outside world. I asked him why no one else
had ever seen them, why there had been no reports of their
existence. Were they in hiding? They're not in hiding, he
told me. They have become invisible.

The next morning I waited for my boy at breakfast, but he
didn't appear. I asked someone working in the kitchen about
him and they said he had checked out early that morning,
that he didn't work there at all, in fact they had never seen

him before. That day I set off on my own and hiked into Glen Affric. It was true, what he said, Miss Swedenborg nodded. They have all become invisible.

Just then the headmaster poked his head through the door. Their time was up. Miss Swedenborg stubbed her cigarette out on the heel of her shoe, threw her bag over her shoulder and walked off without even saying goodbye. Pierre watched through the door as she made a big deal about embracing the headmaster and thanking him for a wonderful afternoon before disappearing in a haze of perfume.

Miss Swedenborg's war paintings have been compared to Constable's seascapes and to Turner's later work. Some argue that her paintings are essentially unpainted, that they are simply primed, and so endlessly receptive, precognitive, even. A painting like *Le Dramont by Night*, it has been argued, anticipates, daily, again and again, until the end of time, the coming night that will, hope against hope, blanket the little seaside town and engulf its sleeping inhabitants once more.

Pierre stood a few inches from the canvas and stared hard. At this point he knew little about art. As with literature, his taste lay with the outliers. He squinted at the canvas, a thick, otherworldly accumulation of blue-greens and blacks, and fancied it squinted back at him. It reminded him more of Rembrandt, a Rembrandt painting of an eye, but an eye that was half closed and not half open and made of glass, maybe. Other paintings added to the feel of a prepared canvas, a painting in a state of anticipation. Seascapes like *From Marseilles Harbour, September 13th, 1940* resembled more a single drop of paint, a tiny pink flame afloat in clear water. First stroke, first light; a perpetual sunrise. Then there were the systematic erasures. What to make of an art that destroys itself in its creation? Except that it must, essentially, be autobiographical.

In keeping with the quality of reception that Miss Swedenborg's war paintings seem to have, the erasures have been described as passages, as tunnels from the past into the future. Could this have been one of the reasons for the military's refusal to have them shown during the war, to secrete them in a vault in the Ministry of Defence? There is no such thing as an 'erasure', Miss Swedenborg insisted in the notes to her catalogue, though by this point she was said to be suffering from the early stages of dementia, her own mind riddled with inexplicable voids and hollows. An erasure, Miss Swedenborg insisted, removes nothing. In fact, it accumulates. By the act of erasure, you are building upon what was there before. There is no way to subtract, she wrote. There is no route backwards. Nothing is undone.

Pierre stared at the indeterminate skylines, at the scabbed and picked-over horizons, and thought of entry points and exit wounds. Is it possible to paint anything that isn't a self-portrait? He caught his own reflection in the glass of a painting purporting to show a military fleet lighting out. It seemed to consist of nothing but shadows and deep gouges yet there was something piercingly sad about it, a purposeless quality of disarray, perhaps, a vision of pointlessness. Pierre lingered over the painting for some time. These are no modern warships, he realised with a start. These ships are ancient. He saw the erasures, the voids and pockmarks that dotted the canvas as a form of rigging, a complex of masts and ropes that rose up and out of the painting to enable it to take sail. And he saw in it his own lighting out, the blank that was yet to come, and all of the forgetting it would take to get there.

In the wake of the exhibiting of Miss Swedenborg's war paintings, Pierre made a decision. He wouldn't go on to college or university. Instead he would set out himself, just as Miss Swedenborg had done. He used the last of his savings from a part-time job to purchase a new motorcycle, an expensive red-and-white Honda. Then he made an appointment to see Miss Swedenborg one more time.

Of course, she had no memory of him. I interviewed you when you came to give a talk at my school, Pierre told her. She smiled and said, that's nice, the way you would compliment a small child on a rudimentary drawing. I would like to take your picture, young man, she said, and she held the old-fashioned camera up in front of her. Pierre posed behind his bike, a delicate flower in his hand. Miss Swedenborg revealed to him the secret nature of flowers and then led him indoors for tea.

She made him sandwiches, though quite unlike any sandwiches he had had before. These are Danish sandwiches, she claimed, buttering a single slice of bread, spreading salmon pâté on it and then crumbling salted crackers on top. This is how they do it in Denmark.

The crowded living room smelled of mints and of beef and of old potpourri and of Calor gas. Despite there being a roaring fire in the hearth, Miss Swedenborg insisted on lighting a small gas heater and rolling it into place next to it. Shouldn't you be careful not to put that too close to the fire?

Pierre asked her. Young man, she said, I lived through the war. I'm not afraid of gas. Now, she said, about that skelf. About what skelf? Pierre asked her. The skelf you were kind enough to call about.

It's in here, she said, and she held out her index finger. I suppose a needle would be best. You can find one in those drawers over there. Pierre got up and rustled through a set of green-painted drawers that were stuffed full of string and wool and small pieces of shredded paper. Does a mouse live in here? he joked. Yes, Miss Swedenborg said, yes, I don't doubt it, and she raised herself from her seat and stood over him so as best to monitor Pierre's retrieval of the needle. A mouse will eat you out of house and home, she said.

Miss Swedenborg gave Pierre her hand. Prick the skin, she said, dredge it out. It feels good to have someone pierce your skin, don't you think? It's never as satisfying to do it to yourself. Pierre removed the skelf, which was actually a piece of strange metal, which caused a trickle of blood to run into Miss Swedenborg's palm. I saw your exhibition at the art gallery, Pierre said, hoping to steer the conversation in the direction of something relevant. He was starting to despair of coming here in the first place. I could've painted Hitler's bunker, she replied.

I could have but I didn't, she said. I snuck in after the war. It was all sealed up, top-secret, hidden treasure. She resumed her place in front of the fire. The Führerbunker, she said, the dream of infiltrators worldwide. There it was. I scaled the fence, prised open a door, took my paints and a foldaway stool and a searchlight and descended into the depths. It had been vandalised. There was extensive flooding. Great desks were upturned; who knows, even the desk that Hitler laid his elbows on and hung his head in despair may have floated past me without concern. I had entered via the stairs to the Foreign Office garden, so I had some ways to go. The central dining passage was like an ark, a cavernous, echoing ark. I thought of everyone drinking wine and gorging on pointlessness in the last days of the war. I descended the stairs to the lower level. All the while I was aware of a presence. Someone was in there, I knew it. I did a quick recce of Goebbels's quarters. There isn't much to tell, an iron bed frame, a filing cabinet, piles of rubble here and there. Not as exciting as you'd think. I crossed the hallway and I held my breath as I prepared to take in Hitler's bedroom and across the way, Eva Braun's quarters. As I passed through Hitler's study, which had been completely gutted, I became aware of a scraping noise. I'll never forget it. It was like the sound of the first man who invented fire, going at it again and again, chit, chit, chit, chit, like a flint that just wouldn't catch. Oh my, I said, we've gone backwards in time. Hitler has sent us all to the Stone Age. I opened the door to his bedroom, which still had a lovely ornate handle on it, and there, in the pitch dark, a figure was sitting on a small stool. Someone had beaten me to it. The sound that I had heard was charcoal. This man was drawing a picture of Hitler's bedroom, in the dark, with a piece of charcoal. We looked at each other for a second, unsure of how to react. Neither of us spoke. I shone my flashlight at him, but he just put his hand up in front of his face. Eventually I simply nodded and retreated. The game was up. He'd beaten me to it. For all I know the paper he was using might even have been black. That would have been the final touch. Think about it, she said.

Another Danish? Miss Swedenborg suggested as she
struggled to her feet and made her way to the kitchen.
Pierre followed behind her. At the far end of the kitchen,
facing the front windows, there was a wicker rocking horse
in the shape of a swan. When we first met you told me about
your walking tour of Scotland, Pierre began, how you went
out in search of something. You inspired me to do the same.
I'm going to bike around Africa and find what's waiting for
me. I suppose I came to get your blessing or mark the start
of the journey somehow.

There is a flower that grows in Africa, Miss Swedenborg
said, as she handed Pierre a tea in a chipped enamel mug,
that only blooms once, for a single summer. After that, never
again. But forever, from that point on, it is a flower that has
bloomed, even when the petals have fallen off and the head
has grown old and died.

Afterwards, in the soft glow of the streetlights, in the
uncanny silence of his youth, Pierre stood outside Miss
Swedenborg's house and watched through the window as
she rocked slowly back and forth on the wicker swan, her
eyes fixed on some newly distant horizon. Then he turned
away, and never saw her again.

BOOK FOUR: CHOIR

I. THE GOSPEL ACCORDING TO FRATER JIM

I have come to rescue all of the disappeared, to reunite all
true loves, to turn history to dust. I write as the captain
of a ship, the ship of my fate, a fate that went down in the
Mediterranean during the evacuation of Crete with everyone
onboard.

There were few deaths during the war, despite all that has
been written, all that has been spoken in lecture halls, in
ministries, in schools and in memorials. Most of us went
missing, were lost, our bodies unaccounted for, our deaths
deduced, implied, though never verified, by our continued
silence.

My own silence lasted thirty years and was facilitated by
fortune or fate, the ship that I sailed on. Then I returned,
I came back, and with me I brought back all of the lost, in
secret, inside of me.

I read the pathetic letters that had been sent, heard the
tear-stained pleas. Dear Sir, they read, Dear Madam, I am
writing to see if you might have any information on the
whereabouts of my husband. He was the captain of a ship
operating out of Malta which was reported sunk in May of

1941. I am pregnant with his son inside of me and would be grateful if you might have any news of his survival or the possibility that he was captured and interned somewhere. I have heard talk of the concentration camps and fear that he may have been sent there. I am writing because I know your husband was returned to you and hold out the hope that mine, too, will one day be back in my arms.

Mumu Corlanis was the name of the rescue ship from Malta. A young man with a beard picked me up from the sea. He saved me, and I am still alive although now near the end of a third life, the one that I returned to after my life in secret, which in turn I was given to from my first life, my first life with marriage and a house in Calderbank and a family too, a father and a mother and a brother, much younger than me and so not eligible for disappearance himself.

My body was received by resistance fighters in Crete. I suffered from burns across my back and my hands and across my right leg. My face was a blackened mess. I was transferred to an improvised field hospital beneath a small town on the south coast of the island that had not yet been overrun by the Nazis. There a doctor attempted, with a modicum of success, to treat my wounds. I spent weeks drifting in and out of consciousness, my body in a tub of ice water beneath flickering strip lights.

Other times the orderlies would wheel me prone in a stretcher to the mouth of the cave. I was in so much pain that the wind felt like it was driving tiny diamonds into my flesh. Why have I been saved? I would ask them. But the words were confused. There were no mirrors in this hospital, this hole in the ground filled with the dead and the dying

and the miraculously born again, and besides, for weeks
afterwards my face was bandaged like the Invisible Man.
My ID card became my reflection and when I wasn't staring
at the sea, that strange green-blue sea of the southern
Mediterranean, now tinged orange with the diluted blood
and the rusted carcasses of everything I had previously
known, I would plumb the depths of myself, my round
mouth the same cave I now emerged from, my eyes sunken,
my memories a great chest of treasure, my marriage, my
garden, my books. To be robbed of your own face is to truly
recognise yourself for the first time.

Listen. Can you hear the sound of your own blood? Can you
feel the force of the life inside of you? Do you dare?

The hospital was raided. They came in the early hours.
They killed most of us. They pulled the bandages from
my face and they marvelled. The first time I saw my true
reflection was in the eyes of a Nazi officer. A golem, he
called me. Not a monster but a golem. A golem is something
that is created from the dust and that is gifted life. I
thanked him for that. He spat in my face in return. A golem
is a Jewish creation.

My eyelids were burned and torn. My eyes are filled with
scum, I said. They beat me to the floor. I put my hand up
to my face. My nose was missing. My mouth was an open
wound. Drown him, they said, drown the golem. Look at
the back of his neck, someone said, there you will find a
letter. They picked me up and scratched at the flesh at the
base of my skull. Omega, I said to myself. Omega. Nothing,
they said, he's already dead, and they pushed me in front
of them. They dragged me to the edge of the cliffs and they

pushed me off. I fell into the water as into a deep sleep. When I awoke I was weightless as an angel.

I floated through schools of jellyfish in the undersea light. I believed I had died and gone to heaven and that the fishes with their divine contorted faces were a manifestation of some final state of grace. Then something told me that I could not be drowned, not in this life, and I started for the surface. I appeared on a beach beneath the high cliffs, where I sat down and wept for the first time. There was no longer anything to stop my tears.

The stars came out. I read something in them, something incoherent. I believed them to be upside down. The world has been inverted, I told myself. Or perhaps it has only just begun. I was still in great pain. I walked by night along the beach. It was as if I could smell the planets. They were huge and they hung in space like my own eyeballs, red, luminous and with storms on the surface. They smelled of sweat and sulphur and of dead fish washed up on a beach. As I walked, the tide snatched my footprints from me. I will leave no trace, I told myself. I will disappear. What is the colour of Venus? I tell you it is red.

My mind began to play tricks on me. Like an unsupervised child with a pair of scissors it began to cut and paste my surroundings so as to appear senseless. A line of German soldiers stood motionless along the cliffs. They held their flashlights high as if they too had become puzzled by the sky. In the distance I could hear explosions. Something has fallen from the sky, I thought, and in my incoherence I believed it to be Wormwood as The Bible had predicted. It was in this state of mania that I encountered an old priest gathering driftwood on the sand. He froze on my approach. Then he raised his right hand in a Nazi salute. I replied with a V for victory and he simply nodded and turned away. I followed him with the hissing of the sea and the roaring of the fallen stars in my ears. I spat in the sand as I went.

He led me to a small white cottage secreted in a cove. He wore a dark-blue robe and a black fez. His eyes were like glassy marbles. Is he blind? I wondered, although unlike me he blinked. Can you see? I asked him. English, he said, English, and he nodded. He put some of the dried wood on the fire. No escape? he said. No, I said, yes, I said, I did escape. Can you see me? I asked him.

He touched my shoulder. Please, he said, please. He handed me a glass jar filled with goat's milk. I had difficulty swallowing and the milk ran from what was left of my mouth and stained my clothes. The man rose and, running his arm along the wall, disappeared into another room. He brought me a robe like his own. I took off my clothes, stained with blood and milk and seawater, and stood naked in front of him. He didn't look away. It is the state of my body that will figure the final judgement, I told him. Please, he said, please, and he handed me the robe. Joshua, he said, and he laughed, Joshua. I thought he was calling me Jesus. But perhaps it was the name of the person who owned the robes. God knows I looked like no one else. We ate fish cooked on the open fire and sat in silence as the bombs rained down and the waves rolled up the beach. Soon I realised it was the sound of the storm inside me.

If your face was taken from you and you washed up as the ghost of yourself in a hermitage on a small island in the middle of a war, what would you do? Would you try to find your way back home? I confess that it never crossed my mind, at first, though exactly why that should be I am at a loss to explain. I am a dead man, I told my companion, and he rolled back his lips in the mockery of a smile. I had taken a step into thin air. I had walked through walls. I had sloughed off my own flesh. I was a monster that even the Germans had no name for and I felt the same distortion in my heart, in my brain, in my capacity for sympathy and love, in my feelings for the past and for the future. Still there is much that goes against the grain.

After many remarkable nights spent in silence with the priest, I left the coast and travelled inland. I made my way like a thief in the night as searchlights poured over the sky and the hum of invisible planes coursed through my veins. I slept in ditches by the side of roads, in clusters of thick trees, once in a chicken coop in a burned-out farmyard. By this time the stars had righted themselves though the moon still appeared as a wound. I developed a taste for rough weeds and roadside flora and also for burglary, although the pickings were scant as most of the dwellings I encountered had been raped and ransacked prior to my arrival. I recall one family home, a small three-room bungalow, where what appeared to be recently extracted human teeth lay scattered across the stone floor. I gathered them up and put them in my pocket. Who knows what currency the future will trade in? I encountered mirrors, too, and I looked upon myself. I was not horrified. I fancied I had the aspect of a shark. Its torn mouth, its rudimentary nasal cavity, its lidless eyes. A shark never blinks, I told myself.

The rain came down and I sought shelter in an old shed.
I could hear a cat calling somewhere, a wounded animal,
horrible, like a torture. Then I realised it was the sound of
someone planing wood. I crossed the courtyard through the
black mud and peered through a slatted door. A man with a
pair of goggles was carving a wooden Madonna. I laughed,
then caught myself. What an occupation, I thought, in all of
this, and I almost raised my arms to the heavens. I fought
the urge to go in, to make myself known, to ask him why he
continued in his task. This is too much, I told myself. This is
like a book. But I couldn't restrain myself. I pushed open the
door and stood there in the frame. The man was startled. It
was my first look of horror. And though there were more to
come, a lifetime's worth, truth told, there was something in
this first look that made me proud, proud of the capacity of
my skin, of the skill with which my body possessed itself, of
my singularity, my ridiculousness. I am a little boy, I said
to the man, and he understood me and was terrified. Until
then the fact of my youth had deserted me. Now it came
flooding back in awe. I advanced upon him like tomorrow.

After you have seen the heavens turned upside down
anything is possible. Every belief is a fairy story. The state
of war, once entered into, offers no possibility of respite. The
whole world is a hospital. The rain came down on the tin
roof. The man backed up against the wall. I held a single
brown leaf in my hand, wet with rain. I held it out to him. I
meant to terrify him. I kept repeating it. I am a little boy.

When he understood I was no threat to him, or more
properly that the threat was to be overthrown by pity, he
pulled himself together. He reached out his hand and took
the leaf. Silently, I marvelled. I felt like the first man on

earth. To me it was like a painting, the man, the leaf, the deformity, the pale light coming through the slats. But what to make of it? My appearance lent every gesture the weight of prophecy. Horror had made me dishonest. Behind the mask of suffering I leered and I leched. He looked at the leaf, now curled in his hand, the little veins that ran through it, and he wept. I had come upon the currency of the future.

An angel touched me on the head when I was born, I told him, and he nodded as if he understood. I felt unstoppable tears run down my face, though inside I felt nothing but a distant rattling, which I realised was what was left of my heart. I began to discourse automatically, vomiting baby words in a torrent. I said things like help me and daddy and small and in the rain, even as the way I looked, the very movement of my body, served to sicken it, to make of it a curse. My wife will be home soon, the man said, in faltering English, we will not betray you. I am the betrayer, my blood boiled, I am the enemy, though outwardly I sighed, and I snivelled, and I appeared as a fallen angel. I cast my eyes over the torso of the wooden Madonna, her tortured form emerging from a section of a gnarled tree. Christ was crucified upon his own mother, I thought to myself. And then he rose again. My own rebirth had been no less painful.

We drank coffee by the light of a single candle. The room is golden now, in my memory. The man has a thick black beard, small eyes, big hands. The coffee tastes of sand and of dirt. We talk of the war in simple sentences. It is a bad thing. It will never end. It is a madness. Some people are still alive. Many people are dead. Hitler is a monster. Giati? we asked. Why?

In the evening the man's wife returned and showered me with pity. We ate bread and cheese and drank ouzo in the kitchen of their farmhouse. We played cards, even as in the distance the sound of shells reminded us of where we were and the pointlessness of our game. Still, there was time to kill. I heard a building crumble to the earth on the other side of the island, a fleet of aeroplanes strafing low across the sand and the dirt. I surveyed my hand. Suddenly I was caught somewhere in my past; fish-hooked, as The Bible would have it, my mouth agape.

My wife stands before me in the darkness of the kitchen. I go to speak, to venture her name, but instead I move up close to her. I place my hands just above her waist, just around her lower belly. I say that word to myself, belly, and I think of a ship, made of skin, and I draw back. She rolls on her toes back and forth. I feel her body tighten, contract. This is a murder mystery, I tell myself, this is a detective story. Then I realise where I am. I'm on an island in the war. I wrap my arms around her waist and I tell her something impossible, something terrifying. In response she tells me she is the three of hearts. Later, in bed, in a nook off the kitchen, she comes to me again. This time she is as sticky as a flower.

I rose in the night and entered the bedroom of my rescuers. By the wound of the moon I was able to make out the man's wife, astonished though unafraid, staring back at me. Without thinking I blew her a kiss, a lipless kiss, though now it seems to me I was caught up in a song, a song that my own wife and I had chosen as ours before I had left on a boat for the war. It was an old song, a sentimental song, a song about saving all your kisses for a future point, for a blessed return. I had determined to spend all my kisses in advance. I helped myself to some provisions from the kitchen which I tied up in a dish towel and I stepped out into a scene from *The Iliad* where the sea lay aslant, like a mirror, or a stately sheet of glass. In the distance I could make out a flotilla of warships, their swastikas raised to the heavens, thin wisps of smoke rising up, behind them the first hint of dawn, war in peace, and it was the most beautiful thing I had ever seen.

I walked the coast roads with no destination in mind other than a circuit of the island and a circuit of the island as though I was tunnelling into the sky. I passed the outskirts of Loutro and lost myself in the forests of the white mountains, where I descended through the clouds to the town of Omalos. I discovered many dead bodies. I slept with goats on the hills as a welcome guest. I sat cross-legged in the mouths of caves in my robes. I stole a pair of jackboots and a water bottle. I passed unseen through Lakkoi. Skines was burning. Vatolakkos too. On the road to Agia Marina I watched from the undergrowth as a convoy of tanks and motorcycles led a wretched group of boys and men to their doom. I saw burned-out houses, twisted metal stretching up, graveyards full of military equipment sunk in the sand like a surrealist vision of hell. I crossed the island once more. Outside Imbros I was shot in the leg from behind and taken prisoner before I could complete a circuit and create a vortex that would have delivered me to another future altogether, or so I had come to believe. Either way my SOS to the gods was not received. I was bundled into a truck and forced to stand in the dank hull of a boat that made the crossing to the Peloponnese. We were packed so tightly that I could feel the erection of the man behind me in my back. It was the first time I had experienced such a thing. An erection in this situation! I shouldn't have been surprised.

The man in front of me was a Scot. My arse is tanned, he said. He had been beaten so badly that he had taken a stroke. One of my bollocks too. A line ran down the middle of his body, bisecting his penis, marking the paralysed half from the half that still had feeling. A divided man. We're all just prawns in their game, he said. Did he mean pawns or sardines? I said prawns, didn't I? he spat. What did they do to you? he asked me. They drowned me, I told him. What happened then? I gained powers. What kind of powers? Prophecy, I told him. ESP. I'm sticking with you, he said. Truth told, it was the first flexing of my new ability, my first glimpse of what the future had in store. What about me? he asked me. What's up ahead? Your arse is tanned, I said. But for your bollocks there's still hope.

In Greece we were handed over to the Italians, whose regime, despite the word of history, was even more baroque and officious than the Germans', except on one count. We were held in a prison in Acronauplia in the city of Nafplion, high on the cliffs, staring out to sea, at the very edge of the world, it seemed to me. Here I committed the first of my identity frauds where I posed as a savant for the authorities, a shell-shocked basket case who in truth held his real identity card wrapped in a plastic bag and stuffed up his anus, which, unlike the Germans, the Italians never searched.

I gibbered and I drooled and I wept, none of which was entirely put on, as a lipless and lidless shark, come ashore. We were ten men to a cell, at first, which wasn't comfortable but was viable, somehow, and amongst them was the paralysed Scot I had met on the boat whose name has eluded me ever since. I sat in the corner like an oracle, which is what I became, a mascot too, a reminder and a there-but-for-the-grace-of-God. The Oddity, they called me. I didn't object. I was the subject of an experiment, by my fellow prisoners and by God Himself. Using sheets of toilet paper and ash from the stove they would draw simple symbols and ask me to read them with my mind. A dot, I said, a circle, a line, a triangle, a square, a heart, a house, a simple church, a penis, a pair of tits; it wasn't hard. The men marvelled.

Outside the window the sea and the sky formed a blue rainbow and it was there that we drew ships from out of the past and out of the future, the flotilla that would rescue us, the ship we went down in, the ship we set out in, ships with names like curses or like books of The Bible, *Exodus*, *Grace*, *Damnation*. We ate cold watery soup with the consistency of freshly melted snow and some of us crumpled paper into balls – salted them, if we could – and dunked them in the soup in place of meat, swallowing miraculous cocks and churches and tits and triangles.

If he can read the future, someone said – they often spoke about me as if I were somewhere else – then surely he knows what's going to happen to every damn one of us. He doesn't read the future, another said, a dark boy with a patch on his eye and no top on, he reads minds. It's not minds, a third one said, an Irishman with thin wiry hair and sullen eyes and permanently pursed lips, it's remote viewing, it's like seeing from a different place, a different angle. So you're saying his mind's up there somewhere, the first one said, up there in the corner of the cell, up there in the sky? Where's your mind? the sullen Irishman asked him. Right here in my head, he said, and he rapped his finger against his skull. Aye, well, two minutes ago it was between the legs of a dirty whore. You're not wrong, the first one said. Looks like we've got another remote viewer, the second one laughed. Seriously, the first one said, let's stop with the games, let's put The Oddity to use. They turned their heads towards me in expectation. I let a long line of drool fall from my mouth. Then I cast my mind into the future.

The war is over, I tell them. It is 1947. I am disappeared, I am dead. I live in a small one-room apartment on the outskirts of Athens, which I pay for with odd jobs and begging. Most days I walk the three miles or so to Syntagma Square in the centre of the city, where I stand motionless for hours on end, my right arm extended, my military ID in my hand, an upturned cap at my feet. This is what I looked like, once, I tell them, though of course I don't speak it. I remain in silence. One day my ID is stolen from me, snatched from my outstretched arm by a passer-by who runs off into the crowd. Now I am a monument, which in Athens makes me a tourist attraction.

The curious flock to see me. They stand some distance off and stare or they sit on a bench and look at me sideways through their sunglasses. Occasionally a small child bursts into tears at the sight of me. I am given a name, they call me The Oddity (the men nod in agreement at this, they knew this already), and soon I begin to attract regulars, silent companions, an old man with blue piss-stained trousers and a beige tank top and a drinker's nose who sits on a bench across from me and nods, occasionally, in my direction, a

pair of swallowtail butterflies that return to me three days
running and that brush my face like eyelashes (but weren't
butterflies only supposed to live for a day?), a young man
who sits on a low wall and sketches me from a distance, a
budding Goya or a Pablo Picasso, though you probably won't
get those references (never heard of them, the men say, get
on with the story), and finally a woman, an older woman, a
graceful woman with prematurely grey hair, a sophisticated
woman, who lights a cigarette and unlike the other ones
looks me in the eye, my blazing eyes, my eyes that are filled
with dust and sand and blood and mucus, my eyes that
are fixed open and that smell like planets (what do planets
smell of? one of the men asks. No idea), and I look back at
her and for the first time in my life I don't see a reflection,
I see something else, another person, for the first time (he's
never seen a person, the men ask themselves, what is he
talking about?) I see something that *is not myself* and it's as
if all my suffering amounted to nothing.

On the way home I feel a silent joy in my guts, in the soles
of my feet, for the first time. Finally, one day, she comes
over to me. She tells me she recognises me. It's far-fetched,
I know, but hear me out. My face was created, I want to
tell her, I wasn't born this way, though surely she knows
that. Then I realise that perhaps she is talking of deeper
things, like when two souls meet or two fated lovers or twins
separated at birth (it's a romance, one of the men nods, I
knew it), and I grant her the possibility that, yes, there
could be some form of recognition, even with my face as it is.

When she leaves she takes my heart, which as I have
intimated was shrunken and in revolt and by this point
the size of a raisin, and leads it up stone stairwells and

along sandy backstreets and past tall apartments with
washing hanging out to dry and secretes it in a studio
on the top floor of a three-storey building that leans into
the sun in Plaka, a great plant-filled conservatory with a
glass roof and with paintings piled up and facing the wall,
she couldn't bear to look at them, her life's work, so she
had turned them away and instead looked to her plants
for solace and companionship, although she was very
beautiful, she could have chosen another life, could have
embraced society, but like me she was chosen, she was
marked somehow and my heart told me (it reported back,
the Irishman with the sullen eyes nodded knowingly) that
this was what she recognised in me, the shark that never
blinks and that never rests, and I returned home to my
own room, which was on the ground floor and which let in
no light, and I lay on my bed, on the dirty white sheets,
and fell asleep with my eyes open beneath a damp cloth and
with the image of this woman fixed on their surface and I
dreamed of the war (damn, said the third man, who had a
tattoo of a harp on his arm, I thought it was all over) and
I saw the war from above, the movement of troops, the
convoys like a shadow on a lung, the burning cities like a
bruise on the thigh of a beautiful woman (that's how it felt,
sometimes, the Irishman with the harp agreed), and I felt
a great sense of gratitude, for every death, for every ship
sunk (wait a minute, the boy with the patch and with no
top on cautioned him), and for a moment, just for a second,
I became reconciled, I let it go completely, I gave up, in
other words, and in that moment my heart came back to
me (a raisin, the Irishman with the harp nodded) and told
me where it had been, told me of its adventures (a talking
raisin, the boy with the patch said, you couldn't make this
up), and I reinstalled it in my chest and boys it was filled

to the brim, let me tell you, it was overflowing, even, and what's more, it was in charge.

The Scot with the tanned arse interrupted me. It's memory that predicts the future, he said. He's doing nothing special. All you need to do is remember. I'm only seventeen, the boy with the eyepatch said, what have I got to remember? Doomed youth, the Irishman with the harp said, there's a poem about that. Not in the hands of boys but in their eyes, he quoted, shall shine the holy glimmers of goodbyes. You can remember that? the boy asked him. I learned it at school, he said. I can hardly remember anything before the war, the boy said. Does that mean I've got no future? What do you see for me? he asked me. I thought for a moment. Liberation, I said. That'll do me, he said, and he clapped his hands. Is that what happened to you? he asked me. Yes, I said, yes, I was liberated by the war. Do you fall in love with the woman? he asked me. Then, putting his hands up to his face: what does she smell like?

At this point I still don't have a nose, I tell him (he grows his nose back, that's something, the Scot says), but her name is Mariella Visconti and she looks the way women used to look before the war (see, he means in our memory, the Scot nods), their cheeks filled with rosy colour, their little bird noses, their fine hair, their delicate wrists, the slow movement of their arms, their perfume, I don't doubt, though at this point in time, in the near future, my olfactory ability is less than nil, but still a cloud hangs around her, a cloud of colour, a lilac mist that she moves around inside.

She takes me home, inevitably, my heart has already all but moved in (a grape, is that what he said it was? the

Scot asks), and I move into a spare bedroom with all of
my possessions, which at this point is a pair of trousers,
a grandfather shirt, a pair of sandals, my old robe, a pot,
a cup, a toothbrush and a sliver of carbolic soap (just like
in jail, the young boy laughs). From my window I can see
people sitting at tables outside the restaurants all along the
street, talking and smoking and drinking wine and eating
fish, couples with their arms round each other, old men in
the sun.

Why are her paintings lying on the floor and pushed against
the wall? the Scot asks me. Why, if she didn't like them,
didn't she just burn them or rip them with a knife and
throw them away? I'm getting to that, I say. It's all tied
up in what we're doing right now. Mariella finds out that
I can see into the future. How does she know? the young
boy with the patch and no top on asks me. Can she hear us
talking? No, I reassure them, don't worry, I'm the only one
that's there. That's not how it feels, the boy shrugs. That's
understandable, I reassure him.

The point is she was interested in spiritualism herself.
Before the war she was involved in a group that practised
what they called 'spirit painting' (sounds weird, the Scot
says), where they would gather in her room underneath
the great glass ceiling of her conservatory with nothing
but the stars up above their heads, nothing but the stars and
the planets, excuse me, and satellites also and comets and
maybe even alien craft who knows and they would attempt
to communicate with disembodied beings (do you mean
the dead? the Irishman with the wiry hair and the poorly
executed tattoo of a harp that might as well have been
the gates of heaven on his arm asked), not just the dead,

there's more than the dead that we can't see, I said, there are things that have never lived or that live on different frequencies from ourselves, frequencies that we are not naturally attuned to but that we can somehow, through will and breathing exercises and sex, even (now we're talking, the Scot with the tanned arse and the half-cock and the paralysed bollock announced), tune ourselves in to, almost like a wireless, if you like.

The point is that when you painted one of these entities, these things from another dimension, which of course did include the dead and the dearly departed as well as strange things that resembled squids and amoebas and octopuses, that was the weird thing, the denizens of the aire, as they called them, that's air with an E, boys, often resembled the denizens of the deep, as if down below were the same as up above (mate, tell me about it, the Irishman with the tattoo that really was quite amateurish shrugged, I used to work in the submarines), and when you painted them, or so the ladies of the group believed (women, the Irishman said, and he nodded and he rolled his eyes), it was all ladies that were involved, ladies only, everyone else was too busy gearing up for war, and they believed that once they had painted the visitor, let's call it, the communicant, let's say, that it became somehow trapped in the painting, imprisoned in the very weave of the canvas, in the frequency of the colours (colours have a frequency? the Scot said, come off it. Light has a frequency, the Irishman said, sound has a frequency, colour has a frequency too, get over it. I wish my bowels had a frequency, the Scot replied), though trapped perhaps is too strong a word, they didn't mean to do violence to this thing from another galaxy, though really it was the same galaxy, just a bit removed, it was more like they provided a field in which it could manifest, it just happened to be static, of course if they could have had access to a movie camera that would have been a whole other thing completely, because that way the entity would at least have had some kind of movement, some kind of space to move around in, even if it was just the same set of movements repeated again and again, though of course it could go backwards and forwards in time, if it wished and if the projectionist was amenable, but with a painting it just sort of sat there and vibrated, which of course is a form of movement, but a subtle one, which is what frequencies do, if you think about it, they vibrate, which is akin to dancing on the spot or more properly around a spot because if you were to zoom in to their movements, if you were to truly get down to their level, you would see that their movements, actually, their dance, was titanic, was earth-shaking, relatively speaking, so what I'm saying is that these things weren't trapped any more than an atom is trapped in a bit of stone, they were as alive as stone (as alive as stone? the boy with the eyepatch burst, that's dead to me!), but the difference is that they had been drawn out from the aire, air with an E, boys, they had been translated into our reality, and that was an act of magic.

But why were they turned to the wall? the Irishman with the crummy harp asked. You haven't explained why she was so forlorn about them. Forlorn? I said. She was heartbroken. She had received messages from the other side, she had seen the obverse of God's plan, she had trafficked in angels, she had seen through the illusion, which is literally to be disillusioned, to be robbed of it, and here she was, on the other side, and nothing had changed. Revelation changes nothing, I said, except to render the past and future irrelevant. She had thought to receive some blessing, some good news, some word of God. But things went on exactly as they had been, even as her apartment came to resemble an otherworldly zoo, an occult aquarium, a diving bell.

What about you, though? the young man with the eyepatch said, now squatted on the floor of the cell and rocking back and forth on his feet. She wasn't expecting that, maybe you were the good news, maybe you were sent by God? Never mind that, the Scot said, turn over one of the paintings, let us see what these things look like. Go on, the Irishman with the harp said, give us an eyeful of the word of God.

I wait until Mariella has gone to the store. It's my first afternoon alone in the apartment. I wander amongst the plants, the cacti, the vines climbing the brick walls. I open a book at random then I put it down. I stare down at the holidaymakers in the street below. I stand in the shower and let it massage the back of my neck (he's playing for time, the Irishman says), my whole body stings. I change into a dressing gown and I walk back to the living room as the rain starts to fall on the glass roof. I stand next to the paintings piled up against the wall. I am assaulted by memories, but I force them back down inside me. I take the first painting and I turn it around.

What is it? the Scot asks. What does it look like? Tell us, man! The men stared at me in silence. It is a painting of a topless young man with an eyepatch. Fuck, that's me, the young man with the eyepatch said. That means I'm fucking dead! I'm fucking dead, he repeated. I'm fucking dead. Wait, he said, you told her about me, you described me to her, and she painted me, right? Or wait a minute, how do I know you didn't paint me and then stash it there and are now pretending it was one of hers? Talk sense, the Scot said, he's making the whole thing up, he could have put any one of us in the painting.

Ask him something else, some historical detail that he couldn't make up, the Irishman said. He could make up anything if it's in the future, the Scot said, how would we even know? The young man with the eyepatch just sat there, he was in shock. Who wins the war? the Irishman asked me. The Allies, I said. What happens to Hitler? Dead by his own hand in a bunker in Berlin. What about Goebbels? Dead, too, in the same spot. Churchill? Victorious. Speer? Arrested. Himmler? Dead in a cell. Göring? Committed suicide the night before he was to be hanged.

He doesn't even pause when you ask him, the young man despaired, he doesn't even blink an eye. Wait a minute, the Scot said, let's ask him something that we can verify, let's ask him what happens tomorrow. Good idea, the Irishman with the pathetic harp said, and he crouched down in front of me and looked straight into my eyes. Tell us, brother, he said, what happens tomorrow? We're in jail, I shrugged, more of the same. Damn, he's got us there, the Scot said, and he ran his hand through his hair and spat on the floor. Tell us something specific that happens tomorrow, the Irishman demanded, something small. Okay, I said, I spill some of my pathetic soup on the floor. Okay, the Irishman said, let's see. Don't be an arsehole, the Scot said, all he'll do now is he'll deliberately spill his soup tomorrow and make it seem like he predicted it. Tell me something I'll do? the Scot said. But then all you'll do is deliberately not do it, the Irishman said, and try to prove him wrong. But if the future is written, the Scot said, then surely there's no way I can

avoid doing it? If you knew you were going to die at a certain
time and at a certain place, then surely you would just not
go there? But avoiding not going there would be exactly
what you were meant to do, the Irishman said, because the
information you were given made you act in a certain way,
which is the way you were supposed to act, which is the
way the future had to be. There is no way of getting out of
it, the Irishman said. If he says that you will do something
tomorrow and then you do it, then he has made you do it. If
he says you will do something tomorrow and then you don't
do it, but you deliberately do something else instead, then
he has made you not do it and do something else instead.
Just like he trapped me in that damn painting, the young
man with the eyepatch said. And now I'm in it no matter
what happens. Okay, okay, the Scot said. From now on,
listen, keep us out of the future. I don't want you making
me do things and making me avoid doing things. Keep it
clean, he said. You asked me to turn over the painting, I
said. Okay, the Scot said, but from now on keep us out of it.
I'll do my best, I said. Tell me, though, the young man with
the eyepatch said, tell me. I'm all tied up in it. Ask the lady
about me, ask her what she knows. I will, I said, I will, I
promised him.

There was an open courtyard in the jail, surrounded by
high stone walls and with the smell of the sea, where the
prisoners would congregate once a day and where new
arrivals were fumigated and deloused and where people
would exchange rumours and trade contraband. Even
then there was talk of the camps. They're shipping people
off, some prisoners maintained, they're running mass
exterminations. Ask The Oddity, someone said, he can see
the future because of his wounds. What happens with the

camps? they asked me. A holocaust, I told them. They stared at me in disbelief.

I stood with the boy in the shadow of the wall. He was trying to remember. His one good eye squinted in the sun. He swept his dark hair up and over his forehead. Perhaps I tell you something remarkable, he said to me. Perhaps that's it. But I didn't paint you, I wanted to say. It wasn't me. Instead I said nothing. But I'm only nineteen years old, he continued, I've nothing remarkable to say. What could I have done so you would remember me? He took a couple of bent cigarette butts out of his pocket and lit one for me and put it in my mouth. My lips burned and my eyes watered. My lungs stood to attention.

He wiped my chin with his shirt. I ran away from home to join the army, he said. Perhaps that's remarkable. My mother died when I was only five from kidney failure. That's something too. My twin brother died when he was only a year old. Wait a minute, he said. What if it's my twin in the painting, what if he still looks exactly like me? I wanted to tell him that when children die they do not grow. What if we're going backwards as well as forwards? What if in the future, in your future, my twin is communicating to me in the past, which is now? I spat the remains of the cigarette onto the ground. That would be remarkable, wouldn't it? the boy said. I nodded. I was beginning to understand the nature of my calling.

One day the boy took me aside in the cell. There was a card game going on. One of the men had procured a set of playing cards, the rumour was that he had 'given sex', that was the phrase that had been used, to a fat Italian guard and now

the whole cell was prospering. Of course the man denied
it, the man who looked a little bit like Mussolini himself,
it had to be said, like a deflated Mussolini, saying that he
had merely been taken under his wing, an unfortunate
euphemism that seemed to imply something much worse
than simply giving sex. Listen, the boy said, I've had an
idea. What if I ask you a series of questions and then, in
the future, but in front of me right now, you ask the same
questions to the graceful woman who has taken you in, Miss
Visconti, if I remember correctly, and we can then find out,
the two of us, exactly what is going on with me and my twin
captured on the canvas in this strange conservatory in a
backstreet in Athens? I looked at him and said nothing. I
made a wretched sound back where my nose would be. Come
on, the boy said, how can you not ask her now? I mean,
when you do meet her in the future and you turn over this
picture you will of course remember this conversation and
how could you not think, to hell with it, what do I have
to lose, let's give it a shot, let's ask the questions that the
boy brought up in the cell during the war all those years
ago. You said yourself that I was implicated, that we all
were. To be honest I couldn't recall saying that and for a
terrible moment I wondered if I was giving up the past, if I
was draining it like a fetid abscess, in exchange for greater
access to the future. I made that noise again back of where
my nose should be, and I nodded. He was right. How could
I refuse? We settled in the corner of the cell. I crouched
down on my knees and for some reason the boy mirrored me,
crouching on his knees in front of me. They'll think we're
praying, the boy said, let's keep the future to ourselves.
Okay, he said, okay, say hi to the woman for me. I looked at
him in silence. Go on, he said, say hi.

I rose early, showered, and walked through to the kitchen wearing the clothes that Mariella had bought me (can't we just jump right into it? the boy sighed), clothes that were suited to a much older man and that were an ill fit, a blazer whose shoulders hung down over my arms, a striped shirt that puffed out of the waist of my trousers, blue slacks with outrageous turn-ups and a hat too, a hat that of course I didn't wear indoors but that hid some of the horror of my face in the sun.

I have someone who wants to say hello to you, I announced. Of course, she was startled. Had I smuggled another deformed refugee into her house? Was I about to present my partner in crime and fleece her, finally reveal the dastardly plan that she had unwittingly played along with? No, I said. It's nothing to worry about. The boy in the painting says hello. Where is he? she asked. Tell her I'm here with you, the boy said. He is here with me now, I told her. Okay, she said, okay. In that case can I ask him something? I looked at the boy, his face which by now had become beautiful in the light of the future, the cell too, which felt illuminated, the circle of men playing cards like a classical painting not of the Last Supper but the last bacchanal, a Rembrandt where the suffering flesh itself lights up in the darkness in celebration of who knows what secret destiny, a Rembrandt, I said to myself, a Rembrandt, as I saw my tortured face from the outside, emerging from the shadows, and I looked to the boy and I mouthed the words 'there is transport both ways' and he beamed back at me, his face beamed and I fancied I saw a tear in the corner of his eye as we kneeled there in the darkness, please, I said to the woman, please, ask us anything, and I referred to the two of us as one for the first time.

After a moment she asked us the question. Why did you
appear? she asked us, a question that sent us back to our
own origins, that sent us spiralling, quite frankly, and that
threw us, quite honestly, in that we had looked to the future
for our answers, for the revelation of our circumstances, for
the word of magic, truth told, and here was the future, in
search of the same revelation, still, in the past.

Then the boy spoke up. I appeared for you, he said, as a
sign. But she couldn't hear him. I saw that there was only
traffic in threes. He appeared for you as a sign, I told her,
translating his words into the currency of the future. A sign
of what? she asked me. The boy paused, then he looked at
me and he smiled. Of the word that was spoken, he said.

You can see into the future, the woman marvelled, and she
leaped from the table and embraced me. You are the one
that has appeared to me as a sign! At last! I stood rigidly
with my arms at my sides. I was still the same monument
she had found in the square. I could have explained that in
the past I could see into the future but in the future I could
only see into the past, but what was the point. The future
has no future, but the past has the past has the past. Yes, I
said, yes, I can tell the future. This is the moment that my
future career reveals itself.

The woman designs me a mask, a leather mask that covers
my features completely and that blocks out the light with
only a small opening for my mouth and a hidden eye slit.
She sets me up as an oracle. At first we perform our tricks
in the conservatory to an invited audience. Mariella spoke in
grand terms. Her English was extravagant. My powers were
omnipotent, she informed our audience, mostly made up of

ex-members of her spiritualist circle. My knowledge of the future was titillating. I sat behind a curtain ready for the great reveal. The mask amplified the sound of my own blood and I began to hear voices, cries, protestations from inside my own body. Perhaps I could do this after all.

More words came from beyond the curtain; redundant, philistine, ectoplasm. As my breathing fell into a particular rhythm, I felt something rise from the base of my spine. Good news, I said, and I spoke the words out loud against my will. I heard the voices outside die down and the sound of footsteps moving towards the curtains. At last I stood revealed, dressed in my dark-blue robe and with a black leather mask and leather gloves. Good news, I repeated, and there were gasps throughout the room.

Come, ladies, Mariella chastised them, this is not a cheap sideshow. He's vibrating, one of them said, he is moving in and out of time. I'm getting a blue triangle, another said, a blue triangle on a plain white background. We have our first question, Mariella said, and I heard a movement of chairs as if one of the women had stood to make her request. My name is Bonnie Ventura, she told me. My husband Frank was lost to me in the liberation of Greece. Do you have any idea of his whereabouts and how I might get a message to him? I turned my mind to the blood and to the bone. He is in the castle of heaven, I told her, and I felt the tears run down her cheek. Is he in pain? she enquired of me. He is held up as though by an ocean, I informed her. With what does he pass his time? she asked me. He is cured of time, I reassured her. Does he think of me dearly? she asked, pathetically. You are his beating heart, I reassured her. What does he look like in heaven? she asked me, and with this she wept once more. He looks like his eternal self, I told her. Can I come to him, when I have to, when I must? Yes, you can come to him, I told her, then I raised my hand as if for the next speaker. There were more questions, questions of lesser and of greater consequence, questions about questions, how they should be asked and why and of whom, questions about animals, animals that were lost and that were ailing, questions about the spread of disease and the accuracy of diagnoses, about ill fate and good fortune, but it was the disappeared of the war that came to occupy our seances, who we looked for in the past and in the future. Where can they be?

In our prison, in the final years of the war, it would sometimes rain for days. The rain would fall into the ocean, where it would rise only to fall back down again. How many times had we escaped across it, imagined ourselves freed and returning home? I don't speak for myself, you understand, but for my cellmates. For me the future was fixed. I saw myself as a great comfort and as a great terror. But for the boys around me I wished them safe passage and I remember them now, so young, as impossible, as a great conundrum, the Irishman with the harp, the Scot with the single functional bollock, the young man with the eyepatch and the tanned chest who one day becomes a painting turned to the wall.

After our seances were over Mariella would lead me back to my room, where I would sit in the silence of my mask and imagine myself as having no head or more properly imagine my head as being like the high branches of a tree, open to everything and with the wind and the air, or like a cup or a chalice, the Holy Grail, I told myself, filled with blood. Once the guests had gone Mariella would enter the room, where she would take off my mask and wash my face in a bowl of hot water. She would wipe my face with one hand while she took slow draws on a cigarette with the other. Everything she did, her movements, the attention of her eyes, the way she would step back as if to examine her work from a distance, had the aspect of a painter. Then she would tuck me into bed in my robe, where she would sit with me for a while, by the light of a candle, me wearing my eye mask, and we would say nothing, but I know that in those moments we both came to doubt ourselves, the validity of what we were doing, the justification for our spurious set-up, the theatricality of our lies. All I can say is that we were compelled to do it, that the dead, who I have already demonstrated were a lie in themselves, who were not truly the dead, conspired with us in order to find a place for themselves in the future, a future that up until the moment of my revelation had never existed.

One day she set up a projector in the living room and showed me the first of several films her husband had made before the war. I didn't realise you had a husband, I told her. I don't any more, she said. I asked her what happened. He died, she said, he died of a broken heart. I didn't press her any further. I had the terrifying idea that she might ask me to forge a contact with him. It says something that I believed we were capable of fooling even ourselves.

The first of the films was a static shot of the ocean coming in and coming out. From the angle and aspect – high up and endless – it could almost have been filmed from the window of my jail cell. I was startled but I kept my composure. This is almost the same view from my jail cell during the war, I told her. It's all the same ocean, she shrugged (tell her we're looking at it right now, the young boy with the eyepatch said to me, tell her there's no doubt), even as I insisted, I would know that view anywhere, I told her, I stared at it day and night for years, but she said, well, this film only lasts three hours, she said, it's slightly sped up, however you do get night and day views, and then I thought, what about the stars, I had a crazy idea that I could place it by the position of the stars, like a sea captain would and I said, okay, where's Orion's Belt, and Orion's Belt, from the window of my cell, was on the horizon, more like a crucifix that had toppled to the ground or a ship that had capsized and that was slowly taking on water, there it is, I said, and I stood up and moved close to the projector, which was a black-and-white projector in those days but which made the stars stand out even more, which illuminated them further and made it possible to pick out Orion's Belt, bobbing on the horizon, being clawed at by the water, and slowly submerging, just as it had looked from our cell, but Mariella made a good point, she said, well, don't you realise that the world keeps turning, don't you realise that people all over the world see the stars fall into the ocean at different times and places, unless what you are trying to say is that my late husband was somehow filming over your shoulder during the war, in the midst of your incarceration, which I think the authorities might have frowned on, I think that they would have legislated against the arrival of a camera crew, because of course my husband didn't work alone, he led a team of experts, of early pioneers in experimental film techniques, and while I admit if he had practised his art in Germany he may well have ended up behind bars, in Italy, which is where he came from, and therefore in Greece, which is where he lived in the years running up to the war and his premature death, there was a more permissive atmosphere, less of a fear of innovation, which thanks to nutcakes like the Futurists had come to be seen not quite as comforting but as something that could be healthily embraced, and of course I stopped her right there and asked her directly, was your late husband a Futurist, and of course as soon as I said that I imagined him, too, living on in some time far up ahead, taking his place, boldly, in what was to come, and inevitably I imagined his disappearance as having something to do with an escape to the future, perhaps, though of course she had already said that he died of a broken heart, which I had to admit did not seem like a typical malady that would affect a Futurist, whose hearts were said to be like cold hard steel, like titanium, I believe, but she brought it back to the stars and ridiculed my attempt to establish a fixed point in my past with a fixed point in the sky and then to presume that everything else could be deduced from there and of course she said, well, think about it, that's what astrology does, so in one sense you are barking up the right tree ('nutcake' and 'barking up the right or the wrong tree' were, of course, phrases taught to her by me in order to add to her armoury of delightfully convoluted and satisfyingly archaic English phrases), but truly, to read the moment, to understand the singularity of its powers you must also track the planets and their relationship with the constellations, so unless you could see the planets from your window, unless you could convincingly map for me the exact state of the heavens at that moment and then somehow overlay it onto the film of my late husband, the melancholy film of my late husband, it seems to me now, your idea that it could possibly be the same view that you yourself internalised, as it were, is impossible to prove, but of course I told her that I didn't insist that it was filmed at the same moment or even during the same years, but that simply the Futurist husband had been there, in that exact same spot as myself sometime in the past, and I asked her when he had died, died is the wrong word, she corrected me, but then she said, 1941, it happened in 1941, and I said, okay, that is the time that I was taken prisoner, so what if he had visited the jail just before then, what if he had been captured, but Mariella insisted, he wasn't captured, she said, he remained at liberty, so okay, I said, what if during peacetime he had visited that same jail cell with a view to shooting precisely that scene, what if he had contacted the authorities, who as you say looked favourably on his experiments with the future, and they had allowed him access to film from precisely the same cell that I ended up in myself, and of course she protested, how would he know precisely what that view was like, she said, he would have to have been in jail before that and to have looked out that same window and said one day I will return here and film this view, this view which had to have been seared onto his mind by a past trauma or a previous visit, a short jail sentence, let's say, or, let's whisper it, he would have to have been a guard who every day visited that same cell and who looked out onto the ocean and thought one day I will come back and I will take this view with me once and for all and of course, as far as I know, he was never in jail, whether as an inmate or as a guard, but I confess that now you have me spooked a little bit ('spooked' I also taught her), exactly, I said, exactly, there are gaps in everyone's lives where they do things that can never be seen or verified and that are never spoken of again, but here's the proof, I said, here's a gap, here is the moment that your late husband the Futurist returned to the scene of some kind of epiphany, and I think it's reasonable to call it that, and of course although you maintain that every ocean is the same ocean, of course every time we encounter the ocean we see it somehow differently and there is so much variation between the form of the waves, the precise combination of sea creatures far beneath, the infinite permutations of sand upon sand, of broken shells and crockery washed up in the tide and, of course, everything that is inside you and that you bring to bear on the ocean, whether you stare out into it as an adult who has lost everything and who longs to be swept away, a suicide who walks out into it and who is rescued by the authorities, a child who wades into it with a bucket and spade for play, a young woman who paints it, two lovers who see it as endlessly romantic, a couple walking a dog who barely notice it at all, we can safely say, I insisted, that this view, this ocean, was significant to your late husband, although it seems a curiously romantic scene for an avowed Futurist, who I would imagine filming in a great factory or during a tank battle or at the very least alongside a motorway as the traffic sped past, and then Mariella corrected me, I didn't say he was a fully paid-up orthodox Futurist, she said, I didn't say that at all, I say, yes, his work paralleled the Futurists (at this I pictured a dual carriageway running all the way into space), his work was partially inspired by the Futurists, his work was co-opted by the Futurists, in some cases, but to say he was a Futurist, plain and simple, although of course really they were extravagant and complicated, would be to simplify things to an intolerable degree ('intolerable degree' is another one of mine, thank you), in fact you have much in common, she said, and I wonder now if that is what I recognised in you in those days when I would pass you by, on those days I was drawn to you in the square as you stood there with your old face held out in front of you, by the way, what happened to that, to the picture of your old face, was it lost or stolen, it was stolen, I told her, it was taken from me, swiped, I see, she said, and what face did you watch the waves with, was that your old

face or your new face, my new face, I told her, the face that I
have now, were you in terrible pain, she asked me, yes, I said,
yes, I was, and still there are issues, repercussions, like what,
she asked me, and I told her about my eyes, they are covered
by a film, I told her, they are like an old pond in the autumn
or in the winter, even, and what else, she asked me, the
sound of my blood, I told her, the sound of my blood is very
loud inside me, like the sea, she asked me, and her own eyes
sparkled, and I said, yes, and I almost laughed, like the sea, I
said, and she shrugged, so the film of your eyes matches the
sound inside of you, I was confused, do you mean the film of
the sea, I said, and then she asked me, do you know the
Roman god that January is named after, it was the beginning
of the year, we had just spent our first Christmas together,
no, I confessed, I'm more up on the Greeks, it's Janus, she
told me, it's Janus with the two faces, one that looks back to
the past and the other that looks forward to the future and in
his head is a door, a gateway, a bridge, a passageway, my
husband wasn't a Futurist, she revealed, my dear husband
was in a fact a Januist, what's a Januist, I asked her, a
follower of Janus, she said, an offshoot of Futurism, she said,
that both pre-dates and supersedes it, listen, she said, while
the Futurists dreamed of dual carriageways running all the
way into space (I had already imagined that, I recalled, with
a shudder), the Januists imagined them in time, tunnels,
sleek passageways, transports, from here to there, in the
firing of a neuron, in the blink, she said, of an eye. I stared at
the film, at the sea, and I felt myself just as the women at the
seance had seen me, flitting in and out of existence, flickering,
slightly, like a projector, I thought.

But wait, I asked Mariella, didn't your late husband talk
to you about his movies, didn't he tell you where they were

filmed, didn't you accompany him on trips to scout locations, didn't you read his storyboards, didn't you discuss his ideas of travelling into the future via the past, and then I had a terrible thought, wait a minute, I said, was he successful, when you say he died of a broken heart is that a cover story, is it because his experiment was successful, is it because he escaped, and Mariella sighed and shook her head and then she said, well, of course, there is a sense that he is immortal, that he has escaped from time, that is true, because cinema says so, and of course I stopped her right there, you mean he starred in his own films, you mean he is in there somewhere, I asked her, you mean there are more films, and she told me there were many more films but that he didn't so much star in them as secrete himself in them, as a stowaway in the hold of an old ship, she said, which of course struck me like a mortar shell, but can cinema really immortalise you, I asked her, well, she said, can a book, can writing yourself into a novel preserve you like an Egyptian, and of course I stopped her there again and reminded her that an embalmed corpse was no more alive than a skeleton in a coffin, whether the gods had their say or not, and that the point was to cross over the dreaded Styx and to make it to the other side, the point was an afterlife, not a death-in-life, which is what art is, and she said to me, you think art is death-in-life, she said, oh ye of little faith, she said, and then of course I brought up the paintings, you too, I said, you too had given up, you too attempted to bring to life something that was between the worlds, something spiritual, some kind of sign from the other side, but you became disillusioned, isn't that true, isn't that the word you used, I asked her, that you somehow lost the illusion that had served as the engine of your experiments with paint, with canvases stretched over the aether like spiderwebs or like netting where you thought you could catch all of these life forms, these entities, and at that I went to walk over to the paintings that lay piled against the wall and to reveal some more but then I remembered how in the cell the men had demanded that I turn over no more paintings, that I somehow avoid showing the hand of the future, which is rich after I have given away so much, and pointless too, but nevertheless I regained my composure and I sat back down and of course Mariella was as frustrated as I was, I don't understand you, she said, you bring me tidings from the past, you in fact tell me that the past is here right now and that we have a captive audience of men in a jail cell during the war that you have somehow transported with you, and yet you tell me art itself is incapable of what you have done, does magic work, she asked me, is this magic that you turn your hand to, it would seem to be, in which case I must ask you simply, does art work, does art work to transform the world, to redraw reality, to rescue moments and ideas and personalities from the stream of time, and I replied with all I knew, I told her that trauma worked best, that suffering was life's truest redeemer, that without it life wasn't worth a scoff and that art, at best, was a Band-Aid, a bandage on an old rotten mummy, and she said, no, I don't accept that, she said, when I told you my husband died of a broken heart, what do you think I meant, and of course I said, well, that he suffered, that his heart fell from a great height and was shattered, and she interrupted me and said, you can die from art too, you know, more than that, you can die into art, and I imagined a film reel covered in dirt and buried in the ground, a watercolour rotting in a cemetery, a paperback spreadeagled in an incinerator, a tomb with a collapsed entrance, afloat, on a stream.

Just then the topless boy with the single good eye interrupted me. We were back in the jail and the war was still on. Were there more films? he asked me. Did you find him, the Featurist? He wasn't a Featurist, I told him. We were in the courtyard, in the shadows, in the middle of summer. Around us men walked in circles, stood naked, rolled improvised cigarettes, lay on the ground half-starved. He was someone who was using art and technology as a means of escape. Do you believe him? he asked me. Do you believe me? I asked in return.

The next film was a film of a zoo, I told him, a visit to the zoo. I believe it was the famous Zoological Garden in Berlin. The cages are empty, the fencing buckled, the compounds collapsed. Again the movie is silent, which makes it seem quite beautiful, somehow, the camerawork is very graceful, it seems to float through the wreckage as if it were on wings. There are no animals to be seen except for the swans and ducks that float serenely on the river. He pauses over an enclosure for polar bears. He zooms in. There is a white paw just visible behind a white rock. There are no signs of life. He crosses a large muddy field that is cratered with bomb blasts. There is a sign, Keep Off the Grass, and an upended picnic table. Behind it there is lion, a beautiful female lion, whose guts have been spilled. Further on there is a field of buffalo, dead, bleached in the sun. It is as if we are going back in time. There are snakes in the shattered remains of their glass cases, their bodies coiled tight, as if they had tried to protect themselves, as if snakes too could sense the future, and there are lizards, tiny insects with their legs held tragically in the air, and there is blood and there is gore where the animals have turned on each other. Outside, in the sunlight, there are dead apes. In the tops of the trees, too, there are bodies. Suddenly there's movement in the distance, a thin dark shadow flitting between the trees. The camera freezes. There it is again. Is it a man on stilts picking his way through the dead bodies? Is it the Featurist? the boy asks me. There it is again. It's some way off. It freezes, and it turns its head slowly and mechanically towards the camera. It is a stork, a solitary black stork. It stands motionless for what feels like an eternity, then it raises one foot after the other in an exaggerated movement and picks its way across the bodies of its companions. Why doesn't it just fly away? the boy asks me. Why doesn't it escape?

There are more men in our cell, men of different nationalities, countless conversations happening at once. With little room to lie down, we sleep on a string tied from one wall to the other that leaves deep indentures in our necks. An escaped prisoner is returned and displayed for all to see in the courtyard. He is given a mock crucifixion by the irreligious guards, one of whom pokes him in the side with an improvised spear in imitation of Longinus, the soldier of Rome. Everyone is forced to attend. The prisoner plays his role perfectly. My God, he cries, at the climactic moment, why have you forsaken me? However, his hands have been tied, not pierced through with nails. He is led off by soldiers with machine guns, but the crucifix is left propped up in the courtyard as a warning. The next time we will use nails, the captain says, and afterwards, in our cell, there is much debate about how painful it would be to have a nail hammered through your hand.

It's not painful, the man with the dreadful harp tattoo on his arm claims, it's the weight of your body when you are suspended from the cross that's the problem. No, another one says, a new arrival with permanent dark-blue stubble and staring round eyes, that's not true, there is a small platform for your feet in order to take some of your weight, he claims, otherwise the body would slide off in seconds due to gravity. Think how easily you can draw a knife through your hand. How easily? someone asked him. Very easily, he replied. Nonsense, the man with the harp tattoo replied, and in the context of the conversation the harp looked even more like a child's drawing of the gates of heaven, they fix your feet with nails too, he said, that's the whole point, have you never been to church? Only the Catholics nail the feet, the Scotsman with the paralysed bollock announced, the Protestants have him sort of hovering in front of the cross. They don't show the nails. Suffering Christ, someone said. The Catholics love their suffering, that's for sure, the Scotsman claimed. That's not true, the tattooed Irishman said, the Protestants are much more attached to it. Then why don't they show the nails? the Scotsman asked him. Because they can't even take any pleasure in pain, he replied. That's no answer, the Scotsman said. The Protestants don't know they're alive, the Irishman said. What, the Scotsman said, you have to be physically impaled on a cross to know you're alive? In that case we're the kings of the castle, he said, and with that there was much hilarity in the cell. Without suffering, the Irishman said, none of us would ever change. Suffering is the engine, he said, and he looked at me. I said nothing. The engine of what? someone asked him. The engine of love, he said, and again there was much mocking and hilarity. In that case I'm fucking Casanova, the Scotsman said, as he blew mock kisses to his cellmates. I felt a great confusion. I sat on the floor with my knees pulled tight against my chest. I took out my ID card and I looked at my old face. I wondered if right now he too was dreaming me, just as I dreamed of my older self and he looked back at me. My God, I said to my younger self, why have you forsaken me? Of course, I knew the answer. It was just hard to take.

There was talk of the war. The Allies have invaded Sicily. Italy is next to fall. Once more we fixed our eyes on the sea, the same sea that I had come to believe had been miraculously fixed years before our own detention, but as in the movie nothing appeared. I searched the horizon for a black stork in vain. Was he the black stork? the boy with the eyepatch asked me, the boy who by this point was wearing a top, a striped pyjama top that he had inherited from a dead man. You know, he said, like a symbol, like when you become something outside of yourself to make a point or to sum it all up? You think you can sum it all up as a black stork? I asked him. I believe so, he said. I wouldn't have believed it years ago, but I do now.

There was more than a stork, I told him. There was a film of a room. A room with no windows or doors or perhaps there was a door behind the camera. What was in the room? the boy with the pyjama top asked me. Nothing, at first, I told him. Or so it seemed. How long was this film? he asked me. Hours, I told him, there were several reel changes. How do you know they were shown in the right order? he asked me. They were numbered, I told him, the film cans were numbered. What if they had been put in the wrong cans? There's no way of knowing, I conceded. But there was an event, a central event, midway through the second reel, which made sense, as it formed the film's axis. That's what they call the Germans and the Italians and the Japs, the boy reminded me. The Axis Powers. How many reels were there in all? the boy asked me. Three in total, I told him. Okay, he said, the first one is Great Britain, the middle one is the Axis Powers and the third one is Russia. Mother Russia, he said, and he looked at me as if he had just said something vitally important and perfectly inscrutable. Okay, I said, so this event, this oddity (that's you, the boy said), takes place in Germany, let's say. Where in Germany exactly? the boy asked me. In the heart of Germany. That would be Berlin, the boy said. Berlin is not the heart of Germany, I told him. Berlin is the pulsating brain of Germany. Where is the heart? he asked me. It is buried beneath a tree in a forest, I told him. The Black Forest? he asked me. No, I said, it's a forest outside Bayreuth that is reached by an unnamed road. Is it a pine forest? Yes, I told him, the kind of pines with high tops and tall branchless trunks covered in lichen. I know the type, the boy nodded, the type of forest you can get lost in and that is uncannily grim. And in this forest in the heart of Germany, which is a room with no doors and windows on a film reel buried beneath a tree and divided between the powers of the war, there is an object. What's the object? A flashlight. A battery-powered flashlight? A battery-powered flashlight. What's it doing? Shining. Shining? Shining in the dark. Shining on and off. Shining on and off? It seems to be set to some kind of programme. Like an SOS? Possibly. Where is it in the room? It's on the floor in the middle of the room. Was it always there and it just became switched on? Impossible to tell, the room is dark, and it's only when the flashlight comes on that you realise it is there. But you don't know for sure? You can tell it's a flashlight but if you look at the other reels featuring the same shot of the room, if you look at Great Britain and Mother Russia, as you said, it's impossible to tell if the flashlight is still there, on the floor, turned off, or perhaps counting down, counting down to the moment where it will send this signal from the heart of Germany. Otherwise the room is dark? It's shot in black and white and with expressionistic shadows. How long does the flashlight send out its signal for? I would say a good twenty-five minutes. Does it have a pattern, or does it vary? It has a simple pattern, though I can't say for certain, because at one point I got up to make a cup of tea. You got up to make a cup of tea after the signal started? I wasn't sure how significant it was, at first. It was the only thing that happened in a film that lasted hours and you weren't sure it was significant? Well, it was the first time I had watched the full thing, how was I to know that there wouldn't be more significant events to come? And there weren't any? No, there was nothing else of significance. Was the movie silent? Yes, the movie was silent. When you came back from making your ill-judged tea, what was happening? The flashlight was still flashing on and off. How long between the ons and offs? Seconds. And what did Mariella say? She said, look, someone has left a flashlight on the floor. She actually used the word someone? Yes, she said someone. Even though her husband had made the movie and it wasn't as if someone else had just wandered through the set and dropped a flashlight on the floor and walked off? Unless her husband hadn't realised there was a flashlight in the dark of the room and he was as surprised as any of us when it made its presence known. Do you think he had asked the room a question and that the flashlight had responded in code? It's possible. In wartime everything speaks in code. And you saw nothing else, you're sure of that? Yes, well, the darkness seemed to settle down a little after the appearance of the flashlight. What do you mean? I mean it was as if the darkness bled back into itself, as if the shadows withdrew slowly, as if there was a retraction somehow, as if the atmosphere slithered, somehow, back into place. You mean like a snake, like a snake in a reptile house? It could just be the flashlight talking. Wasn't The Flashlight the name of a superhero? A comic book? I think that's correct. What was his superpower? A blinding beam of light, I would guess, a light so bright it could stun. Do you think the flashlight just ran out of batteries? What do you mean? When it stopped, I mean, do you think it had just run out of juice? Maybe it's as significant or as insignificant as that. Still, I don't think so, the boy said, I think it's telling us something. Like what? The ocean outside our window, a black stork in a bombed-out zoo, a flashlight in an empty room in the heart of Germany buried in a reptile house beneath a tree in an uncanny forest. I think it's saying we have lost our way. I think it's saying we should never have left the sea.

What if I told you the film was called *Message to the Dead*? That's us, the boy in the striped pyjamas said. No, I told him, we're not the dead, we're the disappeared. Then where are the dead? he asked me. And why are they watching movies? I think it's a film of an attempt to contact the dead, not a film for the dead to watch. Why can't the dead watch movies? the boy protested. I mean, if they can watch an attempt to contact them why can't they watch a record of an attempt to contact them? Who knows if every time the film gets shown they're brought back to life, like a light in a darkened room? Why do we need to speak to the dead and what do we need to tell them? I asked him. Perhaps they're lost, perhaps death isn't clear, perhaps they need directions. To where? I don't know, where do the dead go, to Jerusalem, to heaven, to Timbuktu? It's a place in their mind that has to be resolved, I told him. But where are the minds of the dead? They're in our mind too. So where does our mind need to go? To the fourth film. There's a fourth film? Yes. But it's a porno. No! It's another lengthy one. It goes on for hours. Who's in it, is Mariella in it? Yes, Mariella is in it. How does she look? Immaculate, ravaged. Who else is in it? I think it's the husband, I told him. At last, he said. But I can't be sure. Didn't you ask Mariella? Yes, I said, we watched it together one evening and I said to her, is that your husband who is making love to you? And what did she say? She smiled, her eyes twinkled, end of story. Well, what did he look like? He had a muscular back, I can tell you that much. What about his face? That, unfortunately, is permanently buried in her hair over her left shoulder. You mean he never looks up? Not once. He just keeps going at it. In that one position for hours. Actually, it's a loop, the lovers are caught in a loop, it seems to be a section cut from a much longer piece and then looped for hours. What about his buttocks? Not as tight as you might imagine. His legs? Athletic, a walker. What else? There is a marking on his left arm, some kind of tattoo, a tattoo of a woman, perhaps. So there are two women in the picture? he said. One woman, I told him, and a picture of a woman. A film is a picture too, he said. So it's the missionary position? he asked me. A variant. What about her, how is she looking? Dissipated, enraptured, her hair cast back on the pillow. How long is the looped section? Twenty seconds or thereabouts. What about her legs? One is out to the side, the other is bent over his at a ninety-degree angle. Like The Hanged Man, the boy said, like the Gypsy Tarot? The Hanged Man is upside down, I told him. It's all the same when you are making love, the boy shrugged. What is it they say about the hangman's beautiful daughter, don't the dead ejaculate when they're hanged, something like that? Anyway, I said, interrupting him quite rudely, she's wearing stockings, you'll be pleased to know. What else? Heels, she's wearing high heels. She is dressed for sex. Now we're talking, he said. Does she caress his head, does she run her fingers down his back? No, she stretches her arms back above her head and holds on to the headboard. She's doing a handstand, the boy marvelled, that's acrobatic. What then? The whole thing repeats, I explained to him, he buries his head, he thrusts several times, she crosses her leg at an odd angle over his, she has a look of abandon, she stretches up – or down – and takes hold of the headboard and then we're back to square one. What about her face, what about her lips? She gasps, I can tell you that much. Do we have a title? Yes, I told him. It's titled *Exodus*. Someone is headed in the same direction as the dead, the boy said.

One day I was summoned to a meeting of mid-level British commanders in the courtyard during break. They looked like a gang of toughs. One of them had a scar like an antenna across his chest. Another had an Errol Flynn moustache. We hear you can predict the future, the Errol Flynn moustache said, well, not predict it but at least weigh it up a little, he went on. You've got a feel for it, is what I'm trying to say, he said. They didn't want to believe in it, but they were asking me anyway. It was the closest they were going to get to military intelligence in here. In truth, most of the requests that I had received from fellow prisoners for information from the future had dried up. No one wanted to know. It's better not to know, they said, and they nodded their heads at the wisdom of their words. Knowing what's up ahead is enough to frighten the French, they said, and they nodded again. But this was different. The mid-level British commanders were planning a breakout. In truth, I should

have known they were going to ask me, but there are all
sorts of short-range tributaries running off from the main
thrust of your life, you can't keep your mind focused on all of
them, although you can turn your attention to them, as and
when. One thing I did know, I wasn't going to join them.

I nodded, my expression heavy with the selfsame wisdom
that the people who didn't want to know showed. Yes, I
said, I have a feel for it, I can help. If we were to abseil
from our cell during the night and take off in a small
rowing boat that had been secreted in the rocks down
below, would we make it out? the one with the scar like an
aerial asked me. I thought for a moment. I let my mouth
hang open like a simpleton. I batted what was left of my
eyelids as if I were computing the future. All I could say for
certain is that I was sure I would never see them again. I
predict success, I told them. Only insofar as you are never
captured and returned to this hellhole. I used the word
hellhole deliberately. I thought they might appreciate it.
They sighed, and they nodded. Okay, they said. Then the
one with the scar asked me an odd question. Do you know
how I got my scar? he asked me. I got it in peacetime,
he continued, without waiting for me to respond. That's
surprising, isn't it, everyone is showing off new wounds,
recent damage, whereas my cross – that's what he called,
it, his cross – is purely historical. How can anything be
purely historical, I asked myself, particularly a cross?
But I said nothing. I nodded and then I said, by way of
lubricating the conversation, we all have our cross to bear.
Tell me, friend, he said, how is your feel for the past? My
feel for the past, I told him, is acrimonious. Do you know
how I got this scar? he asked me again. Leave it, the Errol
Flynn moustache said, but he continued to stare at me

nonetheless. It doesn't look like a cross to me, I told him. It looks more like an antenna. He nodded. That's interesting, he said, that's one way of putting it. Is that what happened to you? he asked me. No offence. What do you mean? I asked him. You became a receiver, he said. The second sight, he said. Ask me how I got the scar, he commanded me. I looked at him through the filthy pools of my eyes. You were lovelorn, I told him. And so you spilled your guts. With that I walked away. The next morning, they were gone. That night many more were made transmitters through collective punishment.

But don't get the idea that prison life was eventful. There is a reason that we lived in the future, that we dissected the moments that lay up ahead, that we fantasised about mysterious directors that had died into their movies, that we stared at the ocean for hours on end willing a single miserable ship up from over the horizon. Don't get the idea that there were regular daring escapes, that there were terrible routine punishments, that every day consisted of debating, debating, debating.

I watched my nails grow, broken and crooked as they were, in anticipation of grinding them down once more against the stone floor. I built a huge manor in my head, the kind of manor whose garden we would creep into as children and where we would climb trees and eat berries or steal apples. Now I peopled the room with characters of my own invention and with interesting pieces and with empty rooms, too, empty rooms where I could escape to sit on a single cobwebbed chair and sit there like a jailed Greek god, like the Greek gods of imprisonment, imperious and silent.

I have since come to learn that this is a common strategy for the paralysed and the locked away, to erect a great structure in your head, sometimes a grand ocean liner, other times a humble train travelling through the mountains, even, I have heard tell, a series of hollowed-out caves. Some days I would leave my stately home to wander the imaginary topography of the frozen-in-time, the ghostly canal boats, the boxy caravans, the strange theme parks topped with clown heads, the double-decker buses lighting out, the campsites hidden in the forest, the council houses with their rooms set aside, the abandoned aeroplanes behind high fences, the circus tents with their multiple rings, the tower blocks too, the huge factories, and the prisons too, the prisons and workhouses, prisons within prisons filled with generations past and to come, the Ferris wheels too, running backwards and turning forward and in their compartments faces, blurred faces of groups of people, huddled together, and I would return to my own dwelling where, in a back room at the top of a short flight of stairs, I had, quite deliberately, locked away my own heart.

Other times I would lie with my face to the wall and I would lick it. I would dart my tongue out for no one to see, each time leaving a dark mark on the wall. I would reintroduce parts of my body to itself, I would name my foot, say, and present it once more to my leg or my torso, even, to my hips, my arms to their shoulders, and in doing so I would remake myself on an hourly basis.

Other distractions included urinating on myself – a blessed release – eating paper, as I have said, walking in circles (which only lasted a few months until the cell was too crowded), grinding my nails, as I have said, attempting to

jam my tongue between my teeth, counting the wrinkles
on the roof of my mouth as you would the rings on a tree,
attempting to levitate, to float free into the air, with varying
degrees of success, counting the waves as you would the
rings on a tree, imagining myself dropping from various
heights into the cool spray of the ocean below, mock-
translating people's conversations to myself or sometimes to
the boy with the pyjama top, imagining my face changing,
transforming, imagining that it had once more, like a
baby's, started to grow and to change, and anticipating, up
ahead, what my new face would become and, with it, what
I myself might be, picturing myself as the man lying upside
down on Mariella in the movie, her leg crossed over mine,
the man with no face himself, picturing myself as the man
who breaks out of the loop and who rises and who turns
to the camera and who presents his new face to me for the
approval of his old self, in prison still, his heart locked in a
draughty manor still, in a region of ghosts, still.

But I spent most of the time living in the future, even when
the future was awkward or not to my taste or not as I would
have predicted it, which is odd because of course that was
exactly what I was doing, though if I had predicted it, if I
had chosen it, more properly, I would not have chosen to
turn our parlour games and our spiritualist circle and my
masked persona into a travelling show that played across
clubs and theatres and ballrooms in the dying years of the
1940s and I call them the dying years with no hint of irony
whatsoever.

I was aware, of course, to some extent, that Mariella saw in
me the fulfilment of her husband's quest, as nebulous and
inchoate as it was, although we had established that his

interest lay at the intersection of art, technology, fate and time, not to say the existence of heaven, which is what those films became to me, a sort of extended afterworld, moments of infinity, a love embrace, which is once and forever, heaven is a love embrace, I decided, and the films were too, which was obvious with the fourth one, the one with the lovers in bed, but I came to regard the others, too, as filled with an impossible longing, which is heaven, which is as futile and beautiful as holding on to your lover.

I thought of my own lover, my long-lost lover, who I kept locked in a room that I never visited. I told myself that I fooled people out of love, that I made them believe in heaven, that there was a spark inside a human being that could be activated by hope or fantasy just the same, by lies or by imagination, by flights of fancy, and who would say no to a flight of pure fancy if it's at all a possibility? Why not, I told myself, if it all ends badly, regardless of belief, why not come up with a series of beautiful lies that would transform their relationship to suffering? And there was much suffering in the dying years of the 1940s.

But understand this. A lie is as real as a truth. If a lie, once established, rewrites the world in its wake, then it becomes a truth, if a lie becomes real then it is no longer a lie and tell me, friend, that we are not, already, in receipt of an infinity of lies, are we not balanced, as awkwardly as on a tower of mattresses, on so many lies that were the scales removed from our eyes and we were shown the truth it would appear as the greatest lie of all, indeed, that all the little truths that we have built our lives upon are themselves balanced on an awkward pile of mattresses and if we were to insist on their destruction, if we were to be as idiotic as to stand

up for truth or some such impossibility, all that we would be
left with would be a sad elephant on the back of a tortoise
or whatever grotesque image passes for the first one, a
sad mattress in an empty room, a piss-stained mattress
or a bowl of flowers, a welcoming parent, a sappy cloud, a
rainbow, the tail of a great peacock, a single, silent stone,
so that when the women stood up in their seats in the
great theatres of Greece, in the great run-down theatres,
and asked me what had happened and would there be a
great return, I would tell them, yes, yes there will, yes, and
with that we were one more tear-sodden mattress closer to
heaven, one elephant tusk closer, one sappy cloud away.

What struck me most in our travels across Greece in the
dying years were the tall cranes, the cranes that stood high
above the cities, cranes that stood motionless for the most
part. Everywhere there was rebuilding, but it seemed to
happen when you weren't looking. As soon as your back
was turned a new building sprung up, a new edifice was
completed, a new train station came into view. Cranes can
be made without the aid of cranes, so what is the point of
cranes? The point of cranes is to tower into heaven and
to move majestically slowly. Cranes are dancing about
architecture. We would see them before we saw the city
itself, their thin white bodies, like storks, of course, feeding
in a pool of water. Beneath them, the suddenly completed
houses. The small concert hall where we performed in
Lamia was presided over by four white cranes. What is
the term for a group of cranes; a mirage, a dissonance, a
formation? Inside there was much glass, glass walls, glass
doorways and a high mirrored ceiling. I looked up at myself,
my face a blotch of pink, as we were escorted inside. I saw
the posters on the walls. There, amongst the cabaret acts,

the singers and opera stars, was a crude drawing of my
stage persona. The Oddity, it read, the man from the future:
their words, not my own.

Mariella took care of all business matters. I wasn't to be
approached. Of course, my looks, the extravagance of my
wounds, held most people at a fascinated distance. With
our hosts I would never wear my mask. My face served
as proof of my presence in two worlds at once. At dinner
I would remain silent and all questions were addressed
to Mariella. Is it not a torment, our host at the concert
hall in Lamia asked her, is it not a torture, he said, as he
glanced in my direction, to be with someone who always
knows what's going to happen, who can second-guess, let
us say, your every move? Mariella dabbed her mouth with
a napkin, her pink lipstick staining the white cotton. I
drooled some soup from the corner of my mouth. We never
discuss our own future together, Mariella told him, that is,
we never enquire. Come now, our host's wife demanded of
us, surely when you first met in order to, well, in order to
ascertain his abilities, you must have asked him some test
questions, asked him to provide you with some scenarios
that you could then investigate yourself. Such as? Mariella
asked her. She was expert in the art of turning a question
around. Such as, the lady said, well, such as what shall
we find if we enter the concourse of the train station at 12
p.m. tomorrow? Who shall I meet at the weekend? Is the
notorious murder suspect innocent or guilty? Even better,
who shall win the grand race? How will the price of gold
fare? Will it be a boy or a girl? Before Mariella could reply
I took my hand and placed it across her forearm as if to
prevent her from raising it. She held her knife tight in her
hand. Our hosts exchanged awkward glances. I'm sorry, the

man said, please excuse my wife. Every time, it worked like a charm.

Before the curtain rose we would play a rare 78 recording of Scriabin's 'Étude Op. 8 No. 12' in order to set the scene. I confess I knew nothing of Scriabin's mysticism back then, of his harmonics of colour, his blurring of sight and sound, his own experience of voices, his occult cosmogony, his assumption of godhood, his own black mass, his great negation, his great affirmation. But I knew it to be a music of psychic tumult. The lights would drop in the theatre and with the aid of a rainbow of primitive lighting gels Scriabin would perforate the veil. I sat, masked and robed, in the centre of the stage, the sound of my own blood in my ears. The curtains parted to gasps from the audience. Good news, I would say, and I spoke it as if it were the echo of an echo, I bring good news.

Often we would begin the show with an act of basic hypnotism, in order to presage the greater hypnotism still to come. I would request a volunteer, a young man or a young woman or, on this occasion, a lame old crone. By this point I had developed an elementary but highly effective technique. As the crone approached I would open my arms as if to embrace or console her and then in the second before the love embrace I would strike her arms down and run my fingers, held tight together, quickly and gently across her throat. You have no head, I would tell them, for I have removed it.

The volunteer's body would become limp, and they would stagger, unbalanced, from side to side. I would stand behind them and have them fall back into my arms, a technique that was particularly effective with women. Then I would ask them how, with their head removed, they were capable of thought at all. They would say all sorts of things at this juncture: I don't know; well, what doesn't know; my body; well, where in your body (these answers were often lewd and unintentionally hilarious); something is thinking for me; well, do they have a head (this provoked much laughter); a ghost is thinking; well, does that mean you are haunted (the Headless Horseman, someone shouted one night); my mummy and my daddy dreamed me up; well, would they really have dreamed of a baby with no head (again, much laughter); then I would drop my punchline. You have no head because God is dreaming you, I would tell them. You are a thought bubble in the mind of God. The results, I must confess, were often spectacular.

I am all a bubble, the old crone said. I am set adrift. Isn't that fancy? What did God think of you? I asked her, and at this point I hammed it up a little by turning to the audience and shrugging my shoulders as if to say, what have we got here? He thought me on one of His good days, she said. Then He thought no more of it. Well, who's thinking you now without a head? There was more laughter in the audience, but it was a little more awkward. It's just an echo, she shrugged, as if that were the most natural explanation in the world. Then she started again. Mr Hitler burst a bubble, she said, and she laughed. I heard Mariella cough from the side of the stage, the signal to wrap it up. But I was intrigued, and I couldn't resist one further question. And what do you think God thinks of Mr Hitler? I asked her. Why, He can't stop thinking about him, I would imagine, she said. I clicked my fingers and brought her back to life. There was muffled applause.

The second part of the performance went without a hitch and successfully raised the atmosphere. I reported on the fates of dogs, of sweethearts, of aged parents and of a green parakeet who informed his owner that he had made the journey back to the Azores to be reunited with his family where he had died of old age in a tree. It seemed to satisfy everyone. Traditionally we would end with what we called a 'silent thanksgiving', where for the space of a minute we would praise the creator, however we understood him, the source of all sources, was how we put it in the literature. On this night something wonderful happened. I opened my eyes and it had begun to snow. From the roof of the theatre a blizzard of tiny snowflakes floated to the floor. I looked up to see it and I felt them dissolve into my eyes. Of course it was fake, that was the explanation, that some stagehand had accidentally triggered the fake snow machine. But even so, I realised the truth. It was the first of the miracles that turned me around. Inside me it was snowing for the first time in years.

That night was the first night that we made love, Mariella and I, in the winter, in the snow, in my first summer after the war, my season of romance (boys, it's a sex scene, the young man in the pyjama top announces), we had been drinking wine afterwards, backstage, this time I didn't take off my mask, as there were members of the public swarming all around us, touching my robe, marvelling over me with Mariella, wherever did you find him? they asked her and she said things like, the wind blew him in, or, the sea gave him up, all of which were true, and as she did so she looked at me and she smiled, a wide smile, a toothy grin, that made all the years fall away between us, and as she talked she kept looking at me as if she too was possessed by me completely, as if she had given herself up to my spell, notice that I didn't say I had caught her under my spell, she had given herself up to my spell, which is much sexier, believe me (here we go, boys, the young man nodded), there's a difference, and although she couldn't see where my eyes were, they were on her completely, fixed on her utterly, even as I put up with the pawing of an elderly lady who smelled of potpourri and urine, of musty underwear (here we go, boys, the young man nodded), and I watched Mariella's lips as she drank her wine and I swear they quivered and her cheeks flushed and she smiled self-consciously at that and I thought, love is a power like ESP, and I recalled at that moment that I had known a girl called Mariella when I was at school, a beautiful, unavailable girl outside whose window I had stood in the evening, under a streetlight, outside her empty window, and had willed her to appear, had willed her to break out from her parents' house and float down from the window and make love on the dewy grass right there and then, but who had never appeared, indeed who had dated instead a young man with a squint and a hunchback, you can imagine how that made me feel, and with an eyepatch, for God's sake (hey!), but now here I was, more hideous than he would ever dare, masked up for my own good and for the good of those around me, and with a connection, such a powerful connection, with a woman called Mariella, that I could feel the wine as it trickled slowly, sensuously, down her throat, and into her precious belly, which is where I longed to be myself (here we go, boys, the young man nodded), and I felt myself get an erection (told you, boys, the young man said, let's go), the first spontaneous erection since the war, I'm not saying there had never been a single spontaneous erection since the death of Hitler but then again, who knows, these things

take time, especially after trauma and God knows the whole
continent had been traumatised, so erections were probably
at a premium, remote ones even more so, and besides, that's
exactly what it felt like, an erection rising from the ruins
of Berlin, from the ruins of the Clydeside, and of Dresden
and of Malta and of Oradour-sur-Glane, look it up boys,
when you get out, a filthy erection is what I'm trying to say,
a lascivious erection, an erection like the sun rising on a
battlefield, is what I'm getting at, and of course it began to
stick out beneath my robe and get in the way of old women,
it's big, I might as well tell you, there's no point in lying over
this, it's a big member and it's becoming an obstruction, so
that I push my way through the throng (with his dong! the
guy with the crap tattoo says, who by this point has joined
in) and Mariella sees me moving towards her and she makes
to finish off her conversation and I take her by the arm,
something I had never done before, we never linked arms
or held hands, and I push us through the crowd and out
the emergency exit at the back and down the stairs where
there is a car waiting for us, a car with its engine running,
unbelievably, just like in the movies, and we take off, and of
course outside it isn't snowing, I would love to have said that
we sped through the snow and the dark and all the stars
came out, this time right side up, but it's snowing inside
me, by this point it was a blizzard, a compete white-out, and
we looked at each other and we didn't mention the snow,
even though inside us both we knew, we knew all about it,
and she leaned over and she put her head on my chest and
I thought, she is listening for the snow, she is listening to
the snow falling, but then I thought, does falling snow even
have a sound, doesn't it fall silently, isn't that part of its
magic, that it arranges itself in silence over everything and
transforms it without a sound, so that when you wake up

and throw the curtains back it takes you by surprise and there it is, blanketing everything, transforming everything while slowly dying into it, isn't that what Mariella has said about her husband, about his films, about art, about dying into it, isn't that what she meant?

We measure everything by the past, by the light of the past, we say this is as beautiful as something, as something that happened once that we now think of as the most beautiful time, the most beautiful moment, always in the past, but this is what changed in me and I don't pretend it is anything but a minor miracle, a human impossibility, almost, but for the first time I saw the beauty of the future reflected in the present, it was as if I stepped out of myself, ran a little ahead, and then looked back in amazement, in amazement at the quality of light, the tenderness of the moment (the size of his steaming erection, more like, the man with the crap tattoo said), the miracle of the coincidence of everything, and the cost of it all too, I saw that moments up ahead were just as fixed as moments in the past, that the future sat there in anticipation of your arrival like a host, only I didn't use a word like fixed, I used a word like betrothed, I used a word like reception, but the point is I wasn't up ahead, really, the point is I gained this knowledge, this certainty that the beauty of the moment flows into it from the future, that all that's past is redeemed in the light of the future, I gained it through a connection with another person which in turn connected me to a third truth, in any relationship between two things a third factor is implied which is known as an intercessor, and of course that's when I began to think of my wife once more, my heart in a locked room, was how I described her, if you recall, and how she had appeared to me as the three of hearts, and I wondered if perhaps, somehow, she was the intercessor in all of this, which made me love all the more passionately and with abandon (here we go, boys, the young man nodded) as I dropped my robe to the floor of our hotel room and Mariella kneeled to embrace me (get in there, the young man said), but still I kept my mask on, your mask is sexy, she said, your mask is so sexy, make love to me with your mask on, she said, and I lifted her up and laid her out on the bed, her dress pulled up around her waist (I love it like that, the man with the awful tattoo agreed), and as I slipped her panties off, pink panties would you believe (oh yes, the young man marvelled, perfect, I believe it), I almost went to put them on my head, to wear them like a crown, but at the last minute I thought better of it and instead I tossed them across the room and I watched as they landed, I watched the shape they made, they pooled, to be precise, everything was significant, they pooled in the corner like a puzzled face or like a quizzical face, though maybe that's the same thing, but I don't think so, to be honest, and then I undid her top, her breathing was fast and shallow and rhythmical by this point, and then I unclipped her bra, which clipped at the front, would you believe, I had heard about these bras but never seen one in real life, and at this point I caught myself in the mirror, there was a full-length mirror on the cupboard, and for a moment, just for a second, you understand, nothing significant, but for a moment I was repelled by myself, I was put off, I was disgusted, I saw all the scars on my body, the badly healed wounds, the complications, I remember thinking, though God knows why, but it makes sense, I guess, if you think about it, and my paunch too, I was out of shape, that was another complication, and there I was leaning over this beautiful woman in a state of abandoned undress (you can't beat that, the man with the appalling tattoo agreed), looking like a fiend, there is no other word for it, a Shakespearean fiend with the addition of the mask but a fiend nonetheless, but somehow this only added to my passion, to the lasciviousness of my delivery (nice word for it, the young man laughed), and I felt my back arch uncontrollably in ecstasy and I entered her right there and then as if I were entering heaven's gates themselves, which the unruly tattoo of my cellmate serves to bring to mind, and it felt like my brain was ejaculating, like it was squeezing all its sense down my spine and out into Mariella, who for her own part had started to mutter, to form primitive speech patterns in my ear, and I felt like I was in the movie once more, in all of the movies her husband had made, the one with the couple on the bed, of course, but more than that, the one in the zoo where evolution seems to run backwards, that's what her words said to me, and the one with the light that buzzes on and off in a darkened room and that wakes the dead, and of course the one where the ocean meets the shore.

Cut to the chase, the boy interrupted me, we're in prison, for God's sake, what were her tits like? Her breasts? Her breasts were lined, curiously lined, with thin wrinkles, rivulets, even, as if they had changed size, as if they had once been bigger, in her youth, and they were quite pale. What about the nipples? Let me tell you about her eyes, eyes are best experienced in tandem with the breasts, as we all know. Around her eyes she had the most expressive crow's feet I have ever seen. They were so sexy. It really looked like a crow had stood with one foot planted on either side of her eye while it drank blue milk from her pupil. What about the nipples? Her eye make-up was smoky-grey and combined with her pupils, which, as I say, were the palest whitest blue and which seemed to draw the attention inwards and downwards at the same time, which is to say that making love felt like the equivalent of being a high diver. Were her nipples blue as well? Her nipples were brown and petite, like a freckle stood to attention. Oh wow. What happened next? She took me in her mouth. What was her mouth like? Tight. Endless. Did she say anything else, did she goad you? Not while my cock was in her mouth. Afterwards she just said, fuck me. Oh God. Fuck me? Fuck me. Too much. And did she grab you? She held on to my buttocks. She scratched my back. She bit my neck. You better watch that, the wiseass with the idiot tattoo cautioned, a human bite can be a terrible thing. Did she come? the boy asked me. She didn't say I'm coming or anything. She didn't announce it? No. The muttering became faster and she began thrusting her hips back towards me. Then she sort of melted a little bit. But you kept on at it, right? You bet I kept at it. What did she smell like? Like being pursued through a soft, damp, forest. That'll be the perfume, the young boy nodded sagely. That'll be the womanhood, the clown with the tattoo countered. What next? While I'm fucking her, I spread her buttocks with my hands and I start to tap her asshole, rhythmically, with my finger. Oh boy, that's just like the flashlight going on and off, the kid said. How did she react? She's loving every minute. Then I start to whisper in her ear. Like what? That's between us, boys. But let's just say she's coming back to life all over again. Christ, this is a marathon, the young kid says. What next? I slide my finger in and I keep it there. You keep it there? I keep it there. Then I stop moving altogether. I freeze. Why? I get the feeling that we are being filmed. Impossible, I thought you were in a hotel room in a foreign town? the young man protested. That would have meant someone hiding out in that specific room and having a place to set up a camera and remaining undiscovered and also it would have meant that the hotel staff were in on it too and even the people who presented your performance as they would have had to book the correct hotel and ensure you were given the appropriate room. Nonetheless, I get the feeling, like an arrow through my heart, that we are somehow being captured on film. Captured? I can't explain it but yes, there is no other word that I would have used at that moment. In fact, I believe we are making *Exodus*.

What's *Exodus*? the guy with the unadvisable tattoo asked me. It's a film, the boy said, a film that the woman's ex-husband made of the two of them making love. The two of who? Her and her husband or her and our Oddity? If he's seen the film how can he be in it at a later point? Well, that's just it.

Remember I told you that I couldn't see the face of the man who was making love in the film, I interrupted them, I told you his head was buried over her left shoulder? That's exactly the position I was in when I froze. But also, the film was dark, very dark, it was another silent black-and-white number, so it could have been that the lover was wearing a black leather mask. What about the surroundings? It was a close-up of a bed with nondescript white sheets. Were they in the same position? They could have been. Impossible, they couldn't have replicated every wrinkle, every stain, every fold? I'm saying it could have been the exact same scene. But didn't you say something about Mariella, is that her name, crossing her leg at an angle over the lover? That's just it, as soon as I froze she moved her leg into position as if on cue. No! Yes. Wait, the boy said, I've got it, didn't you say there was some kind of mark on the man's arm, like a

tattoo or something? Yes, I admitted, I did say that. You
don't have a tattoo. No, I don't, but now I think it was a
wound, a scar. Look at my arm, I said, and I pulled up my
sleeve, there was a gash, an injury I had received at the
hands of the Nazis. Okay, but what about your physique, did
it match that guy in the film? I think so, I said, though who
knows, you can't recognise yourself from the back, there's
never the opportunity, everybody knows that. Well, what
happened next, surely now you are aware of the moment you
can disrupt the continuity by doing something unexpected,
something that doesn't take place? But that's just the thing,
I replied, the film I had seen was on a loop, so it doesn't
matter what I do afterwards, I didn't realise where I was,
which is to say I wasn't overcome with a terrible sense of
déjà vu until the action required of the loop had been played
out. Now they could do what they wanted with the footage
and there was nothing I could do to disrupt it. Wait, you
said you slid your finger into her ass and you kept it there.
That's correct. Well, can you tell in the film if he had his
finger up her ass? She's on her back, the arm is beneath her,
the finger could be anywhere, I shrugged. There's no way
of knowing. Anyway, the point is I panicked. I leaped up, I
unplugged my finger from her ass, withdrew my cock, which
was throbbing, still, let me tell you, I was about to come
but I couldn't stay there any longer, ejaculating on cue, in a
film, not me, and I ran over to the painting on the opposite
wall and I yanked it off, fully expecting to find a hole in it, it
was a religious painting, a painting of a woman sitting in a
hallway or an annex or some kind of conservatory, perhaps,
and outside there is another woman, a younger woman who
is kneeling down and looking at her through the window and
offering her something, maybe, I seem to recall something
in her hand like an arrow, maybe, and up above the younger

woman, in the sky, on a cloud, there's God almighty Himself
and He is shooting a beam of light, that's what it looks like,
a beam of desire or longing or will or command, who knows,
he is setting a seed, I thought, which is funny knowing what
comes next, and the beam goes through the window of the
annex and pierces the shoulder of the older woman and I'm
fully expecting to find a window behind it and a camera
crew there, Mariella's own husband, even, with his trousers
round his ankles, getting off, and I realise there's an
unstoppable orgasm building in me, there's no way to head
it off, and I look around at Mariella, she's curled up in the
sheets in a state of confusion, and I'm holding this painting
in front of me and I just shoot, there's nothing I can do to
stop it, I come all over the painting, I'm holding it in front
of me and I look round at Mariella and her mouth's hanging
open, her eyes are wide, those cold blue pools I told you
about, well, the ice has cracked, boys, and then, you couldn't
make this up, it's almost unbelievable, she says to me, that
was fucking amazing.

Seriously. I'm standing there with this painting of God and
His angels or who knows what, and my cum is dripping
off it, there's still dribbles coming out of my jap's eye, the
painting is probably completely ruined, and she says to me,
you are fucking incredible. What a gesture, she says, and
she shakes her head. Then she beckons me over to the bed,
I'm still feeling a bit sheepish, to be honest, and she says, let
me clean you off, and she takes my cock back in her mouth
and cleans up what's left.

No! the young boy gasped. I'm telling you, I said. Then she
lies back on the bed and immediately falls asleep. You're a
fucking nut, the foul-mouth clown with the infantile tattoo

said. What a waste of precious jizz. You could have nailed
that bitch and instead you spent it on a fucking painting.
There's only so much to go round. Even God knows that
much.

Anyway, I continued, ignoring his contribution, now's my
chance, don't think I've given up my hypothesis for the
sake of some post-coital praise. While she's asleep, I comb
through the room. I take down the mirror, I look behind
all the furniture, I run my hand along the wall searching
for spyholes, I examine the elaborate candelabra for tiny
surveillance cameras. Don't be soft, the moron with the
retarded sketch on his arm said, you can't get a camera
that small. You think? I quizzed him. Who knows what the
secret service are up to. Who knows what the Nazi top brass
have dreamed up in secret command bases buried under
huge mountains. And remember, this guy, this husband of
Mariella's, the late film-maker, he was a Futurist, sorry, not
a Futurist but a Januist, which is worse, and so if anyone
could get their hands on the most covert technology, the
latest breakthroughs, tiny pinpoint cameras that could film
your every move, then it was him. So did you find anything?
the curious young man asked me. No, I admitted, there was
nothing I was able to locate. I heard a noise at one point, a
scuffling sound in the wall, but I think it was only rats.

We carried on. Mariella had a new-found appreciation
of me. She looked at me in a new way, full of desire and
bewilderment. We performed in Volos, in Larissa, in
Tsagkarada on the coast. Before the concert it was my habit
to take an early-evening walk around the city, minus my
mask and cloak, obviously, and I was reassured to see that
I could still terrify, that my appearance was still appalling

to the man – or woman – in the street. It was only sex workers, in those years, in the dying years, as I have termed them, who the wounded could turn to. I, too, had my fair share. Often on my evenings alone in an unknown city I would locate the red-light district and buy myself some companionship. Already, even in my secret life, I had deeper secrets. I had an annex and a bunker built in the side of my life that I shared with nameless prostitutes and destitute whores across the length of the country.

In Tsagkarada the whores displayed their wares in a run-down tower block with numbers on the windows. I chose a young blonde in sunglasses on the ground floor. She took her dress off, laid a towel on the bed and sat on the edge of it with her legs spread. Her pussy was perfect, not a wrinkle, not a hair. She asked me to wash my hands, nothing more, and when I removed my underwear she told me that I had a nice cock. I believed her to be earnest. She offered me her asshole to play with and I laid her over my knees like a little girl. When I was about to come, which didn't take long, she said, give me your juice, baby. At the time I thought it was the most beautiful thing I had ever heard.

I single out Tsagkarada and the meeting with the poetic whore because it is there where the visitations began. Let me explain.

Wait a minute, the lout with the cartoon of heaven's gate on his arm interrupted me, why the hell are you seeking out whores when you've got it on tap at home by this point? The idea that I was being filmed had unnerved me, I admitted to him, sex with Mariella now had the aspect of a performance. Whores, in my experience, in other word Greek whores in

the dying years, were not looking to be impressed. My desire
for a quick wank, say, with no kissing on the lips, I was
able to confide in them. They felt the same way themselves.
Besides, love, too, requires its secrets. A transparent love, in
my experience, never lasts. The clown seemed satisfied with
my answer, he gave a low grunt in response.

I took up the story. I'm on stage, I told them, I am
delivering the future. Some old bat has asked some
question about a family member who died, something
typical and tragic and a little bit pathetic like that. I am
about to speak when I catch a figure out of the corner of my
eye, standing on the far side of the stage. It is my father,
my father who died in 1936. He is wearing a light-brown
suit. He has wet himself. I turn to look at him and he looks
right back at me, as alive as he ever was. Then he shrugs.
What's to stop the dead pissing themselves? he asks me.
That's what convinced me it was really him. If he had said,
for instance, who says the dead can't be incontinent, then
I would have had my doubts. But it was my father alright.
There was a silence throughout the room, it was obvious
I was distracted. Could anyone else see him? I wondered.
No bugger can see me or hear me, my father replied, as
if by magic, except for you. Okay, I said, and I attempted
to regain my composure. I am receiving a transmission
from the other side, I announced to the audience. We are
not alone. Fuck it, I thought to myself, he's only going
to disrupt things if I don't include him, so I said to the
crowd, I would like to introduce you to my father. He died
in 1936, I told them, but he has come back from the dead.
Does he bring good news? a voice from the audience asked
me. I looked at the state of him, his stained trousers, his

uncombed hair. He smelled like the grave. Yes, I lied, yes, he brings great tidings.

What was the name of your loved one again? I asked the old dear, who was still standing. His name was Iannis, she said, Iannis Anastas. What can you tell us, Father, I asked him, of the fate of Iannis Anastas of Tsagkarada? How the fuck would I know? my father replied. That's like saying, oh, you live in Scotland, in that case you must know Jimmy McTavish. The afterworld is a fucking big place, you know. Anyway, he said, how are you doing? Not now, I said, and I turned to the audience and told them that some parts of heaven are cut off from others, that the heavens are numbered and that not everyone resides on the same cloud. That's one way to put it, my father mocked. Indeed, I cautioned the audience, the dead often fall into common relation, which can make it hard to recognise them, which is to say they become united, in a sense, with all of the relatives that have come before them, who greet each other with much clamour and joy and who come to resemble each other as one of the tribes of heaven.

I became aware of a tapping, or a rapping, more properly. More spirits, I thought to myself, more ghosts. Then I realised that my father was dancing, performing a tap dance on stage. He started to sing. It was 'My Mammy' by Al Jolson. That's in poor taste, the young boy interrupted me. It was grotesque, I nodded. It was horrific. One of his legs was dragging. His arms flopped by his side. There was some kind of bile or foam coming from his mouth. His head rolled back and forth as he sang in a strangulated voice. As I have already pointed out, there was a huge piss stain on his trousers. What are they doing in heaven today, the old woman asked me, where sin and sorrow are all washed away? I looked to my father, who had fallen to his knees and who was struggling to regain his footing in a pool of his own secretions. They're dancing in heaven, I told her, they're dancing in heaven where everything is forgiven. With that I got to my feet, walked past the pathetic form of my father, now motionless on the floor, and left the building by a rear exit.

The next morning, in a cafe on the waterfront, in the perpetual dust of Greece, in the terrible heat, Mariella quizzed me on the previous night's events. She was wearing a long form-fitting black dress and her now trademark black lipstick. Her black heels were scuffed. The wind blew her hair across her face. The waiter, who I noticed had a limp, brought us two cups of cold water with our eggs. He looked at me and nodded as if to acknowledge our secret brotherhood. Your father was really there, Mariella said, it's true, isn't it? She took a long draw on a cigarette and flicked it agitatedly to her side. Yes, I admitted, he was really there. But he was in a state. I won't lie, I told her, he looked like hell. Yes, she said, and she nodded as if it was no surprise. That's how the dead come back, I'm afraid, she said. Listen, she said, and she tossed her cigarette into the dust and stubbed it out with her heel, do you know what a zombie is? A monster, I said, some kind of voodoo creature that comes back from the dead, a horror show, basically. Do you know what causes zombies? she asked me. I don't know, I shrugged, voodoo priests, curses, hypnotism, some kind of sign or command? No, she said, and she looked at her hand and began to scuff her nails (that's what you do all day in the cell, the young man burst), what causes zombies is love, she said. It's love that brings back the dead. What are you talking about? I demanded.

How can love turn someone into a zombie? This is science fiction, this is fantasy. No, she says, it's all true. As long as we cannot break the bonds with our loved ones they return to us through force of will and incredible sorrow. They rise from the grave and they cannot rest until we ourselves allow them to. This is where the legend comes from. He was in a state, wasn't he, your father? Yes, I told her, he had pissed himself, his leg was dragging behind him, in the end he collapsed on the floor. He is making a supreme effort to come back, she said. There's no love between my father and I, I told her. We were never close. His appearance seems to say otherwise, she said. Look, I told her, you know as well as I do that the whole fucking thing is made up, I don't see these people's relatives in heaven, I don't talk to the dead. Nevertheless, she said, the dead are now talking to you. She lit another cigarette; she was a three-pack-a-day woman at this point. My guess is that your constant focus on them, your constant attempts to get in touch, phoney or not, has made you a target, well, not a target, that's badly put, a point of contact, let's say, a light in the dark. I suspect your father was only the first, she said. After this they'll be climbing heaven's gates to get to you.

At 4 a.m. I woke with a start. Mariella had said it was like a light in the dark, that's what she had said, a light in a dark room. I turned on the lamp next to the bed and she stirred slightly and rolled over onto her side. I confess by this point I was having all sorts of crooked thoughts. She wants to bring her husband back, that's what I thought, the films are like beacons, points of contact, that's what she said, a flashing light in a darkened room. Through her own experiments in mediumship, her own failed experiments, or so she said, she had developed some kind of sixth sense for that power in others, so she had picked me up when she had seen me begging in Athens and set me up in the role of oracle. It was true, now I was attracting the dead, bringing them down, or up. But was there more to it? I slid the covers down and pulled Mariella's black slip up above her waist. I entered her as she slept. Yes, she said softly, yes, but I had the feeling she wasn't talking to me. I looked around the room just in case, searching for what, I wasn't sure, for a camera, for the return of the dead. Eventually I fell back asleep. I had a dream about animals devouring animals, a dog that ate a dog that ate a dog. Everything was significant; isn't that what they say about schizophrenia, that it's like an internal overloading, like everything outside you only serves to further focus the eye inside? I was playing with madness; that much was clear.

In the lobby of the hotel the next morning, as we waited for a lift to the train, Mariella asked me if I had made love to her last night. No, I said to her, it must have been your dream lover, and she laughed, and she stroked my arm, but I could see she was confused and that inside herself there was an eye, casting around for meaning, a bloodshot eye, but an eye all the same.

Volos was uneventful, as was Larissa, except for the moment at the start of the show where I hypnotised and removed the head of a young boy who claimed to be not a thought in God's head this time but something that God had forgotten, that he had escaped from a dream that God Himself had never even realised He'd had. Keep it to yourself, I told him, to much hilarity from the audience, we don't want to go bringing it to his attention, I said to him, this way we can get away with murder.

In Trikala we gave a performance at the house of some kind of local dignitary that Mariella knew, someone with minor local standing who had a grand apartment that looked onto a square where lovers and musicians congregated in the evening beneath the streetlights. I sat in the bedroom, masked and robed, by this point Mariella had embroidered a golden eagle on the back of my robe, and I recalled the man who had given it to me on the seashore at the beginning of my new life. I looked out the window at the lovers coming and going in the square. What if I had washed up here, I thought to myself, what if under the streetlights in the square I was to see myself holding my ID up, begging in the evening? I could live a hundred lives, I told myself, a thousand, even. I knew I was strong enough.

The evening went well; the filthy rich, like the dirt poor, are easily made fools of. I removed a young bureaucrat's head and allowed him to escape from the mind of God. I brought tidings from old uncles and tragic young spouses, all of whom were doing well and thought fondly of the living. As the parents of the young dignitary chastised her from beyond the grave, I noticed a small black dog appear from beneath a chair. I can't say for sure whether anyone else saw it or not. No one seemed to pay it the slightest attention. It walked over to me and sat simply by my side with an expression, if dogs can have them, of sadness, of pity, even. I continued with the message from the parents. What did they miss most about being alive? the young dignitary asked them. They laughed. Not much, they scoffed. The sunlight, the mother said, I miss the sunlight, I suppose. Why, the young dignitary asked her, is it dark where you are? Oh no, dear, she said, don't get the wrong impression, it's just that the sun never rises or sets. The dog cocked its head to one side, and as I looked into its eyes I realised that there was something present in the animal, that the animal was occupied by a twin soul. I realised that my brother, too, had joined the ranks of the disappeared.

What is he on about now? the madman with the single paralysed bollock interrupted us. Dogs have souls, he says, the idiot with the tattoo replied, lots of them. What, the bollocks guy burst, do you mean to say there are dogs in heaven? But the young man with the pyjama top turned on him. Are there tower blocks in heaven? he quizzed him. Is there food in heaven? Can you get a bite to eat in heaven? Are there birds in heaven and do they still sing in heaven? Are there sports in heaven? Is there sex in heaven, is there lingerie in heaven (I fucking well hope so, the bollocks guy said), are there endless orgasms in heaven (you would think so, the man with the solitary functioning bollock nodded), are there beautiful long legs in high strappy heels, is there painting in heaven, is there boxing, is there sparring in heaven, are there clothes in heaven and if so are there cupboards to keep them in, do you need shoes in heaven, is there grass in heaven and how about trees, are there trees in heaven and if so how do they grow, is it all dreamed up in heaven or is there rain in heaven, are there tongues in heaven, are there vocal chords in heaven or is there no need to speak in heaven (okay, okay, the man with the tanned arsehole protested), are there rivers in heaven or mountains, can you even climb a mountain in heaven, is everything achieved in heaven, is there any point in heaven? Are there faces in heaven? If there are faces in heaven there must be prisons too. Don't you see? he said. But dogs, the man with the wretched tattoo said, he's saying people come back as dogs. He's not saying that, the young man contradicted him,

he's saying that animals can become vessels for individual
souls, maybe they're just more porous or something, like
they have less consciousness so there's more room for the
wandering soul to take up residence. What about possession,
the man with the unfortunately permanent scribble on his
arm asked, what about when a man gets possessed by a
ghost or spirit like in voodoo? No one is saying it doesn't
happen, the boy agreed. What I don't get, the man with
the divided genitalia protested, is why the dead don't just
show up as themselves. They do, the boy insisted, but it's
normally terrible.

I saw a ghost once, the man with the obnoxious tattoo
interrupted, steering the story somewhere else completely,
and despite what you say, in my experience, ghosts are
quite beautiful, he continued, and this story, he interjected,
might go some way towards explaining the provenance of
my unfortunate tattoo, which, believe me, I am aware that
you have been clocking the entire time, though I'm surprised
with some of you being sea dogs yourself that you're in any
way perturbed by amateur pinwork, what's the matter, boys,
never seen an unidentifiable on the arm of an old salt, well,
let me tell you how it came about, and what it is, if none of
you have guessed yet, and this requires us going backwards
instead of forwards, but at least that way we're dealing
in verifiable facts, am I right, in things that have actually
taken place rather than flights of fantasy or confidence
tricks, not that I'm saying you can't see the future, and I do
think it's a skill to be able to see the past and see it clearly
and it's true, if you think about it, that there might well
be as many alternate pasts as there are potential futures,
if you were to add up all the eyes that have taken in the
same scene, all the brains too, and all the different parts

of the brain, for that matter, and memory, too, memory too comes into it, I'm not saying anything controversial when I say that no two people remember the same thing in the same way, am I right, lads, memory colours the deal and the colours are often rudimentary, just as this tattoo on my arm is a little, well, a little roughly sketched, I'll give you that, and we'll get to that, believe me, but first just like our faceless friend The Oddity here, he said, and he pointed his chin towards me, his awful chin, it occurred to me, even though I was the one with the hideous face, supposedly, and he continued with a date, it's 1936, he said, and the war hasn't even begun.

Sure, there's unrest here and there, there are signs up ahead, is what I'm trying to say, but back then it was still possible to be romantic, to look to the future with something other than trepidation, you might say, it was still possible to swim naked in rivers and to make love to young girls on the banks, in the grass, in the summertime, without a care in the world.

In 1936 I had decided to do nothing, nothing at all, for the space of a year, which is harder than it sounds, believe me, doing nothing, there's always the urge to be productive, even for a bum, it's hard just to waste and to wander, even though it's not a waste to stop and smell the roses, the weary roses, is that a poem by your man, I think it is, the point being that most people are absolutely terrified of the snail's pace that life moves at, the way one second collapses into another like a slow-motion avalanche, the way that waiting for a whole minute to pass gives you butterflies in your stomach, that a month gives you a terrible sense of vertigo when you have no fixed route through it, that years, well, let's not even talk about years, and so we have these people that we send out to experience the flow of time and to report back to us, you know, when I say us I mean the archetypal Joes, the working stiffs, the timetablists, the nine-to-fivers, the avoiders of time, the sleepwalkers, let's say it, the zombies (I shuddered and looked at the young boy in the pyjama top as he said this), and the people that report back, well, we call them artists, musicians, writers, and we also call them bums, chancers, drop-outs, scroungers, no-goods, derelicts, fools, though secretly we envy their bravery, the courage they have to sit and do nothing for long stretches, their ability to feel the passage of time, because it hurts, let me tell you, but what hurts even more is love, love hurts, boys, let me tell you, let me underline that, you should try being a bum in love, an artist with a broken heart, a derelict with a devotion, a poor pining writer on a bench in a park in the afternoon staring at the newly sprung daffodils, their sad heads nodding pointlessly in the wind, and somewhere else, somewhere out of sight, lost love, well, there is nothing worse, let me tell you, and that summer, well, this is the trap I fell into, and maybe now you are starting to see the significance of my tattoo, that idiot scar, you're thinking, but I doubt it, you're not there yet, though rather you are, you just don't realise it yet, so I mentioned the girl on the riverbank and this is a true story, it really happened to me, but it also seems like a fairy story or what is it they call it, an epic, an odyssey, though on a small scale, you realise, but one day I am lounging on the riverbank, it is the summer of 1936, I have gone to my favourite field, a stubble field, you might call it, a rough field, but nevertheless one that leads down to some beautiful flowing water and one that was secret and one that was unknown to anyone back then except for me and a few lazy cows, one

that was surrounded by trees on three sides and one that
looked out to more fields on the other side of the water and
at one point a ruined castle, its tower just visible above the
tops of the trees, I had spent many afternoons there,
evenings too, whistling to myself, carelessly smoking, under
the eye of God and no one else, that's what I would tell
myself, and sometimes I would get into the water and swim
naked and then lie back down in the grass in the sun and
fall asleep, I had no money, I was dirt poor back then, I had
left a job in the shipyards, a good job, some might say, a job
where you had no fear of time or the future or tomorrow, a
terrible job, others might say, depending on your outlook,
which is to say depending on how you were born, because I
believe that bums are born to be bums just as much as kings
are set to be kings, and here I was naked in the grass, King
Bum, born to it, and it's another one of those endless days,
those glorious processions of hours like a gift, a gift that's
hard to swallow, for some, the gift of eternity, is what I'm
saying, and I lie back, I always remember it, I hear this
splashing noise, soft, splashing water in the silence, and I
sit up on my elbows, at this point I'm smoking a long piece of
dry grass for the hell of it, and I see this figure, this vision,
floating downstream, it's a woman, a girl, and she is floating
on her back, slowly swimming downstream, the angel
stroke, she's doing the angel stroke, I'm telling you this is
for real, and the water is silver in the sunlight and she
doesn't see me, she is looking straight up at the sky, not
even watching where she is going, and I say to myself,
bugger me, it's the ultimate artist, the ultimate bum, and I
marvel a little, she makes me feel like an amateur, and as
she gets closer I can see that she has long blonde hair and
perfect skin, she might be twenty-one, who knows, it's hard
to tell, and I shout out to her, something ordinary,

something banal, like, it's a lovely day, or, watch where you're going, or just, hello there, something that is lost to the mists of time now, and instantly she spins round and stands up in the water, which is above her waist, and she puts her forearm over her breasts, which are small and beautifully formed (now we're talking, the young man in the pyjama top nods), and she looks at me, by this point we're close enough to look into each other's eyes, and her eyes are blue, sapphire-blue, perfect (just like her pert breasts, the young boy nods), and her lips are red and for a moment, for a second, which is all of the space of an avalanche, as I've told you already, her face is frozen, she's caught in the teeth of it, she's in love, I'll go ahead and say it because I believe it to be true, I know they say you can't fall in love in a second, but sometimes a second is all it takes, and now I know, I know from this perfect face and these perfect eyes and lips and I know from the eyebrows, how they arched, and I know from the way she dropped her arm and exposed her breasts to me (go on, the young boy nodded, go on yourself), although exposed is the wrong word, that's too harsh and deliberate, surrendered her breasts wouldn't be right either, revealed, no, displayed, not quite, can we get any closer to the beauty of this gesture with words, is what I'm trying to say (keep trying, the boy nodded, do your best), or even the beauty of her face, for that matter, and this is the incredible thing, that as she walked slowly out of the water towards me I swear it was as if she was flitting backwards and forwards between a naive young girl and a sophisticated older woman, you might say it was the way the sun caught her, the way the shadows fell, the state of my sun-addled brain, you might say it is memory now or you might say it is just the memory of a memory, but I can't take that word, just, I can't reduce it to that, it can't be done, it was there

and it was perfect and that's when I realised we were caught
between past and future, the two of us, we had stepped
outside of time completely or more properly inside of time
completely, we were occupying a second of a second of a
second, which is atomic time, which is cellular time, in my
opinion, you can't put a watch to it, is the thing, and as she
entered my arms and my eyes we fell into the grass and
made love without a word or a sound (what more can you
ask, the young boy nodded) and I tasted her and she tasted
me and of course we tasted of the river and the grass and
the soil but something else too, something that was uniquely
us, that we made between the two of us, and that was also
earthy and divine and afterwards (that's all we're getting?
the boy protested) we ran around in the sun naked and
we chased each other and laughed though we never said
anything, well, anything of consequence, and anything
that we did say is lost to the mists of time just like my
banal introduction, the one that had started it all, and I
never thought to ask her name, that's the crazy thing,
I never thought to ask her anything about herself, and I
think now it was because we were locked in this cell, this
vein, this bubble in time, and the whole outside world had
no consequence, never mind anything as dull as who we
were when we were in it, and we jumped back into the water
and we leaped around and did childish things but then at
other moments we embraced and fell back into the water
and then at one point, as the sun was still high in the sky,
which made it all the more heartbreaking, I let her go, I let
her drift away without a word, she rolled onto her back and
she resumed that stroke, the angel stroke, and she carried
on down the river, and just as I thought she wouldn't say
anything, that she would leave the moment as silently as
she had entered it, she said, goodbye, it's the one word I

remember, oh God, and she waved and she swam away and at first I was in ecstasy, I was overcome, what a remarkable experience, it was perfect, there was nothing you could add to or subtract from the moment that would elaborate it or make more sense or improve it, and I lay back in the grass and I felt myself blessed, King Bum, I told myself, and afterwards I walked for hours, in the shadows of the evening, down tree-lined lanes, and I sat by ponds in the dark, and it was after midnight when I returned home to my old parents' house and I sat on the bed and looked out of the window and peered into the distance and that's when it struck me, and when I say struck me I really mean it, you know what they say about Cupid's arrow, how love pierces your heart, I felt that pain, a pain that is like being shot in the heart with an arrow, yes, but more than that, the heart bleeds, the heart is drained of blood and becomes more like a paper bag, a paper bag inflated by a mischievous child, and I knew I was trapped, I would never be a bum again, I was caught in time, in longing, I dreamed of this girl night after night, I was bereft, I would travel back to our secret spot again and again in the hope of meeting her, but all I ever saw were the flowers swaying pointlessly in the wind, the blurry treetops, the ruined castle, the stubble fields, I had such pain inside me, the minutes were a torture chamber, the hours were like the featureless fields themselves, the weeks and months lined up like an impossible assault course designed by a maniac, and I wanted to harm myself, to let all of my blood pour out, not just from my heart but to become a walking cadaver, a sleepwalker, a zombie (again I shuddered at the word), where is she, I demanded, where can she be, is she out there, is she a dream, is it possible, I couldn't stand it, my peace had been stolen, the thought of doing nothing tied my stomach up in knots, threatened to burst the paper bag in my chest, that's when I knew it was all over, I would never tease out another minute, never enjoy an empty hour, not now that she was gone, and I took a needle and some Indian ink and this is what I did, boys, this is the cap I put on the summer of 1936, this is the scab, can you see what it is now, can you make it out? I'll tell you what it is, boys, it's not a harp, no, it's not the gates of heaven; it's the bars on the window of a prison cell. But look closer, boys. You'll find the bars are made up of arrows. That's how I did it, I imprisoned that moment inside me forever. And then I went and joined the army.

But it doesn't end there. Barracks time was a new kind of time. The years leading up to the war brought up a huge dust storm between myself and that fated year of 1936, the year of the ending of my youth, although I think it was fair to say that everyone's youth was drawing to a close back then, that young boys across the world were saying goodbye to their sweethearts, never to return, and of course I had that moment, sealed inside of me, no matter what else might happen, at least that's what I told myself.

The reality was that I was now a tomb, a walking tomb, with endless clanging depths inside myself where tears were raining into a black void, I felt like a sarcophagus, is what I'm trying to say, with this myth, this god, buried deep inside of me, in the middle of this terrible storm. Of course I ended up in Egypt, in North Africa, that was inevitable. I lay down in the warm sands and remembered the grass of the stubble fields, like it had all been trampled to death. I saw the pyramids, I recognised them. They had withstood time better than any of us. But they weren't tombs, not like me, I could sense that immediately. Then I saw them as

a form of monstrous grammar, does that make sense? Let
me put it another way. They were like full stops in time,
you could feel it, or some were like commas, they checked
the flow of time, some were like semicolons, they were
amazing, and the sentences ran on for aeons, the sentences
were cataclysmic, what force it took to slow them down, to
make of them mortal thoughts, is what I'm trying to say,
without the pyramids history is incomprehensible, without
the civilisation of Egypt, Egypt is the fulcrum, the point
of transmission, the thing that allows the reading of the
past into the future, I realised all this immediately because
of course the pyramids are great centres of condensed
information and it was like they were beaming into me,
into the burial chamber that I carried inside me, and then
of course I realised that hieroglyphs were focused points
of power, not words exactly, but more alive than that, like
living expressions of the possibility of the moment, that time
itself was somehow refracting through them but that it was
the pyramids themselves, the fact of their construction, that
really was what made Egyptian society readable, explicable,
in some dim way anyway, and of course I thought of the
tattoo on my arm, my own personal hieroglyph, and then of
course my place in the sun, the fateful summer of 1936, and
I realised that you can't escape time, try as you might, you
can't even live in it serenely, but you can somehow arrest it,
in moments, you can somehow turn the tide of time, ever so
briefly, ever so minutely, no man is a pyramid, after all, and
I thought, alright, the nameless girl in the stream, then I
thought, you know what, I am completely insane. I stood in
front of the pyramids and I shrugged. Fuck it, I said. Then
I went round the back and urinated on one of them and left
a trail like a dog. Next thing you know I'm half drowning
in the Mediterranean, my ship is blown to pieces and I'm in

another cell, another tomb, looking out through the same damn bars all over again at the water flowing past. What are you gonna make of that? Anyone got any tobacco?

But wait, one more thing before I finish, maybe I'm insane, okay, I give you that, maybe this is madness, but anyone here heard of the tale of the Angel of Mons? Of course you have, every soldier knows it, it's the story of how an angel appeared over a battlefield during the First World War and made it all comprehensible somehow, a wordless angel made sense of all the carnage and horror and destruction and of faceless time itself. Of course they say it was a good-luck sign, that it offered protection to the good guys, who were inevitably us, but that's nonsense, people die regardless of angels, no one is about to legislate death out of existence, never mind God, He thought up the whole deal in the first place, but angels, the appearance of angels at some point in time, at any particular point in time, well, what I'm trying to say is it's never meaningless, even if all they do is float there in the clouds or glide past on their back doing the angel stroke on a river or sit there and point to the heavens, they make things explicable just by their appearance, this is the grammar of the world, I'm trying to say, angels and pyramids and beautiful young girls in the summer of 1936, they make it meaningful somehow, even though really they explain nothing whatsoever.

After the man with the tattoo that had turned out to be the bars of a prison finished his monologue, everyone felt discomfited. We looked around the cell in silence, at our wretched cellmates, at the scrapings on the wall, at the crude signatures and desperate messages, at the sight of the sun coming up – we had talked for most of the night –

at a man with red, swollen eyes and a burned moustache
rocking on the floor in what appeared to be a pool of his
own urine, at another spread out on a bunk, a single line
of drool escaping from his mouth like a determined slug, at
another again, a handsome soldier stood staring into space,
at a crack that ran from the ceiling down most of the wall,
at the inevitable drawings of cocks and vaginas, at a furtive
rat whose snout protruded from beneath the lowest bunk,
at our wretched toenails, at the rust on the metal doors, at
the waves, rising up and rising down, and I can say with
certainty that we all felt a shudder of significance.

Tell us about the Januists, the young boy who by this time
had traded his pyjama top for a small denim jacket that he
wore with a bare chest asked me that evening as we ate our
watery soup with the paper meatballs in it, and the cell fell
into the kind of silence you feel you could touch if you were
capable of being perfectly gentle. Did you ever find out any
more about them? he asked me. I did, I told him, I found
out much more but what I did find out was confusing and
at points contradictory, which might be expected with a
group that is founded on the idea of going in two separate
directions at the same time, you might expect there to be
some internal tension, you might even expect them to be
torn apart, eventually, by contradiction, and that is what
happened, in a way, though not exactly, because in a way
they never disbanded, in a way their final split, which was
more like a disintegration, really, or a timed explosion,
more appropriately, was the ultimate extension of their
programme, which was nebulous, from what I came to
understand, but this nebulousness – is that a word? – was
the engine, if you like, the motor, if you prefer, of their
project, which, as I say, was nebulous.

446

But before I can tell you more about them I have to discover
a book and a photograph, and before I can discover them
both I have to finish our tour, our first grand tour, which
was interrupted by your man's tale of the angels and of the
grand sentences that only made sense with commas and full
stops, a grand tour where we made a packet, quite frankly,
a wedge that set us up for our own experiment in time, our
own contribution to the Januists' cause, in a way, though
we were never officially affiliated or had any real connection
with them outside of Mariella, of course, who had been
married to a Januist herself, and from whom we could claim
some kind of succession, if we were that way inclined, but
really our project was much more personal, in one sense,
although to label the Januist cause, if you could even term
it a cause, as impersonal, well, that's up for debate itself, as
we will find out after I return to our great money-spinning
trek across the theatres and well-to-do parlours of Greece
in those years after the war, the years that, as I have said
before, I have come to term the dying years for reasons
that are not insignificant, in that they were the years of the
dead themselves, they belonged to the dead, and they were
the years when I became acquainted with them, when they
started coming back, which is doubly odd, the dead coming
back is odd in itself, I'm sure you'll agree, but the dead
coming back to someone who pretended, on a nightly basis,
to be in contact with the dead, is odder still, it's like God
appearing to an atheist, a dinosaur appearing to a hellfire
preacher, a beautiful woman giving her hand to a hideous
old deformity, which in my case had already happened, but
still in the towns and the cities that we visited in the dying
years I kept up my dalliances with prostitutes in secret,
it was my only indulgence, the only thing I spent the now
considerable sums we were making on, and I recall some of

them with great clarity and some with fondness and some
are gaps in rooms or ghosts in beds or merely the missing
detail of a morning, I can see the bed with the towel laid
out neatly on top of it, the view over a courtyard with a
mural painted on the wall that depicted a circle of children
of different races dancing together, I can see a block of flats
overlooking a bay, a corridor painted dull lime and cream,
I remember a toilet across the way with no door on it, I
remember a woman with short blonde hair who displayed
her twat for me to examine, I remember another blonde
woman, a blonde silhouette, an older woman, seen through
a window, smiling and waving as I walked away, none of
these women ever felt sorry for me or acted as if I should be
treated gently or lovingly, the myth of the prostitute with
a heart of gold is exactly that, prostitutes, as a rule, don't
care, they don't care and that is the blessing and the mercy
of the oldest profession and why it should be so ancient,
careless sex, men and women meeting and parting without
a thought, barely a glimmer, hardly a memory, goes back
to the creation of the world, there are many kinds of sex,
who can deny it, but silent, wordless sex with an unknown
woman who you will never see again and who you pay for
the pleasure strikes me as the holiest, there are holy whores
in The Bible, we all know that, but there are holy whores in
apartment blocks in Vola and Parga and in Metsovo, too.

I always liked some facial hair, it became, what do you
call it, a tic, a fetish, when I would meet with a girl in an
apartment or hotel and I would see that she was so careless
as not to even pluck the hairs from her upper lip, I would
say to myself, ah, no disguises here, and no thought too,
and little care, and these women would invariably turn out
to be the most passionate, by which I mean unselfconscious

passion, which doesn't mean histrionics but rather a deep
secret enjoyment turned in on herself alone which would
manifest in small things, the licking of the lips, for instance,
the tonguing of her own moustache, the rubbing together of
the feet or ankles, the arching of the back and, of course, the
play of the eyebrows, the most subtly expressive aspect of
womanhood, certainly of whoredom, a kingdom I spent much
of the dying years in as an ethnographer, and not of faces
and names but of secret body parts and backstreets and
bedrooms, although names too, I can give you some names,
almost all of which are now floating free from their bodies,
unanchored by eyebrows, no longer tied to a pair of sad blue
eyes or to a fragile tanned limb, not even to long flowing
black hair or to the beautiful philtrums of the ladies of the
night, again unconnected to names, useless, they tell us, an
evolutionary holdover, but thank God for them as a place to
rest your tongue while in ecstasy, philtrum, philtrum, what
a word you are to me, and Daria and Iantha and Euterpe,
whose name means delight, you too, and I would return
to my hotel or to whatever theatre we were booked into
with their names on my tongue, on my lips, their taste on
my teeth or what was left of them, and sometimes I would
walk straight on stage and summon the dead right then
and there, I bring great tidings, I would announce, and
they would appear and I would thank God or evolution or
whatever force I was caught up in for my position at the
crossroads, which is how I saw it, for my traffic with the
dead and the disappearing and the newly crossed-over.

What's he on about now? the man with the tattoo of the jail
cell on his arm asked the young man in the denim jacket,
rising from his bunk. He's rhapsodising about prostitutes,
the boy told him. That's the last thing you need to hear

about in prison, the tattooed man said, and he shook his head. Angels don't help much either, the boy replied. Anyway, the boy said, where were we, what about the tour, how did it work out, what else did you spend all of that money on, and what about the book and the photograph? Wait a minute, the man with the tattoo interrupted him, what book and what photograph, have I missed something? Don't worry, the young boy reassured him, it's coming up, I hope.

All through the tour the dead return in their masses. Think about it, the legion of the dead all clamouring for attention, imagine that, if you will, all drawn towards this one speck of light that turns out to be a deformed man in a mask on stage at a vaudeville show. Some of them are insulted, some of them are angry, most of them will take what they can get. Often relations between the living and the dead are far from amicable, far from the teary spectacle of lost love returned. Leave me alone, some of them say, let the dead bury the dead, why all this interfering, all this mourning, all this inability to let be? Some of them are cruelly mocking, I never pass this on, some of them are angry, with the knowledge that death has provided them, well, can we even call it death, these are the still-remembered dead and the disappeared, they exist in a kind of purgatory thanks to the thoughts of the living, but in the release of the life force, or rather let us say the transmutation of the life force into another kind of force, in this turning upside down of everything they ever thought they knew, there is some resentment, there is a realisation, in some people, that truly they could have done anything, they could have lived their lives so differently, they could have done so much better, why did they put up with the narrow parameters that their wife or their family insisted was all there was, why did they chain themselves to that particular horizon, a-horizon that seems now more like a bruise, a bloodied sun, an insult to a force that has turned their life inside out as easy as sneezing, and some of them do appear as angels, it is true, but deformed angels, ghastly angels, angels of silent judgement, angels that just stand there and say nothing, with no arms or with half a face or a great gap where their organs used to be, or in one terrible case with their own semi-liquefied organs gathered up in their arms, these were the worst, these silent cases, and they occurred more often than you would think, I would inform the family member that they were there, that these strange angels were there in the room, on stage with me, but that they were silent, and they would think that I meant they were at peace and had now taken up silent guardianship of all that they had left behind, but how wrong they were, how they misunderstood the rancour of the rotten dead, like the presence of a terrible fact, they believed that the dead had duties, that was one of their greatest mistakes, no, the dead do not have duties, my friends, it is only us, down here, or more correctly over here, that make demands of ourselves, the dead resent callings, duties, responsibilities of any kind, that's what bodies are for, let me go, they say, for the most part, aren't we done with this already, but of course, you ask me if the dead have regrets, yes, they do, they regret duty, they often, I'm sad to say, regret the very bonds of love that held them while they were alive, they think to themselves, unbounded love, isn't that a more sane way to be, every life, isn't that a greater goal, to live every life and love every love, that's how the dead feel, in my experience, well, in many cases, let me say, there are more dead than living and it's impossible to account for all of them, of course there are the sentimental dead, the dead that are scared shitless, there are even some souls or some spirits that long for narrow horizons, for small cramped bodies, for suffocating family relationships, I can't deny it, and of course even as the faceless or limbless dead were drawn to the stage every night as if by an usher with a flashlight, my father too returned on a regular basis, not to mention the small black dog with a look of cosmic sympathy on its face, and that I took to be the temporary resting place of my younger brother, some of the dead are too far gone and have to resort to animal possession or synchronicity or coincidence, even, some of them operate by orchestrating our movements ever so subtly, look out for these ones, is my advice, it's happening all the time, in the confluence of a street name, a song played over a cheap tannoy in a gone-to-seed restaurant, in an unaccountable signal from a stranger, in the uncovering of an object, even in the direction of a walk, if you let it take you, and the dog would take its place on the side of the stage or sometimes, brazenly, it would march down the central aisle, once even stopping to urinate on the side of a plush velvet seat (that's like me at the pyramids, the man with the now oddly beautiful tattoo said), and then it would sit and look at me with pity and with understanding, which was quite uncanny, and sometimes they would catch me in a pincer formation and it was my very soul they pinched, let me tell you, my father to the side of me on stage, mercifully, for the most part, no longer dancing but still dragging his leg, his heavy chest heaving, his face fallen and slumped, and he would plead with me, a one-sided pleading unless you call the sad haughty silence of the small dog a sort of plea in its own way, in which case there was pleading on both sides to go home, that's what they wanted me to do, go back home, they said, you're still in the land of the living, leave the dead to the dead, it's not

me that needs you, my father said, it's your mother, it's
your wife, you still have a life there, but there was no way
of telling them I had one foot on the other side, that I had
glimpsed what the dead know, or what many of them know,
that there are endless lives and endless loves, and that I
wanted a part of all of them.

Suffering had opened up a channel with the dead, but
really a person isn't meant to contain death, listen, I'm
talking to you, listen to me, man's lack of any real horizon
beyond day-to-day goals, the impossibility of a truly
cosmic understanding, his brain the size of a pea in the
scheme of things, his nervous system reaching out all of
a few feet in front of him, his sight barely up ahead, his
constant distraction, his picking at himself like a monkey,
don't deny it, his need for a proxy even to experience
anything that could remotely be termed religious, for
a stand-in, or his need for drugs and booze to take him
some of the way there, his petty obsessions, his rivalries
and jealousies, his pathetic ambitions, his body's constant
cravings, all these, I tell you, are a form of mercy; man's
brain isn't commensurate with the universe and thank
God or evolution for it, neither is death something to be
lived with, think of the stars twinkling up above, think
of them blinking, prettily, in the night sky, that's not a
star, that's not a sun, that's a pinprick in your nursery-
rhyme brain, that's what that is, man wasn't made to
encounter stars, never mind terrible planets humming
suspended in black space, never mind mile-long comets
tearing through nowhere forever, mercy is a shutting down
of the possibilities of the universe, mercy is to never fully
understand death, to never believe in it, because who does
except the dying and even then it's never real, who hasn't

sat with someone propped up in a hospital bed with tubes coming out of them and their body pocked with sores and their breathing being done by a machine, their heart the sad paper bag that your man here mentioned, and talked about cleaning the house when they get back home, or the football scores, or a song they once loved, or wondered about the state of their garden and quite right too, if death were to relocate his kingdom – and I say he, it may be ownerless or under the command of a woman for all we know – but if death were to relocate his kingdom down here or more appropriately let's say over here, then every one of us would be on our knees in the streets screaming to heaven, yet here I was, dragging around an entourage of the dearly departed with spirit animals sniffing at my heels, with death inside me, is what I'm trying to say, a death that even after all that I had been through I hadn't truly believed in, even with the gift of precognition, that means seeing the future, boys, even with that death was more like a rumour, a possibility, but its kingdom, unlike the kingdom of whoredom that I mentioned earlier, never impinged on my body, never occupied me in the way that it did now.

By the end of the tour it was hard to put one foot in front of the other. I did what your man here attempted, I did nothing, for a span of time, it might have been months, could have been a year, I did nothing. I stayed indoors. Mariella fed me. We made love to a schedule, we had a routine, I had begun to horrify even her, although it was, of course, the nature of my horror, or the co-ordinates of my horror, the time and place of my horror, the way my face articulated my horror, that had attracted her to me in the first place, that had made her *recognise me*, were the words

she used, yet now I spent most of my days in the mask, of
course we made love in the mask, that was a given, who
could really stand to have a half-eaten face like a gibbous
moon hanging over them, I told you, who wants to get
that close to the planets, really, but now during the day I
would dress in a suit of her husband's, a pale-blue suit or
a double-breasted dark-blue number, and with this black
leather mask on, a mask that constricted my breathing,
my breathing that was already constricted, so that I would
stand by the window and the glass in front of me would
fog up and I would run my fingernails through it and draw
signs in the hot, cold breath, draw signs over people in the
street, spot them down below or across the way and sketch a
quick cross over them or a zero or an out-of-control spiral or
a grave, it's true that for hours on end I would stand by the
window and draw gravestones in my own breath over the
bodies of passers-by and I would glance over my shoulder
and often there would be a queue of corpses, an orderly
queue, who would have dreamed it, waiting for me, standing
in line for me to do what, who knows, more than draw
graves in my own wet breath, that's for sure, but aside from
my father and my brother, the small dog, who implied both
that I had to return, that there was unfinished business at
home, and that I had broken some pact, perhaps, that's how
it felt, some pact that even I, as an emissary of the dead,
had no clear understanding of, besides that the dead offered
no clues, no instruction, not even a pleading half-eaten
expression, they simply stood and waited and occasionally
argued amongst themselves in voices that sounded like the
black bubbling at the bottom of a pond.

Most of the time I read books, I read books in Mariella's
library, which was also her ex-husband's library or her

current husband's library, even, just because he had disappeared didn't mean they were no longer married, and besides, she was unclear herself and would fudge the issue, my long-lost husband, she would say, and I would say, well, is he or isn't he, and she would reply, my long-lost husband, and it would go on forever.

I read books by people like Ouspensky and Blavatsky and people with names like grand citadels in the Himalayas and they would talk about their own contacts with the dead or sometimes they would call them the Ascended, which in my experience made little sense but even so they made me doubt my own experience, perhaps there is an up after all, I said to myself, perhaps it is possible to ascend, perhaps there is more to the brain or perhaps it is possible to go outside it or beyond it but what is the vessel that ascends and if there's no way of experiencing it with your brain, if it takes blowing your brain up or storing it away somewhere else while you take the trip, well, what is the point in that, I had already proven, to myself at least, that there was room in the body for all sorts of crazy wonders but that it involved, as I have explained, a sort of going beyond or doing away with mercy, which is a small-scale blessing but thoroughly worthwhile, believe me, without mercy, it seemed to me, we were nothing but small white mice strapped into spaceships with ridiculous helmets on, but I read these books, these pompous tomes, excuse me but it's true, these douchebag accounts, and somewhere, along the way, there was always an agenda, let's make the world a better place by talking to the big daddies, they would say, and of course I'm paraphrasing, or, even better, the nature of the universe is love; that's the brain of a mouse in a space suit talking right there.

One book was titled *Tertium Organum: A Key to the Enigmas of the World* and made claims of 'beings of the higher world': 'Whether these consciousness in sections of the other than our exist or not, we, *under the existing conditions of our receptivity*, cannot say. They can be sensed only by the changed psyche.' Another book, entitled *The Symbolism of the Tarot*, was housed in an elaborate handmade paper sleeve, a private edition printed in Russia, in St Petersburg, to be precise, in 1913. There was much talk of symbolism, of the triangle in the square, and this is where I came across the card that you had previously mentioned and of course I immediately recalled it from our conversations, The Hanged Man, who crosses his leg over his lover in the Januist feature I had mentioned, and which I had come to believe I had inadvertently starred in a remake of. I noted that it came between Justice and Death, these are the cards that surround it, and truly, in a flash, as it were, or as in the appearance of an angel, more appropriately, I felt something inside me orient itself. But there is more, much more. First, allow me to quote, from memory, what was written of The Hanged Man.

'And then I saw a man in terrible suffering, hung by one leg, head downward, to a high tree. And I heard the voice:-

«Look! This is a man who saw Truth. Suffering awaits the man on earth, who finds the way to eternity and to the understanding of the Endless.

«He is still a man, but he already knows much of what is inaccessible even to Gods. And the incommeasurableness [yes, he really uses this word] of the small and the great in his soul constitutes his pain and his Golgotha.

«In his own soul appears the gallows on which he hangs in suffering, feeling that he is indeed inverted.

«He chose this way himself.

«For this he went over a long road from trial to trial, from initiation to initiation, through failures and falls.

«And now he has found Truth and knows himself.

«He knows that it is he who stands before an altar with magic symbols, and reaches from earth to heaven; that he also walks on a dusty road under a scorching sun to a precipice where a crocodile awaits him; that he dwells with his mate in paradise under the shadow of a blessing genius; that he is chained to a black cube under the shadow of deceit; that he stands as a victor for a moment in an illusionary chariot drawn by sphinxes; and that with a lantern in bright sunshine, he seeks for Truth in a desert.

«Now he has found her.»'

Now, in this booklet, and it may have been a variant or a rejected copy or a misprint, but in this booklet the author had shuffled the order of the cards. The book ends with The Hanged Man. Death and then Justice precede it. So what? the young kid protested, and pulled a cynical face. So you read some nonsense in a book that chimed with you, congratulations, we've all been there. You asked me about the work of the Januists, I replied. I told you I had to finish the tour, I had to go into hiding, I had to discover a book, did I not? I'll give you that, the young boy admitted. But there was one other thing I had to find before our next working, our great experiment in time, could take place. A photograph, the boy recalled. That's right, I continued. And there it was. Slotted into the book, in between the pages for The Hanged Man, there was a photograph, a head-and-shoulders shot of a man, a black-and-white portrait. In that moment I saw who I would become.

Who was it? the man with the radiant tattoo demanded. Tell us, man! It was Mariella's husband. It was the Januist. It was the film-maker.

Well, what did he look like? Unremarkable, archetypal, in one sense, though in his ordinariness, his uniformity, I want to say, there was something uncanny, in the perfect symmetry of his face there was something ungodly and perfect, not beautiful, not handsome necessarily, but something that had been mastered, something that felt like the end of the line, like a man whose children would inevitably start to degenerate, like a specimen at the tip of a strange outlying branch that flowered for the last time before bringing the branch down completely, there was something cold and savage in the parting of his hair, an unearthly radiance to his white skin, he looked like he could have been a banker, an accountant, in one sense, his look was calculated, in other words.

He is wearing a white shirt, a black tie and black blazer jacket. He isn't looking at the camera; rather he is looking beyond it, to the side of it, not at the person taking the picture but at someone or something else, a third presence, on the other side, a presence which is *not himself*. What about his eyes, the young boy asked me, tell us about his

eyes. His eyes, I replied, his eyes, let me tell you about
his eyes. His eyes are the eyes of a high diver.

I looked at the photo some more and as I did I became
aware of the dead, behind me, by this point my constant
companions, in a line, their arms on each other's shoulders,
like the forced march of the blind, a line that stretched off
through the room, through the walls, through the air itself,
a line that might as well have wound up in eternity, if it's
possible for anything to wind up there, boys with missing
ears and black holes for eyes and with torn thighs and
feetless, feetless boys, what a sight, damaged boys, boys
with holes in their bodies where the light shone through,
boys with half-eaten faces, boys with blackened torsos and
with limbless chests, and I looked back at the photograph,
at a face that I described as looking like the end of the line,
and I confronted Mariella, she was in the bedroom, I stood
there like the dead, like my own dead self, like the beggar
in the square, I held the picture of her husband up in front
of me in silence, she came up close, so close that I thought
she might kiss the photograph, it's my husband, she said,
where did you find him, not where did you find it, as you
might say regarding a photograph, and I had the image
of her husband trapped between the pages of a book, his
perfectly symmetrical face pressed like a flower, and a tear
ran down her face and she held her head in her hands and
I felt the violence with which I had confronted her with the
past, with her own past this time, not my own, but all the
time I was starting to see, coming to realise how it would
be, what my role in all of this would become.

She described her husband, she began to describe him using
the kind of extravagant words I had taught her, words that
made everything seem impossible, magical.

We sat in the conservatory as the rain fell on the glass roof.
Mariella smoked cigarette after cigarette. She sat on the
couch with her legs pulled up under her. As the evening
came in she appeared as a simple silhouette, a black bird, its
damp body drying in the heat. He was stupendous, she said,
literate, magnanimous in his vision. He was a sophisticate,
a seeker, a gazer into time and space. He had given his
all for his art, literally, he had given himself up to it.
Imagine an art that would vanquish the artist completely,
she marvelled. And I don't mean these nincompoops,
these fancy-pants, these dope smokers (her language was
confused, partly my fault, I confess) who claim to have
removed the artist from the process of creation, these
crap-eaters are trapped in theory, are lost to ideas, these
tosspots (sorry) have never come close to being torn apart in
the matrix of their own creation, to being dismembered by
their own practice and yes practice is a shite word, that is
why so many artists are using it, but for Donald (she used
his name for the first time, a Donald, I thought, I wasn't
prepared for that) the idea of practice was a sick joke, a
fallacy, a misdirection, there was no practice, this was not
a rehearsal, there were no repeats, no turning back, he
intended to sacrifice himself in order to create a conduit,
an autobahn, a superhighway, between the past and the
future, one that could be accessed via (via is a Roman
road, after all, and another one of mine) a work of art that
was constantly, inevitably, calibrated (mine) to now, in
other words a work of art that held the moment in perfect
equilibrium (mine too, obviously), so much so that both past

and future were implicit (mine) in it, indeed the art was the perfect admixture (mine) of them both so that the moment was not so much interrogated (mine), because interrogation, just like dialogue, is the terrain of the lesser artist, the shit-stirrer, the domain of the masturbatory stain (mine too, I'm afraid), this was no more interrogation than it was analysis than it was critique than it was running commentary, all these wretched excuses for going nowhere, these asswipes (mine too, ha ha), this was not so much interrogation as revelation, but what happened, I interrupted her, where did he go, is he in there somewhere, in his art, and is his art located somewhere specific, is he in another time, is he trapped in a loop, is he dead or alive, and she brought up a god, a particular god, do you recall the god whose body was scattered across time, she asked me, and although I was sceptical I said, yes, I know which one you mean, but in reality I was confused, Jesus's body is, after all, arguably, across all time, though intact, still, perhaps, and then of course there is Osiris who was torn into pieces and whose cock could not be found, Osiris was the god of the dead and resurrection but wasn't Christ also, I was confused but still, despite my doubts, I shrugged and said, yes, I know the one, I understand, though I was far from understanding, and she said, well, okay, now you understand, but think about it, she said, if he is across all time he is immanent in all of it, am I right, and I went to say, I taught you that word, I taught you all of these words, what is your own understanding of them, but instead, again, I nodded, I stood by the window, in the dark, as the rain came down, in my mask, and I nodded, yes, I said, though my voice was muffled, yes, you would be right, and then she said, so there's a power there, there's a power that we can make use of, am I right, yes, I said, in my muffled voice, yes, I said, in my mask, but how, she said,

that is the question, but how, I tried, she said, I admit I
tried, these awful creatures, these amoebas, these jellyfish,
these subaqueous specimens that lie with their faces to
the wall, these canvases that I compared to numinous
nets, this is all that remains of my own experiments, my
own attempts to tap into the stream that Donald gave his
art and life to (Donald, I thought again, Donald, you don't
expect a god named Donald), a mockery, in other words,
mere ectoplasm, comic-book shite, she said, and that's when
I told her about the dead, I have to tell you, I said, I have to
tell you about the dead, they are coming back, I said, and I
compared myself to a lighthouse or to a mayday signal, to
a distress call was what I meant, and I told her that even
as I had kept up the pretence of our psychic sideshows, of
our live communication with the dearly departed, that the
dead, truly, had started to materialise and that even now,
as I stood by the window in the rain, if I were to look over
my shoulder, through the glass, stretched out, floating high
in the air, as far as the eye could see, I would see the dead,
lined up, miraculously suspended, luminous in the sky over
Athens, an endless chain of them snaking far across the
horizon, and with that Mariella broke into tears, don't you
see, she said, don't you see, but I still didn't see, it's all true,
she said, I believed in you from the moment I saw you in the
park, she said, I knew you were special, I knew you had the
power, I never doubted you, it's you, it's you, she repeated,
you've come back to me, don't you see, you are the fulfilment
of the Januist dream, look, she said, look, and she held up
the photograph of Donald in front of her and his eyes met
mine, don't you see, she said, he left you his face.

Back in the courtyard, in the prison, in the years of the
war, I sat with the Scotsman with the tanned arsehole,

in the shade of a sand-coloured wall, and we talked about all the things we would do with a new face, how the world would open up for us like never before. Think about it, he marvelled, the women you could have. What would stop you? You could wear a bow tie and go down to the club and pick them up. You could stand there like fucking Casanova, one hand in your pocket. Or what about going to Africa? I mean, the world would be your fucking oyster, you'd be out there, trading with natives, dining with chiefs, him giving you as many women as you could handle and then you come back, you're society's darling, you write your memoirs and you go off and live on a fucking island. Easy. Basically, with a new face, you live and you learn but the difference is, once you've learned, you get to start all over again. Two shots at this life. It's only fair, if you think about it. You start off unprepared, you're at a disadvantage. He rolled a spitball in his mouth, puckering his lips, and launched it through the air. Then he nodded at his own wisdom. It's only fair, he said. A man should be allowed two faces. Minimum allowance. Three, okay, I wouldn't say no, but then you're getting out of hand, then you'll go chopping and changing your whole life, you'd be with a different woman every day of the week. A second roll of the dice, that's all I'm asking. One face to make all your mistakes with and one to make up for it.

All around us men stood in silence, emaciated, half-starved, their gums swollen, their faces already used up for who knows what.

And what about a career criminal, the palsied Scotsman continued, think about it, dedicating the first half of your life to embezzlement and armed robbery, to rape and destruction, and then bingo, face-swap, ride off into the sunset. But you'd have to know you were due a new face, that God had one lined up for you, and of course this relies on everyone else not knowing and especially on everyone else not getting one too at some point otherwise it would be chaos, everyone would be watching everyone else, seeing what they were up to, what plans they had, what they intended to get away with using their old face. Two-faced, that's what they say, isn't it, duplicitous. Still, a new face is one thing, he continued, your old body is something else, you're still left to drag it around in the wake of your mug regardless. I'd be swanning around like a movie star with a brand-new coupon and I'd be lucky to squeeze a pellet out my old tanned arse at the same time. Still, I'd go back home, I'd go back home all the same, show up looking like laldy, no one suspecting a fucking thing, fire into my wife's sister, fucking do the rounds, new boy in town, my wife would fall for me all over again, I'm willing to bet, even with a new face. It's me, I'd say, but only months later after she thought I was dead, and I was the new man in her life. I came back for you, I'd tell her. Can you imagine that? That's reincarnation right there. Dropping the bomb, know what I mean? Still, as long as God isn't handing out any new pricks my love life is scunnered. Barring any miracles, it's gonna be strictly fondling and looking for me from here on out but fuck it, new faces, new cocks, why not? One day they'll be able to sew a new cock on you, that I believe, and that day we'll all be dancing.

I came back, I told him, I came back, eventually, with a brand-new face. But it worked out completely differently.

I know a surgeon, Mariella told me, an experimental surgeon, a secret operative, you understand, a refugee, in hiding, let's say, and I knew that she meant a Nazi, a Nazi surgeon, a human experimenter. The Nazis are experimenting on humans? the old Scot exploded. The dogs! Yes, they're experimenting on humans, I informed him. They've systematically murdered whole sections of the population, women, children, Gypsies, intellectuals, political radicals, the handicapped and the simple-minded and most of all the Jews. The poor Jews, I said. What about the Jews? the Scot asked me. All gone, I said, six million of them, gone. It's not possible! the Scotsman burst. I mean, I'm not the biggest fan of them myself but shipping six million of them to heaven, well, that would put a strain even on God's resources.

They call it the Shoah, I told him, they call it the Holocaust. They call it Auschwitz and Treblinka and Buchenwald. Doctors inject phenol into the hearts of children in their surgeries in Auschwitz. They make lampshades and soap from their remains. They expose prisoners to experimental diseases. Jews are rounded up and murdered in their millions by gassing. The Nazis have industrialised murder. The extermination camps have become the pyramids of the twentieth century, I informed him. Without them, it would be impossible to read it correctly.

And these are the bastards that you go to for your new face? he asked me. In that case I spit on new faces. Yes, I said, I went to them for a second chance or, more properly, for a third life. This is damnable, he said. I no longer remembered my old face, I continued. I looked in the mirror and felt nothing, a lack, perhaps, but not for a particular configuration of features, not for my old face, which had disappeared along with my ID.

We had nothing to go on, not even the most basic foundation. I would attempt to draw my old face, from memory, but there was nothing left, all of my sketches looked like children's drawings, with triangular noses and round eyes and mouths and a squiggle of hair. My face had gone back to where it had come from, which is the mind of God, and He had forgotten it all over again. God never forgets, the Scot protested. No, I replied, God only remembers once, the rest is down to us humans. That means the gates of heaven themselves were raised by men, the Scot exploded, it's ridiculous. Heaven, I believe, is located somewhere in human memory, I told him. Of course, I continued, there was only one outcome to my story. I could choose to ignore it, or I could choose to take my place. Both seemed, somehow, like an incredible violence. I could live out my days as a man in a mask and a monster in the bedroom or I could adopt a new face, that of Mariella's husband, Donald.

Of course, by doing this, I became part of the Januist experiment. By doing this I made it come true. Or was it that it came true without any volition from me whatsoever? Had everything been set in place by Donald during his original working, had he really succeeded in scattering himself across time through his art and now here he was, in reception of my body, his face restored to him once again?

And you have to think about possession: would a new face take control, would it take over completely, would I be myself any more? Would I become Donald? Or would we share characteristics, would we become some macabre Siamese twin with two personalities warring it out in one body?

Why did I do it? you ask me. Why? Because it offered itself to me, so unequivocally? But it's more than that; it's because I came to understand the nature of my existence, the precise arc of my life, let's say, and the responsibility of my incarnation. It was to lead the dead back home, my friend, it was to rescue all of the disappeared, and for that I needed the face of a dead man come back to life, the face of an ex-corpse.

We arranged a first meeting with an emissary at a small town on the coast some miles from Athens. It may seem abhorrent to you, but I gave my word to keep the precise location of our terrible doctor's practice a secret. I gave him my word. Yes, the emissary informed us, the doctor was skilled in facial rebuilding and in the removal of faces. During the war, in a secret laboratory in a death camp, he'd had a stunning collection of perfectly preserved faces mounted on his wall which had unfortunately, he said, been destroyed by the camp's barbaric liberators.

I removed my mask for him to see. Ah, the emissary marvelled, he will love you! You are a gift, my friend, he said.

The day before we left for the procedure, which took place on a private island off the coast of Greece, I visited my favourite prostitute in Athens for the last time as a monstrosity, or so I believed.

That night I made love to Mariella with a new sense of abandon, although I still wore my mask. Afterwards we lay together in silence for quite some time. A bird sang in the middle of the night, the same three notes, again and again. What can it be? Mariella asked me. I wanted to ask her if she wanted me or if she wanted her husband, but the die had been cast and I knew there was more at stake than simple jealousy or rivalry. A feather on the breath of God, wasn't that the phrase? Besides, I thought, as I stood in front of the mirror in our bathroom for one last time, who was I at this point? A pupa, an indeterminate stage, a man in transition. I stared at myself some more and retired to bed beneath an open window where the night bird continued its forlorn song.

We arrived at the small town on the coast whose name I am sworn not to divulge. There we were met by the pasty emissary, who was wearing a disconcertingly loud dogstooth sports jacket and whose long hair had been greased back with Brylcreem. He believes this is an assignation, Mariella said, he thinks he is in espionage. It will be necessary for you both to be blindfolded, he said, looking at us over the top of his thin spectacles. We climbed onto the boat, a small motorised affair, and the driver, a fat Greek thug, slid a pair of black pillowcases over our heads.

The heat was stifling, and it was difficult to breathe. I tried to track our movements, to estimate the general direction of our approach, but it seemed to me that the fat Greek driver was deliberately out to confuse us, turning back on himself again and again, approaching our island in a series of ever-increasing circles that made it feel more like orbiting a planet.

After what I would estimate was just over an hour he killed
the motor and we floated into a shallow bay. The scene that
greeted us when our blinds were removed was remarkable.
I have never seen such lush, green foliage, such a mixture
of wild and cultivated plants, towering all around us and
running up a steep incline topped off by a building that
I came to find out had originally been a plague hospital
but which now resembled nothing more than a strange
modernist church with high windows and battlements along
the top that looked like stone antennae or crooked crosses.
As we were led up the steep path I was taken aback by the
intense life of the vegetation, which almost felt animal, the
deep green of the grass, the reds and blues of the flowers,
the huge swollen seed heads. The Nazis experimented with
flowers too, I thought to myself.

The doctor, whom I will simply call The Surgeon from here
on, was waiting for us on the wide patio dressed in a white
leisure suit and with a rust-coloured cravat. He rose to greet
us. Ah, he said, I see someone has already unwrapped my
present. I wasn't wearing my mask.

Mariella, he said, it is good to see you. This put me on
guard, I admit. Was this camp old Nazi a friend of hers?
When I asked her afterwards she said I had misunderstood
him, that it had simply been a generic greeting, that there
was no implication of prior knowledge, that was the exact
phrase she used, no implication of prior knowledge. He came
up close to me and offered me his hand. He stared into my
eyes and ran his gaze all over my face as if taking in an old
master. Do you have the photograph? he asked Mariella.
Yes, he nodded, yes, I think we can make this work. A most
excellent choice, he said to me, but before I could explain

that choice really had very little to do with it he put his
hand up and signalled for silence. Really, he said, I regard
this as more of a restoration than a rebuild, you understand.
I didn't, but before I could protest he signalled for silence
again. Have you ever heard of the Turin Shroud? he asked
us. It's a terrible fake, he said, but really that isn't the point.

I gather you were in the war, The Surgeon said as we sat
down to coffee and cake on the patio. Weren't we all? I
replied. Oh no, The Surgeon replied, I wasn't in the war at
all. I took advantage of the war, yes, perhaps, I was on the
sidelines of the war, certainly, but I was never in the war. I
dealt with, how do you put it, the by-products of the war, as
it were. The war was a great opportunity for The Surgeon
to hone his skills, the emissary, whom I will simply call The
Weasel from here on, said. I struggled to get the cake into
my mouth. Eating cake will be a much simpler affair with
your new lips, The Surgeon reassured me. As will kissing
the girls, he said, and with that he winked at me.

When will the operation take place? Mariella asked him.
Oh, in a few days, The Surgeon replied. I will of course
have to take preliminary measurements and I will have to
sketch the rudiments, the basic topography, on our friend's
face here. Those were the words he used, 'rudiments'
and 'basic topography' and 'friend'. In the meantime,
you should make yourself at home. All my hospitality
is at your service. Is it true that this island was once a
plague hospital? Mariella asked him. Yes, that is true,
The Surgeon admitted, but that romanticises it a little,
I'm afraid, or is that just me? In less prosaic terms it was
a hospital for infectious diseases. However, despite my
remodelling I would like to think that some of the original

ethos remains and that we too provide a place of succour for the wounded and the maimed.

I excused myself and The Weasel led me to my room, on the top floor, with its own balcony and a view out across the island and beyond. I had expected to be able to fix my co-ordinates by the islands around us, perhaps even a glimpse of the mainland in the distance, but to my consternation there was only a single other island to be seen, a tiny, uninhabited companion just to the north.

Had we really travelled so far? As I scanned the island I could make out a cluster of semi-industrial buildings somewhere to the east, assembled around another small cove. Why hadn't we come in that way? Elsewhere the island seemed almost impassably rich with huge, fleshy flowers and technicoloured flora, a grotesque bridal bouquet fallen from heaven. I could see The Surgeon down below, seated next to Mariella. They seemed to be deep in conversation, though it was impossible to catch what they were saying from so high up.

Was she crying? At one point she held her hands over her face and shook her long dark hair, at which The Surgeon stood up from the table and went to embrace her. As he embraced her I saw him signal to someone behind her back, just out of sight. I was becoming increasingly unsettled. I snuck from my room and began to explore the rest of the building.

The top floor appeared to be entirely residential, a long corridor running the length of the building with identical doors on either side, although, as I was later to confirm, there only appeared to be windows and balconies on the west side.

A row of windowless rooms facing east on the top floor made no sense.

The second floor was lit up in a pale undersea-blue, giving the impression of being somewhere below sea level while still clearly suspended in the air.

All of the doors I attempted were locked, but as I went to try the final one it opened slowly from the inside, and I secreted myself behind a pillar as The Weasel emerged wearing what appeared to be a bloodied white apron before locking the door behind him.

I've neglected to mention the most striking feature of this second floor – I was stationed on the third, you understand – which was the presence, along its entire length, of perfectly preserved animals in large glass cases.

Some of them I was able to recognise, a red-throated diver or loon, as they are known, who have the most uncanny of mating calls, stood awkwardly upright amidst a diorama of cliffs, seashells and netting, its feet I noticed had both been pierced, as if once upon a time it had been fixed to the spot and there were holes where it had torn free, there were snakes, inevitably, coiled motionless around branches or beneath huge fake rocks, there were larger animals too, a vicious-looking wild boar, owls, a huge pair of deer, and, most unnerving of all, a terrible fake monkey, and by terrible I mean awful, kitschy, cute, macabre, truly awful, propped up in a jungle scene, the kind of monkey a child might win in a raffle, not realistic at all, with a huge dopey smile and big button eyes, the kind of monkey with a name like George, I thought to myself.

I stared at it in morbid fascination. Everything else seemed so particularly realistic, so authentic. I confess that I became troubled by George, as we shall call him for now, this terrible toy monkey in a fake zoo beneath me, beneath the waters, at night. Of course, I thought of the film that Donald had made, the film of the zoo in ruins, but I searched for a black stork in vain.

The first floor was completely sealed – I guessed this was where The Surgeon's operating theatre was located, due to the presence of a light that would go on and off above the door – as was the basement, which appeared fitted with heavy blast doors. Someone intends to sit out the end of the world, I thought to myself, and then it occurred to me that we were on an ark, a great floating ark with every species of fauna and wildlife preserved, and that the rest of the world had disappeared beneath the waves and here we were, two by two, me and Donald or me and George or me and Mariella.

On the ground floor there was a huge indoor swimming pool, lit up from underneath, so that the water appeared electric.

That evening we ate dinner on the patio, served by a pair of elderly kitchen staff who had seemed to appear from out of nowhere.

Where are the kitchens? I asked The Surgeon. Oh, they're on the second floor, he told me, there's a service lift that connects them to a utility room at the back of the manor. That was the word he used, manor. We drank beautiful Greek wine and the main course was a stew of venison and black olives. I drooled the food back into my plate as I ate it. The Weasel seemed particularly disgusted. I was used to it. I wondered if he had slaughtered the deer himself, behind the closed door on the third floor, or perhaps he had simply butchered it. The idea of bringing live animals to the island just to be killed seemed far-fetched, even in the circumstances.

Have you done many of these facial reconstructions? I asked The Surgeon, but I found myself slurring my words even more than usual, unable to articulate even the simplest of phrases. I'm getting worse, I thought to myself, I need this work more than ever. Restoration, my boy, not reconstruction, The Surgeon corrected me, but yes, I have restored many faces. Many faces, he said, and he glanced around the table.

For the first time I felt myself gripped with fear, a fear that ran like a cold liquid injection up through my stomach. I don't feel well, I explained to the table, though the words were disappearing one by one. Don't worry, The Surgeon reassured me, I'm afraid that it's all perfectly natural. We have a big week ahead of us. I took the liberty of dosing you with a slow-release pre-med. It's better this way, he reassured me. You'll find it much more comfortable. I need to lie down, I said, or at least I think I said it, as The Surgeon instructed the two kitchen orderlies to carry me to a lounger on the patio and to lay me flat on my back. I gazed up at the blur of the sun as if I was already beneath the knife.

This is too much, the Scotsman with the tanned arsehole
burst. We were back in the prison yard during the war. I
can't believe all of this is going to happen to you, he said,
aren't you afraid, aren't you nervous, knowing what you
know is up ahead? I'm resigned, I told him. It's hard to
explain, I said. In a way it has already taken place.
That monkey really gets me, the Scotsman said. Fuck that
monkey. I saw The Surgeon talking to the monkey, I told
the Scotsman, I saw him taking tea with the monkey. Fuck
no, the Scotsman said. What was it doing out of its case?
Are you sure you weren't out of your head on the drugs?
I can't be sure of anything, I admitted, but I recall a
conversation between The Surgeon and the monkey.

They were sat at the table, in the afternoon, The Surgeon
and the monkey. There was a single cloud in the sky
and they were arguing about what it best resembled. A
crocodile, George the monkey said. What was his voice like,
the monkey's voice? Like it was filled with sawdust. The
Surgeon disagreed, he said that the cloud best resembled an
idea, not a living thing. Where were you at this point? I was
lying on a deckchair, in the sun, out on the patio. How did
the monkey arrive, was it carried to the table or did it walk
there on its own account? It just appeared but it had soft
feet so there was no way you could have heard its approach.
What did the monkey, sorry, what did George say to that?
He said another word, he said the word alligator. What was
The Surgeon's response? He said, wild geese overhead. What
did George say? I think he asked him if that was some kind
of Chinese poem, admittedly I was in a haze at this point.
It's an idea and a living thing, The Surgeon said. That's a
poem, George told him. Then he pointed to the cloud again,
he raised his stuffed arm, which ended in a rudimentary

hand that best resembled a mitten, being a solid palm with an opposable thumb, and he said another word, he said the word reptile.

Then the cloud began to change, I watched it change in front of me, it seemed to be sprouting legs, it seemed set to scurry off into the blue. The Surgeon raised his arm and pointed at the changes. Cockroach! he said, and both he and George laughed. What was the monkey's laugh like? It wasn't constricted, it was resonant, it wasn't what you would think, it wasn't high-pitched either, like a chimpanzee's, it was a real belly laugh. Then George began playing the fool or acting like a monkey, one of the two.

As he sat up in his chair he began making terrible inarticulate noises with his mouth and scratching himself all over but especially under his armpits. Then he pointed up at the cloud, which was constantly changing shape by this point, and he shouted, fleas! at which both he and The Surgeon collapsed in laughter.

Then all of the life went out of the table and they both just sat there in silence as the cloud dispersed and they were left with the blue of the sky and the blue of the water and nothing in between.

I was drifting out of consciousness and having my own terrible dreams about animals, about white horses and cows, from what I can remember. When I looked around George had gone, had padded off on his silent feet, and it was just The Surgeon who was left and who looked at me with an expression that said, you've been dreaming of animals, haven't you?

Mariella took me upstairs. I told her nothing of what I had seen. We got off at the second floor. Have you checked out the animals? I asked her, and I led her across the huge echoing hall lit up like undersea. Look, I said, and I pointed to the macabre stuffed monkey behind the glass. Look, I said, that surely isn't real. She put her face to the glass. It's a costume of some sort, she said, of course it's not real. Look, she said, you can see fastenings on its back and on its arms, it was made to be worn, by a performer of some sort. A performing monkey. It's probably an antique, she said. You can see where it has been reconstituted, that's the word she used, reconstituted, you can tell by the different qualities of the hair. They've had it stuffed.

The Surgeon is a collector of eccentricities, she said, as she took my hand and led us to our room on the third floor, where I barely slept, not, as you might suppose, due to nerves about the operation that was to take place the next day but truly because the monkey, George, had taken up residency in my brain.

I recalled the empty mansion and the deserted streets that I would walk in my mind through my time of imprisonment during the war, the rooms that stood for memory, and I came to wonder if I hadn't lost myself in a theatre of my own devising, a feeling of space dislocated in time that the drugs undoubtedly encouraged, that I had confused the timelines so completely, with my comings and goings, that they were now breaking down and subject to invasion, from out of the past, from out of mockery, from out of wild speculation.

The next day I was wheeled, alone, into the operating theatre.

Mariella and I said our goodbyes. She put her head on my chest and she wept. She told me things I no longer remember and then waved and blew kisses at me as I disappeared. How had I come to be here? It was all so extravagant. The theatre appeared more like a Victorian observatory or the set of an uncanny funfair than an operating room. Along one wall were arrayed a series of thick pipes that resembled a church organ but with a round, fully movable mirror attached to the end of each. The Surgeon informed me that they were used to focus starlight and moonlight and the light of the planets, that it was crucial that the transformation take place according to the movement of the heavens, according to what he called 'deep time'. After all, he said, every nativity is written in the stars.

What I had taken as crooked crosses or battlements atop the hospital were actually a series of precisely calibrated telescopes. Remember, he said, when we look out on everything we came from, we are looking into time as well as space. He slid the stretcher into place beneath a canopy of bright, almost blinding lights, strategically situated around what appeared to be a run of film projectors.

First, The Surgeon said, we must map the basic topography. The central projector clicked into life and the photograph of Donald appeared on a screen just above my head, superimposed upon my own terrible wounds. I say terrible because it was only in the moment when his face met my own, an elegant ship from the future touched down on Mars, that I realised the extent of my alienation from the ways of men.

I will have to strap you in, The Surgeon informed me,
which will include fixing your jaw shut. We cannot risk the
slightest movement as we plot your new identity. I felt the
straps tight around my throat, pressing my teeth together
and forcing me to breathe through what was left of my
nose. Excuse me while I suit up, The Surgeon said. In the
meantime, my assistant will sketch the preliminaries.

He disappeared into a back room. I heard a door close but
was no longer able to move my head. Then I became aware
of what I can only describe as silent footsteps. I felt a soft
hand, a paw, even, on the top of my head and realised, to
my horror, that his assistant was dressed in the monkey
costume.

His expressionless button eyes looked down through the
eyes of Donald, of the Januist, of the artist and film-maker,
and finally, into mine. In his hand he held a selection of
what looked like coloured pencils. He began to draw lines on
my face, a pencil grasped clumsily in his fist. I was unable to
move or make a sound. I felt like my eyeballs would pop.

Then The Surgeon appeared behind him and put a spike
into my vein and I was flying, high in the air, over this jail,
the very jail we spent the war in, and I looked down and the
roof had been torn off completely, it had been opened like a
tin can and inside it was empty, you could see all the cells
from above, all the individual rooms, the deserted courtyard,
right where we're sitting right now, and everything was
still, there wasn't a sound, not a movement, no birds, even,
nothing, and all around the jail it was the same story,
wreckage, like a great storm had blown through and all the
roofs of the buildings been torn off so that from above you

could see inside them, abandoned rooms, empty streets, churches open to the heavens and debris, debris everywhere, Europe in ruins, it was so lovely, it all ends, I said to myself, it all ends, and I was thankful and I came to a sudden stop in the sky and I hung there, above the ruins, with my arms outstretched for an eternity.

When I came to, I was beneath the telescopes and it was night. I was alone on the first floor. I put my hand to my face. It was bandaged. It's hard to describe but I felt different. I felt the presence of my new face. Not like a mask, not like where you wear a mask and you feel like you have something over your face, something that you have to keep reminding yourself that people are reacting to and that isn't you, it was more like my body, or my will, more amazingly, was under new command.

Still, part of me was nervous. I was divided, that's for sure. How will we get on, I remember thinking, which seems a strange thing to say, but it's true, someone else had taken up residence in my own body and now it was about integrating the two, I realised that. I lay there, beneath the telescopes, and was bathed in starlight. It felt like soft cold rain. After a while I fell asleep. When I woke I was back in my room on the third floor, propped up in bed. Mariella was seated next to me.

I love you, she said, that was the first thing she said, she had never said it before. I tried to speak but my lips and my jaw felt too tight, too heavy to form words. I wanted a cigarette. Isn't that crazy? It was my first thought, it was a craving. I put my fingers up to my lips in a V shape and mimed smoking. Mariella took a cigarette and put it between my lips. I can't describe the feeling. It felt incredible. I gripped the cigarette with my lips, with my new strong lips, I began to lick them, to run my tongue around them inside and out, it was such a thrill. I have big plans for these lips, I thought to myself. With difficulty I began to roll the cigarette from one side of my mouth to the other.

I see you've already started on your physiotherapy, The Surgeon joked as he appeared in the doorway. He sat on the edge of the bed. It went well, he said. It went very well. The stars were propitious. They put on quite a show. You'll have to keep your bandages on until your new face is set – that was the word he used, set – which should take a few weeks. Then we're ready for the big reveal. That's what he called it, 'the big reveal'. I rolled the cigarette around my lips. I felt like Lazarus with a hard-on.

At this point I must mention the presence of the dead. Their presence to me now was more like a constant low-level drone, a distant humming, the sound of a stuffed animal in a case, it occurred to me, as I spent many hours on my own walking the length of the second floor. The dead were waiting for me, stock-still, and as I looked at the wretched animals preserved behind glass I heard the sound of death in momentary abeyance, which is how Mariella described it.

What stills the dead outside of stuffing them and mounting them? Giving in to their demands? Even the dead don't know what they want. But I sensed they had been held at bay, by the island itself, and what went on there.

I can honestly say I began to enjoy our routine, looked forward to our long evening meals out on the veranda, overlooking all of that verdant vegetation and in the distance, in the pale haze, the occasional sailing boat idling by.

The Surgeon began to open up a little about his position 'on the sidelines' of the war, as he would have it. You mustn't be afraid to advance the sum of human knowledge, he insisted one evening, no matter the terms of the situation. Progress remains progress, he insisted, even if it is through the underworld.

After all, he said, what did we have to fear outside of the judgement of God, and surely we had done with that some time ago?

As the servants cleared our plates I sat back in my chair and lit a luxuriant cigarette, held firmly between my lips. I have a question for you, Doctor, and I addressed him like that, as a doctor. I am intrigued, I continued, not to say a little disturbed, by the presence of a strange old stuffed monkey costume in your menagerie – that was the particular word I chose – on the second floor. I confess it has invaded my dreams and, I fear, the operating theatre itself. Am I right in observing that your assistant – and at this I looked pointedly in the direction of The Weasel – wore the suit as he prepared what you yourself described as the preliminary topography of my new face?

The Weasel seemed perturbed, uncomfortable at the suit being brought up, but his reaction confirmed for me that it was indeed he who had sketched the initial outlines of my new face.

Well, The Surgeon said, removing his napkin and pushing it to one side, it's funny you should bring that up, what with this talk of being done with the judgement of God. I confess I am a collector of eccentricities, The Surgeon said, fixing a knowing look at Mariella, and of mementos too. Monkey suits, you call them, and of course you are correct, that is what they increasingly became, improvised to look more and more simian with grafts of fur, stupid button eyes and even, occasionally, a long rat-like tail.

I have come across many variations over the years. However, they did not start out as dressing-up costumes. They were suits worn by specialists, shall we say, in the early days of the camps when the extermination process was, well, a little trying for some. In order to hide their identity from their victims and from the rest of the camp, as well as for reasons of hygiene and safety, some operators demanded an outfit that would cover their body completely and that could be fitted with a respiratory device. These would be worn before, during and after necessary executions of criminals, seditionaries, malcontents and subhumans.

However, this created a schism within the camps as there were soldiers who believed – rightly, I think – that there was no shame in what they did, that the executions themselves were a necessary step towards the cleansing of humanity of the vermin that would drag it down. These were proud soldiers, soldiers who never shirked from their greater duty to humanity, soldiers who did not fear identification, soldiers capable of looking the dead and the dying straight in the eye, soldiers who lived in, and cultivated, an aura of terror and of awe. They looked down on their comrades who sought anonymity, who needed a barrier between themselves and the dying, they mocked these weaklings as being evolutionary throwbacks, as simians still in terror of the judgement of God. They began to modify the costumes to make them look more and more like monkeys in order to humiliate those who would murder covertly, undercover. It's a fascinating development, don't you think?

I have never seen the use of monkey suits in the camps documented in any of the post-war literature, The Surgeon continued. True, they weren't widespread, indeed their usage was probably confined to a handful of camps in Poland, but any that were discovered – and I flatter myself that most of the surviving outfits, in all their strange resplendence (that was the phrase he used, strange resplendence) are in my own personal collection – were probably destroyed or discarded as improvised clothing, something to keep the cold out, just another purloined wardrobe.

Why did The Weasel find it necessary to wear one when operating on me? I asked The Surgeon, refusing to address so much as a glance towards The Weasel himself. Old habits die hard, The Surgeon shrugged. Besides, they retain their surgical function. Still, he admitted, I couldn't resist having one stuffed and displayed alongside my menagerie, he said, just to make the point, you understand. At which The Weasel, with a look of real shame, excused himself from the table and disappeared inside the house. The Surgeon watched him go. He has the temperament of an artist, The Surgeon said, before turning back towards the table. Let me reassure you both, he said. I was never one to wear a monkey suit.

I was never to share the story of my 'big reveal' to the Scotsman with the tanned arsehole. That day that we sat in the sun, in the courtyard, our backs against the wall, that day I told him of my arrival on the verdant island in the middle of the ocean, that day during the war was the last day of his life.

That evening he died of a second stroke in our cell, which by this point was filled well beyond capacity, as a result of which his dead body, which had first been sick over itself and then had cried out in terror and then had drifted into incoherence and finally silent spasm, was left to cool down, as it were, between three living bodies on a bunk, one of which was my own, and with nowhere to move the corpse and, besides, nowhere to resituate ourselves to in the morning, despite much calling out and clamour in our cell, we were forced to spend the night with it, my friend that had by now become an it, an it that nevertheless we were forced to come to intimate terms with, to wrap our arms around and to rub our legs up against, even as it became moist and caused a puddle of its own previously sound liquids to pool beneath us, even then we still struggled to sleep and to toss and to turn, if occasionally to groan and to cry out and protest, protestations that were silenced by the rest of our cellmates, determined to sleep through whatever the night dealt, be it death or putrefaction, as night is a blessed release to all prisoners, regardless of its terrors, as we all know, and here is where I first, truly, it might be said, communed with the dead and the recently departed, which I would compare to a miasma, rising from a swamp, which bears the same relation, only in more corporeal terms, to the spirit passing from the body, which is to say the ghost of the dead, that which remains, in my

first experience of its possible ascendance, of its puzzling
new freedom, the freedom of the dead, which is only truly
freedom, as I have come to learn, once the dead have been
forgotten about completely, in other words once the living
cease to make any demands of them whatsoever, which
can take generations, inevitably, generations of unquiet
dead, and which for famous people and for people of great
standing may even mean a restless eternity, which may go
some way towards explaining why there is a preponderance
of famous ghosts and why the psychics of today claim, in
seemingly unlikely numbers, to be in contact, so regularly,
with the great and the good, and I say miasma as I wish to
conjure to your mind the idea of an unpleasant emanation
and I also want you to recall the bit in The Bible, early on,
when God talks – if it was truly Him – about the separation
of the waters, a word, waters, that is repeated three times,
in God's words, where He says 'Let there be a firmament in
the midst of the waters, and let it divide the waters from the
waters', and it occurred to me, that night, as we ourselves
lay in a pool of the lower waters, a fetid pool, mind, that
another water, a miasmic water, a water heated to the point
of a miasma, rose up, took itself off from the firmament of
the body – my friend's old useless body that had so suddenly
become an it – and the firmament, if I'm right in saying, was
originally supposed to be a great solid dome that held in the
world and that separated it from space and here was the
world now, leaking down into our bedclothes and rising up
too, rising up to whatever was beyond the firmament, and
which may well have been heaven, or one of the heavens, as
there appear to be stations, as I said, beyond which the dead
disappear forever or before which they are forced to answer
to the sorrows of the living, but what I'm trying to say is
that in the death of my friend I witnessed the primal act,

the separation of the waters, and came to realise that every death re-enacts the beginning of the world and that we have the whole thing ass-backwards.

Right there, you see, truly, is the beginning of my tale.

In the morning the body was removed, and I suppose it was burned or buried in a pit.

In the courtyard people would quiz me for news of the war and I would give them the vaguest outline of what I would later glean from books and newspapers, the war on two fronts, the Bulge, the terrible Russian winter, the bunker, the chancellery in ruins . . . Hitler is dead, the rumour went round, although at that point, of course, he was still very much alive.

The young boy, who was back wearing a regulation striped pyjama top after losing his smart denim jacket in a brawl, would ask me questions about the far future, about the possibilities of the fantastic, things that were beyond the reach of my own terrible powers, things that were outside the span of my own life, but nonetheless I would entertain his fascination with speculation that I would present as vision and soon we had two parallel futures that we spent much of our time in, one that would unfold and that would come around and that would pass just as surely as the sun would continue to shine, and one that we would never enjoy outside of anticipation and fantasy, a world where they landed on the moon, they really did that? the young man burst and yes, I told him, yes, they really did, the Germans were working on the technology in secret, I claimed, and after the war they moved over to the American side and they came up with a great saucer, a round disc with retractable legs, which could move so fast it was almost invisible and they kept it inside a mountain and it would take off vertically and soon they were sending fleets of these ships to the moon to conquer it, though when they got there they found there was nothing to conquer, that it was in fact just a dead stone floating there, but nevertheless it was some kind of achievement, but how did they prove it, the young man asked, how did they prove they were on the moon, and I told him that they took photographs, that films were made, and the young boy said, well, they can make a film of anything they like, he talked about a film he had seen where a race of aliens conquer the earth, and I said, yes, okay, but what happens is they put a huge flag on the face of the moon, a flag so big that it can be seen from everywhere on earth, that's how they prove that they get to the moon, but what's on the flag, he asked me, surely it isn't just the flag of a country, surely people would protest across the world about having to look at another country's flag every night stuck in the moon and towering over them, like an advert, an advert for a country, and of course he was right, and I had to think, what would they put on a great flag that wouldn't even flap on the moon, a flag that would stand motionless, a flag that would, of course, attract attention from all sides, from out there in the solar system, in the depths of space, as much as from the people of earth, and I was stumped for a minute and then I said, well, what they come up with is, what they decide would best represent the achievement of man, what would best represent him to the cosmos, in a way, is, well, what do you think they chose, I asked the young man, who at this point had stopped shaving with a rusty razor that he would borrow from an emaciated Italian who described himself as a prisoner of conscience and had therefore sprouted the beginnings of a soft beard and who was also sporting a bloodshot eye and cuts across his hands as a result of the fracas over his purloined denim jacket, and the boy thought a while and said, well, a flag is ruled out, we know that much, people across the world don't want to look at the same flag flapping every night in their face, even though you point out that it wouldn't flap, I think we get the point, so I would guess that they would put something on it like a picture of a man, a drawing of an earthman, no, well, in that case, a man and a woman, you know, that's how we get along down here, why not up there, any aliens can check us out, we can see ourselves in space, everyone wins, no, okay, I see, I guess there are many types of people on God's earth so it was too hard to decide, you know, should they be fat, should one of them be fat and the other tall and beautiful, but who wants to look at an ugly fat person flapping on the moon, which I know they wouldn't flap but you get what I'm saying, but I suppose the whole thing became too fractious, too complicated, like should the man have a beard, should the woman have long hair or short hair, this is the human race we are representing here, after all, and we're all going to have to look at it, though in what detail I'm really not sure, could you make out their genitals from the earth, for instance, or would you need a telescope, should they even be naked in the first place, but you know if you put them in clothes that, well, fashion keeps on changing, they will be out of date in no time, but maybe that doesn't matter too much as although in the short-term they will become a bit of an eyesore, kind of an embarrassment, with people looking up at the moon incredulously and thinking, did we really dress like that, I mean, we could get to the moon but we couldn't figure out just how off the mark women's fashions were, but of course eventually, in time, they will come to seem quaint and then historical and that of course lends them a certain air of gravitas, a certain authenticity that we can all be proud of, even if we wouldn't be seen dead looking like that today, and of course how do they stand, do they stand like statues, heroic, mythic-looking, or is that all too much, should they slouch around, touch each other, appear casual, and of course we haven't even brought up the race thing, never mind what age these two should be, should they be at their peak, which I read somewhere for men it's twenty-one and for women thirty-two, which puts us out of sync, I've always felt, and a twenty-one-year-old man, let's call him, with a thirty-two-year-old woman on a flag on the moon, well, that's too much reality for anyone, I fear, should she expose her breasts, of course, being a breast man I would say yes, and wouldn't that be a healthy attitude, there's a voluptuous naked woman on the moon for all to see at any age, but then I'm a freethinker, well, I regard myself as one, and there are lots of religious people who would not be happy with a buck-naked woman on the moon, never mind a guy with his penis hanging down, that'll inevitably offend someone, you can imagine whole areas of the world where they would have to lock themselves in at night just to make sure they didn't catch an inadvertent eyeful, religions that would be forced into fear of the moon, which is fear of women, if you think about it, which would give women a nice feeling of revenge for all that they've had to put up with over the years, yes, I'm rather coming round to the idea of a giant naked woman on the moon, if women were able to be reasonable with each other and agree on basics then they all could get a lot out of a development like that, but I know, as I say, I'm a freethinker, and there are men to think about too, aliens might think it was a race of women, for a start, and think we were a pushover or an ideal conquest, more likely, and of course men would feel left out, it wouldn't be the whole story unless, of course, you could plant a flag in the sun and have the man on that, but that's never going to happen, let's face it, and of course what colour skin should the woman have, should she have oriental eyes, should she have those hips, those great wide hips, or what about the women with the long necks and the eyes all askew, I'm partial to those myself but what's wrong with a blonde, a traditional blonde, or a Scandinavian blonde, if you really want to push the boat out, and of course what about South Americans, what about Latino women, the most beautiful women in the world, some might say, and sometimes it's hard to disagree, at least that is until you get into Eastern Europe and then it's all over, for me anyway, at any rate, it's all over when confronted by the beauties of the near East, Polish women, oh my God, the women of Czechoslovakia and Hungary and Romania, okay, hear me out, this could be out in the realm of fantasy but how about a painting, a painted flag, with five women on it, a Japanese woman, an African woman, a great Eastern European beauty, a Latino honey and an Arabian woman – a Persian would be my first choice – and the painting, the way I'm seeing it right now, which is with my mind's eye, it looks like something by Marc Chagall, do you know him, he's a great Russian painter, though God knows where he is now, with all of this turmoil, what has it done for the arts, who knows, will they ever recover, though the arts are resilient, we all know that, you didn't know I had a background in the arts myself, I'll bet, you took me for one of those kids that run off to the army straight from school, well, no, not quite, but I was that oddity, a patriotic artist, well, not so odd if you think of it as an artist with a social conscience, if you twist it like that, but that was never me, I

kept politics out of art but I loved my country, loved
England, and of course loved Poland and loved the women of
Poland, which is what drove me to enlist, those terrible
animal Germans stomping all over Poland then threatening
England into the bargain, what a thought, and so I
abandoned my painting, which, as you might have guessed,
was very influenced by my discovery of Chagall, and so I'm
imagining this flag, this flag on the moon with a painting by
Chagall on it, a painting of five women and the women are
standing in a ring in a garden and they might be dancing,
they might be twirling around, a leg is lifted here, a heel
kicks out, a thigh curves in the way that only Chagall can
make a thigh curve, the quality of his brushwork, which is
what makes a great painter, ultimately, look closely and tell
me I'm wrong, and if you think about it, Chagall's paintings,
if you've never seen them let me tell you, they have the
quality of moonlight, that is of reflected light, that is of the
memory of the sun, the memory of colour, they are
illuminated, like stained glass in the cold dark of an old
church, something that he also dabbled in, or so I heard, so I
was told at art school where we would marvel at his works,
how they were illuminated from elsewhere, the colours like
a fantasy of colour, an uncomplicated supernatural aspect,
that's what they said, and of course Chagall was a Jew,
which makes me wonder if he is still alive, after you told us
of the fate of the poor Jews in this war, have we lost Chagall
with his wonderful light, even more reason to memorialise
him and his women on the moon, though I'm sure, like
myself, he would have opted for five women from Eastern
Europe, five dark beauties with pale skin like the light of
the moon itself, translucent skin and dark eyes and with
their breasts exposed, let's say, let's compromise, with their
nipples of scarlet and of darkest brown, dancing in a circle,

of course what would have been even better, if you ask me, would have been to erect a church on the moon, a church with huge panels of stained glass that could be seen from the earth, one that stood on the surface of the moon as a sign that mankind had been there with reverence, which is the correct attitude with which to approach the moon, I believe, and the windows filled with dancing women in the style of Chagall, in the style of the late Chagall, I almost said, and who can say for sure that he hasn't been murdered already, shot in the back of the head with a single bullet, thrown into a communal grave, what a loss to mankind, will the world ever really be the same, tell me, think of all that we have lost, a holocaust of books and paintings and ideas and thoughts and visions and great buildings rising up on other planets, all the different colours, all the gradations of light, that we will now never experience, people call the light in Chagall's paintings otherworldly and of course that's understandable, I said myself that it resembled bright moonlight, but moonlight is of the world, Chagall's colours are of the world so completely that there is something ridiculous about them, it's colour reflected through a small eye, a tiny pupil that longs to be the size of a planet, that longs to have the surface of the ocean at its disposal, that longs to reflect the expanse of the sky but that is hemmed in, that is concentrated on a tiny surface, and of course Chagall's paintings, forgive me my passion for him, but Chagall's paintings have no depth of colour, his paintings place colour next to colour, never so much colour on top of colour, everything has risen to the surface in a painting by Chagall, everything has risen in the paintings of Chagall, which again is a good enough reason to have his paintings on the moon, in a great church on the moon is how I would have done it, and of course there is something simple about the moon, in my opinion, something that is happy just to be, but even so it makes its demands, it makes its demands of women and of the oceans and of gravity too, there are days of the moon when you can move faster than others, days of the moon when you can jump higher, days of the moon, as we all know, where you can make love all night, days of the moon where you can go a bit crazy and drink yourself till you're poisoned, it makes demands of birds and of moths and, who knows, of insects too, I'm willing to bet, and wouldn't that be something, a painting of a moth, a great moth landed on the moon, wouldn't that be humorous and kind of touching too, the dream of every poor raggedy moth fulfilled, would it confuse the moths of the earth, though, that's impossible to say, and a moth painted by Chagall, inevitably, if he's still around in the future to paint them, and I pray that he is and I pray that as well as women, as well as Chagall's dark and, inevitably, tragic women, that he lives to paint moths, who better, who better to paint their translucent wings, their splashes of eerily simple colour, the way they too become besotted by the reflection of light and fly towards it and burn up, and think of all the light that's burned and buried already, but we go to the moon anyway, we never lose that attraction, that's reassuring, somehow, that we have enough leisure time, that there's a cessation of conflict long enough to facilitate going to the moon and planting a big flag there, even if it doesn't have a painting by Chagall on it, even if it's not, inevitably, a ring of happy and sad women dancing on the moon, or a great moth hovering in happy silence above it, even if it took a war and a holocaust to get there, even if it took a battlefield to invent a UFO, which according to what you are telling me is how it went down, that the Nazis invented UFOs as weapons, at first, and then afterwards for a short trip to another planet,

and of course there's the matter of your new face, which
came to you through the experiments of the Nazis, so some
good came out of it, as least that's how it seems, we're still
waiting to hear how that goes, though it would seem like the
possibility of a fresh start, and that's something, that's
something we would all love to have, a life all over again,
rising up, like the colours in a Chagall painting, how
incredible, but first, okay, put me out of my suspense, what
was it that they put on the huge flag that they raised on the
moon and that everyone could see from space and from down
here on the earth, it wasn't the earth itself, was it, the earth
in space, no, okay, that might have been too uncomfortable,
like looking in a mirror all the time, plus you might get
vertigo, depending on the scale, okay, in that case I give in,
what did they decide in the end, after all the back and forth,
the inevitable complaints and pressure groups and special
interests and lobbyists and international law, I'm sure that
must have come into it, as the moon knows no borders and
so the flag would have to reflect that, wait a minute, wait a
minute, a perfect reflection, of course, after all is said and
done what else could they possibly do, don't tell me, I think I
have it, it's outlandish, but I think I have it, in the future,
when they land on the moon, in order to prove they have
been there they erect a huge flag that has a picture of the
moon on it, am I right, yes, am I right, wow, okay, I guess
there was no other option, really, though I don't suppose it
was painted by Chagall, was it, that's asking for too much,
isn't it.

Of course I thought about the portrait of the young man in
the pyjama top, a portrait that I still hadn't come across
but one that waited for me, deliberately, in the future.
Although the content of my days up ahead, tomorrow and

tomorrow and tomorrow, remained vague – the future I had been given was the future up ahead, my gift for prophecy medium-term – I was able to say with certainty, or near-certainty, more appropriately, that the painting I had claimed to reveal in Mariella's parlour, the painting of the young man in the pyjama top, was actually a self-portrait, though I hadn't said so at the time, in order not to force the hand of chance, a self-portrait in the style of Chagall, even, and that it too functioned as a marker in time, as a flag on the moon, even, though more impossible still, a flag in the future, yet still there were things that I couldn't say, things that I was unsure of, of the fate of the young man with the pyjama top, of his disappearance from my own life, of the circumstances of the painting of the picture, although I was fully aware of the circumstances of its discovery, which was not, as I had claimed, amongst the paintings of otherworldly ectoplasm and deep-sea creatures that Mariella had painted as part of her spiritualist group, rather it waited for me in a curiosity shop in the Plaka area of Athens in the dying years of the 1940s.

I had been taking an afternoon's stroll around Plaka, occasionally sitting down to a coffee or a glass of wine, most of which were provided for free by the gracious and occasionally terrified landlords and restaurateurs who would hurry me to a shady corner in the back of the room in order not to put off the rest of the customers with my face like a soft-boiled egg, when I came upon a shop that I was never able to find again, a shop the size of a long walk-in cupboard that was filled to the ceiling with old green filing cabinets, hat stands, toys, cups and plates, and with paintings hung along the wall and piled up on the floor.

The paintings were the usual garbage, a mix of amateur studies and mass-produced tat, two bright foxes staring out of a green earthen den, a sad horse in a field, a bowl of fruit, the Acropolis, inevitably, beach scenes, seascapes, but there amongst them, luminous, in a box beneath a table, was my young friend from the years of the war, my cellmate in his striped pyjamas, right on cue. I asked the proprietor where he had acquired the painting, if he knew anything about the artist, but he shrugged and said he had no idea, that he got all of his stuff through house clearances, which of course made me suspect that my young friend had died alone in a house in Athens, in the dying years of the 1940s, he had survived the war only to die alone, survived to paint his own portrait and then, as if in a dream, to deliver it to me, who, in turn, would deliver it back to him, in his past.

Why had I not told him the truth about the painting and our remarkable rendezvous in years to come? I had merely set the seed. I pictured him in his garret, in his lonely attic room, coming to the realisation that it was he himself who had painted the picture I had prophesied in our years together in the prison, that there was an aspect of destiny that had fallen into his own hands, and also, I confess, I lied about the painting because I didn't want it to seem as if he was dead, as if he would ever die, and I set it up, in a way, to make it seem that perhaps someone had painted him, that he had merited that, somehow, but also to say that he was remembered and to leave open the possibility, perhaps, of some kind of afterlife, of some kind of communication from the dead, as if Mariella herself had channelled the young man, as if he had never truly disappeared, and of course, to make it real, to anchor it in reality, I placed the painting facing the wall, amongst Mariella's paintings of

the 'denizens of the aire', her 'sidereal visions', that's how
she described them, and like a magician presenting 'the big
reveal', the very words, the very words that The Surgeon
had used to describe the revelation of my new face, I turned
the painting around, as I had predicted I would, as if to an
invisible camera, as if to a rapt audience, though truly I was
the only person in the room, and felt myself part of a chain
of events fixed forever in heaven's unchanging heart.

Soon after the young man's vision of the church of Marc
Chagall on the moon, he was moved to another cell.
Actually, it wasn't a cell but rather the abandoned stables
that had been opened to take an overflow of prisoners. My
own cell became a little more commodious, we now only
had to sleep three abreast, but it became more dangerous
with the arrival of a crook named Malodie with the stupid,
wide-open face of an overgrown child, who immediately
established a vicious hierarchy in which, inevitably, I was
somewhere near the bottom, due to the state of my features.

I realised that in order to secure my own safety I would
be forced to institute something dramatic, a scene of wild
unpredictable violence, and so one evening, as he lay
with his arms around his charge, an Italian boy of barely
seventeen years, I fell upon him in a frenzy and bit a hole
in his neck. Guards were called, and we were both removed
and beaten in front of each other. Malodie called me a
monster, the beast, he cried, the beast, but I knew I had
made my point. From that day on he avoided me, and I was
sent to the stables myself after a brief period in solitary
confinement, a dark windowless room that confused night
and day and that resulted in an uncanny feeling of being
able to levitate, a feeling that prefigured my dream on the

operating table where I had hung suspended above the ruins of the prison itself. I became aware of my potential to horrify because after all, without a mirror, and only the pain of your own wounds to guide you, it is easy to forget the appalling visage you present to the world, and with my certainty of the gift of a new face up ahead I decided to make the most of what I now thought of as a temporary mask, an aberration with which I would institute my own heinous hierarchy.

I'm going to act cracked, I told the young man in the pyjama top when I was returned to the stables, we can blame it on the solitary, I told him, but it's time to make the most of my temporary features. Although the nights were even colder in the stables than they were in the cells, due to the flimsy wooden roof that was badly splintered, it allowed a spectacular view of the night sky, and so night came to seem as a double blessing, as we occupied the wee small hours by naming stars and constellations and enjoying the benediction of the planets. Sometimes the moon was so bright that it would illuminate the entire room and I would look around and realise that no one was sleeping, that everyone was flat on their back, bathed in its light, lost in its simple mystery, looking up.

The moon is the church of Marc Chagall, the young man said to me one night, that's why there's no point in painting anything on it but the moon itself. He seemed satisfied with this and then he went to sleep.

By day I would often spy my nemesis, as I had come to regard him, sly Malodie, at some distance in the courtyard, his young charge by his side, his neck wrapped in heavy bandages where I had done the deed, his eyes fixed on mine

in a kind of revulsion, always orbiting me and the young
man at a precise distance, so much so that I began to believe
that there was between the two of us some kind of fixed fate
or relationship, one that had somehow eluded me in my
plotting of the future, some strange tributary that ran off
from the main course of my life, but a key one nonetheless,
even as it refused navigation from so far off. Indeed, as I
looked at the two of them, sly Malodie and his young charge,
it occurred to me that they were a malevolent reflection of
myself and the boy, and not only that but a taunting of my
powers, my ability to see what was up ahead. Then what of
us? the pair of them seemed to ask me, a pair of vagrants
that not only had the power to unnerve me by day but
that had taken up residence in the mansion of my dreams,
even, where previously I would travel in my mind as a
necessary restorative, the same mansion where I kept my
love imprisoned under lock and key and where I would now
encounter these two as inexplicable trespassers, eyeing me
from the stairs, seated on twin chairs at the far end of the
empty dining room, stood behind a hedge at the bottom of
the garden, only sly Malodie's eyes, those eyes of revulsion,
visible above the phantom green foliage, illuminated as if,
once more, in back of the scene, lay a dream of the moon.

I ventured to tell my young companion none of this. To him
I maintained my new front of reprobate terror. I hollered
and I screamed and I forced unpronounceable words
from my deformed mouth. This, in combination with my
looks, and the tales of me feasting on the thin neck of sly
Malodie, afforded us our own area in the stables as well as
small favours from the more obsequious and superstitious
prisoners. In this way I established the time and the leisure
to continue my story relatively unmolested.

You mentioned the big reveal, the young man prompted me. Yes, I said, yes. In the weeks leading up to it I often walked on my own around the island, the island of the plague, following secret paths to elaborate grottoes with wooden steps leading up to clifftop views, or cutting my way through groves of fleshy flora that felt alive, to me, in a way that was more animal than plant, it's hard to relate, the heads of the flowers seemed to pulse with life, the greens were the chthonic greens of the insides and of the beginnings of life, the foliage would press in on you as if possessed of independent life, as if it would bend to sample your bouquet as you passed.

I investigated the small harbour I had spied on the opposite shore and found a motley collection of small boats tied up there, bobbing silently in the tide, motorboats for a speedy escape, I told myself, and discovered a pair of large metal doors set into the face of the rocks that I surmised led to a tunnel that ran beneath the island and that connected to the sealed basement of the manor. I sat on a rock amongst the outbuildings, which were actually rusting metal shipping containers, and spent most of that afternoon, and the afternoons to come, smoking silently, staring at the sea, thinking thoughts, making predictions, though, of course, I cannot now know what those predictions might be because, as I have taken pains to explain to you, it is impossible to tell the future through a prophecy of the future, you can't pile the futures on, is what I am trying to say, because that would simply result in confusion. But I can sketch for you my feelings at that moment, as they are contemporary with my story.

I felt a surge of power running through my body. The future was a source of almost sexual anticipation. I wanted to mount it and tame it and dominate it. The nicotine lit me up inside. I pictured the parting of the sea as the parting of the legs of a woman as the surrendering of the future. At this moment I had forgotten about the dead that plagued me, the dead that waited for me on the opposite shore, as if it is ever truly possible to live without the dead, walled in by all of the dead that have passed and all of the dead that are to come, but as I sat there the prospect of my new face had lightened life, if only for a season, and I pictured myself as a seducer, and the seal on the future no longer the bars of a prison cell but a huge smacker on the lips, as I puckered my own, again and again, as I brought my lips down, strong, on my own fingers, as I developed an appetite, once more, and I pictured future events as swooning before me, the man who was gifted a second chance, the man who disappeared and came back anew, the man who sidestepped fate, was it possible, was it truly possible, no, it was impossible, I was impossible, which is why I imagined all the time that was yet to come as trembling in fear and excitation at a new possibility, one that had never been reckoned with before.

I saw the future from two standpoints, then, from the stables in the jail and from the mournful harbour towards the east of the island, and in both I pictured the havoc I would cause. The new man, I told myself – for that is how, for a season, I saw myself – will appear as an aberration, as a disease, as a modern in a village in the rainforest. He will infect the future and cause it to chaos.

Even now, in my wartime confinement, I felt the force of the future, travelling back, and I ranted and I raved and I drooled and I fought and I pillaged and I stole. I attacked those near me in a fury, a fury that sent me to isolation and then returned in a greater fury still. I ran rackets, pitiful rackets, we were in jail during the war, after all, but rackets all the same, rackets that made enough noise to establish me as the ruler of an improvised fiefdom based around the terror of my appearance and the instability of my moods, a fiefdom based around the trade of tobacco and of rusting razor blades and of extra portions and of crumpled pin-ups and of carbolic soap and access too, access to the oracle, access to The Oddity that I was now and which I was yet to become and in the possibilities of which I took a new-found delight.

You mentioned the big reveal, the young man prompted me again. Yes, I said, yes. We returned to the theatre with its cluster of telescopes, its wall of lights and film projectors, its wood and brass and silver, its gleaming surfaces, its abandoned trolleys and its tools, its smell of ammonia, its white tiles, its unearthly glow, its position between the swimming pool, which we had never used and I had never seen lit up since the day we arrived, and the menagerie, which every night took its place in my dreams, and they wheeled me once again in front of the projectors and the lights and they sat me up straight, Mariella took my hand, and they started the film projector, they wanted to capture the moment, it was a historic moment, the apex, The Surgeon said, though of what he wasn't clear, and then The Weasel appeared, this time not dressed as a monkey, it wasn't necessary, apparently, and The Surgeon stood back and asked me if I was ready and I said yes, yes I was, but curiously I didn't feel the sense of moment that I had anticipated, which of course, if you think about it, makes some kind of sad sense, that anticipation and the moment should be mutually exclusive, anticipation cannot live in

the moment, it always looks ahead, and it's true to say that
I was already somewhere else, literally and in my mind,
I wasn't there, and I thought about the picture of Donald,
the picture that my new face had been based on, and I
recalled his eyes, the eyes of a high diver, and The Weasel
handed me a mirror and began to unwind the bandages
from my head, and first I saw the forehead, unremarkable,
you might think, but no, you would be wrong because the
thing that was remarkable about the forehead, when seen
alone, without the accompaniment of the eye socket and the
nose and the lips, was its remarkable lack of wrinkles, it
was completely smooth, baby-smooth, I thought, there were
no markings at all, no spots or freckles or blemishes, and
I thought to myself, it's a blank slate I've been given, and
then the eyes, oh Lord the eyes, there they were, eyes that
weren't deep, necessarily, eyes that were shallow, perhaps,
but eyes that projected, eyes that went out, eyes that were
capable of penetrating the depths, the eyes of a high diver,
with these eyes, I said to myself, I can see through walls,
and then the nose, it wouldn't have been my first choice,
I'll be honest, but it had to go with the eyes, small, a little
bulbous at the end, and there, right at the tip, the first
blemish, a single brown freckle, that was artistic, I thought
to myself, if a little precocious, and the cheeks, well, they
were worried cheeks, cheeks that had been worried hollow
but without any of the actual worry, pre-worried cheeks,
sunken, there to cast a shadow on the rest of the face,
to balance the button nose and the eyes searching out,
hollowed cheeks and the philtrum, oh yes, now that was
created with me in mind, exaggerated, with sharp lines, one
of the first things I'll do is I'll lick that, I said to myself, I'll
tongue my own philtrum, I thought, with delight, and then
the lips, okay, I might have gone a little plumper but again,

I could see the logic, plump lips with that nose and those
eyes, well, it would have been too cute, thin lips are hard-
boiled, I told myself, thin lips are a black-and-white movie, I
said, and of course, if I looked to the left I could see my face,
on the projector, in a real black-and-white movie, this is a
monochrome face, I said to myself, true enough, and then
the jawline, again, I would have exaggerated it a little bit
but it's testament to the artistry of The Surgeon that it's not
all cliché, I'll give him that, besides, I thought, it's nothing
that some stubble won't cure, and then of course it crossed
my mind whether my face could even grow hair, could it
sweat, even, could it bruise in a fight, how would my tears
be, I was flooded with questions like that, but then I noticed
the eyebrows, I had completely passed them by, they were
thick and bushy, slightly curved, okay, there's the proof,
I said to myself, though of course they could be implants,
which would mean they would never have to be trimmed,
and then the chin, a little sharp compared to the jawline but
it's these kinds of combinations, these intricacies, that are
the work of God, traditionally, and The Surgeon seemed well
versed, I'll give him that, but then I realised, with a start,
that the face on the projector wasn't moving at all, that it
was completely still, and then, with a shock, I realised that
it was Donald's face on the projector that I had mistaken for
my own, but then, with a greater start still, I realised that
the face in the mirror was exactly that, that The Surgeon
had remodelled Donald's face perfectly on top of my own,
that I was literally wearing another man's face, and for a
second, a split second, but nevertheless, I felt the briefest
collision between anticipation and moment, the tiniest
frisson as their paths crossed and I felt what I had never
expected to feel, that truly I was wearing a mask, that I
was undercover, that yes, I really was in a black-and-white

movie, and when Mariella hugged me and started to cry she called me Donald, Donald, she said, and she wept and I held her and I said nothing, I'm not Donald, I thought to myself, but I said nothing, I held her as if I was, as if I was her old love come back to life in a black-and-white movie, and The Surgeon too wiped a tear from his eye and marvelled at what he had done and The Weasel too, he embraced The Surgeon, and I found out about my own tears because they rolled down my cheek as if it were the most natural thing in the world.

Of course there was still some bruising around my face, some swelling here and there, and I still had my own hair, which didn't prove to be a problem as it was as dark as Donald's, as dark as a sparrow's, Mariella said, and she insisted on combing it into his style, that same cold parting that he had in the photograph, and of course I assented, what would be the point of refusing a final detail at this stage, and The Surgeon advised me to take it easy, to indulge in rest and recuperation in order to let my face set, that was the word he used, set, but when a man is presenting a new face to the world he is inexhaustible, his appetite is insatiable, for food, for sex and for encounters, and so once more I spent the days circuiting the island, offering up my face to the curious flora, awed at my own reflection in the water as I swam in the mournful harbour on the other side of the island, my reflection, I repeated it softly to myself beneath my breath, my reflection, my reflection, and the salt water made it sting and contract, like a newborn held tight to its father, and of course there was the incredible sex, the death-defying sex, that's what it was for both of us, in our own way, mine in that I no longer had the sense of being observed, of being covertly watched, that the third component I had been somehow aware of had been internalised and now we made love as three, which is the perfect number for sex, and for the sea, as it turns out, that's something else I read in Donald's library, which was really, to all intents and purposes, my own library now, that the sea has the number three for certain thinkers, certain initiates, which is what I now considered myself, an initiate of the supreme mysteries incarnate, and when Mariella and I made love we possessed the three, incarnated the three, and we bit and tore at each other in the process and then of course there were the meals, the endless meals on the patio, the meat that I held fast behind my lips and tore apart with renewed vigour, the wine that I never drooled, the cigarettes that I smoked between courses, I was drunk, many nights I was drunk, sodden drunk, and had to be carried up to my room, and I would insist that we visit the menagerie on the way, which as I have said was lit up with a light like undersea, and I saw my reflection in the glass of the animals, my reflection, I would repeat softly to myself, my reflection and my tears would come again on cue and I would feel a great sense of relief and I would be led up to my bed where I would laugh maniacally to myself on my back as Mariella undressed at the foot of the bed and the cycle would begin all over again with the three of us wrapped in each other's arms, struggling to be inside each other, and in the morning the ocean and the great sky and the feel of salt around my face, setting the mask, sealing me in.

This is when the second thing happened, I told the boy. We were seated in our corner of the stables, given a wide berth by the rest of the inmates. Some crooked constellation was visible through the broken wood of the ceiling. What's

the second thing? the boy asked me. I inherited Donald
Visconti's memories, I told him.

It was after lunch on the island, on the kind of glorious
afternoon when it was almost impossible to prise the sea
and the sky from the horizon. I sat out on the patio, lit a
cigarette and sent a long arc of spit through the air, one
of my favourite things I liked to do with my new lips. The
Surgeon laid a card folder on the table, looked to Mariella,
then back at me. I bring great tidings, he said, and he
winked and pushed the folder towards me. Inside was
a sheaf of typed pages with Donald Visconti's name on
the top. What is this? I asked them both. It's your story,
The Surgeon said, if you want it. Mariella looked at me
expectantly. I scanned the first sentence. 'In the event of
the success of our experiment,' it read, 'I am providing these
notes in order that you or that I or that the two of us should
be better able to orient ourselves in our new role.' I closed
the folder and took a long, silent draw on my cigarette. This
whole thing was planned, wasn't it? I said to Mariella. But
by whom? The Surgeon interjected. By you, I replied, by
her, I nodded. That was the word I used, her, in order to
wound her. We helped facilitate it, that is true, The Surgeon
responded. But like I said, it's your story, if you want it. I
picked up the folder, pushed my chair back from the table
and walked away without a word.

What follows is what I read and reread and then read again,
in awe, and in disbelief.

'I want to attempt to trace the genesis of this notion, this
fascination that took me quite early on in life and that
indeed paralleled the experience or dreams or a combination

of the two more properly of a diverse group of people, people who were to all outward appearances geographically and culturally unconnected, in the early years of the 1930s, a period that I will hereafter refer to, for reasons that will soon become transparent, as the dying years of the 1930s.

'As a young man I shed many tears over the prospect of death, over the deaths of my mother and father and the children all around me. At night, as something in my heart was unlocked by the familiar sounds drifting up the stairs, the sound of the grill sliding into the cooker, the smell of toasted bread and scones, the low murmur of the wireless, the soft padding footsteps, the sound of distant conversation, all of this conspired to rouse me from the sanctuary of my bed and to appear in front of my bemused, long-suffering parents, from whom I would demand to know the true secret of death and whether, in my own precocious way, it was irrevocable, or that there was anything to be done. They would lift me up and assure me that death was something that should be no concern of mine, that surely its time would come, but that time was so far off as to cast not even the slightest shadow on the quiet comfort of my childhood. Our lives, or at least a section of them, would remain impregnable to the storms of time. This all changed rapidly and quite suddenly with the death of George, our tortoise, who passed frozen on the spot in the garden where the soft of his insides had been eaten away by a worm, and which inadvertently – or, more probably, in full knowledge – provided the perfect metaphor for what did away with my father, soon after, on a sudden Sunday afternoon, and my mother, too, who followed him to the grave not six months later, as well as for the wretched condition of myself thereafter, whose worm-eaten heart continued to put up a semblance of effort even as it was riddled with holes and sad tunnels and cast over with dark shadows that worked to frustrate all of its best efforts.

'My father was well known locally and served his time both in the military and in local government, and later in his life, though God knows the forties aren't later in any man's life, no matter the span, he became the kind of local dignitary who attends dinners at film festivals and whom old women accost in the street in order to have their photograph taken. According to local custom, a custom that goes back centuries, albeit with a big gap in the middle when no one paid it any heed whatsoever, a death mask was made of my father as he lay on his dying bed, a mask that was then displayed, alongside the supposed great and good, in the town hall, high on the wall in the tiled reception area so that it appeared to me, with the worm I had inherited in my heart, as if centuries of the once-living were forever attempting to break the bonds of the tomb.

'In my heart-rotten state, and especially after the death knell of our happy escape from time sounded with the subsequent death of my mother, God rest her soul, I became obsessed with the black arts, thanks to a local library that presented a great stock of diabolism, fortune telling, mesmerism, Tarot and demonology. I also became very interested in the classical arts, especially sculpture, and I am sure there are many amateur psychologists who deal in the workings of the life and death urges who could uncover a sublimated longing to rescue my father from the marble tomb that held him high in the tiled reception area of the town hall. However, as I have intimated, my subject matter was more classical, though assuredly of a necromantic bent, as I resurrected dark gods and uncovered fair nymphs from mute monoliths of stone.

'In classic storybook style I was given up to the care of a cruel uncle, a bachelor himself, but one who had the means not just on occasion to beat me senseless but to fund my education on the side, and once again I call on any psychologist who might want to uncover another, although this time barely sublimated, association that I have long wrestled with between creating and suffering, between art and punishment, between vision and pain. As soon as I was old enough I left home, and this terrible uncle provided the means with which I was able to formalise my studies in sculpture and, behind the scenes, the black arts, as I attended an art school on the outskirts of Athens that at the time was considered to be at the vanguard of new thought.

'I read about the attempts to make contact with the other side and also the attempts at transmutation, lead into gold, clay into flesh, and I dreamed of ways of empowering my sculptures with some rudimentary form of life. I carved signs on their bodies, made chants over them, prayed to them with little success. I befriended a fellow student from a separate faculty, that of engineering and technology. Previously I had enjoyed little but my own company, preferring to spend weekends at art galleries and museums or recreating strange solitary rites from the books I read. He introduced me to nightlife and to women and to alcohol and to the pleasures of driving in fast cars. He lived his life at an accelerated pace. His name was W___.

'He also introduced me to the Futurists. He mocked my classical leanings, he called me a relic, he said the moving image was the future, not the static painting, not the immobile sculpture. Sculpture must be kinetic, he insisted, the visual arts dynamic, music cacophonous. We began to work together, to make art together, and early on we created a series of mechanical men capable of moving at their own volition.

'At first we had a pair of legs and a pelvis attached to wires that was capable of writhing on the ground as if it had been shocked into existence. But there was something so uncanny and repellent in its movements and in its sickening form that we destroyed it and from then on we made whole bodies or at least semblances of full figures because animated anatomy, divorced from the human figure, is too macabre and unnatural, even for a would-be Futurist.

'The Futurists revelled in noise, in war, in the sound of industry, in speed, in scale, in brutality and lack of sentiment. At first, I confess, I was interested, chiefly because of their name, a name that suggested a process that rendered time itself pliable and that tied in with my own experiments in diabolism and theurgy. My understanding of Futurism was as an art form that made objects or created ideas that would only make sense in time, art that anticipated its place in the future, for instance we imagined an army of mechanical soldiers, of automatons, swarming across the European continent, the sound of their metal limbs like thunder, the smell of oil and industry replacing that of flesh and blood, war as a spectator sport, a savage board game, a mechanised theatre.

'We exhibited our mechanical men in leftfield galleries in Athens, where they attracted much comment; war machines as kinetic sculpture. But really, we were no more in the future than the classicists themselves. We were caught up in the times, more properly, we were of the moment, Futurism, truly, had little facility with time and looking back, I am sure, it will come to seem as quaint and as daft and yes, just as dated, as any other outmoded school of art practice. But the point is this: we took Futurism at its word. We abandoned our steel dream of robotic men, leaving them in a lock-up in an Athenian suburb where I suppose they remain to this day, and began to formulate something a little more ambitious, something that had its roots in a misunderstanding of the Futurist creed and that then took it somewhere else completely.

'Look, W___ said, magic doesn't work, everyone knows that, magic is dated, it has no power, science and technology point towards the only hope of travelling through time, of escaping backwards and forwards. That's as may be, I said, but it was then that I had the first of my epiphanies, the first of my revelations that would lead me to you or you to me, however you choose to understand it, I said to W___, okay, well, does art work? You say magic doesn't work any more, that it worked once, perhaps, but that today we require a new magic that is in line with our deepest-held beliefs, well, what about art, think about it, there are no objective proofs about the facility of art to change anything, to work on the world, to transform and transport, yet ask anyone and they will confess their belief that art works, that art, really, can do anything, and what a reservoir of belief lies behind that, what a potential source of power, there, right there, is the engine for our great experiment in time, we will become artists and we will take art at its word. But every artist needs tools, W___ said, I propose we marry art and technology, the moving image and a commitment to the potential of art to raze and rebuild reality, I say we use the latest technology, the moving picture, the film camera, the projector, as our transport in and out.

'Of course, we were playing with fire, the great artists were naive, there should be protections in place, safeguards, ways out, just as in the practice of magic, there should be banishings, magic circles, purifications, ritual offerings, an understanding of correspondences, of propitious times, of the movement of the stars and planets, but like the great artists before us we were naive ourselves and so exposed ourselves to much peril.

'We were able to secure the use of an unwieldy film camera, a prototype, a Zagrab C20, that shot in black and white and without sound, which for us was perfect as there had to be a distance to the work, it had to reflect a different world, a silent world, a world of simple tones, a stark world, a world of shadows. We had no idea what we were doing, at first. We shot long, stationary portraits of the two of us, one after the other, then we took turns sitting in front of our own image, which we projected on a wall of the flat I had rented in Plaka. We created primitive loops across two spools, we called them time capsules, and we would set ourselves up in the room and immerse ourselves in the contemplation of our own shadow in the dark for hours or days or weekends at a time, the other taking time, according to a schedule, to deliver food and water or cigarettes to whoever was taking the transport.

'The results were extraordinary. There was a form of osmosis between our present and past selves that resulted in what felt like the raising of a third personality. He is risen, we would announce to each other as we left the room after a successful session, a future self, is what it felt like, like the communion between the two somehow attracted the third, all of whom, of course, were surely one. My studies in magic and experimental psychology and of course alchemy suggested that the goal of magical practice, which had become the goal of art practice, was a reuniting of fractured selves across time, an attempt at wholeness, is what it seemed to suggest, and in our early experiments this feeling of union, of union with the past, the present and the future, in a place that was outside of time, well, it was palpable, to say the least. And true to our beliefs, our gamble with art changed everything.

'Contemporary with our experiments in killing time dead using art and technology we were contacted by a group of researchers based in Germany who claimed to be fugitive Futurists themselves. However, their interests lay more in biology and technology, a sideways interest to our own. Specifically, they had been experimenting on animals. They had written to the gallery where we had shown our mechanical men and the gallery had forwarded the letter to us. It explained that they had been disassembling living animals, that was the word they used, disassembling, an ominous word when used in connection with a living thing, and then attempting to reanimate them. Really, what they had been doing was mutilating them. They would literally skin an animal, remove all of its identifiable features until all that was left was pale pulpy flesh and sinew and nerve endings and bone, and then they would attempt to rebuild it using artificial materials. It was terrible and incredible at the same time. They're practising the art of The Creator, W___ said.

'They wanted our help in mechanising the bodies, in lending them a semblance of new life. Until we find the elixir, they wrote, and it was impossible to tell whether they were joking or not, electricity will have to suffice. We explained in a letter of return that we had moved on, that our interest now lay in film and art and the possibility of a transport through time and a raising of the dead via focused experiments on the two. They replied in kind that it seemed our motivations were held in common. They confessed that they had never experimented with the moving image, however, but they said that if we had access to a film recorder then they would be happy for us to document their experiments and they even used the term "art and magic" in regard to the specifics of our own contribution, so that I exclaimed to W___ that somehow they must have made the same intuitive breakthroughs that we had and that their work, although admittedly more macabre than our own, took a belief in art and the possibilities for ingress, into the future, into the dark of our past, into the work of creation, to a fevered extreme. That was the word I used, fevered, for that is how I felt. We wrote back, and a meeting was arranged, in Düsseldorf, for October, in the first of the dying years of the 1930s.

'Before we left I had an uncanny experience of prophecy. I was listening to the wireless, a habit that I had maintained from the blessed years of my childhood, to a popular general knowledge quiz. I swear this is true and that it really happened and I'm not just misremembering it. It could have been a prankster or an ideologue or a bloody-minded National Socialist but every question that was put to them was answered with two words: Adolf Hitler. Who is the inventor of the telescope? Adolf Hitler. What is the name of the longest river in Africa? Adolf Hitler. How many books are there in the Old Testament? Adolf Hitler. Which of Shakespeare's plays is referred to by the euphemism "the Scottish play"? Adolf Hitler. Which famous modern composer was born in Leipzig in 1813? Adolf Hitler. Who holds the record for running the fastest mile? Adolf Hitler. What form did Zeus take in order to seduce Leda? Adolf Hitler. Can you name their offspring? Adolf Hitler, Adolf Hitler, Adolf Hitler, Adolf Hitler. The quizmaster made no comment about this and made no attempt to correct him. This remains inexplicable to me to this day.

'True to form, when we touched down in Düsseldorf, we quickly came to realise that our correspondents were themselves under the spell of Hitler, that indeed they were in his employ. The two men, whom I will simply refer to as X___ and Y___, claimed that the Nazis were truer to the esoteric principles of Futurism than even the Italians and that they held in great esteem art's ability to transform reality and to rewrite history. Of course I quizzed them about decadent art, as we had all heard the rumours that Hitler and his cronies were philistines. Decadent art, X___ explained, and I can still hear his irritatingly nasal Low Countries accent as I recount this, decadent art, my friend, is art that does nothing for humanity beyond simply revelling in its hopelessness.

'Y___ was the odder of the two. Under the name The Unicorn he presented private piano performances in the top floor of the tower block they occupied in the warren of streets behind Düsseldorf train station, where he would "rape" the piano, climbing inside the guts of a grand Bösendorfer with an erection and engaging in violent copulation with it. The piano, he informed me at one of these covert gatherings, should be played as if it has been accosted and assaulted in a back alley. If you closed your eyes and ignored The Unicorn's increasingly frenzied vocal exhortations, it could almost be Scriabin.

'Still, the pair's main artistic focus lay in the flaying and the restoring of the recently deceased. I will never forget the scene that greeted us when W___ and I first entered their studio on the second floor. There in front of us, held upright by chains strung from the ceiling, was the body of a horse whose skin had been removed and whose blood had been drained. Look at the technology, X___ marvelled as he ran his fingers along the striated muscle and sinew, what madman dreamed this up? The studio stank of ammonia and of preserving fluids and of the insides of things. W___ made the mistake of making a flip comment about taxidermy and X___ exploded. The flesh remembers, he burst, the flesh remembers! Taxidermy is hollow, he said, empty shells. The Jews have a word for it, he said, Qliphoth, the impure husks, the shells. The life of an animal transforms the viscera, remodels the muscle, and so deepens the eye, he said. The eye, he said again, pointedly, with a manic expression on his face. The organs, the muscles, the blood veins, he said, these all become imbued with time. That was the phrase he used, "imbued with time". The flesh remembers, he repeated, the flesh remembers, and he stared at me with his eyes like egg whites, his pupils like birdseed.

'But their experiment – their art – was more terrible and incredible than we had been led to believe. They were creating hybrids. They had started on dogs, stray dogs that they captured roaming the streets by night, dogs whose

faces had been changed. Y___, with great surgical skill,
had perfected the process of removing the face of a dog,
preserving it perfectly, and transplanting it onto another.
I have to tell you that some of these dogs were alive during
the process. W___ and I were implicated.

'We filmed the work. We would begin just after midnight.
We placed the camera in the back of a van on which we had
painted a red cross in order to dissuade suspicion, and we
drove through the outer reaches of Düsseldorf. We travelled
with poisoned meat, enough to knock the dog out for a
few hours at least. We would spot our prey, a thin waif, a
haggard black dog whose eyes lit up in the darkness, and we
would open the doors of the van and switch the camera on,
placing the meat on the floor.

'Come on, boy, we would say, you can see X___ mouth it
on the camera, he pats his thigh and waves the dog into
the back of the van. The dog turns around, looks up, it
is so dark, it is black and white, the dog's eyes are like
tadpoles on the surface of a pond, it thinks for a second, it
is motionless, then it leaps, it leaps into the back of the van
and it starts to eat. The effect is almost instantaneous. X___
holds the dog, it slumps into his arms, it knows something is
wrong and it looks into the camera in fright. It wants to hold
on to life. It was unaware of what life felt like, living its life
in happy ignorance of the life force until the moment when
it felt it draining away, a moment that it seemed to me X___
took a peculiar pleasure in, as he held the dog in his arms
and as he whispered to it, who knows what, you can see it
in the films, it looks like a religious painting, W___ said,
a religious painting in the dark, *The Passion of the Dog
Saint, The Annunciation of the Street Bitch*, and as we drove

back in the dark I let the camera run and it was obvious that X___ had been affected, he was upset, or no, he was filled with emotion, yes, and at that moment he was almost tender.

'Back home Y___ would immediately begin work. The dog was laid out on a trolley, X___ had carried it in his arms, and Y___ would begin the removal of the face. He made it appear no more difficult than the skinning of a rabbit by a teenager. As he made the final cut he held the face in his hand and displayed it for the camera. It hung down over his fingers like thin dough. Then he turned to the dog whose face he had removed and he greeted what was underneath, and you can see it clearly on camera, you can see him mouth the word hello, that was what he said to the bloody mess on the table, to the revelation of muscle and blood and vein and bone showing through, hello, he said, and of course you might say it could be any word, the film is silent, after all, it could be any exclamation of two syllables, "my God" might have been more appropriate, but I was there and I heard it with my own ears. He clearly said hello.

'X___ walked to one of the pressurised containers that lined the wall and that looked like silver tombs. There was a low hiss and a puff of dry ice as the door opened out and X___ appeared with what looked like a goldfish bowl or a space helmet in his hand. He placed it on a surface next to the faceless dog. Y___ put on a huge pair of gloves and put his hand into the bowl, removing what looked like some kind of thin animal-print material. He looked between W___ and me with an expression of manic glee. Then he held up the material for us to see. I got it from a young giraffe with a broken neck, he boasted. I froze behind the camera. We have an arrangement with the Zoological Gardens, he explained. He began to smooth the lineaments of the face over the dog's head. He held the head towards the camera. This is the future of painting, he said.

'There had been many previous experiments. Afterwards, as the dog lay sedated in a cage, X___ showed us around a back room of macabre exhibits, of hybrid animals in grotesque transformations. In a series of glass cases there was a collection of birds with the faces of rats. Y___ seemed embarrassed about those ones. Indulge me, he shrugged. There were horses with camel humps and small, rudimentary wings. Pegasus, X___ laughed. There was a cat with the tail of an overgrown monkey and the snarling face of a ferret, snake heads on turtles, a small rhino with the head of a donkey (we just grafted that straight on, Y___ explained), a donkey with the head of a rhino (likewise, Y___ explained). Until now the artists have only interpreted the world, X said as we walked along in the gloom. The point is to change it.

'Of course, these are early models, Y___ said, practice runs. Nothing has survived the surgery, so far. That is why we moved on to street dogs and to facial grafts. And why we invited you here, X___ added. The organs must remain intact. Our art must have integrity. That is where the Egyptians got it wrong, even with their great cooling towers and funerary palaces. But it's understandable in a land where the sun is all-devourer and all-begetter and corruption moves fast. In the cold heart of Germany, however, we have, let us say, more options. We propose, in cases that don't survive the transformation, to replace the skeleton with one of your mechanical structures. To reanimate the dead, to better them, even. What is the point of all this? W___ finally burst. We wouldn't be the ones to ask, X___ replied, with a smile, and a shake of his head.

'That night, when we returned alone to our quarters – thankfully we were billeted in a separate building far from our colleagues' experiments – I sat on my bed in the dark with Düsseldorf lit up beneath me and felt completely undone.

'I dreamed of more fantastic creatures still, of terrible transformations, of mocking animals with talking assholes, with horrid lips on their anus, moving and forming mute words, of ghastly distended stomachs lined with sharpened teeth. This is all nonsense, I told myself, this is all a pointless nonsense. But what had I expected of magic and of art? Magic, it had seemed to me, bypassed gristle and blood and bone, or at least merely symbolised it in passing, as results came straight out of the clear air. Sculpture idealised the body, its clean lines, its lack of viscera. Was it all an escape from the body, from its ghastly possibilities? And why had I been called here? It is the body that allows us to travel from the past into the future, I told myself. To modify the body, in that case, modifies our relationship with the past and the future. But what about continuity? Without continuity we are simply mocking life and death and we are simply less than it. How does one man, one living thing, exchange its appearance for another, while remaining that first thing, while to all intents and purposes appearing as another, even believing itself to be another? This was the conundrum that we breakaway Futurists came to wrestle with and which came to be symbolised by Janus, from whom we took our name, the two-headed god – I almost said dog – of beginnings and endings.

'The poor sick dog lolled in its cage, clawed at its new face, bled on its sheets. Food drooled from its mouth, its eyes were obscured by its new sockets. We held a mirror up in front of its cage and it just looked through it. After all, dogs don't care for their own reflections at the best of times. So, we mutilated a living being, W___ said, so what now? Do we put it on display, do we boast of our achievements? Can this really be the pathway to the future?

'X___ protested. Brueghel's first painting was a mess, he shrugged. It had to be. Because he couldn't display it in a gallery should he have given it all up there and then? But how much suffering, how many abortions before we make the perfect hybrid? How much suffering? X___ burst. How much suffering? Is that what you think the great artists sought, an end to suffering? No, X___ continued, no. There is no end to art because there is no end to suffering.

'We continued with the kidnap of dogs, reluctant though we were. We travelled across Düsseldorf in the black of the van, with a single light that would flash on and off at random, why can't we fix that, I asked X___, it's driving me mad, and for a second I would catch his silhouette and the outline of the animal in his lap, the poor dog, and then we would plunge into darkness once more. And we continued to document it, to film our midnight runs, for some purpose that continued to evade us and that we thought of as the future. Still, even the dogs that lived, briefly, a week, two weeks, the best part of a month, with a new face, the face of another creature entirely, the face of the dead of the zoo, even those dogs died, eventually, and even when they were alive experienced a death-in-life that was unjustifiably sad. Y___ narrowed his approach. From now on, he said, we will focus on the exchanging of faces between two dogs, dogs of the same breed, even. We will reel in our ambitions, we will start small. We will practise face-swapping. From there, he said, who knows, though I am guessing now, as you read this, possibly, in the circumstances that I imagine you reading it in, that is to say, that you can see where we went, and what the outcome was.

'Suffice to say that our early face-swaps were a success, the dogs were uncomfortable, for a while, undoubtedly, but we kept them sedated and well fed until the face had taken and then, a decision we made between ourselves, we set them free, we let them go, on their way, out, into the world. There was something about that, something about having all of these dogs with surreptitious new faces, out in the world, interacting with reality, that really struck me. To me, it was the equivalent of a radical new perspective in art, where the scene is altered, subtly, where the plane is recalibrated, so subtly that at first, or perhaps at all, you do not realise that you are seeing something new, something that is almost impossible, even as it barely registers on your attention. Yes, it was a contagion, as all great art is, yes, we had so uncannily altered reality that it felt like things would never be the same. I began to have ambitions for all of God's creatures.

'We began the process of mechanisation. W___ and I worked on the birds, the birds with the faces of rats. Y___, as I have explained, was embarrassed about these. When I quizzed him further he claimed that he had plagiarised them, which made no sense to me, where, in the world, are there birds with the faces of rats to copy? We soon came up against our first obstacle. The presence of the organs, perfectly preserved as they were, militated against us installing a full mechanical skeleture. We followed the original skeleture as much as we could, but the presence of the organs meant that we simply didn't have enough room to build in the kind of strength that would facilitate convincing movement. We came to a compromise. For now, X___ said, for now we can remove the peripheral organs; the lungs, the bowels, the intestines, the offal; but the heart remains, he said, the heart must have its place. To tell you the truth, I thought it was a very poetic compromise. I imagined these birds with their rat faces let loose in the forest of Germany, a single still heart in their breast. I confess it almost brought a tear to my eye.

'Then came the incident that nearly got us shut down. I have explained that Y___, under the guise of The Unicorn, would present what he described as "piano actions" once a month in the studio of our building. We would invite forward-thinking members of the Nazi elite, radicals, avant-gardists, freethinkers, Futurists and their ilk. We would also invite prostitutes from the building opposite ours, a tower block where the models sat in the windows with numbers and were picked out by customers from the forecourt below. W___ and I had made friends with many of the women due to the proximity of our working environments and our monthly actions provided them with some extra trade and us with future credits that we quickly spent in the building next door. I had a fair appetite for the women of the night, so much so that I pray that I get to indulge it, once again, and forever, in my next life. If you get my point.

'Anyway. On this particular night the crowd were rowdier and more drunken than usual. There were faces

I didn't recognise. There had been drinking at a beer hall beforehand and one of the regulars had invited a group of young SA men. These boors were manhandling the women and generally making a shame of themselves. Y___ made his appearance as The Unicorn, naked and with a startling erection. He had added a yellow cape to his repertoire so that he appeared as an X-rated comic-book hero. The young men began to heckle him. There were shouts of Es ist Übermensch! With the help of a small ladder he climbed into the innards of the piano. Then he began. He bucked, and he wailed, and in his own words "fucked the shit out of it". It was a tempestuous performance. There were shouts of Es Ist Wagner! as he hammered his penis against the bass strings. People gathered around the piano drinking beer and spilling it on The Unicorn. No, he cried, Es ist Unicorn! as he came to a climax and ejaculated all over the strings with a sound like a small frog plopping into a pond. The drunken SA men took it in good spirits and raised their glasses and toasted his performance. They seemed most impressed by the potential ruination of the piano. That piano cost a fortune, no doubt, I heard one philistine say, what a laugh. Then he let out a large belch and slapped one of the prostitutes on her ample rear. Soon the sounds of muffled lovemaking could be heard from the corners of the studio and I heard doors being opened and closed as couples sought out secluded locations for trysts while a gramophone played obscure piano music from Y___'s collection.

'A cry of anger erupted from one of the back rooms and I realised I had forgotten to secure the room that housed our hybrids. A young SA man of high rank came charging through the door with the shout that we were engaged in experimenting on animals. There was general uproar.

You will be reported for this, you degenerates, he spat.
Throughout, Y___ and X___ remained startlingly calm. The
party's over, X___ announced to the room, this reactionary –
that's the word he used, reactionary – this reactionary has
overreached himself in his attempt to appreciate the new
vanguard of contemporary art. There is no room for small
boys here, he continued, in what I thought was an inspired
retort, no room for the pea-brains of yesterday, he said, no
room for the Untermensch, he said, piling it on, go back
to being foot soldiers, he spat, while behind closed doors
the elite of the party, that's what he called us, the elite of
the party, while behind closed doors the elite of the party
make the kind of art that greets the new dawn on hind legs
and with brave faces, while we, my friend, the elite of the
party, he repeated, for effect, the elite of the party continue
to push the boundaries of what man and animal, together,
are capable of, which is a Reich that will last forever, that
is where our experiments point, not to the conscience of
animal-lovers, perhaps, of sheep, perchance, but to the
establishment not of a thousand-year Reich, he insisted,
not of a thousand-year Reich, but of an eternal Reich, in
heaven as it is on earth, what a flourish, the crowd were
cowed and dazzled, they were beating a retreat, they were
walking backwards towards the door, their hats in their
hands, some of the girls were marvelling, when the war
comes, he continued, like a madman by this point, when the
war comes, he boomed, as we know it will, who will be there
to gather the broken limbs from the battlefield and put you
back together, will it be puppies, will it be cuddly dogs that
graft the skin from your arm or the arm of your brother onto
your shattered torso, will it be sentiment that will protect
us against storm and steel or will it be the elite, once again,
the elite, behind closed doors, experimenting, yes, creating,

yes, appalling, well, possibly, and in that case don't go
trying closed doors, if you're not sure what you will find, if
your tiny brain won't let you, because we are after nothing
less than the philosopher's stone of old, the vital elixir, the
source of all life, the Holy Grail, what's more we are under
orders to find it, so get out of the way of the future, my
friend, and one more thing, before you go, he said, and with
a final flourish saluted the air, Heil Hitler, he boomed, Heil
Hitler! By this point the SA contingent were out the door
and making their way hurriedly down the stairs and into
the night. What was left of the inner circle, the close group
of avant-garde thinkers and cultural and political radicals
that regularly attended our events, burst into spontaneous
applause. I looked around at X__ and Y__ who stood there
in mock triumph. Still, I knew in my heart that we were in
trouble. I knew that we were far from being thought of as
the Nazi elite. No more SA, X__ said, scanning the people
in the room. No more SA, is that understood? They cannot
be trusted. They're too soft, he said. They're sentimentalists.

'A week later we were called on by a devious-looking man
with a thin lip. He announced himself as belonging to a
National Socialist group known as The SIRK. X__ bundled
him into his office and I went next door, to the adjoining
room, and stood with my ear to the wall. It was impossible
to make out the whole conversation, words escaped me,
sentences came and went. He said something about being
careful. He repeated the word sentimental, the word
that X__ had used himself. He warned him; he used the
words warning and advice a lot. He spoke of time and art
and reality, again and again. He used the German word
fadenscheinig. Flimsy art, flimsy reality, flimsy time, I
couldn't tell. Then he left.

'X___ called us together. We are on the verge of war, he said. Poland will fall first. The nature of our tasks, the future of our experiments, will change. New opportunities will assert themselves, therefore we must do what we can in order to bring this phase of the work to a head. We are taking on new staff to help us, he announced, people that we can trust. Also, W___ and I were gifted with German passports assigning us new identities. We were too caught up to turn back, caught up in the sweep of the future, the gravity of the past.

'An Italian woman by the name of Mariella came to work for us. We fell in love, our courtship was a whirlwind, we were married soon after. Who knew what the coming war would do to any of us? Bring this phase of the work to a head, X___ had advised us. Prepare for new possibilities. Mariella I will say no more about, in order that you – or I – or the two of us, might rediscover her all over again.

'We worked on the animals together, the mechanised hybrids. The future of painting meant that we were to release them across the country, these mechanised monstrosities, these grotesque works of the imagination that would turn the whole country into some fantastic fable, into some kind of dreamland: the Reich as the mind of the artist.

'War broke out. Poland fell. The project was to be closed. We were reassigned by the man from The SIRK to an internment camp in Poland. You can better work in secret there, we were told, plus the facilities were cutting-edge, the opportunities unsurpassed. We began to deposit our creations in the wilds around Düsseldorf.

'In the hills around Wuppertal we left a flock of bird-rats hidden amongst the trees, to be found, to decay, to confuse and to amaze. The last of our dogs we loosed in Düsseldorf itself, in Essen and in Dortmund. We left a particular monstrosity in Münster just for the poetry of it and for the future of cryptozoology. Turtles with moving limbs and mechanical snake heads we left by a secret lagoon north of Cologne. Larger animals, big cats, extravagant horses, mythical creatures, fabled beasts, we secreted in caves, transported to the bottom of rocky gorges, once, even, just as a teaser, left at a bus stop in Solingen.

'Then we were done; we locked the building and drove across a newly risen Germany more fantastic than any painting. Poland was more incredible still. In a matter of months they had transformed this dull little country into a setting better suited to the playing out of history, as fantastic as art itself. Flames rose up from villages in the snow. The tracks of articulated combat vehicles lay thick in the mud and across the roofs of collapsed houses. Dead horses laid out like letters across a field. Convoys of uniformed foot soldiers walked this way and that. Off in the distance we could hear the symphonic sounds of heavy artillery redrawing the map. We were euphoric. The Futurists were right: what a sound, what a scene lay in the guiltless embracing of the full possibilities of tomorrow.

'We were stationed at an internment camp in the north-east of the country. We marvelled at the great alliance between war, art and technology that the Nazi party had mobilised across the space of a few short years. Our quarters were basic – bare rooms with a desk and some chairs and a screened-off bed behind a curtain – but our facilities were advanced. There will be much raw material for your experiments, The Kommandant told us, as doctors there will be much to marvel at. He called us doctors; is that what he thought we were, is that what he had been told? None of us made to protest. We had immediately acquiesced to the undercover nature of our work, perfect secret agents. Something else was driving us along. Besides, there was a whole medical team in the wing next to ours, we wouldn't be treating cold or typhoid or whatever it was that mass gatherings of criminals and the war wounded and the most wretched sections of humanity brought down upon themselves. But who were we working for? The SIRK? We called it the future and thought no more of it.

'Artists seeking the elixir of life in a death camp, I'm sorry, it sounds ridiculous now. I can't explain how it felt. We were caught in the teeth of it. The bodies began piling up. We worked in shifts. What are we to do with all this flesh? W___ asked. We proposed tests, idiot tests. Stress tests on dead bodies, strategic removal of body parts, and soon, of course, the grafting began. The grafting of human tissue is a complicated business. Imagine a fleet of mechanised corpses turned against the enemy! X___ marvelled. Imagine the legions of the walking dead! It wasn't hard to imagine. A walk round the camp revealed the legions of the walking dead in ever-swelling numbers. Our art, what was left of it, seemed even more of a cruel mockery. But X___ argued that if we could perfect the process of facial transference we could use it for good, we could rebuild damaged faces, replace limbs with new mechanised constructions, whereas I began to feel we had lost the plot; what about our dream of immortality, our dream of waking the dead, our dream of travelling through time using art? Here we were, elbow-deep in viscera, rearranging the corpses of poor children like jigsaw puzzles.

'W___ and I began to film the day-to-day working of the camps. Our credentials as artist-doctors gave us complete access. Why film suffering? For history, for one, but even then we continued to nurse an idea that by using the moving image we could perform some kind of alchemy, that some kind of escape could still be facilitated through the manipulation of signs and symbols. While X___ and Y___ continued to expand their experiments, Mariella, W___ and myself focused on capturing the scene forever. We shot hours of film, hours of terrible footage. Guards casually and brutally beat men and women and children in front of us. They held up emaciated bodies and forced them to perform, we closed in on the faces of the dead and of the dying. There is a way out through art, I continued to believe it, continued to believe it, continued to believe it, even as the empty eyes of hopelessly lost prisoners stared back at us in disbelief.

'The camera isn't a key. I became more and more despondent. Mariella spent more time on her own in our quarters. She had taken to knitting obsessively, knitting clothes that we would gift to the prisoners and we would film them as they tried them on, pathetic attempts to capture a few short frames of joy and hopefulness, when we knew as soon as the camera turned away the prisoner would be beaten and his clothes stolen or removed.

'Then Y___ achieved a breakthrough. First, he successfully brought a dog back to life, a dog that had belonged to a camp warden, a faithful companion. Working with X___ and W___, they had succeeded in giving it a new face and reinforcing its frame with mechanics. But what of the spark of life? They had used arte, they said, art with an E, they said, the ancient artes, the black artes. Magic was afoot.

'Then they successfully transplanted the face of a dead boy onto one whose face had been eaten away by the pox. After several weeks with his face held in a cage we were able to conclusively say that the face-swap was a viable option. This will be our redemption, X___ said, our first step towards a form of immortality. Would the face age as normal? Would it break down? Would it eventually reject or be rejected by its new owner? What were the psychological ramifications? The boy was twenty-one years old and had the face of a fourteen-year-old. Who knew? He himself seemed grateful, though he spoke a Gypsy dialect that was difficult to understand. But he had trouble using his new lips at first. He should be freed, I insisted, he should be let go. What is the point of a new face if every day is spent in a camp counting down your own doom? But it was impossible. We were artist-doctors, we were not the jailers; really, we were as trapped by this point as they were. Our animals, our art, we were forced to set free, our early experiments in new life, in kinetic sculpture, in savage new art, we gave up to the elements, and even now they are crawling in awkward circles or rotting in the rain or haunting dark forests, and here, new life, a human being with a blank slate for a face, we were forced to hold behind bars. It was no better than a zoo.

'Soon I was initiated into the artes myself. The process involved a form of transubstantiation that Y___ had chanced upon and that is subtle and that is difficult to achieve but one that must take place on all the planes simultaneously. Part of the living must be gifted to the dead. Sacrifice, the making of an offering, was key. I began to vision myself as an animal.

'Then the systematic killing of prisoners began. Previously there had been beatings, even executions, but there was always an attempt to keep some kind of order. Now, as the population of the camps filled to bursting, and with the majority unfit for work or incapable of being productive, the decision had been made, by whom I don't know, Hitler himself, perhaps, or Himmler, more likely, to begin a programme of mass extermination. One by one, prisoners were led into a specially constructed compound with a series of rooms. In the central room they were left alone with their head against the wall. A slot was pulled back and the executioner delivered a single bullet to their head. The door in the furthest room opened and closed as the body was removed for future burial.

'Everyone in our unit was assigned to help with the digging of the mass graves. The graves were at the north end of the camp but could be clearly seen by prisoners in certain sectors. The guards would force them indoors, but you could still make out their ghostly disembodied faces, pressed to the glass with a look that was beyond horror. People became uncomfortable being seen entering what everyone knew was the extermination block and being seen shovelling corpses, so much so that a special masked uniform was instituted, although not everyone insisted on wearing it. I did. X___ and Y___ and W___ chose not to. I didn't judge them. Rather, I judged myself.

A pecking order soon established itself. People looked down on those whom they deemed cowardly enough to disguise their faces. Comments were made. Soon, when it became our turn to dig a new grave, we would notice that our suits had been doctored. Bits of fur had been attached to them, long tails. Monkey suits, they called them. Some people protested but to no avail. The upper echelons felt the same. With our sentiments we were evolutionary throwbacks, mere animals, monkeys of men. I imagined the view from the barracks, a fleet of monkeys digging a mass grave for everyone you ever knew. I felt sick. But still I practised the arte. The monkey was the first step, I told myself, the arte was working, and by night I worked long, solitary hours re-editing my films until I had the perfect loops, the perfect repeating moments. I isolated single sections, single sections that I felt manifested a certain power, demonstrated a certain gravity, but that were also gaps, gaps that I could escape through, gaps that I believed offered ingress, that uncovered tunnels, that revealed the subterranea of the moment, the very scaffolding of reality, just briefly, just in the corner of the frames, frames that were the equivalent of the mythic tree that falls in the first forest without anyone seeing or hearing it.

'Then I told the others of my plans. I am going to escape, I told them. But first I must become a new animal. At first they were horrified. This is too much, Mariella protested. This is insane, W___ said. I will redeem this project if it is the last thing I do, I told them. Though honestly, if we succeeded, I knew it would be the first thing that I would do. Then I explained what would happen on the other side, once I had successfully disappeared, once I had made my escape. Everyone marvelled, they couldn't believe the audacity of my belief. I thought we had lost you with our work, X___ said, but truly you have taken it further than any of us. I arranged for the removal and the storage of my face. We had the facilities to make it possible. I gave instructions for the final film, how it was to be made, what it would consist of, the perfect document of my escape, the capturing of it, if you like, of what I had become and why. I am writing this the night before I intend to submit to the knife. I hail you over the years. Hail, brave friend. I am making my way towards you even now. We are reunited at last, you and I, while the rest of me I send off as a black stork picking its way through the wreckage of the dying years.'

That's a heavy story, the young man with the patch said to me. We'd just delivered a solid beating to a pair of punks who were trading cigarettes on our territory in the stables. We were back in prison, again. It is heavy, I said to him. It is heavy. I feel privileged to see your face the way it is right now, he said. Knowing it will change, I mean. Knowing you will be stuck with a new face. Stuck with a new face, that's the exact phrase he used, stuck with a new face and that's exactly how it felt. That is, he said, presuming you don't have it removed or replaced again, he said, I mean who knows what's up ahead. That was exactly what he said. Who knows what's up ahead. I know what, I said to him. I know what's up ahead. What have I been doing this entire time but telling you what's up ahead. I raised my fist and brought down a crashing blow upon his head. He fell to the ground and whimpered for a bit. Then he clung to my leg for dear life. What's up ahead is escape, I informed him in no uncertain terms. What's up ahead is escape.

I gathered my belongings together. I rose early. I told Mariella I was taking a walk with my new face, not my new eyes, I didn't say my new eyes, but with my new face, my

new face in the terrible flora and fauna of this nightmare
island. I had a bagful of painkillers. I was still in much
pain. I walked through this terrible flora and fauna, flora
that seemed alive, the way flesh is alive, like a zombie, a
zombie come back from the dead again and again. I made
my way to the harbour, the harbour with the boats bobbing
almost silently, almost silently but not quite, my new
ears told me, my new ears, although of course not really, I
listened with the same ears, the same eardrum, the same
auditory ossicles, the same cochlea, the same cochlea curled
like a snail in the auditory canal, I thought, but there was
no denying it, it was as if a new level of silence had been
revealed to me, because it was clear that the boats were
moving silently, not rubbing up against each other, not
caught in a breeze, but all the same the silence of their
movement made itself heard, quietly, of course, which is
the speech of silence, quiet, quiet speech but without wind,
without a breeze, what was it that troubled the waters,
something deep, it could only be, something deep below
the waters troubled the waters and moved the boats in the
waters, something below spoke silently as I moved towards
the boats, as I clambered into one of the small boats and
laid my pack down, my pack filled with food and drugs
and money, I had gone through Mariella's purse and I had
stolen her money, and I had a knife, I had a knife with me
because after all who knows, though really I know, really,
I know, I know what's up ahead and up ahead is an island,
up ahead is an island, a twin island, an island like a mirror
of the first island only completely denuded of flora and
fauna, an island that does not include a plague hospital,
an island that has no surgeons or monkeys, an island that
does not have a great mansion in its heights, a converted
mansion with a dark swimming pool, lit up from below,

in its depths, an island whose waters are silent, whose waters speak in the voice of silence, an island whose quiet waters deposited me on a sandy shore not two hours later, an island from which the original island could be seen, an island that provided a vista from which the first island could be viewed, an island from which, on the third day of my vigil, my solitary vigil eating fish on an island, eating fish and surveying an uninhabited island, eating fish and planning, planning my next move, though not thinking, not thinking too deeply, waiting, more like waiting, that was the plan, an island from which on the third day I was able to observe smoke rising, smoke rising from the first island, the mirror island as I have come to call it, smoke rising in great black funnels, flames following in great torrents, flames taking off for the heavens and flora burning, flora burning too, and fire spreading, fire spreading across the mirror island, an island which I became aware was not entirely uninhabited, an island that I had the uncanny feeling I was sharing with what could only be described as *disembodied entities, disembodied entities* that seemed to crowd around me to watch the razing of the mirror island, disembodied entities that seemed cheered at the sight, cheered at the sight in the same way that silence was capable of speaking, in the same way disembodied entities were cheered at the sight of this island in flames, this mirror island, sinking beneath the waves, which is how it appeared to me, as if the island would go down, in flames, like a ship, like the ship that I had been captain of myself, like the ship that went down in the beginning, I told myself, which was my fate, which was the name of my fate, I said, as I was rescued once more, as I was rescued by a ship that had been drawn to the smoke and the flames and that had passed close by the island I was on, a small fishing boat with a crew of three men who were amazed to find me in such good repair, that was what they said, such good repair for a castaway, they said to each other as they looked me up and down, and I explained that I had lost my way, that I had taken a small boat out from Athens for the day and become disorientated and they said, that is impossible, that is practically impossible, that we were a day's sailing from Athens at this point, unless the tides got him, one of them said, unless he was taken by the tides, they said, and were you alone, they said, and what became of your companions, but I told them I was alone even as the three of them looked around themselves and sniffed the air and stared back into the trees as if my companions would reveal themselves and overthrow them at any minute, even as I felt the entities swarm all around me, even as I felt the return of the dead, who have yet to overthrow anyone, I thought to myself, but then I had a sudden swooning feeling like the beginnings of vertigo and I changed my tune, my companions are dead, I told them, my companions died in the fire on the island, I told them, and they asked me to accompany them, come with us, they said, we can look for survivors, and I climbed into the boat and we made for the island, which was now a smoking husk, with clumps of blackened vegetation floating out to sea and on the top of the hill the grand mansion, now a skeletal ruin, and I told them there was no hope, that no one could have survived, and to push on to the mainland, where we could best avail ourselves of help, and as we went to push away from the island the mangled body of an animal could be seen floating silently towards us, an animal that was impossible to identify, and one of my shipmates said, it must have been some kind of zoological gardens, he said, it must have been one of these rich men's follies, and he looked at me and I nodded, grimly, and we turned away from the island and made our own way silently back to port.

Wow, you could do anything at this point, the young boy said to me, as we sat up late at night in the stables in the dying years of the war with the prison silent all around us. What do you intend to do with your new face? Try it out, he said. Try it out on the ladies. I had no money, I reminded him, no documents of my own. I returned to Mariella's apartment and climbed through a high window on the landing. I bathed and changed my clothes. I took what was left of the money that Mariella kept hidden in a drawer in the kitchen. Take my painting with you, the boy said, go on. It stays where it is, I snarled at him, and he quickly dropped the matter. I took a train through Greece and having no identity papers I got off just before the border and made my way across a dusty mountain pass and into Albania. From there I was able to secure passage on a boat to Lecce in the heel of Italy. This is when my face came into its own (at last, the young boy said, some kind of pay-off). I was picked up by a young woman at the train station (here we go, he said), a local whore with a kink (yes!), and we returned to her apartment, which was in a stunning old building with wide colonnades and turreted windows and with a rooftop garden where the residents met to dine beneath the stars and to play with their dogs.

How is it to make love with the face of another man? the boy asked me. It is as emboldening as with a mask, I told him. You mean like S&M? he asked me. There is an element of performance to it, I said to him. An element of showing off or of self-display, rather.

You mentioned she had a kink, he said to me. Yes, I told him, yes, she was a dog-lover. This whore was known as a dog-lover. She and her lover would parade the streets together, this black dog, this old black Labrador, the dog wearing leather studded collars and a harness of silver chains while she wore an auburn wig and red stilettos and heavy make-up and with a cane and a see-through umbrella.

Hardly a kink, the boy said, you led me on. Plenty of women are dog-lovers. Dog-fuckers, I said to him, are plenty of women dog-fuckers? Oh shit, he said to me. Oh wow. Did you see them do it? I saw them do it, I told him. I saw them do it in pictures at first. She was a fetish star, she appeared in the magazines alongside her dog. What was the name of her dog? Amour. Amour? Amour is a female name. Not on this dog, I said. How did they do it? the boy asked me. Doggy style, I said. Were you appalled? No, I told him. I was amazed and in awe at the things that were being presented to my new face. I was able to watch them from behind a mask so that it did not seem disgusting to me. Did she blow the dog? She blew the dog most artfully, I told him. Then the dog mounted her. It mounted her and dominated her. She had taught it well. Can a woman become pregnant with a dog? he asked me. It's a biological impossibility, I told him. But biological impossibilities were now my field, if you understand me.

And did you both fuck her? Not at the same time, I couldn't bring myself to. Ah, so there are limits even to a new face. It would seem so. And how did you feel about putting your penis where a dog's penis had been, if you don't mind me asking? the young boy said. I enjoyed it, I said to him. I confess that I enjoyed it. I asked her if it was degrading, do you enjoy degradation? I asked her. It is ennobling, she said to me. It is elevating, she said. Wait, the young boy said to me, is this because of the war? Do women take to dogs because all of the men have been killed in a holocaust? No, I told him, this is the preserve of the elite.

But then a terrible thought came to me. What? I began to suspect that I had in fact created this dog. That I was, in fact, its maker. What? She had found the dog as a stray, as a stray that had come to her on the street one day. I imagined that it was one of the dogs that I had loosed, one of the dogs that I had loosed in my other life, my life as a Januist. I thought, these are hybrid dogs, these are dogs that have developed a taste for humans and for human sex and for the female. These dogs are anomalies. What dogs, I thought there was only one dog? One dog that I had come across, I told him. But what of all the dogs that we had set free? What of all the dogs we had reanimated? I thought that the experiments were a failure, on the whole? Yes, but we had never given them time, we had never monitored their behaviour, we had never seen how they readapted to the wild. You mean dogs with the faces of rats? What was this dog's face like? As seamless as my own, I told him. But I had to know. I had to know.

One day while my companion was out whoring on her own I fed Amour some steak with a sedative in it. I lifted its body into the bath and I cut open its belly. You did what?! I cut open its belly and I slid my arm into its innards, all the way to the elbow. What on earth were you looking for? Parts. Evidence. I cut slits in its paws and peeled back its skin. That was when I discovered it. Amour had a metal construction around one of its legs and a steel plate in its side. But that tells you nothing, the young boy protested.

It was a stray dog, I said to him, why would someone put a steel plate inside a stray dog? From kindness, the boy said to me. It must have had an injury at some point, perhaps its first owner had beaten it and someone had looked on it kindly and had it rebuilt. I know all about that kindness, I told him. I built it myself. Then I left the dead dog in the bath and I fled the apartment. Perhaps you will think me insane, I said to the young boy. He said nothing in reply. He didn't dare to.

I made my way to Germany. How? Things are becoming blurry. There is a storm in the future. Clouds coming down. I made my way to Germany in time for the Passion play. What? The Passion play in Oberammergau. The Passion play that lasts one whole day. Bavaria was cursed by the bubonic plague, overrun by rats infected with a mutant strain and with the bodies piled up in mounds. To be done with the judgement of God, and in order for Him to spare Oberammergau, the residents of the village promised to put on a Passion play that depicted the final days of Jesus Christ on earth. Since the seventeenth century they have performed this play repeatedly over the course of five months in every year that ends in the numeral zero. What year is this? 1950.

Do you understand what a tableau vivant is? I asked the young boy. He had extorted a packet of cigarettes from a group of dying soldiers. Yes, he said, it is a vivid picture. You are merely repeating what I am saying, I said to him. Repeating is not understanding. Then why repeat the Passion play every day for five months? Because there is no understanding in the judgement of the Lord. Have you come with judgement? the boy asked me. Have you come to bring

judgement down on the world? I have come to rescue all
of the disappeared, to unite all true loves. Would that you
could, the young boy said, and he spat into the dirt. But I'm
too young to have had a love to return to. My parents threw
me out when I was a kid. I'm beyond rescuing. A tableau
vivant is a picture that has come to life, I told him.

I stood in front of a group of small children gathered around
a cross. The children were completely motionless. I was able
to observe them from all sides. I was able to ascertain that
they did not even blink. Not one of them. They did not shake
or fidget or scratch at themselves the way young monkeys
are prone to. Not once did their gaze leave the cross at
their centre. They call this the Adoration, and this is how
it begins. I looked closer at the children. I surreptitiously
poked one of them in the arm, a dark girl with freckles and
with thick curly hair. No response. The child seemed fixed
to the spot. Don't tell me, the young man said, you had your
suspicions that you were their creator. I had my suspicions,
I admitted. But no longer that I myself was their creator.
Rather, that in the wake of the war, simulacra were the
order of the day. That truly we had been prophets. After
all, a Januist is a man who is capable of seeing both ways.
I made my way to the stalls. Great crowds were all around.
They replay the Passion, day in day out, for the space of
five months, I said to myself. Truly these are mechanical
men. Then it dawned on me. Is that not what God Himself
demands of us? The mechanising and regulating of His own
creation? Were we not prophets? The play had begun.

I took a part-time job as an orderly at a mental home on
the outskirts of a small town in order that the dead, whose
chosen representative I had become, might converse more

freely with the living or the touched or the half-dead, more appropriately, the kind of maniacs who had been locked away for hearing voices or for following commands, as I intended to put my theory to the test, my theory that the war had given birth to a new race of mechanised men, a hybrid who now wore a new face, a theory that had become confused in my mind with Christ's promise of rebirth through suffering, a promise that I had become the living personification of, even as it exiled me from the company of my fellow men, even as I came into the confidence of madmen and was brought to the understanding that a single gesture, obsessively repeated, as by a man who has taken leave of his senses, as by a black stork in the remains of a bombed-out zoological garden, might contain all of the hope and dread that the world affords.

The inmates were suffering from shell shock or, as it is referred to in the modern world, post-traumatic stress disorder. Something in their brains had been broken, as a hymen, by the force of their own experience, which said to me that we stood at a key moment in evolution, as the love play between what was out there and what was in here had toppled into an overwhelming one-sided assault which consciousness had been slow to take up, in which consciousness played the part of the unwilling sub, to put it in a way that would have held the attention of my fellow jailbirds. And so, the rebuilding of man, in the second half of the twentieth century, became the responsibility of the dead and the dying, the insane and the blind, who stood as its crowning achievement.

I am organising a march, I told them. I am organising a great homecoming. Are you with me? A repeated phrase, an involuntary spasm, an obsessive tracking of the room. One man spoke to me as if I was his returned son, always with the same circular conversation. Heinrich, what time is it? What time is it, my boy? Father, it is Christmastime. Is it Christmastime yet? Father, it is Christmastime. Then go tell your mother that you are home for Christmas. Go tell her you are home for Christmas and that the shop is open. Another drew pictures of a man on stilts who with three strides could cover all of Germany. A third clacked the stumps of his arms together in a frenzy.

I worked under a doctor named Strindberg who claimed a distant relation to the melancholy Swedish playwright of the same name. We shall cure them with the aid of a metal bed frame secreted in the attic, the doctor would joke, a reference to the playwright's belief that he had been controlled by a bed frame of similar design during an extended experience of mesmerism and possession documented in his books *Inferno* and *From an Occult Diary*. Strindberg also had a very pretty wife, the real Strindberg, my Dr Strindberg, although unlike his distant relation he enjoyed real sex with her, not conjugation with her spirit form, as his namesake had enjoyed or more accurately suffered from when his third wife, Harriet Bosse, thirty years his junior, would invade his dreams and make spectral love to him. Can you be possessed by your relations? I asked the doctor. Is biological inheritance not a form of possession? he asked me in return. Is heredity not another name for the ghost in the machine?

Strindberg quoted Strindberg: 'Who was the artificer who forged the links in these infernal syllogisms? Where was he? "There would be nothing for it but to kill the gold-maker."

That was the last thought which my tortured mind could retain before I fell asleep about sunrise.'

What did you do during the war? I asked him. I sat it out on the sidelines, he said. I continued to practise, in secret, even though psychiatry itself was looked down upon by the regime in Germany at the time. But what an opportunity, he marvelled, a whole continent of the insane, he said, no end to the varieties of madness, be boasted. And yourself? I too practised in secret, I told him, though my process was more invasive.

?

I was involved in experimental surgery.

?

I was a pioneer of facial transplants.

?

I was the gold-maker.

I laughed and made light of it. Facial transplants are an impossibility, he said. Exactly, I said to him.

My quarters were situated on the second floor of the hospital, a converted nineteenth-century tenement in the north of Wuppertal. Truly, I had drifted. I had followed suggestions, associations, the fugitive signings of chance, in order to find myself where I was. I had been recognised, once, and now I led a furtive existence, careful not to wear

my face fully uncovered, concerned, somehow, that my face
or the other life that I had inherited was somehow directing
me back to its old haunts, intent to resume the Januist
experiment of the past, even as I had become the living
embodiment of its dream, its vision of the two-faced man.

I had been recognised in the street, whilst walking in the
pedestrian precinct and taking one of our mental cases
for a run in his chair, which was something we tried to
do as often as possible, Dr Strindberg believing firmly
in the display, if not the full integration, of a society's
madmen, just as psychiatry pushed for a form of cathartic
wellness by the uncovering of the mind's tightest knots and
deepest complexes, so we too believed in the uncovering
and the exposure of its tortured bodies, its drool-soaked
overgarments and its fevered hallucinations.

I had been approached by an older gentleman who had
greeted me as Donald and who had grasped both my hands
and shaken them vigorously. Donald, he said. I thought that
we had lost you. I denied any such thing. I'm afraid I have
no idea what you are talking about, I told the man, and
made to push the wheelchair we had improvised from the
mangled frame of an old rusted bike further down the street.
But he had blocked our progress. What are you doing? he
said to me. And who is this man? The madman in the chair
clanked his handless stumps together and looked up at our
interlocutor with a tortured expression. Our interlocutor
passed his gaze between me and the madman. Is this . . .
he started, but before the sentence was out we had pushed
through him and away. The man shouted something after
us, something, I fancied, about making contact or staying
in touch. By the time I returned to the hospital I was

shaken. Had a rendezvous been arranged in another life? I wondered. Was there a point of contact? Had I arranged for my own great return, in secret? I was a man possessed by a mission, a mission that I could only be dimly aware of. In the meantime, I gave bed baths to cripples and cleaned up their mess and talked in riddled conversations to men with shattered memories.

And what of the dead? I hear you ask. I kept them in a room at the top of the hospital where they were least likely to cause a commotion.

As our friendship progressed I would often dine at the weekend with Dr Strindberg and his pretty wife, herself a budding artist. As I examined them across the table at a tacky beach-themed bar in a Wuppertal backstreet that had become a favourite due to its experimental cocktail list and its mix of low-class and eccentric clientele, I saw them as a reflection of everything that Mariella and I might have been, or more properly could have been, once. Which is to say I could feel the past of my face colonising the present of my body.

What do you paint? I asked her. Animals, she said. Chimeras, she said. Invented animals. Of course, I said. Why of course? she asked me. I was about to say, because you are a reflection of what I once was myself, but instead I merely hinted that I too, in the wake of the Great War, had become interested in cryptozoology. Why in the wake of the Great War? she asked me, and I explained that the war had flattened zoological gardens across Europe, meaning that we had inadvertently seeded the continent with all sorts of previously unseen animal life, animal life that remained furtive and that kept away from human beings but animal life that was recombining and cross-breeding in all sorts of unimaginable ways. I paint more from myth, she said to me, I'm thinking more of Pegasus the flying horse than some kind of gruesome backstreet hybrid. Flying horses, I said to her, that too.

My plans were confused. I was waiting around for something to happen, for this rendezvous that I felt sure would take place, while at the same time avoiding it, hiding myself away, burying myself in the endlessly repeated complexes of our patients. It only occurs to me now that I had fled one madhouse for another, all the time dragging the dead with me, the unresolved dead, the silent dead.

At lunch breaks and in the early evenings I would steal into the room at the top of the hospital that I reserved for the dead, the dead, the dead, and I would scan their ranks. My family no longer pursued me. I hadn't seen the hideous cadaver my father had become since our days touring the drawing rooms and theatres of the great and the good, never mind the small dog that now hosted the soul of my brother. For these were the disappeared, the never dead, forever. What was my role in all of this? What was I to do with them? They shuffled towards me as soon as I unlocked the door, gathering around me and pushing up against me, their faces to the floor, or at least what was left of them. I was never afraid. Instead it was a vague sense of mission that tied me to them. A mission that was soon to be revealed.

You have been talking to yourself all night, the young boy said to me. I woke in the stables of the jail, in a pool of my own sweat. Summer had arrived and with it a change in our fortunes. The winter had killed off many and now the prison seemed semi-abandoned. There were stories of jailers walking away, of soldiers absconding in the middle of the night. The war was turning. Soon it was as if we were a walled-in city-state, a strange experiment in barbarous living, more than just another internment camp for the dead and the dying.

Didn't you put your face to better use than hiding away in a mental institute? the young boy asked me as he took a leak from a terraced walkway that ran high above the central courtyard. Think about it, he said. You know that you will be freed from this prison one day, you know that your face is rebuilt, you know that once again you can take your place amongst the living, in the heart of life, and this is what you do with it, this is to be your fate, a hospital orderly, a bed-cleaner, an ass-wiper? I struck the boy hard around the head and he urinated all down his leg. Some things are fixed and have to be, I said to him. Would you deny the workings of gravity? He looked down at the stain on his trousers and shook his head. So, did you make love to Dr Strindberg's wife? he asked me. Did you fire right in there? he said. Come on, he said. For God's sake. Live a little.

Dr Strindberg was ill with the beer. He would go on benders that meant he was often blacked-out unconscious or recovering in a darkened room, so that he would send his pretty wife to do the rounds on his behalf. His was a private practice, with no ties to the state and so answerable, essentially, to no one. This is before the days of reform and redress, when there was no one to complain to and no one to expect anything different than that a catatonic might be left in a bed encrusted with his own faeces for days on end.

We would meet in her private quarters, on the floor below the doctor's apartment, they maintained separate living arrangements within the same building, and some of my greatest memories are of entering her on the divan with the headboard in the shape of a half-sun, as if we were capable of fucking the sun into the sky while all around us lay artefacts and collectibles and items of clothing that seemed to speak to us in our passion, a bowl of fruit slowly rotting in the darkness, a wicker chair that held a large potted fern, a swan made of glass that sat on the ledge in front of the mirror, a silk glove hanging limp from a shelf, the old-fashioned wallpaper with designs like octopuses or orchids, and her curly auburn hair and the dark of her eyes, the feel of her teeth on my shoulder (go on, get in there!), and her white chiffon dress pulled up around her waist and her panties down around her ankles (oh Lord!) and her pussy (go on . . .) and her pussy, delicately shaved to a thin strip of hair (f-me, I have never seen that before, what wonders the future has in store for you, didn't I tell you?), and every fuck felt like a reunion, every orgasm a reconstituting of the way things were (stick to the graphic sex descriptions, come on now), so that I began to feel that perhaps my mission was with the living and not the dead (don't get distracted now, get back to the action), so that as she climbed up onto me one more time (here we go . . .), so that as she guided me inside her (her trim little pussy, think about it, wow), so that as we exploded together (damn, no, seriously, is that what it feels like?) I began to feel that the rendezvous that my new face had set for me, the rendezvous for whom the dead waited in abeyance upstairs, was a simple love story, a simple boy-meets-girl tale, could it be that trivial, that profound (and did she say anything to you when you fucked her, did she say things like, give me your juice, baby?), and when we made love she would say, give me your juice, baby, as she lay with her ass on my face (wow, didn't see that coming!), and I came to believe that we were in love and that our assignation across time was a form of poetry that came from the love play of space and time (back to the action, baby, come on), for love itself is a kind of sixth sense, is a kind of immediate or sometimes slowly dawning revelation that you are stood, right here, right now, in the presence of the future, it is a recognising of something that hasn't happened yet and with that knowledge in my heart I was overwhelmed when Strindberg's pretty wife revealed to me that she was pregnant and that I was, indeed, the father, as we lay on the divan with the half-sun, whether setting or rising I was unaware, at that time, only that it marked a star's transit of the sky (and why does she have no name, this pretty wife?), and I said to myself, true love, true love secretes itself in history, true love is untold in time, true love, my friend, is just as soon forgotten.

I was walking with one of our madmen strapped to an improvised wheelchair when I noticed something odd. Across the street, some way off, I glimpsed what appeared to be a lynch mob kicking and lashing out with sticks against something that lay huddled in their midst. As I approached with my madman someone broke from the crowd and ran up to us and warned us to keep our distance. There's a spell upon it, he said. Keep back. It has been suckled on the witch's tit. Don't be insane, man, I said to him. This is the twentieth century. The tits of witches have long dried up. The crowd parted as I drove towards its centre, pushing my madman in front of me. There I found a hybrid animal, a chimera, possibly one of our own, lying bloody on the ground, its grotesquely outsize arms and hands held tight around a gaping wound in its head. Its back leg circled and pawed with an automatic motion. It had pissed itself. It's the work of the Devil, someone in the crowd cried. A curse on Wuppertal, someone else said. The end of days! Get back, I said. I'm a doctor. I undid the straps on my madman and lifted him into the arms of a stranger. Hold him for me, I said to her, as he drooled all down her dress. Then I gathered the chimera into my arms and tied it to the chair. The beast was unconscious. You, man, I instructed one of the navvies in the crowd, pick that madman up and carry him back to the asylum for me. He followed behind us as our macabre convoy made its way down a cobblestone street to much jeers and fear and taunting.

I threw some sheets across a wide table in a back room and laid out the beast. Dr Strindberg's pretty wife came to the door and gasped. What is it? she said. One of yours, I said to her. One of your creations come to life. Bring me my tools, oxygen and some sedatives, I said to her.

For four hours I worked on the beast. I opened up its chest and probed inside. Its construction was far beyond our own abilities. Inside it there was tiny circuitry, like a tag, almost, and its entire skeletal system had been bolstered with a metal that seemed perfectly soft and pliable. The face fit perfectly, the transplant as seamless as my own, although much more grotesque, an ancient, amphibious mask that was cold and rubbery and that spoke of the depths, the depths of evolution, the depths of the sea. At either side of the neck there were pale fleshy gills. Yet its body seemed that of a fat, stunted dog, a sea lion that had grown hair and sprouted thin, muscular legs, each of which ended in long curled claws like a hawk or griffin's. I sewed it back up and did my best to repair that gaping wound on its head. Then I left it to recover.

I went to speak with Dr Strindberg's pretty wife and I found her weeping in her study. Where are these terrible things coming from? she demanded of me. I have been assailed by them, she told me. My mind has been invaded by these hybrid creatures, she told me. And now they crawl along our streets, now they bleed down from our mountains. I thought it a strange phrase, to bleed down, as if they poured forth from a wound.

Excuse me, the young boy interrupted me, but have you started speaking funny? You know, like old-fashioned funny, like in an old book or a different century? The century is regressing, I told him, time is running backwards as we progress, I said to him, time's wingèd chariot hurrying near. Just wondering what it was all about, he said. Sorry, keep going.

The creature awoke with a start. (Wow, okay.) Then it made the strangest sound. I had it tied to the table and covered in a bloodied sheet and it turned its thick neck to look at me, with eyes of helpless terror, and it made this sound: Ah-Eh-Oxt. (What?) Ah-Eh-Oxt. (It's just a groan, just an inarticulate animal groan of pain.) But no, it repeated the phrase, again and again. Ah-Eh-Oxt. Ah-Eh-Oxt. It was language. The beast was trying to communicate, or so I convinced myself. (An exit, it's saying an exit.) No, you're just repeating what it is saying, that's not what it means. (It's saying it's exhausted, it's saying it doesn't want to live any more, it's asking you to end it.) No. It's saying something else.

Dr Strindberg's pretty wife fetches him from his quarters and he arrives a little worse for wear. He stares in horror at the beast strapped to the table. Gad, he says, it's some kind of evolutionary throwback! That's where you're wrong, I tell him. This thing comes from the future. I explain how we found it in the marketplace being set upon by an angry mob. You repaired the wound? he asked me. You stitched up the belly? Yes, I said. Where did you learn your surgical skills? I was apprenticed to a radical surgeon as a young man. A radical surgeon? What does that mean? A surgeon who pioneered experimental techniques. You mean a surgeon who could have come up with this? he said, gesturing towards the thing on the table, which was now unconscious and breathing in a slippery, laboured manner. What makes you think it was surgically engineered? I asked him. Come on, man, he said, this kind of hybrid makes a mockery of any creator! I wanted to say to him that we were the creators and that it was we who had made a mockery but instead I nodded slowly and held my peace.

Just then there was the sound of a fracas outside the building (a fracas?). An angry mob was chanting and demanding the death of the devil we were protecting. Stones and handfuls of dirt rained down on the shutters. I accompanied the doctor out into the street. He stood on the steps and addressed the rabble (the rabble?). We have a poor wounded creature in here, the doctor said. Cease with these protests immediately. As doctors we have taken a solemn oath to protect the life, and where possible alleviate the suffering, of all sentient beings. It's not a sentient being, it's a monster, someone shouted. The whole building is a collection of monsters, someone else shouted. You'll bring curses down upon our town, someone else said. The beast must be destroyed. God demands it. He won't stand for mockery, the doctor whispered to me, and gave me a look. Listen, the doctor said. We need to get to the bottom of this. We need to find out where this creature has come from and if there are more of them. We need to examine it. Then we'll put it to the stake, someone else cried. Time, the doctor said, and he raised up his hands, all we need is time. Please. There were mutterings in the crowd and they slowly began to disperse.

An hour later a military convoy came tearing into the yard. Soldiers dressed in protective full-body suits stormed the hospital. In every ward the madmen were screaming and harming themselves and weeping silently in the corners. They came to the room with the beast. They made us stand outside in the corridor at gunpoint. From inside the room I heard that same word, that same sound. Ah-Eh-Oxt. Then the sound of a gunshot. And another. And another. A group of soldiers emerged from the room with the thing in a body bag. Behind them came the one with the gun. I was unable to see his face through his tinted visor, but I swear as he turned to go I saw a thin ratty tail attached to the back of his suit.

I went upstairs to the dead and I sat with them. I was looking for a sign, an intimation of what was to be. (That's ironic since you seem to know exactly what is going to happen.) Shut up. They looked at me, and then they held their heads to the ground. I went back to work.

We treated a man for a syndrome where he would obsessively predict the time at which various things would take place, various trivial things. For instance, at ten o'clock, he would say, I will proceed to enter the bath. At approximately 5.24 p.m. the sun will go down on another blessed day. At 8.10 I will remove my slacks and hang them over the back of a chair there to await my rendezvous with them at 6.10 the next morning. But then he began to predict other things, greater things. He had been an officer in the German army during the war and had served on the Russian front, where he had taken a head wound and deteriorated from there. His family had washed their hands of him. But like me, his wound or the terror of his service or a combination of both had gifted him with prophecy. I looked into his eyes, which were glazed over and somewhere else, somewhere in the future, and I thought that prophecy, too, is a way of keeping terror in abeyance, and I felt fuzzy, like the connection to myself, myself in the prison, this wretched self right here in front of you, was shaky, and that it would be possible, with a great effort of will, to up and break the connection and to strand myself in the past and in the future. To split myself in two. But there was something else, something in the telling of it that insisted on maintaining the link. For now. Okay. Okay. We carry on.

Stories circulated around Wuppertal, sightings of mythical beasts come down into the valley, rumours that secret Nazi experiments had resulted in hybrid life forms, that the Allies had introduced monsters into Germany, that the house of madmen was really a front for the creation of basilisks. We experienced suspicion and outright hostility on the streets.

While wheeling two of our madmen around the park in the afternoon I was once more approached by the elderly gentleman who had first called me Donald, the gentleman

I had disabused and denied, but here he was again, and he approached quickly and grasped my hands and he said to me: I know. You said this would happen, he said to me. But you must accept that I know. Dr Strindberg's pretty wife had accompanied me. By this point she was starting to show. She had led Dr Strindberg to believe that the baby was his. The elderly gentleman looked towards her bump and then back at me. Everything has been prepared, he said. For the influx. This time I nodded. I acted as if I understood. Yes, I said. The influx.

The Estimator, the madman who announced the forthcoming time and date of everything, began to make obsessive drawings on bits of scrap paper in the day room, covering sheets of toilet paper, the edges of newspapers, the envelopes of the sad letters his relatives would occasionally send him. I showed them to Dr Strindberg's wife. He had drawn a great hotel, a great haunted hotel, whose rooms were peopled by monsters. I told her, I have this hotel in my head. I explained to her how when I was a prisoner in Italy during the war I had created a towering mansion in my head whose rooms I would wander for hours and where at the top of a set of stairs, in a lonely room with one window, I had secreted my young wife. You are married? she asked me. I was married, I corrected her, once. But I am carrying your child, she said. Listen, I said to her. I have something to confess to you. My face is not my own, I told her. I was given this face and this future as a second chance. I came back. But now I believe I have come back for you. Do you believe in fate? I asked her. Do you believe in destiny? But something is out of joint, I told her. I feel as if I have failed to keep an assignation with myself. You saw the man who accosted us in the street? Well, I feel I am in conspiracy with him, somehow. I feel myself to be like a blind man who has been told that he is at the centre of all events. And now the contents of my head, the contents of the life that I have inherited, are invading the present. I prophesied all this, I said.

Who are you talking to? the young boy asked me. Where are you right now? I am escaped, I said to him. I am disappeared.

I am disappeared.

I am returning home. I am booked into a private hotel built high on the cliffs above the River Calder. I am eating in its handsomely appointed dining room. Above the fireplace there is a painting of a young man. He has the same face as you. Seated across from me there is my son. He has the same face as me. The face of Donald, that is. The face of a Januist. I have brought him back home. Though, really, I have secreted him in my past. We crossed Europe in the space of three months. Germany–Belgium. Belgium–France. France–England. I returned to staging my own travelling psychic review in order to fund our trip. Many impossible things have taken place. The dead too have followed in my wake. The disappeared have returned. I cross to the viewing gallery and I peer down into the gorge. The bilious flora and fauna twist up towards me. The trees are alive with the sound of exotic birds. The sun is high in the sky. Across the river the spires of Chapelhall are hazy in its light. The animals wander in the shade of the grove and children hold them in their arms and are not afraid. Animals that have the aspect of lambs and of lions. Animals with tiny bodies and long ponderous legs graze on the highest branches. Creatures with the face of silly fishes and with hairy bodies like cattle or yaks roll over to expose their tender undersides to the light. We watch them, the dead, as one. I take my son's hand, my son who wears the same impossible face as myself, and we walk towards the village. Calderbank, too, has become a great grassland, a verdant field with clusters of houses scattered here and there. We cross the green grass and send up a cloud of tiny whirring insects, their bodies completely covered in eyes. It is as if nature cannot evolve fast enough to take in all of this wonder. We pause in the shade of a tree. This whole world was stone, I tell my son, once upon a time this whole world was dead stone. Grass grew from the wound, I tell him. Flowers grew from the corpses.

Something is moving in the undergrowth. It bursts past us, pursued by a man with an old-fashioned blunderbuss over his shoulder. He looses several shots into the air and the animal bounds off, its long tongue wagging, its face with an expression of simple joy. The man stops us and asks us where we are from. An outlandish pair, he calls us. Yes, we tell him, we have travelled from Germany, that once we lived here, long ago, we say, and have come back. It's very busy in Germany, he marvels. I know everyone around here, he says, and I can't say I can place your faces. Oh, we have returned with different faces, I say to him. That'll be it, he says, before continuing his leisurely pursuit of the strange creature who waits for him, pretending to hide. In the distance the sound of church bells can be heard.

Wait, the young man interrupts. Wait. I remember, too. What? I remember the crossing, do you remember? We crossed the sea on a great ship, a great ship of rust and of rope and of old black wood. Don't you remember looking down, looking down through the pale-blue water? You said it was the colour of blood, the true colour of blood. Yes, I tell him. Yes. I remember. Do you remember the horses? Yes. Now I remember. Now I remember the horses. The waters were as quiet as can be, except for some froths, except for some froths of water. The froths were being sent up by the horses. The horses were walking at the bottom of the water. The horses were walking on the bottom of the ocean, all with wounds in their stomach. They were marching blind at the bottom of the water and they were bleeding there. They were bleeding an ocean. An ocean of pale-blue blood flowed from the wounds on their chest and submerged them completely. This was the separation of the firmament. This was the first act of God. Now I understand. We are walking in the stuff of our own wounds. That is what the horses said. We are walking in the rends of our own flesh.

The man who called me Donald returned. He returned to the mental hospital one evening when Dr Strindberg's pretty wife had fallen into labour. He delivered you to us in secret. Who? You. My son. He delivered you to us with the face of the disappeared. He looks just like you, the man who delivered you exclaimed, a man who from now on I will refer to as Richard Snow. I looked like you? You looked like me, like my new face. An impossibility. Exactly. We hid you in the attic with the spectres of the disappeared. Richard Snow informed me of his true identity. He claimed to be a Januist. The one that was left behind, he said. Then one night he appeared with a film camera and a projector. He appeared with a film camera and a projector and told me that he had come with great tidings. He said that he had come to put on a show for the dead and the disappeared. We set up a

projector in the loft space against one wall. We gathered
the missing all around us. We held our little baby in our
arms. With everyone's eyes we watched as the Januist
project flickered back into life. A horsebox stood by the edge
of the ocean. One by one a series of huge oversized horses
fitted with elaborate black leather blinds walked down the
gangplank and straight into the ocean.

But it was impossible. The horsebox had room for two
or three horses at most but still they came, one after
the other, in their tens and twenties, and now in their
hundreds, never-ending. The dead stood there in silence
as the horses filed into the water and walked up to their
bellies through the water and disappeared beneath the
water. I stood up and shouted in protest at Richard Snow.
He laughed and nodded and confessed to me. It is all done
with the aid of a simple loop, he said. The drowning of
horses is achieved by means of a loop? I demanded. The
horses don't drown, he told me. These are our horses, he
said. But there is a loop. Haven't you realised yet? he said
to me. Can't you work out where the loop is set? You mean
I am caught up in the same loop? I asked him, and I felt
the dead huddle around me, I felt them as if to say, cut this
loop, and free us, let us go, even if just to lie prone at the
bottom of the water, even if only to be swept away by the
tide. You are that loop, Richard Snow told me. You are the
one that can never drown.

I recalled my rescue from a sinking ship. My fleeing from
the island. My crossing of the ocean with the horses down
below. But for what reason? I demanded of him. Of your own
choosing, he said to me. But why are we bleeding? I asked
him. Why are we wounded? You're the only one who can

answer that, Richard Snow told me. You are the one who came back in blood.

The soldiers burst into the cell.

You're free, they tell us. Hitler is kaput! You're free to go.

This is the book, I tell them.

I have come to rescue all of the disappeared, to reunite all true loves, to turn history to dust, I tell them.

I am the one who came back in blood, I tell them.

I get up, and I take your hand, and together we walk out into it.

SEDILIA

APPENDIX CELEBRANT: *VICTORY GARDEN,* A SCIENCE FICTION BY PAIMON

(translated from the French by David Keenan)

EARTH'S ORBIT, 2099

Adam Aros watched from the observation deck as the *New Jerusalem* disengaged with a gentle puff and began its slow descent to earth. Spaceships make silent music, he thought to himself, and for a moment a hymn came back to him, and a singer too. A feather on the breath of God; that was it. But who was the singer? That eluded him. Are we down below or up above, he often wondered, in all of this space. The changeover wasn't particularly perilous; there were safeguards in place all along the Victory Gardens. But the symbolism was hard to miss. The chain had been broken. Just like water, time will find the weakest point. After that, the deluge. Still, he could already see its replacement, suspended high above the sea and climbing, a creature without eyes, approaching slowly but surely, blind to the folly of climbing out of the sea in the first place. He caught the words of another song. There was something haunting in its delivery. But who was the singer? It eluded him still. He looked to his WordPool and drew up an entry.

WordPools aren't predictive; at least, that's what they maintain. But it was impossible not to read something into the spontaneous texts they delivered. In the twenty-first century they had come to replace astrology and Tarot cards, geomancy and divination, or at least to rival them, although they had initially been designed as a tool for creative writing. Then some scholar, some wayward academic, had announced them as the future of literature. Now nearly everyone carried one. Well, everyone with a brain. The more you used them, the more their stories became living counterparts to your own, as key words and obsessions, sudden inspirations that struck during the day, dreams, fears and fantasies, characters and observations from your own life were fed into the device and algorithms turned them into an ongoing saga, a second internal dialogue, once removed, the voice of the conscience or a consciousness, a daemon or the very word of God, according to just how far-out you wanted to get about it.

Ook. That was what it read. Ook. Okay, that was weird. But sometimes it happened. A ghost in the machine. Adam shrugged, though there was no one here to see it outside of his reflection in the glass of the observation deck, as lonely in space as the earth itself.

WordPool time was strictly rationed for Victory Gardens staff and crew. It had to be. Safety, flight protocol and environmental information had to override all other potential sources of instruction or command, even, or more especially, divine inspiration. But they couldn't outlaw it altogether. That would have been like banning literature.

Gazing out at the infinity of stars and the light of distant planets brought to mind his friend Robert Scott and his fantastical ideas about man's new place in the universe. No Prince of Peace up here, Scott had insisted, and as Adam scanned the dark from his single bubble of light it was impossible not to agree. Out here the sole arbiters were elementals, gas giants, impossible gravities; our true heavenly nature stood revealed as fire unsound. Earth is monotheistic, Scott had claimed. Space is pagan. Yet here we are, Adam thought, fighting to preserve the ancient balance of life and death.

Scott was back on earth now and his replacement was already on his way, now a small speck, spinning slowly in the sun, a single bright teardrop, rising up. Adam couldn't resist another look at his WordPool, although he was nearly at his ration point for the day. It is me, man, who will be judge at the end of the count, it read. He recognised the quote, but he couldn't place it.

□

Who could remember their entire story, who could ever hope to put it all back together, to make perfect sense of it? When the WordPool had first taken off, an unexpected development for its bookish creator Dr Crevasse, there had been much debate over its function of auto-forgetting. How to remember where we were in the story, everything that had come before? There had been a movement to replace the single sentences, instantly deleted and wiped from memory, written over again and again, with immediate back-ups and endless scrolling. Pirates and entrepreneurs rushed to issue hacks and patches that facilitated the creation of marathon texts that allowed you to search through time-dated pronouncements. But who had the time to constantly reread a book that would never end? Or is that the definition of a classic?

Crevasse held out, refused to legitimise the upgrades, even as rival companies issued their own handhelds with massively improved functionality. Still, a superstition held around the original WordPool, an irrational belief that somehow it, and only it, had access to something that was supra or subconscious, something spectacular that had been loosed, or more properly channelled, by Crevasse, something that had been looking for a voice and that had used Crevasse as the medium. His media-shy reputation, his refusal to give interviews, his reported antipathy towards his own invention: all of this led to much rumour and speculation. There was an aura to Crevasse's creation, a magic to his algorithms, a purity – a naivety, even – to his creation, that no marketing team was capable of divining. Sure, you could write every line down, and many people did keep WordPool diaries, but it was hard to dispute that the readings most truly made sense in the moment they were issued, as if somehow they were intimately caught up with the precise co-ordinates of now, as if the very nuance, the freewheeling dance of time and space, had been for a moment stilled or mirrored, more precisely, in their gnomic utterances, in the endless, coterminous play of the alphabet.

□

The Earth Got Fucked and She Knows It, That's Why She Winks in Space. No, that won't do. How about *Y'All Have Knocked Her Up?* Pointless, no one else is gonna get that.

How about *Been Up So Long It Looks Like Down to Me*?
Ditto.

What the fuck – excuse me – but what the fuck was a
performance poet, an amateur painter, an amateur explorer,
an all-round amateur never-been-paid-for-a-thing-in-his-life
guy like Peter Muldoon doing as artist-in-residence on the
Victory Gardens?

That's what everyone wanted to know. Friends were
jealous, colleagues bemused, peers furious, at least they
would have been except that he had few friends, zero
colleagues, and the concept of peers was a complete
fantasy. He had only been in space once before and that
was illegally, during the protests over the construction of
the new spaceport in the Sea of Tranquillity. Back then you
could see it from earth without a telescope, this terrible
metal construction surrounded by high floodlights, this
awful wound. They'd have concreted over the whole of the
moon if they thought they could get away with it. Muldoon
had hitched a ride on a small interplanetary Snowdrop
commandeered by a gang of radical geodesics who had
talked Helpless Clairvoyants into playing a protest gig
inside a pop-up bubble somewhere in the region of the
original Apollo 11 touchdown. The idea was that afterwards
they would record an album on the dark side of the moon,
the first music ever made by humans out of sight of the
earth and face-on to the outlands – who knew what it would
sound like? – but in the event most of the attendees had
been arrested after protesters surrounded the spaceport
with a series of domes and tunnels and tried to proclaim it
a Free State. Clairvoyants' lead singer, Firth Column, was
last seen heading for the dark side on a moon buggy with

nothing but a guitar and amplifier, a pair of wraparound shades and a DIY dome kit. Since then a number of solo recordings had appeared purporting to be new work, most of them collections of lonely tones like the sound of foghorns from ships at sea or of interstellar shortwave, singing softly to itself, but they were patently a put-on. I mean, he was obviously dead, right?

Things were different now. Governments could no longer ignore the facts. Ecological disaster was no longer disputed, no longer the domain of cranks and hippies and psychedelic guitarists. Now the freaks were taking over. Even so, Peter Muldoon in residence at the Victory Gardens? Give me a fucking break.

□

In the end The Bible got it right, right at the very end, that whole bit about revelation through destruction, apocalyptic gnosis, rising up in rapture as the planet goes up in flames. It's ironic but it was there all along, the story of our future, the great mess of our tenancy on earth. The earth used to be the centre of the universe. Now it felt more like a fortified island.

It was environmental destruction, our trashing of the precious gift, that marked humanity's adulthood, its coming to some kind of terms with its place in the universe. Which had coincided, ironically, with a new sense of occupying the planet, a new tenancy, if you like. Now we would have to negotiate with beings and forces that absolutely transcended the kind of fantasy figures we had spent much of our time on earth bartering with. The equinox of the gods, the twilight of the idols, it had been coming for some time. Still, it was a lot to take in.

Robert Scott was much occupied by the role of the new priestly caste and what form it would take in the future. He was just back from the Victory Gardens, where he had used his residency to argue that Jesus and the Apostles and the saints were characteristic by-products of a certain era, a certain time and place. That didn't make them any less real or any less eternal. It was just that the axis had shifted, humanity had stepped out of the frame and with it the suffering of Christ was finally at an end. The lighting out had begun. Still, all of this was for the more advanced members of society, you understand. Scott went about his days on earth as though nothing had changed. He still gave communion, he still absolved sins, he still attended flower shows and garden fetes, even as he denied Christ in space. But he was occupied, that much was obvious, and friends and members of his diocese began to make comment on it. He heard them talk. It only encouraged a feeling of contempt that had been building, contempt for these sheep without a master, these pathetic children who were unable to take responsibility for a single stray thought or action.

He was rude at the flower show. He couldn't help himself. He always maintained that daffodils stank, that there was something of the grave to them, and he told them so. These flowers are cadaverous, he insisted. Get them out of my face. His judgement was ruled invalid. He left early. I'm a born negotiator, he told himself. I should be up there, bartering for the next man. He stood in the street in front of the church hall and stared up at the ring of steel that circled the earth. He caught himself out and laughed under his breath.

The earth is in the sky already. Why do priests always insist that we need to die to get there? We came close, we came damn close. But then we woke up and looked about us. Then we established where we were. The earth, it turns out, is in heaven.

☐

Welcome to space. Adam Aros held out his hand and Peter Muldoon reluctantly took it. It's not my first time, Muldoon said. Oh, we know, Aros replied, we know. Who the fuck is this we? Muldoon thought. He imagined a group of boffins scrolling through a secret file that tracked all of his actions and that listed him as a crackpot artist and hopeless seditionary. Hopeless as in crap. He still had no real idea of why he was here, but why blow a lucrative gig? He vowed to say nothing. This could change everything. You're probably wondering why you're here, Aros said. Not really, Muldoon shrugged. I knew the time would come. Very well, Aros said, though he seemed vaguely puzzled himself. I'll take you to your quarters.

Aros led him around the curving observation corridor, dotted with glass portals on either side. Two-headed, Muldoon thought. The twins, diastole and systole, suspended in time and space, drawn back towards earth while pushing deep into the future. The architecture of the Victory Gardens held the echo of the moment. Muldoon went to say as much. He knew he had better turn up the poetry. Gnomic utterances and extravagant proclamations would be the order of the day if he was to pull this off. The Dark Continent, he said, and he motioned towards the stars. What do you mean? Aros said. We've been here before, Muldoon said, that's all. He shook his head. Aros shrugged. Leave it at that, Muldoon said to himself. That's the trick.

This far out the stars seemed closer to suns, to blazing fires, than they had ever done from earth. Man's fascination with fire, his internal relationship to it, has driven him to the edge of the universe and given birth to the technology to get him there, Muldoon thought. Reunited. Voluntary exile and a great return. That was a good one. He'd save that for later.

Muldoon was presented with his quarters. When was the last time he had slept the night, undisturbed, curled up in peace? Truthfully, not since his early thirties. He scanned around the room, the simple bed, the skylight with the stars up above, the bookcase, already filled, and saw himself for a strange split second curled, once again, in the warmth of possibility, in the womb of the future. Thank you, he said to Aros, and he sealed the door behind him. Then he took off his clothes and lay back on the bed; newborn, chosen, and perfectly confused.

□

Life is clingling, dwindling. The same sentence three times. Life is clingling, dwindling. Aros shut down his WordPool and pulled it up again. Each time it read the same. Nonsense in, nonsense out, wasn't that the mantra? But Aros had been scrupulous, had built up his own WordPool as he would his diary, had obsessively tracked stray thoughts, articulated vague urges, detailed his relationship with his parents, reviewed every film he had seen, every book he had read, included every person who had ever meant anything to him. Yet now the machine was sighing, as if to fade away, making sounds to itself like a retiree in a home rolling words around their mouth in memory of their tongue.

Life is clingling, dwindling. Of course, it was common for people to read augurs of illness or omens of sudden death in the machinations of the WordPool. It was the same kind of ignorance that had made people start when the Death card was drawn during a Tarot reading, or The Hanged Man.

Life is clingling, dwindling. He said it softly to himself. It seemed to make everything slow down. The people passing him in the corridor appeared diminished. Outside, in the starfield, the distant suns seemed no longer scintillating but nodding and heavy-lidded, running, finally, on empty.

He reached his quarters, where he updated the WordPool with the events of the day. He profiled Muldoon, his own take on him. It wasn't flattering. He added a line from a poem that seemed apposite, a poem from the twentieth century. He confided his own fear of dying, far away from everyone he once knew and loved, in another life altogether. Then he punched it in himself. Life is clingling, dwindling. Now it was canon. Now, it was under control.

There comes a period in every person's life, a season, best perhaps, where it would seem that he is most open to influence. Where this influence might be seen as coming from, or emanating out from, more properly, depends on the cultural vagaries of the moment, the psychological status of the person receiving it, the position of the stars, the flight of the birds, or the name of God Himself. A modern man might most likely locate it in the machinations of the WordPool.

Life is clingling, dwindling. It appeared as a song to Aros, but when did he ever attribute anything meaningful to songs, when had he last cast his fate to music or read in a lyric the direction of his life?

He rose from his bed and flipped listlessly through Peter Muldoon's file. He shook his head. A crackpot artist and hopeless seditionary. How the hell had he stumbled over this? He reread an account of an exhibition that featured paintings of a series of couplings that Muldoon claimed were various 'accidental' sexual positions lifted from Jackson Pollock paintings. A Japanese woman being painfully entered from behind; a woman with an enormous ass smothering a small-limbed boy; endless cocks ejaculating; a group of men urinating on a woman's body; doggy style embraces; on-your-knees fellatio; mass couplings that appeared as multi-limbed gods and goddesses. Chaos always tends towards sensuality, towards the sexual and the procreative, Muldoon had maintained. That was the point. Then he had begun to locate the sex positions in the sky. Muldoon's next exhibition had tied in with the creation of the Victory Gardens. Muldoon redrew the constellations as hermaphroditic gods, intuiting new connections between the stars and renaming them himself. Or so he said. Then he painted them, as a sort of cosmic Kama Sutra, as an orgy of stars.

□

Thing is, he was onto something. He had given them names, rechristened them as hermaphrodites, constellations of suns making love to themselves, weird names, sexy names like Xstabeth, Qbxl, Lalino, intersexed names that seemed to collapse in the middle only to reappear again, as if there were a black hole in their centre. That was quite possibly true. Because now Xstabeth was in touch. He, she, it, had started communicating via the British Victory Gardens WordPool. And it was asking for Muldoon.

☐

You're using a WordPool at the Victory Gardens? Muldoon burst. This is madness. What are you using it for? He had been called to a briefing in a meeting room situated in a bubble on the outer curve of *The Advance*, the British link in the Victory Gardens. He had been introduced to the project manager, a Mr Clyde Evans, alongside a representative of the government of the United Kingdom who declined to give his name. You do realise that everything that is revealed in this room is top-secret, the nameless man repeated. That you are sworn by oath not to reveal anything you are told here. I realise that, Muldoon said, but seriously, I'm blown away by this. Are you actually making decisions based on WordPool results? I was under the impression that access to WordPools on the Victory Gardens was strictly controlled according to international agreements. Now you're telling me there's an actual project WordPool? The three men looked at each other. Evans spoke. We've been making decisions based on the WordPool for much longer than this, he revealed. Where do you think we got the idea for the Victory Gardens in the first place?

☐

The Victory Gardens had been conceived as a last-ditch attempt to head off – or at least regulate – environmental catastrophe, a ring of steel that would serve to artificially regulate the atmosphere, recomposing weather systems and managing temperature fluctuations while recalibrating mankind's relationship with the universe. The project had been the brainchild of the British, who had named it after the attempts to make gardens and grow food in the craters and potholes that had dotted the country in the wake of the Second World War. What at first had been written off as the utopian fever dream of a bunch of science fiction-addled hippies somehow, due to the rigour of the planning, the detail of the blueprints, the desperation of the situation, had attracted the interest of the major world powers and soon the powers of the new colonial axis – all twelve of them – had committed funding, technology and their finest scientific minds to the creation of what many began to speak of as a new Eden, with earth as the first garden planet.

The Advance had been the first ship to take its place, closely followed by Israel's *New Jerusalem* and Spain's *Aboyos*. Right from the start there had been a strange undercurrent of religious fervour to the project, a new millenarian dream. Although in one sense the horizons had really been narrowed – earth was now the mission, not deep space – to many it felt like the vanguard in mankind's eventual lighting out, in its sailing to the stars and its leaving of the planet altogether.

Already the skies had changed. The Victory Gardens had become as familiar as the stars and the planets in the sky, as the links of the chain spun slowly by, the shimmering blue steel of *Aboyos*, bright, hopeful *Praetoria*, gentle *Gyrus*, summoning the rains, bringing food to the hungry, and all the flora of the earth seemed to rise up in salute to the bounty of the skies.

□

The priesthood is nothing but a temperance society, an
organisation dedicated to the policing of the sex urge,
Robert Scott fumed. He gazed at himself in the mirror.
Isn't it ironic, he thought to himself, that the one thing the
Church is incapable of dealing with is revelation, is actual
experience of the unveiling of the divine? All we have to
offer are rules, codes of behaviour, terrors and frights. The
birth of Christ damned us to the future and we gave up on
the present. But suffering is at an end. Isn't that what he
had told the audience that had gathered to hear him on the
Victory Gardens? But why invite a theologian into space if
not to ridicule his faith?

He had fielded questions, barbed comments, all set-ups,
obviously. If heaven is a state of mind, they asked him, then
whose brain are we in now? That got a laugh alright. You
mistake me for a liberal, he came back at them. Heaven
is somewhere we have arrived at. Our new vantage point
demands that we rethink the specifics of our location. Look,
he said, and he pointed back at the earth, now a point
among points, a circle within circles. The earth is in heaven.
And we are among the gods. What of Christianity? someone
asked him. What of Islam? We still have many believers
amongst the crews. As a representative of the Church, what
do you have to say to them? Will there be a new revelation?
Scott felt a fury rise in his veins. A new revelation? Another
fairy story, is that what these infants require? We stand
face to face with the very depths of ourselves and we ask for
revelation? Where will it end? When will it begin?

Instead he held his breath. He felt his pulse rise to his
temple. He put his hand on his head. He mopped his brow.
He kept at it. These clowns think I'm receiving the word
of God right now, he said to himself, and he continued the
charade some more, even going so far as to close his eyes
and mutter under his breath. Give them some glossolalia, he
said to himself. Why the hell not. He held out for as long as
possible. He milked the silence of every nuance, sustained
every pathetic hope and dream with jaw-dropping amateur
dramatics. Then he spoke.

The book has been written, he said. The stars are in place.

There were gasps, nods of approval, thankful blushing faces
staring out amidst the usual impassive science types. The
believers will swallow anything, Scott thought to himself.
So long as it is empty. But truly, there is no such thing as
empty space. Not any more. Now there is only time. And
those who would set sail in it.

He steadied himself on the lectern. He gazed out at all the
faces, staring back at him. Have you ever looked out at the
world and recognised yourself, he asked them, seen the work
of your own hand, in the soft, warm rain, in the green of
the grass and the blue of the sky, in men and women, and
in sex, and the idea of it, and the dressing for it, in the past
and the future and in the moving through it, in the rising
and falling, the coming and going, in the idea of dreams,
of tastes and experiences and desires, in the existence of
biographical facts? How unlikely it all is, and how specific;
who else could have thought of it?

They think God is coming, he thought to himself. They think the whole thing has a punchline.

Let me tell you a story, he began. This is some years ago, he said, as if to distance himself from the person he was about to describe. But really, it was distance and time that had conspired to make of it a lesson, an edifice, a commandment written in stone. That's what these idiots need, he muttered, and he cursed them beneath his breath, they need a stone tablet, they need a set of dos and don'ts, a law to live by, and a past and a future to be torn apart between.

I was serving time, he admitted, and he shook his head. Best thing that ever happened to me. I was careering, out of control. I ran with a gang, he said. Hardnuts with big kick-your-cunt-in faces.

There were gasps all around. This isn't a man of the cloth speaking any more, he told them. Make your peace. He stared down his critics and continued with his talk.

These men had faces to terrify you, faces all out of proportion with their bodies, which is the criminal type, I'm afraid, and which comes, I believe, from a certain form of mental pressure, an isolation, if you like, a social maladjustment, that results in the expansion of the head as the centre of consciousness – hear me out – and the concomitant thickening of the features, the fortification of the face, which can be willed or caused by belief and circumstance. A big kick-your-cunt-in face, he repeated. That was gratuitous, he could admit that much.

My own features changed, he admitted. You might not
believe it, but I was a different man. The more you
look in the mirror, the more you fix your own face. The
vanity of the criminal classes is beyond reckoning. In
prison everyone is working out, haven't you ever noticed
it? Everyone is squatting and grimacing and dropping
suddenly to the floor and pushing up or grabbing hold of a
door frame and suspending their entire body weight from
it. Just to experience a little resistance. You go into a jail
an island and you come out of it a fortress. I went down for
GBH. I rearranged someone else's face. Then I took a chisel
to their privates, so they couldn't go making any new ones.
I'm not proud of it. It's who I was, at least who I thought I
was.

I shared a cell with a man with one hand. We all had our
deformities, it was unremarkable. He told me he was an
oracle. That was remarkable. At first I ridiculed him. Then
you knew you would end up here, I told him. Yes, he said.
I knew that already. Then he told me that the moon was
being dreamed by a great lake beneath its surface, a lake of
blood and water, somewhere near the centre. I asked him
where his other hand was. It's out there, he said, and he
pointed out the window.

Later he wrote a book about the water of the moon and its
dreaming of itself as a lonely satellite, a barren rock ejected
from the earth like an egg. But really it was a great expanse
of blood and water, which is exactly what the moon needs, if
you think about it, which is what would solve the moon, in
a way. Some of you may have read it. I don't know. I can't
remember what it was called. *The Stone Afloat*? It was a
science fiction or something. Years later, when I heard he

had published a book, I used to picture him reading it in his lap and struggling to turn the page with one hand.

In prison I would lie in my bunk at night, unable to sleep, and sometimes the moon would shine through the window so bright and my bunkmate would sing under his breath, I could never make out the words, but in the morning the floor would be wet and the guards would accuse him of soiling our cell and we would be given a work detail and made to mop it up.

The other remarkable thing is he could stand on his hand, he could do a handstand with one hand. It's not impossible, I've seen it happen. I thought of all these goons hanging from door frames and lifting weights above their heads when I would see my cellmate – whose name was Adolphus but whom everyone called Banjo because of his wiry hair and his hollow, empty face – upside down, with such ease, such lightness and grace, that I thought that he must be from the moon, or at least have some insider knowledge about gravity.

At the same time, I had started attending church services in prison. I can't say why, the light of the moon, who knows. At that time there was a Father Sacraviscera who led confessions and who was available for counselling and questions of faith.

Sacraviscera, I said to him, that's not an Irish surname, is it? No, he said. It's not Irish. It's my confirmation name. He said he had taken it in order that everything might be holy, even the most appalling soft organs of the body, those most vulnerable to clots and blows and sharp objects. He told me that he had received a vision where all of his internal organs, all of the cells, all of the corpuscles in the blood, all of the forces that push out the nails and sprout the hair, yes, even those that deal with the asshole and the gonads, the sweat glands and the beating of the heart, all of these, he said, rose up in a great salutation, a great yes which he described as a sort of cosmic orgasm, a great rushing climax, which he realised, right then and there, was man himself, and woman herself, a great symphonic climax, the very raiment of infinity, was how he described it. There are more possibilities in the brain, he said, more combinations in the body, than there are atoms in the universe. That's where I first got religion. I found it up my ass.

There were gasps throughout the room. That was gratuitous, he had to admit.

Of course, there were inmates who drank, he continued. Who raged in their solitude, as if a mere cup of this or that, a good dose, would lead to the heart, would open up the thing in things. I did my fair share. I caned this, shotgunned that. I threw my guts up. I passed out unconscious. But there was no revelation, no transport between here and there. Narcotics, stimulants, are where the dream of time travel comes from. But time is not a prison, he said, time is not an exercise yard. There is nothing to escape from and nowhere to go.

That was my mistake. As a young man I went in search of revelation, of guidance, and I saw it in the future, in an apocalypse, so to speak. This is the promise of Jesus misunderstood. That at some future point there will be change, a revealing of the thingness of things, the same thingness that we wish alcohol and drugs and sex and achievement to reveal to us, the same promise of the future. I joined the Church. I stood in line. I practised good deeds. There was a mathematics of eschatology, a kind of adding up, and once you passed this certain point – people saved, good deeds done, prayers recited, beads counted, sufferings suffered – you would be granted a truth, given a bird's-eye view of how it all went down. I was deluded. All we have to do is look up, look out, at ourselves and there we stand, revealed, beyond explanation.

You have asked me here, I can only presume, in order that a man of the cloth can give you his take as to where humanity stands, in relation to the gods, in relation to Christ's revelation, to the love of God, as we stand on the cusp of infinite space, staring out but also staring back, at the planet we have destroyed, at the catastrophe we are now attempting to put right. And I tell you: down there is Eden; out there is Eden.

On the long nights when I lay in my cell after Banjo had been released, I thought about what he'd said. The water and the blood that coursed deep inside inanimate matter or what we thought was inanimate matter, cold stone, dead stone, and I thought about his missing hand. Where is your hand? I had asked him. And he had pointed out there. Just as I ask you to look out into space, to fix your gaze on eternity, and to see if you don't find part of yourself there. Time is not a prison. We are not escapees who have somehow smuggled ourselves, in birth, out of the universe, in opposition to it. We are it; we are the epiphany of matter, the play of time, the thingness in things. Yes, we must continue to fecundate the earth, the precious womb, the mother of us all. But the age of earthly deities is at an end. Christ will not resurrect. The turn of the seasons is at an end. Environmental catastrophe has so altered the rhythms of the planet that Jesus himself has been forsaken. It's no bad thing. Humanity's childhood is at an end. And with it all sense of guilt. Through our misadventure we burned all of our bridges. Through strife we have been given the opportunity to find ourselves again. Through recombination and division we have been brought to nought. And this, before us, this emptiness which is really fullness, and which holds all of the stars and planets at their precise distances, in the perfection of their orbits, the glory of their revolutions, is the great gift. Here we will encounter new gods, an endless pantheon of powers, written in the pattern of the stars themselves. Our original heavenly nature is fire unsound, he said. And now, as we stand here, in orbit, suspended hundreds of miles above the earth, with the whole of space and time in front of us, at the beginning of a great adventure, I say to you, our new masters are no masters at all. Our new masters are the heavenly fires themselves.

□

Back in his quarters, Muldoon's head was spinning. They had been in touch. They were real. Xstabeth had spoken first. She had given her name. Then Qbxl. Then Lalino. They had identified themselves as menwomen. Then as gods. Then as the light of the stars themselves. The British Victory Gardens had been receiving these broadcasts for some time. It was as if their mission had somehow forced the gods into revealing themselves. This is impossible, Muldoon told himself. This is insane. I dreamed them up. I created them. I made them out of nothing. The Controller, that was the name they had given for the British government's WordPool operative, had recognised the names, the figures in the stars, and had pointed them out to Muldoon. Then the gods had asked for him by name. Now the British government wanted Muldoon as the new Controller. Or did they? Paranoia was rife, that much was certain. Were the gods playing the missions off against each other? What of the other nationalities? Were they using WordPools? Were they in touch with the same gods? Different ones? Or had someone hacked into the WordPool? They said it wasn't possible. The construction of the WordPool was so simple, so straightforward, it would be like hacking into a Hoover. Besides, what exactly was the WordPool, really, outside of an extended conversation with yourself?

You're staying here, they told Muldoon. No one else knows, outside a small coterie. Not even Adam Aros, who believes he brought you here. This can't get out. We need to trace the source of these messages. Had they been guiding the Victory Gardens project from day one? Had Muldoon?

What's to prevent me telling everyone? Muldoon said to them. How can I even be trusted? You're so tied up in it already, he was told. Besides, they told him, aren't you curious? Don't you want to get involved? Don't you want to know?

Why did the project even have a WordPool? Because it was actually making breakthroughs; it was providing creative solutions to problems. Under the guidance – that was the term they used – of a series of Controllers, the WordPool had detailed every step of the way in terms of managing the environment and shielding the earth. It had been consistently offering solutions that worked. No one knew that the solutions were coming from the WordPool. The project was passed off as the result of the UK's own brainstorming. But it was true. The WordPool was responsible for all of the breakthroughs, all of the technological know-how that had helped save the planet – or at least preserve it – and that had taken humanity back into space.

But what of other links in the Victory Gardens, Muldoon quizzed them, what of other nationalities? The Spanish had pushed for full colonisation of the moon, was that coming from a WordPool? And what exactly was the legislative situation? We all knew that WordPools couldn't be outlawed, instead being simply time-locked when you passed through spaceport control on the way up. But governments needn't enforce their own agents, although of course they had long played with the idea that the WordPool could be used to work against them as well as for them, a tool for sedition, suggesting other allegiances or loyalties, promoting megalomania or paranoia or alternative agendas.

But works of rogue imagination: they were impossible to police. Muldoon shook his head. There had long been alternative theories that the WordPool itself was in fact a propaganda tool, complete with subtle ideological algorithms, and that its creator was in fact a government stooge, something that Dr Crevasse had strenuously denied. Though of course he would, wouldn't he? But it was all too personal, all too specific in its response, in its extrapolations and intimate revelations, to fit one interest, one ideological aim, wasn't it? Now I know how God feels, Muldoon thought to himself, and he lay back on his bed and stared out at the moon. He could have sworn that it winked.

□

As a boy Adam Aros had dreamed of becoming a sailor.
Either that or a lawyer. Somehow the arc of his life had
encompassed the two. He had been a map-maker, a
navigator, part of the team that had worked on the Galactic
Map, a three-dimensional imaging of the solar system and
its environs that could be scaled up or down according to
where it was to be installed: a gallery; a country park; a
wilderness; the span of an entire country.

Looking back, it seemed more like a first tentative
pilgrimage, a dry run through the Stations of the Cross
in preparation for man's entrance into the universe. It
had been an art project and an educational tool but now
it seemed like an imperative, too, a first dim realisation
that new concepts of scale would have to be internalised.
Together the team had created a series of gigantic
holograms that they would set up in precise relationship
with each other, the solar system scaled to fit Scotland, say,
and they would publicise the locations, so that it became
a contemporary pilgrimage, so that you could walk the
distance between Jupiter and Saturn.

He had done it himself during the summer that the solar
system came to Scotland. Who could forget the rings of
Saturn rising in an arc above the mountains at night, the
eye of Jupiter whorling above the council estates, now
shadowed in a temporary blackout, lonely Pluto, just off the
coast of the Hebrides, as if it had risen from the waters, and
beyond that, the endless sea.

Of course, it had been a propaganda exercise too, in a way, classic shock and awe. The team had been peopled by environmentalists, utopians, hippies and progressives who read mankind's future in the stars. It had felt like the war, after the passing of the temporary dark skies legislation that the team had campaigned for. That way the planets could be seen in all their glory. And who would want to stay in, in the dark of a council estate, when Jupiter came down to earth? People had stood out in the streets, had sat up all night around bonfires and with music and food. A mass regression had taken place, a regression towards the future, as if Palaeolithic man were to take his place among the stars.

It was uncanny, too, on balmy summer evenings, to see Jupiter rise behind Jupiter, as if projecting itself onto earth, or for Venus to appear as a bright light on Venus, a campfire, as if to reflect the ceremonies on the ground.

In the wake of the rolling out of the Galactic Map across the world, the first of the Victory Gardens had taken to space, and had been greeted with flag-waving and applause, as if mankind was simply taking its preordained place, as if up was down. The earth would be fructified, and space would yield like a new bride. It was a time of great hope.

In the end they toured the Galactic Map across all twelve of the Victory Gardens signatories. The UK, the USA, Spain, Israel, Sudan, Mexico, Germany, France, Australasia, India, Russia and Japan, signatories who later formed ecological, technological and economic blocs with their neighbours and allies, a series of treaties that made the project feasible. It seemed like a coincidence at the time, or maybe there really was something in the Galactic Map itself, which was hard to dispute when you first glimpsed Neptune, huge across the snowy tundra of Siberia, or Mars turn the Nile blood-red.

Besides, was it really possible to be a propagandist for space? Space was a fact, we were already in it; the Galactic Map was just a reminder. Still, there was an element of deception written in, if you really thought about it. People spent days or weeks or even months tracking a series of holograms, a series of optical illusions, an empty spectacle, while up above them the real thing revolved regardless.

Well, isn't that art? Aros asked himself. Isn't that meaning? And isn't there something quite beautiful about it? About emptiness and futility and pointlessness on that kind of scale? Plus, if it really had led to the creation of the Victory Gardens, or at least contributed to the kind of atmosphere that was more conducive to it, wasn't that justification enough? Now we could control the rains, manipulate the temperature, fix what came in and what came out with this huge global shield that covered the earth, this incredible collaborative project that had brought governments and populations together.

Still, sometimes it was hard to fight the feeling that we had simply built ourselves a new prison. That we had actually sealed ourselves off from the rest of the universe. What was that song again, that piece of music? 'Die ganze Welt ist ein Krankenhaus'. 'The Whole World is a Hospital'.

Aros had volunteered for the Victory Gardens as soon as the announcement went out. Having worked on the Galactic Map, he was fast-tracked into the role of cultural co-ordinator for the UK project ship *The Advance*. Here he had been initiated into an inner order calling itself The SIRK (Secret Interstellar Reconnaissance Kommando, he was told) that saw the Victory Gardens not so much as a holding position to be maintained for the future of the earth but as a first step towards mankind's place amongst the stars. Quite a few of the Galactic Map team were involved, but politically it was mixed, and there was a certain degree of distrust and many counter-agendas at work. After all, there are many reasons to want to get away.

Aros had been responsible for booking Scott and it had been his idea to follow up with Muldoon as artist-in-residence. He had expected to come up against some kind of protest from the top brass; after all, Muldoon was hardly a household name. But his arrest during the protest against the new spaceport on the moon gave him common cause with many of the radical ecologists on board, even if his opposition to further colonisation put him at odds with them. Still, this was new science, and they were making it up as they went along; dissenters were welcomed, artists embraced, priests, well, barely tolerated, to be honest, after Scott's infamous foul-mouthed rant. Fuck them, Aros said to himself. It's hard truths we're after up here. If they can't take it, send them back to the hospital.

□

Muldoon's first request was for a complete transcription of every interaction with the *Advance* WordPool, every input, every response, right from the start. That's out of the question, Clyde Evans told him. They had met in Evans's private quarters, which were all rigged up like a television

set from a 1970s sci-fi serial. A personal indulgence,
Evans told him, forgive me, as he offered him a seat in a
white bubble chair suspended from the ceiling. I feel like
a monkey, Muldoon said. Baboons in space, Evans joked.
That's all we are at this point.

Do you think we're going to meet our maker? Muldoon asked
him.

Well, as far as I can see, Evans replied, as he took a stubby
cigarillo from a stainless-steel case on the table and offered
Muldoon one, you're the closest thing to a creator that we've
uncovered.

What have you actually uncovered?

That's the thing, Evans said. It has all been redacted.

So what exactly am I supposed to work from?

We can give you the last four interactions; that's all.

I feel like I'm being set up. That this is some kind of
experiment. Is this part of the WordPool's plans? Is this
what happens next?

The WordPool has no plans, per se, Evans went to reassure
him. It is we who have the plans.

At least that's the official line, Muldoon replied.

That is the official line, I admit, Evans nodded. But you're
on the inside now. Quite literally.

Have you tried asking the WordPool, simply asking it questions, straightforward questions? Muldoon suggested.

Questions beget questions, Evans replied. Listen, he said. Have you ever heard of The SIRK?

Muldoon blew a ring of smoke from his mouth and it settled above Evans's head like a stinky halo. Should I have? he replied.

Probably not, Evans said. It stands for the Society of Inveterate Recidivist Knights. I'm one of them.

Is this like the Masons? Muldoon asked him.

Well, we're dedicated to the brotherhood of man, put it that way.

And what are you doing up here?

We've always been here, Evans said. We've been behind the space programme since day one, give or take a few Nazi scientists and all of the stooges we had working for us. Thing is, we have been receiving messages for much longer than this. This is the tip of the iceberg. Only this time, the iceberg has a name. And it's talking back.

Each planet has a frequency, a tone that it emits, Evans continued. We know that much, right?

The music of the spheres, Muldoon shrugged. It's old hat.

Yeah, it's old hat alright. It has been going on forever. Thing is, we decoded it some time ago.

And what's it saying?

It's a piece of music.

Must be pretty avant-garde, Muldoon joked.

It's a piece of classical music, actually. 'BWV 25', to be precise.

Bach?

Yes.

Bollocks, Muldoon spat. You're trying to tell me that no one ever noticed that the planets were playing classical music in space? Who's the conductor?

Well, exactly, Evans said. It was as if something, some object, some event, was working on the solar system and somehow massively but subtly affecting the speed and scale of the planets' revolutions. The reason that nobody noticed it before is that it was only a snatch, played once, over a certain period of years. And it was played so slowly, a single phrase spread across twelve months, then another, that it was only when we sped up the signals, accumulated over the period of a decade or so, that someone recognised it as the opening bars from 'BWV 25'.

There is nothing sound in my body, Muldoon said.

You know the piece? Evans asked him.

I know it well, he said. Then he looked out the window. A small fleet of supply ships were fanning out, moving towards the Victory Gardens, like the slow opening of a peacock's tail. The stars hung noiselessly in space. Clouds covered the earth. It was night-time down below. He looked back at Evans. What's nothing sound? he asked him.

□

Robert Scott owned a small wooden shack built up on stilts on the banks of Loch Awe in Argyll in Scotland. He stood there on the deck, in the dim light of the evening, and listened to the silence, a final silence, he thought to himself. Despite all the talk, time was running out. The storms had swept away the diving gantry he had built running into the loch, this crazy wonder, and now it lay there, tormented, half submerged, as in the final resting place of a gargantuan fossil.

They say they have control of the weather, he thought. They say the climate is in our hands. But for that they would need to seize control of the sun. His wife joined him on the deck. His loyal wife who for so long he had hidden in the background. He had lived the life of a man of the cloth for all to see. But privately he had raged and roared and tormented them both. Barbara bore the scars. She was like a little white mouse. You got the worst of me, my darling, Scott said, and he ran his hands through her hair. She stared back at him without blinking, her green eyes now dimmed and untroubled, her dark curly hair now loose and long let go.

They had met long ago, in another life, and now they were here. What happened to us? she asked him. Whatever it was, he said, we should never have let it. It will take another planet to put us back together. We don't have that much time, Barbara said. And besides, there's no way back.

I dreamed that you died, she said. I dreamed that we rose too early and it caused your collapse. She walked to the edge of the deck and looked down at the dark water scattered with shattered wood and pieces of flotsam. I kneeled over your dying body on the floor and I said you were the best husband ever, the most perfect partner, how much I loved you, and forever. Then you recovered and got back up. That was embarrassing, you said. Now you'll have to do that all over again the next time.

What does it say in The Bible, Scott said, something about how for one kiss we must be willing to sacrifice all? I don't think that's in The Bible, Barbara said. Think of it, Barbara, he continued, ignoring her. For just one tender moment we must be willing to say yes to all of it, all of it forever, running back into the past, streaming out into the future, the sum of every suffering and joy. A great secret river, a storm-tossed loch, a single bright teardrop, rising up. It feels awkward to kiss you now, Barbara said. We know each other too well. Don't worry, Scott said, don't worry, darling, we can forget each other and find each other all over again. At which Barbara started to cry.

☐

The last four interactions with the *Advance* WordPool read:

Peter Muldoon painted the gods and gave them their names.

He set a fountain of tears in my eyes.

Why and wherefore?

All throughout the book, all throughout time, all vainglorious.

What do you think? Evans asked him.

It's hard to know, what are the stakes?

Incalculable.

It feels like Consequences. You know, like the surrealists would use, where you would add words to a sentence that you hadn't seen. Who wrote 'Why and wherefore'?

The Controller.

That feels like a really strange thing to say.

Evans poured each of them a glass of wine. A Polish wine, from one of the new producing regions.

It's a little poetic, I'll give you that, he said.

Why would naming the gods or rendering them in some kind of visual form cause them to weep?

Idolatry? Wasn't God always against that, or one of the gods, anyhow?

It all feels a little Old Testament. But with names like Xstabeth, menwomen, that's really how they announced themselves?

Basically.

Then there's 'vainglorious'. Great vanity. That feels like another warning. An imprecation.

Against what? Evans asked him.

Who knows, something that's omnipresent, something throughout.

It could be drawing a line under the thing, you know, like this is where the mission terminates.

Is it?

If you're asking me whether the results could have any effect on us pushing forward into space then, no, I would say it couldn't. There's too much momentum behind it now. Besides, what would we do, say that we had been hearing voices and they had told us to stop?

Did the WordPool always talk like this?

Talk? In voices? At first it was used in a completely technical manner, you know, it started off as a journal that we would add to.

Who's we?

The SIRK. We would add to it communally. It was kept
under lock and key and at meetings we would update it
with our plans and any relevant developments and then
we would take note of its replies. At first it was more like a
secretary, taking minutes, making suggestions using a fairly
transparent dialectic, that sort of thing. But once we got into
space, well, it began talking more like this.

Which is?

You know: oracular, poetic.

Have you ever read the Song of Solomon? Muldoon asked
Evans. In it they talk about fountains stopping and fountains
flowing.

Evans pulled the Song of Solomon up onto his screen.

Here it is, Muldoon said. 'A garden enclosed is my sister, my
spouse; a spring shut up, a fountain sealed.' And here: 'A
fountain of gardens, a well of living waters, and streams from
Lebanon.'

'Let my beloved come into his garden,' Evans read, 'and eat his
pleasant fruits.' He turned to Muldoon. Have you ever heard of
a priest and writer named Robert Scott? he asked him.

□

There are countless fountains in The Bible, Robert Scott
confirmed, and he shook his head. But everyone's a sucker for

the Song of Solomon. Clyde Evans had arranged a meeting between the two of them back on earth. Muldoon had insisted on meeting his predecessor. He looked ill, Muldoon thought. Troubled, certainly.

Scott sat on the porch of his hut, bent over an old wooden table where he was rolling a small joint of home-grown marijuana with one hand. He was dressed in a dark-blue silk dressing gown embroidered with golden planets, his thin grey beard speckled with Viking red. Muldoon fancied that his puffy eyes and his emaciated face made him look like an old jazz pianist, beaten down from smoke and drink and all-night performances in titty bars. Titty bars, Muldoon thought to himself, and he sighed. That was a blast from the past.

The wine was from a vineyard in Perth in central Scotland, now one of the most praised grape regions in Western Europe. The sun was up, high in the sky, and they sat on wooden chairs on the porch as the gentle waves lapped against the supports. Someone had taken a boat out onto the water, its sail a small triangle of light that rippled in the heat. Scott's arm was bandaged after a drunken fall. Night swimming, he joked, is a perilous activity.

Have you ever heard of pathetic fallacy? he asked Muldoon. It was coined by some artist or other, but it has come to signify a kind of grotesque error, a kind of unforgivable presumption. Listen to the soft sound of the waves, he said to Muldoon. Muldoon listened. Wouldn't you say they were gentle? Wouldn't you say that they were almost caressing the supports? As if they were half in love with their own dispersal onto the land and into space? That would be pathetic fallacy. Waves aren't gentle or fond of caresses or half in love. At least, that's what they say. You see, when you start to interpret the actions of matter as having characteristics that can only really be ascribed to humans, then you have erred. When you pick out patterns in nature, patterns that are entirely arbitrary and entirely reliant on the specifics of your observation of them, then you have fallen. Matter functions without motive, a flower flowers for no other reason than its flowering.

Isn't rising up towards the sun a motive? Muldoon asked him.

You might think so, Scott said. When you are confused and upset the sky itself can seem to rage.

I'm confused right now, Muldoon said, and yet the sky seems unconcerned.

You might think so, Scott said. But consider this. The best sex you ever had. Think of it. It wasn't just fucking, I'm willing to bet. It was more like fucking and being fucked at the same time. Am I right?

Scott took a huge, triumphant draw on the joint and they both burst out laughing. He poured them both another glass of wine. Did you ever work in a titty bar? Muldoon asked him, and they both broke up all over again.

Where was I? Scott said. Okay, fucked and being fucked. Now think about lying in bed in the morning in that blissful post-coital state. Your wife gets up, say, or whoever it was you were fucking, I'd hate to presume, and you can hear them next door, perhaps they're singing to themselves under their breath or putting away last night's dishes. You turn over in bed and you feel the weight of the mattress, holding you up, the way it curves around the shape of your body, the feel of the blanket, the soft weave of the wool, the delightful cold silk of the trim, you feel it wrap itself around you. Where are you?

There is a form of mutual exchange here, between what you think of as you and what you think of as not you. Really there is one experience, but that one experience, which is really nothing, if you want to get deep down into it, relies on two, on duality, on duplicity. Really, when you are lying in bed after sex and feeling that beautiful warm, cosy sensation, it is like a duet, between what we have come to term animate and inanimate. One facilitates the experience and – this is the thing – vice versa. The blanket is given its particular characteristics by this incredible opportunity of communion, which the coming together of both 'you' and 'it' have facilitated. Do you see what I mean? Experience isn't one-way. We think it is, we have fallen for that, but no experience is divisible from the components of that experience. The blankets truly are warming, are comforting, are gentle. You are being covered and they are covering you. And there is something else born in their mingling.

Let me put it another way. When you look back, say, when you remember, what is it that you remember, and where are you? Memories do not contain you. Most times you are nowhere to be found. Memories do not consist of you seeing yourself, there, in the centre, cut off from everything all around you, sealed in. You don't look back and see yourself standing there. You recall what was around you, what was outside you, and how that chimed with what was inside at the time. Yet you say, that was me, I remember. What are you remembering? Are you putting your body back together, piece by piece? Or are you reassembling the world, as it was? So, you see, you, when you think about it, tend to find yourself out there. And it's just as correct to say that out there finds itself in you. Is the water gentle as it ripples against the pier? Well, I think so. But you know, he said, laughing, I'm a perfect fool.

Scott stood up and untied his dressing gown. The light, transparent days of summer, which now reliably spanned May to October, had transformed Scotland into an earthly paradise. The dark hills stood illuminated in the distance, the trees like crystals seen through pure, clear water. Scott's torso criss-crossed with scars. He looks like a cadaver, Muldoon thought. But he talks like he's the happiest man alive. Scott walked, with some difficulty, it appeared, and stood staring down into the water. The light played across his features, his face now translucent, and clear, in the light of the water. Then he turned to face Muldoon and fell backwards, grinning, into the water.

My favourite thing is to urinate on myself when I'm in the water, Scott announced. It's the most futile fun you can ever have. Muldoon started to laugh, and he took off his own clothes and leaped in beside him. Scott's wife Barbara appeared on the deck, carrying a tray with salad and bread and cheese. Oh, you're in the water, she said, and she took a seat at the table and stared out at the two of them.

Scott lay on his back, floating in the sun, but Muldoon suddenly felt self-conscious. We must look like two boys to Barbara, he thought to himself. What is a boy to a woman?

Is a boy the grace of men? Some kind of gentle consolation for all the layers of armour in a man's life?

These were the kind of thoughts that went through his head as he stood with his feet on the soft sand, the water caressing his shoulders. He looked at Scott and at Barbara and he pictured a man's life lived backwards, beginning in carefree senility, and with the blessings of old age, and progressing through manhood and marriage and questions of purpose, and ending in the easy dissolution of all bonds, in simple pleasures and naive communion, girls restored to their mystery, boys gifted with disinterest.

But frontways forward life had its own graces: the grace of senility, the grace of the shutting down of memory, the grace to slowly dull the sex drive, to reduce the possibilities, the grace of unconsciousness and coma, the grace of the blood slowly seeping from the brain, the grace of the ruptured vein and the slow, soft dissolving of all that we were. That's how his own father had died; softly, bit by bit, in an ambulance.

You were asking about fountains, Scott said, as they dried off. It had taken him an age to climb out of the water, with Muldoon and Barbara both helping him. Yet he had seemed so light, so weightless, that Muldoon had pictured him climbing straight up the ladder to the heavens, like an Indian rope trick, until from below he simply appeared as a speck in the sky, a child's balloon.

In the occult literature, fountains are everywhere, Scott said. They're up there with peacocks. And gardens, of course. Do you know much of the sixteenth-century occultists John Dee and Edward Kelley?

They travelled the aethers in communion with heavenly and infernal powers. How they ever got the idea of the aethers is anyone's guess. Aether means pure sky, the very air that the gods themselves breathe. Dee and Kelley travelled on God's breath, which is probably the closest you can get to the tip of his tongue and of course on his breath were other words, which in turn combined as intelligences, or intelligibles, if you like. Many of these intelligences appeared as fountains. Life itself appeared as a fountain, an eternal upflowing or outflowing. The fountain was flanked by light and by fire. These are the three worlds, according to Dee: the super-celestial world from which comes the light of the spirit, the second celestial world, where we have the fountain of life and the soul, and the elemental world, from which Dee says comes 'the Invincible, heavenly yet sensible fire by which is digested and ripened that which is comprehensible'.

Now, let me ask you this, Scott said in a voice that seemed a little uneasy, have you ever heard of Area 47?

Is that the place where the American government was supposed to have kept all its aliens?

Scott broke into laughter. Ha ha, well, yes, you might say that, but no, that's not what I'm talking about. Area 47, or so they say, is an area of the brain the size of a small finger that seems to relate to what they call creativity within constraints, whatever constraint might mean to you: the outline of an idea, a diagram, a sketch, a novel, a poem, a song, a notational system or a deadline, perhaps, a timescale.

You see, and this is counter-intuitive, but the less information you have, the closer you get to only having very bare bones with which to work, the more likely it is to result in inspired extrapolation. Too much information results in breakdown or gridlock. Even though we, as humans, think that more information is beneficial, we want more of it, we presume it will help. Constraints, you see, inspire a form of loquaciousness. Skeletons are what we hang things on. Area 47 is a place of bare bones and it is also an island battlemented by stone. You want to understand the significance of fountains and peacocks and gardens and stones? Find yourself an island. Fortify it.

□

Adam Aros pulled up his WordPool and started to type: The first impact was felt all along the Victory Gardens when the Spanish ship, *Aboyos*, came under attack on Saturday 20 April 2099 at approximately 3.14 SST, he wrote. There are books on Saturdays, it came back. There is a lore of days.

There had been a series of impacts. For almost three minutes the hull of the *Aboyos* had been assaulted with what staff variously described as high-impact weapons, meteors the size of cannonballs, intensely focused beams of light, a rain of marbles, terrible hands and fists, a torrent of debris, space junk, industrial jackhammers, catapults, slingshots, cluster bombs, guided missiles, drones, nuts, bolts and machinery. The British-designed hull had survived intact, but on a spacewalk afterwards a delegation described it as looking uncannily like the moon: pocked and cratered and with deep hollows that resembled dead oceans. There hadn't been enough time to scramble any defences and, besides, the Victory Gardens, the earth itself, had never experienced, or fully prepared for, an attack from without.

At first cameras appeared to reveal nothing but streaks of light, travelling at incredible speeds, emerging, seemingly, from nowhere. Further out, however, a pattern could be discerned, a series of lights that came to be known as the Luna Armada, not just because they resembled a ghostly naval fleet when blown up to maximum resolution, but also because they resembled moths, their 'sails' or 'wings' a pale translucent green, moths rising up, or angels, their wings extended behind them and on their wings what appeared as eyes, Horus-like whorls of colour, of black and red and pale yellow and white, and there, in the centre, a chthonic, pond-scum green. They appeared to rise up, slowly, moving in and out of formation until they cohered in a single point like the foggy film of a planet, before disappearing altogether.

The Victory Gardens were set on a war footing with no idea when or from where they might strike next. But not everyone was preparing for an assault. Aros gave a speech, an impassioned one. He argued that they had no right to treat the Luna Armada as unequivocally hostile. Think of a moth, he said, attracted by the light, hurling its broken body, again and again, against a bulb, against the glass of a window. We have made our presence in the universe known; we have signalled our interest in becoming full galactic citizens. With the ring of the Victory Gardens we have lit up the earth. Think of wild horses. Think of dolphins. Who would have believed that one day we would harness and ride on the backs of these incredible creatures, separated from us by a gulf of biology and physiognomy? A gulf that truly is as vast as the great distances between the stars. Who first thought to swim with dolphins? Remember, he insisted, they did no serious damage, they took no lives. This is first contact. How did we picture it? That they would arrive bearing gifts, following our star, like the three wise men? That they would knock on the door and ask for passage? Well, they knocked alright. Now we must be very careful how we answer.

Of course, there were dissenting voices. What of wolves, some said, what of lions? Would you have us make of them as dogs? There were suspicions, too. What about Spain? someone asked. Why them in particular? It may just have been their position at the zenith, their place in the wheel at that moment. But the rumours resurfaced. What of Spain's ongoing petitioning for full lunar colonisation? Hadn't the impact been compared to a map of the moon? That was far-fetched, Aros came back. People see what they want to see. It's the equivalent of staring at the sun up here; after a while you start to see the moon superimposed on everything. Besides, in that case, why did this Luna Armada not go straight for the moon itself?

Perhaps they came from there, someone said.

Look, Aros said, the whole world is right now mobilising its combined military might in anticipation of an attack. We're here on the front line. We have a great opportunity. Let them worry about the military logistics, the potential for catastrophe. Let us stay true to our guiding principles. What do we have to lose? This is the moment. Let us welcome them as brothers.

Or tame them as animals, someone else joked. But it wasn't funny.

Back in his quarters, Aros put a call through to his wife. Hi, baby, he said. Baby, she said, is everything okay up there? I heard they were sending up the military. And what are they going to do up here? In space the military are helpless. They should stay down on earth, out of our way, where at least their guns work, instead of gurning out the window up here. We're all helpless right now, it's like being born. They're going to have to get used to it. What's the atmosphere like down there?

Oh, you know: euphoria, mass panic, jubilation, paranoia, religious fervour, civil unrest.

So, business as usual?

Ha ha. That's funny. There was a huge revival meeting on Glasgow Green. They think it's the beginning of the rapture. Your friend Robert Scott was on television. He was quite good, actually. He was on some talk show alongside some politicians and religious figures and philosophers and scientists. They billed him as a defrocked priest and he burst out laughing. He said the events of the past few weeks have effectively defrocked every single member of this panel. It's funny: it's the scientists that are the most flummoxed. And they admit it. I always thought when we first encountered intelligent life that it would be religion that would take the hit. But they think it's holy war up there. They think it's judgement coming down.

What else did Scott say?

He said we need a new mind. He said that approaching the future with a mindset from the past is like dreaming inside a dream. That's how he put it.

Dreaming inside a dream, Aros said. But that's it exactly. There's something on the tip of my tongue, a song, a piece of music. I can't shake it. I'm telling you, Sarah, I've had this feeling ever since I arrived up here. It's as if what is taking place is somehow written over what's come before. As if back of here there is another sequence of events holding everything in place, a scaffolding or a skeleton structure, but like an arrangement of music, that's what I keep feeling, like a melody on top of a melody, but a forgotten melody, somehow, like this is some kind of strange counterpoint to a melody that has somehow been dismembered, transposed by time. Yet somehow, inexplicably, it remains harmonious. It's as if the Victory Gardens themselves, this circle around earth, is just another layer of the dream. And there are gaps, openings, where the Luna Armada came through, a pause, a second's cessation that works as a kind of tunnel. When you watch the footage of the Armada, these distant lights, these luminous wings moving in this grand distant formation, intertwining with each other and floating up, it's impossible not to think of silent music, not to see it as dance. But who is the dreamer?

Who is the composer, you mean? Sarah said.

Who is the creator? Aros replied. But really, think about it, is a dream dreamed? Who dreams dreams? There is only the dream.

☐

Over the weeks and months that followed first contact
Adam Aros was visited by a series of unnerving waking
dreams. He would rise from sleep to a succession of short-
lived blanks, of subtle erasures and momentary removals.
At first it was a framed painting that hung on the wall of
his bedroom whose subject had been replaced by a rectangle
of blank, piercing white. It took several moments before the
peasants, busy at harvest, were returned to the scene, as in
the lifting of an all-enveloping blizzard. Other nights it was
his obsessively organised book collection that disappeared
from the shelves, replaced just as suddenly as if by some
supernatural sleight of hand. Then the planets themselves
went out and came back on. Through his window the moon,
for the blink of an eye, or more properly the beating of a
great wing, became a black hole in the sky.

As always, when moments of breakdown threatened to
overwhelm him, Aros resorted to painting his way out.
He painted the ghost moths of the Luna Armada, their
translucent wings, their invisible eyes.

In order to internalise his experiences of nocturnal
dislocation he painted the moths as white on white, their
delicate wings as see-through veils, as though they lay
draped like a thin film across the eyeballs themselves.
He dressed his sleeping quarters with these compulsive
portraits, these deep seeings.

He wondered if, when waking from sleep, whether the
moths themselves might appear, might rise from the canvas
– from the eye – and make themselves known. Form from
out of nothing, he reasoned, and nothing from out of form.
But they never rose. Of course not, Aros told himself. He

rose from his bed and pulled up his WordPool. I painted the moths but they never rose, he wrote. They are trapped, it said. They are imprisoned inside of me.

◻

Robert Scott's condition was deteriorating. Three days ago he had suffered a stroke in his cabin at Loch Awe. Barbara had found him on the floor in front of the couch, unable to move. Get some nets and some ropes, he had instructed her, you can haul me in with that. He was clearly confused. Barbara called an ambulance, but it took an hour to get there after they arrived on the opposite shore by mistake. Barbara stood helpless on the deck, her poor husband talking to himself inside, giving constant instruction on how best to raise him from the floor, the flashing lights of the ambulance across the dark water, turning the night sky blue. It's an ice cream van, Scott said. It's my brother Gregor in an ice cream van. He has come to rescue me. She looked at Scott, curled on the floor, his legs pulled up tight against his chest. He looks like a little boy, she thought. They took him out on a stretcher and he asked her for water and she filled a baby's bottle for him. How else could he drink it lying down? The ambulance sat outside for some time. Barbara watched from the window. Now she was unable to move. Is he dying out there? she wondered. Is he dying out there in the ambulance? Still she didn't move. The medics told her to follow the ambulance in her car when they left. Until then she stood at the window and imagined her husband, pictured the interior of the ambulance, tried to imagine the loosening of his thoughts, his face from above, the wonder and terror inside him, the harsh light, the green uniforms of the medics, bent over him, the coded conversation. You have become a little boy, she told him, and she held the ambulance in her arms.

By the time she arrived at the hospital Scott was no longer conscious. He had been awake when he arrived, the nurse said. She had asked him if he knew where he was. She declined to say if he replied.

The sheets were pulled up to his neck so that he appeared as a disembodied head. His face was lost in the white of the pillow; translucent, painted on. There was a halo like a pale shadow around him. He's dwindling, the doctor said. It sounded like an errant schoolboy, Barbara thought, deliberately wasting time. They asked her if he required a priest to perform the last rites. Best to cover all bases, she thought, and she agreed. He was the most miserable priest she had ever encountered: gruff, unpleasant and with a monotonous way of talking. Not the best argument for the priesthood, she thought.

He laid his hands on Scott's head, Scott's papier-mâché head, she thought, don't crush it. He began the Commendation of the Dying. Barbara didn't recognise any of the passages he quoted. Then he walked off and left the two of them alone. Barbara touched his face. Then she leaned over and kissed him. He still smelled like himself. Every so often his leg would kick. He could be paralysed down one side, the nurse had told her. My baby, she said, and she cradled his head in her breast, my poor little baby. Don't die yet, she said. Please come back to me. But secretly, in her heart, she knew that now was as good a time to die as any.

□

When Peter Muldoon was only twelve years old he developed a terrible stammer that lasted until he was a young adult. Stammer is a word that is used to encompass many different and unrelated difficulties with the articulation of words. In Muldoon's case, or so he claimed, he had actually developed an allergy against a certain letter of the alphabet. It made him sick. It was the letter D. Words that ended in D were especially problematic. The end, say. This made things difficult, as you can imagine. Many words ending with the letter D signify things that have happened or that are over. Respired is to have already taken a breath. Retired is to be all over. Hammered is to be already drunk. Convinced is to have fallen for the argument. Perplexed is to have not understood. However, minus the ability to articulate a D, Muldoon could never have completed the first half of this sentence. So the absence of a D in his vocabulary, or, more properly, on the tip of his tongue, meant that he lived – or more properly, live – in an eternal present. Respiring, retiring, hammering, convincing, perplexing, all of these were no problem. But a word like dead, as you can imagine, became a complete impossibility. Should he attempt to articulate it, most people would believe that he was instead merely pausing in his speech: ea, eh, eh?

As an artist, which is what Muldoon became by the age of seventeen, his condition presented him with myriad opportunities. His friends encouraged him. They compared his condition to that of a young castrato. Your voice could break at any moment, they told him, make the most of it.

At this point Muldoon made the decision to remove the letter D from his writing. He became, if you like, Peter

Muloon. If Peter Muloon ha written this sentence then it woul rea like this. Or more like this.

Of course, his art tutors thought he was faking it. They believed him cannier than he was in reality. There were many artists who had made the decision to live in the past. There were many students at the art school who dressed in tweeds and wore plus-fours and who went home to garrets without heating or electricity. Who scorned cars and who walked everywhere, who wrote with calligraphic pens dipped in inkpots. Who used Brylcreem on their hair and who wore moustaches.

But it would be difficult to name an artist who chose – or was chosen, arguably – to live in the present. However, Muldoon himself rejected the use of the word present. Rather, he claimed, I was force to be prior. Either way the lack – or forfeit – of one letter seemed to make all the difference.

In order to incorporate this perpetuating lack, which is what Muloon called his early paintings, perpetuating lacks, he began to work in text-based pieces, primarily. At first he would paint odd gnomic phrases, black on white, things like 'Efuse /Unphase', and of course people would read them as though a phantom D had been dropped. A perpetuating lack, Muloon explained, is something that even when it isn't invoke is implie or transpose through the very knowlege of the existence of the lack. It's like having a club foot, he said, or a eforme face, an everyone interpreting everything that happene in your life in the light of that. They will make lepers of all of us, he said. That was hard to misinterpret. But had he said, I believe in me, people would immediately assume he was having a crisis of faith in himself. The perpetuating lack would add a D where it could and send all of Muloon's self-belief packing into the past.

Of course, there were many amateur psychologists amongst his friends and family who attempted to account for Muloon's horror of the letter D. It wasn't difficult to seek out a David or a Donald in the family or at school or in the vicinity of where he had grown up whose very presence, it was then implied, had been toxic to the young boy. The usual explanations were bandied about: sexual abuse; fear of castration; domineering father; suffocating mother; the pitfalls of toilet training. Muloon himself pointed to his obsessive reading habits. I didn't like to finish a book, he said, when in reality he said, I in't like to finish a book. This made little sense, really, as books don't always end in D. Indeed, E may be just as common. The last book of the Old Testament, for instance, ends in an E, with a curse. The last book of the New Testament ends with an N, with an amen, predictably. Moving to literature, *Lolita*, by Vladimir Nabokov, of course ends, unsurprisingly, with an A. James Joyce's *Ulysses* ends with an S. So you see, from this brief examination of literature, that Muloon's claim is unlikely. Unless he was primarily reading pulp. Of course, he could simply have meant that he didn't like to get to the en. Which, if you think about it, is how the New Testament ens.

Muloon's breakthrough piece was when he was commissioned, at the age of twenty-three, to contribute a public artwork that would be displayed on the side of a building next to the motorway just outside the centre of Glasgow. At first the city council proposed the use of the wall of a large warehouse to the west of the city. But Muloon petitioned to have his work displayed on one of the huge gasometers at Provan gas works to the east of the city. He imagined a work that would expand and contract, rising up and down according to the volume of gas stored inside. The city agreed, somehow, and in the summer of his twenty-third year, on a particularly wet and stormy afternoon, the art was unveiled. In huge black letters on a white rectangle, Muloon had written 'You Too Will Isappear'.

□

In the wake of Robert Scott's death many characters came out of the woodwork with tales to tell, the most controversial of which was a previously unknown first wife who claimed that Scott had been a child abductee. Sophia Clark was a professional violinist and amateur novelist who had published a series of UFO 'romances' with titles like *The Hovering Heart, I Won't Let You Down* and *Three Times a Lady.* She did not claim to be an abductee herself, rather that throughout her life abductees had been hopelessly attracted to her, 'like a moth to a flame,' she laughed, and winked her eye.

Still, it was her first time in space. Adam Aros had invited her to give a presentation on Robert Scott's previously undocumented early years after Scott's widow Barbara had confirmed her description of three circular 'burn marks' on Scott's chest, which Barbara said Scott had claimed were caused by a boiling kettle that someone had thrown at him during a dispute in jail. Sophia, inevitably, disputed Barbara's account, claiming that Scott had told her that he had received these same burns during some kind of investigative experiment aboard a flying saucer.

Space makes me giddy, Sophia announced. But luckily I brought along my giddy pills. She offered Aros a small blue pill. What are these? he asked her. Betty Hills, she said, and she shrugged. Aros declined. Stick, bubbly, she said. Sophia was five foot one with a shock of black wiry hair. And she had a mouth on her. What have you been up to since you arrived on *The Advance*? Aros asked her. Not much, she said. I got the grand tour and all that shit. Mostly I've been sleeping and having sex.

Who she had been having sex with wasn't exactly clear.

I have to ask you a question, Aros said. We want to know if you will submit to hypnosis.

What the fuck is the point in that? I've never been on a flying saucer. I'm not the one with the experiences.

It's just to verify your story. There are a lot of rumours about Scott doing the rounds since his death, as I'm sure you are aware. Your story could be of seismic importance to our own mission.

And what is your mission? Sophia asked him.

Listen, Aros said. I knew Scott a little myself. Before he died we became friends. It was me that invited him to give a talk to *The Advance*, a new vision of man in space. I thought of him as a religious man, true, but a freethinker nonetheless. He talked about new gods. He talked about the final death of Christ. But he never mentioned aliens. I want to know why not.

Think about it, Sophia said. His death coincided, almost perfectly, with the arrival of alien life.

Yes.

Well, think about it.

I am thinking about it.

Think some more. Maybe he was a cocoon.

That doesn't make any sense.

Maybe I'm a cocoon.

That make even less sense.

Well, in that case, why do you want to open me up? Why do you want to get inside me? You want to hypnotise the hell out of me so that there's no one home while you poke about inside, see what's secreted itself in there, see what's growing.

Something's growing inside you?

Something's always growing inside you, honey, she said. Otherwise there'd be nothing new under the sun. Listen, she said. I took a vow, I can't go into the specifics, but I was involved, let's say, with a group where we had to take a vow never to allow ourselves to be hypnotised. Never. Under any circumstances. And you know, I never have. I don't engage with television. I don't use mobile technology. I don't care about interactive movies or sex games. I have a filter on my brains, she said. I only let in what I decide to let in. Plus all that other stuff that you have no choice over. But I'm going to let you in. Hypnotism is when you're all caught up in someone else's game. And you couldn't possibly play me.

□

There are a lot of cats in here, Sophia said, though she more droned it than said it. Ever since Evans had put her under she had been talking in a weird robot voice that everyone thought was a put-on.

Cat shit everywhere, she said, in a steady, monotonous voice. The place needs a good clean.

Where are you? Evans asked her.

Good question, she droned. I'm . . . She paused. I would say that I was back in the garden.

Where is the garden?

Everywhere. No, wait a minute. Paris.

Who's in the garden?

Good question, she droned. I would say that there are three people in the garden.

Who are they?

That's difficult to say. At a guess I would say they are father, mother and son.

Who are you?

Stupid question.

I'll ask it anyway.

The daughter, obviously. Listen, she said in a hollow, automatic voice. This isn't about you.

Are you talking to me? Evans asked her.

You're the only voice.

Where am I?

Good question. In the kitchen, perhaps?

Where's Scott?

With his mother and father.

In the garden?

Obviously.

Okay. I want you to ask Scott something.

He's speaking already. Can't you hear him?

I thought you said I was the only voice?

That is correct.

But it isn't about me.

That's true.

What is Scott saying?

How far is it to heaven?

How far is it to heaven?

Yes.

How far is it to heaven?

How far is it to heaven.

Okay, well, that's unanswerable.

Next question.

Ask Scott about his abduction.

You just did.

Scott was taken to heaven?

Our true heavenly nature is fire unsound.

I don't understand.

That is why our lives and loves are ruled by heavenly fires.

You mean fate?

Fate is a blimp, a weather balloon.

Did Scott have contact?

Yes, he touched it. There were burns on his body. And on his penis.

On his penis?

Yes. They removed it and they put it back on again.

In heaven?

If you like.

You said you were Scott's sister.

I am the sister of all the disappeared.

☐

This excerpt from Sophia Clark's *The Hovering Heart*:

Amanda's cruel parents forbade her to go to the beach after dark. The lights of the previous three nights were the talk of the village. And the outlandish man that had appeared from beneath the waters. He had appeared naked for all to see but not as a man might. It was more that he radiated his maleness than wore it. To Amanda, who encountered him first, beneath the tree on the beach, he appeared as a god. All my life I have dreamed of you, she told him, as he held her head to his chest. To be returned to you, my prince.

My darling, he said, in a strange, uninflected voice, I have crossed the great divide to be with you. In that time, I have seen stars rise up and fall from the skies to their doom. I have travelled through cold wastes, through timeless heat. I have seen the old gods pass and be renewed. All the while you were the ship of my heart. He ran his curiously translucent hands through Amanda's long dark hair.

In his fingers she could hear the rushing of his blood, louder than the tide that stormed across the sand.

Even the wind, it seemed, raged in protest against their meeting. Some will call it unnatural, our love, the man revealed. They will say that we defied the order of things just to meet like this, this once, forever. Oh, don't say it is only once, Amanda cried. You are the first man I have ever loved. And I recognised you immediately, as soon as you emerged from that great ball of light that hovered over the ocean and threatened to turn back the tide. I knew you were meant for me and always have been from the beginning of time! Oh, my man, she swooned, and she wept. I cannot stay for long, the man confided. A heavenly love like ours must destroy us in the end. For this moment I have given my all. Now be gone from me, my darling. We have three more nights in which to celebrate our love, three storm-tossed days to dream of it. At which he let her go and she appeared to fall down, softly, into the warm, wet sand, like a butterfly, or a leaf.

But they had been seen. Bascomb, the village idiot, whose head, rumour had it, had been caught in a heavy door as a little baby, and whose eyes had been forced to either side of his head like a seal, had followed the lights during one of his nocturnal navigations and had spied the couple's unearthly embrace from behind a tree.

The next morning rumours were afoot. The stars come 'own, Bascomb told his father, who at first slapped him around the head and damned him for being a retard. The man hel' the woman in his light, he cried, which drew another blow from his father and an upping of his condition to the level of spastic. The hovering heart, he wept, the hovering heart came 'own and kisse the girl! And what girl would this be? his father asked him. It were Amana, Bascomb cried. It were Amana with the long hair hanging 'own. That harlot, his father spat. Now he was interested. He made enquiries with the neighbours. Oh aye, Mrs Bustard said. There were lights in the sky alright, over by the beach, they were; didn't you hear my dogs barking? Had them in a terror of a fright, it did.

I'm afraid I sleep with my ears bunged up and my eyes blindfolded ever since the passing of my good wife, Bascomb's father explained to her. As a result, I saw and heard nothing. My beloved son, however, saw everything.

Bascomb's father made his way to Amanda's parents' house and told them the terrible news. They were grief-stricken and the fear was in them. I suspect witchery, Bascomb's father told them, but with the powers of the priesthood invested in me, we may still have time to turn back the advance of Satan's hordes and their possession of your daughter's tender body. These are wild claims, Amanda's father returned. And all turning on the word of, if you'll excuse my pardon, a simpleton that looks like a fish. An angel touched him on the head when he was born,

Bascomb's father corrected him. And now he has the power. God drew him to that storm-wracked beach last night for a reason. To witness the fall of your daughter and her wanton congress with demons! Where is she? Bascomb's father demanded. I tell you there is still time. I only want to help her.

She is asleep, Amanda's father explained. Come, he said, let us confront her together. Amanda's mother wept, Amanda's sister moaned. Together the two fathers entered the girl's bedroom, where they found her naked on the bed, asleep in a shallow pool of water, her pale white skin covered in a thin layer of seaweed and sand, her long wet hair spread across the pillow and with a small garland of flowers now wilting in her hand. Why, if I had not known it was your daughter, Bascomb's father turned to him, I would have reckoned it was Ophelia herself. Turn away your eyes, man, Amanda's father demanded of him, lest you too are tempted by the light! It's not my eyes that must be stopped, Bascomb's father returned, but young Ophelia's here. We must tear out her eyes and put in two eyes of wood.

Amanda woke with a start and leaped from the bed, throwing the blankets around her naked body. She stood in the corner of the room, panting and silent. We have not come to ravish you, Bascomb's father announced, at which point Amanda's father began to sob, silently, in sympathy with his daughter and in horror of the situation. But something must be done. You were seen in congress with a demon last night, lit up in all descended fires. No, Amanda protested, it's not true! Who says this against me?

My son, the seer, encountered you both on the beach, locked in an unearthly embrace. You intend to deny it when the light of your passion lit up the entire village and drove the very dogs to distraction?

Your son, Amanda replied, is a human vegetable. Better take the dogs' word than his.

Very well, we shall take the word of the dogs. In which case we must still put out your eyes.

Father, Amanda burst, and she ran to her father's side and begged him to soften his heart. She was wet to the touch and smelled of the depths. It was as if her body were turned inside out, her father thought, and he couldn't bring himself to hold her. He pictured the viscous texture of newly exposed organs, the mucus of the heart, the terms of the womb, and he felt himself overcome. My darling, he said, what have we done to you that you would seek solace in the arms of Satan's infernal army?

I bathed in moonlight, swam in the fire of the stars, that is all!

And what of the glowing man in whose embrace you appeared to expire?

A phantom, a trick of the light, an escapee from the collapsed maze of Bascomb's mind!

And what of the lights, the testimony of the dogs?

Father, it was the brightest night of the year, is it not
the peak of midsummer? The stars were joyous in their
revelling, the moon itself pregnant with delight! I was
drawn to their frolic, it is true. But no more did I embrace
a man fallen from the sky than I gave myself up to
wantonness.

At the very least this is idolatry, paganism, Bascomb's
father spat. Confine her to her room. We will take a group
to the sands tonight and we will make vigil for the return of
the creature ourselves, God help us.

With that, a mob was raised. Donnelly, Gilhooley, McIntyre,
Peebles, Washington, Robinson, Bart, Peterson, McPheat,
all gathered under the leadership of Bascomb's father. They
stood outside in the dwindling light and they watched the
skies with trepidation. It was decided that Bascomb himself
would lead them to the spot and as a precaution they fixed
a long, heavy rope around his waist. That way we can safely
use him as bait, his father explained, and everyone agreed it
was a splendid idea.

At the last minute Amanda's father joined them, to see, face
to face, 'the author of her fate'.

As the sky grew dark they made their way through the
trees, Bascomb out ahead, connected to the mob by the
length of rope. The women of the village huddled in circles
to watch them go, this strange silhouette, now lost in the
woods.

They came to the beach. It was true what Amanda had
said, all of the stars were out, and the moon lit up the

tempestuous water. The mob stopped at the edge of the trees and fed the rope out. Bascomb walked to the edge of the water and then into the water until he was knee-deep in the water. Then he looked up. Above him the figure of an oversized man hovered in the air, although his genitalia did not identify him as such. Behind him, attached to a sort of silver umbilical, spun a huge globe of light.

Bascomb began to cry, softly, and the man descended a set of invisible stairs and embraced him.

Don't worry, my darling, he said. There was nothing you could have done. With a blood-curdling scream the mob burst from the trees and set about him. They pierced his side with a pitchfork and his guts fell out. They hacked at his neck with an axe. They wounded where his genitals should have been. He fell into the shallow waters, whereupon Amanda's father straddled his body and repeatedly thrust a large broken knife into his chest. Just as suddenly everything was still. The body of the man from hell lay mutilated in the shallow waters, unnameable viscera bobbing in the tide, the waters now a fetid electric-blue. Suddenly there was an ear-splitting roar and the great globe of light that hung above the ocean seemed to contract inwards and swallow itself with a sound like the sky being torn apart. Locked up in her room, several miles away, Amanda heard the sound and felt that her own heart had been rent in two. She threw herself down on her bed and she tore at her hair and bit the inside of her mouth.

We're finished here, Bascomb's father announced, but not before he took a stick and speared one of the misshapen organs that washed up on the shore like jellyfish. Blue blood, he said, and he pointed to the deformed mass as it released its terrible cargo. This man was not one of God's chosen. At which they turned and headed back to the village, this time dragging Bascomb, in tears, behind them.

The next day the body was gone. There was no trace of the crushed and speared organs, of their uncanny electric-blue secretions, nothing to mark the scene of the crime except a series of oversized footsteps that almost seemed burned in the sand and that appeared to lead out of the water and through the trees and back towards the village. That was when the stories began.

□

Peter Muldoon paced the corridors and viewing galleries of *The Advance* alone. In space everything echoes, he thought as he passed looping corridors that turned on themselves like strips of spaghetti, bubbled windows like the eyes of amphibians, deserted hallways like underground car parks. And then there were the stars: oppressive, omnipresent.

Tomorrow he would give his first talk as 'artist-in-residence'. It seemed even phonier now, more futile, in the light of the Luna Armada and in the revelation of his own gods. But what to say? I stand at the centre of the world, something portentous like that. It was true. But then, hadn't it always been? Every artist wants to redraw the universe so it more closely orbits themselves, or their conception of it, as it stands, right?

That's all you are now, he laughed to himself, a successful artist.

He made his way to the canteen and ordered an Irish coffee. Through the window small ships came and went, bringing military reinforcements, evacuating civilian personnel. There were soldiers stationed all around, even in here, pointlessly displaying their weapons. It was all so ridiculous, what did they intend to do?

Here you are, he heard a voice from behind him burst. It's you, oh my! Muldoon turned in his seat. A small woman with an explosion of black curly hair put her hand on his shoulder. She looked Jewish, he thought, bookish. A little eccentric, but with the buzzing energy of a small planet. An unravelled red scarf hung round her neck like the frazzled tail of a comet. Look at me, she laughed. Here I am!

And you would be? he said.

Oh, I'm sorry, I forgot we haven't been introduced yet. I'm Sophia, I'm the secret wife, she beamed. I appeared out of nowhere after the death of Robert Scott. I was his partner, his confidante, his co-conspirator. She took a seat across from him. And I'm a lover of abductees, she winked.

I met his last wife, Barbara, Muldoon said. That bitch, Sophia mock-spat. Then she cracked up laughing. I was just about to say, how do you like it in heaven, she laughed. But we're not there yet! How do you like it in space, is what I meant to say. Every little boy dreams of being an astronaut, right? Of walking on the moon, of speeding through the galaxy in a sexy space suit.

I've walked on the moon, Muldoon said.

How was it?

It was weird, actually. It was almost kind of a let-down.

How can the moon be a let-down?

I think it's because I was there.

You mean your very presence gave it a sense of bathos?

Yes, in a way. Muldoon laughed, awkwardly.

Sophia nodded and looked at him with understanding.

There was some kind of disturbance at the bar, some kind of argument going on. He saw the soldiers move in and separate two elderly men. That's what it has come to for the army, he thought, breaking up disputes between pensioners.

Feelings are running high, Sophia said. There's a lot at stake. Some of the stories that people have lived their entire lives are about to come undone.

It feels like that, Muldoon said. Then he paused. It's true that you can't escape from yourself, even when you are on the moon. I've had this feeling my entire life, in a way. But I could never bring myself to admit it. It would be like cancelling the future, it would be like saying there is nowhere to go and nothing will ever get better.

You could just as easily say that nothing will ever get worse.

That's the thing, Muldoon said, and Sophia watched as a thin trickle of coffee ran down his beard, it sometimes feels like things are going one way, or, wait, let me put it this way, that things, outcomes, moments, are hanging on a precipice, are teetering at the very edge of . . . something . . . the edge of the end or the edge of a descent, the end of something, like when you come to the end of the land, and you're in a vehicle and the vehicle stops halfway over the cliff. There's either stability, or there's collapse. And stability, temporary stability – because the wind is whipping up and the cliffs are giving way – is all you can hope for.

How did you become so gloomy?

Through good fortune, Muldoon smiled. Through achievement, through success, through finding myself at the centre of the world. You know when you're on holiday, and you've looked forward to it for so long, and you're escaping your day-to-day worries, you're getting away from your hellish job, from bad weather, from dull day-to-day strictures like you shouldn't drink that much, or you shouldn't spend that much? You know when you look forward to it so much, so much, and then, when you're there, in the back of your mind you realise that really you don't feel any different, even with all this free time, even with your worries far away in another country, on another planet, that in the midst of happiness there's this same underlying condition, this . . . boredom. This constant desire to be other than you are, which comes up against this feeling that is impossible to change, this growing realisation that there is nothing worth running towards and that nothing can be held in your hand, at least nothing that will make any difference. People drop out, they disappear, and we envy them. They gave up, we think, maybe that's the key. Giving up, letting go, becoming one of the invisible.

Like a feather on the breath of God, Sophia said.

That's a nice way to put it. People always envy successful people, famous people, celebrities, pop stars. And no one can understand it when, again and again, they go insane, they take an overdose, they hang themselves in the garage. But achievement is the worst thing that can happen to you, because you find there's nothing there, it means nothing, there is nothing to be achieved and there is nothing beneath your feet but a long, long drop. At least if you never get to where you're going, you never realise it was a phantom all along. You're left believing there was a point, a stopping point, a destination. You just never reached it.

You're talking about heaven, Sophia said. It's no wonder we had to dream it up. It's either that or endlessness. An ocean without an island: what a thought! Tell me, Sophia said, and she leaned in closer to Muldoon, would it be any easier to be dreamed? Think about it. To be dreamed up means there is ground, down there, somewhere, the ground of the dream is the dreamer itself, right? That's why the dream is so seductive, right?

Do you believe the WordPool is real? she asked him.

Muldoon sat up in his chair. What? Of course it is.

You think it really works?

I'm really not sure. I always avoided getting one myself, at first. I was superstitious about it, I guess. Everyone is, even those that use it.

What if I told you I invented the WordPool? Sophia asked him. What if I told you that I wrote the book in which the WordPool appears?

Muldoon froze in his chair. He felt his memory turn itself inside out. Then he felt like he was drowning. He crossed his arms and held hard to his own body. He caught his breath. Finally he asked her. Are you Xstabeth? he said.

I made you so you couldn't say my name, she said. Then she stared at him without a word.

But I painted you, he said.

Say my name, she said.

Go, he said.

Down below, just behind her, the earth turned in silence.

Sophia got up from the table, pushed her chair back, and walked away.

□

The glow of Adam Aros's handheld WordPool lit his face like a vampire in a bad movie. Godforsaken island, it read, a great earthly love is all that will sustain you. Aros had been at it all night, freestyling, mind-blowing, trying to get to the bottom of it. And this is where he wound up. A godforsaken island. He had dreamed of being unable to walk forward, of the effort being crippling, and in his dream he turned around and walked backwards towards his goal, suddenly released from the weight of the future. He climbed through trapdoors, crawled through tiny impossible tunnels on the edges of things, scaled ladders at uncanny angles. In his dream his home was an impossible trapdoor in the sky that he was forever approaching, backwards. Something had broken, in the WordPool, in Aros's brain. Just like water, he wrote, time will find the weakest spot. After that, the deluge. So I step from my ship into my own city, came the response, which is the kingdom of heaven, where I with all the righteous shall enter out of so great a tribulation. Where is the locus of control? he asked it. Area 47, it read. Where is Area 47? The whole world is a hospital, it returned. Where is the entranceway to play? he asked it. Then it went dead. I've exhausted it, Aros thought, I've killed it, and in a triumphant fever he lay back on his bed and laughed and laughed and laughed.

□

Aros met Muldoon in the antechamber of the great debating hall, which was more of a bubble than a hall, really, a great transparent bubble with nothing but endless space above or below. Muldoon's presentation was to take place in an hour. Aros looks ill, Muldoon thought, Muldoon looks haunted, Aros thought. What's the story with Sophia? Muldoon asked him. A fraud, he said, a fruit loop. Evans had a team put her under, and there was nothing there. She seems to have made up the whole thing.

I've remembered something that happened on the moon, Muldoon said. That's what I'm going to talk about.

The moon is a balloon, Muldoon announced to a half-empty auditorium. After all, who cared about the thoughts of an artist and poet, now that reality itself had the veneer of the fantastic? The moon is a balloon, he said, the earth's plaything, let go, the toy of our childhood. When we first looked up, there it was, staring back down, into our cot, into our hospital bed. It was easy to mistake it for our father or our mother. Back then there was no difference. But really, it was we who gave birth to it. Just as in the story where the earth gives birth to the moon through its side. The earth is made fertile by the stars. I chose to paint the stars. I painted them in new formations, I gave them new names. But I first saw them, first realised them, when I visited the moon. Because of the moon, every child dreams of colonisation and of sexy space suits. There were some laughs around the room. I was unremarkable in that regard.

I travelled to the moon, illegally, to join a protest against the building of a second spaceport in the Sea of Tranquillity. There was the promise of riots and of some good bands on the bill, which is what every adolescent dreams of.

Again, there were some awkward laughs.

The Treaty of Twelve had attempted to close the moon to civilian traffic after the first wave of protesters arrived, but the moon wasn't a nation state with borders and boundaries and fixed entrances and exits – at least not yet! – and so there was really no way to stop the fleets of handmade ships

– Snowdrops, they called them – swarming across the face of the moon.

We touched down in the south-west of the Sea of Fecundity. I'll never forget that first journey across the lunar landscape, the great arcing steps of our convoy, this feeling of endlessness, of incredible clarity, of scale revealed, the epic poetry of distance, it was impossible to fit it into your eyeball, whatever you could cram in there became the horizon. The movements, the soft gentle movements in zero gravity, felt more like swimming, as if we had regressed somehow, returned to the sea, like wise dolphins, and as we moved across the surface it was as if we were dancing at the bottom of the ocean. Still, there was something wrong, something disappointing, as if the idea I had of myself walking on the moon would forever outstrip the reality of it, like distance or remove was part of its magic. Once you get there, walking on the moon is just walking on the moon, not the . . . I don't know, not the revelation that the idea of you walking on the moon would seem to contain or imply.

And that's when I first saw the stars, really saw them. Their figures were so clear, yet nothing like we see them on earth. This slight shifting of the centre, a mere 200,000 miles or so, had resulted in a radically new perspective. The stars seemed to gather themselves in powers. We all walked with our heads up, or down, straining, as if we were hanging from the moon in space. I felt alive, finally, free of past and future. As we approached the Sea of Tranquillity we could already make out all the lights from the new spaceport, there was something quite beautiful about it, this explosion of light on the horizon, this fiery white corona, reaching up, but of course we all groaned and said it was ugly, a pluke on the face of the moon, someone said, industrial debris, a dumping ground, they're blotting out the stars, someone else said, but it wasn't true, the stars were clearer than they had ever been.

It made me think of a campfire, a single great bonfire, signalling our presence, like here we are on this lonely stone, stranded. Come and get us. There was something brave and forlorn about it. Still, no one wanted to see the moon turn into another shopping mall, another multi-storey car park, which is surely what would happen, in the end. Protesters had erected a series of huge geodesic domes around the area where the Apollo 11 mission had touched down and there were small buggies parked around them filled with amplifiers and small PAs and portable generators. Inside the domes they had managed to create artificial atmospheres thanks to salvaged military equipment and a few renegade government scientists who had become hippy drop-outs due to environmental concerns. This was the beginning of the movement, in a way. It really was like a music festival, they wanted to call it Moonstock but that was in poor taste, I thought, I mean, it made it feel like just another fucking teenage bacchanal.

We set up our own accommo-dome on the outskirts of the camp and then a few of us took a walk – though it was more of an arcing bounce – over to the spaceport construction site. Why do they even need a second spaceport? No one was clear. The first one had resulted in the placement of new telescopes, a new lunar study centre and some minor excavation work. Why a second one? All that anyone could think was that it was the first step in lunar colonisation, something that certain nation states had increasingly been calling for in the wake of impending environmental catastrophe. Of course, the creation of the Victory Gardens, thanks to the good work of all of the people gathered here, made colonisation irrelevant. But back then it really looked like it might take place.

I saw people with patches on their space suits: Keep the Moon Wild; Nicht Auf Luna Lebensraum, which Helpless Clairvoyants had coined, and which joined the dots to the Nazis' land grab; Space Is Feral; Grow Up!; Use Your Imagination; Moon First; The Lunatics Are Taking Over the Adytum; all this kind of stuff.

And of course, with hippies involved, there was much talk of lunar forces that would come to our aid, sightings of inexplicable lights, reports of invisible presences, of shadowy life forms flitting around the boundaries of the spaceport and committing random acts of industrial sabotage. And, of course, there was a faction amongst the protesters that clung to the belief that the moon had once been occupied. Outings were arranged for groups to visit notorious craters like Eratosthenes, in the Sea of Rains, where the astronomer W.H. Pickering claimed to have seen the movements of migrating life forms. Of course no one was ever able to find this mythical moon tribe again. It was as if they had become invisible.

There was something eerie about the moon, which I'm sure many of you in the audience have visited and will probably have experienced yourself. There were murmurs in the audience, a few people said yup, and sure. It's almost as if this eternal migration was always taking place, Muldoon continued, and of course, here we all were, protesting against another.

The full military might of the Council of Twelve was out
in force. When we first cased the perimeter of the new
spaceport we could see lines of guards with riot equipment
assembled behind rings of steel fencing and barbed wire.
Obviously on the moon you can jump a lot higher, so fences
weren't the best means of defence, and of course, try firing
a gun up there. So there was a real sense of unease on both
sides, like we were coming up against possibilities, against
new modes of conflict that neither side had ever imagined
before. People began talking about a mass assault on the
spaceport, a spontaneous act of liberation. They talked
about how, back in the day, during a protest against the
Vietnam War, a group of heads had attempted to levitate
the Pentagon. Up here, some people said, levitation was
a real possibility. Others proposed a sort of co-ordinated
mass leaping where fleets of protesters would be propelled
into the air while attached to ground umbilicals and
would rain down on the spaceport from the skies while
attack buggies rammed the fences and forced their way
through. Someone else suggested that we declare our
raggle-taggle collection of geodesics a Free State and stage
a full occupation. It was all pretty vague, which made it
incredibly exciting.

When Helpless Clairvoyants touched down it really began to
have the feel of a genuine happening. I knew Firth Column,
the Clairvoyants' lead singer and guitarist, from art school.
We had been in the same year together. I saw him coming
down the ramp from their Snowdrop, which was shaped like
a pear and painted to look more like a single bright tear,
come to fertilise the moon, and I laughed when I saw that he
was wearing a pair of black shades beneath his visor. The
rest of the band followed, and roadies began wheeling out

stacks of Marshall amps. The Clairvoyants refused to play through anything else.

There were a number of bands on the bill, but no one was in any doubt that the Clairvoyants were the main event. They rarely played live, rarely gave interviews, and when they did they spoke only in German, even though they were all French. Sometimes their gigs consisted of a single chord, endlessly inflected, while Column played FX-destroyed guitar solos all over the top. On the day of the concert I took acid.

There were some whoops in the room, a few people even applauded.

Thank you very much, Muldoon said. I appreciate it. It wasn't a particularly heroic dose, but I hadn't taken it in years and it was a trip, for sure. I sat on the floor of this huge dome they had erected, and it was all lit up in pale whites and oranges and deep reds so that it felt as if I was behind a great eyelid or inside one of the organs of the body, even. I swear at one point the dome itself began to breathe, pulsing in and out like a great lung or a heart, more like, a heart that had been spilled on the moon. It was crazy. I watched a group of women on stage who were all dressed up in black skintight rubber space suits. They appeared to be singing backwards over the sounds of hacked transmissions from the earth to the moon played at ear-splitting volume, and every so often one of the women would leave the stage and float up in the air towards the roof of the dome and the rest of them would take out these long whips, like long lizard tongues, and whip her back down. At least, that's how I remember it.

There were a few laughs in the audience, a few jokes about the effects of LSD.

All of the Helpless Clairvoyants' roadies looked like they were tripping. They wore black all-in-one space suits with Nicht Auf Luna Lebensraum T-shirts. When the group played they formed a wall by locking arms at the front of the stage, so no one could get past. It looked amazing.

The gig was unbelievable; massively over-amped acid punk with endlessly reverbed vocals that seemed to consist of single syllables, simply exhaled. It was incredibly violent, when they played 'Krankenhaus Blues' the guitars sounded like they were tearing the sky apart, but there was something easy, inexorable, about the way the music progressed, like they were four receivers, channelling the music of the spheres. It was as if the stars above us were the score and Helpless Clairvoyants were simply reading it, or being played by it, more properly. It was elemental. I began to wonder about the genesis of their name. It made sense all of a sudden. And of course, back then, well, that was probably the moment that Xstabeth was born, somewhere in my mind, and her brother-sisters Lalino and Qbxl, all the paintings that I later made.

After they played, the atmosphere was really charged. People began chanting, Free the Moon, Free the Moon, and I imagined the moon severing its connection with earth and sending us all hurtling off into space. I wanted it to happen. It seemed like a good idea. I was peaking and ready to ride a dead stone through the cosmos at out-of-control speed.

I went to see the group backstage, but it was almost impossible to get near them; so many people were mobbing them. Then the bassist, Tomnado, spotted me and waved me over where a couple of roadies whisked me down this tunnel and into the inner sanctum. There were some girls around and Firth Column and the rest of the guys were spread out across a series of packing crates that were draped with Indian rugs and fabrics. Of course, they were all talking in German. When Column saw me, he raised his alco-pac and he toasted me. Heute ist Die Welt Tag! he said, and everyone cheered. Then he had his roadies clear the room of any hangers-on. Sorry, he said, I only speak in German in public.

I told him I loved the gig. That's phase one, he said. Phase two is the assault. The guitarist, Yacob Yacob, fell back prone across the packing crates at this point and he remained like that, immobile, for the rest of the evening. I was beyond impressed.

You're planning an assault? I asked him. Tomnado replied. We have information, he said. Intercepts that suggest there's a lot more going on here than any of us might have guessed. There's an entire subterranean complex, a bunker, beneath the new spaceport.

The spaceport isn't the point, Column underlined. It's only necessary for what lies beneath.

What do you think it is? I asked them. Dig this, Tomnado said. I think they found life. Beneath the surface. Or maybe the remains of a civilisation, Column added. Maybe there's a whole new world down there. The point is, for us, the assault on the spaceport is only an excuse, a necessary diversion. We have the plans; we know where the entrance is. We're going in, under cover of a riot.

Just then someone knocked on the door. A beautiful blonde girl stuck her head into the room. Glückliche Tage sind wieder da! Column burst, and the girl danced her way over to him and curled up in his lap. Das ist Candy, he said, vom Himmel. I took another hit, and the whole night dissolved.

The assault on the spaceport is something that I'll never forget, the spectacle of it. On the moon everything takes place in slow motion. You can see the future before it happens. A fleet of handmade Snowdrops took off from locations all across the Sea of Fecundity, just behind us, and passed over our heads, like a black cloud or a murder of crows. There were handmade junkers, primitive planet-hoppers, ships in the shape of strange birds, metal crocodiles, imperfect globes, even some with primitive sails with markings on them like red crosses or black suns. Around the perimeter fencing, makeshift ramps were rushed into place, and eager cosmonauts launched themselves over the wires, some tumbling gleefully head over heels, others raining down hand in hand, some rebounding hopelessly against the tall metal mesh. They came from the other side too, and in the distance you could make out all of these little dots, human snowdrops or petrified tears, falling from the skies.

Finally, there was the moon buggy assault battalion. I rode alongside the rest of Helpless Clairvoyants, with their drummer The Doom driving, and at first we held back, looking for a gap in the fence, for the weakest point. Then

we saw this small ship, this ball of light, hovering high
above the railings in front of us. It was pandemonium
by this point, like a stop-motion explosion all around us,
but this single light seemed unconnected somehow, as if
it was back of the whole scene. Then it lowered down two
claws, it seemed like, two hooks hanging down, and it tore
the fencing from the ground. The Doom stepped on the gas
and suddenly we were inside. But there was no one around.

The place looked abandoned. There were some buildings
that looked as if they had been blown up. There were great
holes where the runways had been. And there was no
military response. It was as if the place had been evacuated,
late last night perhaps, during the Helpless Clairvoyants
gig. But it seemed impossible. Something's going on,
Tomnado said, stick to the plan.

Space is silent, for the most part, but I swear there was
some kind of constant background noise going on the whole
time we were in the abandoned spaceport, some kind of
music. It's a set-up, I kept telling myself, but we pushed on
regardless, if with great trepidation.

The entrance to the subterranean complex appeared to be
at the far side of the spaceport, near one of the collapsed
observation towers. We came to a short stairwell obscured
by a pile of rubble and were able to force the steel door at
the bottom. We made our way inside, with only the lights
on our helmets illuminating the darkness. The rooms were
opulent but long gone to seed. This is history, Yacob Yacob
said, this isn't now, which is the only sentence I ever recall
him saying. We came to another set of stairs and descended
to a complex of rooms that were knee-deep in water.

There were gasps throughout the audience, mutterings of disbelief. The waters of the moon? someone said. Hold your peace, Muldoon said. Let me continue.

There were large wooden bureaus floating upturned in the water, battered metal filing cabinets, bits of broken statuary. Let's split up, Column said. We may not have much time. Back here in twenty minutes, he said. We all fanned out.

I went through one room and then another until I came to one that was completely gutted except for a single chair in the centre. Around the walls you could see where paintings had hung, now disappeared, nothing left but their outline, a discoloured stain on the wall. I sat down on the chair and I took out a small piece of paper and a bit of soft rock that I had picked up from the surface of the moon and I began to draw. I switched off my helmet light and I drew the gaps on the wall, in the dark.

At one point someone came in, I don't know if it was one of the Clairvoyants, but they shone a light at me, just for a few seconds. It lit up the room like a small sun, obscuring the figure behind it, dark black on black, but I swear that it looked like they weren't wearing a space suit. I held my hand up to my face, the light was blinding, but they left as quickly as they came, closing the door behind them and without saying anything. I went on sketching for a few minutes, and then I started to make my way back to the meeting point. There was nothing to be found. Whatever was here, once, was long gone.

Everyone was waiting in the central room except for Firth Column. No one had found anything of interest, just empty room after empty room. The Doom showed me a scrap of paper he had found in a drawer. On one side it had a hastily drawn map showing the way to a forest, on the other showing the way to a river. We waited in the darkness, in our own circle of light, for what seemed like an eternity.

Five more minutes, The Doom said, and we stood there and listened to the sound of our own breathing mingling with the constricted sound of the pipes above our heads that once must have brought oxygen to the various parts of the bunker. At one point it felt as if we were floating in space with no walls around us. Then Column appeared. We could see him in the distance: a beam of intense white light that seemed like it was miles away, dancing, looping in the air, describing a figure of eight, two noughts, and then falling back. It didn't seem possible. None of it did: the scale, the distance, the blinding brightness of the light; it was as if Column was floating towards us, slowly, through the air, rising up on a beam of pure white light. We held our breath and braced ourselves. The light and the dark were playing tricks with us. As Column got closer we could see that he was actually carrying a bright white cube in his arms. It seemed to be giving out light. I found something, he said as he ran towards us. We need to get out of here.

We turned and fled. We stumbled up the stairs, tore through the great black vaulted spaces and came to the steel door. Bury it, Column said as soon as we were clear, and we rolled as much rubble as we could back down the stairs and re-covered the entranceway. Outside it was chaos. The authorities had arrived from out of nowhere. There were small recon shuttles hovering over the ruined spaceport, their searchlights casting this way and that. It's a set-up, Tomnado said. They planned it from the start. They let us overrun the spaceport and then they come in and hoover us up. But it made no sense and it still doesn't. Of course, later they claimed that rioters had forced their way into the spaceport and that staff and security had been forced to retreat in the face of concentrated acts of mass destruction, only finally routing the protesters when military reinforcements turned up. But everyone had seen the huge military presence the night before, which, when you did bring it up, only gave credence to the doubters who said that the spaceport had never been evacuated, that it had been fully staffed and operational before the onslaught of the rioters had reduced it to echoing ruins.

I remember I looked at Column at this point, with this white cube in his arms, and he had an expression of absolute panic on his face. I'm a stooge, he kept saying. I'm a stooge. This was all meant to happen. They've played every one of us right from the start.

We made our way across the spaceport in the black shadows of the ruined buildings, shadows that appeared as scorch marks burned into the surface of the moon. The lights of the recon shuttles danced and spun all around us. Militarists in black space suits patrolled the grounds. Through the fences we could see captured protesters forced to stand in lines behind the barbed wire. Of course, many of them never came home. The disappeared, they call them. Firth Column was one of them.

We came to the broken-down fence. The Helpless Clairvoyants' moon buggy was still there, still loaded with music equipment and supplies for constructing a basic survival dome. I can't go back, Column said, and he turned and looked at us. I'm not going to play my part. They might have orchestrated it this far, who knows, but no more. What's in the box? I asked him. It's singing, he said, and in the glow of the searchlights I thought I saw a tear glisten on his cheek, and in the tear the whole of the moon. Where will you go? Tomnado asked him. Further, he said, and they laughed and embraced each other. Then Column put the box in the back of his buggy and set off north across the Sea of Tranquillity. Do you think he's heading for the dark side of the moon? The Doom said, and we all laughed, and then stood there, and watched until he was nothing but a pinpoint of black atop a brilliant white cube. Then the soldiers came.

☐

Adam Aros took Peter Muldoon to one side. Great speech, he said. But where is it? Where's what? Muldoon replied. The white cube. You've got it, haven't you? You don't expect me to believe that crap about the made-up rock group and the dark side of the moon. I didn't make them up, Muldoon claimed. But they don't exist, Aros said. I've checked the records. There are no recordings, no photographs, no interviews. The interviews were all in German, Muldoon said. Nonsense, Aros replied. Look, why the hell do you think you are here? Do you really think your crappy art and your clichéd hippy drop-out bullshit is of any interest to us up here, at the vanguard of the future, on the edge of the goddamn universe?

I know why I'm here, Muldoon said. He was becoming
increasingly frustrated. Come with me, he said, and grabbed
Aros by the arm and dragged him out to the observation
corridor. They asked for me, he said, and he pointed to
the stars. And who's they? Entities, new configurations,
hermaphroditic gods, we don't know. And who's we? The
SIRK. That's us, Aros replied. We're The SIRK.

Did you know that The SIRK have written the whole of the
Victory Gardens using a WordPool? Muldoon asked him.

Aros looked at him in horror. Bullshit, he said. That's
insane, that's unethical, that's . . . impossible. Well, it's true.
And it asked for me. By name. The real reason I'm here, my
friend, is to take over the writing of the story. I'm the new
author. Be careful I don't relegate you to a bit player. Like I
did with Robert Scott.

Who's Robert Scott? Aros asked him. His expression was
genuinely blank. You don't remember him? The machine is
running down, Muldoon said. The letters are isappearing.
Life is clingling, winling, Aros said. Say that again, Muloon
aske him. It's what the WorPool says. Life is clingling,
winling.

Look, Aros says. The white cube is here, the white light.
The Luna attacks, the moth creatures, the entities, they are
coming for the light. In the box. This isn't first contact. We
know of them.

Who's we? The SIRK. They are coming in through gaps. Who
are? The SIRK? The moths are moving to the light. Think.
The attacks only began once you got here. I am The SIRK.

Then remember. I'm trying to. Can you hear music? What's that song? The one we sang? Where's the WorPool? It's here, it's blank. No, it's waiting to begin again. Quick, we haven't much time. Type this in. I am Peter Muloon. Say it. I am Peter Muloon. Say it. I am Peter Muloon. There's no one left. I am Peter Muloon. o you rea me? o you rea me? Sen help, please sen help. The Victory Garens are uner attack.

ea, ea.

En.

APPENDIX DEACON: AN ATTEMPTED PAIMON BIBLIOGRAPHY

A SIRK publication © The Flashlight/Token Bob, 1995

Victory Garden (short story, originally published in *Plus de Choses Dans le Ciel et la Terre* #3, 1982)

Pirates of the Universe Divide (novelisation of an unmade *Doctor Who* script submitted to Douglas Adams in the summer of 1979, published by Tara, 1983)

Belly of the Fish of Christ, Ship (credited as a 'found' text, though textual analysis reveals, we feel, although we are not accredited textual analysts, we are fans, and deep readers, but nevertheless we feel close readings reveal it as a Paimon text, maybe *the* ur-Paimon text, in a way, maybe the *Two Way Mirror* of Paimon texts, actually, due to the quality it has of peering in, or peering out, at you and, of course, the opportunities for textual ingress it provides. We are not textual analysts, but we are ingressers, infiltrators. The first of the Holy Books, issued as a limited-edition chapbook with no publication details, though seems likely 1983, self-published)

I am the Lion of Judah (credited as a 'channelled' text,
though, again, we identify this as a Paimon working,
possibly. The second of the Holy Books, issued as a limited-
edition letterpress chapbook with no publication details,
though, again, seems likely 1983, self-published)

*Proceeds From the First Synod of the Church of the Stone
of First Witness* (a Paimon text, certainly, though perhaps
with input from 'Frater Jim', issued as a limited-edition
broadside by the press that Paimon set up in Grez-sur-Loing
and which was run out of the converted barn/garage that
also housed Hildegard von Strophe's ceramics workshop; the
first of the Vanguard! broadsides, 1983)

If Unto the Red Planet, A Traveller (oddly precognitive
short story about a man who returns from the first-ever
manned expedition to Mars, all his companions left dead
across its surface, and his memory wiped, so that he believes
himself the first Martian to arrive on earth and writes the
book *If Unto the Earth, A Traveller* about his experiences
with an alien race who have mistaken him for one of their
own because, he believes, Mars is a mirror planet, in fact
all planets are, which is the whole basis of astrology and
planetary hours and goetia and the raising of the dead;
Vanguard! #2, 1983)

Crossing the Abyss (fictional/real (?!) account of a weekend
binge on cocaine where 'the author' believed himself to be
John the Baptist as he took a ferry across a river and had
basically a psychotic episode in public which resulted in, he
claims, an encounter with his Holy Guardian Angel, who it
turns out is a complete and utter fiction and only there as
a pair of armbands to get you to the other side of yourself,

which is Abyss, as it turns out, which is the name of your
Holy Guardian Angel, buddy, and not fucking Raphael;
Vanguard! #3, 1983; nice hand-stitched edition with every
copy stamped with the Vanguard! logo, which varied
but was mostly based around the letter V on a stem or a
pedestal like a cocktail glass with two bars or scores across
it, thus: ¥. Edition of 127 copies, and yes, I am packing.
1983, natch)

Mathematics of the Asteroid Belt (short story, elementary
potboiler about some educated bozos living in caves on
spinning asteroids to hold off the end of the world or such
saintly behaviour, and then getting attacked by aliens. The
first experiment in 'gridlocked' text by Paimon, as we have
christened and identified it; also, a quote from Lou Reed
in the text, from the song 'Some Kinda Love'. Published in
Regardez le Ciel #24, 1983, of course)

Cry Me A Way (cut-up text, or one written while nodding off
and waking up on horse, just as likely, with words spilled
up into phonemes so that the text appears like Braille, or
machine code, and printed with upraised letters, too, as
if it could be fed into the mouth of a machine as a set of
instructions, or enter through the fingertips of a beautiful
blind girl sat in the sun, on the steps of her house, in the
summertime; a deluxe edition and perhaps the high point of
the Vanguard! issues. 1983, summer of, what do you think,
edition of 33 copies: #need)

Caress Me A Waterfall (as above; variant)

Cover Mission As Wonderful (as above; variant)

Capable Mirage Age Wakens (as above; variant) (possibly more)

If You Expect the Antithesis of Venus You Are Gifted, That, in the End (another smacked-out/cut-up production, beautifully realised, but now more like text-sound experiments à la Richard Kostelanetz; Vanguard!, 1983. Bob Dylan and Philip K. Dick quotes in acrostics throughout the text – it's true, have a look – which can't be accidental, but seems more impossible than any crossword)

Appealing for Calm is the Way of a Mass Catastrophe (privately printed photobook featuring photographs, by Paimon, I think we can safely say, of Hildegard von Strophe, often graphic, and abstract, 1983?)

The Uncollected Escapologist (unpublished manuscript, believed lost, 1983)

Our Original Heavenly Nature is Fire Unsound (the breakthrough book and the first commercially successful Paimon outing, published by Nebula Books, 1983, about Star Gods, warring with ideas, vying to convince each other of their non-existence, until only one Star God remains, who has to start the whole thing again, for fear of loneliness, and an eternity of idle hands, and then his people fall in love with him, his creations, his flock, his church, and he models himself after their love, which means he has to bring all of the arguing Star Gods back again, because he now believes himself to be a loving, merciful, nostalgic and repentant god, as well as all of the normal god attributes, and of course the same old arguments start, and then what happens is an unknown starship turns up that none of the

gods can even remember making, that none of them are
willing to take credit or responsibility for, and inside the
spaceship is a dead body, a dead body of something that has
never died before, and the gods are amazed, a first death,
out of nothing, is a miracle, even to the gods, they agree, and
they are united in wonder, at the infinity of creation that
even gods partake of, of the unsoundness of fire, and then
it basically turns into a space opera of gods and men and
goes downhill from there, in this humble reviewer's opinion,
but still, as with genre in general, it is textually unpoliced
and provides multiple exit and entrance points for ingress,
which may be a large part of its success, that people could
disappear in it, easily)

The Coral of Heaven (deep space as undersea, the sound of
seashells, on the seashore, as spaceways; Orizon, 1983)

The Metal-Plated Dream Inc. (robotics in the far future
mechanise the dreamspace and lucid dreaming becomes
'the fastest-growing market' in technologies, the noumenon
is colonised, by advertisers, and becomes a mall, so as
imagination must purchase attributes, equipment, and
adventure holidays; Orizon, 1983)

Out Lilith! Oil Skin of the Dark! (Follow-up to *The Metal-
Plated Dream Inc.*, earth-abound; Orizon, 1983)

A History of Religious Ideas (space opera theatre-of-war
grandiosity; Orizon, 1983)

Phantom Our Town, Africa (which is where a mirror planet
is found in perfect orbit next to ours and we remodel it so
completely, at war, it ends up as the moon; Orizon, 1983)

Imitation of a Shadow (retro 50s noir where the murderer is revealed as a many-tentacled, semi-translucent alien who lives inside our own brain and feeds on our thoughts like a dog with a tapeworm; Orizon, 1983)

Man and Underground Man (essay on 'potentialities', on 'directions', literature as psychic topography; Orizon 1983)

Kazimir is Emerald for Forever (trouble at the court of the gods, as gods dream up new skills with which to assail gods and all of their subjects suffer, classic space opera, really, were it not for the semaphoric lines of punctuation that stand in for the speech of the gods, one of the weirdest successes of the 80s sci-fi 'boom' and further proof that reality is for people who can't handle science fiction; Nebula Books, 1984)

Rot (a sequel to *If Unto the Red Planet . . .*, in a way, *Rot* documents an invasion of aliens who are colour itself, and it's like a parable of when movies went coloured and more fantastic in the 50s and horror and sci-fi benefited the most, you can be sure they did, alongside porn, but also to say there are multiple incomprehensible forms of life that will eradicate you without a single thought of your existence because they simply is, or are; Nebula Books, 1984)

Today is Die Welt Day (alternative-history Nazi sci-fi Third-Reich-as-Atlantis short story, anthologised in the epochal collection edited by Arnaud Pierrepont, *L'Age d'Aura*, 1984)

Phantom Aros: Dream River: Tia Rio (full textual gridlock; the opening of the channels, the uncovering of the tunnels:

still selling, but on this form it can't last forever. Nebula
Books, 1984)

APPENDIX SUBDEACON: PROCEEDS FROM THE FIRST SYNOD OF THE SOCIETY OF IRREGULAR RESEARCH AND KNOWLEDGE (SIRK) 1993

Originally published in *Roll Away the Stone* (2008)

I. AS ABOVE

We came together through a love for subterranea, for the great mysterious battlements that line the east coast of Scotland and the abandoned complexes beneath; the stone sound mirrors, no longer cupped to the drone of the brave young German fighter pilots as they crossed the water on their way to an assignation with fate, our fate, their fate, God love us both; abandoned railway tracks; old tunnels that ran deep into the past; shortwave patterns decoding the night; the topography of the invisible world; abandoned madhouses; old aircraft hangars; military wrecking yards; lost rivers; dark drains and Victorian sewage systems; air raid shelters; nuclear bunkers; secret command posts where steely generals made their last stands; rooms that were more like suits of armour or tombs, as if they were built to be worn rather than to be lived in; second skins; bandages; anything with a funerary aspect.

We rolled our eyes at Blake, scoffed at Rimbaud, whose deathbed lament for an eternal place in the sun we took as a confession of poetic incontinence. Instead we sought out the dark, surveyed the mausoleums, and felt ourselves truer poets than any of them.

The world seemed fuller then, somehow, less populated by explanations. Now I see it as a lifetime's worth, a lifetime of love, of loving and of being loved, which I am still, mercifully, unable to explain. Nevertheless, I remain helpless in the face of sentiment or nostalgia for the sublime darkness of our youth, our happy companionship with inhuman scale and our shared commitment to scaring ourselves half to death.

I have long nursed a secret joy in disappointment, the frisson that only perfect failure can supply, a silent satisfaction in defeat. I should like very much to be diagnosed with a fatal illness, a slow death, preferably, so that I may conduct my body like a circus master, like those handsome circus masters of old who would set up tent on the football fields outside Calderbank and who would crack the whip over fierce animals that would eventually, inevitably, decapitate them; dreamy mermaids who would betray their love; midgets who would stab them in their sleep; dogboys that would turn on them in the dead of night. But still to be the master of ceremonies, the very seal of God, which is the seal of fate, on my forehead, the whip in my hand and with the horses long since bolted.

Old age has, however, held out against my fantasy of coasting into twilight on a mutinous vessel, and going by family history I am more likely to be taken down in the night while on lookout duty than to pilot the ship into the depths. And although I believe in reincarnation, I suspect I am about to play my final turn.

Are people markers of time? Is landscape alive like people? Is context conscious? These are the kinds of questions that haunt me in my dotage, me, a man for whom answers were like so much candyfloss, things you gave to children on the beach once a year to shut them up, to fill their idiot cakeholes. To pose a question, to propose any kind of lack or absence, is to get further from the truth. That's why we always assumed that ghosts were here right now and that even disappearing was present. But now all I have is absence, the absence of my daughter, the lack of my wife, the loss of my dear partner, all, finally, written out. The questions have long since been posed.

If, like Dante, I could walk once again in the fulcrum of my life, and so of history itself, one foot in the morning of my wedding, the other in the night of my ravishing, I would find myself in attendance at the Burntisland Conference, that fateful day, that most auspicious date, 20 April 1993, with my wife still asleep in a hotel along the coast, our beautiful daughter still four months secret, the holidaymakers lining the front in deckchairs and the air so perfectly still.

Anyone who has heard the rumours about Burntisland, the stories of an underground city, the mirror of the one above, built during the Second World War as a war room or a resistance cabinet office or even as a munitions factory, the whole town once reputed to be sitting on enough dynamite to land it on the moon, cannot fail to be spellbound by the atmosphere of the place, all of which points towards some kind of occult construction. There's something indisputably *hollow* about the town – no other word will do – as if the buildings are a mere facade, as if you could walk behind them and they would be held up by nothing but wooden planks. The seagulls look as if they have been etched hurriedly into the air and the pavement itself seems to echo, lending even a leisurely early-morning stroll the gravitas of a funeral parade or a wedding march.

A few months before my arrival, sometime in late December, there had been the widely reported Double A disaster, where the floor of an old school hall that had been hosting an all-ages discotheque had suddenly given way, resulting in the deaths of five youngsters. Though I have little sympathy for disco dancers and their ilk I took an interest in the story when a pen pal, Token Bob, sent me a newspaper clipping showing the carnage that coincidentally provided a tantalising glimpse of the subterranean tomb that had claimed the partying idiots. He had included a blown-up photostat of a tag on the wall of the complex, the letters S I R K alongside a number that remained indecipherable, and in the accompanying note – written, I might add, with all of the letters slanting to the left – he claimed that SIRK was a well-known acronym used by special military ops that stood for Secret Initiatory Realm of Knights, who were in charge of constructing and maintaining an entire hidden infrastructure, almost a mirror image of everything that exists around us up here on the ground, only down there, beneath our feet, ready, in the event of disaster, to go to ground and repopulate.

At the time Token Bob – that's how he was known, named after his wife's attitude to him or a wound he received through unpaid gambling debts, it was never clear which – was an up-and-coming star of the discipline, a discipline now given a veneer of academic respectability through the increasing exposure of the work of tedious lefties like Guy Debord and Raoul Vaneigem (not to say the rediscovery of the work of John Dee and Edward Kelley, in reality our truest guiding spirits), but back then one that would have got you laughed out of the changing rooms, if you know what I mean. Still, here's Token Bob filling A5 stapled journal after A4 fold-out poster book with some of the most groundbreaking fieldwork of the day, mapping the course of subterranean streams, writing letters on behalf of sorry twentieth-century defence architecture, shimmying his way up chimneys or burrowing down tiny sewage pipes in search of lost worlds, or, more accurately, temporarily forgotten domains. So his word held a lot of clout (this was some years before the whole 'Dark Lochnagar' UFO flap that effectively destroyed his reputation), and as the papers circulated amongst the community the decision was made to host the first-ever societal AGM of the Second Church of the First Stone at Burntisland, as we named ourselves in tribute to the secret society founded by our favourite subterraneans, the architect Pierre Melville and author Max Rehberg.

As I walked along the front, as I travel there once more in my mind, I am struck by three characters, three still lives, more appropriately, that have stayed with me to this day and that I still struggle to make sense of.

The first was a girl in a long flowing skirt and a crop top dancing with a hula hoop. Every so often she would raise one of her hands in the air and manoeuvre the hoop until it was spinning around her wrist. To say I was both captivated and repelled would be accurate, but not quite. I stood there watching her for some time, spellbound, you might say, like a detective at a crime scene. I recall that I began to sweat slightly and I fancy that my heart may even have skipped a beat – it may have been the caffeine, I had treated myself to a black coffee from a small seafront cafe along the way – when I realised that the girl was in fact blind, that what I had taken for the kind of obnoxious oversized sunglasses favoured by disco dancers was in fact a cover for her dead eyes. Right then her mother, at least I presume it was the girl's mother, put her hand out and through the hoop in order to stop her gyrations – is she deaf too? I wondered – and guided her into taking a cup in her hand.

At that moment I looked away, over towards the grass verge that runs along the promenade, and saw a homeless person asleep with a filthy rucksack for a pillow, his shoes by his side but still wearing socks, ghastly woolly socks more suited to mountainsides than seasides.

And then along from him a young couple, the girl lying on her back in a green bikini, the boy leaning over her, his body raised up on one elbow, the pair of them kissing in the keen way that is the preserve of the eternally young. At that moment I felt as if all three tableaux were related, like I was being shown three potential futures: the blind dancer, the sleeping hobo, and the young lovers. I hope it would be obvious which one I chose.

The conference was big news amongst the community. Up until that point we had all existed as a faceless network of typed or handwritten pseudonyms: Chubby Nightstick, The General, Token Bob, whom you have met, Approximately Toxic, sometimes simply XX, The Plug, The Flashlight, The Grey Wolf, The Lightning Bolt, cursed Jack Frost, The Pink Panzer . . . My own pseudonym I choose to withhold. Arthur McManus – I still refuse to call him Aha – was, of course, The Grey Wolf.

Token Bob and The Flashlight were in charge of proceedings. Going by their list of conquests, everything from the large sinkhole behind Niagara Falls – very much the 'holy grail' of waterworks enthusiasts and, until their infiltration and privately circulated field report, reputed to be physically impregnable, though now it's a tourist attraction, good God – through the mapping of the abandoned artificial islands off the East Neuk of Fife that provided cover for what at the time were some of the most advanced undersea battle stations ever invented by the crackpot wing of the British army, I had half expected a pair of geeky hyperactive teenagers. But as I arrived at the church hall that had been hired to host the proceedings – an unfortunate architectural monstrosity that should have been shipped directly to the Western Isles – I caught my first sight of the pair of them in the lobby and was relieved to see that they were in fact conservatively dressed, almost to the point of invisibility, the kind of people that can disappear in the corner of your eye or pass you by without ever impressing themselves on your memory. Magicians, I thought to myself.

The Flashlight was smoking a pipe – they were both wearing name tags so I knew who was what – while Token Bob combed what was left of his hair in a hand-mirror and pulled at the lapels of an oversized tweed jacket. And you might be? The Flashlight asked me. Token Bob's huge face peered over his shoulder, sizing me up, trying to get my number, a wolf or a star or a sword or a sudden darkness? I'm William Scotia, I announced. They both nodded in approval. We meet at last, Token Bob said. This is a great honour. He extended his hand in greeting. I'm a fan of your work, The Flashlight informed me. I've read all of your publications. Likewise, I said, cursing myself for such an idiotic reply and for so immediately surrendering the higher ground. I made a mental note to regale him with one of my adventures as soon as the opportunity presented itself and then to walk away with a leer on my face.

Once inside I was greeted with the expected mix of dark tragic poets, plumbers of the depths, middle-aged explorers, social misfits and even a few young people – an unfortunate rarity in this profession, a calling that most commonly has its first stirrings in the black hole that opens up (I should say reveals itself) in the mid-thirties – most spectacularly Jack Frost, who was either an extremely malnourished ancient or an anorexic child, probably the latter, I decided, due to the constant presence on his cranium of an oversized baseball cap.

He caught my eye immediately. There was something in the curve of his spine that made me think of the shrivelled corpse of Tutankhamen, and in our company that was worth more than gold. For a second it crossed my mind that he was the living embodiment of what we were all searching for, a tomb dweller, a true subterranean. At the same time, he projected a grotesque appearance, a crippled man-child whose sole purpose was to make a mockery of us all. Aside from a notorious series of letters published in *The Complex* that attacked the upper echelons of established fandom as a bunch of armchair explorers, I knew nothing of his work.

Then there was The Grey Wolf. At first, I confess, knowing nothing of his current proclivities, I likened him more to a Grey Owl, someone with an intimate knowledge of the dark but with the kind of equivocal attitude that comes with eyes that you could watch the moon rise in. I hadn't seen him since 1991, when he had seemingly disappeared, into the dark of his own researches, into his quest for the perfect timeless abyss, after warning me to watch my body for any signs of loose talk.

At one point during the round-table debate – we were discussing that perennial chestnut, Arbitrary Division, a token-based monetary system that had been the darling of the political fringe during the 1930s and which was once more experiencing a revival (we saw ourselves as social revolutionaries as much as tomb raiders; sincerely, what is the difference?) – Jack Frost stood up, teetering on frail legs, and made a stand. He called us nostalgists, accused us of being practitioners of kitsch. Next you'll be issuing a manifesto, he said, looking pointedly in my direction. At the other extreme, The Plug argued for a statement of ideology – not a manifesto, he insisted, under pressure from Frost – that had less to do with national renewal than with national decay. I'm expounding the politics of rot, he exclaimed, to much hilarity. But his basic tenets were sound: full colonisation of the underground, the widespread creation of mirror cities, veneration of the war machines, the equilibration of the gods, etc. All the time The Grey Wolf, The Silent Owl, sat between them. Occasionally he would glance over at one or the other with a look that I can only describe as imperial pity, a haughty emotion that was beyond sorrow, love or anger. Later he told me it was the child of suffering that had raised up its hand and instructed him to remain silent.

Recess was called, and we made our way along the front to an old-fashioned tavern that at first glance appeared to be someone's house. Our hosts reassured us that it was in fact a drinking establishment and that a table had been reserved for our party in the garden.

Along the front I spotted the same young lovers as before, but now they had been joined by an older man wearing nothing but a pair of pink bikini bottoms. He was lying on his back in the grass while the young girl balanced on his leg in the air, her arms spread out as if she had taken flight. The boyfriend looked on approvingly. I looked around at my comrades but no one else seemed to have noticed them.

As we seated ourselves around a large wooden table, there was much jostling for position and I could see that already alliances were forming and hierarchies were falling into place. I vowed to have nothing to do with it. Instead of fighting for a seat I opted to walk inside the bar and peruse the taps.

Sure enough, there was a fine selection of ales: milds, stouts, porters, a wee heavy or two. A figure perched on a stool next to me – I didn't deign to turn around – made some comment about the presence of the riding cap on my head, so I took my walking stick and laid it on the bar in the way that I would a weapon. Typically, I heard no more from him. Right then The Grey Wolf appeared at my shoulder. I recommend a low-alcohol beer, he said. You might want to keep your senses about you. I nodded, silently, and suppressed a shudder.

Outside, the discussion, somewhat inevitably, had turned to childhood epiphanies. If you leave these people alone for five minutes with nothing but a pouch of tobacco and a bar tab, the talk will almost certainly stray towards an analysis of what exactly it was – in their DNA, in the circumstances of their youth – that first set them on the path. The sound of artillery, the air raid warnings, the smell of old gas masks, the sight of bombed-out buildings, the solitary walls raised up to heaven with single panes of glass still tantalisingly preserved but forever out of reach, I've heard it so many times that the birth canal itself might as well be a hastily dug escape tunnel.

It was the Clyde Blitz that did it for me, The Pink Panzer said. Fifteenth of March 1941. It's the incendiary devices I remember the most, the huge warehouses on fire by the water. The whole of my childhood had been spent waiting for a meteor to come screaming through the skies and wipe out my entire family, flatten the rotten lot of them, he said. In comparison Glasgow at war had been like a playground, a place of unpredictable adventure. I remember when the grain silos were hit, he said, we lived on Dumbarton Road in Partick and had a bird's-eye view. The rat population had fled, some of them still on fire, flaming rats coming in this wave from the Clydeside. The next day I found one asleep, still smouldering, in my father's shoes, which he would leave outside the door in the close each night.

I saw the water on fire, The Lightning Bolt said, an older
man with a jowly, liver-spotted face and flat cap. It was
just like the Styx, the waters of hell, all of the fuel from the
depots had leaked into the Clyde and erupted in this wall
of impenetrable flame, but even so there would be these
young daredevil fighters, these plucky Germans, who would
deliberately swoop down and tear through the fire. Back
then I thought to myself, they're thinking of the children,
they're putting a display on just for them. It was marvellous,
this acrobatic release of energy, and being a child that was
how I saw it, the best fireworks night of my life.

Token Bob posed the question. Do you remember your first
night underground? The topic was passed around the table.
The Grey Wolf remembered the silence, he said. You all
talk about explosions, bombs, detonations, but what of the
aftermath, he said, what is it that you're really after?

What you are really seeking – correct me if I'm wrong
– is some kind of death-in-life, some kind of perpetual
profanity. What more, then, than the silence of the tomb?
That's what I recall most of all in my time spent in the
buried subterranean complexes, he continued, in the
bunkers and bomb shelters, miles deep in the abandoned
munitions depots and underground railways, running off,
an infinite silence, the eternal presence of nothing: eternal
life. Isn't that the reason we have chosen to spend our lives
desecrating graves? We may go down, he insisted, but don't
forget, we take the world down with us.

An awkward silence fell upon the room, a silent bruise,
like he'd smacked us backwards into the grave right then
and there. I looked over as he swatted a fly off his arm

with a grand gesture. It was precisely the kind of spiritual melodrama I had been looking for.

That night my wife and I dined at our hotel along the front. Next to us an elderly Japanese couple complained about the steak. Too black, they said. After several bottles of wine and a few surreptitious whiskies supplied by the doorman, who beckoned us into his den at the back of the hotel – more of a glorified shed, really, complete with nude pictures cut out of magazines and pinned on the wall and a single bed that seemed as if it was designed to fit a small child curled up like a shell – we took an evening walk along the promenade.

My wife seemed upset. It was that man, she said. You mean the Japanese? I asked her. No, she said, the doorman. He was staring at me the whole time he had me in his den, she said. At one point he flicked his tongue out at me. I told her I had noticed nothing of the sort. You're naive when you're drunk, she told me. I love you, but sometimes it's difficult. I changed the subject and told her about the young lovers – keeping the rest of the day's tableaux to myself – how the girl had balanced on the foot of the older man like a mermaid. We combed the beach for the best part of an hour in search of them, but they had long since disappeared.

The morning's activities were scheduled to start at 8.15 a.m. We were told there would be a tour of the disaster scene, the hollow shell of the Double A, with the tantalising possibility of a glimpse of the bunker below. For some reason no one else at the conference seemed to be staying at our hotel, despite it being recommended in the brochure. In fact, the majority of attendees had opted for a gone-to-seed hovel in the backstreets which they had dubbed The Land Without a

Name because the landlady was suffering from early-onset dementia and so would regularly forget where she was and who she was welcoming. I dubbed our hotel Uncle Stephen's in retaliation, but no one got the joke.

I arrived outside the venue at 8 a.m. sharp and was surprised to find that I was the first person in attendance. I went for a coffee and came back and soon I was joined by the rest of the group, most of whom seemed a little worse for wear. The Plug and The Lightning Rod arrived arm in arm. Fun night? I asked them. One of them made a sign with his hands that I won't repeat. The other sniggered. Is this what the hobby's come to? I thought to myself.

Then The Grey Wolf appeared, no longer acting like a wolf or an owl but more like a bat, his great cape billowing behind him. He swept past the main group and fell into concerned conversation with The Flashlight. It was apparent that there was a problem. Our appearance in the village had not gone unnoticed. The Pink Panzer mentioned something about a protest, a blockade. That's when the abuse began. Vultures, someone shouted, and as if from out of nowhere a battalion of locals, mostly purple-haired old women but with a few village toughs and what I was later led to believe were concerned parents, began to bear down on our party. Grave robbers, someone shouted, murderers, someone else said. At one point a young man with sticky-out ears picked up a handful of sand and threw it at us but thankfully it dispersed in mid-air. The Flashlight stepped forward. Hear me out, he said. The entire crowd collectively inhaled. We are here because we believe that military negligence resulted in the death of your children.

He was well versed, I thought to myself.

We are here because we believe that the disco was built on unstable ground, he said. We have come to conduct a fully independent investigation into the circumstances surrounding the deaths of your loved ones. Now, if you will allow us to proceed, perhaps we can get to the bottom of this tragedy. There were murmurs within the crowd. Someone shouted out, you don't look like detectives! That's why we're so successful, The Flashlight countered. Then the crowd opened up, still with some muttering, and we made our way towards the bunker.

The whole scene was a mess, still cordoned off with police tape and with the great letter A toppled sideways so that it looked like a Soviet spaceship beached on the moon. There is a certain protocol, Token Bob reminded us, and he stopped us in our tracks. We cannot change a single iota; we should not remove a single jot. We nodded to one another, then we descended into the gloom.

In the end it was a disaster, mirroring the original catastrophe like an aftershock or a bellyache. No sooner had we crossed police lines and started lowering ourselves, man by man, through the gaping hole in the floor, than the authorities showed up. Down below you could hear the snap of camera shutters like the report of a machine gun. The officers called, cease and desist, and we threw our hands in the air, half in love with the idea of our own outlawry, as the police moved in and began to politely manhandle us out of the door. I thought about what The Grey Bat had said about staring nothing right in the face and for a moment I felt as if I recognised it. But where had he gone? I had clearly seen him disappear through the hole in the floor, this splintered wound with twisted boards stretching up, leaping feet first into this vat of darkness, this historical question. But he never reappeared. The Flashlight winked at me and pointed to the floor and made a signal like he was taking a photograph with a camera. Okay, I said, okay, we have one of us down there, we have infiltrated the bunker, mission accomplished. I nodded but I was already starting to feel excluded.

Later that night all the talk was focused on The Grey Bat, The Grey Owl, The Grey Fox. He was the real deal, someone said, a commitment above and beyond, someone else added. If anyone can turn this around, he can, The Pink Panzer insisted.

When I got back to our hotel my wife was reading in bed, a book I had recommended to her, *Jersey Under the Jackboot* by R.C.F. Maugham. She was at the bit about the ban on excessive tobacco cultivation. This book is depressing me, she said. Can't we just cuddle up? I stripped down to my vest and underwear and climbed into bed. Outside the window we could see the silhouettes of people passing back and forth along the front. In the distance someone was flying a kite. I told her about the events of the day, how The Grey Bat had disappeared beneath the floor on a reconnaissance mission, how we had fooled the police. I will never understand it, she said. What's wrong with being up here in the light? I was about to tell her how we believed in exploring every possibility, how there was light in darkness, a black sun behind the bright one, but in the end I gave up. How could I explain to her that we find our origins in blood and in darkness on an unimaginable level? I reached over, switched off the lamp, and lay with my arms around her.

The next day the conference continued as usual but there was no sign of The Grey Wolf. In the morning there were various presentations: Scotland's Secret Runways, a somewhat dry topography of Scotland's longest and straightest roads; The Corsham Mirror, an interesting attempt to map the secret thirty-five-acre city buried beneath Wiltshire complete with man-made lake, sixty miles of road, a BBC recording studio and a paper messaging system facilitated by tubes filled with compressed air; Flat Earth: Notes Towards a Lexicon of Luftwaffe Targets, a potentially interesting talk that included a slideshow of rare Luftwaffe reconnaissance photographs taken from the air in Fife in the closing years of 1939 but which was marred by a pronounced stammer and a complete failure to get to grips with the technology of overhead projectors; Grim's Graves, a tedious account of some godforsaken Neolithic flint mine (we do tend to attract them); and – most interesting of all – Here is Bunker of Upon Bunker, an attempt to map what for many of us was the underground site with the most significance, the ultimate prize, the dream of infiltrators worldwide, the place where Hitler made his last stand and his last exit via a pill and a bullet in the head, the Führerbunker.

It was the closest any of us could hope to come to walking in the footsteps of Dante or John Dee. The speaker – a Polish émigré whose name unfortunately translated as The Cold Fish – had drawn up several maps that included the location of Hitler's study and living room, Eva Braun's bedroom, Goebbels's bedroom and the quarters of his wife and family – whose bodies the Bolsheviks discovered – even the quarters of the dog Blondi and its fated litter, alongside lists that were mind-boggling in their detail and scope, lists of

the wines cellared in the basement of the Reich Chancellery
and indiscriminately consumed during that fateful week
in April, the single gramophone record that accompanied
the tragic dance parties in the Vorbunker – a sentimental
and effeminate recording of Bach's *Brandenburg Concertos*,
according to The Cold Fish – the cakes favoured by Hitler,
sometimes three servings at a time, the paintings that
decorated the walls (everyone knows about the portrait of
Frederick the Great, but how about the lesser-known *Grey
Lady*, the painting of an unknown woman with a face like
granite and arched eyebrows that seemed to contain all the
sorrow and pain of the world?).

It was a stunning feat of scholarly exegesis that was
somewhat undermined by the revelation that he had
personally uncovered a Nazi interrogation and torture
chamber in the basement of a property in Greece, where
he kept a holiday home, a room filled with bloodied sheets
and dentist's chairs, he insisted, a common fantasy among
crackpots of a certain bent.

Still, there was enough material there that we all quite
forgot about The Grey Wolf and instead spent the bulk of
the morning wandering the bunker in our minds, the noise
of constant bombardment up above, the sound of boots on
concrete steps, the asthmatic drone of the air conditioning,
the smell of wet dogs, the secret files, the wooden pews
and the subterranean light, the rusting blast doors
opening and closing like the gates of heaven.

The afternoon was set aside for a field trip around the
defence architecture of Fife; the Secret Bunker – back then
still very much a secret other than to those 'in the know' –

and the pillboxes that dotted the coast; the fortified islands; the anti-tank cubes; the abandoned airstrips; the sound mirrors; the nightside that had come to lord it over our lives. Truth is: I had seen it all before.

Incredibly, The Sightless Head, the modernist seminary designed by Pierre Melville just along the coast, wasn't even on the itinerary. Back then it was still a functioning theological school. Its lack of mystery, its lack of a patina of decay, its refusal, back then, to become ruins, made it inexplicably unattractive to my fellow subterraneans, which seems crazy, now that it's abandoned, and in the past, and haunted.

Let the neophytes have their day, I said to myself, and began to make my way back to the hotel, imagining a spot of lunch with my wife and perhaps even a game of chess and a short nap. I always carried a travel set with me but had yet to convince my wife to join me in a full game. She said she knew me too well, whatever that meant, and besides, she kept forgetting the rules, her rooks would become bishops, her castles like kings, and the next thing you knew she would be in tears over what she described as my 'territorial aggression'. It's not Austria, I would say to her, it's not Poland!

As I passed along the front – it was another glorious summer's day with highs in the mid-seventies – I spied a queue developing outside a seafront cafe. Never being one to pass up a spectacle, I immediately attached myself to the throng. The man in front of me, a man with tightly curled black hair and the swollen nose of a perpetual drug addict, turned and grinned up at me. You're into it too, he said to me.

Let me assure you, I replied, I am most certainly not 'into it'. You're here, he said, you're into it. I am most assuredly 'into' nothing, I informed him. Then why are you here? he said. I merely came to see what all the fuss was about. It's Mascaroni, he said, Elizabeth Mascaroni, she's in the ice cream shop. And who might she be? I asked. Elizabeth Mascaroni is a star, he said, a child star. She's come back to Burntisland to visit her family and meet her fans.

Just then I noticed Jack Frost a few people ahead of us in the queue. I ducked behind my new-found acquaintance. What was he doing here? I could see that he was holding something, a photograph, perhaps, was he queuing in order to obtain a signature? Right then a beggar appeared from out of nowhere, a negro, itself a rarity in Burntisland, never mind a blind one. As he made his way along the queue, an awkward silence descended upon us. What's the matter? he asked. Hasn't anyone ever seen a blind person before? Every so often he would poke someone in the leg or rap a child on the head with his stick, but no one had the nerve to say anything. I recommend the Mexican Vanilla, he announced, while facing the wrong way altogether, and with that he disappeared towards the beach.

That was the moment I decided to set a trap. I broke off from the queue and took a seat on a bench across the way, directly facing the door of the cafe. I crossed my legs, loaded a pipe and waited for the confrontation. It took no more than twenty minutes.

There he was, clutching his prize in one hand and with an expression that said, look at me, God Herself just kissed me on the forehead. I stood up as he approached. What's that

you've got there? I asked him. He was cool as a cucumber.
It's a signed photograph of your mother, he said to me.
That was below the belt. I would have thought you would
have been on the tour this afternoon, I said to him. After
all, there's a lot to learn. There's only one person that could
possibly have anything to teach me, he said, and right now
he's six foot under. That stung. So, in the meantime we
line up for autographs from pop stars? I asked him. I'm
surprised you even know who she is, he said. I don't, I said,
someone informed me of the level of mass idiocy that was
taking place here. You obviously don't get out much, he said.
A bachelor, I'm guessing? On the contrary, I informed him,
my wife is waiting for me right this minute in a hotel along
the front. So how come you're hanging around outside here?
he countered. It was a good question.

I spied you, I said, and I wanted to get to the bottom of
it. I'm flattered, he said, I had no idea that I had made
such an impression. My feeling is that you are shocked, he
continued, that you are shocked by my interest in things
that aren't over with already. You mistake my interest in
graveyards for nostalgia or for some kind of refusal of the
present. In this you are wrong. I heard your memorialising
of the dead the other night (in truth I had no idea what
he was talking about), your conviction that the past had
somehow been buried and the present was just a pale ghost.
Well, the poorer for you. For me, the ruins, the abandoned
bunkers, the secret plans, are precisely the things that I
have moved beyond. When I look in the mirror, I see
everything that I have cast off. I come here, to this meeting,
this pathetic AGM, and all that I see are dead men,
skeletons preparing their own resting place and already
nostalgic about it, nostalgic about death itself. You remind

me of alcoholic novelists or the kind of pill-popping nut jobs that work the nightshift in bakeries or that have miserable paper rounds and save their pathetic manuscripts in chests or in shoeboxes under the bed in the hope that the future will deign to throw them some scraps, preferably, conveniently, once they have long vacated the scene.

I took a nervous step backwards. At first I feared he would assault me. But I kept my cool. You, sir, are an ignoramus, I informed him. And a rat to boot. You're the rat, he spat back. I know the game you're playing. I was shaken. I was most assuredly not playing any games but somehow the accusation hit home. Is that how I was coming across? Aside from a self-confessed badly fluffed intro, I had thought my entrance to the conference a masterclass in subterranean disdain.

I dismissed him with a shake of the head and walked off. However, I had been disturbed by the vehemence of his attack and I may have stumbled once or twice on my way back to the hotel. The temperature was rising, and the afternoon had become doubly uncomfortable. In a side street I caught sight of the same blind beggar as before, this time walking down the middle of the road and into the path of oncoming vehicles. I watched as a concerned middle-aged woman took him by the arm and led him back to the pavement. It's a con, I said to myself. It's all a rotten con.

The next day I was booked to headline afternoon proceedings with my presentation – I should really say unveiling – of The AntiMatterist Manifesto. I prayed that The Grey Owl would return by then.

That night I sat up until dawn, revising the manifesto, reading it softly to myself, tuning it, as it were.

I wrote by the light of a candle while the hearth crackled and my wife occasionally changed sides beneath the soft sheets the hotel had provided us with. I watched figures pass by in the night, silhouettes. The blind beggar, perhaps, who knows? Then the sky moved from grey to blue and finished on a burst of silver that felt magnetic, like it was the colour of the future itself, dawning on me.

The talk was a triumph. What if you were to say yes to no? I asked them. I threw out points like a machine gun.

Afterwards I asked about The Grey Owl. He's back in town, Token Bob said. The word is, he intends to make a headlining speech. It felt like someone had dropped my heart down an elevator shaft. Had he attended my talk? I asked him. He had. In fact, he had been seen taking notes. I envisioned a great collaboration, him quoting me at length, Jack Frost curled over in his seat in the front row like a rotten question mark. We're onto something, I said to myself.

Right then I had my first premonition, my first flash of the future, like a camera that takes a shot of a pitch-black room and for a second illuminates a body, slumped awkwardly in a chair, and all around it nothing, no explanation, no context, just the future plain and simple. There had been a discovery, I was sure of that, and it had coincided with my AntiMatterist declaration.

I rushed back to my wife, who was in bed reading, this time Hugh Trevor-Roper's *The Last Days of Hitler*. This one is better, she said, this one is real literature. I felt impossibly moved. I fell to my knees and clasped my hands to my chest before presenting her with a bunch of carnations that I had pilfered from a field behind a petrol station. My love, I said to her. My angel.

Then I told of her of the reception of my speech, my feeling of impending deliverance to the future. We'll be there any minute, she laughed, and put her arms around my neck. I lifted her from the bed and the blankets slid from her like the skin of a snake that lives beneath rocks in the desert and that rarely feels the contact of another living being except through a skin that has been left behind and trampled under feet. I fixed her in her chair and wheeled her onto the balcony. We looked out over the beach as the silhouettes of the ice cream ladies made their last rounds and families in swimwear walked home. I asked her if she remembered how we were when we first met. Barely, she said. But I miss them, those two. Then she said it again, those two, like a simple repeat was all that it would take.

I arrived back at the conference at 6.15 p.m. The evening programme wasn't scheduled to start until seven, but I intended to waylay The Grey Wolf before then and quiz him over the reception of The AntiMatterist Manifesto. He was nowhere to be seen. He's on stage at 10 p.m., The Lightning Rod confirmed. But he was acting like he had been sniffing cocaine, so I disregarded his information completely. It was only when Token Bob turned up that I gleaned the real story. That The Grey Owl had driven to Edinburgh in order to have a reel of film express-processed in time for that evening's talk. We're all hanging by our balls, Token Bob said. He was uncouth. But I got the message.

I could barely contain a feeling of exultation, even as I sat through a series of interminable lectures with titles like If This Be a Plan: The Enigma of the Dunglass Frigidaire – the report of a ruin situated on an outcropping of water near the mouth of the Clyde that had a sealed room deep in its basement that was filled by an impossibly modern fridge that opened like a trapdoor – The Minotaur: A Genealogy; Provocation: The Ground Beneath Our Feet; and, finally, Jack Frost's London Flatlands: A Refutation. Evidently, they had saved the colons for last.

Frost's speech began in his usual manner, with much coughing and the forming of white foam in the corners of his mouth, much subconscious genuflecting, at one point even kneeling on the stairs as he made his way on stage, although some people maintained that he briefly collapsed or perhaps suffered a breakdown, which makes sense, knowing what comes next.

He started off on a familiar line, expanding on the idea that there weren't any true depths at all, that everything lay on the surface. At first he came across like a witchfinder. Then he changed tack, arguing that the idea of the below – which was always a concept, he insisted, as it's impossible to be below where you are, which means below is permanently inaccessible, which means you are nowhere, not even at a crossroads – was a practical creation, a bin-hole, the exit and entrance for so much rubbish in people's brains. Poor soul, I thought to myself. Poor suffering soul.

Then he began to talk about reconnaissance missions he had undertaken around London, the tunnels he had discovered that led in and out of the moment at certain points in the city, distinct collusions between time and space. He moved on to his investigations of potentiality. His talk took a magical turn. Magic is the activation of potentialities, he said. Then he came down on us all. He spat foam from the sides of his mouth. You have let yourselves down, he proclaimed. You mistake the catacombs for a different place. He took out a cigarette paper and began to roll it in his fingers. This went on for about ten minutes. An awkward silence crept over the audience. Every so often he would purse his lips and stare at the paper like it had eluded him and then he would start all over again, rerolling this one endlessly delayed cigarette. At one point someone coughed. Token Bob nudged me on the shoulder. He's not mental, he said, he makes origami animals, at which point Frost perched the model of a small paper deer on the edge of his lectern and walked – some say staggered – off the side of the stage and straight out the door of the auditorium.

There were a few gasps from the more gullible members of the audience. Someone said it was like Freddie Mercury. Someone said Rimbaud but someone else said it was more like Verlaine. Someone mentioned a dyspeptic Polish writer who had written one great book and then killed himself. I maintained that he was more like a punctuation mark, an * or a & or a ? on a broken typewriter where the figure was smudged and barely legible. That's grammar, someone said, there's more to it than that. I wasn't so sure.

I approached Token Bob for an update. No word. By this point it was 9.45 p.m. A few of us stepped outside for a smoke but in reality to keep watch along the front for the return of our hero.

An hour passed. There were quotes. What is here is made perfect, someone said, that's what Jack Frost was trying to say. It's imperfect, someone else maintained, if not then why would it require a royal art to fix it? There's only one royal art, another one said.

Two hours passed. Someone screened footage from an air show at Leuchars to pass the time, blurry shots of Lancaster bombers, Spitfires, even a Focke-Wulf Ta 154 Moskito. Bomb us all to hell and back, I thought to myself.

At midnight the decision was made to close the conference. The Grey Wolf had failed to return. The plan was to retire to the bar at The Land Without a Name and salvage what was left of the weekend.

As we walked along the front, a substantial group of us, at least twenty people, I caught our reflection in the windows along the way, some lit up with ironing boards and television sets, some with bookcases, some with solitary couches and bare walls, some with husbands and wives and children grouped around a single table, some with newspapers piled up to the ceiling, and I felt a silent terror take hold of me, as if each scene was like a card drawn from the pack at random. I began to feel faint and stopped to take a seat on the wall and to fan myself with a handkerchief. The Iron Giant, a good-natured ex-serviceman from Calderbank, sat down next to me. Is everything alright? he said. I didn't know what to say.

Later, at the bar, he bought me a pint of heavy and we
compared notes. Jack Frost, I said, he was the worst.
The Opening Invocation was the worst, he insisted. What
Opening Invocation? I asked him. I hadn't been invited to
any Opening Invocation and it didn't appear anywhere on
the programme. It was more of a word-of-mouth thing, he
said. It had been at The Grey Wolf's suggestion, he said.

They had been told to gather in his room just after two.
The door had been answered by a dishevelled girl who kept
referring to him as Art. Art will be with you in a minute,
she kept saying, and it seemed like she was suppressing a
laugh, she had that kind of face, a delighted face, he said,
but devious, like the joke was on you.

Inside, the room was a mess. It didn't seem as if he had been
expecting us. There was underwear on the floor, crumpled
shirts across the bed, empty bottles on the dresser, a half-
eaten tray from room service with the remains of a BLT.
And there were books spread all across the bed, all lying
opened and facing down. The poor spines, I thought to
myself. What were the books? I asked him. Tell me what
the books were. I didn't look closely at them, The Iron Giant
said, I couldn't give you names.

One of them had a picture of an eye on the front, he said, the
drawing of an eye in the sky, gazing down on what looked
like a seaside town in Europe with great beams or tentacles
or eyelashes, I couldn't tell you which.

Another had a picture of a man smoking a cigarette with a
face so pockmarked you could have landed on it and planted
an American flag.

692

One book said something about Empire.

Another had artwork that seemed to show people growing up from the ground like plants. That's what it looked like, but I could be wrong.

Then there were the magazines. There was porno there, he said, and he nodded gravely. There was a lot of porno there. What kind? I asked him. The explicit kind, he said.

We all filed in, it was awkward, none of us wanted to look each other in the eye. We lined up at the end of the bed, five or six of us. There was a balcony that looked out to the sea, it seemed like an executive suite or something, I had no idea they were even available in this hotel. That's when he made his appearance. He was wearing a white bathrobe and smoking a cigarette. It looked like he hadn't shaved in days. He gestured to the girl to leave us in peace and flicked his cigarette into a bin. I didn't sleep with her, he said, just in case you're wondering. Then he told us to clear some space and to watch him. He took off his robe to reveal an athletic build and a pair of swimming shorts. He took a few steps back and then propelled himself up the side of the wall, performing a last-minute backflip in order to bring himself back to earth. He looked around at us, lined up at the bottom of the bed. Can any of you do that? he said. Then he sniffed the air like that: sniff, sniff. Did one of you just shit yourself? he said. Then he lit a cigarette. Let's take it to the balcony, my friends, he said, that's how he referred to us, his dear friends.

The balcony was large, running around the entire top level of the house and with a panoramic view over the beach.

By this time there were only stragglers left outdoors. The Grey Wolf pointed out across the sea. What's down there? he asked us. You ever think about that? Of course we did, who doesn't think about fishes now and then? People call it the Abyss, he said. Yet it's teeming with life. But somehow, to us, it feels more like a regression or an inversion. Ask yourselves, he said, what kind of subterranea would you have us map? Shadows have less substance, it's true, he continued, but substance precludes depths, just as form gets in the way of nothing. I'm paraphrasing here, The Iron Giant said. But bear with me. Essentially, he seemed to be saying, we're plotting shadows. We're wasting our time. Then he challenged us once again. Ask yourselves, he said, whether it wouldn't be better to be buried alive than to chase after your own shadow. Then his mood turned irritable, he became argumentative, culminating in him snatching at a bottle of whisky that one of the boys had been helping himself to for the best part of half an hour and ushering us out of the room.

I stood for a time outside his door, listening in, and I almost fancy that the lights in the hallway were flashing on and off but that could just be because sometimes I think I live in a movie. I couldn't make out what was going on, but it sounded like he was wolfing down the entire contents of the minibar, shortbread included. The next time I saw him it was at the round-table debate with Frost and The Plug. He didn't seem himself.

Just then, interrupting our conversation, Frost entered the snug. He made a big deal of banging and wiping his shoes on the mat, like he was an Arctic explorer come in from the cold, and then he crept forward like an upright centipede and ordered two pints of his finest from the landlord, which is an idiotic way to order beer. I stared him straight in the face. I wasn't afraid.

That's when The Grey Wolf made his entrance, striding up to the bar and receiving a pint from a beaming Frost. Then he turned to his audience and proposed a toast. This is the beginning of a great adventure, he said. Henceforth we shall be known by a new name. We shall follow in the shadows of our forefathers. We shall regain our memories. We shall never surrender to ourselves. My heart leaped; the birth of The AntiMatterists!

I christen us The Society of Irregular Research and Knowledge, he announced, reborn from the ashes of the Second Church of the First Stone. Everyone joined glasses and there was much frivolity. My heart sank. I made my way back to the hotel and slept until noon.

Over the weeks that followed, The Grey Wolf played things close to his chest. My life almost returned to normal. Token Bob kept me updated through regular telephone conversations and the occasional letter or circular printed on paper bearing the acronym of the newly formed society. I made some overtures, suggested the drawing up of a formal constitution and proposed the acceptance of my manifesto as a broad outline, though really I saw it as a Holy Book and unalterable by a single letter.

Bob said he would forward it to The Grey Owl for approval. Bob seemed to have taken up the role of The Grey Owl's secretary, PR expert and bodyguard, all rolled into one. It was now impossible to contact The Grey Owl except through

the offices and goodwill of Bob. I repeatedly asked him to
spill the beans on exactly what The Grey Owl had seen
down there and the contents of the photographs but every
time I brought it up he assumed a grave tone and talked
about potentialities and possible outcomes, so much so that
I began to suspect the presence of Jack Frost's shrivelled
hand behind the scenes, resting on Bob's shoulder like a
stroke victim or covering the mouthpiece of a second phone,
listening in silence.

I returned to my job of counting beans for an educational
establishment in Monklands. It was a school with a good
disciplinary record, the region's high-flyers in calligraphy.
I had retired from History – though not history proper, I
hasten to add – after only a few years in the game. I had
prematurely aged. Not physically but there had been some
kind of recompense taken out on my soul, my heart had been
branded, so to speak, with a light so bright that it drove me
deep into darkness.

I occupied the building at the back of the school, a single
bungalow surrounded on three sides by tall trees so that
it felt as if I lived inside an empty aquarium, the only
architecture at the bottom of the pool a sad castle, long since
abandoned.

I subsisted on the smell of old stationery, the lustre of rusty
grey filing cabinets, the quiet spell of pencil holders, wire
bins filled with balls of crumpled paper, the yellow strip
light that made me feel like a salamander or a chameleon
behind glass, I took on the colour of brown elastic bands,
of coffee-stained folders, I was a writer, a secret novelist
who had fallen in love with the tools of the trade, every day

I gathered information, cross-referenced facts, processed every transaction that took place, every new arrival, every child lost in the woods, every dux medallist, every bruised head, every proud parent, every temporary illness, so that I said to myself, this is one of the classics, this is *The Iliad* right here, and I began to feel like a great writer, which is to feel like the only writer, the only one who has broken the silence, the only one who has dared to sacrifice his life to the mapping of this shape of consciousness.

I had put together a group of young male students that I particularly favoured and often during playtimes they would gather in the bungalow and I would lecture them on the kind of temptations they should avoid when they graduated to secondary school.

Tattoos, I said. The wearing of earrings. Hair dye. Then I would pass round toffees and we would debate the subject of the day, chosen by myself in advance. Outdoor skills, tying knots, Greek poetry, *The Silmarillion*, M.R. James, the ghost stories of Vincent O'Sullivan, the Ouija board, chess, the Second World War, Caldey Island, D.H. Lawrence, standing stones, maps and orienteering, *Tarka the Otter*.

I began to organise field trips, all with the parents' permission, of course, days out to view the barracks in Maryhill where Rudolf Hess had been imprisoned or to walk the tunnel that ran beneath the Clyde at Finnieston or even just to visit the parks, the secret parks of the East End, like Tollcross Park, where I first experienced the silence that lies beneath the city itself, the beautiful stillness perfectly maintained, as though above was below, the negative of the true mirror city, or Sighthill

Park, in the north, with its mysterious stairways that
led nowhere, its Hill of Mementos, so-called, an area of
skeletal scrub that had become an unofficial bulletin board
for the shadows of the city, with calendars left strapped
to standing stones and opened at a summer month, long
passed, highlighted in pen, a gesture that came across
as more breath-taking – more dramatic in scope, and in
possibility – than any novel.

My concern was for ideas, that certain ideas could fall by the
wayside if not properly serviced, and I set out to train the
students as I would an army of monks. Our activities spilled
over into the weekends. The boys turned into dinner guests
and confidants and they would present my wife with tragic
tokens of affection: chipped porcelain birds, postcards from
the Museum of Transport, suspect fossils, bug-infested pine
cones.

One afternoon I was seated at my desk in the cottage,
sniffing erasers and chewing old pencil-tops, as was my
wont, as I went through the school's accounts, trying to
make sense of all of its comings and goings in this terrible
heat, who could forget that summer, when a note presented
itself, a note that purported to be a contract for a new
history teacher. This was extremely irregular. The history
department was at capacity, my own recently vacated
position having been taken up by a carnaptious bitch by the
name of Miss Harriet. The name on the new contract was
Arthur McManus.

Art! I rose from my desk and rushed across the playground,
arriving at Mr Archibald the head teacher's office out of
breath and with a thin sliver of sweat across my top lip. I

burst through the door without bothering to knock and there in front of me stood The Grey Wolf, resplendent now as The Grey Bat, his black cloak billowing over his light-grey suit. Doesn't he feel the heat? I said to myself.

Can I help you? Mr Archibald asked me. I apologised while attempting to explain my position. You must understand, I said, how difficult it is for me to balance the books when I am no longer privy to staffing decisions. Mr Archibald nodded portentously while The Grey Bat remained silent. Then he looked me straight in the eye. It was unforeseeable, Mr Archibald said. It was a spur-of-the-moment appointment. Meet Mr McManus, the headmaster said, our new head of history.

What are you doing here? I asked him as we swept into the corridor. There's no time for that now, he said, in fact there's very little time at all. How about a school trip? he said. I feel a school trip coming on. I've always wanted to visit the trenches in Ypres, he said. What do you say? Get a nice guesthouse along the front at Ostend. Why don't we get some of the boys together and make a weekend of it?

Forty-eight hours later we were booking ourselves into a tall white guesthouse just off the promenade in Ostend by the name of Julio's but which we later heard referred to by the locals as Rabbit's Wedding for reasons we were never able to get to the bottom of. We had four of our best boys with us.

Breakfast was a disaster. The boys had refused the classic Belgian breakfast and insisted on baked beans to a man. After I had procured us a raft of tins from a nearby supermarket, I gave them to Julio, who turned them out

cold in their bowls. We laughed and rolled our eyes. A
Europe of unrepentant idiots.

Our first port of call was to the war graves, which in a
way were more fascinating than the trenches, especially
when seen in motion, from a tour bus or a car, the effect
of the endlessly repeating lines seemingly planned with
the automobile in mind, in other words with an eye to the
future, and so destined, ultimately, to be relics. I thought of
populations uncovering them hundreds of years from now
and having no understanding of the speed at which they
were intended to be read.

The afternoon we spent at the trenches. We visited the First
World War trenches at Sanctuary Wood, Hill 62 still intact
but now overgrown with grass and foliage. The boys ran riot
amongst the channels, leaping from one side to the other
and pursuing each other through the tunnels. They might
as well be furrows in the brain, The Grey Wolf said.

The boys had been eager to try their hands at European
athletics and they convinced us to check in on a gymnasium
on the way back. I was always very fond of gymnasiums.
This particular gym hall was built in the shape of an
octagonal dome at the end of a blank concrete walkway
and when we entered they were playing loud electronic
music over the speakers. This music is too much for me,
I confessed, and I left The Grey Wolf in charge, and I
walked out and sat next to the railings, where I lit a pipe.

I had the urge to call my wife. I made my way to a payphone
across the way. Melanie, I said to her, Melanie my darling,

I'm calling from Belgium. I made it to the trenches.
Everything is okay.

Everything's fine at home, she said. Nothing to report. What
have you been doing, darling? I asked her. I wanted to say
something else, something loving and intimate, to praise her
playfulness or her dedication or her fortitude in the face of
all of her misfortune, but the conversation came to nothing.
I realised I was being forced deeper and deeper into silence.

As I made my way back to the gymnasium I staggered under
the assault of the sun. I held my hands up to my face and
made my way by looking through my fingers. I sat on the
stairs in order to steady myself. An attendant emerged and
put his hand on my shoulders, a young black man with a
distasteful goatee beard and a shaved head. Is everything
alright, he asked me, is there a problem? His tone a mix of
faux concern and obvious distaste. I raised myself up with
the aid of the banister. I have loved, I announced. I have
suffered. I have nothing more to say beyond that.

The Grey Owl emerged into the sunlight. I need a drink, he
said. I don't know about you. We gathered up the children
and made for a seafood bar along the front. He ordered
ouzo and Belgian beer for the two of us, half-pints of beer for
the children. The boys sat with their shoes off and their feet
up on the table, their muscular legs already, maddeningly,
turning brown. I searched for a sign of the sun in ourselves.
I looked to The Grey Wolf. What did you think of the
trenches? I asked him. They didn't go deep enough, he said.

Later, after we'd put the boys to bed, he suggested we go see
the sights. Let's make for the heart of the city, he said.

Ostend is the queen of the Belgian seaside resorts. Even in its earliest form, as seen on surviving maps, the city has the appearance of an open heart, a vulva or a rose. Late-night bar gave way to late-night drinking den gave way to illicit basement joint until it felt as if we were pursuing a point at the very end of the night, a particle of an impossible density and of the colour cobalt, the light at once dimming and coming up.

We arrived at what appeared to be an abandoned bar on the very fringes of the city, though its distant silhouette had made it seem more like a ruined castle or a secret rock formation in the depths of a forest. There was a poster on the wall advertising some forgotten concert by an emaciated singer dressed completely in black who looked like the living dead and who wore a wide-brimmed hat that cast a shadow over his face. The Grey Wolf led us to the back of the building, where we descended a flight of stairs to a subterranean bunker. At the door we were instructed to remove all of our clothes except for our undergarments and our shoes.

I was filled with silence, and with not speaking. I removed my clothes.

When we reached the bottom of the final set of stairs, this set of stairs that plunged and spiralled through endless darkness, The Grey Wolf stepped forward and parted the black curtain in front of us.

Three men and a woman, all of them in nothing but underwear and shoes, stood drinking at the bar. The men wore surly expressions while the woman gazed straight ahead, her elbows planted on the edge of a table, as she made some kind of emphatic point.

The Grey Wolf ordered for both of us. I confess, for a second, I wondered whether the glassware was sanitary. But as we drank the mezcal I felt the light inside me equilibrate, somehow, the goings-on around us, so that I was able to soak in the scene without concern. I thought of the pulque gods, I had seen them in a book, how their bodies were two colours, mirrored, as was their function inside the body itself, to mirror, and to forgive, and I thought of Melanie, too, my other half.

The Grey Wolf took my arm and ushered me into a back room. It was like I could hear the wind from a long way away, and a bird, singing, somewhere a final bird is singing, I said to myself, somewhere in back of things, I told myself, and I told myself, it takes you all of your life to hear it, even though it has been pursuing you since the beginning of time, I said to myself, I am that, I said to myself, who knows, my spike had been drinked, I had woken up, I was beyond words, who knows, if a head speaks and there is no one there to understand that it has spoken, I said to myself, then has it spoken at all, and yet I heard it with my own two ears, and if a flower blooms, once, and no one ever notices it, I said to myself, and I wondered, then, has it bloomed at all, and I thought, the world is reliant on invisible flowers, on lonely dares on precarious clifftops, and in the corner there was a single white cubicle, and open the door, I heard him say, but when I looked around he had disappeared, though his voice remained in my head, this voice, that it occurred to me had been making its way towards me from the beginning, like a long-range spacecraft,

tumbling, rapturously, into orbit, which is open the door, it
said, and I crept forward, slowly, like I was crossing cracked
ice but underneath it was nothing, emptiness, this same
silence that held me up threatened to drown me forever,
and I pushed the door open and it swung back slowly on
its hinges, the rust the colour of old flames, the cubicle the
stained off-white of military barracks

~^~*~^~

The next morning we hired bikes and drove along the promenade. We struggled with the gears and several times swerved into oncoming traffic.

We made our way to a seawater swimming pool that had been dug out of the rocks and that The Grey Owl had read about in a brochure. One hardly gets the time to read, being a full-time adventurer, he protested, before falling asleep with a copy of the *Reader's Digest* spread out on his ample chest.

The sight of the boys leaping from the rocks reminded me of a painting of young boys along the cliffs of St Andrews Bay.

In the evening we hired a taxi to take us to a memorial for forces killed in the Second World War that The Grey Wolf claimed included members of his own family. Our taxi driver spoke no English and confused the word harbour with memorial and so kept driving us to empty marinas and windswept bays where we would pace the ground, fruitlessly, before getting back in. At one point we pulled up on the beach and the driver got out and pointed towards the moon. Maan, he said. Then he pointed to the water. Meer, he said. Maanmeerial, he said, maanmeerial.

On the way back, as we walked along the seafront, one of the boys started acting up. At first he complained about the taxi ride, claiming it had made him seasick. You mean motion sickness, The Grey Wolf corrected him. No, he said, I mean seasick. I hate Belgium, he said. My legs are burned. The Grey Wolf turned him around to reveal a pair of badly sun-scarred legs. How could we have let this happen? he asked, lifting the boy over his shoulder. Let's get this boy home, he said. What were we thinking?

Back at the guesthouse things escalated when a fellow boarder alerted the authorities to the boy's moaning. They thought someone was being abused, they said. In the event they took the boys away from us and lined them up in the corridor outside while they questioned The Grey Wolf and myself, both of us at this point in nothing but our dressing gowns.

They asked us what we were doing here, whether the children were our children or if they had legal permission to be with us. We had no proof, nothing to show parental consent or to confirm our status as teachers. But out in the corridor the boys were giving them no quarter. Call my mother, one of them said. She'll confirm everything. They called the number and got his sister on the phone. Yes, he lives here, she said. Yes, everything's fine. They asked her about The Grey Owl and she claimed she knew him, calling him De Schrijver. He's covered all the bases, I thought to myself, and I marvelled at his foresight. We have all the information we need, the authorities said, handing the boys back into our care.

Nevertheless, there was a feeling of paranoia, and as soon as the lights went out we packed our bags and fled, checking into a single room above a bar with several double beds and with net curtains that opened to reveal the beach in silence and the tide temporarily stilled.

This is more like it, The Grey Wolf said. Now we're talking. You boys should know about alcohol, he said, and he opened a bottle of vodka and poured us all a shot. Look out there, he said, you think that's down below, that it's underneath or beyond you. It's right here, he said, pointing to his chest, and he raised his glass, although I fancy he was moved beyond anything he had expected, as his eyes glazed over while he proposed a toast to deep-sea creatures, to those without eyes, he said, wherein the boys all clinked their glasses and vowed to never leave the sea, even though we had all left it long ago, and forever.

There was a small terrace bar below our room and once we had put the boys to bed I joined The Grey Wolf for a nightcap. He seemed preoccupied. The sea has got to him, I thought to myself. Do you have any idea where we are? he kept asking me. Of course, back then, I thought it was a silly question. We're here, I said, we're in Belgium. But now I think he was trying to tell me that we had escaped into time and further, that we were safe there. He put his hand on my leg. I felt like we were military commanders and the sea our frontier and somewhere beyond the horizon a battle taking place, a battle whose strategy consisted of every move we had ever made in our lives, every sickness, every pleasure, every stirring urge.

I have unlocked the tunnels, he said. I have gone deeper than any man has gone before. That's how I came to be here. I walked in the garden, he said. I entered the abyss.

I fancied that in the distance I could hear explosions, see flares going up, the way the light caught it was as if the sea itself was on fire. I had to pull myself together. What do you mean? I asked him. Where are these tunnels?

What am I doing here right now? he asked me. I shook my head.

I have uncovered a passage from the past to the future, he told me, only one that runs both ways.

What do you intend to do with it? I asked him.

I came to get you, he said.

I was taken aback.

I came back because I wanted to ask you what it was all about, he said.

All what is about?

Time, he said, the universe, he said, everything. And then he sighed, and placed his hand on my thigh.

That was so like The Grey Owl; who else would even ask that? That combination of earnestness and naivety. I turned the question over in my mind. The life and death of every cell, the thoughts blowing through my mind like leaves, the memories whose only proofs were chemical, this light that now seemed to fill me and to make me brave, and complete.

It is the state of my body, I said to him. It just came to me, a dimly remembered quote, who knows where from. It is the state of my body that will figure the final judgement, I said to him.

The body in the cubicle in the dark? he asked me. The body of knowledge? The body of history? The body of Jesus Christ himself?

What was it that you stole through the tunnels? I asked him, warming to my theme. It was your body. The body is the vessel that travels through time.

That's true, he said, but only in a limited sense. The body travels forward in time. There's no reverse, no backwards gear. The body is like a time machine with the rudder jammed. But there are tunnels, in the head, tributaries, if you like, that lead off from consciousness, and these are the true highways, the only way of travelling backwards and forwards.

Yet they are part of the body, I said, they're chemical, biological.

That's well observed, he said. But ask yourself this. Is mathematics chemical? Is logic? Is fate and destiny? Is literature?

Nothing makes sense, I said to him, and I sat back in my chair, in silence.

I'll tell you something that makes sense, he said, leaning forward conspiratorially. Putting your foot on the gas and getting the fuck out of here.

I resigned from my job. As soon as I got back home I resigned. I took my darling wife out for a sad dinner in a dimly lit Italian restaurant. I have to leave you, my darling,

I told her. Then I got down on one knee and laid my head on her lap. I could feel the pulse of our unborn baby, a broadcast from another world, now.

The next day the journal arrived, the one with The Grey Wolf's pictures from the mirror city beneath Burntisland. There were photographs of three-wheeled tricycles piloted haphazardly along the seafront; of empty gym halls and of boys on trampolines; of endless lines of military graves; and in one picture, a blurry Polaroid that was so out of focus it was impossible for anyone else to identify the man in question, I recognised the contours of my own visage, somewhat the worse for wear, in a subterranean nightspot somewhere on the continent.

I telephoned Token Bob. When had the pictures been handed over? As soon as The Grey Wolf had emerged from the underworld, he insisted. It was impossible, I said. These things have only just taken place, I told him. He laughed at me then, but this was before the whole UFO incident when he still saw himself as rigorous, the poor fantasist bastard.

A second meeting was called, a return to Burntisland scheduled for two weeks' time. In the meantime, I focused on the disposal of my particulars. I signed the house over to my wife. I cashed in my savings plans and used them to pay for a round-the-clock carer. I called what was left of my family and lied, signed off, bid them au revoir.

They had never understood me, my passions had remained secret, my triumphs untranslatable. I manufactured a series of lies, one per family member. That I was fleeing debts; that I was moving to a political commune in Natividad,

Bolivia; that I was being taken into the witness protection programme after exposing a communist terror plot; that I had given myself up to a life of outlawry; that I had 'gone native', so to speak; that there had been several attempts on my life that had forced me to go underground; that I was about to kick the bucket and was heading off to the Scottish mountains to have my entrails eaten by birds of prey; that I had a job driving trains through underground munitions plants whose location I could never reveal (in truth a long-cherished fantasy); that I had fallen in love all over again.

The last one I saved for my father, who was so far gone that his personality had been erased to the point of complete forgiveness for everything. I fell in love with a man, I told him. A wonderful man. Your uncle Sam was a wonderful man, he said. Many men were in love with him. I'm leaving my wife, I said, my poor suffering wife with her shrivelled legs, her once lovely legs, now hidden beneath a permanent tartan blanket. Legs change, my father said. I have been part of a time travelling experiment, I told him, only this time going backwards as well as forwards. You remind me of someone I used to know, he said, but I can't quite put my finger on it. Goodbye, I said to him. Of course, he said. Goodbye.

On the night before my departure, the bulk of the tears having already been shed, my wife joined me for a last vegetarian meal that we ate together in silence. In the distance we could see the tall blocks of flats that would soon become my home. Will you be able to see me from there? she asked me as I cleared the plates. With the aid of binoculars, I would expect so, I said. Will you zoom in on me now and then? she said. Just so I know there's a pair of eyes out there looking? We could arrange times, I suggested. We could arrange times where I would definitely look, and you could be right there at the window. You'll see me, but I won't see you, she said. It'll be like acting. I feel like I'm acting right now, I confessed. You can't choose your part, she said. But you can empathise with it, I said. I feel sorry for my part, she said. It was a very small role.

I brought up Rilke's *Diaries of a Young Poet*; in my opinion they have the answer to everything. I talked at length about the section where Rilke writes of the idea of demanding you of yourself. Think about that, I said. But I could see that it had little effect.

We sat for a time in silence, only interrupted by the ticking of a clock in an empty room, before I carried her to bed, an old four-poster with a high view out to the river and in the distance a row of trees that in the darkness resembled the spine of a dinosaur. I turned the radio on, the shipping forecast, inevitably, and I went into the room next door to pack.

I packed a few suits, two pairs of shoes, a basic toilet bag, a paperback edition of *The Collected Poems of A.E. Housman*, a small hip flask, a George V knuckleduster made by my father when he was in jail in Ireland, and an anonymous flat cap that I intended to use as a disguise when moving around above ground.

In my head there was music, piano music, accompanying the radio in the background, and when my wife began to sing from the bed next door it was as if she was accompanying the song in my mind, not so much in the words but in the melody, which was alternately nostalgic and strident. It made me think about the possibility of life on other planets.

2. SO BELOW

The Grey Owl, like many of us, was preoccupied with the Jewish Question. We sat on the balcony with the lights out, the city laid out like a war map in front of us. The Jewish Question is as important as ever, he said. It boils down to this. What place compassion? To take the side of the Jews is to say live and let live, let God be the judge of history. To take the anti-Semitic stance is to reject all appeals to outside authority, to colonise consciousness with the rapacity of a Roman legion or an Egyptian dynasty or a German Reich, and to wake up to history as the men who direct it. The choice is that, or to count yourself to sleep inside it.

The Jewish Question must be answered, Julius Streicher said. What he meant was that there was a frontier of consciousness that was both individual and historical that had yet to be fully explored. They intended to lay siege to Semitic reality, this people – these time travellers, these heralds of a new aeon, really, in their repercussions – and to expose it as nothing more than a series of props or facades no more convincing but every bit as seductive as the Hollywood sign itself, which, of course, was built by international Jewry. This manifested itself in the destruction of compassion.

Hans Frank called them lice. For Hugo Höppener it meant sterilisation. But Erhard Wetzel brings up guilt. He says extermination of the Polish population would result in guilt. Why wouldn't the extermination of the Jewish race result in guilt? Because they were envisioned as *the source of guilt itself*. The Nazi assault was nothing more than a storming of heaven, which is every possibility under the sun. After the destruction of the Jews, guilt would henceforth manifest itself as a form of ennui, a simple falling short of possibility. In the face of that, an armed Jewry is a terrible thing, I said. Think about it, The Grey Owl said. A sea of misfortunes.

Together we began to prepare for the Burntisland Conference. The idea was that we would present our experiment with time as a refutation of Semitic ideas. The liberating of time meant that compassion and love were sundered. As players in the show we came, and we went, in rapture. History itself was a great game, a theatre: of war; of love; of endings and beginnings; but still a theatre. And man, the new man, the subterranean man, the man who travelled in the backroads of history, at will, was its only fit judge. Now that history was self-directed, and could be corrected, now that it was indistinguishable from the machinations of man himself, guilt was at an end. We made history as men. And we judged it accordingly.

I told The Grey Owl about Jack Frost's love of pop music, the idiot girls whose autographs he sought, his passion for costume and camp. We can use that against him, I said. We can expose him as a decadent fairy. No, he said. He could be useful to us. When you came back from the past, when you emerged from the mirror city, I said, Jack Frost was the first person you contacted. He was waiting for you at the bar when you made your entrance. Haven't you read any Shakespeare? The Grey Owl asked me.

It was the night of the conference. We came on stage in long
black robes, by this point The Grey Owl's trademark. We
faced down our opponents, those that pooh-poohed us. We
presented date-coded blow-ups of the photographs, then
followed up with the kind of inspirational rhetoric that would
enshrine them as the founding documents of our assault
on Semitic slavery and our philosophy of lighting out into
the past and into the future. Death, The Grey Owl said,
and the reports that he stammered when he said this are
true, as though his body was unconvinced and in fact was
actually protesting, death provides the momentous energy
of expanding creation, he said, which means that when we
make battle – inside our bodies, inside our minds, or upon the
world – we are at the bridgehead of creation. But the doctrine
of 'as above so below' means that it is not a sacrifice, as the
Semitic races would have us believe, rather, an eternal taking
part, and a coming into being, guilt-free, forever.

We stood at the front of the stage, our toes gripping the edge
like a pair of upside-down bats, and leered at our audience.
This is what it's all about, I said to myself.

We fell in love with the subterranean monuments, the
night-time of Europe, I told them, because the basic
architecture of our souls was pagan. A simple gravestone,
a cross, a church no longer had any significance. We
demanded antechambers, tunnels, bunkers, lost rivers,
deserted airfields, caverns, caves, secret ladders, tributaries,
shadows, abandoned railroads, underground factories,
deserted quarries, deep pools, hollow mountains, noise,
bonfires, crisis, war, secret files, as truer reflections of the
endless shadowland of the soul, yet none of us realised
what our demands would ultimately lead to: that ours was

the great psychic revolt of the age, and that our insistence on the existence of subterranea, and our determination to sound their depths, would open up parallel tunnels in the mind and in time and space.

Of course there were critics, contradictors. You opened up nothing, The Green Beret said, the mirror city was built by the government who were obviously involved with time travel experiments, you just stumbled upon it, and what exactly was the technology, someone else shouted, a small man with a comedy nose and an over-large suit with no name tag, what did it consist of, was there a portal, did you step into something, were there buttons, what did it feel like, did it hurt, did it feel like you were taken apart atom by atom and rearranged somewhere else, did it turn you on, Token Bob shouted, a low blow, for sure, and I looked around at The Grey Wolf and it's true that his head was in his hands and he was bent over in his chair, although the reports that he was trying to cover up his tears are simply offensive, he had just travelled backwards through time, he was beyond the astronauts at this point, beyond the so-called psychedelic adventurers, beyond the brains of the greatest men of the twentieth century, because after all no one was coming back in time to say hello to him, and so he was moved, it's true, but not to tears, if anything, he told me later, and it was unlike him to open up in this way, it was a sudden dizziness, he said, like looking down on a dark lake from up above and suddenly the lake winks at you, he said, like an eyelid shoots across it, however briefly, and you realise that when you thought you were staring into nothing you were in fact staring straight into an eye, an eye with no pupil, so how were you to know, but an eyeball, nonetheless, brave traveller.

The synod afterwards was dramatic; the first official
synod of the newly christened SIRK. Ranged around the
table there was Token Bob (homeland security), The Iron
Giant (secretary), The Plug (propaganda), The Flashlight
(archivist), The Lightning Bolt (away team) and Jack Frost,
whom The Grey Owl had insisted we bring onside (logistics).
There were also two secretaries, whose conflicting minutes
speak of the feeling of something going on in the room that
was protean on the very deepest of levels. The Grey Wolf
had insisted on booking them at the last minute. What great
man in history, he had asked me, what great man since the
invention of the nib or the quill hasn't looked towards his
biographers? What great man ever went unrecorded?

At points the noise of the typewriters was deafening,
marking rounds with their bells like a boxing match, and
several times I had to shake myself from a trance as I felt
the individual letters impressing themselves on the soft grey
of my brain as if my thoughts were being spelled out letter
by letter, at incredible speed, and for long minutes I had to
grip the desk and hold on for dear life.

Jack Frost stood up and gesticulated, his body contorted
like he was standing on his hind legs for the first time ever,
like he had only just staggered up and out of the sea. Token
Bob was laughing, hysterically. The Iron Giant rose to calm
things. The Grey Wolf pushed back his chair. At length he
made a show of removing a small hip flask from his inside
pocket with a jewelled engraving of a headless man on the
side, biting the top off with his teeth, pushing the chair back
with his legs and while balancing precariously with his feet
on the edge of the table taking a long drink and spitting the
contents out in a great arc across the table.

Everyone was stunned. The typists froze. I sat bolt upright in my chair.

Tell me, he said, when was the last time anyone in this room got rat-arsed?

I had a few ales last night, The Iron Giant offered. Me too, Token Bob said. And I'm paying for it this morning, I can tell you. I'm not talking about a few pints of an evening, The Grey Wolf said. I'm taking about systematic derangement. I'm talking about visionary excess.

Once, back when I had just left school, I drank a half-bottle of whisky in my bedroom on a summer's afternoon while reading a book of Wordsworth's poetry, The Iron Giant said. Who on earth reads Wordsworth in this day and age? I thought to myself. That's as may be, The Grey Wolf said. But let me get to my point. What takes place in the inner sanctum, the holy order – at which he made a point of looking each and every one of us square in the eye – stays in the inner sanctum. Let us drink to knowing, to daring, to willing, and yet to remaining silent. Then he passed around the hip flask so that each of us in turn could swear and drink from the same cup. Some of them, I won't name any names, had obviously never tasted alcohol in their lives before, as there were numerous oohs and aahs and oh my Christs as they forced this green-golden mixture down their throats like they were sucking it straight from The Grey Wolf's prodigious member itself. Later I found out that it was absinthe that we had been drinking, from an old family stash. The Grey Wolf had dosed us.

No sooner had we finished drinking than an argument broke out. The Plug described The Pink Panzer as an entertainer. A crowd-pleaser, he called him. It was true that The Pink Panzer had a flamboyant style. His reports were riddled with brackets, columns, colons, semicolons, subsections, clauses, footnotes, indexes, asides, digressions, subtexts, elaborations, underlinings, diagrams, doodles and marginalia, drawings, like once where he drew a walking map of the twenty-two districts of the underground city of Burlington and colour-coded it like a Tube map, all painstakingly footnoted, the first map ever to come to light before its decommissioning, or the time he produced a fold-out supplement in the shape of a concertina for *Passing Through Doubt*, a literary magazine run by a priest with a philanthropic taste for the esoteric that I'm told is now very collectable and that consisted of *Notes Towards an Introspective Vision of Subterranea*, where he had argued – I can't be clear as I'm not well versed in the subject myself – for something along the lines of extending, or rather inverting, the poet Charles Olson's vision of projective verse and his notions of scale in time and space wherein he posited that Olson had failed to anticipate that the birth of his idea would result in a dark twin, which implied a contraction, an introspecting of language, a shortness of breath, a gulping, gasping-for-air poetry of being buried half-alive, and a language that had more to do with grammar – structural, organisational – a language that would be as implacable, now, as those first stone circles, in time, as inexplicable, too, and as unconcerned by meaning, as the tightening of a fist.

For his *Notes Towards . . .* essay, The Pink Panzer had letterpressed a fold-out visual poem that he claimed was empty of any content outside of suffocatingly dense relationships of structure and tone, like a tuning fork for the whole of reality, in fact he compared it to the Kabbalistic Tree of Life, a glyph was how he described it, though to most people it looked more like an early computer print-out or a supermarket receipt, and of course his publishing in what many aficionados still flippantly derided as 'the pink press' gave him both his handle and his reputation as a performer. Token Bob, so the rumour went, was his partner, in secret.

On hearing this slander, this bald-faced accusation of playing to the balcony, Token Bob first made a big deal of stubbing his cigar out on the sole of his shoe, a brown brogue with a small leather tassel on the front that he invariably wore with dark, variously striped socks, a brogue that had seen better days in a charity shop on Dumbarton Road, if we're being honest. Then, moving in a deliberately exaggerated fashion, he seemed to flit across the room, and just as it looked like he was going to grab The Plug in some kind of death grip, he inserted a single finger into The Plug's hair and wound it to a tight curl, then he grabbed a knife from the kitchen drawer that was lying open right next to him and with a single slicing motion he cut The Plug a new bald spot. And The Plug burst into tears, somewhat miraculously, as no one had ever heard him express anything that could be termed an emotion outside of obsession or excitement or resentment.

It was true that he was often seen to resent, whether another rising star in the group or a new subterranean find, the mapping of a new ruin, the giving of a speech, he was one of those people, I suspect, and they're more common than anyone cares to admit, because if we did admit it, what then,

there'd be no one to be successful for, all it would create
would be enemies and God knows a man has enough of those,
the kind of people who see their failure in anyone else's
success, a quality which of course was actually desirable in
our own line of research, the ability to always see the reverse,
to picture the opposite, but which in The Plug's personal life,
it was said, had brought him nothing but grief, treating his
daughter like an aged crone, his wife like an enemy or more
properly an agent provocateur, his friends as combatants, his
parents as ghosts, a subterranean who turned his own world
upside down in some kind of futile attempt to balance the
scales, the avant-garde, truly, for he was at the very edge of
the avant-garde, and had much in common with the most
far-out practitioners of the radical art he claimed to despise,
in that he refuted almost any kind of artistic practice
altogether, hated poetry, condemned painting, disdained
novels, rejected film, put up with photography on account
that it was uncreative, despised sculpture, all except for
the strange sculpture that was the figure of his letterhead,
this strange Romanesque statue of a man with two heads, a
muscular Janus or a mischievous Gemini, it was never clear,
and of course he claimed he had moved beyond art altogether,
more, that he had *cured himself* of art and come out the other
side, he said, and he went so far as to maintain, in fact, that if
he was a fascist dictator his first order of the day, even before
banning training shoes and leisurewear, would be to ban art
altogether, to announce a moratorium on expression, whether
of the self or of 'the universe', to turn the imagination into the
very same deep, dark lochs that dotted the Highlands of
Scotland, which would constitute a radical rewilding of art,
these places of perfect stillness and infinite mystery,
untouched by humanity, a virgin darkness, the kind of
spiritual conservatism that posited a hymen in the brain and

a corresponding concept of mental chastity, and now here he
was in tears while Token Bob continued to interfere with his
hair, now taking two strands and pleating them together
until there were two circular bald patches surrounded by thin
dreadlocks, so that someone, The Iron Giant, I believe, said
that he looked like an analemma, which is the empty figure
eight that the sun traces in the sky across the space of a year,
and at this The Plug wept, this drain-clearing noise that had
obviously given him his name along with his dedication to
Victorian sewage works, lost rivers, floodgates, anything to do
with the subterranean transport of water, and then he began
to recant everything, confessing through the tears, explaining
how he was still in thrall to opinion, he admitted, in other
words he was sentimental, he said, God damn that word, and
then he broke down again, dismissing all of his opinions, the
very minutiae of his arguments, arguments that had been
debated over and subscribed to and that had consoled and
alienated in equal measure, confessing that every one of them
had been conceived with the service of the identity that had
come to possess him in his mind, he recanted everything, his
creed, his allegiance, his membership, I'm spooked, he said,
I'm haunted, forget your abandoned buildings, I'm the very
ghost of place, insisting that everything had been done in
service to this phantom child, this demon, he called it, this
terrible dictatorial image inside his head, I have fallen for
ideas, he confessed, and all the while the typists were still
typing, these two young girls, one of whom I saw look up
when The Plug said the word demon with an expression of
actual delight, a secret gambler with an illicit run on the
horses, at which point I fancied she slid a single hand into the
warmth between her legs, the transcription clearly shows
that she was typing with one hand from this point on, you can
see the impact on the paper of the individual letters, craters, I

thought to myself, as if they had been dropped like bombs
into an empty no man's land, and of course I thought of the
trenches, and I flitted back there in my mind, via the secret
tributaries that tunnel beneath the page, and I imagined
a literary underground, a book as a tomb for language and
of a literary Valley of the Kings, a vast subterranean network
connected across time and space and all that would entail, the
empty bunkers, the daring passageways, the perpetual lack of
sunlight, at which point The Grey Owl turned to face us, The
Grey Bat, because he may as well have been hanging upside
down from the ceiling, or scaling the walls with a backflip,
and I felt myself caught in this rush of language that felt
more like a palpitation, like balancing on a precipice, and I
was overcome with fear, not that my heart would pop, more
that it would let me down, at which point The Grey Bat
dropped a large book onto the table with a bang that woke the
entire room from this strange fugue, this atmosphere of teary
disassociation that he had somehow orchestrated (with the
aid of some occult family-brewed absinthe, we now know),
and he announced our founding text, *The Tomb of the Song*,
he said, a Jewish parable, he admitted, to slow gasps and
popping sounds, but from one who got away, he insisted, from
one who woke up, and a few people breathed a sigh of relief, a
few people shook their heads, the room was divided almost
fifty-fifty between people who believed in the reality of the
Jewish Question and its relationship to our own interests and
people who thought we were bats but who were caught up in
the eccentricity of the venture regardless, and then he started
to read from the text and I was caught up almost
immediately, I confess, I recognised myself in its very
cadence, I felt myself transported, as he described a song that
had once been heard in the distance by three wise men, three
wise men that had pronounced the correct words, the precise

spell, that would turn a wounded animal to stone, and they drowned that animal, and that was the first turning to stone, and whose reward, after the animal had passed through the final waters, was the song of the birds from some way off, a song that was as beautiful as the first morning, according to historical accounts, though some translations and various dubious adaptations – it remains one of the most 'bootlegged' of the Kabbalistic literature, if contradictorily the least studied, or perhaps the best studied, should I say, by people who understood the great silence at its centre – describe it as being more like the purring of a cat, the sound of an old motorcycle in the mountains, of the sky in Greece at night, of the echo of an abandoned swimming pool in California – and it's true there is a barren Jewish 'Mem' emblazoned on the cover, which means Abandoned Echoing Swimming Pool – of a child's foot cracking very delicate ice, if fish could sing, someone else said, and the result was horrifying rather than cute, a nursery rhyme you have convinced yourself you always knew, someone else suggested, and best of all, the sound of a light being switched off while holding your breath, and I thought, wait, though, if the song is of a bird, in the distance, if this is the sound of the first moments of creation, then what is that bird perched on, and where does it nest, and I thought of high clifftops, and I visioned lonely stones that the sun could rise above, at last, and we all looked around at each other and I knew we were thinking the same thing, that in our hearts we were subterraneans, and as soon as we felt that great space open up beneath us our first urge was to run down ropes and risk never coming back up, that was when we realised the earth-shaking nature of our mission and felt our membership as a calling, as medieval knights, as blind moles digging tunnels, into the depths of our own obsession and all of its repercussions, in our thoughts

727

and in our lives, and once more felt like masters of our fate, and afterwards I approached Jack Frost and he used much the same language, comparing us to a sacred growth in a backstreet in a small town, risen up in the crack between the stones, in the concrete seam of some invisible wall, this organism, this entity that finally understood its own importance, though honestly he repelled me still, I'm no part of that organism, I said to myself, no part of Jack Frost, even as our fate and our beliefs held us together, still I refused him, idiot, I said, crippled, full of malice, bitter, broken down, troublemaker, at one point I called him all of these, I confess, and he deserved every one of them, yet now I wonder why I would abuse someone that was such an integral part of my own life while the other side of my brain convinces me it was my part to play and there was no other way for us to relate, that the script had been written with us in mind, and that in some book written deep beneath the world there was a small room, a tiny chapel, consigned to rumour, barely locatable, that was dedicated to our interactions regardless, well, the chapel had already been built, I told myself, the structure assigned its place deep inside ourselves and inside history, which is a darkness that awaits explorers like ourselves, and I feel excited when I say that, and proud of the hobby that had made of us brave explorers, we had started out as amateurs, enthusiasts, back then we felt it was more about ourselves, the unspeakable frisson of being lost underground in secret bunkers or in abandoned industrial architecture, how time had tamed even the most grotesque excesses and made them beautiful, even terror, even scale, we were pioneers, a privileged avant-garde who lived down below and not up above and who were the lucky witnesses of this hidden grandeur, this secret pleasure in the reverse, whereas now it was clear that it was the architecture that looked to us, these secret rooms, these memories entombed against the past and the future that longed to be burgled, that thrilled at the lifetime's dedication it took to map their position and the scale of the logistics and the adventure, so that even the curses associated with the desecration of graves seemed more like self-scarification or symbolic twinings, the sex play of a witchy lover, we believed in lovers not victims, lovers in pain and lovers in torment and lovers buried deep beneath the earth, even as we felt ourselves bugged, wired, put upon, pushed to the margins of society due to our insistence on the lie that sustained the truth, our eyes wide open and cast down, tightrope walkers, even as we were bent crooked on canes and couldn't read a damn menu or look up a book at the library or like The Pink Panzer took to writing experimental prose in obscure journals, some of which, it is alleged, were funded by the CIA, which proves that wherever a frontier is being fought the secret service are never far behind, in other words they patrol the perimeter of the mind, has it ever struck you that the reality that mind insists on, and by this I mean the mind of sleepwalkers, of dogs, of shoppers, is that of a concentration camp, wired off, compartmentalised, with gas chambers and death camps for all that it refuses to accommodate, work details for interlocutors who cross the line, punishment blocks for new arrivals, ablutions for the filth, guards to beat lifers black and bloody, unable to see the view from the other side of the fence, forced to carry great weights on their backs, falling like dominoes, ready, at any moment, to respond to orders, no matter how distasteful, then imagine digging a hole, going underground and so avoiding all of their defences and their traps, the searchlights at night and the barbed wire, the early-morning roll call, naked in the square in the mist, the flea-bitten beds, the endless soup, that was how we answered the Jewish Question, we broke out and formed our own society, and in our personal lives people asked questions about us, who was that writer that walked off into the snow, and they would occasionally see us at the cafeteria at Safeway in the afternoon and would lament our wasted potential, he was a boy genius, they would say, a lovely kid, and look at him now, we were the disappeared, though really the escapees, now fugitives, forced into clandestine activities, and so wretched myths survived about us, that we had gone down, that we were personae non gratae, and of course it was a bluff perpetrated by the security services, which is half the people in your life, half, who am I even kidding, most of the people in your life wish to convince you that there is nothing beyond the border of their own minds but abortion and madness and fantasy, and a pile of corpses, ultimately, so as to dissuade any escape bids, and after the reading, which had been very powerful and moving, we exited the building, squinting in the early-evening sun, a historic committee, the vanguard of a new subterranea, though to the people around us we were dreary old men, dodderers, in love with Latin, calligraphic purists, wearers of hats, and as we came out onto the beach, an uninviting part of the coast due to our forced relocation, The Grey Owl made his dramatic speech about walking on water, where he claimed that stone was a component of all elements, there was stone in the sea, in the sky, stone in our souls, that's what supports you, he said, then he went into this vision of the sea being covered with stone, like a fake stone lake in Eastern Europe dreamed up by communists, and he came up with a whole back story to accompany it, a great feat of imagination, the submarines going in and out, the thickness of the stone – fourteen feet – the lights beneath it so that it was illuminated like an underwater city, by this point we had made our way to the beach and we stopped at the foot of the waves and sure enough there was the sound of huge stones moving in the silence somewhere down below, shipwrecks suffering in the deep, scuttled vessels grinding against each other, I thought to myself, when all at once the water seemed to still and solidify, I remember the reflection of the sun on it like a galleon from a dream of the beginning of the world, and The Grey Bat made his move, turning and tearing at his mackintosh while walking straight towards the water, by this point the typewriters have been abandoned though we still have the girls' testimonies as they followed us across the sands and they describe it as 'balancing', which has subsequently been twisted and taken to mean that The Grey Bat, this athlete that could hang from his toes over a drawbridge if he felt like it, somehow balanced on an underwater prop or a sunken wall in order to generate the illusion of stone, of walking on water, when it was plain to everyone who saw it, and there were seven independent witnesses, not including the girls, that he never once looked down, never for a second faltered or even looked around himself, rather he strode out across this paralysed sea and afterwards he drew a blade across his finger and he never bled, I have stilled the waters, he said, look here, and he gave us his thumb, cut open but with no sign of life inside, and I thought of the Witkiewicz painting *Suicide-to-be Three Seconds Before Pulling the Trigger*, a painting that my wife clipped out of a dearly held collection of his work, a fact I only stumbled across many years later when I went to look it up in order to show a fellow connoisseur who was already in love with Rudolf Bauer and Austin Osman Spare, and couldn't locate it, began in fact to wonder if I had made it up or dreamed it or perhaps even painted it myself, a thought that triggered an evening's frenetic cross-checking across various periodicals in order to ascertain its existence, and of course I lost my wife to suicide in the end so I was doubly spooked, it was my first experience of what I might called cursed art, art that speaks so particularly it can lure you into death or disaster, art that demands some kind of existence in the world beyond itself, or that implies it, rather, art that isn't a mirror but a simultaneity, a necessary part of the unfolding, and that enters your life as a catalyst, a catalyst of sorrow, often, a day-old flower already trodden, a young girl who catches her shadow in a vision of death taunting the living, it's a collision, there's no point in trying to pretend otherwise, and right at that moment I saw the same painting in front of me, the gun pressed against The Grey Bat's head, only shooting blanks, these terrible echoes through time, echoes through empty swimming pools, through tunnels, which even at this point I am subjected to daily, on my own out here, and I saw him that night, like the painting come to life, all of himself, in his death-defying bravery, in the spell of his mania, his walking on water, his refusal to bleed, I give him three years tops, I said to myself, three years spent together, and from then on it was a romance, a speedboat that went careering into the future with the two of us onboard like handsome playboys but with no one at the helm.

3. SONS OF THE DESERT

We spent our evenings in a square in Athens painting
tourists, and sometimes beggars, who still longed to see
themselves fixed, on the page, and sometimes monsters,
too, whose longings are the same, for there were monsters
on the street in that time too, and soon we were making a
small fortune, which The Grey Owl channelled into daily
supplies of the best freshly caught salmon, which was
perverse, what don't you like about our sea bass, our red
porgy, the stallholders asked us, what's wrong with our
fucking lobster, some guy said, and The Grey Wolf made
them wrap the salmon in newspaper rather than take it
home in a bag with ice, and we would grill it in the back
garden, really a concrete courtyard the size of a small WC
with high, whitewashed walls on three sides and a dead
vine creeping up, where one day we found a secret note, a
piece of folded-up paper that at first looked like a fag end
so that we wondered if some ne'er-do-well hadn't scaled the
walls and smoked some cannabis in our back porch before
stubbing it out on the wall and getting a clear eyeful of
our belongings through the window, which at this point
amounted to three or four books, a few cloaks, a pocket-
size shortwave radio, a men's magazine The Grey Owl
had bought and then discarded down the side of the bed,
a typewriter that was so heavy that when working in the
field we would take turns strapping it on our backs like a
rucksack, a small paraffin lamp for cooking should we sleep

through the day, and the tools of our new trade – chalks, quills, pens and paintbrushes, along with masking tape and fixing spray, a few easels made out of a combination of metal hangers and wooden chairs, Charles Sims had no better at St Boswells, The Grey Owl said – but then The Grey Owl unrolled the paper like a tiny scroll and we realised that it was in fact a love letter; we had moved into the room two months before, and now it seemed like the previous occupant had an estranged lover, one who was now leaving us poetry and flowers and even one night, impossibly, a painting of a small bird.

S.W.A.L.K., the letter read, and there were rhymes, lewd rhymes, and The Grey Owl urged that we should be careful, that there could be rival operatives, he hinted, others could have made ingress, he suggested, our adventure in time and space could have brought us to the attention of the Axis Powers, he said, and I said to him, isn't that the Nazis, isn't that Stalin and the Japanese, but he said, no, there is a greater axis, and there are powers set to police it, and the visitations became creepier and creepier, to the point that we became convinced that our belongings had been moved around, The Grey Owl's men's magazine now rescued from the side of the bed, a pair of trousers hastily abandoned on the floor now in folded repose upon the bed – what was he thinking, that his love, who was clearly addressed as a female throughout, had taken to cross-dressing, that she was subletting a single room to two ageing astronomers, that the smell of her 'almond curls' had turned to a kind of deflated musk? – then one day we received the invite, a letter addressed to 'The Occupiers' that invited us to an event, a special happening that was to take place in an old lane on the nightside of the city, just behind an abandoned car park, to be there at eight, it said, where 'blank' would take place and where we would 'blank', going on to promise us 'blank', and on the night we made our way by a circuitous route that took us through the fish market, eventually opening out onto a series of dusty paths that wound gradually upwards towards the Acropolis until the whole of the city lay beneath us like scattered pottery and we came to the lane in question, which from a distance had looked like a nondescript loading bay but which as we approached took a turn as the lane narrowed to a tunnel until we were walking in almost complete darkness, our arms held out in front of us, eventually stepping in what seemed to be a huge pile of horse manure – we had seen some mounted policemen earlier, though it was hard to believe that a horse could actually fit through a space so enclosed – and soon we came out on the other side, the tunnel opening onto a row of ordinary shops, all of which were closed for the night, and so we made the decision to pass back through the tunnel one more time, just in case anything had eluded us, just in case we had overlooked this promised 'blank', and sure enough, halfway along we discovered a small antechamber inside which there had been a ritual abandoning of old clothes, broken bottles, cardboard boxes and plastic bags, and as we turned back we caught a sudden movement and pressed ourselves flat against the wall and heard something large and formless approaching us and saw the glow of a cigarette and the silhouette of a man holding what appeared to be some kind of small child or struggling creature in his arms, and upon its head what looked like a series of twisted wire receivers or a crown of thorns, even, a homunculus, was what sprang to mind, even though afterwards The Grey Owl said, no, it was a monkey, it was a monkey with the top of its skull removed, it was a vivisected monkey, he said, are they sending monkeys through time, are there operatives reporting back, were these the first nascent experiments in time travel of some kind of rival organisation, he said, and we attempted to follow this pair, this man and his awful child, this tortured monkey, these Axis Powers, maybe, but when we emerged onto the main street there was no sign of them, and instead we were accosted by two drunken teenagers in sunglasses and an innocent passer-by who warned us to stay away from the tunnel, telling us that only drug addicts used it, and that in fact human beings had been known to defecate in there, and again we wondered about the horses, and when we returned home we realised that we had in fact misconstrued the date and that the event was actually scheduled for the next night, the realisation of which succeeded in sending us both into a rapture of having inadvertently penetrated the inner sanctum, of having seen deeper, and clearer, into the mechanism of the moment, we saw it as the sublime artistic gesture, the total work, this bracketing off of a section of reality, and we realised that this, truly, was the role of The SIRK, to excavate time and space and to reveal the underground that was right there in the moment, we rethought the movement as an art movement, essentially, which at first alienated the scientific wing until it became clear that science was in fact more important in the fostering of a particular illusion or the establishing of a reality set than art had ever been, and we committed ourselves to our actions – we called them nocturnal actions whether we staged them in full daylight or at night – with the detachment and exactitude of scientists we calculated, we inferred, we devised, we studied ambiences, moods, we looked to the areas of the city that were not under surveillance, the artistic equivalent of genre movies, where the exaggerated characters live and where you shake your head at the illusion-shattering walk-ons, the overly earnest extras, the fact that the damn set wobbles, and although you realise the audience figures are nil or nearly nil and that almost everyone who has seen it will instantly forget it or never take it seriously, you are somehow able to view it as a portrayal of everything that it is not, a literal negative, and you realise that it is a fiction that holds us up, just as it is a fiction that takes us down.

We had a series of calling cards printed that we distributed at random across the city of Athens, sliding them under the doors of widows and through the letter boxes of families and into the pigeonholes of hostels, possessed of a sudden mania, cards that had things printed on them like If You Are Reading This You Have Just Been Drugged, and that had small print that confirmed that the card they were now holding had been exposed to an experimental toxin and that included the phone number of a 'helpline' that connected you to an answer-machine message from a deadpan female we had hired off the street and who confirmed that the caller had been exposed to an experimental drug that had been stolen from a top-secret government laboratory and seeded at random to the public, going on to describe its effects, all of which were entirely positive: the euphoria; the increased sexual appetite; the reports of X-ray vision; the feeling of timelessness and of intellectual superiority; and which is how Jack Frost rumbled us, I believe, which is how Jack Frost found a way in, which is to say how Jack Frost discovered a portal, a point of ingress into the story that we thought we were writing ourselves, and this contact from Jack Frost, this signalling that he was in on the story, began when The Grey Wolf first took leave of me in Athens,

I have business to attend to, he said, and I asked him, but why now, we have all the time in the world, but he remained silent, except to say something about the axis, how the axis (which at that point, honestly, I visioned as a cross, as the place where a cross meets) was always shifting, and how constant adjustment was the only way to keep giving birth to the future, that there are certain checks and balances required, certain sacrifices, he said, and I started and I said, what, to hear you use that word, it's disconcerting, but he calmed me and he explained to me that there were certain historical inevitabilities, was how he might better describe them, that simply had to take place, and under his watch too, he felt, you can imagine the sense of responsibility he must have felt, and I said to him, but take me with you, I want to travel in time with you too, I want to cross the great divide with you, but he said, no, no, he said, the toll it would take upon you is too great, he said, and then he said to me, would you have me fix this moment, in time, he asked me, as he held me by my arms, and looked into my eyes that he had always told me were beautiful and blue, and my nose, too, he said was unique, and of course I said, yes, yes, my prince, I said, yes, and he said, in that case I must love you and leave you, and with that he bid me adieu, farewell, my summer love, he said to me, and we held each other before we let each other go, into the past, into the future, in order that he could better fix the two of us forever.

And in my loneliness and confusion (weeks passed, without a word, without a sign, why, if he could travel the subterranean tunnels would there even be a gap in our story, why could he not simply travel back to wherever he had left off, like when he appeared in the wreckage of the Double A after our adventure across Europe, and

I shed a tear at the thought of his return, and in answer
to his disappearing) I took a lover, a lover who presented
himself to me at the door of our apartment, a beautiful boy
who claimed to be searching for his own true love, who he
claimed had lived in the exact same room, in the exact same
apartment, in Plaka, in the years after the war, and I said
to him, no, we are the lovers here, I said, and I asked him if
he had sent us the mysterious love letters, whether they had
been meant for his original love, and he said, yes, he was
looking for his true love, he said.

I had to go, he said. I had to go, and now I am returned
in search of my one true love, and I said to him, is it you,
and he said, is it me what, and I said, nothing, sorry, for
a second, I said to him, I thought my own true love had
returned to me in disguise, and he blushed, I had never
made a boy blush before, I was becoming aware of my own
powers, perhaps, in the absence of The Grey Wolf, and
we became lovers, inevitably, and I let my guard down, I
confess, I was so proud of my prince that I told my lover
one night as we lay in bed that my prince claims to have
travelled through time, I told him, and I met him there, on
the other side of time, he laughed then, you think time has
another side, he joked, time is locked on some infinite zero
point that it is constantly moving towards and retreating
from, I told him, as I stroked his hair and ran my finger
through his tight curls, time implies a relationship with
something that is not it, just as an above to a below – I
felt like I was back at the convention hall, wooing the
crowds – and what did you do with yourselves there in
this paradox, he asked me, this beautiful boy come out of
nowhere, we cycled along the front, I told him, we took a
school trip to the trenches, we went to illicit nightclubs,

that sort of thing, then he asked me if I really believed that he had travelled in time and what proof I had and why didn't he do something more dramatic with it and I told him that the nature of enlightenment is shining light on precisely the same situations that take place every day, it is simply more angles on the same things, and that nothing is gained and nothing changes, so that The Grey Wolf's behaviour seemed especially enlightened in that respect, and besides, what were the alternative explanations, that he had somehow survived in a subterranean complex for days on end on his own with no munitions, that he had escaped from the complex without any witnesses and lain low, and what about the photographs that he had emerged with and immediately had developed, the photographs are the least interesting element to me, George said, the most easily faked, whenever technology comes into the picture we're all savages, he said, did he ever describe what the experience was like, he said, the actual feeling of travelling through time, the only thing he said was that you ended up wet, a little damp, was what he said, like being in a sauna with your suit on, and how he literally had to wring out his trousers when he first arrived, nipping behind a hedge in an avenue lined with council houses painted washed-out pink, and drying his suit in the blazing sun while he lay on his back in nothing but a pair of briefs and a vest, when suddenly he heard this sound, not a wolf whistle, exactly, more a kind of ironic alarm, and down the path came this old dear, Miss Sweden, she called herself, and she asked him what he was doing sunbathing behind a hedge in this old avenue all but cut off from the world and hidden amongst circuitous backstreets and what in the world could have brought him here – he was virtually naked but the old dear seemed to have no problem with nudity, it didn't terrify

her – and he told me he was in the mood for truth, having
just been delivered of a fair dose of it himself, so he told
her straight out that he had arrived from the recent past,
just arrived, briefly, via a subterranean military complex
somewhere on the east coast of Fife, and she winked at him
and told him how her husband had been in the army and so
she understood these kinds of operations and was willing
to admit that the boys upstairs, as she referred to them,
were onto more than anyone ever suspected, eventually
inviting The Grey Wolf indoors where she offered him tea
and biscuits and that was when The Grey Wolf discovered
a funny thing, that time travel confuses your senses, as
when he first helped himself to a caramel wafer and it
tasted like a sound, well, what sound was it, George asked,
I don't know what sound it was, I said, he didn't tell me, the
point is he said that for a while it was as if time itself was
confused about how it was supposed to express itself, as if
it had forgotten everything but where it was supposed to be
right then, so that the presence of this traveller out of time
had forced it to establish new connections and so for The
Grey Shark taste was much like playing a prepared piano,
the dead notes, the sudden crescendos, the atonal clusters,
he began to stuff his face so that it tasted like something
by Scriabin, and Miss Sweden took a chair across from him
next to the fire and asked him what he intended to do with
these precious hours and minutes snatched from the hands
of the clock, and he replied that the last thing he intended
to do was to report back, now that he had all the time in the
world there was nothing to be gained, and so he intended
to take it easy, finally, to live the retirement that should
have been his middle age, was how he put it, and he asked
Miss Sweden what she would do if she had all the time
in the world, this is what he told me, and she said that if

she had all the time in the world she would go back and witness the first awkward dates between her mother and her father, even though she wasn't biologically related to either, she added, somewhat cryptically, I would hide in the bushes outside the bedsit in Kirklee Circus on the day my father moved in, she said, I would linger at the window of their first house together, a ground-floor flat on Willowbank Street, in Glasgow, and hope to catch a glimpse of my beginnings.

But would you give yourself away? he asked her. No, she said, never, and The Grey Wolf stayed for dinner, mince pie and steamed vegetables followed by homemade Florence cake, and already the sounds in his mouth were starting to die off, just an occasional sound like a patch of dead leaves disturbed by a blackbird (that was the mince pie), and of course his hearing was equally odd, as was his vision and his sense of smell, his sense of touch he said never varied, outside of a vague buzzing in all of his extremities, while in his head he experienced what he described as being akin to a radio ham tuning across frequencies and occasionally coming upon bursts of inexplicable noise or distant foreign languages, sudden snippets of someone else's reality altogether, I felt like the British Telecom Tower, he said, and of course it wasn't lost on either of us that Rimbaud had once stayed in a building on the very spot of the tower's construction in London, lending The Grey Wolf's description the feel of poetry, like it was a mental space that had been conquered by fellow explorers, people who experimented with time, and after they finished dinner they took a walk together in Miss Sweden's overgrown garden, ducking beneath oversized rose bushes and crooked monkey trees until they reached a shaded clearing where the old woman

had buried several generations of cats, what do you intend
to do about them, she laughed, and he told her, nothing,
I intend to do absolutely nothing about any of it, he said,
except perhaps enliven it, he said, and by coincidence Miss
Sweden occasionally worked as cover for Saturday-morning
art lessons at the school in which I worked myself, though
I confess I had never heard of her, and so she was able
to facilitate The Grey Wolf's admission to staff, it will do
the children much good, she said, to be assisted by a time
traveller, and so he presented himself to me, as a new
master, and I can't think how else he could have done it,
unless he had set the seeds of the whole affair so far in the
past that it qualifies as time travel still, either way I find
myself willing to accept the hypothesis of time travel and
the surety that our time together was spent, at various
points, out of sync, out of time, that our relationship was
a form of defiance that went beyond time and space itself,
because that's exactly how it felt.

I thought of The Grey Owl and I wondered who he was
seducing and in what time. The Grey Owl is behind all of
this, I said to him. He could be anywhere in time. He is
waiting for us. I came up with an idea. Let's say The Grey
Owl has travelled into our past or fast-forwarded into our
future, I said to George. That means he has rewritten our
own stories. Which means that we can pretty much treat
everything that happens to us as having been penned by
The Grey Owl himself. Which means what? he said. It just
means that everything is significant, I told him. Because it
has been written. Knowing The Grey Owl, he would have set
in place a labyrinth of tunnels and subterranean passages,
endless clues and wormholes that would lead us in and out
of the story.

We wandered, and we allowed our wandering to pass for deliberate action. Of course, we came across tunnels and secret entrances; but it seemed too heavy-handed, too obvious a set-up. We held off for something innocuous. We made a determined turn away from significance. Let's find him here, we said, let's read the small print, we said, let us uncover his hand.

We swam in slow-moving rivers on summer afternoons. In the evening my boy would lie down to nap in the grass, the sun upon the high sides of white-brick houses like in old photographs, the same blue skies, the same puffs of cloud. We read the landscape as a form of prophecy, the prophecy, of course, of His coming. And at night he sang me songs, my beautiful boy come back, soft ghostly songs, on his guitar.

Have you ever read Camus' *The Stranger*? my boy asked me as we ate dinner on the terrace of a restaurant in Plaka, still alert for signs of ingress and for intrusions from the past and future. I told him I had, only the edition I had read had been translated as *The Outsider*. He produced a scrunched-up paperback edition from an inside pocket and began to read from the section in which Meursault mentally lists his possessions while spending time in jail, but the translation was like no other edition I have ever read, in this edition Meursault's possessions included a stuffed owl, a small pewter canister, a boat made of matchsticks, a pint glass, a black scarab framed behind glass, four pairs of brown socks, a single suit, a three-wheeled bicycle found abandoned in a lane, a collection of letters from a first love, an unfortunate plastic chess set, two hidden bottles of wine, and a single key, pinned imperiously and mysteriously – I can see it in my mind's eye now – on the kitchen wall. A key is always associated with unlocking, my boy said, never with locking up.

Suddenly I was struck by a terrifying thought. Was it possible for books to dream? Could it be that every time a book was closed it fell into a deep slumber wherein it dreamed itself as something else? I considered myself an erudite man, well read, able to discourse at length on the classics. Could it be that I was simply a victim of fancy and fate? That all I had remembered and studied and was able to quote at length, all that I had in fact lived by, was nothing but the night-time reveries of books dreaming themselves? In that case the history of literature was nothing but a phantom; no one had ever read the same book. I held on to the table to steady myself as I felt something lurch beneath me, as if the scenery was being moved about, like in a cheap theatrical production where the characters remain, awkwardly, taking up space, milling about, as the scene transforms around them.

That night the dream I had went like this. First I was a long streak of cloud, like the arc of an aeroplane at evening, and I was climbing up through the sky, but somehow I could still see myself from the ground and the trail that I was leaving. It wasn't very graceful. Then I was a swan, a widowed swan, and I was looking back over my life and I was mourning. I recalled the still, distant lochs that we had sailed across together, my partner and I, the sound of our wings over the water, so that people often mistook us for geese, his voice, too, the quality of his voice, which was more like the sound of a plane in the distance, a small biplane, or a generator heard from the top of a hill, a vibration in his throat, and his eyes, my God his eyes, black as hell's gates, eyes that told me he had been here before, that he knew the whole deal backwards.

In the dream his eyes appeared to me again. The eyes of a swan are inscrutable under normal circumstances. But in the dream I could make out a dark pool ringed by light. If you would raise a monument to our love, it said, my dear departed love, it called me, his lost love, his dearly departed, as if I was in a graveyard, laying flowers on our grave, when in the dream I was a swan, floating with the tide past long-abandoned mansions and great chateaux overgrown with trees and thick vines.

I fancied I was in the French Riviera and at one point we pull up to a landing bay and there is another sort of bird there, one that I recognise, somehow, and the bird moves to greet us, a respectable bird and affectionate, with a wide wingspan, as though we had been expected for a long time, and we are taken along a path in the shadow of tall fir trees and of course it's awkward, we're swans, what do we need with a mansion house, with a butler and a maid, even if they're ghosts, or strange adult birds, and we are led into a library and we look around and on the shelves there is everything we have ever dreamed of reading, biographies of friends, confessions of parents, poetry collections from our brothers and sisters, accounts of the war from our grandparents, wild journals from friends who walked away from it all aged seventeen, poets who stabbed themselves in the heart and lived to tell the tale, or who fell asleep on the couch and never woke up, and we turn to each other and it's like a joke, a terrible sad joke, that we were turned to swans, and had no way of making sense of any of it.

Swans can't read, I say to my lover. Then he looks at me with those eyes of his, and he asks if he could be turned into a book. But I won't be able to read it, I say to him. I won't be able to read you, my love.

And we're back in the air, high above a lake, a magnetic lake, a secret stopping point in all our migrations, forgotten, now, forever, with no location on any map, and we land on the water, and it's soft between our legs and we sail off, silently, and without a thought.

And now there is an accumulation of moments.

We are in bed together. We have just made love. I am reading from a collection of Hebrew poetry entitled *Zaddak Torosh Mem*, which I recognise as a reference to the artist Michahim Bengt, who was said to have recorded camels speaking a particular brand of Hebrew that was described as 'the masticating of the words', in other words the regurgitation of words, and so Bengt had come up with a form of Hebrew poetry that regurgitated itself, in other words a poetry that saw a form of evolution in rephrasing, in reformulating, or rather infinitely recycling, really, but it was these letters, repeated in endless configuration for eternity, that was poetry, was the point: ZTM. TMZ. ZMT. MTZ.

We are lingering in bed; to linger afterwards, to lingerie, I always said, which meant to bask in the glow of love, to chat about novels, to compare passions. My boy was in love with science fiction novels, novels with paintings of mile-long interstellar cruisers on the cover, preferably by Chris Foss, and where the aliens were bent-over hybrid-monstrosities

like Blake's flea, crippled horrors that made me think of
Jack Frost, stalking a universe that was cold and immense
and romantic and full of secrets.

My boy tells me about a story from one of his favourite
writers. Listen to this, he says.

This story is called *Today is Die Welt Day* and it's about a
time traveller who has lost his memory named Paimon. He
has come out of Africa, which is how he arrived, and up until
now he has been invisible within this timeline. He takes a
job as a trigger man. And at first he is a success, and then
a rising star, and then a legend, even, so that eventually
he rules the streets, but he's sweet too and takes truants
by the ear and gives them a good talking-to and is polite to
women, you never heard a swear word come out his mouth,
he is a non-drinker, a teetotaller, and you'd see him in
church every Sunday, he settles down to his new role, but
then he gets leaned on, I don't know who by, the concept is
that it's fate, I suppose, some impersonal god has got his
mark, without even holding a grudge, even, just leaning
his elbow on him until he pops, and he experiences strange
visitations and time seems all out of joint, the rules of the
universe he exists in become all messed up, the timelines,
especially, culminating in the night where he wakes and is
surrounded by frosted glass and the whole scene is lit up
from behind so that it may be aliens that have abducted
him, he sees the perfect straight hair of the females running
down to their thighs, the males who look like monkeys, who
look like grotesque stuffed monkeys, moving around, and
he is paralysed on this stretcher, he is tied down, in this
alien operating theatre, and he hears a chattering noise that
might be in his brain but could just as well be the snapping

of pincers or the gnashing of teeth, tiny teeth, midget blades capable of dismembering thoughts, that's how the author described it, so that the middle part of the book becomes almost incoherent, the thoughts themselves impossible to articulate, and the only thing that breaks the spell is when he looks out of his window and sees this flashing red light over a bar, this bum hotel cliché, this classic noir set-up, and now he's killing time in genre, and the double letters A flash into the air, AA, as in before in the beginning, and he loses consciousness & then wakes up again and this time he's making his way through a series of abandoned caravans beneath tall trees with tiny pyramids of greenery on the top, and it's a foggy evening, and the sun comes muddled through the trees like a bruise at a crime scene, and in each of the long-abandoned caravans, now lit up like a grand finale, an astral caravan park, there is a body, sometimes two bodies or three bodies, sometimes whole families; children dead in their bunk beds; adults who have kicked the bucket in the bathroom; overweight men in wigs who have snuffed it; flamboyant young boys who have carked it; waxwork lesbians long since crossed the Styx; middle-aged intellectuals and landowners now wandering the Elysian Fields; strange dwarves off to a better place; young girls six feet under; parents no longer with us; artists riding into the sun; and at first he thinks it's all of the people he killed come back to haunt him, but then he starts to recognise some of the bodies & they are famous figures of the day, the day of 1983, which to a modern reader feels more like night than day.

Somehow, in the corridors of his dreams, he has stumbled upon a secret dumping ground for a cosmic killer who is literally taking people out of history. The hero dedicates his life to the solving of this mystery and the way he goes about it is that he employs various eccentrics: nudist painters from out in the sticks; slum-dwelling occultists; a taxidermist from Bethnal Green; the famous Siamese twins from Upper Clapton, The Clapton Clique, as they were known, due to their insular nature and their tendency to shun the attentions of fascinated strangers; but it isn't until he makes the acquaintance of a certain Jack Frost that he begins to make serious inroads in his investigation.

I shuddered when I heard his name, although I knew it was coming. Everyone who reads it gets a shiver, my boy said, not like somebody has walked over their grave, more like someone else was in their grave in place of them. But he's not in the grave, I said. Jack Frost has gained entrance to the book.

I asked him what Frost's contribution to the narrative was, what background details were given. Not much, he said. He is described as looking like a shrivelled child, like a smudged punctuation mark, a comma, perhaps, or an ampersand, a semicolon, a question mark, an empty set of brackets, I can't remember exactly what, his body seems to curl in on itself, like he has a deformity, which in the book gives him a contradictory ability to be invisible, like he isn't noticed, and of course every time you come across a comma in the book you think maybe that's him, maybe he's so grotesque as to be able to disguise himself as actual punctuation right in front of your eyes as an ampersand like this & or as a semicolon like this; oh my days, I said to myself, Jack Frost has only gone and done it; he's penetrated the tunnels that lie beneath literature itself.

A smart move to enter via genre, I thought to myself. The place is riddled with secret pathways and yawning chasms and mysterious openings that are stranger than fiction itself, not to say possessed of a certain timelessness that forgives these kinds of grand gestures. It made sense. It all made too much sense. Jack Frost on the trail of The Grey Bat. My nemesis and my great love, at war, in the subterranea of certain fringe novels.

Can you hear that? I said suddenly. I thought it was an owl, but it was a siren. I'm shaken up, I said. I admit it. Then I turned to George. Everyone wants you to die, I said. In your life you will meet two or three people at most who truly want you to live, I said. The rest will instruct you in how to die. That includes your family and your friends. My boy nodded. I owe him so much, I told him.

I acted quickly. Who knows where else in the story these words are speaking. I realised that in order to stay the advance of Jack Frost, in order to save the life of The Grey Owl, in order to build a definitive bridgehead in this battle that was raging across time, across literature, across grammar itself, I had to write the next chapter of the story myself. The Grey Owl had made the ultimate sacrifice. He had given up authorship of his own story. In doing so he had given me the opportunity to rescue him.

I turned to my boy, and without thinking, without an idea in mind, I began. Let me tell you the story of a man who tries to build himself a time machine, I said to him.

He decides that he will take note of a certain period in time and space, I began, a certain phase of reality, and attempt to document and measure every last aspect of it, from the soft pink clouds above the tops of the trees through specifics of wildlife and flora and temperature – all this in relation to a flat on the seventeenth floor of a tower block in the north of Glasgow, where our would-be explorer has lived in almost complete isolation for the past six months, streamlining his life to the bare necessities in order to keep potential variables to a minimum – the exact placement of everything in the room, the precise angle of the sunlight, the food that he ate that evening, the people he interacted with, all scripted, set in stone already so as to be more easily replicable, obviously he had a team of assistants and was a man of independent means, even the thoughts he thought, which he had pre-decided and mentally trained himself not to deviate from via years of extreme yogic training that included a night spent alone in the catacombs beneath Edinburgh's Old Town which were reputed to be haunted, his reasoning being that if every detail can be recovered, every single variable that came together in a single moment in time and space, and if we can document that to the point that we can recreate it, given a team of volunteers from the university and a playboy budget, though not quite a full playboy budget as during the preparation and despite his extreme mental training the explorer had caught alcoholism – as if you can catch alcoholism like you catch measles – and so his daily alcohol regime had to be factored into the equation, which actually wasn't at all problematic and in fact its routine aspect was gold dust, really, to the team of researchers and volunteers who worked on the project, if he drinks himself insane every night, someone said, all the easier to replicate it, but what about his thoughts, someone else said, won't they wander under the influence of the drug, won't they fluctuate and change, but if we can do that, if we can make it work, then surely we will have conquered time itself, or at least set a flag inside it that we can artificially orientate ourselves to again and again, someone else said, and someone else said, well, why this moment as opposed to any other moment, and of course they were forced to admit that money had the upper hand and that money facilitated time travel even better than mind control, that's the conclusion some of them came to as they watched this mad monk drink himself to death in precisely the same fashion every night, with every detail rehearsed and meticulously watched over, like you've stained your shirt, monk explorer, you need to change it, or your right leg was crossed over your left one, brave friend, to the point that they decided that drinking himself unconscious was in fact the only foolproof way of cheating time, but what about nightmares, someone else said, what about obsessive thoughts, incoherent shapes, sounds that you can taste in your mouth, strange premonitions, a feeling of sinking, of rising up, what about paranoia or half-remembered stories from books passing for memory? Consciousness has a baseline, they say, but not exactly in those words, they say something like, there's always the reptile mind, by which they mean the idea that the serpent is the only creature that truly travels in time, through the particular construction of its own mind, and that through the extreme and sudden application of alcohol it was in fact possible for a man to access that mindset, to cast himself down into the slime of his preconscious, which is the phlegm and venom and saliva of his maker, the seed of his worm, and so to defeat time by mimicking its fluctuations, a secret combination of poetry and objectivity was how the monk explorer described it, which could just as well describe the movement of the planets and the immensity of space itself, and so the experiment came to be more about an experience of eternity over travelling through time, and of course someone mentioned the positions of the stars, the transit of the planets, they can never be replicated, what about the movement of birds, earthworms eating soil and excreting their young, someone said, but the monk explorer shot him down, they are all cycles, he said, they are all looping, endlessly, saying that we could replicate anything on a smaller scale, even the secret stars behind the stars, the moon behind the moon and the sun that held the sun itself in its power, that's ridiculous, someone said, if we had the powers of infinite suns here on earth then we would be as gods – some of the prose was awkward, like a biblical comic book – and it was here that the monk turned silent and asked for a bottle of premium vodka and a diet soda, and as the experiment began at first everything went according to expectations and they were transported via sound effects and stage props and complex logarithms and alcohol and mind control to a nondescript day, an event actually outside of the day itself, but still a part of it, although, as someone remarked, deadly dull, all the same, and they watched as this secret warrior monk crossed the threshold, passed through the iron vault of heaven itself, eventually dropping the glass bottle of vodka to the floor, a carpeted floor in order to prevent it from breaking, unpredictable shards of glass would have been a headache all round, and by this point the way he dropped the bottle to the ground, how he rolled it down his forearm, expertly, it had come to seem to the experimenters like a classical painting, like a romantic death, and he slumped to the bed as if in slow motion but still in perfect formation, there were gasps from amongst the onlookers, this is ballet, someone said, this is classical dance, this is art, someone said, a perfectly nuanced revisitation, they pronounced it, and they too felt themselves travel back in time, even though they had none of the mind training of the warrior monk, who by this point was their hero, what must it be like in there, they said, to re-enter a moment for a second time, someone gasped, and when they turned back around, the monitoring equipment confirmed it, it was right there on videotape, on hissy audio tape, on smudged amateur snaps from a disposable camera, in a transcription from a secretary that reads more like hieroglyphics than shorthand but that makes clear that what took place was undeniably real, that the warrior monk disappeared from the bed, that the bed disappeared from beneath the warrior monk, and that all that was left, hovering in a void – a depth, someone said, which better communicates the sense of cosmic endlessness and dread it conveyed, the contemporary accounts are more like whirlpools, madmen's faces, dilated eyeballs – was a series of tall black towers set around a stone encampment in the shape of a hexagon, a mighty fortress, a prison camp, someone suggested, Colditz, someone else said, the Ark, the grail castle, someone else said, a classical scholar, perhaps, or a practising magician, but it was impossible to see what was inside, the walls seemed to climb before your eyes and subsequent analysis of the film revealed nothing, it was literally impenetrable, which is what made the experimenters agree that the vision of the abyss, as they dubbed it, a borrowed phrase but pertinent in the extreme, was the only permissible evidence of time travel, and the theory came about that the abyss was in fact a holding station, a full stop, a first stone holding time in check while the pilot travelled through the tunnels of Set, the tunnels of the RAF, the tunnels of the SS, the tunnels of The Kommandant, the tunnels of The SIRK, and afterwards, on his return, he seemed embarrassed, like a drunken teenager with a next-day hangover, materialised back on his bed, they asked him what it was like, this travelling in time, this storming of heaven, and it was like he wanted to change the subject, like it was something he would rather avoid, like sex talk with your parents, he brushed away questions about vertigo, about visions and demons but not about penis size, someone thought it might shrivel, someone else thought it might grow, and oddly enough he laughed at that one and answered it directly, it's bigger, boys, he said, in fact it's a monster, indeed his talk became increasingly sexualised, like smut was less embarrassing than scientific fact or mystical experience, and every time he would steer them away from the facts by introducing an unsophisticated sexual metaphor, doing the dirty, he would say, gardening up hill, tossing the chicken, strangling the cat, swimming the channel, riding a three-speed, which caused gasps all around, living the vida loca, breaking the hymen, busting the cherry, the beast with two backs, he said, and he winked at that one, the love that dare not speak its name . . . That night he used them all and invented a fair few besides, of which my favourite is still wolfing it, for obvious reasons.

He was the anti-Houdini, that's how one of his followers described it, and by now they were all followers, disciples, witnesses to his turning back the power of the tide, and the decision was made to go public, to report the startling results of the experiment, and despite the recorded evidence, the floating towers, the stone of in the beginning, the comparisons to Treblinka and Belzec and Colditz, they were widely guffawed. The experimenters were called everything from mystics and psychic investigators to crackpots and poofters, alongside hints that they were actually a secret boys' club that had more to do with bringing back the glory days of Rome than fighting for equal opportunities in time travel. Yet amidst all of the moral hysteria, which really was a terror of the past opening up and becoming accessible to anyone, from the authorities and the police through the widowed and the wounded, a concern that the first use of time travel would be to right rights and to avenge wrongs, and so the establishment closed ranks and science turned its back on them, and it was left to the counterculture – a culture that to all intents and purposes the warrior monk despised – to propagate his views and to campaign for government funding for further experiments. Soon he rose to the status of a cause célèbre in the underground press, on the level of a Mel Lyman or an R.D. Laing or a Sun Ra, where he lashed out at the scientific establishment and instead courted artists and musicians and poets, poets most of all, now rethinking his experiment as an exercise in poetry.

Gentle, fearless life, he said, and at this point he took out a handkerchief that was actually a Buddhist prayer flag and dabbed his eyes and blew his nose on it and then he went on like a poem, at least according to the transcript that appeared in *Cold Hand* # 5 where some longhair reporter spent twenty-four hours in his company, dogging him across the borough of Hackney, where he had relocated from Glasgow 'in order to be closer to the eye of the storm', he had said, and of course his followers read that as some kind of code, like he had located a secret vortex or a time tunnel somewhere in the East End of London, and indeed he made cryptic references to nineteenth-century authors and alcoholic poets, claiming that he had picked up the trail through initiated interactions with their works, and so the longhair threw out some names, Machen, Dowson, O'Sullivan, and he claimed never to have heard of any of them, and despite all the literary talk, and the moment where he seemed to recite a poem made of single adjectives stated boldly – imaginary, nauseating, obsequious, hallowed, numberless – which the longhair described as a moment of delirium, brought on, he believed, by his experiences in the time vortex and the effect of the alcohol that he was consuming, and despite all of the eccentricity and the one-way conversations and the talk of this citadel that stood in for time, this Eagle's Nest, the reality of his day-to-day existence was regimented and ordinary, he would visit this particular bagel shop on Northwold Road every day where he would order exactly the same thing, a bagel with cheese and an apple strudel, all the while dressed like he had stepped out of a Perry Como album, the creased sporty trousers, the salmon-pink shirt, the jumper tied casually across the shoulders, grey side-lacing shoes, white socks, regimental side-parting, a stray cigarette behind the ear, sometimes large brown sunglasses, or sandals, even, dressed for another jet-set entirely, a dark musky aftershave – never a cologne, he told the long-haired reporter – but still he comes across well; so he visited the launderette at one every afternoon and spun the same pair of trousers, so he stood on the platform at Clapton every 8 a.m. and refused to get on, so he sat by an open window and dreamed of foxes snatching children in the heat of the dark summer evenings, every evening, all summer long, wearing a dark-blue blazer, pale chinos, and smoking a cigarette in a bay window just by the sorting office while thinking of his father?

At one point in the interview, which was alternately fascinating and repulsive in its focusing on the minutiae

of his life, as if the compulsion of his habits was being
presented as a mania, and so his experiment in time a form
of obsessive-compulsive overcompensation, a form of autism,
say, that was lucid enough to build itself an environment
that seemed, on that particular wavelength, what is it
they call them, children of a lesser god, is that the phrase,
when they would more profitably use the phrase from The
Bible, sons of the desert, but really the implication was
these idiots, these soft-headed children, had put together an
environment that appeared inviolable to time out of a terror
of time itself, and of course the longhair goes into this long
discourse about how he was a social worker – inevitably –
and how he worked with young men who suffered from a
form of Asperger's that meant they were unable to stand
their own reflection in the mirror, and he recalled having to
cover every mirror in the care home – the young men lived
independently and had their own flats in the East End of
London, not far from Abney Park Cemetery – wrapping
some of them in towels, others with bubble wrap and gaffer
tape, some again with blankets from the storeroom – he
makes a point of listing them all, his own feeble attempt
at poetry – and then he compares the warrior monk to
one of these unfortunates and goes into this whole thing
about how the dream of outwitting time comes down to a
fear of reflections, 'A Retreat from Echoes', which is the
title of the piece, a poor title but one that conveys the gist
of his argument, and then he quotes Norman O. Brown
(inevitably) and Albert Camus (wrongly) and André Breton
(completely out of context) as well as assorted Kabbalists
from the thirteenth century with names like gardens of fruit
or garlands of flowers, and at this point the warrior monk
becomes very emotional and the longhair is taken aback, ah,
he says, the weary flowers of time, and he lets out a great

sigh and the longhair thinks he's referring to the Kabbalists
with their names like elaborate bouquets or shaded arbours
but really he's talking about the autistic boys, fellow
travellers, he calls them, fallen angels. You describe it as a
reflection, he says, but what these boys experience is a world
divided and it horrifies them.

And as we move away from the page, zooming out from a
clumsy closing paragraph that would have the warrior monk
framed on the horizon like a shot from a John Ford movie,
we start to imagine his movements on the other side of this
profile, this puff piece for cynical longhairs to laugh over, we
see him go into a chemist's on the high street and pick up a
prescription for God knows what secret terror, we see him
clip his nails, in his pyjamas, his feet on the very edge of the
toilet bowl, which from this angle looks like the notorious
sinkhole behind Niagara Falls, and we observe the bruise on
his calf and the hard skin on his feet, the white lines on the
nails, and watch as the nails fall in perfect half-moons into
the dark water, each one breaking the surface and sending
out waves like stones into flooded quarries, or single bright
tears, all accompanied by this impossible silence that the
warrior monk has entered into, and watch as he boards
a train to Devon on a summer's morning to attend the
showing of some newly recovered experimental films, one
of which consists of a loop of two people making love, some
art film that went on forever, only they are upside down,
with their bodies entwined around each other, this eternal
love, the warrior monk thought, this fuck forever, this
upside-down embrace where only the woman's features were
visible, the man is on top of her, her left leg wrapped around
his, his face buried in the pillow, over her shoulder, are they
coming, are they caught up in coming, again and again, the

warrior monk wondered, the two of them fused, in passion,
forever, and he thought of all the little deaths inside the
body, and how crucial they were, it was a factor he could
never control in his experiments, this state of ceaseless
sacrifice, this interior force, in time, although it may well
be an exterior force, this sacrificial power, he allowed, or
perhaps language itself wasn't really up to the job, and as he
looked from interior to exterior he felt the same bottomless
terror of the fallen angels stood in front of their mirrors in
care homes at night and all he is able to do is to run a little
drool from the side of his mouth and put his hands to his
forehead, where the skin has suddenly become too tight, and
he starts to rub his temples in order to relieve the pressure
and to loosen the skin, and as the lovers repeat, in the
flickering light of the film, in its perfect black and white,
he passes his fingers over his crown and comes to feel it for
the first time as endless, skin, no shortage of it in the world
to come, impossible to map, this creation, and as the lovers
repeat he staggers out, into the night, and lights a cigarette
– he hasn't smoked in months – and stands on the balcony
of the picture house, a little shaken up, it has to be said,
and in the distance he watches as a small boat, transformed
by perspective into a simple cube, disappears beneath the
horizon, a stone, afloat on the water, is the moon, and this
is the Valley of the Kings, he thinks to himself, lover, kind
lover, as the lovers, repeat, forever.

Another summer.

APPENDIX NEBULA: CATHEDRAL OF ALL SUMMERS

- Abandoned Robotic Men in a Lock-Up in Athens – choristers.
- Actual Frenchman in an Actual Beret with an Actual Goatee Who Plays Atonal Acoustic Guitar Between Serving Overpriced French Artisanal Beers and Shaking His Head Over His Lack of a Single Fucking Word of English – proprietor of a bar in Bourron-Marlotte.
- Douglas Adams – *Doctor Who* producer whom Paimon submitted the (rejected) script for *Pirates of the Universe Divide* to.
- Adolphus – aka Banjo, prisoner with one hand (and who could stand on it), intimate of the moon, cellmate of the late Robert Scott.
- Adults Who Have Kicked the Bucket in the Bathroom – choristers.
- Advertisers – choristers.
- African American Tank Commander – liberator of Mauthausen.
- African Woman – chorister.
- Ageing Astronomers – choristers.
- Alarmed Fellow Boarder – chorister.
- Albigensians – self-suicide in perfection, for transmigration is wanderings in the desert of eternity and the body of Christ is a lie.
- Pope Alexander II – threatened William the Conqueror and his wife with excommunication for marrying without his permission.
- Pope Alexander VII – Bernini's wretched pope.

- Muhammad Ali Pasha – led the raid against the fort of Gereif on the Blue Nile. Betrayed and set upon by black demons on that very same Nile, his body was never recovered.

- Aliens – choristers.

- Dante Alighieri – walking, once again, in the fulcrum of his life, in the summer of his years.

- All of the Disappeared – choristers.

- Amanda – lover of the outlandish man.

- Amanda's Father – chorister.

- Amanda's Mother – chorister.

- Amateur Psychologists – choristers.

- Amour – old black Labrador.

- Iannis Anastas of Tsagkarada – a loved one, lost.

- Angel of Mons – supernatural entity that was seen above the battlefield during the Battle of Mons in Belgium on 23 August 1914, possibly inspired by the Arthur Machen story 'The Bowmen'.

- Angelic Children with Wide Reflective Eyes – choristers.

- Kenneth Anger – film-maker and occultist, author of the classic *Hollywood Babylon*.

- Angry Mob in the Marketplace in Wuppertal – choristers.

- Anne – boring Swedish Robert Creeley-lookalike's cute girlfriend, resident in Grez-sur-Loing for a summer long ago, went on to become a semi-famous Swedish pop star.

- Anonymous Donor – forgotten, now, except in the mind of the architect Pierre Melville, who entombed him.

- Anonymous Espagnol – composer of 'Guárdame las vacas' circa 1550. Chorister.

- Another Nameless Black Man in a Novel – chorister.

- Saint Anselm – God is a thing that nothing could be greater than. Therefore he must exist, because a thing that is greater than everything else but that does not exist would be a lesser thing than a thing that is greater than everything else and that does exist.

- Saint Anthony of the Flowers – the headless body of Goya resides in his hermitage in Madrid, where Goya lies buried in his own art. The Madonna Flower is the *Lilium candidum*.

- Anti-Democrats – choristers.
- The AntiMatterists – manifesto written by young William Scotia but in the end they went for The SIRK all the same.
- Approximately Toxic – aka XX. Subterranean.
- Thomas Aquinas – faith and reason are not opposed, faith takes up where reason ends, and reason can help to elucidate faith by metaphor and example, for can you, truly (ask yourself), reason to the end?
- Arabian Woman – chorister.
- Mr Archibald – headmaster at the school where young William Scotia works.
- Adam Aros – first river. Part of the team that worked on the Galactic Map. Chief cultural liaison officer on *The Advance*, the British link in the Victory Gardens.
- Sarah Aros – wife of Adam.
- Art Tutors – choristers.
- Antonin Artaud – it is the state of his body.
- Artists – choristers.
- Artists Living in the Past – choristers.
- Artists Who Fell Asleep on the Couch and Never Woke Up – like Jack Rose. Choristers.
- Astronauts – choristers.
- Atlas – another summer. Raise it.
- Audience in Space – choristers.
- Audience Members Joking About the Effects of LSD – choristers.
- Saint Augustine – a shining example of man's corruption, redemption and continued imperfection.
- The Authorities – choristers.
- The Axis Powers – the Nazis, the Russians and the Japanese.
- The Axis Powers – adjustment.
- Babette – French woman with long curly hair, owner of Ook, the dog, lover of Flower, my Flower. Striking red birthmark on her face in the shape of a small island. Briefly signed to the same modelling agency as Carla Bruni. Later married a roadie for French rock bands who fell from a lighting rig, and retired from

life to look after him in his paralysed state. I hear they still live together in a cottage in L'Isle-sur-la-Sorgue, in south-east France.

- J.S. Bach – resident composer in the castle of heaven.
- Bald Guy with Big Ears – chorister.
- Bald Unremarkable Tenor – chorister.
- J.G. Ballard – author of the classic *The Unlimited Dream Company*. Looked like Frederick Delius in a painting.
- Baphomet – (bisexual) talking head worshipped by the Knights Templar in the subterranean tunnels of Cugny.
- Catherine Barjansky – sculptor, author and artist, born in Odessa, in the Ukraine, in the dying years of the nineteenth century. Sculpted Delius as a ghost in beeswax.
- Baroque Music Trio – bass recorder, lute and bass viol, with the unforgettable singer who is my sister in another life.
- Bart – chorister.
- Bascomb – village idiot.
- Bascomb's Father – chorister.
- Battalion of Locals in Burntisland – choristers.
- Rudolf Bauer – avant-garde German artist who was a big influence on film-maker, artist and occultist Harry Smith. Painted portals, tunnels, transmitters.
- The Beach Boys – endless summer.
- Beautiful Blind Girl Sat in the Sun – chorister.
- Beautiful Girl Whose Tiny Pink Bikini Is the Colour of Pale Flesh Made Rosy by the Sun – chorister.
- Hans Bellmer – artist of the disarraying of the body, the erotic disarticulation of the limbs.
- The Beloved – in his garden.
- Michahim Bengt – said to have recorded camels speaking a particular brand of Hebrew that was described as 'the masticating of the words', in other words the regurgitation of words, and so Bengt had come up with a form of Hebrew poetry that regurgitated itself, in other words a poetry that saw a form of evolution in rephrasing, in reformulating, or rather infinitely recycling, really, but it was these letters, repeated in endless configuration for eternity, that was poetry, was the point: ZTM. TMZ. ZMT. MTZ.

- Benzillah of Diagoras – aka Benzillah the Low to the Earth, author of *The Qutub* aka *The Tomb of the Song*.
- Jean Pierre Bernard – built a house, once, in Larchant, in the summer of 1792, with his wife, Adelaïd Hamelin.
- Saint Bernard of Clairvaux – was it in vain that the Wisdom of God hid what we are unable to see?
- Gian Lorenzo Bernini – seventeenth-century Italian sculptor and architect credited with the creation of the baroque style.
- Joseph Beuys – artist, Nazi, Marxist, hypnotised parrot, circumcised squirrel.
- Biographers – choristers.
- The Birds of the Air – choristers.
- Black GIs at Normandy – choristers.
- Black Slaves from the Valley of the Blue Nile – choristers.
- Black Soldiers Holding Up the Bullets They Dodged and Grinning – choristers.
- Black Soldiers Lying in a Field Hospital – choristers.
- Black Soldiers Pictured with Their New Extended Families with the Lovers They Took in France and the Babies They Made Together – choristers.
- Black Soldiers Tending to the Survivors of a Nazi Time Bomb on a Street in Coutances, France – choristers.
- Black Stork in a Bombed-Out Zoo –
- Saint Blaise-des-Simples – simple is a Flower.
- William Blake – as alive today as he ever was.
- Blake's Flea – crippled horror that makes you think of Jack Frost?
- Madame Helena Blavatsky – author of the classic *The Voice of the Silence*.
- Blind Girl Dancing with a Hula Hoop – chorister.
- Blind Man Being Led on a Rope Through the Night of Khartoum – chorister.
- Blind Man in Burntisland – chorister.
- Blondi – Hitler's dog, and perhaps the true love of his life.
- Bodies of Decapitated Men with Signs Carved into Their Flesh Like This: '#' – choristers.

- Bodies of Mutilated Women – choristers.
- The Body in the Book Tower – outlandish knight.
- Antoine Boësset – composer. Superintendent of music at the *Ancien Régime* French court. Chorister.
- Bolsheviks – choristers.
- Jorge Luis Borges – claimed the last sound was a bird, left nothing to no one, turned history to dust.
- Boring Swedish Artist Who Looks Like Robert Creeley – resident in Grez-sur-Loing all those years ago in the past now. He also wore an eyepatch, which might have been what made him look like Creeley, who, like James Joyce before him, also wore an eyepatch. Famous in Sweden for his boring still lifes, he shot himself in the head and he didn't even die, how boring.
- The Bornless One – the deathless one.
- Harriet Bosse – long-suffering object of obsession for August Strindberg (see: *Letters to Harriet Bosse* by August Strindberg).
- David Bowie – station to station.
- Boys on a School Trip to Belgium – choristers.
- Boys on Trampolines – choristers.
- Boys Playing Frisbee by the River Loing – choristers.
- Boys with Asperger's – choristers.
- Boys with Half-Eaten Faces – choristers.
- Boys with Holes in Their Bodies Where the Light Shines Through – choristers.
- Boys with Missing Ears and Black Holes for Eyes – choristers.
- Lee Brackstone – editor.
- Eva Braun – Hitler's lover aka Eva Hitler, whom he married in the Führerbunker the day before she swallowed a cyanide pill and he put a bullet in his head.
- Brave Young German Pilots – crossing the water on their way to an assignation with fate, our fate, their fate, God love us both.
- André Breton – author of the classic *Arcanum 17*, The (Lovely) Star.
- Brothers – choristers.
- Norman O. Brown – author of the classic *Life Against Death*.

- The Brown-Skinned Virgin – came down to earth and fucked a man silly so that the image of her was left on his heart, and on his skin, beneath the veil where she fucked him.
- Anton Bruckner – composer of the classic Symphony No. 7, the music that accompanied the announcement of Hitler's suicide on German radio.
- Burly Young French Youth Pulling His Girlfriend's Hair – chorister.
- Mrs Bustard – chorister.
- Cadaver with Its Own Semi-Liquidised Organs Gathered Up in Its Arms – chorister.
- Albert Camus – author of the classic *The Stranger* aka *The Outsider* aka *The Outlandish Knight*.
- Candy – beautiful blonde groupie.
- Captain of a Ship Operating Out of Malta Reported Sunk in May of 1941 – chorister.
- Casanova – chorister.
- Cats in a Hypnotised Dream – choristers.
- Marc Chagall – the great Russian painter, architect of the First Church of the Moon.
- Child Crying in the Distance – chorister.
- Children Dead in Their Bunk Beds – choristers.
- Children Holding Animals in Shaded Groves in Calderbank Who Are Not Afraid – choristers.
- Children Lost in the Woods – choristers.
- Children on the Beach – choristers.
- Children Trying to Steal Bird Eggs at a Cafe and Getting Chased Off by a Patron During the Siege of Khartoum – choristers.
- Children with Phenol Injected into Their Hearts – choristers.
- The Chimera – escaped creation of the Januists?
- Jesus Christ – Christ Jayzus.
- Chubby Girl in a Purple One-Piece Bathing Costume with the Word Disco Written on It in Lurid Green Paddling Past – chorister.
- Chubby Nightstick – subterranean.

- Winston Churchill – prime minister of the United Kingdom.
- CIA – never The CIA.
- Cico and His Wife – Italian proprietors of a cafe in Villiers-sous-Grez who moved back to Lecce shortly after, the rumour was that they had been called back by the Mafia, geez.
- Circus Master in the Fields Outside Calderbank – chorister.
- Cistercians – silent stone, speaking.
- City Councillors – choristers.
- The Clapton Clique – the famous Siamese twins from Clapton, London.
- Clara – white Spaniel lost in the rain outside Montigny.
- Sophia Clark – professional violinist and author of the classic UFO 'romances' *The Hovering Heart*, *I Won't Let You Down* and *Three Times a Lady*.
- Claude – one-time secretary of Pierre Melville.
- Henry Clews – American artist who left for France who can blame him. Sculpted Delius as a grub, come out a cocoon, in blind bliss and silent agony.
- Cloud of Tiny Whirring Insects in Calderbank in the Summer – choristers.
- King Clovis – 'Worship what you burn, and burn what you worship.'
- Jean Cocteau – is buried beneath your feet.
- The Cold Fish – subterranean, unfortunate name, but he did present a brilliant account of the Führerbunker near the end.
- Firth Column – lead singer and guitarist with legendary French psychedelic rock group Helpless Clairvoyants, last seen heading for the dark side of the moon on a moon buggy with nothing but a basic survival dome, the band's music equipment and what was reputed to be a head, singing, inside a white cube.
- Perry Como – never swore, never drank and was always faithful to his wife. Singer of the classic 'Make Love to Life'.
- Concerned Attendant – chorister.
- Concerned Middle-Aged Woman – chorister.
- Conductor at Saint-Étienne de Villiers-sous-Grez – piloting a dread ship through the dark.

- John Constable – English landscape painter.
- Contemptuous Young Man Who Shakes His Head – chorister.
- Contented Spaced-Out Fat Village Rocker's Wife and Children – choristers.
- Convoys of Uniformed Soldiers Moving East – choristers.
- Corpses of Poor Children – choristers.
- Julio Cortázar – author of the classic *Hopscotch*.
- The Counterculture – choristers.
- Couples with Their Arms Around Each Other at Restaurants – choristers.
- The Court of the Gods – classic space opera shit.
- Crackpot Wing of the British Army – choristers.
- Crackpots – choristers.
- Crap Poofs – choristers.
- Creatures with the Face of Silly Fishes – choristers.
- Robert Creeley – poet. 'The Figure of Outward', according to Charles Olson.
- Dr Crevasse – creator of the WordPool.
- Crew of Three on a Small Fishing Boat – choristers.
- Silvia Crompton – copyeditor.
- Aleister Crowley – 'The word of sin is Restriction. O man! refuse not thy wife, if she will! O lover, if thou wilt, depart! There is no bond that can unite the divided but love: all else is a curse. Accursed! Accursed be it to the aeons! Hell.'
- The Crusaders – the Holy Land forever rearranged in their stead.
- Curious Onlookers in Athens After the War – choristers.
- Cynical Longhairs – choristers.
- Damaged Boys – choristers.
- Daredevil Fighter Pilots – choristers.
- Dark Boy with a Patch on His Eye and No Top On in an Italian Prisoner-of-War Camp Near the End of the War – a lost painting, now.
- Dark-Eyed Sweetie in the Sexy Librarian Glasses – chorister.
- Dark Tragic Poets – choristers.

- David – Christ is of his house.
- David – wonderful evidence that, apart from other kinds of worship, music in particular was commanded by the Holy Ghost through David.
- Davide – Flower's ex-boyfriend, that prick.
- Cait Davies – head of marketing.
- The Dead – choristers.
- The Dead and the Dying – choristers.
- The Dead and the Dying and the Miraculously Born Again – choristers.
- Dead Bodies Piled Up in Mounds – choristers.
- Dead Bodies Outside Omalos in Crete – choristers.
- Dead Children Buried in a Calamity – choristers.
- Dead Horses Laid Out Like Letters Across a Field – choristers.
- Dead Loved Ones – choristers.
- Dead Parents – choristers.
- Dead Sweethearts – choristers.
- Deadpan Female Hired Off the Street – cold automatic voice on the end of the line.
- Deaf Boy Looking Up and Pointing – the true name of Holy Maximilian Rehberg.
- Guy Debord – tedious leftie.
- Deceased Green Parakeet – chorister.
- John Dee – court astronomer to Elizabeth I, spoke with angels in their original Enochian via his scryer, Edward Kelley, who later reincarnated as Aleister Crowley.
- Daniel Defoe – author of the classic *Robinson Crusoe*.
- Delightful Eccentric Friends from That Summer in Grez-sur-Loing – choristers.
- Frederick Delius – composer who went blind at the end of his life after seeing and doing everything that was worth doing. Resident of Grez-sur-Loing in the house that would later be occupied by the Church of the Stone of First Witness. Set music to Nietzsche's *Thus Spoke Zarathustra* and titled it *A Mass of Life*. Author of the dream poems *The Last Voyage* and *Songs of Farewell*. Telepath.

- Frederick Delius's Sisters – ten sisters, all are my sisters.
- Jelka Delius – Frederick's wife, who maintained an invisible garden in the mind of her husband, all painted pink.
- Dervishes of Gereif – routed, for now.
- Desolate Whores – choristers.
- The Devil – is delight in what God gone done.
- The Devil – is the eroticising of change.
- Devious-Looking Man with a Thin Lip – chorister.
- Devious Midgets at the Circus – choristers.
- Danny DeVito – shortarse actor. Looks exactly like the bastard who runs the rip-off restaurant in Grez-sur-Loing.
- Disembodied Entities – choristers.
- Dishevelled Girl – chorister.
- Disinterested Boys – choristers.
- Dissenters – choristers.
- Dissenting Voices – choristers.
- DJs Playing Reggae on the Football Fields Outside Villiers-sur-Grez – choristers.
- Doctor in a Hospital – chorister.
- Doctor in an Improvised Field Hospital in Crete – chorister.
- Dog Breaking Free of Its Owner and Pursuing a Duck Across the Water – chorister.
- Dogboys – choristers.
- Domineering Father – chorister.
- Dominicans – the keepers of the true faith have nowhere to lay their heads.
- Donnelly – chorister.
- The Doom – drummer with Helpless Clairvoyants.
- Doris – friend of the older Swedish couple in Grez-sur-Loing all those years ago now.
- Fyodor Dostoevsky – author of the classic *Notes from Underground*.
- Doubles of Dubai – warriors with second skins.

- Ernest Dowson – author and poet who died at the age of thirty-two in 1900 and who once proposed to an eleven-year-old (unsuccessfully).
- Arthur Conan Doyle – author of the classic 'The Adventure of the Final Problem'.
- Dreamy Mermaids – choristers.
- Dreary Old Men in Love with Latin – choristers.
- Drug Addicts – choristers.
- Drummer with an Awful Head Mic – this is France.
- Drunken Doorman – chorister.
- Drunken Finnish Poet – resident in Grez-sur-Loing long ago now in the past. I forgot to say she was a midget.
- Drunken French Rocker with Swollen Calves and a Precocious Beer Gut – chorister.
- Drunken Teenagers in Sunglasses – choristers.
- Bob Dylan – off his tits at the 'We Are the World' recording session.
- Dyspeptic Polish Writer – chorister.
- The Early Church Fathers – God became man in Christ in order that man might become God.
- Eccentric Collector of Old French Bottle Tops – chorister.
- Meister Eckhart – union with the ultimate nothing is the highest goal of man.
- Educated Bozos Living in Caves on Spinning Asteroids Trying to Hold Off the End of the World – choristers.
- Elderly Japanese Couple at a Restaurant – choristers.
- Elderly Kitchen Staff – choristers.
- Elderly Lady Who Smells of Potpourri and Urine – chorister.
- Emaciated Italian Prisoner of Conscience – chorister.
- Emaciated Singer Dressed Completely in Black – Paimon.
- Emaciated Street Whore – chorister.
- The Emissary – aka The Weasel.
- The Emperor – the wound that is given birth to must be greater than the wound that gives birth. It is Frater Jim's father.
- Encouraging Friends – choristers.

- Endless Cocks Ejaculating – choristers.
- Desiderius Erasmus – the suffering of Christ was not necessary, as God, in His infinite love and mercy, has more than enough forgiveness of His own, and so the crucifixion was no true sacrifice.
- Escaped Prisoner Recaptured and Given a Mock Crucifixion – echoes of Hans Bonarewitz.
- Katie Espiner – managing director and chief breaker of balls.
- Saint-Esprit – holy ghost.
- Estate Agent in the Employ of God Forever – chorister.
- The Estimator – inmate in a nuthouse in Wuppertal.
- The Estranged Lover – chorister.
- Saint-Étienne – Saint Stephen.
- Mr Clyde Evans – project manager on *The Advance*, the British link in the Victory Gardens. SIRK.
- Joan Evans – author of the classic *Monastic Architecture in France*.
- Exaggerated Characters – choristers.
- Fallen Angels – choristers.
- Families in Swimwear Walking Home from the Beach – choristers.
- Families Laid Out on Towels by the River Loing – choristers.
- Famous Figures of the Day – choristers.
- Fascist Bastards – any word but is.
- Fascists – choristers.
- Fat Girl with an Off-the-Shoulder Dress and Appealing Sunburn Drinking from a Hip Flask – chorister.
- Fat Greek Thug – chorister.
- Fat Village Rocker – ready to get back in the game.
- Father and Son at a Table in Bourron-Marlotte on National Music Day – choristers.
- Father of the Saintly Children with a Rotten Ear – chorister.
- Father of the Unknown Narrator During the Siege of Khartoum – a shadow cast by the sun.
- Feetless Boys – choristers.

- Female Villager with a Lazy Eye – first to roll away the stone.
- Female Villager with Facial Scarification Like Tiny Tears – second to roll away the stone.
- Female Villager Who Remains Unrecorded – third to roll away the stone.
- Females with Perfect Straight Hair Running Down to Their Thighs – choristers.
- Eric Fenby – Delius's amanuensis, telepath.
- Jessie Ferguson – wife of William Ferguson, bride of all of the disappeared.
- William Ferguson – in memoriam. Disappeared during the evacuation of Athens when his boat was sunk by a German bomb in April 1941. He was twenty-nine years old. Husband of Jessie Ferguson, of Calderbank, who held out all her life for his return; perhaps he had lost his memory, and was still alive, somewhere. Jessie died aged eighty-one and never saw her true love again.
- Figure Perched on a Stool – chorister.
- The Filth – the pigs.
- Five Women from Eastern Europe – choristers.
- Five- and Six-String Bassist – this is France.
- Flamboyant Young Boys – choristers.
- Flaming Rats Coming in Waves from the Clydeside – choristers.
- The Flashlight – subterranean, founding member of the reconstituted Church of the Stone of First Witness aka The SIRK, archivist and pipe smoker, but where did he get that name.
- Fleet of Handmade Snowdrops Taking Off from the Sea of Fecundity – choristers.
- Fleet of Monkeys Digging Mass Graves – choristers.
- Flower Flower – a Flower, is a Flower, is a Flower (is).
- Biraggo Fonte – of Khartoum.
- John Ford – director of the classic *The Searchers*.
- Isa Forsyth – in memoriam. Beloved wife of Joseph Tosh, returned from the war. Dead at the age of thirty-two from kidney failure.
- Chris Foss – sci-fi artist.

- The Fourth Lateran Council – when the priest at the altar utters the words hoc est corpus meum (this is my body), the wine and bread is transformed into the blood and body of Christ (wow).

- Franciscans – poverty, renunciation and joy is the true cathedral.

- Hans Frank – Nazi, head of the General Government in Poland during the Second World War, overseer of four concentration camps; Belzec; Treblinka; Majdanek and Sobibor. Besides Albert Speer he was the only Nazi at the Nuremberg Trials to show anything approaching remorse for his crimes. He converted to Catholicism while awaiting trial and wrote a memoir, *In the Face of the Gallows*. Executed on 16 October 1946, he asked that God grant him mercy. His ashes were drowned in the River Isar and now he is in every waterway in the world.

- Frater Jim – co-founder of the Church of the Stone of First Witness. Januist. Returned after the war with a new face and remarried his wife in secret.

- Frater Jim's Brother – a small black dog now.

- Frater Jim's Father – undead.

- Frater Jim's Wife – he came back, years later, and remarried her, in secret, with a new face, before she died in a tragic accident, never knowing that her true love had come back to her, in secret.

- Frederick the Great – Prussian king and military leader.

- Ellie Freedman – editorial assistant.

- Freemasons – who put the first stone.

- French Boys Leaping from a Bridge in Grez-sur-Loing – choristers.

- Friends and Family – choristers.

- Friends and Neighbours from That Summer in Grez-sur-Loing – choristers.

- Friends Who Walked Away from It All Aged Seventeen – choristers.

- Full Military Might of the Council of Twelve – choristers.

- Fundamentalist Pigs – we may reason to the end.

- Futurists – sculpture must be kinetic, the visual arts dynamic, music cacophonous.

- Jean-Pierre Galezot – architect of the Curious Collared Dove Fallen From Heaven.

- A Garden Enclosed – my sister, my spouse.
- Paul Gauguin – painter of a nude African woman named *Evermore*.
- The General – subterranean.
- George – beautiful boy lover in Plaka.
- George the Monkey – terrible toy monkey in a fake zoo.
- George V – king of the United Kingdom.
- A Ghost – chorister.
- Ghostly Disembodied Faces in the Camps – choristers.
- Gilhooley – chorister.
- Cecilia Giménez – much-maligned restorer of that awful 1930s fresco *Ecce Homo*, true fosterer of Christ in time.
- Girl in a Dark-Blue Bikini with the Most Perfectly Pert Young Teenage Ass (a Rarity in France, as We Have Established) Moving Her Towel into the Sun – chorister.
- Girls of Another Summer – choristers.
- Gislebertus – GISLEBERTUS HOC FECIT. Architect of the Cathedral of Saint Lazarus, in Autun, patron saint of our stone-cold hearts.
- William Gladstone – prime minister of the United Kingdom.
- God – to the glory of.
- Joseph Goebbels – Nazi minister of propaganda, died by suicide in the Reich Chancellery on 1 May 1945, after Hitler shot himself.
- Gordon of Khartoum – Charles Gordon, Chinese Gordon, Heart's True Gordon, Defender of the Empire, Unbowed Gordon.
- Hermann Göring – Nazi military leader, First World War fighter pilot ace, and convicted war criminal. Committed suicide on 15 October 1946, the night before he was to be hanged. His ashes were drowned in the River Isar, and now he resides in all the waterways of the world.
- Francisco Goya – artist whose *The Third of May 1808 in Madrid*, painted in 1814, is one of the great masterpieces of religious painting. Most everything in the picture is lit by an impossible moon, it would appear, which in turn is lit by way of an impossible sun, except for the hero, the central hero whose body is lit by a mysterious cube, a lantern, it seems, but a mysterious

illuminated ark all the same, and its light takes up the hero of the body, except for his head, which remains in the moon, and inside the box is death, which is spoken in light, inside of which is a head, a disembodied head, which is the body of the hero, projected. Picasso considered the painting to be under a spell, a supernatural spell, and he compared the crucified stance of the hero to the skeleton of a bat, which is the ancient of nightmares. Goya's headless corpse is buried inside his art. No one knows where his head is. Supposedly.

- Grandparents – choristers.

- The Grass of the Field – choristers.

- Great Crowds at the Passion Play in Oberammergau – choristers.

- Great Eastern European Beauty – chorister.

- The Greatest Men of the Twentieth Century – choristers.

- Greek Nuns in Bloodied Habits Treated Like Circus Animals – choristers.

- Greek Whores in the Dying Years – choristers.

- The Green Beret – smart-ass subterranean.

- Frank A. Greenhill – author of the classic *Incised Effigial Slabs*, published by Faber & Faber at, one imagines, considerable expense, and, surely, with little hope of recouping their costs, in the year of 1976.

- Gregory of Tours – 'Worship what you burn, and burn what you worship.'

- The Grey Lady – unknown woman with a face like granite and arched eyebrows that seem to contain all the sorrow and pain of the world.

- The Grey Wolf – aka Arthur McManus aka The Grey Bat aka The Grey Owl aka The Silent Owl aka The Grey Fox aka The Grey Shark aka De Schrijver aka Aha aka Art.

- Grez-sur-Loing History and Village Preservation Society – choristers.

- Group of Avant-Garde Thinkers and Cultural and Political Radicals in the Years Before the War in Düsseldorf – choristers.

- Group of Black Men in Full Uniform Shopping for Gifts at a Market Stall for Their Sweethearts Back Home – choristers.

- Group of Heads Attempting to Levitate the Pentagon – choristers.

- Group of Men Urinating on a Woman – choristers.
- Group of Mid-Level British Commanders in an Italian Prisoner-of-War Camp – choristers.
- Group of Villagers on a River of Africa – choristers.
- Group of Women Dressed in Skintight Rubber Space Suits – choristers.
- Group of Young SA Men in Düsseldorf – choristers.
- Groupies Backstage on the Moon – choristers.
- Groups of Villagers Who Stop Talking as Soon as Jim and Max Appear – choristers.
- Guards Casually Beating Men and Women – choristers.
- Guards Holding Up Emaciated Bodies and Forcing Them to Perform for the Camera – choristers.
- Che Guevara – your corpulent Scoutmaster.
- Guy in a Baseball Cap and a Turquoise T-Shirt with the Number 10 on It Trying to Tempt His Dog into the Water with a Tennis Ball – chorister.
- Guy in a White Trilby, Knee-Length Shorts and an Unbuttoned Purple Shirt Who Was Also Spotted Roaring Drunk in Nemours – chorister.
- Guy with a Pair of Chiselled-Off Privates – chorister.
- Guy with a Rearranged Face – chorister.
- Gypsies – choristers.
- Gypsy Boy Whose Face Had Been Eaten Away by the Pox – chorister.
- Johnny Hallyday – 'Le Rocker Originel'. On the wall of the bar in Bourron-Marlotte.
- Adelaïd Hamelin – built a house, once, in Larchant, in the summer of 1792, with her husband Jean Pierre Bernard.
- Handsome Soldier Staring into Space – chorister.
- Mary Hanna – the legendary Mary Hanna; bassist for Memorial Device, member of Dark Bathroom, secret sculptor.
- Hardnuts with Big Kick-Your-Cunt-In Faces – choristers.
- Miss Harriet – carnaptious bitch.
- George Harrison – does he even appear in the 'We Are the World' video?

- Hateful Jeans and No-Top Guy Talking on the Payphone – chorister.
- The Headless Horseman – aka the Headless Hessian of the Hollow, a trooper killed at the battle of White Plains who came back headless.
- Heinrich – someone's lost child.
- Helpless Clairvoyants – legendary French rock group who only spoke German in interviews and who played endless FX-destroyed jams w/stone-cold vocals and who split up after headlining a protest gig on the moon.
- Helpless Clairvoyants Roadies – choristers.
- Henry V – king of England. Had the flesh boiled off his bones so he could be sent in the post.
- Hercules – stands at the gate of the Mediterranean and seals passage in, and out.
- King Herod – wanted Jesus dead.
- Philippe Herreweghe – Belgian conductor of the classic *St Matthew Passion*.
- Hildegard of Bingen – a feather on the breath of God.
- Betty Hill – abducted by extraterrestrials alongside her husband for three days in September of 1961 from a town in rural New Hampshire.
- Carl Fredrik Hill – madman painting.
- Heinrich Himmler – Reichsführer of the SS and architect of the Holocaust. Committed suicide when captured by the Allies on 23 May 1945.
- Hippies – opened their heart to the whole universe and found it was loving.
- Hippy Convoy Across the Sea of Fecundity – choristers.
- Historical Fantasists – any word but is.
- Adolf Hitler – leader of the Nazi Party and of the Third Reich (1933–1945). Architect of the Second World War. Author of *Mein Kampf*. Shot himself in the head in the Führerbunker on 30 April 1945, ten days after his fifty-sixth birthday.
- Holidaymakers in the Streets of Athens After the War – choristers.
- The Holy Ghost – chorister.

- The Holy Guardian Angel – knowledge of, and conversation with, your very own HGA represents the culmination of the Abramelin working.
- Holy Whores – choristers.
- Homeless Person Asleep in the Grass with His Awful Socks – chorister.
- Bishop Honorius of Rome – anathematised heretic who believed that although Christ had two natures and was, essentially, divided, in his humanity and in his divinity, yet in this division, precisely because of this division, in fact, he was united in one will, which was the will of God, the Father, who made this world, Maximilian Rehberg claims, in an updating of Honorius's heresy, in order that Christ, and all of the Christs to come (for, in his argument, anyone who enters history is incarnated as a Christ), could *Run Wild In It*.
- Hopelessly Lost Prisoners with Empty Eyes – choristers.
- Hugo Höppener – aka Fidus. Artist, Lebensreform advocate, virulent anti-Semite.
- Horses Walking on the Bottom of the Ocean with Great Wounds in Their Stomachs – the separation of the firmament, the first act of God. We are walking in the stuff of our own wounds.
- Host at a Concert Hall in Lamia – chorister.
- Host's Wife at a Concert Hall in Lamia – chorister.
- Jacques Hotteterre – French composer and flautist. Chorister.
- A.E. Housman – poet, author of the classic *A Shropshire Lad*.
- Huge Old Man with a Mediterranean Tan Who Looks Like Kenneth Anger – chorister.
- Huge Old Man's Wife – chorister.
- Husbands and Wives and Children Grouped Around Tables – choristers.
- Idiot Girls – choristers.
- Idiot in a Red Headband – chorister.
- Ignominious Human Torso Turning Somersaults in Khartoum – chorister.
- Ignorant Moderns – it's just chemicals, and atoms, and evolution.
- Illiterate Thugs – choristers.

- Inchoate Voices in the Distance in the Night of Khartoum – choristers.
- Initiates – choristers.
- Inmates Suffering from Shell Shock – choristers.
- Inmates Who Drank – choristers.
- Intellectual Spiritual Aristocratic Types – choristers.
- Interlocutors – choristers.
- *The Invisible Man* – a science fiction by H.G. Wells.
- Irishman in an Italian Prisoner-of-War Camp Near the End of the War – with a badly executed tattoo that everyone thought was a harp, maybe, but that turned out to be a prison cell where the bars on the window were actually Cupid's arrows that had imprisoned him ever since he had made love to a ghost come out of a river.
- The Iron Giant – ex-serviceman from Calderbank. subterranean, co-founder of the revived Church of the Stone of First Witness aka The SIRK, secretary, fan of Wordsworth when he's had a few.
- Irritating Finnish Doodler – resident at Grez-sur-Loing one summer long ago now in the past. Looked Chinese, but claimed he was a Finn right enough. Later joined the army and renounced art altogether, thank God. Only but then he died, which was a pure sin.
- Italian Boy of Barely Seventeen Years – chorister.
- Jack Frost – ?
- M.R. James – ghost story writer. Author of the classic 'A View from a Hill'.
- Januists – offshoot of Futurism that both predates and supersedes it.
- Janus – god of passage, doors, gateways, tunnels, transmitters, beginnings and endings.
- Japanese Woman – chorister.
- Japanese Woman Being Painfully Entered from Behind – chorister.
- Jean-Marc – Babette's partner who trains attack dogs. Master of Ook. Wore a Mohican like an old-school punk. Later I heard that he was a member of the French experimental rock group

Soixante Étages. Went on to make his fortune in the French 'dot-com bubble'. These days I hear he is pals with Sarkozy.

- Saint Jerome – translated The Bible into Latin, the Vulgate. Took to studying Hebrew in order to circumvent an obsessive desire for masturbation.
- John of Damascus – Christian monk who coined the term 'the Books of the Unlearned'.
- John the Baptist – traditionally portrayed as headless, or bodiless, more properly, for a great and secret reason.
- Al Jolson – 'king of blackface'.
- Joseph – Christ's earthly father returned to Bethlehem, his hometown, from Nazareth, because there was a census on, which is why Jesus was born there.
- James Joyce – author. 'Near to the wild heart.'
- Julio – proprietor of Julio's in Ostend aka Rabbit's Wedding.
- Carl Gustav Jung – magician and psychoanalyst. Dreamed of a phallus on a throne.
- D.K. – D.K.
- D.K.'s Father – drowned in all the rivers of the world, now.
- D.K.'s Mother – D.K.'s mother.
- H.K. – D.K.'s sister.
- P.K. – D.K.'s brother.
- Kabbalists from the Thirteenth Century with Names Like Garlands of Flowers or Gardens of Fruit – choristers.
- Giovanni Girolamo Kapsberger – German/Italian baroque composer and performer.
- Karo Man Bursting from the Crowd with a Blade the Size of His Goddamn Forearm – primitive weaponry.
- Karo Man with a Long Kimono and a Bullet Belt – he has drawn Death.
- Karo Man with a Single Glass Eye (Is It?) Wearing a Cap with What Looks Like a Spark Plug On It (Is It?) – chorister.
- Karo Men of Ethiopia – aloof, and distant.
- Karo Village Elder – chorister.
- Karo Woman with the Crucified Christ Dangling from Her Nose – chorister.

- Karo Women of Ethiopia – their constellated faces as if the suffering stars themselves have come down and are risen, in the flesh.
- Katarina the Bitch and Her Husband Thierry – obviously swingers. Both had red hair, which was the weirdest thing ever. Now run a 'painting retreat' in the mountains outside Malaga, in Spain.
- David Keenan – author of *This Is Memorial Device, For The Good Times, The Towers The Fields The Transmitters* and *Xstabeth*.
- Edward Kelley – John Dee's scrying partner who conversed with angels and who witnessed great fountains, rising up, and who was commanded to swap his wife with Dee's wife, by these same angels, and who was later reincarnated as the occultist Aleister Crowley.
- Thomas à Kempis – God is best pleased with adoration, not theological speculation.
- Kid Leaping Off a Bridge and Landing on His Back in the Water – chorister.
- B.B. King – banging blues guitarist on the wall of the bar in Bourron-Marlotte.
- Kitchen Attendant in a Hostel Near Glen Affric – chorister.
- Knights Templar – worshipped a (bisexual) talking head named Baphomet in the catacombs of Cugny.
- The Kommandant – unknown artist whose works have been identified, and verified, as being from the same hand – Lord knows how – in concentration camps around Poland, appearing in the early to mid-1940s, like environmental art with pointless tunnels that turned in on themselves to nowhere but that were miles long despite themselves, or the inexplicable three-tiered target signs, cut into barbed-wire fences around the camps, like an RAF sign or the three layers of hell, and of course the only person with the ability to create that kind of art is a Kommandant, is a prison guard, is an insider. Isn't it?
- Tadeusz Kościuszko – Polish/Lithuanian military leader and national hero, whose heart and body were divided at death and whose ghost now walks the subterranean pathways of the black ash forest of La Route de la Grande Vallée, which links Montigny-sur-Loing with Bourron-Marlotte.

- Richard Kostelanetz – American artist, publisher of *Assembling*.
- Ladies of the Night – choristers.
- Ladies-Only Spiritual Art Group in Athens – choristers.
- R.D. Laing – absolute clown.
- Lalino – sexy star goddess.
- Lame Old Hypnotised Crone in a Grand Theatre in Greece – chorister.
- Rachael Lancaster – designer.
- Landlady with Early-Onset Dementia – chorister.
- Large Group of Men Watching a Woman Slowly Dancing Through the Night of Khartoum – choristers.
- Latino Honey – chorister.
- Saint-Laurent – Christian martyr.
- D.H. Lawrence – author and poet, author of the classic 'Fish'.
- Saint Lazarus of Autun – back from the dead, Christ's biggest fuck-up.
- Lead Guitarist in a Hawaiian Shirt – barely audible.
- Lead Singer – in yoga pants.
- Led Zeppelin – legendarily loud rock band.
- Leda – Aetolian princess, raped by Zeus in the guise of a swan, in return.
- Legions of the Walking Dead – choristers.
- Heather Leigh – photographer.
- Leonine Bass Straight Out of Amateur Dramatics – chorister.
- Lesbians – choristers.
- Liberators of Auschwitz – choristers.
- The Lightning Bolt – subterranean, away team, co-founder of the revived Church of the Stone of First Witness aka The SIRK.
- The Lilies of the Field – choristers.
- Lilith – Out! Oil Skin of the Dark! Earth Abound!
- Limbless Boys with Blackened Torsos – choristers.
- Limping Waiter in a Cafe in Greece – chorister.
- Line of German Soldiers Stood Motionless Along the Cliffs – choristers.

- The Lion of Judah – ravish me, in the moment, extinguish me, now.
- The Little Girls of France – how their fathers kiss them.
- Little Kid in White Briefs Holding His Nose as He Jumps into the Water – chorister.
- Little Punk with a Backwards Baseball Cap – chorister.
- Little Sparrow Who Cannot Sing – for God has stopped her throat.
- Local Dignitary from Trikala – chorister.
- Long-Lost Love – chorister.
- Long-Necked Women in Khartoum – choristers.
- Longinus – soldier of Rome.
- Lord Lucifer – chorister.
- Lost Old Inmate – chorister.
- Lotus Eaters – legendary travelling band, part missionary, part Gypsy bandit.
- Luke – one of only two Gospel accounts that mention the miracle of Christ's virgin birth.
- The Luna Armada – mysterious moth-like formation of spectral entities or crafts which made assault on the Victory Gardens as moths drawn to the moon on Saturday 20 April 2099 at approximately 3.14 SST. There is a lore of days.
- Martin Luther – For I am dust, and ashes, and full of sin, and I am speaking to the living, the eternal, and the true God, and there is no bargaining with him.
- Mel Lyman – cult leader who laid holy siege to America and cut a brilliant album with his Family called *American Avatar* and who died, at the age of forty, of no cause of death whatsoever.
- Arthur Machen – author of the classic 'The Bowmen'.
- Sainte-Marie-Madeleine de Vézelay – abbey that presents the most imperturbably alien manifestation of the unknown God in Romanesque sculpture.
- Madman Breaking from the Crowd – chorister.
- The Madonna – Mary Mother of God.
- The Mahdi – prophesied redeemer of Islam.

- Yasser Mahmoud – aka The Ostrich due to his preferred mode of execution, which alternated between upside-down crucifixions over firepits and being buried alive, head first.
- Malodie – sly Malodie, Frater Jim's prison camp nemesis.
- Man Carving a Wooden Madonna During the Invasion of Crete – chorister.
- Man Clacking His Stumps Together in a Frenzy – chorister.
- Man Drawing a Man on Stilts – chorister.
- Man in Black Trunks Applying Suntan Lotion to a Blonde Woman in a Turquoise Bikini Who Is Complaining That He Is Too Rough with His Hands – choristers.
- The Man on Stilts – ghastly omen of Khartoum.
- Man Returned from Mars with His Memory Wiped – chorister.
- Man Smoking a Cigarette with a Pockmarked Face on the Cover of a Book – got to be Blaise Cendrars on the cover of the hardback of *Selected Writings* published by New Directions.
- Man Spread Out on a Bunk – chorister.
- Man Standing in the Street Smoking Kif in Khartoum During the Siege (Occasionally He Licks His Lips and Scratches His Face) – chorister.
- Man Who Runs an Eccentric Bookshop in France – chorister.
- Man with an Old-Fashioned Blunderbuss – chorister.
- Man with Red Swollen Eyes and a Burned Moustache Rocking on the Floor in What Appears to Be a Pool of His Own Urine – chorister.
- Man with Tightly Curled Hair and the Swollen Nose of a Perpetual Drug Addict – chorister.
- Man with Two Mangled Stumps for Legs Dancing on the Spot – chorister.
- Claude Mann – from Chicago, Illinois. Tank Battalion driver at Normandy. Killed in the battle for Bezange-la-Petite on 8 November 1944. Ecce Homo.
- Many-Tentacled Semi-Translucent Alien – feeds on our thoughts like a dog with a tapeworm.
- Mark – like any good biographer, Mark skips over the circumstances of Christ's birth altogether, because everyone

knows that is always the least interesting bit in biographies (except with Jesus, woops).

- Martha of Bethany – poor Lazarus's sister who complained to Christ that surely, by this time, her brother's corpse would stink.
- Saint Martin – Martin of Tours, patron saint of France.
- Mary – gave birth to Jesus in Bethlehem.
- Marxist Scum – any word but is.
- Elizabeth Mascaroni – some crap pop star.
- Mass Couplings That Appeared as Multi-Limbed Gods and Goddesses – choristers.
- Samuel Liddell MacGregor Mathers – co-founder of the Hermetic Order of the Golden Dawn, translator of The Bornless One aka The Headless One. Deathless, too, as his death certificate lists no cause.
- Saint Mathurin – patron saint of madmen.
- Matilda of Flanders – in Normandy, William the Conqueror and his wife Matilda of Flanders built two abbeys in order that they could be reconciled with the Church after they married without the Pope's consent: the Abbaye aux Hommes and the Abbaye aux Dames.
- Matthew – one of only two Gospel accounts that mention Christ's virgin birth.
- R.C.F. Maugham – author of the classic *Jersey Under the Jackboot*.
- McIntyre – chorister.
- Arthur McManus – aka The Grey Wolf aka The Grey Bat aka The Grey Owl aka The Silent Owl aka The Grey Fox aka The Grey Shark aka De Schrijver aka Aha aka Art.
- 'Tusky' McPheat – chorister.
- Jimmy McTavish – for example.
- Blind Willie McTell – bluesman, singer of the classic 'Delia'.
- Herman Melville – author of the classic *Pierre; or, The Ambiguities*. Likened the cries of the wounded leviathan to the sounding of the atomic pain at the centre of the world.
- Mr Melville – Pierre's father. The Outlandish Knight?
- Mrs Melville – Pierre's mother, resident in the village of In The Beginning.

- Pierre Melville – author of *Lonely Caravan*, *White Marble* and *Full Length Mirror*, co-founder of the Church of the Stone of First Witness, architect, theologian, adventurer, lover of Hildegard von Strophe, one summer. One half of the science fiction pseudonym Paimon.
- Men in Cloaks with Horned Helmets in the Forest Around Villiers-sous-Grez – choristers.
- Men of Little Faith – choristers.
- Men Passing Around Water and Smoking Kif and Speculating During the Siege of Khartoum – choristers.
- Men So Shrunken and Sunbeaten They Appeared as Children – choristers.
- Men Stood in Silence – choristers.
- Men Walking in Circles, Stood Naked, Rolling Improvised Cigarettes and Lying on the Ground Half-Starved – choristers.
- Men Who Look Like Grotesque Stuffed Monkeys – choristers.
- Mental Case in a Chair – chorister.
- Freddie Mercury – what a showman. Stole the show at Live Aid.
- Tarquinio Merula – early baroque Italian composer and instrumentalist. Chorister.
- Meursault – lead character in Albert Camus's *The Stranger* aka *The Outsider* aka *The Outlandish Knight*.
- Meursault's First Love – chorister.
- Saint Michael – archangel.
- Middle-Aged Explorers – choristers.
- Middle-Aged Intellectuals – choristers.
- Militarists in Black Space Suits – choristers.
- Miserable Priest in a Hospital – chorister.
- Marilyn Monroe – on the wall of a bar in Bourron-Marlotte.
- Claudio Monteverdi – Italian composer, instrumentalist and priest. Chorister.
- Moses – wrapped in swaddling clothes and sent down the river, in the blood of Egypt.
- Mother of the Unknown Narrator During the Siege of Khartoum – delicate, impossible.
- Mounted Policemen – choristers.

- Charles Mouton – French lutenist and composer. Chorister.
- Peter Mul(d)oon – artist. Painted the gods and gave them names.
- Mummified Head That Speaks in the Voice of the Lion of Judah – silence, for belief to me is abhorrent.
- Muttering Touched Woman – chorister.
- Mysterious Girls – choristers.
- Mysterious Girls Borne Upon a River – lover of the Irishman with the suspect tattoo and the ghost that imprisoned him.
- Mystics – choristers.
- Mythologists – life feeds on life.
- Vladimir Nabokov – author of the classic *Lolita*, which ends, unsurprisingly, with the letter A.
- Nameless Children Burned and Eaten by Wildlife in the Desert – choristers.
- Nameless Hunk in the Night – was to be my own name, once.
- Nameless Prostitutes – choristers.
- Nazi Doctors in Auschwitz – choristers.
- Nazi Officer in Crete – chorister.
- Nazi Party Members in Düsseldorf – choristers.
- Nazi Wives Backstage at Nuremberg – choristers.
- Nazi Women at a Party – choristers.
- Nazis – choristers.
- Neophytes – choristers.
- New Arrivals Being Fumigated and Deloused in an Italian Prisoner-of-War Camp – choristers.
- New Prison Camp Arrival with Permanent Dark-Blue Stubble and Staring Round Eyes – chorister.
- Friedrich Nietzsche – philosopher and author of the classic *Ecce Homo: How One Becomes What One Is*. Claimed Christianity had failed to make suffering sacred.
- The Nile – 'Let not the dwellers in Thebai and the temples thereof prate ever of the Pillars of Hercules and the Ocean of the West. Is not the Nile a beautiful water?'
- Nudist Painters Out in the Sticks – choristers.
- Will O'Mullane – publicist.

- Vincent O'Sullivan – writer of ghost stories, author of the classic *Master of Fallen Years*.
- Obnoxiously Fat Woman with No Top On – chorister.
- Obvious Drug Dealer Stood Next to His Bike Propped Up Against the Public Toilets – chorister.
- The Odd Hot Daughter – chorister.
- The Odd Young Couple – choristers.
- The Oddity – Frater Jim, the man from the future.
- Old Blonde in Silhouette – chorister.
- Old Dear with a Grotesque Face – chorister.
- Old Dog-Fucking Whore in Lecce – author of the photobook *I Am the Best*.
- Old Grey-Haired Fishermen in Canoes Loaded with Bucketfuls of Live Bait – choristers.
- Old Man with Blue Piss-Stained Trousers and a Beige Tank Top and a Drinker's Nose Sat on a Bench – chorister.
- Old Men in the Sun in Athens Back in the Day – choristers.
- Old Priest Gathering Driftwood on the Sand – Frater Jim's second rescuer, gifted him the name 'Joshua'.
- Old Uncles – choristers.
- Old Woman Admiring a Lovely Dog – chorister.
- Older Gentleman in the Street – chorister.
- Older Man Wearing Nothing But a Pair of Pink Bikini Bottoms – chorister.
- Older Swedish Couple – painters, retired doctor and chemist, resident in Grez-sur-Loing all those years ago now. Claimed to be distant relations of John Donne. Seemed unlikely.
- Charles Olson – poet. Author of the classic *The Maximus Poems*.
- Ecco Omar – from the Garden of Eden, to Khartoum, in order to secure the head of the Mahdi and re-fructify the garden with it. Leader of the Yezidis.
- One-Legged Sun Watcher – wife of Biraggo Fonte.
- Ook – dog.
- Oracular Bookseller and Her Husband: collect books on islands and anything to do with penguins. Like King Crimson. I think they were originally from Germany.

- Orderlies in an Improvised Field Hospital in Crete – choristers.
- The Original Galactic Map Team – worked together on a three-dimensional imaging of the solar system and its environs that could be scaled up or down according to where it was to be installed: a gallery; a country park; a wilderness; the span of an entire country.
- Organist with His Face Reflected in a Small Mirror – chorister.
- Agha Khalil Orphali – Gordon of Khartoum's bodyguard and top physician, a vegan and an ascetic.
- Osiris – Egyptian god whose Body is scattered across time and whose Cock cannot be found.
- P.D. Ouspensky – author of the classic *The Symbolism of the Tarot: Philosophy of Occultism in Pictures and Numbers, Pen-Pictures of the Twenty-Two Tarot Cards by P.D. Ouspensky. Translated by R.L. Pogossky. St Petersburg (Russia). 1913.*
- The Outlandish Knight – has drifted out of sight. Pierre's father?
- The Outlandish Man – who rose up from the waters only to be with you, my Love.
- Overweight Men in Wigs – choristers.
- Paimon – hermaphroditic goetic demon who rides on a camel across a desert of Africa.
- Paimon – outsider real-people DIY blues psychonaut.
- Paimon – pseudonym for the science fiction authors Pierre Melville and Maximilian Rehberg.
- Paimon – a time traveller who has lost his memory in the book *The Tomb of the Song.*
- Painting Class on the Opposite Bank of the River in Grez-sur-Loing – choristers.
- Pair of Friendly Drunks – choristers.
- Pair of Punks Trading Cigarettes – choristers.
- Palaeolithic Man – takes his place in the stars.
- Papus – aka Gérard Encausse, that occult fraud.
- Parents – choristers.
- Parents of a Young Dignitary – choristers.
- Partying Idiots – choristers.
- Pascal – you would not be looking for me had you not already found me.

- Passing Stranger with Tattoos Around His Mouth in Khartoum – chorister.
- The Path of the Birds Through the Air, Diving – chorister.
- Paul – no inkling of Christ's virgin birth whatsoever.
- Peebles – chorister.
- Pegasus – the flying horse.
- Imogen Pelham – agent.
- People Sleeping Upright on Crutches in the Night of Khartoum – choristers.
- People Smashing Wooden Doors to Splinters for Firewood During the Siege of Khartoum – choristers.
- People Whooping and Applauding – choristers.
- People with the Words Nicht Auf Luna Lebensraum on Their Space Suits – choristers.
- Perplexed Stallholders at the Fish Market in Athens – choristers.
- Peterson – chorister.
- Philosophers – choristers.
- Pablo Picasso – the greatest artist, with no style, like God.
- W.H. Pickering – astronomer who witnessed the movement of migrating life forms across Eratosthenes, in the Sea of Rains, on the Moon.
- Pierre's Old Headmaster – chorister.
- Pierreists – a blind man sits on a bench next to the river on which a stone is held afloat. He raises his rifle to his blind eyes and takes a shot at it, regardless.
- Arnaud Pierrepont – compiler of the epochal science fiction short story collection *L'Age d'Aura*.
- Pill-Popping Nutjobs Working the Night Shift in Bakeries – choristers.
- The Pink Panzer – author of *Notes Towards an Introspective Vision of Subterranea*, where he argued for something along the lines of extending, or rather inverting, the poet Charles Olson's vision of projective verse and his notions of scale in time and space wherein he posited that Olson had failed to anticipate that the birth of his idea would result in a dark twin, which implied a contraction, an introspecting of language, a shortness of breath, a gulping, gasping-for-air poetry of being buried half-alive, and

a language that had more to do with grammar – structural, organisational – a language that would be as implacable, now, as those first stone circles, in time, as inexplicable, too, and as unconcerned by meaning, as the tightening of a fist.

- The Plug – subterranean, propagandist, co-founder of the revived Church of the Stone of First Witness aka The SIRK.
- The Plug's Daughter – agent provocateur.
- The Plug's Friends – combatants.
- The Plug's Parents – ghosts.
- The Plug's Wife – an aged crone.
- Plumbers of the Depths – choristers.
- Poetic Young Blonde Whore in Sunglasses – chorister.
- Poets Who Stabbed Themselves and Lived to Tell the Tale – choristers.
- The Police – choristers.
- Police in Grez-sur-Loing – choristers.
- Politicians – choristers.
- Poofters – choristers.
- The Poor Jews – choristers.
- Pregnant Wife of a Ship's Captain Lost at Sea – chorister.
- Elvis Presley – still The King, on the wall of a bar, in Bourron-Marlotte.
- Priest with a Philanthropic Taste for the Esoteric – chorister.
- Priests – choristers.
- Prison Guards – choristers.
- Prisoner Who Looks a Bit Like Mussolini, Actually, 'Giving Sex' to an Italian Guard – chorister.
- Prisoners Shot in the Head – choristers.
- Prisoners Trying On Clothes – choristers.
- The Proprietor and His Wife – run the rip-off restaurant in Grez-sur-Loing. Avoid.
- Prostitutes in Düsseldorf – choristers.
- Protesters on the Moon – choristers.
- Proud Parents – choristers.

- Marcel Proust – author of the classic *Remembrance of Things Past*.
- Psychic Investigators – choristers.
- The Pulque Gods – custodians of deep time.
- Purple-Haired Old Women – choristers.
- Qbxl – sexy star goddess.
- The RAF – choristers.
- Gerry Rafferty – singer of the classic 'Baker Street'.
- Raggle-Taggle Collection of Geodesics – choristers.
- Randar and Fitchin – Yezidis from the Garden of Eden.
- Raphael – archangel.
- Rastafarians – Marcus Garvey has come to pass.
- Jean-Féry Rebel – French baroque composer and violinist. Chorister.
- Red-Faced, White-Haired Ex-Sailor – sells home brew from his cottage with a thatched roof in Villiers-sous-Grez.
- Maximilian Rehberg – soldier of fortune, religious polemicist, co-founder of the Church of the Stone of First Witness, lover of Hildegard von Strophe, one half of the pseudonymous science fiction author Paimon, author of the pamphlets *To Run Wild In It* and *Worship What You Burn and Burn What You Worship*. Thank you for your persistence, Maxi x.
- Maximilian Rehberg's Aunt – chorister.
- Maximilian Rehberg's Father – begging Max to suicide him.
- Maximilian Rehberg's First Wife and Child – disappeared now, into history, in order, one presumes, to run wild in it.
- Maximilian Rehberg's Mother – naked and passed out unconscious in the bath, drunk and dying of cancer, Max curled there beside her, upside down.
- Maximilian Rehberg's Three Wives – two dead, one completely off her tits.
- Religious Figures – choristers.
- Rembrandt – the loneliest paintings in the history of religious art because they are suffused by the shadow of death, and none of its lighting.
- Saint Remi of Reims – 'Worship what you burn, and burn what you worship.'

- Resistance Fighters in Greece – choristers.
- Pierre Reverdy – French religious poet.
- Kenneth Rexroth – poet of the Sierras.
- Rhythm Guitarist – sings Bob Marley in a Rasta Hat.
- Lionel Richie – starting to despair of ever getting a useable vocal take out of Dylan during the 'We Are the World' recording session.
- Rainer Maria Rilke – poet, author of the classic *Diaries of a Young Poet*.
- Arthur Rimbaud – poet who cured himself of art at the age of seventeen and who walked out the other side into life and who on his deathbed lamented his exile from the sun, forever.
- Justin Robertson – artist.
- Robinson – chorister.
- Angela Rippon – TV presenter, though she never presented *Pebble Mill at One*, as far as I can ascertain.
- The Ruling Elite – choristers.
- Father Sacraviscera – mentor to Robert Scott, in order that everything might be holy, even the most appalling soft organs of the body, those most vulnerable to clots and blows and sharp objects.
- Saxophonist Out of Nowhere – clearly drunk.
- Science Fiction-Addled Hippies – choristers.
- Scientists – choristers.
- Scientists – heat and cold come together on planet earth to create life.
- Mr Scotia – calligrapher, astronomer, local Airdrie historian, collector of maps, inveterate sniffer of bouquets.
- Mr Scotia – William Scotia, son of Mr William Scotia, of Airdrie, school secretary, subterranean, co-founder of the revived Church of the Stone of First Witness aka The SIRK, lover, and redeemer, of The Grey Wolf aka Arthur McManus.
- Mr Scotia's Uncle Sam – many men were in love with him.
- Mrs Scotia – Melanie Scotia, wife of the son of Mr William Scotia, of Airdrie, abandoned by her husband long ago, dead now.
- Mr and Mrs Scotia's Daughter – abandoned by her father, long ago.

- Scotsman with a Tanned Bollock in an Italian Prisoner-of-War Camp Near the End of the War – a tanned arsehole, too.
- Barbara Scott – Robert Scott's wife.
- Gregor Scott – here comes Robert's brother in an ice cream van.
- Robert Scott – hip priest.
- Robert Scott's Father – held the ambulance in his arms.
- Alexander Scriabin – Russian composer of the classic 'Étude in D-Sharp Minor', performed perfectly, and differently, by the pianist Vladimir Horowitz near the beginning, and again, near the end, of his incredible career.
- Seagulls Etched Hurriedly into the Air – choristers.
- The Secret Service – choristers.
- Alexander Selkirk – Scottish castaway who became the real-life inspiration for the classic *Robinson Crusoe*.
- Sentries Lying Exhausted in the Sand – choristers.
- Set – (tunnels of).
- Seth – the disharmonious brother.
- Seven Boys and a Single Girl in a Black Bikini Stood Around an Inflatable Ring, Waist-Deep in the Water – choristers.
- Seven Independent Witnesses – choristers.
- The Sex Pistols – punk group whose second single, 'God Save the Queen', was the soundtrack to the summer of 1977.
- Sex Workers in the Dying Years of the 1940s – choristers.
- William Shakespeare – author of the classic *Scottish Play*.
- Ariel Sharon – Israeli military general who led an invasion of Egypt in 1973. Eleventh prime minister of Israel, 2001–06.
- Sheik el Obeid – dervish master.
- Shoppers – choristers.
- Silhouette of a Man Holding What Looks Like a Small Child or a Monkey Maybe – chorister.
- Silhouettes of Ice Cream Ladies – choristers.
- Charles Sims – painter who ended up in the madhouse.
- The SIRK – Secret Initiatory Realm of Knights.
- The SIRK – Secret Interstellar Reconnaissance Kommando.
- The SIRK – Society of Inveterate Recidivist Knights.

- The SIRK – Society of Irregular Research and Knowledge.
- Sister of All the Disappeared – chorister.
- Sisters – choristers.
- Sleepwalkers – certainties of.
- Slowly Dancing Woman Through the Night of Khartoum – chorister.
- Slum-Dwelling Occultists – choristers.
- Small Black Dog with a Look of Cosmic Sympathy on Its Face – Frater Jim's brother back from the dead.
- Small Child Weeping in a Square in Athens After the War – chorister.
- Small Children Gathered Around a Cross – choristers.
- Small Conductor with All the Martial Kinetic Intensity of a Picasso – chorister.
- Small Dog on a Pew – chorister.
- Small Man with a Comedy Nose – chorister.
- Richard Snow – the Januist that was left behind.
- The So-Called Psychedelic Adventurers – choristers.
- Social Misfits – choristers.
- Soldiers Bursting into a Cell – choristers.
- Soldiers in Protective Full-Body Suits – choristers.
- Soldiers Separating Two Elderly Men – choristers.
- Solitary Sleepers Pressed Up Against the Walls Through the Night of Khartoum – choristers.
- Solomon – even he was not arrayed like the lilies in the field.
- Some Athletic Meathead Leaping to Catch a White Rugby Ball – chorister.
- Some Idiot in a Bunny Costume Acting the Goat – chorister.
- Some Nut Who Looks Like a Junkie – chorister.
- Some Old Bat – chorister.
- Someone Leaping from a Bridge – splash!
- Someone's Mother on the Phone – chorister.
- Sophisticated Older Woman – chorister.
- Sophisticated Older Woman's Dweeby Husband – chorister.
- Soprano as White as a Mime – chorister.

- Soprano Who Looks Like a Cross Between Germaine Greer and Barbara Dickson – chorister.
- Austin Osman Spare – painted nightmares.
- Albert Speer – Hitler's architect. Prisoner Number Five in Spandau after the war, he was released in 1966 and died of a stroke in 1981, in London, where he had travelled to appear on the BBC *Newsnight* programme.
- Spiritual Libertarians – choristers.
- The SS – choristers.
- John Stainer – English composer, organist and idiotic old fart.
- The (Lovely) Star – dip a toe, and allow yourself to be swept away.
- Star Gods – with sexy man-woman names, come down.
- Starship – sang the classic 'We Built This City'.
- The Starved and the Dissolute Lying Entangled in Each Other in the Street in Khartoum – choristers.
- Steely Generals Making Their Last Stand – choristers.
- Stone Angel in the Cemetery at Église Saint-Martin de La Genevraye – chorister.
- Strange Angels – choristers.
- Strange Dwarves – choristers.
- Stranger in Khartoum Who Talks of Prophecy – chorister.
- Stray Drunk from the Night Before in Grez-sur-Loing – chorister.
- Julius Streicher – Nazi Party member and founder of the virulently antisemitic newspaper *Der Stürmer*. Executed by hanging at Nuremberg Prison on 16 October 1946. His last words are reputed to be 'Adele, my dear wife.'
- Stressed Waiters at the Bar in Bourron-Marlotte – choristers.
- August Strindberg – Swedish playwright, occultist, resident of the Hotel Chevillon in Grez-sur-Loing long ago now in the past, one hell of a man. Author of the classics *Inferno* and *From an Occult Diary*.
- Dr Strindberg – doctor at a mental home in Wuppertal who employed Frater Jim as an orderly.
- Dr Strindberg's Pretty Wife – Frater Jim's lover, mother of his son.

- Hildegard von Strophe – aka Penny Apostrophe aka Penny Apo'strophe aka Penny von Strophe, artist, stripper, ceramicist, lover of Maximilian Rehberg and Pierre Melville, co-founder of the Church of the Stone of First Witness, named after the woman who was as soft as a feather on the breath of God.
- Simeon Stylites – extravagant Syrian monasticist who sat on top of a pillar for thirty-seven years.
- Suffocating Mother – chorister.
- Sufi Master from Garnethill – gives the gift of ejaculating with no hands (in secret).
- Sufis – practitioners of Qutub meditation.
- Sunbather in a Bikini on the Opposite Bank of the River in Grez-sur-Loing – chorister.
- Sun Ra – it's after the end of the world, don't you know that yet?
- Sun Watchers – believe that women experience the caress of the sun much more vividly and sensuously than men. Therefore, the solar current is more easily transfused throughout the woman's body. Deaf women, blind women, mute women, paralytics, the socially ostracised, the incomplete, these women are favoured amongst the Sun Watchers as being more adapted to bathing in the sun's rays through forfeiting the traditional roles of women.
- Super-Cute Alto with a Wide Face – chorister.
- The Surgeon – Januist.
- Clarissa Sutherland – project editor.
- The Swallows of Summer – choristers.
- Swans – in return.
- Miss Sweden – perfectly unfazed old dear who facilitates The Grey Wolf's new job as a history teacher in Mr Scotia's school after he traverses time.
- Miss Sweden's Husband in the Army – dead now, but it meant that she understood these kinds of top-secret assignations and was willing to admit that the 'boys upstairs', as she referred to them, were up to more than anyone ever imagined.
- Miss Sweden's Mum and Dad on Their First Awkward Date – in a bedsit in Kirklee Circus, in Glasgow.
- Juliette Swedenborg – uncanny French war artist, could have painted Hitler's room in the Führerbunker, only someone beat her to it.

- Tall Karo Man with a Semi-Automatic Pistol – chorister.
- Thomas Tallis – composer of the classic *Spem In Alium Nunquam Habui* aka *Hopelessly Devoted To You*. Great architect of the empty music.
- Taxi Driver with no English – hopeless.
- Taxidermist from Bethnal Green – chorister.
- Team of Assistants on an Experiment in Time Travel – choristers.
- Terrified Landlords and Restaurateurs in Athens – choristers.
- That Writer Who Walked Off into the Snow – probably Robert Walser.
- Three Boys Goading Each Other to Jump Off a Bridge – choristers.
- Three Crippled Brothers – vengeful cripples, choristers.
- Three Dumb Shepherds – God hates shepherds, believe me.
- Three Giggling Japanese Girls Launching a Canoe into the Water – choristers.
- Three Great Tzaddikim – witness to the doe that passed through three iterations of water.
- Three Men and a Woman in Nothing but Underwear and Shoes – choristers.
- Three People in the Garden – choristers.
- Three Wise Men – wise enough to attend the birth of the Christ child in time.
- Tiny Girl in a Red Swimming Costume Turning Cartwheels on the Opposite Shore – chorister.
- Token Bob – Scotia's pen pal, fellow hobbyist, subterranean, co-founder of the revived Church of the Stone of First Witness aka The SIRK, co-organiser of the Burntisland Conference alongside The Flashlight, partner, so the rumour went, of The Pink Panzer. Homeland security.
- J.R.R. Tolkien – author of the classic *The Silmarillion*.
- Tomnado – bassist with Helpless Clairvoyants.
- Joseph Tosh – of Calderbank. One of the first British troops into Berlin, where he found the enemy gone. Worked at the Organon factory in Chapelhall. Lost his young bride, Isa Forsyth, to kidney failure at the age of only thirty-two. After the war

travelled across Europe using his free rail pass in order to attend the Passion play in Oberammergau. Died at the age of sixty-four from a heart attack. Beloved memories.

- The Tower – the whole edifice of personality when it becomes like a suit of armour that protects you from reality, from the fullness of experience of the world, from speaking your secret name.
- Trader of Small Phalluses and Marital Toys – chorister.
- Tragic Young Spouses – choristers.
- Hugh Trevor-Roper – author of the classic *The Last Days of Hitler*.
- Truants – choristers.
- J.M.W. Turner – English Romantic painter.
- Tina Turner – not Dionne Warwick.
- Tutankhamen – boy king at the nebula.
- Two Guys Stroking Each Other's Arms on a Bench – choristers.
- Two Madmen on Wheelchairs in the Park – choristers.
- Two Muscular Young Men Bringing a Coffin Down a Thin Flight of Stone Stairs Between Two Buildings – choristers.
- Two Old Bedouins Who Keep Using the Word Thahab for Gold – choristers.
- Two Old Women – choristers.
- Two Police Officers by a River in Africa – first witness.
- Two Secretaries – choristers.
- Two Sisters from the Art School Who Had an Orgy with Maximilian Rehberg and Who Smoked Cigarettes in Their Pussies and Made Sounds Like Owls – choristers.
- Two Soldiers Walking Slowly Along a Dust Track Near the Marshes – choristers.
- *Uncle Stephen* – by Forrest Reid.
- The Unicorn – aka Y___.
- Unknown Body Come Down a River in Africa – *Genesis* by Pierre Melville.
- Unknown Members of the Public – choristers.
- Unknown Serving Girl – spat in the face by Biraggo Fonte.
- Unnamed Ambulanceman – chorister.
- Unnamed Men in an Italian Prisoner-of-War Camp – choristers.

- Unnamed Representative of the British Government – SIRK.

- Unnamed Witness to the Siege of Khartoum – chorister.

- Raoul Vaneigem – another tedious leftie.

- Vendor Selling Battered Flower Petals Fried in Oil During the Siege of Khartoum – chorister.

- Bonnie Ventura – wife of Frank, writer of tearful letters.

- Frank Ventura – disappeared during the liberation of Greece, reappeared in dreams, never returned.

- Paul Verlaine – mad poet shot by Rimbaud.

- Village Toughs – choristers.

- Mr Visconti – chorister.

- Mrs Visconti – chorister.

- Donald Visconti – Januist.

- Donald Visconti's Cruel Uncle – chorister.

- George Visconti – Donald Visconti's childhood tortoise.

- Mariella Visconti – wife of Donald Visconti, lover of Frater Jim, Januist?

- Robert de Visée – singer, instrumentalist and composer at the court of the French kings Louis XIV and Louis XV. Chorister.

- Voices Calling from Windows in Grez-sur-Loing – choristers.

- Voodoo Priests – choristers.

- W___ – Futurist, Januist, Donald Visconti's first collaborator.

- Richard Wagner – German composer overly concerned with his bud Nietzsche's intemperate wanking.

- Waldenses – live in an unheated shed in the garden of your mother all the better to feel the kiss of his mouth.

- Warrior Monks – choristers.

- Dionne Warwick – not Tina Turner.

- Washington – chorister.

- Danny Watson – Hildegard von Strophe's poet boyfriend with his sexy unbuttoned shirt, hot boy in a council house to a soundtrack of the Stranglers, before Maximilian Rehberg calls him a crap poof with dreadlocks and steals her from him right under his eyes.

- Waxwork Lesbians – choristers.

- Wet Dogs – choristers.

- Erhard Wetzel – worked for the Nazi chief ideologist Alfred Rosenberg as 'Judenreferent' and wrote the infamous 'gas chamber' letter which provides the earliest paper trail to the formulation of the Final Solution. Sentenced to house arrest for twenty-five years, he was pardoned, his prison sentence was reduced and he was eventually released. Died on 24 December 1975 of, we can only assume, natural causes.
- White Dog Lying in the Sun and Yawning in Blissful Boredom and with Great Skill – chorister.
- White-Haired Man Who Runs the Boulangerie in Grez-sur-Loing – chorister.
- White Marble – every day is marked with a white stone.
- White Poodle That Looks Crazy Thrown into the Water by Its Owner Swimming Back to Shore in a Terror – chorister.
- White Teenager with Dreadlocks – chorister whose name is God's Own Singer of Songs.
- Whole Families Wading Through the Nile by Night – choristers.
- The Widowed and the Wounded – choristers.
- Wife of Man Carving a Wooden Madonna During the Invasion of Crete – chorister.
- William the Conqueror – in Normandy, William the Conqueror and his wife built two abbeys in order that they could be reconciled with the Church after they married without the Pope's consent: the Abbaye aux Hommes and the Abbaye aux Dames.
- Henry Williamson – author of the classic *Tarka the Otter*. Tarka really was a terrific otter.
- Witchy Lover – chorister.
- Stanisław Ignacy Witkiewicz – Polish artist, author, philosopher, that cold star of the inter-war period, painter of the classic *Suicide-to-be Three Seconds Before Pulling the Trigger*.
- Woman in Nemours Hacking Off the Claws of a Poulette – chorister.
- Woman Shouting at a Man with a Walking Stick During the Siege of Khartoum – chorister.
- Woman Who Is Obsessed with Black GIs – specifically their presence, or not, at Normandy.
- Woman with an Enormous Ass Smothering a Small-Limbed Boy – chorister.

- Woman with Short Blonde Hair Who Displayed Her Twat – chorister.
- Women and Children Who Cross the Nile by Night – choristers.
- Women Dressed as Sorceresses in the Forest Around Villiers-sous-Grez – choristers.
- Women in the Great Rundown Theatres of Greece After the War – choristers.
- Women of the Village – choristers.
- Women with Facial Hair – choristers.
- William Wordsworth – poet. Author of the classic 'The Prelude'.
- Would-Be Initiates – choristers.
- Wretched Cellmates – choristers.
- Wretched Derelict in Khartoum – chorister.
- Wretched Group of Boys and Men Led to Their Death by a Convoy of Tanks and Motorcycles – choristers.
- X___ – Nazi Futurist.
- Xstabeth – Gordon of Khartoum's talking mouse made up of the stars aka Elizabeth of the Cross who has no time for tales.
- Xstabeth – sexy star goddess.
- Y___ – Nazi Futurist aka The Unicorn.
- Yacob Yacob – guitarist with Helpless Clairvoyants.
- W.B. Yeats – we have come to give you metaphors for poetry.
- Yezidis in Khartoum – choristers.
- Young Black Man in a Training Session in the Woods in France – chorister.
- Young Boy Believing Himself to Be a Forgotten Thought of God – chorister.
- Young Boy in Oversized Yellow Armbands Leaping from the Bank – chorister.
- Young Boy Limping into the Palace During the Siege of Khartoum – chorister.
- Young Boys Leaping from Rickety Piers – choristers.
- Young Bureaucrat – chorister.
- Young Couple in Swimwear Kissing Keenly on the Beach in Burntisland – choristers.

- Young French Kid Selling Hard Rock LPs from the Boot of His Car – one-time lover of Flower, once.
- Young Girl Catching Her Shadow – chorister.
- Young Girl in a Black Swimming Costume – chorister where God begins.
- Young Girl on a Fold-out Bed at the Foot of a Row of Terrible Rusting Gas Tanks – chorister.
- Young Girls – choristers.
- Young Girls in Flesh-Pink Bikinis – choristers.
- Young Girls Slipping Their Bikinis Down in Order to Avoid Tan Lines – choristers.
- Young Girls Spread Out on Towels – choristers.
- Young Man Fellating an Older Man Against a Wall with His Robes Pulled Up During the Siege of Khartoum – chorister.
- Young Man Sat on a Wall Sketching in a Square in Athens – chorister.
- Young Man with a Beard on a Rescue Ship from Malta – chorister.
- Young Man with Sticky-Out Ears – chorister.
- Young Mother and Baby Posing for the Camera – choristers.
- Young People – choristers.
- Young SA Man of High Rank – chorister.
- Young Teen on the Timpani – who are these people?
- Zeno of Elea – Greek philosopher who claimed nothing can be achieved ever except in the impossible mind of God.
- Zeus – sky god, father, protector, spirit, air. Raped Leda in the guise of a swan, in return. Perfect foolishness.

Monument Maker was completed in Grez-sur-Loing in the summer of 2018 thanks to a Robert Louis Stevenson Fellowship awarded by Creative Scotland.